W9-AAW-386

POE'S CHILDREN

Poe's Children

✠ THE NEW HORROR ✠

An Anthology

PETER STRAUB

DOUBLEDAY

New York   London   Toronto   Sydney   Auckland

DD

DOUBLEDAY

PUBLISHED BY DOUBLEDAY

Published in the United States by Doubleday, an imprint of The Doubleday
Publishing Group, a division of Random House, Inc., New York.
www.doubleday.com

Book design by Caroline Cunningham
Title page photo of haunted tower © Shutterstock

Library of Congress Cataloging-in-Publication Data
Poe's children : the new horror : an anthology / [edited by] Peter Straub. — 1st ed.
p. cm.
1. Horror tales, American. 2. Horror tales, English. I. Straub, Peter, 1943–
PS648.H6P58 2008
813'.0873808—dc22
2008003013

ISBN 978-0-385-52283-0

PRINTED IN THE UNITED STATES OF AMERICA

1   3   5   7   9   10   8   6   4   2

First Edition

CONTENTS

Introduction

I could say: Kelly Link created a world, and it then had been there all along. Or: John Crowley entertained the possibility of a grand possibility, and after that it had always been in place, available for use. Something similar could be said of all the superb writers in this book, which category includes every one of its contributors, from Dan Chaon to Rosalind Palermo Stevenson. Each of these writers either came through to the recognition, or were permitted by a generous environment early on to understand, that the materials of genre—specifically the paired genres of horror and the fantastic—in no way require the constrictions of formulaic treatment, and in fact naturally extend and evolve into the methods and concerns of its wider context, general literature. Yet most professional reviewers of fiction instinctively tend to protect the categories that simplify their tasks. Therefore, when faced with work that, while indisputably though perhaps even in some not-quite-definable sense connected to a genre like sf or horror, also possesses literary merit, they tend to fall back on the convenient old shell game of expressing their admiration by saying that the work in question transcends its genre.

Now, let us be clear about this. Claiming that a work transcends its genre is almost exactly like saying, as people once were wont to do, that an accomplished African-American gentleman, someone say like John Conyers or Denzel Washington, is a credit to his race—the unstated assumption of course being that the race in question needs all the help it can get. (One day I'd like to hear an after-banquet introducer describe some silver-haired New England WASP as a credit to his race.)

By my own ground rules, then, I have been called a credit to my race maybe half a dozen times, directly or indirectly, and about half of those times I was dumb enough to feel flattered. These days, publishers market a product they are happy to call "literary horror," but when I first appeared everyone understood that horror was inherently trashy, unliterary to the core, actually rather shameful, literature's wretched slum. Teenaged boys and other degenerates were its natural demographic. Of course Poe had somehow crept into the canon, maybe because Baudelaire's translations had fooled the French into mistaking him for a reputable figure; hints and echoes of the supernatural filled Hawthorne's books; Henry James had written "The Turn of the Screw" and "The Jolly Corner" and other great ghost or horror stories; and Edith Wharton had written many wonderful ghost stories. These figures, so important to me that in my 1979 novel *Ghost Story* I had not only named two principal characters James and Hawthorne but inserted into its first part what I called a "junked-up" version of "The Turn of the Screw," were nonetheless safely in the past. During the late seventies, when you thought of horror, you did not think of the Master of Lamb House, Rye. What came to mind instead were paperbacks with graphics of broken dolls, severed heads, or minimalist mouths letting slip single drops of blood.

(When at a lovely, crowded party in London in 1977 I complained about the dripping severed head on the newly released paperback of my latest book, its publisher told me, "Peter, that book isn't for people like *you*." Too stunned to reply, I turned around and aimed for the bar.)

Really because of the marketing approach reflected in those gaudy paperback covers, which included packing the newly popular category with far too many titles by authors whose ambitions went no further than that market, "horror" as a category overflowed its banks during the late eighties and flooded the chain-stores' shelves with malevolent orphans, haunted brownstones and haunted farms and haunted subway cars, ancient curses, things in bandages, evil toddlers, zombies at play, Nazi vampires—"underwater lesbian Nazi vampire turtles," my now-deceased friend Michael McDowell joked while impaneled at a genre convention in Rhode Island. In the early nineties, in a Guest of Honor speech at a World Horror Convention in New York, I responded to the decaying world I saw around me by saying that horror was a house that horror had already moved out of.

The statement earned me some hostile glances during the evening's celebrations, for far too many younger writers present had trusted that their extravaganzas about back-country zombies or teenaged vampires were one day going to settle them on or near the best-seller lists, in the vicinity of their favorite books by V. C. Andrews, Ann Rice, Stephen King, Dean Koontz, and a few others. It never happened. None of these twenty- and thirtysomethings who had plotted Regicide and Koontzicide while the well-padded target at the podium dispensed urbane twaddle about Emer- son and All Things Glittering and Gleaming (or whatever it was; he was having an Emersonian moment) into the microphone ever got near any best-seller list, and over the next decade a lot of them faded from view.

Which helped prove my point of view. The process has nothing to do with best-seller lists, but time has a tendency generally to support the proposition that very good work survives, while work that is not very good does not. Who now reads, to pick three of the best of the pack, Ken Eulo, Robert Marasco, or Frank deFelita, all of whom once had great success with books that now seem more than a bit, well, gestural?

What I had not anticipated, though, was that over the next ten to fifteen years there would appear a number of writers of fantasy, science fiction, and horror—among them, Kelly Link, M. Rickert, Graham Joyce, Elizabeth Hand—who had far more in common with one another and per- petual wild cards like John Crowley and Jonathan Carroll than they did with those writers who were supposed to epitomize their fields. They were literary writers and genre writers at the same time. When Bradford Mor- row invited me to guest-edit *Conjunctions 39: The New Wave Fabulists* (2002), I accepted on the spot, thinking that his much-respected, smart, and intrepid journal would provide the perfect showcase for these writers, most or all of whom would be unknown to its regular subscribers. The ben- efits of such an encounter should, I thought, flow both ways. And so, as far as I can determine, it proved: the issue was widely reviewed, much praised, and it went into three or four printings. It also inspired a couple of other anthologies edited by people who understood exactly what we were trying to do.

Poe's Children very much continues on from *The New Wave Fabulists*, and this time I am free to include work by breathtaking "literary" writers, who in this newly liberated atmosphere have no problem embracing their inner Poe, or to put it another way, no problem making use of the strengths and insights made available to them from their own personal engagements with horror and sf. (For reasons having to do with length, along with many other people I wanted to include, Michael Chabon and Jonathan Lethem are not represented in this volume, but they fall into the same category.) This crossover is entirely welcome, I think, as it erases boundaries and blurs distinctions that sometimes seem designed mostly to keep everyone in their proper place.

In November 2003, when Stephen King was awarded the National Book Award's Medal for Distinguished Contribution to American Letters, he went out of his way to invite the resplendent audience before him to read the latest fiction by a number of his writer friends. He went on to praise the books. Not long afterward, the distinguished novelist who had just won the NBA for Best Novel, and whom until that moment I had admired, included in her acceptance speech the remark that she did not think those present needed to be given a reading list. At that moment, Stephen King and I had the same thought: you're wrong, lady, you could really use that reading list.

The beautiful, disturbing, fearless stories in *Poe's Children* make up a kind of reading list for anyone who wants to experience what I think is the most interesting development in our literature during the last two decades. It has been taking place in small presses, genre journals, and year's best compilations, and it has been gathering steam as it goes. You have to be open-eyed and flexible as to category to get what is going on, but some vital individual breakthroughs are in the wind. We are all fortunate, readers and writers alike, to participate in a moment of such amplitude, luxury, and promise.

Peter Straub
New York City

The Bees

Dan Chaon

Gene's son Frankie wakes up screaming. It has become frequent, two or three times a week, at random times: midnight—3 A.M.—five in the morning. Here is a high, empty wail that severs Gene from his unconsciousness like sharp teeth. It is the worst sound that Gene can imagine, the sound of a young child dying violently—falling from a building, or caught in some machinery that is tearing an arm off, or being mauled by a predatory animal. No matter how many times he hears it he jolts up with such images playing in his mind, and he always runs, thumping into the child's bedroom to find Frankie sitting up in bed, his eyes closed, his mouth open in an oval like a Christmas caroler. Frankie appears to be in a kind of peaceful trance, and if someone took a picture of him he would look like he was waiting to receive a spoonful of ice cream, rather than emitting that horrific sound.

"Frankie!" Gene will shout, and claps his hands hard in the child's face. The clapping works well. At this, the scream always stops abruptly, and Frankie opens his eyes, blinking at Gene with vague awareness before settling back down into his pillow, nuzzling a little before growing still. He is sound asleep, he is always sound asleep, though even after months Gene can't help leaning down and pressing his ear to the child's chest, to make sure he's still breathing, his heart is still going. It always is.

There is no explanation that they can find. In the morning, the child doesn't remember anything, and on the few occasions that they have managed to wake him in the midst of one of his screaming attacks, he is merely sleepy and irritable. Once, Gene's wife, Karen, shook him and shook him, until finally he opened his eyes, groggily. "Honey?" she said. "Honey? Did you have a bad dream?" But Frankie only moaned a little. "No," he said, puzzled and unhappy at being awakened, but nothing more.

They can find no pattern to it. It can happen any day of the week, any time of the night. It doesn't seem to be associated with diet, or with his activities during the day, and it doesn't stem, as far as they can tell, from any sort of psychological unease. During the day, he seems perfectly normal and happy.

They have taken him several times to the pediatrician, but the doctor seems to have little of use to say. There is nothing wrong with the child physically, Dr. Banerjee says. She advises that such things were not uncommon for children of Frankie's age group—he is five—and that more often than not, the disturbance simply passes away.

"He hasn't experienced any kind of emotional trauma, has he?" the doctor says. "Nothing out of the ordinary at home?"

"No, no," they both murmur, together. They shake their heads, and Dr. Banerjee shrugs. "Parents," she says. "It's probably nothing to worry about." She gives them a brief smile. "As difficult as it is, I'd say that you may just have to weather this out."

But the doctor has never heard those screams. In the mornings after the "nightmares," as Karen calls them, Gene feels unnerved, edgy. He works as a driver for the United Parcel Service, and as he moves through the day after a screaming attack, there is a barely perceptible hum at the edge of his hearing, an intent, deliberate static sliding along behind him as he wanders through streets and streets in his van. He stops along the side of the road and listens. The shadows of summer leaves tremble murmurously against the windshield, and cars are accelerating on a nearby road. In the treetops, a cicada makes its trembly, pressure-cooker hiss.

Something bad has been looking for him for a long time, he thinks, and now, at last, it is growing near.

When he comes home at night everything is normal. They live in an old house in the suburbs of Cleveland, and sometimes after dinner they work together in the small patch of garden out in back of the house—tomatoes, zucchini, string beans, cucumbers—while Frankie plays with Legos in the dirt. Or they take walks around the neighborhood, Frankie riding his bike in front of them, his training wheels recently removed. They gather on the couch and watch cartoons together, or play board games, or draw pictures with crayons. After Frankie is asleep, Karen will sit at the kitchen table and study—she is in nursing school—and Gene will sit outside on the porch, flipping through a newsmagazine or a novel, smoking the cigarettes that he has promised Karen he will give up when he turns thirty-five. He is thirty-four now, and Karen is twenty-seven, and he is aware, more and more frequently, that this is not the life that he deserves. He has been incredibly lucky, he thinks. Blessed, as Gene's favorite cashier at the supermarket always says. "Have a blessed day," she says, when Gene pays the money and she hands him his receipt, and he feels as if she has sprinkled him with her ordinary, gentle beatitude. It reminds him of long ago, when an old nurse had held his hand in the hospital and said that she was praying for him.

Sitting out in his lawn chair, drawing smoke out of his cigarette, he thinks about that nurse, even though he doesn't want to. He thinks of the way she'd leaned over him and brushed his hair as he stared at her, imprisoned in a full body cast, sweating his way through withdrawal and D.T.'s.

He had been a different person, back then. A drunk, a monster. At nineteen, he'd married the girl he'd gotten pregnant, and then had set about slowly, steadily, ruining all their lives. When he'd abandoned them, his wife and son, back in Nebraska, he had been twenty-four, a danger to himself and others. He'd done them a favor by leaving, he thought, though he still felt guilty when he thought about it. Years later, when he was sober, he'd even tried to contact them. He wanted to own up to his behavior, to pay the back child-support, to apologize. But they were nowhere to be found. Mandy was no longer living in the small Nebraska town where they'd met and married, and there was no forwarding address. Her parents were dead. No one seemed to know where she'd gone.

Karen didn't know the full story. She had been, to his relief, uncurious about his previous life, though she knew he had some drinking days, some bad times. She knew that he'd been married before, too, though she didn't know the extent of it, didn't know that he had another son, for example, didn't know that he had left them one night, without even packing a bag, just driving off in the car, a flask tucked between his legs, driving east as far as he could go. She didn't know about the car crash, the wreck he should have died in. She didn't know what a bad person he'd been.

She was a nice lady, Karen. Maybe a little sheltered. And truth to tell, he was ashamed—and even scared—to imagine how she would react to the truth about his past. He didn't know if she would have ever really trusted him if she'd known the full story, and the longer they knew one another the less inclined he was to reveal it. He'd escaped his old self, he thought, and when Karen got pregnant, shortly before they were married, he told himself that now he had a chance to do things over, to do it better. They had purchased the house together, he and Karen, and now Frankie will be in kindergarten in the fall. He has come full circle, has come exactly to the point when his former life with Mandy and his son, DJ, had completely fallen apart. He looks up as Karen comes to the back door and speaks to him through the screen. "I think it's time for bed, sweetheart," she says softly, and he shudders off these thoughts, these memories. He smiles.

He's been in a strange frame of mind lately. The months of regular awakenings have been getting to him, and he has a hard time getting back to sleep after an episode with Frankie. When Karen wakes him in the morning, he often feels muffled, sluggish—as if he's hung over. He doesn't hear the alarm clock. When he stumbles out of bed, he finds he has a hard time keeping his moodiness in check. He can feel his temper coiling up inside him.

He isn't that type of person anymore, and hasn't been for a long while. Still, he can't help but worry. They say that there is a second stretch of craving, which sets in after several years of smooth sailing; five or seven years will pass, and then it will come back without warning. He has been thinking of going to A.A. meetings again, though he hasn't in some time—not since he met Karen.

It's not as if he gets trembly every time he passes a liquor store, or even as if he has a problem when he goes out with buddies and spends the evening drinking soda and non-alcoholic beer. No. The trouble comes at night, when he's asleep.

He has begun to dream of his first son. DJ. Perhaps it is related to his worries about Frankie, but for several nights in a row the image of DJ— aged about five—has appeared to him. In the dream, Gene is drunk, and playing hide and seek with DJ in the yard behind the Cleveland house where he is now living. There is the thick weeping willow out there, and Gene watches the child appear from behind it and run across the grass, happily, unafraid, the way Frankie would. DJ turns to look over his shoulder and laughs, and Gene stumbles after him, at least a six-pack's worth of good mood, a goofy, drunken dad. It's so real that when he wakes, he still feels intoxicated. It takes him a few minutes to shake it.

One morning after a particularly vivid version of this dream, Frankie wakes and complains of a funny feeling—"right here"—he says, and points to his forehead. It isn't a headache, he says. "It's like bees!" he says. "Buzzing bees!" He rubs his hand against his brow. "Inside my head." He considers for a moment. "You know how the bees bump against the window when they get in the house and want to get out?" This description pleases him, and he taps his forehead lightly with his fingers, humming, "zzzzzzz," to demonstrate.

"Does it hurt?" Karen says.

"No," Frankie says. "It tickles."

Karen gives Gene a concerned look. She makes Frankie lie down on the couch, and tells him to close his eyes for a while. After a few minutes, he raises up, smiling, and says that the feeling has gone.

"Honey, are you sure?" Karen says. She pushes her hair back and slides her palm across his forehead. "He's not hot," she says, and Frankie sits up impatiently, suddenly more interested in finding a Matchbox car he dropped under a chair.

Karen gets out one of her nursing books, and Gene watches her face tighten with concern as she flips slowly through the pages. She is looking at Chapter 3: Neurological System, and Gene observes as she pauses here and there, skimming down a list of symptoms. "We should probably take him back to Dr. Banerjee again," she says. Gene nods, recalling what the doctor said about "emotional trauma."

"Are you scared of bees?" he asks Frankie. "Is that something that's bothering you?"

"No," Frankie says. "Not really."

When Frankie was three, a bee stung him above his left eyebrow. They had been out hiking together, and they hadn't yet learned that Frankie was "moderately allergic" to bee stings. Within minutes of the sting, Frankie's face had begun to distort, to puff up, his eye welling shut. He looked deformed. Gene didn't know if he'd ever been more frightened in his entire life, running down the trail with Frankie's head pressed against his heart, trying to get to the car and drive him to the doctor, terrified that the child was dying. Frankie himself was calm.

Gene clears his throat. He knows the feeling that Frankie is talking about—he has felt it himself, that odd, feathery vibration inside his head. And in fact he feels it again, now. He presses the pads of his fingertips against his brow. *Emotional trauma,* his mind murmurs, but he is thinking of DJ, not Frankie.

"What are you scared of?" Gene asks Frankie, after a moment. "Anything?"

"You know what the scariest thing is?" Frankie says, and widens his eyes, miming a frightened look. "There's a lady with no head, and she went walking through the woods, looking for it. 'Give . . . me . . . back . . . my . . . head. . . .' "

"Where on earth did you hear a story like that!" Karen says.

"Daddy told me," Frankie says. "When we were camping."

Gene blushes, even before Karen gives him a sharp look. "Oh, great," she says. "Wonderful."

He doesn't meet her eyes. "We were just telling ghost stories," he says, softly. "I thought he would think the story was funny."

"My God, Gene," she says. "With him having nightmares like this? What were you thinking?"

✝ ✝

It's a bad flashback, the kind of thing he's usually able to avoid. He thinks abruptly of Mandy, his former wife. He sees in Karen's face that look Mandy would give him when he screwed up. "What are you, some kind of idiot?" Mandy used to say. "Are you crazy?" Back then, Gene couldn't do anything right, it seemed, and when Mandy yelled at him it made his stomach clench with shame and inarticulate rage. I was *trying*, he would think, I was *trying*, damn it, and it was as if no matter what he did, it wouldn't turn out right. That feeling would sit heavily in his chest, and eventually, when things got worse, he hit her once. "Why do you want me to feel like shit," he had said through clenched teeth. "I'm not an asshole," he said, and when she rolled her eyes at him he slapped her hard enough to knock her out of her chair.

That was the time he'd taken DJ to the carnival. It was a Saturday, and he'd been drinking a little so Mandy didn't like it, but after all—he thought—DJ was his son too; he had a right to spend some time with his own son. Mandy wasn't his boss even if she might think she was. She liked to make him hate himself.

What she was mad about was that he'd taken DJ on the Velocerator. It was a mistake, he'd realized afterward. But DJ himself had begged to go on. He was just recently four years old, and Gene had just turned twenty-three, which made him feel inexplicably old. He wanted to have a little fun.

Besides, nobody told him he *couldn't* take DJ on the thing. When he led DJ through the gate, the ticket-taker even smiled, as if to say, "Here is a young guy showing his kid a good time." Gene winked at DJ and grinned, taking a nip from a flask of peppermint schnapps. He felt like a good dad. He wished his own father had taken him on rides at the carnival!

The door to the Velocerator opened like a hatch in a big silver flying saucer. Disco music was blaring from the entrance and became louder as they went inside. It was a circular room with soft padded walls, and one of the workers had Gene and DJ stand with their backs to the wall, strapping them in side by side. Gene felt warm and expansive from the schnapps. He took DJ's hand, and he almost felt as if he were glowing with love. "Get ready, Kiddo," Gene whispered. "This is going to be wild."

The hatch door of the Velocerator sealed closed with a pressurized sigh. And then, slowly, the walls they were strapped to began to turn. Gene tightened on DJ's hand as they began to rotate, gathering speed. After a moment the wall pads they were strapped to slid up, and the force of velocity pushed them back, held to the surface of the spinning wall like iron to a magnet. Gene's cheeks and lips seemed to pull back, and the sensation of helplessness made him laugh.

At that moment, DJ began to scream. "No! No! Stop! Make it stop!" They were terrible shrieks, and Gene grabbed the child's hand tightly. "It's all right," he yelled jovially over the thump of the music. "It's okay! I'm right here!" But the child's wailing only got louder in response. The scream seemed to whip past Gene in a circle, tumbling around and around the circumference of the ride like a spirit, trailing echoes as it flew. When the machine finally stopped, DJ was heaving with sobs, and the man at the control panel glared. Gene could feel the other passengers staring grimly and judgmentally at him.

Gene felt horrible. He had been so happy—thinking that they were finally having themselves a memorable father and son moment—and he could feel his heart plunging into darkness. DJ kept on weeping, even as they left the ride and walked along the midway, even as Gene tried to distract him with promises of cotton candy and stuffed animals. "I want to go home," DJ cried, and "I want my mom! I want my mom!" And it had wounded Gene to hear that. He gritted his teeth.

"Fine!" he hissed. "Let's go home to your mommy, you little crybaby. I swear to God, I'm never taking you with me anywhere again." And he gave DJ a little shake. "Jesus, what's *wrong* with you? Lookit, people are laughing at you. See? They're saying, 'Look at that big boy, bawling like a girl.'"

This memory comes to him out of the blue. He had forgotten all about it, but now it comes to him over and over. Those screams were not unlike the sounds Frankie makes in the middle of the night, and they pass repeatedly through the membrane of his thoughts, without warning. The next day, he finds himself recalling it again, the memory of the scream impressing his mind with such force that he actually has to pull his UPS truck off to the side of the road and put his face in his hands: Awful! Awful! He must have seemed like a monster to the child.

Sitting there in his van, he wishes he could find a way to contact them—Mandy and DJ. He wishes that he could tell them how sorry he is, and send them money. He puts his fingertips against his forehead, as cars drive past on the street, as an old man parts the curtains and peers out of the house Gene is parked in front of, hopeful that Gene might have a package for him.

Where are they? Gene wonders. He tries to picture a town, a house, but there is only a blank. Surely, Mandy being Mandy, she would have hunted him down by now to demand child support. She would have relished treating him like a deadbeat dad, she would have hired some company who would garnish his wages.

Now, sitting at the roadside, it occurs to him suddenly that they are dead. He recalls the car wreck that he was in, just outside Des Moines, and if he had been killed they would have never known. He recalls waking up in the hospital, and the elderly nurse who had said, "You're very lucky, young man. You should be dead."

Maybe they are dead, he thinks. Mandy and DJ. The idea strikes him a glancing blow, because of course it would make sense. The reason they'd never contacted him. Of course.

He doesn't know what to do with such premonitions. They are ridiculous, they are self-pitying, they are paranoid, but especially now, with their concerns about Frankie, he is at the mercy of his anxieties. He comes home from work and Karen stares at him heavily.

"What's the matter?" she says, and he shrugs. "You look terrible," she says.

"It's nothing," he says, but she continues to look at him skeptically. She shakes her head.

"I took Frankie to the doctor again today," she says, after a moment, and Gene sits down at the table with her, where she is spread out with her textbooks and notepaper.

"I suppose you'll think I'm being a neurotic mom," she says. "I think I'm too immersed in disease, that's the problem."

Gene shakes his head. "No, no," he says. His throat feels dry. "You're right. Better safe than sorry."

"Mmm," she says, thoughtfully. "I think Dr. Banerjee is starting to hate me."

"Naw," Gene says. "No one could hate you." With effort, he smiles gently. A good husband, he kisses her palm, her wrist. "Try not to worry," he says, though his own nerves are fluttering. He can hear Frankie in the backyard, shouting orders to someone.

"Who's he talking to?" Gene says, and Karen doesn't look up.

"Oh," she says. "It's probably just Bubba." Bubba is Frankie's imaginary playmate.

Gene nods. He goes to the window and looks out. Frankie is pretending to shoot at something, his thumb and forefinger cocked into a gun. "Get him! Get him!" Frankie shouts, and Gene stares out as Frankie dodges behind a tree. Frankie looks nothing like DJ, but when he pokes his head from behind the hanging foliage of the willow, Gene feels a little shudder—a flicker—something. He clenches his jaw.

"This class is really driving me crazy," Karen says. "Every time I read about a worst-case scenario, I start to worry. It's strange. The more you know, the less sure you are of anything."

"What did the doctor say this time?" Gene says. He shifts uncomfortably, still staring out at Frankie, and it seems as if dark specks circle and bob at the corner of the yard. "He seems okay?"

Karen shrugs. "As far as they can tell." She looks down at her textbook, shaking her head. "He seems healthy." He puts his hand gently on the back of her neck and she lolls her head back and forth against his fingers. "I've never believed that anything really terrible could happen to me," she had once told him, early in their marriage, and it had scared him. "Don't say that," he'd whispered, and she laughed.

"You're superstitious," she said. "That's cute."

He can't sleep. The strange presentiment that Mandy and DJ are dead has lodged heavily in his mind, and he rubs his feet together underneath the covers, trying to find a comfortable posture. He can hear the soft ticks of the old electric typewriter as Karen finishes her paper for school, words rattling out in bursts that remind him of some sort of insect language. He closes his eyes, pretending to be asleep when Karen finally comes to bed, but his mind is ticking with small, scuttling images: his former wife and son, flashes of the photographs he didn't own, hadn't kept. *They're dead,* a firm voice in his mind says, very distinctly. *They were in a fire. And they burned up.* It is not quite his own voice that speaks to him, and abruptly he can picture the burning house. It's a trailer, somewhere on the outskirts of a small town, and the black smoke is pouring out of the open door. The plastic window frames have warped and begun to melt, and the smoke billows from the trailer into the sky in a way that reminds him of an old locomotive. He can't see inside, except for crackling bursts of deep orange flames, but he's aware that they're inside. For a second he can see DJ's face, flickering, peering steadily from the window of the burning trailer, his mouth open in an unnatural circle, as if he's singing.

He opens his eyes. Karen's breathing has steadied, she's sound asleep, and he carefully gets out of bed, padding restlessly through the house in his pajamas. They're not dead, he tries to tell himself, and stands in front of the refrigerator, pouring milk from the carton into his mouth. It's an old comfort, from back in the days when he was drying out, when the thick taste of milk would slightly calm his craving for a drink. But it doesn't help him now. The dream, the vision, has frightened him badly, and he sits on the couch with an afghan over his shoulders, staring at some science program on television. On the program, a lady scientist is examining a mummy. A child. The thing is bald—almost a skull but not quite. A membrane of ancient skin is pulled taut over the eye sockets. The lips are stretched back, and there are small, chipped, rodentlike teeth. Looking at the thing, he can't help but think of DJ again, and he looks over his shoulder, quickly, the way he used to.

The last year that he was together with Mandy, there used to be times when DJ would actually give him the creeps—spook him. DJ had been an unusually skinny child, with a head like a baby bird and long, bony feet, with toes that seemed strangely extended, as if they were meant for gripping. He can remember the way the child would slip barefoot through rooms, slinking, sneaking, watching, Gene had thought, always watching him.

It is a memory that he has almost, for years, succeeded in forgetting, a memory he hates and mistrusts. He was drinking heavily at the time, and he knows now that alcohol had grotesquely distorted his perceptions. But now that it has been dislodged, that old feeling moves through him like a breath of smoke. Back then, it had seemed to him that Mandy had turned DJ against him, that DJ had in some strange way almost physically transformed into something that wasn't Gene's *real* son. Gene can remember how, sometimes, he would be sitting on the couch, watching TV, and he'd get a funny feeling. He'd turn his head and DJ would be at the edge of the room, with his bony spine hunched and his long neck craned, staring with those strangely oversized eyes. Other times, Gene and Mandy would be arguing and DJ would suddenly slide into the room, creeping up to Mandy and resting his head on her chest, right in the middle of some important talk. "I'm thirsty," he would say, in imitation baby-talk. Though he was five years old, he would play-act this little toddler voice. "Mama," he would say. "I is firsty." And DJ's eyes would rest on Gene for a moment, cold and full of calculating hatred.

Of course, Gene knows now that this was not the reality of it. He knows: he was a drunk, and DJ was just a sad, scared little kid, trying to deal with a rotten situation. Later, when he was in detox, these memories of his son made him actually shudder with shame, and it was not something he could bring himself to talk about even when he was deep into his 12 steps. How could he say how repulsed he'd been by the child, how actually frightened he was. Jesus Christ, DJ was a poor wretched five-year-old kid! But in Gene's memory there was something malevolent about him, resting his head pettishly on his mother's chest, talking in that sing-song, lisping voice, staring hard and unblinking at Gene with a little smile. Gene remembers catching DJ by the back of the neck. "If you're going to talk, talk normal," Gene had whispered through his teeth, and tightened his fingers on the child's neck. "You're not a baby. You're not fooling anybody." And DJ had actually bared his teeth, making a thin, hissing whine.

He wakes and he can't breathe. There is a swimming, suffocating sensation of being stared at, being watched by something that hates him, and he gasps, choking for air. A lady is bending over him, and for a moment he expects her to say: "You're very lucky, young man. You should be dead."

But it's Karen. "What are you doing?" she says. It's morning, and he struggles to orient himself—he's on the living room floor, and the television is still going.

"Jesus," he says, and coughs. "Oh, Jesus." He is sweating, his face feels hot, but he tries to calm himself in the face of Karen's horrified stare. "A bad dream," he says, trying to control his panting breaths. "Jesus," he says, and shakes his head, trying to smile reassuringly for her. "I got up last night and I couldn't sleep. I must have passed out while I was watching TV."

But Karen just gazes at him, her expression frightened and uncertain, as if something about him is transforming. "Gene," she says. "Are you all right?"

"Sure," he says, hoarsely, and a shudder passes over him involuntarily. "Of course." And then he realizes that he is naked. He sits up, covering his crotch self-consciously with his hands, and glances around. He doesn't see his underwear or his pajama bottoms anywhere nearby. He doesn't even see the afghan, which he'd had draped over him on the couch while he was watching the mummies on TV. He starts to stand up, awkwardly, and he notices that Frankie is standing there in the archway between the kitchen and the living room, watching him, his arms at his sides like a cowboy who is ready to draw his holstered guns.

"Mom?" Frankie says. "I'm thirsty."

He drives through his deliveries in a daze. The bees, he thinks. He remembers what Frankie had said a few mornings before, about bees inside his head, buzzing and bumping against the inside of his forehead like a windowpane they were tapping against. That's the feeling he has now. All the things that he doesn't quite remember are circling and alighting, vibrating their cellophane wings insistently. He sees himself striking Mandy across the face with the flat of his hand, knocking her off her chair; he sees his grip tightening around the back of DJ's thin, five-year-old neck, shaking him as he grimaced and wept; and he is aware that there are other things, perhaps even worse, if he thought about it hard enough. All the things that he'd prayed that Karen would never know about him.

He was very drunk on the day that he left them, so drunk that he can barely remember. It was hard to believe that he'd made it all the way to Des Moines on the interstate before he went off the road, tumbling end over end, into darkness. He was laughing, he thought, as the car crumpled around him, and he has to pull his van over to the side of the road, out of fear, as the tickling in his head intensifies. There is an image of Mandy, sitting on the couch as he stormed out, with DJ cradled in her arms, one of DJ's eyes swollen shut and puffy. There is an image of him in the kitchen, throwing glasses and beer bottles onto the floor, listening to them shatter.

And whether they are dead or not, he knows that they don't wish him well. They would not want him to be happy—in love with his wife and child. His normal, undeserved life.

‡ ‡

When he gets home that night, he feels exhausted. He doesn't want to think anymore, and for a moment, it seems that he will be allowed a small reprieve. Frankie is in the yard, playing contentedly. Karen is in the kitchen, making hamburgers and corn on the cob, and everything seems okay. But when he sits down to take off his boots, she gives him an angry look.

"Don't do that in the kitchen," she says, icily. "Please. I've asked you before."

He looks down at his feet: one shoe unlaced, half-off. "Oh," he says. "Sorry."

But when he retreats to the living room, to his recliner, she follows him. She leans against the doorframe, her arms folded, watching as he releases his tired feet from the boots and rubs his hand over the bottom of his socks. She frowns heavily.

"What?" he says, and tries on an uncertain smile.

She sighs. "We need to talk about last night," she says. "I need to know what's going on."

"Nothing," he says, but the stern way she examines him activates his anxieties all over again. "I couldn't sleep, so I went out to the living room to watch TV. That's all."

She stares at him. "Gene," she says after a moment. "People don't usually wake up naked on their living room floor and not know how they got there. That's just weird, don't you think?"

Oh, please, he thinks. He lifts his hands, shrugging—a posture of innocence and exasperation, though his insides are trembling. "I know," he says. "It was weird to me, too. I was having nightmares. I really don't know what happened."

She gazes at him for a long time, her eyes heavy. "I see," she says, and he can feel the emanation of her disappointment like waves of heat. "Gene," she says. "All I'm asking is for you to be honest with me. If you're having problems, if you're drinking again, or thinking about it. I want to help. We can work it out. But you have to be honest with me."

"I'm not drinking," Gene says, firmly. He holds her eyes earnestly. "I'm not thinking about it. I told you when we met, I'm through with it. Really." But he is aware again of an observant, unfriendly presence, hidden, moving along the edge of the room. "I don't understand," he says. "What is it? Why would you think I'd lie to you?"

She shifts, still trying to read something in his face, still, he can tell, doubting him. "Listen," she says, at last, and he can tell she is trying not to cry. "Some guy called you today. A drunk guy. And he said to tell you that he had a good time hanging out with you last night, and that he was looking forward to seeing you again soon." She frowns hard, staring at him as if this last bit of damning information will show him for the liar he is. A tear slips out of the corner of her eye and along the bridge of her nose. Gene feels his chest tighten.

"That's crazy," he says. He tries to sound outraged, but he is in fact suddenly very frightened. "Who was it?"

She shakes her head, sorrowfully. "I don't know," she says. "Something with a 'B.' He was slurring so bad I could hardly understand him. B.B. or B.J. or..."

Gene can feel the small hairs on his back prickling. "Was it DJ?" he says, softly.

And Karen shrugs, lifting a now teary face to him. "I don't know!" she says, hoarsely. "I don't know. Maybe." And Gene puts his palms across his face. He is aware of that strange, buzzing, tickling feeling behind his forehead.

"Who is DJ?" Karen says. "Gene, you have to tell me what's going on."

But he can't. He can't tell her, even now. Especially now, he thinks, when to admit that he'd been lying to her ever since they met would confirm all the fears and suspicions she'd been nursing for—what?—days? weeks?

"He's someone I used to know a long time ago," Gene tells her. "Not a good person. He's the kind of guy who might...call up, and get a kick out of upsetting you."

They sit at the kitchen table, silently watching as Frankie eats his hamburger and corn on the cob. Gene can't quite get his mind around it. DJ, he thinks, as he presses his finger against his hamburger bun, but doesn't pick it up. DJ. He would be fifteen by now. Could he, perhaps, have found them? Maybe stalking them? Watching the house? Gene tries to fathom how DJ might have been causing Frankie's screaming episodes. How he might have caused what happened last night—snuck up on Gene while he was sitting there watching TV and drugged him or something. It seems farfetched.

"Maybe it was just some random drunk," he says at last, to Karen. "Accidentally calling the house. He didn't ask for me by name, did he?"

"I don't remember," Karen says, softly. "Gene..."

And he can't stand the doubtfulness, the lack of trust in her expression. He strikes his fist hard against the table, and his plate clatters in a circling echo. "I *did not* go out with anybody last night!" he says. "I *did not* get drunk! You can either believe me, or you can..."

They are both staring at him. Frankie's eyes are wide, and he puts down the corn cob he was about to bite into, as if he doesn't like it anymore. Karen's mouth is pinched.

"Or I can what?" she says.

"Nothing," Gene breathes.

There isn't a fight, but a chill spreads through the house, a silence. She knows that he isn't telling her the truth. She knows that there's more to it. But what can he say? He stands at the sink, gently washing the dishes as Karen bathes Frankie and puts him to bed. He waits, listening to the small sounds of the house at night. Outside, in the yard, there is the swing set, and the willow tree—silver-gray and stark in the security light that hangs above the garage. He waits for a while longer, watching, half-expecting to see DJ emerge from behind the tree as he'd done in Gene's dream, creeping along, his bony hunched back, the skin pulled tight against the skull of his oversized head. There is that smothering, airless feeling of being watched, and Gene's hands are trembling as he rinses a plate under the tap.

When he goes upstairs at last, Karen is already in her nightgown, in bed, reading a book.

"Karen," he says, and she flips a page, deliberately.

"I don't want to talk to you until you're ready to tell me the truth," she says. She doesn't look at him. "You can sleep on the couch, if you don't mind."

"Just tell me," Gene says. "Did he leave a number? To call him back?"

"No," Karen says. She doesn't look at him. "He just said he'd see you soon."

⊹ ⊹

He thinks that he will stay up all night. He doesn't even wash up, or brush his teeth, or get into his bedtime clothes. He just sits there on the couch, in his uniform and stocking feet, watching television with the sound turned low, listening. Midnight. One A.M.

He goes upstairs to check on Frankie, but everything is okay. Frankie is asleep with his mouth open, the covers thrown off. Gene stands in the doorway, alert for movement, but everything seems to be in place. Frankie's turtle sits motionless on its rock, the books are lined up in neat rows, the toys put away. Frankie's face tightens and untightens as he dreams.

Two A.M. Back on the couch, Gene startles, half-asleep as an ambulance passes in the distance, and then there is only the sound of crickets and cicadas. Awake for a moment, he blinks heavily at a rerun of *Bewitched*, and flips through channels. Here is some jewelry for sale. Here is someone performing an autopsy.

In the dream, DJ is older. He looks to be nineteen or twenty, and he walks into a bar where Gene is hunched on a stool, sipping a glass of beer. Gene recognizes him right away—his posture, those thin shoulders, those large eyes. But now, DJ's arms are long and muscular, tattooed. There is a hooded, unpleasant look on his face as he ambles up to the bar, pressing in next to Gene. DJ orders a shot of Jim Beam—Gene's old favorite.

"I've been thinking about you a lot, ever since I died," DJ murmurs. He doesn't look at Gene as he says this, but Gene knows who he is talking to, and his hands are shaky as he takes a sip of beer.

"I've been looking for you for a long time," DJ says, softly, and the air is hot and thick. Gene puts a trembly cigarette to his mouth and breathes on it, choking on the taste. He wants to say, *I'm sorry. Forgive me.* But he can't breathe. DJ shows his small, crooked teeth, staring at Gene as he gulps for air.

"I know how to hurt you," DJ whispers.

Gene opens his eyes, and the room is full of smoke. He sits up, disoriented: For a second he is still in the bar with DJ before he realizes that he's in his own house.

There is a fire somewhere: he can hear it. People say that fire "crackles," but in fact it seems like the amplified sound of tiny creatures eating, little wet mandibles, thousands and thousands of them, and then a heavy, whispered *whoof,* as the fire finds another pocket of oxygen. He can hear this, even as he chokes blindly in the smoky air. The living room has a filmy haze over it, as if it is atomizing, fading away, and when he tries to stand up it disappears completely. There is a thick membrane of smoke above him, and he drops again to his hands and knees, gagging and coughing, a thin line of vomit trickling onto the rug in front of the still chattering television.

He has the presence of mind to keep low, crawling on his knees and elbows underneath the thick, billowing fumes. "Karen!" he calls. "Frankie!" but his voice is swallowed into the white noise of diligently licking flame. "Ach," he chokes, meaning to utter their names.

When he reaches the edge of the stairs he sees only flames and darkness above him. He puts his hands and knees on the bottom steps, but the heat pushes him back. He feels one of Frankie's action figures underneath his palm, the melting plastic adhering to his skin, and he shakes it away as another bright burst of flame reaches out of Frankie's bedroom for a moment. At the top of the stairs, through the curling fog he can see the figure of a child watching him grimly, hunched there, its face lit and flickering. Gene cries out, lunging into the heat, crawling his way up the stairs, to where the bedrooms are. He tries to call to them again, but instead, he vomits.

There is another burst that covers the image that he thinks is a child. He can feel his hair and eyebrows shrinking and sizzling against his skin as the upstairs breathes out a concussion of sparks. He is aware that there are hot, floating bits of substance in the air, glowing orange and then winking out, turning to ash. For some reason he thinks of bees. The air thick with angry buzzing, and that is all he can hear as he slips, turning end over end down the stairs, the humming and his own voice, a long vowel wheeling and echoing as the house spins into a blur.

And then he is lying on the grass. Red lights tick across his opened eyes in a steady, circling rhythm, and a woman, a paramedic, lifts her lips up from his. He draws in a long, desperate breath.

"Shhhhh," she says, softly, and passes her hand along his eyes. "Don't look," she says.

But he does. He sees, off to the side, the long black plastic sleeping bag, with a strand of Karen's blond hair hanging out from the top. He sees the blackened, shriveled body of a child, curled into a fetal position. They place the corpse into the spread, zippered plastic opening of the body bag, and he can see the mouth, frozen, calcified, into an oval. A scream.

Cleopatra Brimstone

Elizabeth Hand

er earliest memory was of wings. Luminous red and blue, yellow and green and orange; a black so rich it appeared liquid, edible. They moved above her and the sunlight made them glow as though they were themselves made of light, fragments of another, brighter world falling to earth about her crib. Her tiny hands stretched upwards to grasp them but could not: they were too elusive, too radiant, too much of the air.

Could they ever have been real?

For years she thought she must have dreamed them. But one afternoon when she was ten she went into the attic, searching for old clothes to wear to a Halloween party. In a corner beneath a cobwebbed window she found a box of her baby things. Yellow-stained bibs and tiny fuzzy jumpers blued from bleaching, a much-nibbled stuffed dog that she had no memory of whatsoever.

And at the very bottom of the carton, something else. Wings flattened and twisted out of shape, wires bent and strings frayed: a mobile. Six plastic butterflies, colors faded and their wings giving off a musty smell, no longer eidolons of Eden but crude representations of monarch, zebra swallowtail, red admiral, sulphur, an unnaturally elongated hairskipper, and *Agrias narcissus.* Except for the *narcissus,* all were common New World species that any child might see in a suburban garden. They hung limply from their wires, antennae long since broken off; when she touched one wing it felt cold and stiff as metal.

The afternoon had been overcast, tending to rain. But as she held the mobile to the window, a shaft of sun broke through the darkness to ignite the plastic wings, blood-red, ivy-green, the pure burning yellow of an August field. In that instant it was as though her entire being was burned away, skin hair lips fingers all ash; and nothing remained but the butterflies and her awareness of them, orange and black fluid filling her mouth, the edges of her eyes scored by wings.

As a girl she had always worn glasses. A mild childhood astigmatism worsened when she was thirteen: she started bumping into things, and found it increasingly difficult to concentrate on the entomological textbooks and journals that she read voraciously. Growing pains, her mother thought; but after two months, Jane's clumsiness and concomitant headaches became so severe that her mother admitted that this was perhaps something more serious, and took her to the family physician.

"Jane's fine," Dr. Gordon announced after peering into her ears and eyes. "She needs to see the ophthalmologist, that's all. Sometimes our eyes change when we hit puberty." He gave her mother the name of an eye doctor nearby.

Her mother was relieved, and so was Jane—she had overheard her parents talking the night before her appointment, and the words *CAT scan* and *brain tumor* figured in their hushed conversation. Actually, Jane had been more concerned about another odd physical manifestation, one which no one but herself seemed to have noticed. She had started menstruating several months earlier: nothing unusual in that. Everything she had read about it mentioned the usual things—mood swings, growth spurts, acne, pubic hair.

But nothing was said about eyebrows. Jane first noticed something strange about hers when she got her period for the second time. She had retreated to the bathtub, where she spent a good half-hour reading an article in *Nature* about Oriental Ladybug swarms. When she finished the article, she got out of the tub, dressed, and brushed her teeth, then spent a minute frowning at the mirror.

Something was different about her face. She turned sideways, squinting. Had her chin broken out? No; but something had changed. Her hair color? Her teeth? She leaned over the sink until she was almost nose-to-nose with her reflection.

That was when she saw that her eyebrows had undergone a growth spurt of their own. At the inner edge of each eyebrow, above the bridge of her nose, three hairs had grown remarkably long. They furled back towards her temple, entwined in a sort of loose braid. She had not noticed them sooner because she seldom looked in a mirror, and also because the odd hairs did not arch above the eyebrows, but instead blended in with them, the way a bittersweet vine twines around a branch. Still, they seemed bizarre enough that she wanted no one, not even her parents, to notice. She found her mother's eyebrow tweezers, neatly plucked the six hairs, and flushed them down the toilet. They did not grow back.

At the optometrist's, Jane opted for heavy tortoiseshell frames rather than contacts. The optometrist, and her mother, thought she was crazy, but it was a very deliberate choice. Jane was not one of those homely B movie adolescent girls, driven to Science as a last resort. She had always been a tomboy, skinny as a rail, with long slanted violet-blue eyes; a small rosy mouth; long, straight black hair that ran like oil between her fingers; skin so pale it had the periwinkle shimmer of skim milk.

When she hit puberty, all of these conspired to beauty. And Jane hated it. Hated the attention, hated being looked at, hated that other girls hated her. She was quiet, not shy, but impatient to focus on her schoolwork, and this was mistaken for arrogance by her peers. All through high school she had few friends. She learned early the perils of befriending boys, even earnest boys who professed an interest in genetic mutations and intricate computer simulations of hive activity. Jane could trust them not to touch her, but she couldn't trust them not to fall in love. As a result of having none of the usual distractions of high school—sex, social life, mindless employment—she received an Intel/Westinghouse Science Scholarship for a computer-generated schematic of possible mutations in a small population of viceroy butterflies exposed to genetically engineered crops. She graduated in her junior year, took her scholarship money, and ran.

She had been accepted at Stanford and MIT, but chose to attend a small, highly prestigious women's college in a big city several hundred miles away. Her parents were apprehensive about her being on her own at the tender age of seventeen, but the college, with its elegant, cloisterlike buildings and lushly wooded grounds, put them at ease. That and the dean's assurances that the neighborhood was completely safe, as long as students were sensible about not walking alone at night. Thus mollified, and at Jane's urging—she was desperate to move away from home—her father signed a very large check for the first semester's tuition. That September she started school.

She studied entomology, spending her first year examining the genitalia of male and female Scarce Wormwood Shark Moths, a species found on the Siberian steppes. Her hours in the zoology lab were rapturous, hunched over a microscope with a pair of tweezers so minute they were themselves like some delicate portion of her specimen's physiognomy. She would remove the butterflies' genitalia, tiny and geometrically precise as diatoms, and dip them first into glycerine, which acted as a preservative, and next into a mixture of water and alcohol. Then she observed them under the microscope. Her glasses interfered with this work—they bumped into the microscope's viewing lens—and so she switched to wearing contact lenses. In retrospect, she thought that this was probably a mistake.

At Argus College she still had no close friends, but neither was she the solitary creature she had been at home. She respected her fellow students, and grew to appreciate the company of women. She could go for days at a time seeing no men besides her professors or the commuters driving past the school's wrought-iron gates.

And she was not the school's only beauty. Argus College specialized in young women like Jane: elegant, diffident girls who studied the burial customs of Mongol women or the mating habits of rare antipodean birds; girls who composed concertos for violin and gamelan orchestra, or wrote computer programs that charted the progress of potentially dangerous celestial objects through the Oort Cloud. Within this educational greenhouse, Jane was not so much orchid as sturdy milkweed blossom. She thrived.

Her first three years at Argus passed in a bright-winged blur with her butterflies. Summers were given to museum internships, where she spent months cleaning and mounting specimens in solitary delight. In her senior year Jane received permission to design her own thesis project, involving her beloved Shark Moths. She was given a corner in a dusty anteroom off the Zoology Lab, and there she set up her microscope and laptop. There was no window in her corner, indeed there was no window in the anteroom at all, though the adjoining lab was pleasantly old-fashioned, with high arched windows set between Victorian cabinetry displaying lepidoptera, neon-carapaced beetles, unusual tree fungi, and (she found these slightly tragic) numerous exotic finches, their brilliant plumage dimmed to dusty hues. Since she often worked late into the night, she requested and received her own set of keys. Most evenings she could be found beneath the glare of the small halogen lamp, entering data into her computer, scanning images of genetic mutations involving female Shark Moths exposed to dioxin, corresponding with other researchers in Melbourne and Kyoto, Siberia and London.

The rape occurred around ten o'clock one Friday night in early March. She had locked the door to her office, leaving her laptop behind, and started to walk to the subway station a few blocks away.

It was a cold clear night, the yellow glow of the crime lights giving dead grass and leafless trees an eerie autumn shimmer. She hurried across the campus, seeing no one, then hesitated at Seventh Street. It was a longer walk, but safer, if she went down Seventh Street and then over to Michigan Avenue. The shortcut was much quicker, but Argus authorities and the local police discouraged students from taking it after dark. Jane stood for a moment, looking across the road to where the desolate park lay; then, staring resolutely straight ahead and walking briskly, she crossed Seventh and took the shortcut.

A crumbling sidewalk passed through a weedy expanse of vacant lot, strewn with broken bottles and the spindly forms of half a dozen dusty-limbed oak trees. Where the grass ended, a narrow road skirted a block of abandoned row houses, intermittently lit by crime lights. Most of the lights had been vandalized, and one had been knocked down in a car accident—the car's fender was still there, twisted around the lamppost. Jane picked her way carefully among shards of shattered glass, reached the sidewalk in front of the boarded-up houses, and began to walk more quickly, towards the brightly lit Michigan Avenue intersection where the subway waited.

She never saw him. He was *there,* she knew that; knew he had a face, and clothing; but afterwards she could recall none of it. Not the feel of him, not his smell; only the knife he held—awkwardly, she realized later, she probably could have wrested it from him—and the few words he spoke to her. He said nothing at first, just grabbed her and pulled her into an alley between the row houses, his fingers covering her mouth, the heel of his hand pressing against her windpipe so that she gagged. He pushed her onto the dead leaves and wads of matted windblown newspaper, yanked her pants down, ripped open her jacket, and then tore her shirt open. She heard one of the buttons strike brick and roll away. She thought desperately of what she had read once, in a Rape Awareness brochure: not to struggle, not to fight, not to do anything that might cause her attacker to kill her.

Jane did not fight. Instead, she divided into three parts. One part knelt nearby and prayed the way she had done as a child, not intently but automatically, trying to get through the strings of words as quickly as possible. The second part submitted blindly and silently to the man in the alley. And the third hovered above the other two, her hands wafting slowly up and down to keep her aloft as she watched.

"Try to get away," the man whispered. She could not see him or feel him though his hands were there. "Try to get away."

She remembered that she ought not to struggle, but from the noise he made and the way he tugged at her, she realized that was what aroused him. She did not want to anger him; she made a small sound deep in her throat and tried to push him from her chest. Almost immediately he groaned, and seconds later rolled off her. Only his hand lingered for a moment upon her cheek. Then he stumbled to his feet—she could hear him fumbling with his zipper—and fled.

The praying girl and the girl in the air also disappeared then. Only Jane was left, yanking her ruined clothes around her as she lurched from the alley and began to run, screaming and staggering back and forth across the road, towards the subway.

The police came, an ambulance. She was taken first to the police station and then to the City General Hospital, a hellish place, starkly lit, with endless underground corridors that led into darkened rooms where solitary figures lay on narrow beds like gurneys. Her pubic hair was combed and stray hairs placed into sterile envelopes; semen samples were taken, and she was advised to be tested for HIV and other diseases. She spent the entire night in the hospital, waiting and undergoing various examinations. She refused to give the police or hospital staff her parents' phone number, or anyone else's. Just before dawn they finally released her, with an envelope full of brochures from the local rape crisis center, New Hope for Women, Planned Parenthood, and a business card from the police detective who was overseeing her case. The detective drove her to her apartment in his squad car; when he stopped in front of her building, she was suddenly terrified that he would know where she lived, that he would come back, that he had been her assailant.

But, of course, he had not been. He walked her to the door and waited for her to go inside. "Call your parents," he said right before he left.

"I will."

She pulled aside the bamboo window shade, watching until the squad car pulled away. Then she threw out the brochures she'd received, flung off her clothes, and stuffed them into the trash. She showered and changed, packed a bag full of clothes and another of books. Then she called a cab. When it arrived, she directed it to the Argus campus, where she retrieved her laptop and her research on Shark Moths, then had the cab bring her to Union Station.

She bought a train ticket home. Only after she arrived and told her parents what had happened did she finally start to cry. Even then, she could not remember what the man had looked like.

She lived at home for three months. Her parents insisted that she get psychiatric counseling and join a therapy group for rape survivors. She did so, reluctantly, but stopped attending after three weeks. The rape was something that had happened to her, but it was over.

"It was fifteen minutes out of my life," she said once at group. "That's all. It's not the rest of my life."

This didn't go over very well. Other women thought she was in denial; the therapist thought Jane would suffer later if she did not confront her fears now.

"But I'm not afraid," said Jane.

"Why not?" demanded a woman whose eyebrows had fallen out.

Because lightning doesn't strike twice, Jane thought grimly, but she said nothing. That was the last time she attended group.

That night her father had a phone call. He took the phone and sat at the dining table, listening; after a moment stood and walked into his study, giving a quick backward glance at his daughter before closing the door behind him. Jane felt as though her chest had suddenly frozen, but after some minutes she heard her father's laugh: he was not, after all, talking to the police detective. When after half an hour he returned, he gave Jane another quick look, more thoughtful this time.

"That was Andrew." Andrew was a doctor friend of his, an Englishman. "He and Fred are going to Provence for three months. They were wondering if you might want to housesit for them."

"In *London*?" Jane's mother shook her head. "I don't think—"

"I said we'd think about it."

"*I'll* think about it," Jane corrected him. She stared at both her parents, absently ran a finger along one eyebrow. "Just let me think about it."

And she went to bed.

She went to London. She already had a passport, from visiting Andrew with her parents when she was in high school. Before she left, there were countless arguments with her mother and father, and phone calls back and forth to Andrew. He assured them that the flat was secure, there was a very nice reliable older woman who lived upstairs, that it would be a good idea for Jane to get out on her own again.

"So you don't get gun-shy," he said to her one night on the phone. He was a doctor, after all: a homeopath not an allopath, which Jane found reassuring. "It's important for you to get on with your life. You won't be able to get a real job here as a visitor, but I'll see what I can do."

It was on the plane to Heathrow that she made a discovery. She had splashed water onto her face, and was beginning to comb her hair when she blinked and stared into the mirror.

Above her eyebrows, the long hairs had grown back. They followed the contours of her brow, sweeping back towards her temples; still entwined, still difficult to make out unless she drew her face close to her reflection and tilted her head just so. Tentatively she touched one braided strand. It was stiff yet oddly pliant; but as she ran her finger along its length a sudden *surge* flowed through her. Not an electrical shock: more like the thrill of pain when a dentist's drill touches a nerve, or an elbow rams against a stone. She gasped; but immediately the pain was gone. Instead there was a thrumming behind her forehead, a spreading warmth that trickled into her throat like sweet syrup. She opened her mouth, her gasp turning into an uncontrollable yawn, the yawn into a spike of such profound physical ecstasy that she grabbed the edge of the sink and thrust forward, striking her head against the mirror. She was dimly aware of someone knocking at the lavatory door as she clutched the sink and, shuddering, climaxed.

"Hello?" someone called softly. "Hello, is this occupied?"

"Right out," Jane gasped. She caught her breath, still trembling; ran a hand across her face, her fingers halting before they could touch the hairs above her eyebrows. There was the faintest tingling, a temblor of sensation that faded as she grabbed her cosmetic bag, pulled the door open, and stumbled back into the cabin.

Andrew and Fred lived in an old Georgian row house just north of Camden Town, overlooking the Regent's Canal. Their flat occupied the first floor and basement; there was a hexagonal solarium out back, with glass walls and heated stone floor, and beyond that a stepped terrace leading down to the canal. The bedroom had an old wooden four-poster piled high with duvets and down pillows, and French doors that also opened onto the terrace. Andrew showed her how to operate the elaborate sliding security doors that unfolded from the walls, and gave her the keys to the barred window guards.

"You're completely safe here," he said, smiling. "Tomorrow we'll introduce you to Kendra upstairs, and show you how to get around. Camden Market's just up that way, and *that* way—"

He stepped out onto the terrace, pointing to where the canal coiled and disappeared beneath an arched stone bridge, "—that way's the Regent's Park Zoo. I've given you a membership—"

"Oh! Thank you!" Jane looked around, delighted. "This is *wonderful*."

"It is." Andrew put an arm around her and drew her close. "You're going to have a wonderful time, Jane. I thought you'd like the zoo—there's a new exhibit there, 'The World Within' or words to that effect—it's about insects. I thought perhaps you might want to volunteer there—they have an active docent program, and you're so knowledgeable about that sort of thing."

"Sure. It sounds great—really great." She grinned and smoothed her hair back from her face, the wind sending up the rank scent of stagnant water from the canal, the sweetly poisonous smell of hawthorn blossom. As she stood gazing down past the potted geraniums and Fred's rosemary trees, the hairs upon her brow trembled, and she laughed out loud, giddily, with anticipation.

Fred and Andrew left two days later. It was enough time for Jane to get over her jet lag and begin to get barely acclimated to the city, and to its smell. London had an acrid scent: damp ashes, the softer underlying fetor of rot that oozed from ancient bricks and stone buildings, the thick vegetative smell of the canal, sharpened with urine and spilled beer. So many thousands of people descended on Camden Town on the weekend that the tube station was restricted to incoming passengers, and the canal path became almost impassable. Even late on a weeknight she could hear voices from the other side of the canal, harsh London voices echoing beneath the bridges or shouting to be heard above the din of the Northern Line trains passing overhead.

Those first days Jane did not venture far from the flat. She unpacked her clothes, which did not take much time, and then unpacked her collecting box, which did. The sturdy wooden case had come through the overseas flight and customs seemingly unscathed, but Jane found herself holding her breath as she undid the metal hinges, afraid of what she'd find inside.

"Oh!" she exclaimed. Relief, not chagrin: nothing had been damaged. The small glass vials of ethyl alcohol and gel shellac were intact, as were the pillboxes where she kept the tiny #2 pins she used for mounting. Fighting her own eagerness, she carefully removed packets of stiff archival paper, a block of Styrofoam covered with pinholes; two bottles of clear Maybelline nail polish and a small container of Elmer's glue; more pillboxes, empty, and empty gelatine capsules for very small specimens; and last of all a small glass-fronted display box, framed in mahogany and holding her most precious specimen: a hybrid *Celerio harmuthi Kordesch*, the male crossbreed of a Spurge and an Elephant Hawkmoth. As long as the first joint of her thumb, it had the hawkmoth's typically streamlined wings but exquisitely delicate coloring, fuchsia bands shading to a soft rich brown, its thorax thick and seemingly feathered. Only a handful of these hybrid moths had ever existed, bred by the Prague entomologist Jan Pokorny in 1961; a few years afterward, both the Spurge Hawkmoth and the Elephant Hawkmoth had become extinct.

Jane had found this one for sale on the Internet three months ago. It was a former museum specimen and cost a fortune; she had a few bad nights, worrying whether it had actually been a legal purchase. Now she held the display box in her cupped palms and gazed at it raptly. Behind her eyes she felt a prickle, like sleep or unshed tears; then a slow thrumming warmth crept from her brows, spreading to her temples, down her neck and through her breasts, spreading like a stain. She swallowed, leaned back against the sofa and let the display box rest back within the larger case; slid first one hand then the other beneath her sweater and began to stroke her nipples. When some time later she came, it was with stabbing force and a thunderous sensation above her eyes, as though she had struck her forehead against the floor.

She had not: gasping, she pushed the hair from her face, zipped her jeans and reflexively leaned forward, to make certain the hawkmoth in its glass box was safe.

Over the following days she made a few brief forays to the newsagent and greengrocer, trying to eke out the supplies Fred and Andrew had left in the kitchen. She sat in the solarium, her bare feet warm against the heated stone floor, and drank chamomile tea or claret, staring down to where the ceaseless stream of people passed along the canal path, and watching the narrow boats as they plied their way slowly between Camden Lock and Little Venice, two miles to the west in Paddington. By the following Wednesday she felt brave enough, and bored enough, to leave her refuge and visit the zoo.

It was a short walk along the canal, dodging bicyclists who jingled their bells impatiently when she forgot to stay on the proper side of the path. She passed beneath several arching bridges, their undersides pleated with slime and moss. Drunks sprawled against the stones and stared at her blearily or challengingly by turns; well-dressed couples walked dogs, and there were excited knots of children, tugging their parents on to the zoo.

Fred had walked here with Jane, to show her the way. But it all looked unfamiliar now. She kept a few strides behind a family, her head down, trying not to look as though she was following them, and felt a pulse of relief when they reached a twisting stair with an arrowed sign at its top.

REGENT'S PARK ZOO

There was an old old church across the street, its yellow stone walls overgrown with ivy; and down and around the corner a long stretch of hedges with high iron walls fronting them, and at last a huge set of gates, crammed with children and vendors selling balloons and banners and London guidebooks. Jane lifted her head and walked quickly past the family that had led her here, showed her membership card at the entrance, and went inside.

She wasted no time on the seals or tigers or monkeys, but went straight to the newly renovated structure where a multicolored banner flapped in the late-morning breeze.

AN ALTERNATE UNIVERSE:
SECRETS OF THE INSECT WORLD

Inside, crowds of schoolchildren and harassed-looking adults formed a ragged queue that trailed through a brightly lit corridor, its walls covered with huge glossy color photos and computer-enhanced images of hissing cockroaches, hellgrammites, morpho butterflies, death-watch beetles, polyphemous moths. Jane dutifully joined the queue, but when the corridor opened into a vast sun-lit atrium she strode off on her own, leaving the children and teachers to gape at monarchs in butterfly cages and an interactive display of honeybees dancing. Instead she found a relatively quiet display at the far end of the exhibition space, a floor-to-ceiling cylinder of transparent net, perhaps six feet in diameter. Inside, buckthorn bushes and blooming hawthorn vied for sunlight with a slender beech sapling, and dozens of butterflies flitted upwards through the new yellow leaves, or sat with wings outstretched upon the beech tree. They were a type of Pieridae, the butterflies known as whites; though these were not white at all. The females had creamy yellow-green wings, very pale, their wingspans perhaps an inch and a half. The males were the same size; when they were at rest their flattened wings were a dull, rather sulphurous color. But when the males lit into the air their wings revealed vivid, spectral yellow undersides. Jane caught her breath in delight, her neck prickling with that same atavistic joy she'd felt as a child in the attic.

"Wow," she breathed, and pressed up against the netting. It felt like wings against her face, soft, webbed; but as she stared at the insects inside, her brow began to ache as with migraine. She shoved her glasses onto her nose, closed her eyes, and drew a long breath; then took a step away from the cage. After a minute she opened her eyes. The headache had diminished to a dull throb; when she hesitantly touched one eyebrow, she could feel the entwined hairs there, stiff as wire. They were vibrating, but at her touch the vibrations like the headache dulled. She stared at the floor, the tiles sticky with contraband juice and gum; then looked up once again at the cage. There was a display sign off to one side; she walked over to it, slowly, and read.

CLEOPATRA BRIMSTONE

Gonepteryx rhamni cleopatra
This popular and subtly colored species has a range which extends throughout the Northern Hemisphere, with the exception of Arctic regions and several remote islands. In Europe, the brimstone is a harbinger of spring, often emerging from its winter hibernation under dead leaves to revel in the countryside while there is still snow upon the ground.

"I must ask you please not to touch the cages."

Jane turned to see a man, perhaps fifty, standing a few feet away. A net was jammed under his arm; in his hand he held a clear plastic jar with several butterflies at the bottom, apparently dead.

"Oh. Sorry," said Jane. The man edged past her. He set his jar on the floor, opened a small door at the base of the cylindrical cage, and deftly angled the net inside. Butterflies lifted in a yellow-green blur from leaves and branches; the man swept the net carefully across the bottom of the cage, then withdrew it. Three dead butterflies, like scraps of colored paper, drifted from the net into the open jar.

"Housecleaning," he said, and once more thrust his arm into the cage. He was slender and wiry, not much taller than she was, his face hawkish and burnt brown from the sun, his thick straight hair iron-streaked and pulled back into a long braid. He wore black jeans and a dark-blue hooded jersey, with an ID badge clipped to the collar.

"You work here," said Jane. The man glanced at her, his arm still in the cage; she could see him sizing her up. After a moment he glanced away again. A few minutes later he emptied the net for the last time, closed the cage and the jar, and stepped over to a waste bin, pulling bits of dead leaves from the net and dropping them into the container.

"I'm one of the curatorial staff. You American?"

Jane nodded. "Yeah. Actually, I—I wanted to see about volunteering here."

"Lifewatch desk at the main entrance." The man cocked his head towards the door. "They can get you signed up and registered, see what's available."

"No—I mean, I want to volunteer here. With the insects—"

"Butterfly collector, are you?" The man smiled, his tone mocking. He had hazel eyes, deep-set; his thin mouth made the smile seem perhaps more cruel than intended. "We get a lot of those."

Jane flushed. "No. I am not a *collector*," she said coldly, adjusting her glasses. "I'm doing a thesis on dioxin genital mutation in *Cucullia artemisia*." She didn't add that it was an undergraduate thesis. "I've been doing independent research for seven years now." She hesitated, thinking of her Intel scholarship, and added, "I've received several grants for my work."

The man regarded her appraisingly. "Are you studying here, then?"

"Yes," she lied again. "At Oxford. I'm on sabbatical right now. But I live near here, and so I thought I might—"

She shrugged, opening her hands, looked over at him, and smiled tentatively. "Make myself useful?"

The man waited a moment, nodded. "Well. Do you have a few minutes now? I've got to do something with these, but if you want you can come with me and wait, and then we can see what we can do. Maybe circumvent some paperwork."

He turned and started across the room. He had a graceful, bouncing gait, like a gymnast or circus acrobat: impatient with the ground beneath him. "Shouldn't take long," he called over his shoulder as Jane hurried to catch up.

She followed him through a door marked AUTHORIZED PERSONS ONLY,

into the exhibit laboratory, a reassuringly familiar place with its display
cases and smells of shellac and camphor, acetone and ethyl alcohol. There
were more cages here, but smaller ones, sheltering live specimens—pupat-
ing butterflies and moths, stick insects, leaf insects, dung beetles. The man
dropped his net onto a desk, took the jar to a long table against one wall,
blindingly lit by long fluorescent tubes. There were scores of bottles here,
some empty, others filled with paper and tiny inert figures.

"Have a seat," said the man, gesturing at two folding chairs. He settled
into one, grabbed an empty jar and a roll of absorbent paper. "I'm David
Bierce. So where're you staying? Camden Town?"

"Jane Kendall. Yes—"

"The High Street?"

Jane sat in the other chair, pulling it a few inches away from him. The
questions made her uneasy, but she only nodded, lying again, and said,
"Closer, actually. Off Gloucester Road. With friends."

"Mm." Bierce tore off a piece of absorbent paper, leaned across to a
stainless steel sink, and dampened the paper. Then he dropped it into the
empty jar. He paused, turned to her, and gestured at the table, smiling. "Care
to join in?"

Jane shrugged. "Sure—"

She pulled her chair closer, found another empty jar, and did as Bierce
had, dampening a piece of paper towel and dropping it inside. Then she
took the jar containing the dead brimstones and carefully shook one onto
the counter. It was a female, its coloring more muted than the males'; she
scooped it up very gently, careful not to disturb the scales like dull green
glitter upon its wings, dropped it into the jar, and replaced the top.

"Very nice." Bierce nodded, raising his eyebrows. "You seem to know
what you're doing. Work with other insects? Soft-bodied ones?"

"Sometimes. Mostly moths, though. And butterflies."

"Right." He inclined his head to a recessed shelf. "How would you label that, then? Go ahead."

On the shelf she found a notepad and a case of Rapidograph pens. She
began to write, conscious of Bierce staring at her. "We usually just put all
this into the computer, of course, and print it out," he said. "I just want to
see the benefits of an American education in the sciences."

Jane fought the urge to look at him. Instead she wrote out the information, making her printing as tiny as possible.

Gonepteryx rhamni cleopatra
UNITED KINGDOM: LONDON
Regent's Park Zoo
Lat/Long unknown
21.IV.2001
D. Bierce
Net/caged specimen

She handed it to Bierce. "I don't know the proper coordinates for London."

Bierce scrutinized the paper. "It's actually the Royal Zoological Park," he said. He looked at her, then smiled. "But you'll do."

"Great!" She grinned, the first time she'd really felt happy since arriving here. "When do you want me to start?"

"How about Monday?"

Jane hesitated: this was only Friday. "I could come in tomorrow—"

"I don't work on the weekend, and you'll need to be trained. Also they have to process the paperwork. Right—"

He stood and went to a desk, pulling open drawers until he found a clipboard holding sheaves of triplicate forms. "Here. Fill all this out, leave it with me, and I'll pass it on to Carolyn—she's the head volunteer coordinator. They usually want to interview you, but I'll tell them we've done all that already."

"What time should I come in Monday?"

"Come at nine. Everything opens at ten, that way you'll avoid the crowds. Use the staff entrance, someone there will have an ID waiting for you to pick up when you sign in—"

She nodded and began filling out the forms.

"All right then." David Bierce leaned against the desk and again fixed her with that sly, almost taunting gaze. "Know how to find your way home?"

Jane lifted her chin defiantly. "Yes."

"Enjoying London? Going to go out tonight and do Camden Town with all the yobs?"

"Maybe. I haven't been out much yet."

"Mm. Beautiful American girl, they'll eat you alive. Just kidding." He straightened, started across the room towards the door. "I'll see you Monday then."

He held the door for her. "You really should check out the clubs. You're too young not to see the city by night." He smiled, the fluorescent light slanting sideways into his hazel eyes and making them suddenly glow icy blue. "Bye then."

"Bye," said Jane, and hurried quickly from the lab towards home.

That night, for the first time, she went out. She told herself she would have gone anyway, no matter what Bierce had said. She had no idea where the clubs were; Andrew had pointed out the Electric Ballroom to her, right across from the tube station, but he'd also warned her that was where the tourists flocked on weekends.

"They do a disco thing on Saturday nights—Saturday Night Fever, everyone gets all done up in vintage clothes. Quite a fashion show," he'd said, smiling and shaking his head.

Jane had no interest in that. She ate a quick supper, vindaloo from the take-away down the street from the flat, then dressed. She hadn't brought a huge number of clothes—at home she'd never bothered much with clothes at all, making do with thrift-shop finds and whatever her mother gave her for Christmas. But now she found herself sitting on the edge of the four-poster, staring with pursed lips at the sparse contents of two bureau drawers. Finally she pulled out a pair of black corduroy jeans and a black turtleneck and pulled on her sneakers. She removed her glasses, for the first time in weeks inserted her contact lenses. Then she shrugged into her old navy peacoat and left.

It was after ten o'clock. On the canal path, throngs of people stood, drinking from pints of canned lager. She made her way through them, ignoring catcalls and whispered invitations, stepping to avoid where kids lay making out against the brick wall that ran alongside the path, or pissing in the bushes. The bridge over the canal at Camden Lock was clogged with several dozen kids in mohawks or varicolored hair, shouting at each other above the din of a boom box and swigging from bottles of Spanish champagne.

A boy with a champagne bottle leered, lunging at her.

"'Ere, sweetheart, 'ep youseff—"

Jane ducked, and he careened against the ledge, his arm striking brick and the bottle shattering in a starburst of black and gold.

"Fucking cunt!" he shrieked after her. "Fucking bloody cunt!"

People glanced at her, but Jane kept her head down, making a quick turn into the vast cobbled courtyard of Camden Market. The place had a desolate air: the vendors would not arrive until early next morning, and now only stray cats and bits of windblown trash moved in the shadows. In the surrounding buildings people spilled out onto balconies, drinking and calling back and forth, their voices hollow and their long shadows twisting across the ill-lit central courtyard. Jane hurried to the far end, but there found only brick walls, closed-up shop doors, and a young woman huddled within the folds of a filthy sleeping bag.

"*Couldya—couldya—*" the woman murmured.

Jane turned and followed the wall until she found a door leading into a short passage. She entered it, hoping she was going in the direction of Camden High Street. She felt like Alice trying to find her way through the garden in Wonderland: arched doorways led not into the street but head-shops and blindingly lit piercing parlors, open for business; other doors opened onto enclosed courtyards, dark, smelling of piss and marijuana. Finally from the corner of her eye she glimpsed what looked like the end of the passage, headlights piercing through the gloom like landing lights. Doggedly she made her way towards them.

"Ay watchowt watchowt," someone yelled as she emerged from the passage onto the sidewalk, and ran the last few steps to the curb.

She was on the High Street—rather, in that block or two of curving no-man's-land where it turned into Chalk Farm Road. The sidewalks were still crowded, but everyone was heading towards Camden Lock and not away from it. Jane waited for the light to change and raced across the street, to where a cobblestoned alley snaked off between a shop selling leather underwear and another advertising "Fine French Country Furniture."

For several minutes she stood there. She watched the crowds heading towards Camden Town, the steady stream of minicabs and taxis and buses heading up Chalk Farm Road towards Hampstead. Overhead, dull orange clouds moved across a night sky the color of charred wood; there was the steady low thunder of jets circling after takeoff at Heathrow. At last she tugged her collar up around her neck, letting her hair fall in loose waves down her back, shoved her hands into her coat pockets, and turned to walk purposefully down the alley.

Before her the cobblestone path turned sharply to the right. She couldn't see what was beyond, but she could hear voices: a girl laughing, a man's sibilant retort. A moment later the alley spilled out onto a cul-de-sac. A couple stood a few yards away, before a doorway with a small copper awning above it. The young woman glanced sideways at Jane, quickly looked away again. A silhouette filled the doorway; the young man pulled out a wallet. His hand disappeared within the silhouette, reemerged, and the couple walked inside. Jane waited until the shadowy figure withdrew. She looked over her shoulder, then approached the building.

There was a heavy metal door, black, with graffiti scratched into it and pale blurred spots where painted graffiti had been effaced. The door was set back several feet into a brick recess; there was a grilled metal slot at the top that could be slid back, so that one could peer out into the courtyard. To the right of the door, on the brick wall within the recess, was a small brass plaque with a single word on it.

HIVE

There was no doorbell or any other way to signal that you wanted to enter. Jane stood, wondering what was inside; feeling a small tingling unease that was less fear than the knowledge that even if she were to confront the figure who'd let that other couple inside, she herself would certainly be turned away.

With a *skreek* of metal on stone the door suddenly shot open. Jane looked up, into the sharp, raggedly handsome face of a tall, still youngish man with very short blond hair, a line of gleaming gold beads like drops of sweat piercing the edge of his left jaw.

"Good evening," he said, glancing past her to the alley. He wore a black sleeveless T-shirt with a small golden bee embroidered upon the breast. His bare arms were muscular, striated with long sweeping scars: black, red, white. "Are you waiting for Hannah?"

"No." Quickly Jane pulled out a handful of five-pound notes. "Just me tonight."

"That'll be twenty then." The man held his hand out, still gazing at the alley; when Jane slipped the notes to him he looked down and flashed her a vulpine smile. "Enjoy yourself." She darted past him into the building.

Abruptly it was as though some darker night had fallen. Thunderously so, since the enfolding blackness was slashed with music so loud it was itself like light: Jane hesitated, closing her eyes, and white flashes streaked across her eyelids like sleet, pulsing in time to the music. She opened her eyes, giving them a chance to adjust to the darkness, and tried to get a sense of where she was. A few feet away a blurry grayish lozenge sharpened into the window of a coat-check room. Jane walked past it, towards the source of the music. Immediately the floor slanted steeply beneath her feet. She steadied herself with one hand against the wall, following the incline until it opened onto a cavernous dance floor.

She gazed inside, disappointed. It looked like any other club, crowded, strobe-lit, turquoise smoke and silver glitter coiling between hundreds of whirling bodies clad in candy pink, sky blue, neon red, rainslicker yellow. Baby colors, Jane thought. There was a boy who was almost naked, except for shorts, a transparent water bottle strapped to his chest and long tubes snaking into his mouth. Another boy had hair the color of lime Jell-O, his face corrugated with glitter and sweat; he swayed near the edge of the dance floor, turned to stare at Jane, and then beamed, beckoning her to join him.

Jane gave him a quick smile, shaking her head; when the boy opened his arms to her in mock pleading she shouted, "No!"

But she continued to smile, though she felt as though her head would crack like an egg from the throbbing music. Shoving her hands into her pockets she skirted the dance floor, pushed her way to the bar, and bought a drink, something pink with no ice in a plastic cup. It smelled like Gatorade and lighter fluid. She gulped it down, then carried the cup held before her like a torch as she continued on her circuit of the room. There was nothing else of interest; just long queues for the lavatories and another bar, numerous doors and stairwells where kids clustered, drinking and smoking. Now and then beeps and whistles like birdsong or insect cries came through the stuttering electronic din, whoops and trilling laughter from the dancers. But mostly they moved in near-silence, eyes rolled ceiling-ward, bodies exploding into Catherine wheels of flesh and plastic and nylon, but all without a word.

It gave Jane a headache—a *real* headache, the back of her skull bruised, tender to the touch. She dropped her plastic cup and started looking for a way out. She could see past the dance floor to where she had entered, but it seemed as though another hundred people had arrived in the few minutes since then: kids were standing six-deep at both bars, and the action on the floor had spread, amoeba-like, towards the corridors angling back up towards the street.

"Sorry—"

A fat woman in an Arsenal jersey jostled her as she hurried by, leaving a smear of oily sweat on Jane's wrist. Jane grimaced and wiped her hand on the bottom of her coat. She gave one last look at the dance floor, but nothing had changed within the intricate lattice of dancers and smoke, braids of glow-lights and spotlit faces surging up and down, up and down, while more dancers fought their way to the center.

"Shit." She turned and strode off, heading to where the huge room curved off into relative emptiness. Here, scores of tables were scattered, some overturned, others stacked against the wall. A few people sat, talking; a girl lay curled on the floor, her head pillowed on a Barbie knapsack. Jane crossed to the wall, and found first a door that led to a bare brick wall, then a second door that held a broom closet. The next was dark red, metal, official-looking: the kind of door that Jane associated with school fire drills.

A fire door. It would lead outside, or into a hall that would lead there. Without hesitating she pushed it open and entered. A short corridor lit by EXIT signs stretched ahead of her, with another door at the end. She hurried towards it, already reaching reflexively for the keys to the flat, pushed the door-bar, and stepped inside.

For an instant she thought she had somehow stumbled into a hospital emergency room. There was the glitter of halogen light on steel, distorted reflections thrown back at her from curved glass surfaces; the abrasive odor of isopropyl alcohol and the fainter tinny scent of blood, like metal in the mouth.

And bodies: everywhere, bodies, splayed on gurneys or suspended from gleaming metal hooks, laced with black electrical cord and pinned upright onto smooth rubber mats. She stared openmouthed, neither appalled nor frightened but fascinated by the conundrum before her: how did *that* hand fit *there*, and whose leg was *that?* She inched backward, pressing herself against the door and trying to stay in the shadows—just inches ahead of her ribbons of luminous bluish light streamed from lamps hung high overhead. The chiaroscuro of pallid bodies and black furniture, shiny with sweat and here and there red-streaked, or brown; the mere sight of so many bodies, real bodies—flesh spilling over the edge of tabletops, too much hair or none at all, eyes squeezed shut in ecstasy or terror, and mouths open to reveal stained teeth, pale gums—the sheer *fluidity* of it all enthralled her. She felt as she had, once, pulling aside a rotted log to disclose the ant's nest beneath, masses of minute fleeing bodies, soldiers carrying eggs and larvae in their jaws, tunnels spiraling into the center of another world. Her brow tingled, warmth flushed her from brow to breast...

Another world, that's what she had found then; and discovered again now.

"Out."

Jane sucked her breath in sharply. Fingers dug into her shoulder, yanked her back through the metal door so roughly that she cut her wrist against it.

"No lurkers, what the fuck—"

A man flung her against the wall. She gasped, turned to run, but he grabbed her shoulder again. "Christ, a fucking girl."

He sounded angry but relieved. She looked up: a huge man, more fat than muscle. He wore very tight leather briefs and the same black sleeveless shirt with a golden bee embroidered upon it. "How the hell'd you get in like *that*?" he demanded, cocking a thumb at her.

She shook her head, then realized he meant her clothes. "I was just trying to find my way out."

"Well you found your way in. In like fucking Flynn." He laughed: he had gold-capped teeth, and gold wires threading the tip of his tongue. "You want to join the party, you know the rules. No exceptions."

Before she could reply he turned and was gone, the door thudding softly behind him. She waited, heart pounding, then reached and pushed the bar on the door.

Locked. She was out, not in; she was nowhere at all. For a long time she stood there, trying to hear anything from the other side of the door, waiting to see if anyone would come back looking for her. At last she turned, and began to find her way home.

Next morning she woke early, to the sound of delivery trucks in the street and children on the canal path, laughing and squabbling on their way to the zoo. She sat up with a pang, remembering David Bierce and her volunteer job; then recalled this was Saturday not Monday.

"Wow," she said aloud. The extra days seemed like a gift.

For a few minutes she lay in Fred and Andrew's great four-poster, staring abstractedly at where she had rested her mounted specimens atop the wainscoting—the hybrid hawkmoth; a beautiful Honduran owl butterfly, *Caligo atreus*; a mourning cloak she had caught and mounted herself years ago. She thought of the club last night, mentally retracing her steps to the hidden back room; thought of the man who had thrown her out, the interplay of light and shadow upon the bodies pinned to mats and tables. She had slept in her clothes; now she rolled out of bed and pulled her sneakers on, forgoing breakfast but stuffing her pocket with ten- and twenty-pound notes before she left.

It was a clear, cool morning, with a high pale-blue sky and the young leaves of nettles and hawthorn still glistening with dew. Someone had thrown a shopping cart from the nearby Sainsbury's into the canal; it edged sideways up out of the shallow water, like a frozen shipwreck. A boy stood a few yards down from it, fishing, an absent, placid expression on his face.

She crossed over the bridge to the canal path and headed for the High Street. With every step she took the day grew older, noisier, trains rattling on the bridge behind her and voices harsh as gulls rising from the other side of the brick wall that separated the canal path from the street.

At Camden Lock she had to fight her way through the market. There were thousands of tourists, swarming from the maze of shops to pick their way between scores of vendors selling old and new clothes, bootleg CDs, cheap silver jewelry, kilims, feather boas, handcuffs, cell phones, mass-produced furniture, and puppets from Indonesia, Morocco, Guyana, Wales. The fug of burning incense and cheap candles choked her; she hurried to where a young woman was turning samosas in a vat of sputtering oil, and dug into her pocket for a handful of change, standing so that the smells of hot grease and scorched chickpea batter cancelled out patchouli and Caribbean Nights.

"Two, please," Jane shouted.

She ate and almost immediately felt better, then walked a few steps to where a spike-haired girl sat behind a table covered with cheap clothes made of ripstock fabric in Jell-O shades.

"Everything five pounds," the girl announced. She stood, smiling helpfully as Jane began to sort through pairs of hugely baggy pants. They were cross-seamed with Velcro and deep zippered pockets. Jane held up a pair, frowning as the legs billowed, lavender and green, in the wind.

"It's so you can make them into shorts," the girl explained. She stepped around the table and took the pants from Jane, deftly tugging at the legs so that they detached. "See? Or a skirt." The girl replaced the pants, picked up another pair, screaming orange with black trim, and a matching windbreaker. "This color would look nice on you."

"Okay." Jane paid for them, waited for the girl to put the clothes in a plastic bag. "Thanks."

"Bye now."

She went out into the High Street. Shopkeepers stood guard over the tables spilling out from their storefronts, heaped with leather clothes and souvenir T-shirts: MIND THE GAP, LONDON UNDERGROUND, shirts emblazoned with the Cat in the Hat toking on a cheroot. THE CAT IN THE HAT SMOKES BLACK. Every three or four feet someone had set up a boom box, deafening sound bites of salsa, techno, "The Hustle," Bob Marley, "Anarchy in the UK," Radiohead. On the corner of Inverness and High Street a few punks squatted in a doorway, looking over the postcards they'd bought. A sign in the smoked-glass window said ALL HAIRCUTS TEN POUNDS, MEN AND WOMEN CHILDREN.

"Sorry," one of the punks said, as Jane stepped over them and into the shop.

The barber was sitting in an old-fashioned chair, his back to her, reading the *Sun*. At the sound of her footsteps he turned, smiling automatically. "Can I help you?"

"Yes please. I'd like my hair cut. All of it."

He nodded, gesturing to the chair. "Please."

Jane had thought she might have to convince him that she was serious. She had beautiful hair, well below her shoulders—the kind of hair people would kill for, she'd been hearing that her whole life. But the barber just hummed and chopped it off, the *snick snick* of his shears interspersed with kindly questions about whether she was enjoying her visit and his account of a vacation to Disney World ten years earlier.

"Dear, do we want it shaved or buzz-cut?"

In the mirror a huge-eyed creature gazed at Jane, like a tarsier or one of the owlish caligo moths. She stared at it, entranced, then nodded.

"Shaved. Please."

When he was finished she got out of the chair, dazed, and ran her hand across her scalp. It was smooth and cool as an apple. There were a few tiny nicks that stung beneath her fingers. She paid the barber, tipping him two pounds. He smiled and held the door open for her.

"Now when you want a touch-up, you come see us, dear. Only five pounds for a touch-up."

She went next to find new shoes. There were more shoe shops in Camden Town than she had ever seen anywhere in her life; she checked out four of them on one block before deciding on a discounted pair of twenty-hole black Doc Martens. They were no longer fashionable, but they had blunted steel caps on the toes. She bought them, giving the salesgirl her old sneakers to toss into the waste bin. When she went back onto the street it was like walking in wet cement—the boots were so heavy, the leather so stiff that she ducked back into the shoe shop and bought a pair of heavy wool socks and put them on. She returned outside, hesitating on the front step before crossing the street and heading in the direction of Chalk Farm Road. There was a shop here that Fred had shown her before he left.

"Now, that's where you get your fetish gear, Jane," he said, pointing to a shop window painted matte black. THE PLACE, it said in red letters, with two linked circles beneath. Fred had grinned and rapped his knuckles against the glass as they walked by. "I've never been in, you'll have to tell me what it's like." They'd both laughed at the thought.

Now Jane walked slowly, the wind chill against her bare skull. When she could make out the shop, sun glinting off the crimson letters and a sad-eyed dog tied to a post out front, she began to hurry, her new boots making a hollow thump as she pushed through the door.

There was a security gate inside, a thin, sallow young man with dreadlocks nodding at her silently as she approached.

"You'll have to check that." He pointed at the bag with her new clothes in it. She handed it to him, reading the warning posted behind the counter.

SHOPLIFTERS WILL BE BEATEN,
FLAYED, SPANKED, BIRCHED, BLED
AND THEN PROSECUTED
TO THE FULL EXTENT OF THE LAW

The shop was well lit. It smelled strongly of new leather and coconut oil and pine-scented disinfectant. She seemed to be the only customer this early in the day, although she counted seven employees, manning cash registers, unpacking cartons, watching to make sure she didn't try to nick anything. A CD of dance music played, and the phone rang constantly.

She spent a good half hour just walking through the place, impressed by the range of merchandise. Electrified wands to deliver shocks, things like meat cleavers made of stainless steel with rubber tips. Velcro dog collars, Velcro hoods, black rubber balls and balls in neon shades, a mat embedded with three-inch spikes that could be conveniently rolled up and came with its own lightweight carrying case. As she wandered about, more customers arrived, some of them greeting the clerks by name, others furtive, making a quick circuit of the shelves before darting outside again. At last Jane knew what she wanted. A set of wristcuffs and one of ankle-cuffs, both of very heavy black leather with stainless steel hardware; four adjustable nylon leashes, also black, with clips on either end that could be fastened to cuffs or looped around a post; a few spare S-clips.

"That it?"

Jane nodded, and the register clerk began scanning her purchases. She felt almost guilty, buying so few things, not taking advantage of the vast Meccano glory of all those shelves full of gleaming, somber contrivances.

"There you go." He handed her the receipt, then inclined his head at her. "Nice touch, that—"

He pointed at her eyebrows. Jane drew her hand up, felt the long pliant hairs uncoiling like baby ferns. "Thanks," she murmured. She retrieved her bag and went home to wait for evening.

It was nearly midnight when she left the flat. She had slept for most of the afternoon, a deep but restless sleep, with anxious dreams of flight, falling, her hands encased in metal gloves, a shadowy figure crouching above her. She woke in the dark, heart pounding, terrified for a moment that she had slept all the way through till Sunday night.

But of course she had not. She showered, then dressed in a tight, low-cut black shirt and pulled on her new nylon pants and heavy boots. She seldom wore makeup, but tonight after putting in her contacts she carefully outlined her eyes with black, then chose a very pale lavender lipstick. She surveyed herself in the mirror critically. With her white skin, huge violet eyes, and hairless skull, she resembled one of the Balinese puppets for sale in the market—beautiful but vacant, faintly ominous. She grabbed her keys and money, pulled on her windbreaker, and headed out.

When she reached the alley that led to the club, she entered it, walked about halfway, and stopped. After glancing back and forth to make sure no one was coming, she detached the legs from her nylon pants, stuffing them into a pocket, then adjusted the Velcro tabs so that the pants became a very short orange and black skirt. Her long legs were sheathed in black tights. She bent to tighten the laces on her metal-toed boots and hurried to the club entrance.

Tonight there was a line of people waiting to get in. Jane took her place, fastidiously avoiding looking at any of the others. They waited for thirty minutes, Jane shivering in her thin nylon windbreaker, before the door opened and the same gaunt blond man appeared to take their money. Jane felt her heart beat faster when it was her turn, wondering if he would recognize her. But he only scanned the courtyard, and, when the last of them darted inside, closed the door with a booming *clang*.

Inside all was as it had been, only far more crowded. Jane bought a drink, orange squash, no alcohol. It was horribly sweet, with a bitter, curdled aftertaste. Still, it had cost two pounds: she drank it all. She had just started on her way down to the dance floor when someone came up from behind to tap her shoulder, shouting into her ear.

"Wanna?"

It was a tall, broad-shouldered boy a few years older than she was, perhaps twenty-four, with a lean ruddy face, loose shoulder-length blond hair streaked green, and deep-set, very dark blue eyes. He swayed dreamily, gazing at the dance floor and hardly looking at her at all.

"Sure," Jane shouted back. He looped an arm around her shoulder, pulling her with him; his striped V-necked shirt smelled of talc and sweat. They danced for a long time, Jane moving with calculated abandon, the boy heaving and leaping as though a dog was biting at his shins.

"You're beautiful," he shouted. There was an almost imperceptible instant of silence as the DJ changed tracks. "What's your name?"

"Cleopatra Brimstone."

The shattering music grew deafening once more. The boy grinned. "Well, Cleopatra. Want something to drink?"

Jane nodded in time with the beat, so fast her head spun. He took her hand and she raced to keep up with him, threading their way towards the bar.

"Actually," she yelled, pausing so that he stopped short and bumped up against her. "I think I'd rather go outside. Want to come?"

He stared at her, half-smiling, and shrugged. "Aw right. Let me get a drink first—"

They went outside. In the alley the wind sent eddies of dead leaves and newspaper flying up into their faces. Jane laughed, and pressed herself against the boy's side. He grinned down at her, finished his drink, and tossed the can aside, then put his arm around her. "Do you want to go get a drink, then?" he asked.

They stumbled out onto the sidewalk, turned, and began walking. People filled the High Street, lines snaking out from the entrances of pubs and restaurants. A blue glow surrounded the streetlights, and clouds of small white moths beat themselves against the globes; vapor and banners of gray smoke hung above the punks blocking the sidewalk by Camden Lock. Jane and the boy dipped down into the street. He pointed to a pub occupying the corner a few blocks up, a large old green-painted building with baskets of flowers hanging beneath its windows and a large sign swinging back and forth in the wind: THE END OF THE WORLD. "In there, then?"

Jane shook her head. "I live right here, by the canal. We could go to my place if you want. We could have a few drinks there."

The boy glanced down at her. "Aw right," he said—very quickly, so she wouldn't change her mind. "That'd be aw right."

It was quieter on the back street leading to the flat. An old drunk huddled in a doorway, cadging change; Jane looked away from him and got out her keys while the boy stood restlessly, giving the drunk a belligerent look.

"Here we are," she announced, pushing the door open. "Home again, home again."

"Nice place." The boy followed her, gazing around admiringly. "You live here alone?"

"Yup." After she spoke Jane had a flash of unease, admitting that. But the boy only ambled into the kitchen, running a hand along the antique French farmhouse cupboard and nodding.

"You're American, right? Studying here?"

"Uh huh. What would you like to drink? Brandy?"

He made a face, then laughed. "Aw right! You got expensive taste. Goes with the name, I'd guess." Jane looked puzzled, and he went on, "Cleopatra—fancy name for a girl."

"Fancier for a boy," Jane retorted, and he laughed again.

She got the brandy, stood in the living room unlacing her boots. "Why don't we go in there?" she said, gesturing towards the bedroom. "It's kind of cold out here."

The boy ran a hand across his head, his blond hair streaming through his fingers. "Yeah, aw right." He looked around. "Um, that the toilet there?" Jane nodded. "Right back, then . . ."

She went into the bedroom, set the brandy and two glasses on a night table, and took off her windbreaker. On another table, several tall candles, creamy white and thick as her wrist, were set into ornate brass holders. She lit these—the room filled with the sweet scent of beeswax—and sat on the floor, leaning against the bed. A few minutes later the toilet flushed and the boy reappeared. His hands and face were damp, redder than they had been. He smiled and sank onto the floor beside her. Jane handed him a glass of brandy.

"Cheers," he said, and drank it all in one gulp.

"Cheers," said Jane. She took a sip from hers, then refilled his glass. He drank again, more slowly this time. The candles threw a soft yellow haze over the four-poster bed with its green velvet duvet, the mounds of pillows, forest-green, crimson, saffron yellow. They sat without speaking for several minutes. Then the boy set his glass on the floor. He turned to face Jane, extending one arm around her shoulder and drawing his face near hers.

"Well then," he said.

His mouth tasted acrid, nicotine and cheap gin beneath the blunter taste of brandy. His hand sliding under her shirt was cold; Jane felt goose pimples rising across her breast, her nipple shrinking beneath his touch. He pressed against her, his cock already hard, and reached down to unzip his jeans.

"Wait," Jane murmured. "Let's get on the bed . . ."

She slid from his grasp and onto the bed, crawling to the heaps of pillows and feeling beneath one until she found what she had placed there earlier. "Let's have a little fun first."

"*This* is fun," the boy said, a bit plaintively. But he slung himself onto the bed beside her, pulling off his shoes and letting them fall to the floor with a thud. "What you got there?"

Smiling, Jane turned and held up the wrist cuffs. The boy looked at them, then at her, grinning. "Oh ho. Been in the back room, then—"

Jane arched her shoulders and unbuttoned her shirt. He reached for one of the cuffs, but she shook her head. "No. Not me, yet."

"Ladies first."

"Gentleman's pleasure."

The boy's grin widened. "Won't argue with that."

She took his hand and pulled him, gently, to the middle of the bed. "Lie on your back," she whispered.

He did, watching as she removed first his shirt and then his jeans and underwear. His cock lay nudged against his thigh, not quite hard; when she brushed her fingers against it he moaned softly, took her hand, and tried to press it against him.

"No," she whispered. "Not yet. Give me your hand."

She placed the cuffs around each wrist, and his ankles, fastened the nylon leash to each one, and then began tying the bonds around each bedpost. It took longer than she had expected; it was difficult to get the bonds taut enough that the boy could not move. He lay there watchfully, his eyes glimmering in the candlelight as he craned his head to stare at her, his breath shallow, quickening.

"There." She sat back upon her haunches, staring at him. His cock was hard now, the hair on his chest and groin tawny in the half-light. He gazed back at her, his tongue pale as he licked his lips. "Try to get away," she whispered.

He moved slightly, his arms and legs a white X against a deep green field. "Can't," he said hoarsely.

She pulled her shirt off, then her nylon skirt. She had nothing on beneath. She leaned forward, letting her fingers trail from the cleft in his throat to his chest, cupping her palm atop his nipple and then sliding her hand down to his thigh. The flesh was warm, the little hairs soft and moist. Her own breath quickened; sudden heat flooded her, a honeyed liquid in her mouth. Above her brow the long hairs stiffened and furled straight out to either side: when she lifted her head to the candlelight she could see them from the corner of her eyes, twin barbs black and glistening like wire.

"You're so sexy." The boy's voice was hoarse. "God, you're—"

She placed her hand over his mouth. "Try to get away," she said, commandingly this time. *"Try to get away."*

His torso writhed, the duvet bunching up around him in dark folds. She raked her fingernails down his chest and he cried out, moaning, "Fuck me, God, fuck me . . ."

"Try to get away."

She stroked his cock, her fingers barely grazing its swollen head. With a moan he came, struggling helplessly to thrust his groin towards her. At the same moment Jane gasped, a fiery rush arrowing down from her brow to her breasts, her cunt. She rocked forward, crying out, her head brushing against the boy's side as she sprawled back across the bed. For a minute she lay there, the room around her seeming to pulse and swirl into myriad crystalline shapes, each bearing within it the same line of candles, the long curve of the boy's thigh swelling up into the hollow of his hip. She drew breath shakily, the flush of heat fading from her brow; then pushed herself up until she was sitting beside him. His eyes were shut. A thread of saliva traced the furrow between mouth and chin. Without thinking she drew her face down to his and kissed his cheek.

Immediately he began to grow smaller. Jane reared back, smacking into one of the bedposts, and stared at the figure in front of her, shaking her head.

"No," she whispered. "No, no."

He was shrinking: so fast it was like watching water dissolve into dry sand. Man-size, child-size, large dog, small. His eyes flew open and for a fraction of a second stared horrified into her own. His hands and feet slipped like mercury from his bonds, wriggling until they met his torso and were absorbed into it. Jane's fingers kneaded the duvet; six inches away the boy was no larger than her hand, then smaller, smaller still. She blinked, for a heart-shredding instant thought he had disappeared completely.

Then she saw something crawling between folds of velvet. The length of her middle finger, its thorax black, yellow-striped, its lower wings elongated into frilled arabesques like those of a festoon, deep yellow, charcoal black, with indigo eye spots, its upper wings a chiaroscuro of black-and-white stripes.

Bhutanitis lidderdalii. A native of the eastern Himalayas, rarely glimpsed: it lived among the crowns of trees in mountain valleys, its caterpillars feeding on lianas. Jane held her breath, watching as its wings beat feebly. Without warning it lifted into the air. Jane cried out, falling onto her knees as she sprawled across the bed, cupping it quickly but carefully between her hands.

"Beautiful, beautiful," she crooned. She stepped from the bed, not daring to pause and examine it, and hurried into the kitchen. In the cupboard she found an empty jar, set it down, and gingerly angled the lid from it, holding one hand with the butterfly against her breast. She swore, feeling its wings fluttering against her fingers, then quickly brought her hand to the jar's mouth, dropped the butterfly inside, and screwed the lid back in place. It fluttered helplessly inside; she could see where the scales had already been scraped from its wing. Still swearing, she ran back into the bedroom, putting the lights on and dragging her collection box from under the bed. She grabbed a vial of ethyl alcohol, went back into the kitchen, and tore a bit of paper towel from the rack. She opened the vial, poured a few drops of ethyl alcohol onto the paper, opened the jar, and gently tilted it onto its side. She slipped the paper inside, very slowly tipping the jar upright once more, until the paper had settled on the bottom, the butterfly on top of it. Its wings beat frantically for a few moments, then stopped. Its proboscis uncoiled, finer than a hair. Slowly Jane drew her own hand to her brow and ran it along the length of the antennae there. She sat there staring at it until the sun leaked through the wooden shutters in the kitchen window. The butterfly did not move again.

The next day passed in a metallic gray haze, the only color the black and saturated yellow of the *lidderdalii's* wings, burned upon Jane's eyes as though she had looked into the sun. When she finally roused herself, she felt a spasm of panic at the sight of the boy's clothes on the bedroom floor.

"Shit." She ran her hand across her head, was momentarily startled to recall she had no hair. "Now what?"

She stood there for a few minutes, thinking, then gathered the clothes—

striped V-neck sweater, jeans, socks, jockey shorts, Timberland knockoff shoes—and dumped them into a plastic Sainsbury's bag. There was a wallet in the jeans pocket. She opened it, gazed impassively at a driver's license—KENNETH REED, WOLVERHAMPTON—and a few five-pound notes. She pocketed the money, took the license into the bathroom and burned it, letting the ashes drop into the toilet. Then she went outside.

It was early Sunday morning, no one about except for a young mother pushing a baby in a stroller. In the neighboring doorway the same drunk old man sprawled, surrounded by empty bottles and rubbish. He stared blearily up at Jane as she approached.

"Here," she said. She bent and dropped the five-pound notes into his scabby hand.

"God bless you, darlin'." He coughed, his eyes focusing on neither Jane nor the notes. "God bless you."

She turned and walked briskly back towards the canal path. There were few waste bins in Camden Town, and so each day trash accumulated in rank heaps along the path, beneath streetlights, in vacant alleys. Street cleaners and sweeping machines then daily cleared it all away again: like elves, Jane thought. As she walked along the canal path she dropped the shoes in one pile of rubbish, tossed the sweater alongside a single high-heeled shoe in the market, stuffed the underwear and socks into a collapsing cardboard box filled with rotting lettuce, and left the jeans beside a stack of papers outside an unopened newsagent's shop. The wallet she tied into the Sainsbury's bag and dropped into an overflowing trash bag outside of Boots. Then she retraced her steps, stopping in front of a shop window filled with tatty polyester lingerie in large sizes and boldly artificial-looking wigs: pink afros, platinum blond falls, black-and-white Cruella De Vil tresses.

The door was propped open; Schubert lieder played softly on 32.

Jane stuck her head in and looked around, saw a beefy man behind the register, cashing out. He had orange lipstick smeared around his mouth and delicate silver fish hanging from his ears.

"We're not open yet. Eleven on Sunday," he said without looking up.

"I'm just looking." Jane sidled over to a glass shelf where four wigs sat on Styrofoam heads. One had very glossy black hair in a chin-length flapper bob. Jane tried it on, eyeing herself in a grimy mirror. "How much is this one?"

"Fifteen. But we're not—"

"Here. Thanks!" Jane stuck a twenty-pound note on the counter and ran from the shop. When she reached the corner she slowed, pirouetted to catch her reflection in a shop window. She stared at herself, grinning, then walked the rest of the way home, exhilarated and faintly dizzy.

Monday morning she went to the zoo to begin her volunteer work. She had mounted the *Bhutanitis lidderdalii* on a piece of Styrofoam with a piece of paper on it, to keep the butterfly's legs from becoming embedded in the Styrofoam. She'd softened it first, putting it into a jar with damp paper, removed it, and placed it on the mounting platform, neatly spearing its thorax—a little to the right—with a #2 pin. She propped it carefully on the wainscoting beside the hawkmoth, and left.

She arrived and found her ID badge waiting for her at the staff entrance. It was a clear morning, warmer than it had been for a week; the long hairs on her brow vibrated as though they were wires that had been plucked. Beneath the wig her shaved head felt hot and moist, the first new hairs starting to prickle across her scalp. Her nose itched where her glasses pressed against it. Jane walked, smiling, past the gibbons howling in their habitat and the pygmy hippos floating calmly in their pool, their eyes shut, green bubbles breaking around them like little fish. In front of the Insect Zoo a uniformed woman was unloading sacks of meal from a golf cart.

"Morning," Jane called cheerfully, and went inside.

She found David Bierce standing in front of a temperature gauge beside a glass cage holding the hissing cockroaches.

"Something happened last night, the damn things got too cold." He glanced over, handed her a clipboard, and began to remove the top of the gauge. "I called Operations, but they're at their fucking morning meeting. Fucking computers—"

He stuck his hand inside the control box and flicked angrily at the gauge. "You know anything about computers?"

"Not this kind." Jane brought her face up to the cage's glass front. Inside were half a dozen glossy roaches, five inches long and the color of pale maple syrup. They lay, unmoving, near a glass petri dish filled with what looked like damp brown sugar. "Are they dead?"

"Those things? They're fucking immortal. You could stamp on one and it wouldn't die. Believe me, I've done it." He continued to fiddle with the gauge, finally sighed, and replaced the lid. "Well, let's let the boys over in Ops handle it. Come on, I'll get you started."

He gave her a brief tour of the lab, opening drawers full of dissecting instruments, mounting platforms, pins; showed her where the food for the various insects was kept in a series of small refrigerators. Sugar syrup, cornstarch, plastic containers full of smaller insects, grubs and mealworms, tiny gray beetles. "Mostly we just keep on top of replacing the ones that die," David explained, "that and making sure the plants don't develop the wrong kind of fungus. Nature takes her course and we just goose her along when she needs it. School groups are here constantly, but the docents handle that. You're more than welcome to talk to them, if that's the sort of thing you want to do."

He turned from where he'd been washing empty jars at a small sink, dried his hands, and walked over to sit on top of a desk. "It's not terribly glamorous work here." He reached down for a Styrofoam cup of coffee and sipped from it, gazing at her coolly. "We're none of us working on our PhDs anymore."

Jane shrugged. "That's all right."

"It's not even all that interesting. I mean, it can be very repetitive. Tedious."

"I don't mind." A sudden pang of anxiety made Jane's voice break. She could feel her face growing hot, and quickly looked away. "Really," she said sullenly.

"Suit yourself. Coffee's over there; you'll probably have to clean yourself a cup, though." He cocked his head, staring at her curiously, then said, "Did you do something different with your hair?"

She nodded once, brushing the edge of her bangs with a finger. "Yeah."

"Nice. Very Louise Brooks." He hopped from the desk and crossed to a computer set up in the corner. "You can use my computer if you need to, I'll give you the password later."

Jane nodded, her flush fading into relief. "How many people work here?"

"Actually, we're short-staffed here right now—no money for hiring and our grant's run out. It's pretty much just me, and whoever Carolyn sends over from the docents. Sweet little bluehairs mostly, they don't much like bugs. So it's providential you turned up, *Jane*."

He said her name mockingly, gave her a crooked grin. "You said you have experience mounting? Well, I try to save as many of the dead specimens as I can, and when there's any slow days, which there never are, I mount them and use them for the workshops I do with the schools that come in. What would be nice would be if we had enough specimens that I could give some to the teachers, to take back to their classrooms. We have a nice website and we might be able to work up some interactive programs. No schools are scheduled today, Monday's usually slow here. So if you could work on some of *those*"—he gestured to where several dozen cardboard boxes and glass jars were strewn across a countertop—"that would be really brilliant," he ended, and turned to his computer screen.

She spent the morning mounting insects. Few were interesting or unusual: a number of brown hairstreaks, some Camberwell Beauties, three hissing cockroaches, several brimstones. But there was a single *Acherontia atropos,* the Death's head hawkmoth, the pattern of gray and brown and pale yellow scales on the back of its thorax forming the image of a human skull. Its proboscis was unfurled, the twin points sharp enough to pierce a finger: Jane touched it gingerly, wincing delightedly as a pinprick of blood appeared on her fingertip.

"You bring lunch?"

She looked away from the bright magnifying light she'd been using and blinked in surprise. "Lunch?"

David Bierce laughed. "Enjoying yourself? Well, that's good, makes the day go faster. Yes, lunch!" He rubbed his hands together, the harsh light making him look gnomelike, his sharp features malevolent and leering. "They have some decent fish and chips at the stall over by the cats. Come on, I'll treat you. Your first day."

They sat at a picnic table beside the food booth and ate. David pulled a bottle of ale from his knapsack and shared it with Jane. Overhead scattered clouds like smoke moved swiftly southwards. An Indian woman with three small boys sat at another table, the boys tossing fries at seagulls that swept down, shrieking, and made the smallest boy wail.

"Rain later," David said, staring at the sky. "Too bad." He sprinkled vinegar on his fried haddock and looked at Jane. "So did you go out over the weekend?"

She stared at the table and smiled. "Yeah, I did. It was fun."

"Where'd you go? The Electric Ballroom?"

"God, no. This other place." She glanced at his hand resting on the table beside her. He had long fingers, the knuckles slightly enlarged; but the back of his hand was smooth, the same soft brown as the *Acherontia's* wingtips. Her brows prickled, warmth trickling from them like water. When she lifted her head she could smell him, some kind of musky soap, salt; the bittersweet ale on his breath.

"Yeah? Where? I haven't been out in months, I'd be lost in Camden Town these days."

"I dunno. The Hive?"

She couldn't imagine he would have heard of it—far too old. But he swiveled on the bench, his eyebrows arching with feigned shock. "You went to *Hive*? And they let you in?"

"Yes," Jane stammered. "I mean, I didn't know—it was just a dance club. I just—danced."

"Did you." David Bierce's gaze sharpened, his hazel eyes catching the sun and sending back an icy emerald glitter. "Did you."

She picked up the bottle of ale and began to peel the label from it. "Yes."

"Have a boyfriend, then?"

She shook her head, rolled a fragment of label into a tiny pill. "No."

"Stop that." His hand closed over hers. He drew it away from the bottle, letting it rest against the table edge. She swallowed: he kept his hand on top of hers, pressing it against the metal edge until she felt her scored palm begin to ache. Her eyes closed: she could feel herself floating, and see a dozen feet below her own form, slender, the wig beetle-black upon her skull, her wrist like a bent stalk. Abruptly his hand slid away and beneath the table, brushing her leg as he stooped to retrieve his knapsack.

"Time to get back to work," he said lightly, sliding from the bench and slinging his bag over his shoulder. The breeze lifted his long graying hair as he turned away. "I'll see you back there."

Overhead the gulls screamed and flapped, dropping bits of fried fish on the sidewalk. She stared at the table in front of her, the cardboard trays that held the remnants of lunch, and watched as a yellowjacket landed on a fleck of grease, its golden thorax swollen with moisture as it began to feed.

+ +

She did not return to Hive that night. Instead she wore a patchwork dress over her jeans and Doc Martens, stuffed the wig inside a drawer, and headed to a small bar on Inverness Street. The fair day had turned to rain, black puddles like molten metal capturing the amber glow of traffic signals and streetlights.

There were only a handful of tables at Bar Ganza. Most of the customers stood on the sidewalk outside, drinking and shouting to be heard above the sound of wailing Spanish love songs. Jane fought her way inside, got a glass of red wine, and miraculously found an empty stool alongside the wall. She climbed onto it, wrapped her long legs around the pedestal, and sipped her wine.

"Hey. Nice hair." A man in his early thirties, his own head shaven, sidled up to Jane's stool. He held a cigarette, smoking it with quick, nervous gestures as he stared at her. He thrust his cigarette towards the ceiling, indicating a booming speaker. "You like the music?"

"Not particularly."

"Hey, you're American? Me too. Chicago. Good bud of mine, works for Citibank, he told me about this place. Food's not bad. Tapas. Baby octopus. You like octopus?"

Jane's eyes narrowed. The man wore expensive-looking corduroy trousers, a rumpled jacket of nubby charcoal-colored linen. "No," she said, but didn't turn away.

"Me neither. Like eating great big slimy bugs. Geoff Lanning—"

He stuck his hand out. She touched it, lightly, and smiled. "Nice to meet you, Geoff."

For the next half hour or so she pretended to listen to him, nodding and smiling brilliantly whenever he looked up at her. The bar grew louder and more crowded, and people began eyeing Jane's stool covetously.

"I think I'd better hand over this seat," she announced, hopping down and elbowing her way to the door. "Before they eat me."

Geoff Lanning hurried after her. "Hey, you want to get dinner? The Camden Brasserie's just up here—"

"No thanks." She hesitated on the curb, gazing demurely at her Doc Martens. "But would you like to come in for a drink?"

He was very impressed by her apartment. "Man, this place'd probably go for a half mil, easy! That's three quarters of a million American." He opened and closed cupboards, ran a hand lovingly across the slate sink.

"Nice hardwood floors, high-speed access—you never told me what you do."

Jane laughed. "As little as possible. Here—"

She handed him a brandy snifter, let her finger trace the top part of his wrist. "You look like kind of an adventurous sort of guy."

"Hey, big adventure, that's me." He lifted his glass to her. "What exactly did you have in mind? Big game hunting?"

"Mmm. Maybe."

It was more of a struggle this time, not for Geoff Lanning but for Jane. He lay complacently in his bonds, his stocky torso wriggling obediently when Jane commanded. Her head ached from the cheap wine at Bar Ganza; the long hairs above her eyes lay sleek against her skull, and did not move at all until she closed her eyes, and, unbidden, the image of David Bierce's hand covering hers appeared.

"Try to get away," she whispered.

"Whoa, Nellie," Geoff Lanning gasped.

"Try to get away," she repeated, her voice hoarser.

"Oh." The man whimpered softly. "Jesus Christ, what—oh my God, what—"

Quickly she bent and kissed his fingertips, saw where the leather cuff had bitten into his pudgy wrist. This time she was prepared when with a keening sound he began to twist upon the bed, his arms and legs shriveling and then coiling in upon themselves, his shaved head withdrawing into his tiny torso like a snail within its shell.

But she was not prepared for the creature that remained, its feathery antennae a trembling echo of her own, its extraordinarily elongated hind spurs nearly four inches long.

"Oh," she gasped.

She didn't dare touch it until it took to the air: the slender spurs fragile as icicles, scarlet, their saffron tips curling like Christmas ribbon, its large delicate wings saffron with slate-blue and scarlet eye-spots, and spanning nearly six inches. A Madagascan Moon Moth, one of the loveliest and rarest silk moths, and almost impossible to find as an intact specimen.

"What do I do with you, what do I do?" she crooned as it spread its wings and lifted from the bed. It flew in short sweeping arcs; she scrambled to blow out the candles before it could near them. She pulled on her kimono and left the lights off, closed the bedroom door and hurried into the kitchen, looking for a flashlight. She found nothing, but recalled Andrew telling her there was a large torch in the basement.

She hadn't been down there since her initial tour of the flat. It was brightly lit, with long neat cabinets against both walls, a floor-to-ceiling wine rack filled with bottles of claret and vintage burgundy, compact washer and dryer, small refrigerator, buckets and brooms waiting for the cleaning lady's weekly visit. She found the flashlight sitting on top of the refrigerator, a container of extra batteries beside it. She switched it on and off a few times, then glanced down at the refrigerator and absently opened it.

Seeing all that wine had made her think the little refrigerator might be filled with beer. Instead it held only a long plastic box, with a red lid and a red biohazard sticker on the side. Jane put the flashlight down and stooped, carefully removing the box and setting it on the floor. A label with Andrew's neat architectural handwriting was on the top.

DR. ANDREW FILDERMAN
ST. MARTIN'S HOSPICE

"Huh," she said, and opened it.

Inside there was a small red biohazard waste container, and scores of plastic bags filled with disposable hypodermics, ampules, and suppositories. All contained morphine at varying dosages. Jane stared, marveling, then opened one of the bags. She shook half a dozen morphine ampules into her palm, carefully reclosed the bag, put it back into the box, and returned the box to the refrigerator. Then she grabbed the flashlight and ran upstairs.

It took her a while to capture the moon moth. First she had to find a killing jar large enough, and then she had to very carefully lure it inside, so that its frail wing spurs wouldn't be damaged. She did this by positioning the jar on its side and placing a gooseneck lamp directly behind it, so that the bare bulb shone through the glass. After about fifteen minutes, the moth landed on top of the jar, its tiny legs slipping as it struggled on the smooth curved surface. Another few minutes and it had crawled inside, nestled on the wad of tissues Jane had set there, moist with ethyl alcohol. She screwed the lid on tightly, left the jar on its side, and waited for it to die.

‡ ‡

Over the next week she acquired three more specimens. *Papilio demetrius*, a Japanese swallowtail with elegant orange eyespots on a velvety black ground; a scarce copper, not scarce at all, really, but with lovely pumpkin-colored wings; and *Graphium agamemnon*, a Malaysian species with vivid green spots and chrome-yellow strips on its somber brown wings. She'd ventured away from Camden Town, capturing the swallowtail in a private room in an SM club in Islington and the *Graphium agamemnon* in a parked car behind a noisy pub in Crouch End. The scarce copper came from a vacant lot near the Tottenham Court Road tube station very late one night, where the wreckage of a chain-link fence stood in for her bed-posts. She found the morphine to be useful, although she had to wait until immediately after the man ejaculated before pressing the ampule against his throat, aiming for the carotid artery. This way the butterflies emerged already sedated, and in minutes died with no damage to their wings. Left-over clothing was easily disposed of, but she had to be more careful with wallets, stuffing them deep within rubbish bins, when she could, or bury-ing them in her own trash bags and then watching as the waste trucks came by on their rounds.

In South Kensington she discovered an entomological supply store. There she bought more mounting supplies, and inquired casually as to whether the owner might be interested in purchasing some specimens.

He shrugged. "Depends. What you got?"

"Well, right now I have only one *Argema mittrei*." Jane adjusted her glasses and glanced around the shop. A lot of morphos, an Atlas moth: nothing too unusual. "But I might be getting another, in which case . . ."

"Moon moth, eh? How'd you come by that, I wonder?" The man raised his eyebrows, and Jane flushed. "Don't worry, I'm not going to turn you in. Christ, I'd go out of business. Well, obviously I can't display those in the shop, but if you want to part with one, let me know. I'm always scouting for my customers."

She began volunteering three days a week at the insect zoo. One Wednesday, the night after she'd gotten a gorgeous *Urania leilus*, its wings sadly damaged by rain, she arrived to see David Bierce reading that morn-ing's *Camden New Journal*. He peered above the newspaper and frowned.

"You still going out alone at night?"

She froze, her mouth dry; turned and hurried over to the coffeemaker. "Why?" she said, fighting to keep her tone even.

"Because there's an article about some of the clubs around here. Apparently a few people have gone missing."

"Really?" Jane got her coffee, wiping up a spill with the side of her hand. "What happened?"

"Nobody knows. Two blokes reported gone, family frantic, sort of thing. Probably just runaways. Camden Town eats them alive, kids." He handed the paper to Jane. "Although one of them was last seen near Highbury Fields, some sex club there."

She scanned the article. There was no mention of any suspects. And no bodies had been found, although foul play was suspected. (*"Ken would never have gone away without notifying us or his employer...."*)

Anyone with any information was urged to contact the police.

"I don't go to sex clubs," Jane said flatly. "Plus those are both guys."

"Mmm." David leaned back in his chair, regarding her coolly. "You're the one hitting Hive your first weekend in London."

"It's a *dance* club!" Jane retorted. She laughed, rolled the newspaper into a tube, and batted him gently on the shoulder. "Don't worry. I'll be careful."

David continued to stare at her, hazel eyes glittering. "Who says it's you I'm worried about?"

She smiled, her mouth tight as she turned and began cleaning bottles in the sink.

It was a raw day, more late November than mid-May. Only two school groups were scheduled; otherwise the usual stream of visitors was reduced to a handful of elderly women who shook their heads over the cockroaches and gave barely a glance to the butterflies before shuffling on to another building. David Bierce paced restlessly through the lab on his way to clean the cages and make more complaints to the Operations Division. Jane cleaned and mounted two stag beetles, their spiny legs pricking her fingertips as she tried to force the pins through their glossy chestnut-colored shells. Afterwards she busied herself with straightening the clutter of cabinets and drawers stuffed with requisition forms and microscopes, computer parts and dissection kits.

It was well past two when David reappeared, his anorak slick with rain, his hair tucked beneath the hood. "Come on," he announced, standing impatiently by the open door. "Let's go to lunch."

Jane looked up from the computer where she'd been updating a specimen list. "I'm really not very hungry," she said, giving him an apologetic
smile. "You go ahead."

"Oh, for Christ's sake." David let the door slam shut as he crossed to
her, his sneakers leaving wet smears on the tiled floor. "That can wait till
tomorrow. Come on, there's not a fucking thing here that needs doing."

"But—" She gazed up at him. The hood slid from his head; his gray-
streaked hair hung loose to his shoulders, and the sheen of rain on his
sharp cheekbones made him look carved from oiled wood. "What if somebody comes?"

"A very nice docent named Mrs. Eleanor Feltwell is out there, *even as
we speak*, in the unlikely event that we have a single visitor."

He stooped so that his head was beside hers, scowling as he stared at
the computer screen. A lock of his hair fell to brush against her neck. Beneath the wig her scalp burned, as though stung by tiny ants; she breathed
in the warm acrid smell of his sweat and something else, a sharper scent,
like crushed oak-mast or fresh-sawn wood. Above her brows the antennae
suddenly quivered. Sweetness coated her tongue like burnt syrup. With a
rush of panic she turned her head so he wouldn't see her face.

"I—I should finish this—"

"Oh, just *fuck* it, Jane! It's not like we're *paying* you. Come on, now,
there's a good girl—"

He took her hand and pulled her to her feet, Jane still looking away.
The bangs of her cheap wig scraped her forehead and she batted at them
feebly. "Get your things. What, don't you ever take days off in the States?"

"All right, all right." She turned and gathered her black vinyl raincoat
and knapsack, pulled on the coat, and waited for him by the door. "Jeez,
you must be hungry," she said crossly.

"No. Just fucking bored out of my skull. Have you been to Ruby in the
Dust? No? I'll take you then, let's go—"

The restaurant was down the High Street, a small, cheerfully claptrap
place, dim in the gray afternoon, its small wooden tables scattered with
abandoned newspapers and overflowing ashtrays. David Bierce ordered a
steak and a pint. Jane had a small salad, nasturtium blossoms strewn across
pale green lettuce, and a glass of red wine. She lacked an appetite lately, living on vitamin-enhanced, fruity bottled drinks from the health food store
and baklava from a Greek bakery near the tube station.

"So." David Bierce stabbed a piece of steak, peering at her sideways. "Don't tell me you really haven't been here before."

"I haven't!" Despite her unease at being with him, she laughed, and caught her reflection in the wall-length mirror. A thin, plain young woman in shapeless Peruvian sweater and jeans, bad haircut, and ugly glasses. Gazing at herself she felt suddenly stronger, invisible. She tilted her head and smiled at Bierce. "The food's good."

"So you don't have someone taking you out to dinner every night? Cooking for you? I thought you American girls all had adoring men at your feet. Adoring slaves," he added dryly. "Or slave girls, I suppose. If that's your thing."

"No." She stared at her salad, shook her head demurely, and took a sip of wine. It made her feel even more invulnerable. "No, I—"

"Boyfriend back home, right?" He finished his pint, flagged the waiter to order another, and turned back to Jane. "Well, that's nice. That's very nice—for him," he added, and gave a short harsh laugh.

The waiter brought another pint, and more wine for Jane. "Oh really, I better—"

"Just drink it, Jane." Under the table, she felt a sharp pressure on her foot. She wasn't wearing her Doc Martens today but a pair of red plastic jellies. David Bierce had planted his heel firmly atop her toes; she sucked in her breath in shock and pain, the bones of her foot crackling as she tried to pull it from beneath him. Her antennae rippled, then stiffened, and heat burst like a seed inside her.

"Go ahead," he said softly, pushing the wineglass towards her. "Just a sip, that's right—"

She grabbed the glass, spilling wine on her sweater as she gulped at it. The vicious pressure on her foot subsided, but as the wine ran down her throat she could feel the heat thrusting her into the air, currents rushing beneath her as the girl at the table below set down her wineglass with trembling fingers.

"There." David Bierce smiled, leaning forward to gently cup her hand between his. "Now this is better than working. Right, Jane?"

He walked her home along the canal path. Jane tried to dissuade him, but he'd had a third pint by then; it didn't seem to make him drunk but coldly obdurate, and she finally gave in. The rain had turned to a fine drizzle, the canal's usually murky water silvered and softly gleaming in the twilight. They passed few other people, and Jane found herself wishing someone else would appear, so that she'd have an excuse to move closer to David Bierce. He kept close to the canal itself, several feet from Jane; when the breeze lifted she could catch his oaky scent again, rising above the dank reek of stagnant water and decaying hawthorn blossom.

They crossed over the bridge to approach her flat by the street. At the front sidewalk Jane stopped, smiled shyly, and said, "Thanks. That was nice."

David nodded. "Glad I finally got you out of your cage." He lifted his head to gaze appraisingly at the row house. "Christ, this where you're staying? You split the rent with someone?"

"No." She hesitated: she couldn't remember what she had told him about her living arrangements. But before she could blurt something out he stepped past her to the front door, peeking into the window and bobbing impatiently up and down.

"Mind if I have a look? Professional entomologists don't often get the chance to see how the quality live."

Jane hesitated, her stomach clenching; decided it would be safer to have him in, rather than continue to put him off.

"All right," she said reluctantly, and opened the door.

"Mmmm. Nice, nice, very nice." He swept around the living room, spinning on his heel and making a show of admiring the elaborate molding, the tribal rugs, the fireplace mantel with its thick ecclesiastical candles and ormolu mirror. "Goodness, all this for a wee thing like you? You're a clever cat, landing on your feet here, Lady Jane."

She blushed. He bounded past her on his way into the bedroom, touching her shoulder; she had to close her eyes as a fiery wave surged through her and her antennae trembled.

"*Wow*," he exclaimed.

Slowly she followed him into the bedroom. He stood in front of the wall where her specimens were balanced in a neat line across the wainscoting. His eyes were wide, his mouth open in genuine astonishment.

"Are these *yours*?" he marveled, his gaze fixed on the butterflies. "You didn't actually catch them—?"

She shrugged.

"These are incredible!" He picked up the *Graphium agamemnon* and tilted it to the pewter-colored light falling through the French doors. "Did you mount them, too?"

She nodded, crossing to stand beside him. "Yeah. You can tell, with that one—" She pointed at the *Urania leilus* in its oak-framed box. "It got rained on."

David Bierce replaced the *Graphium agamemnon* and began to read the labels on the others.

Papilio demetrius
UNITED KINGDOM: LONDON
Highbury Fields, Islington
7.V.2001
J. Kendall

Loepa katinka
UNITED KINGDOM: LONDON
Finsbury Park
09.V.2001
J. Kendall

Argema mittrei
UNITED KINGDOM: LONDON
Camden Town
13.IV.2001
J. Kendall

He shook his head. "You screwed up, though—you wrote 'London' for all of them." He turned to her, grinning wryly. "Can't think of the last time I saw a moon moth in Camden Town."

She forced a laugh. "Oh—right."

"And, I mean, you can't have actually *caught* them—"

He held up the *Loepa katinka,* a butter-yellow Emperor moth, its peacock's-eyes russet and jet-black. "I haven't seen any of these around lately. Not even in Finsbury."

Jane made a little grimace of apology. "Yeah. I meant, that's where I found them—where I bought them."

"Mmmm." He set the moth back on its ledge. "You'll have to share your sources with me. I can never find things like these in North London."

He turned and headed out of the bedroom. Jane hurriedly straightened the specimens, her hands shaking now as well, and followed him.

"Well, Lady Jane." For the first time he looked at her without his usual mocking arrogance, his green-flecked eyes bemused, almost regretful. "I think we managed to salvage something from the day."

He turned, gazing one last time at the flat's glazed walls and highly waxed floors, the imported cabinetry and jewel-toned carpets. "I was going to say, when I walked you home, that you needed someone to take care of you. But it looks like you've managed that on your own."

Jane stared at her feet. He took a step towards her, the fragrance of oak-mast and honey filling her nostrils, crushed acorns, new fern. She grew dizzy, her hand lifting to find him; but he only reached to graze her cheek with his finger.

"Night then, Jane," he said softly, and walked back out into the misty evening.

When he was gone she raced to the windows and pulled all the velvet curtains, then tore the wig from her head and threw it onto the couch along with her glasses. Her heart was pounding, her face slick with sweat—from fear or rage or disappointment, she didn't know. She yanked off her sweater and jeans, left them on the living room floor, and stomped into the bathroom. She stood in the shower for twenty minutes, head upturned as the water sluiced the smells of bracken and leaf-mold from her skin.

Finally she got out. She dried herself, let the towel drop, and went into the kitchen. Abruptly she was famished. She tore open cupboards and drawers until she found a half-full jar of lavender honey from Provence. She opened it, the top spinning off into the sink, and frantically spooned honey into her mouth with her fingers. When she was finished she grabbed a jar of lemon curd and ate most of that, until she felt as though she might be sick. She stuck her head into the sink, letting water run from the faucet into her mouth, and at last walked, surfeited, into the bedroom.

She dressed, feeling warm and drowsy, almost dreamlike; pulling on red-and-yellow-striped stockings, her nylon skirt, a tight red T-shirt. No bra, no panties. She put in her contacts, then examined herself in the mirror. Her hair had begun to grow back, a scant velvety stubble, bluish in the dim light. She drew a sweeping black line across each eyelid, on a whim took the liner and extended the curve of each antenna until they touched her temples. She painted her lips black as well and went to find her black vinyl raincoat.

It was early when she went out, far too early for any of the clubs to be open. The rain had stopped, but a thick greasy fog covered everything, coating windshields and shop windows, making Jane's face feel as though it were encased in a clammy shell. For hours she wandered Camden Town, huge violet eyes turning to stare back at the men who watched her, dismissing each of them. Once she thought she saw David Bierce coming out of Ruby in the Dust, but when she stopped to watch him cross the street it was not David but someone else. Much younger, his long dark hair in a thick braid, his feet clad in knee-high boots. He crossed the High Street, heading towards the tube station. Jane hesitated, then darted after him.

He went to the Electric Ballroom. Fifteen or so people stood out front, talking quietly. The man she'd followed joined the line, standing by himself. Jane waited across the street, until the door opened and the little crowd began to shuffle inside. After the long-haired young man had entered, she counted to one hundred, crossed the street, paid her cover, and went inside.

The club had three levels; she finally tracked him down on the uppermost one. Even on a rainy Wednesday night it was crowded, the sound system blaring Idris Mohammed and Jimmie Cliff. He was standing alone near the bar, drinking bottled water.

"Hi!" she shouted, swaying up to him with her best First Day of School Smile. "Want to dance?"

He was older than she'd thought—thirtyish, still not as old as Bierce. He stared at her, puzzled, then shrugged. "Sure."

They danced, passing the water bottle between them. "What's your name?" he shouted.

"Cleopatra Brimstone."

"You're kidding!" he yelled back. The song ended in a bleat of feedback, and they walked, panting, back to the bar.

"What, you know another Cleopatra?" Jane asked teasingly.

"No. It's just a crazy name, that's all." He smiled. He was handsomer than David Bierce, his features softer, more rounded, his eyes dark brown, his manner a bit reticent. "I'm Thomas Raybourne. Tom."

He bought another bottle of Pellegrino and one for Jane. She drank it quickly, trying to get his measure. When she finished she set the empty bottle on the floor and fanned herself with her hand.

"It's hot in here." Her throat hurt from shouting over the music. "I think I'm going to take a walk. Feel like coming?"

He hesitated, glancing around the club. "I was supposed to meet a friend here . . ." he began, frowning. "But—"

"Oh." Disappointment filled her, spiking into desperation. "Well, that's okay. I guess."

"Oh, what the hell." He smiled: he had nice eyes, a more stolid, reassuring gaze than Bierce. "I can always come back."

Outside she turned right, in the direction of the canal. "I live pretty close by. Feel like coming in for a drink?"

He shrugged again. "I don't drink, actually."

"Something to eat then? It's not far—just along the canal path a few blocks past Camden Lock—"

"Yeah, sure."

They made desultory conversation. "You should be careful," he said as they crossed the bridge. "Did you read about those people who've gone missing in Camden Town?"

Jane nodded but said nothing. She felt anxious and clumsy—as though she'd drunk too much, although she'd had nothing since the two glasses of wine with David Bierce. Her companion also seemed ill at ease; he kept glancing back, as though looking for someone on the canal path behind them.

"I should have tried to call," he explained ruefully. "But I forgot to recharge my mobile."

"You could call from my place."

"No, that's all right."

She could tell from his tone that he was figuring how he could leave, gracefully, as soon as possible.

Inside the flat he settled on the couch, picked up a copy of *Time Out* and flipped through it, pretending to read. Jane went immediately into the kitchen and poured herself a glass of brandy. She downed it, poured a second one, and joined him on the couch.

"So." She kicked off her Doc Martens, drew her stockinged foot slowly up his leg, from calf to thigh. "Where you from?"

He was passive, so passive she wondered if he would get aroused at all. But after a while they were lying on the couch, both their shirts on the floor, his pants unzipped and his cock stiff, pressing against her bare belly.

"Let's go in there," Jane whispered hoarsely. She took his hand and led him into the bedroom.

She only bothered lighting a single candle, before lying beside him on the bed. His eyes were half-closed, his breathing shallow. When she ran a fingernail around one nipple he made a small surprised sound, then quickly turned and pinned her to the bed.

"Wait! Slow down," Jane said, and wriggled from beneath him. For the last week she'd left the bonds attached to the bedposts, hiding them beneath the covers when not in use. Now she grabbed one of the wristcuffs and pulled it free. Before he could see what she was doing it was around his wrist.

"Hey!"

She dove for the foot of the bed, his leg narrowly missing her as it thrashed against the covers. It was more difficult to get this in place, but she made a great show of giggling and stroking his thigh, which seemed to calm him. The other leg was next, and finally she leapt from the bed and darted to the headboard, slipping from his grasp when he tried to grab her shoulder.

"This is not consensual," he said. She couldn't tell if he was serious or not.

"What about this, then?" she murmured, sliding down between his legs and cupping his erect penis between her hands. "This seems to be enjoying itself."

He groaned softly, shutting his eyes. "Try to get away," she said. "Try to get away."

He tried to lunge upward, his body arching so violently that she drew back in alarm. The bonds held; he arched again, and again, but now she remained beside him, her hands on his cock, his breath coming faster and faster and her own breath keeping pace with it, her heart pounding and the tingling above her eyes almost unbearable.

"Try to get away," she gasped. "Try to get away—"

When he came he cried out, his voice harsh, as though in pain, and

Jane cried out as well, squeezing her eyes shut as spasms shook her from head to groin. Quickly her head dipped to kiss his chest; then she shuddered and drew back, watching.

His voice rose again, ended suddenly in a shrill wail, as his limbs knotted and shriveled like burning rope. She had a final glimpse of him, a homunculus sprouting too many legs. Then on the bed before her a perfectly formed *Papilio krishna* swallowtail crawled across the rumpled duvet, its wings twitching to display glittering green scales amidst spectral washes of violet and crimson and gold.

"Oh, you're beautiful, beautiful," she whispered.

From across the room echoed a sound: soft, the rustle of her kimono falling from its hook as the door swung open. She snatched her hand from the butterfly and stared, through the door to the living room.

In her haste to get Thomas Raybourne inside she had forgotten to latch the front door. She scrambled to her feet, naked, staring wildly at the shadow looming in front of her, its features taking shape as it approached the candle, brown and black, light glinting across his face.

It was David Bierce. The scent of oak and bracken swelled, suffocating, fragrant, cut by the bitter odor of ethyl alcohol. He forced her gently onto the bed, heat piercing her breast and thighs, her antennae bursting out like flame from her brow and wings exploding everywhere around her as she struggled fruitlessly.

"Now. Try to get away," he said.

The Man on the Ceiling

Steve Rasnic Tem and Melanie Tem

*E*verything we're about to tell you is true.

Don't ask me if I mean that "literally." I know about the literal. The literal has failed miserably to explain the things I've really needed explanations for. The things in your dreams, the things in your head, don't know from literal. And yet that's where most of us live: in our dreams, in our heads. The stories there, those fables and fairytales, are our lives. Ever since I was a little boy I wanted to find out the names of the mysterious characters who lived in those stories. The heroes, the demons, and the angels. Once I named them, I would be one step closer to understanding them. Once I named them, they would be real.

When Melanie and I got married, we chose this name, TEM. A gypsy word meaning "country," and also the name of an ancient Egyptian deity who created the world and everything in it by naming the world and everything in it, who created its own divine self by naming itself, part by part. Tem became the name for our relationship, that undiscovered country which had always existed inside us both, but had never been real until we met.

Much of our life together has been concerned with this naming. Naming of things, places, and mysterious, shadowy characters. Naming of each other and of what is between us. Making it real.

The most disturbing thing about the figures of horror fiction for me is a particular kind of vagueness in their form. However clearly an author might paint some terrifying figure, if this character truly resonates, if it reflects some essential terror within the human animal, then our minds refuse to fix it into a form. The faces of our real terrors shift and warp the closer they come to us: the werewolf becomes an elderly man on our block becomes the local butcher becomes an uncle we remember coming down for the Christmas holidays when we were five. The face of horror freezes but briefly, and as quickly as we jot down its details, it is something else again.

Melanie used to wake me in the middle of the night to tell me there was a man in our bedroom window, or a man on the ceiling.

I had my doubts, but being a good husband I checked the windows and I checked the ceiling and I attempted to reassure. We had been through this enough times that I had plenty of reason to believe she would not be reassured no matter what I said. Still I made the attempt each time, giving her overly reasonable explanations concerning the way the light had been broken up by wind-blown branches outside, or how the ceiling light fixture might be mistaken for a man's head by a person waking suddenly from a restless sleep or an intense dream. Sometimes my careful explanations irritated her enormously. Still mostly asleep, she would wonder aloud why I couldn't see the man on the ceiling. Was I playing games with her? Trying to placate her when I knew the awful truth?

In fact, despite my attempts at reason, I believed in the man on the ceiling. I always had.

As a child I was a persistent liar. I lied slyly, I lied innocently, and I lied enthusiastically. I lied out of confusion and I lied out of a profound disappointment. One of my more elaborate lies took shape during the 1960 presidential election. While the rest of the country was debating the relative merits of Kennedy and Nixon, I was explaining to my friends how I had been half of a pair of Siamese twins, and how my brother had tragically died during the separation.

This was, perhaps, my most heartfelt lie to date, because in telling this tale I found myself grieving over the loss of my brother, my twin. I had created my first believable character, and my character had hurt me.

Later I came to recognize that about that time (I was ten), the self I had been was dying, and that I was slowly becoming the twin who had died and gone off to some other, better fiction.

Many of my lies since then, the ones I have been paid for, have been about such secret, tragic twins and their other lives. The lives we dream about, and only half-remember after the first shock of day.

So how could I, of all people, doubt the existence of the man on the ceiling?

My first husband did not believe in the man on the ceiling.

At least, he said he didn't. He said he never saw him. Never had night terrors. Never saw the molecules moving in the trunks of trees and felt the distances among the pieces of himself.

I think he did, though, and was too afraid to name what he saw. I think he believed that if he didn't name it, it wouldn't be real. And so, I think, the man on the ceiling got him a long time ago.

Back then, it was usually a snake I'd see, crawling across the ceiling, dropping to loop around my bed. I'd wake up and there would still be a snake—huge, vivid, sinuous, utterly mesmerizing. I'd cry out. I'd call for help. After my first husband had grudgingly come in a few times and hadn't been able to reassure me that there was no snake on the ceiling, he just quit coming.

Steve always comes. Usually, he's already there beside me.

One night a man really did climb in my bedroom window. Really did sit on the edge of my bed, really did mutter incoherently and fumble in the bedclothes, really did look surprised and confused when I sat up and screamed. I guess he thought I was someone else. He left, stumbling, by the same second-story window. I chased him across the room, had the tail of his denim jacket in my hands. But I let him go because I couldn't imagine what I'd do next if I caught him.

By the time I went downstairs and told my first husband, there was no sign of the intruder. By the time the police came, there was no evidence, and I certainly could never have identified him. I couldn't even describe him in any useful way: dark, featureless. Muttering nonsense. As confused as I was. Clearly not meaning me any harm, or any good, either. Not meaning me anything. He thought I was someone else. I wasn't afraid of him. He didn't change my life. He wasn't the man on the ceiling.

I don't think anybody then believed that a man had come in my window in the middle of the night and gone away again. Steve would have believed me.

Yes, I would have believed her. I've come to believe in the reality of all of Melanie's characters. And I believe in the man on the ceiling with all my heart.

For one evening this man on the ceiling climbed slowly down out of the darkness and out of the dream of our marriage and took one of our children away. And changed our lives forever.

Awake.

Someone in the room.

Asleep. Dreaming.

Someone in the room.

Someone in the room. Someone by the bed. Reaching to touch me but not touching me yet.

I put out my hand and Steve is beside me, solid, breathing steadily. I press myself to him, not wanting to wake him but needing enough to be close to him that I'm selfishly willing to risk it. I can feel his heartbeat through the blanket and sheet, through both our pajamas and both our flesh, through the waking or the dream. He's very warm. If he were dead, if he were the ghostly figure standing by the bed trying to touch me but not touching me, his body heat wouldn't radiate into me like this, wouldn't comfort me. It comforts me intensely.

Someone calls me. I hear only the voice, the tone of voice, and not the name it uses.

Awake. Painful tingling of nerve endings, heart pumping so wildly it hurts. Our golden cat Cinnabar—who often sleeps on my chest and eases some of the fear away by her purring, her small weight, her small radiant body heat, by the sheer miraculous contact with some other living creature who remains fundamentally alien while we touch so surely—moves away now. Moves first onto the mound of Steve's hip, but he doesn't like her on top of him and in his sleep he makes an irritable stirring motion that tips her off. Cinnabar gives an answering irritable trill and jumps off the bed.

Someone calling me. The door, always cracked so I can hear the kids if they cough or call, opens wider now, yellow wash from the hall light across the new forest-green carpet of our bedroom, which we've remodeled to be like a forest cave just for the two of us, a sanctuary. A figure in the yellow light, small and shadowy, not calling me now.

Neither asleep nor awake. A middle-of-the-night state of consciousness that isn't hypnagogic, either. Meta-wakefulness. Meta-sleep. Aware now of things that are always there, but in daylight are obscured by thoughts and plans, judgments and impressions, words and worries and obligations and sensations, and at night by dreams.

Someone in the room.

Someone by the bed.

Someone coming to get me. I'm too afraid to open my eyes, and too aroused to go back to sleep.

But we've made it our job, Melanie and I, to open our eyes and see who's there. To find who's there and to name who's there.

In our life together, we seem to seek it out. Our children, when they become our children, already know the man on the ceiling. Maybe all children do, at some primal level, but ours know him consciously, have already faced him down, and teach us how to do that, too.

We go toward the voice by the door, the shape in the room. Not so much to find the vampires and the werewolves who have been seen so many times before—who are safe to find because no one really believes in them anymore anyway—but to find the hidden figures who lurk in our house and other houses like ours: the boy with the head vigorously shaking nonono, the boy who appears and disappears in the midst of a cluttered bedroom, the little dead girl who controls her family with her wishes and lies, the little boy driven by his dad on a hunting trip down into the darkest heart of the city, and the man who hangs suspended from the ceiling waiting for just the right opportunity to climb down like a message from the eternal. To find the demons. To find the angels.

Sometimes we find these figures right in our own home, infiltrating our life together, standing over the beds of our children.

"Mom?"

A child. My child. Calling me, "Mom." A name so precious I never get used to it, emblematic of the joy and terror of this impossible relationship every time one of them says it. Which is often.

"Mom? I had a bad dream."

It's Joe. Who came to us a year and a half ago an unruly, intensely imaginative child so terrified of being abandoned again that he's only very recently been willing to say he loves me. He called me "Mom" right away, but he wouldn't say he loved me.

If you love someone, they leave you. But if you don't love someone, they leave you, too. So your choice isn't between loving and losing but only between loving and not loving.

This is the first time Joe has ever come for me in the middle of the night, the first time he's been willing to test our insistence that that's what parents are here for, although I think he has nightmares a lot.

I slide out of bed and pick him up. He's so small. He holds himself upright, won't snuggle against me, and his wide blue eyes are staring off somewhere, not at me. But his hand is on my shoulder and he lets me put him in my lap in the rocking chair, and he tells me about his dream. About a dog that died and came back to life. Joe loves animals. About Dad and me dying. Himself dying. Anthony dying.

Joe, who never knew Anthony, dreams about Anthony dying. Mourns Anthony. This connection seems wonderful to me, and a little frightening.

Joe's man on the ceiling already has a name, for Joe's dream is also about how his birthparents hurt him. Left him. He doesn't say it, maybe he's not old enough to name it, but when I suggest he must have felt then that he was going to die, that they were going to kill him, he nods vigorously, thumb in his mouth. And when I point out that he didn't die, that he's still alive and he can play with the cats and dogs and dig in the mudhole and learn to read chapter books and go to the moon someday, his eyes get very big and he nods vigorously and then he snuggles against my shoulder. I hold my breath for this transcendent moment. Joe falls asleep in my lap.

I am wide awake now, holding my sleeping little boy in my lap and rocking, rocking. Shadows move on the ceiling. The man on the ceiling is there. He's always there. And I understand, in a way I don't fully understand and will have lost most of by morning, that he gave me this moment, too.

I was never afraid of dying, before. But that changed after the man on the ceiling came down. Now I see his shadow imprinted in my skin, like a brand, and I think about dying.

That doesn't mean I'm unhappy, or that the shadow cast by the man on the ceiling is a shadow of depression. I can't stand people without a sense of humor, nor can I tolerate this sort of morbid fascination with the ways and colorings of death that shows itself even among people who say they enjoy my work. I never believed horror fiction was simply about morbid fascinations. I find that attitude stupid and dull.

The man on the ceiling gives my life an edge. He makes me uneasy; he makes me grieve. And yet he also fills me with awe for what is possible. He shames me with his glimpses into the darkness of human cruelty, and he shocks me when I see bits of my own face in his. He encourages a reverence when I contemplate the inevitability of my own death. And he shakes me with anger, pity, and fear.

The man on the ceiling makes it mean that much more when my daughter's fever breaks, when my son smiles sleepily up at me in the morning and sticks out his tongue.

So I wasn't surprised when one night, late, 2 A.M. or so, after I'd stayed up reading, I began to feel a change in the air of the house, as if something were being added, or something taken away.

Cinnabar uncurled and lifted her head, her snout wrinkling as if to test the air. Then her head turned slowly atop her body, and her yellow eyes became silver as she made a long, motionless stare into the darkness beyond our bedroom door. Poised. Transfixed.

I glanced down at Melanie sleeping beside me. I could see Cinnabar's claws piercing the sheet and yet Melanie did not wake up. I leaned over her then to see if I could convince myself she was breathing. Melanie breathes so shallowly during sleep that half the time I can't tell she's breathing at all. So it isn't unusual to find me poised over her like this during the middle of the night, like some anxious and aging gargoyle, waiting to see the rise and fall of the covers to let me know she is still alive. I don't know if this is normal behavior or not—I've never really discussed it with anyone before. But no matter how often I watch my wife like this, and wait, no matter how often I see that yes, she is breathing, I still find myself considering what I would do, how I would feel, if that miraculous breathing did stop. Every time I worry myself with an imagined routine of failed attempts to revive her, to put the breathing back in, of frantic late night calls to anyone who might listen, begging them to tell me what I should do to put the breathing back in. It would be my fault, of course, because I had been watching. I should have watched her more carefully. I should have known exactly what to do.

During these ruminations I become intensely aware of how ephemeral we are. Sometimes I think we're all little more than a ghost of a memory, our flesh a poor joke.

I also become painfully aware of how, even for me when I'm acting the part of the writer, the right words to express just how much I love Melanie are so hard to come by.

At that point, the man on the ceiling stuck his head through our bedroom door and looked right at me. He turned, looking at Melanie's near-motionless form—and I saw how thin he was, like a silhouette cut from black construction paper. Then he pulled his head back into the darkness and disappeared.

I eased out of bed, trying not to awaken Melanie. Cinnabar raised her back and took a swipe at me. I moved toward the doorway, taking one last look back at the bed. Cinnabar stared at me as if she couldn't believe I was actually doing this, as though I were crazy.

For I intended to follow the man on the ceiling and find out where he was going. I couldn't take him lightly. I already knew some of what he was capable of. So I followed him that night, as I have followed him every night since, in and out of shadow, through dreams and memories of dreams, down the back steps and up into the attic, past the fitful or peaceful sleep of my children, through daily encounters with death, forgiveness, and love.

Usually he is this shadow I've described, a silhouette clipped out of the dark, a shadow of a shadow. But these are merely the aspects I'm normally willing to face. Sometimes as he glides from darkness into light and into darkness again, as he steps and drifts through the night rooms and corridors of our house, I glimpse his figure from other angles: a mouth suddenly fleshed out and full of teeth, eyes like the devil's eyes like my own father's eyes, a hairy fist with coarse fingers, a jawbone with my own beard attached.

And sometimes his changes are more elaborate: he sprouts needle teeth, razor fingers, or a mouth like a swirling metal funnel.

The man on the ceiling casts shadows of flesh, and sometimes the shadows take on a life of their own.

Many years later, the snake returned. I was very awake.

I'd been offered painkillers and tranquilizers to produce the undead state which often passes for grieving but is not. I refused them. I wanted to be awake. The coils of the snake dropped from the ceiling and rose from the floor—oozing, slithering, until I was entirely encased. The skin molted and molted again into my own skin. The flesh was supple around my own flesh. The color of the world from inside the coils of the snake was a growing, soothing green.

"Safe," hissed the snake all around me. "You are safe."

Everything we're telling you here is true.

Each night as I follow the man on the ceiling into the various rooms of my children and watch him as he stands over them, touches them, kisses their cheeks with his black ribbon tongue, I imagine what he must be doing to them, what transformations he might be orchestrating in their dreams.

I imagine him creeping up to my youngest daughter's bed, reaching out his narrow black fingers and like a razor they enter her skull so he can change things there, move things around, plant ideas that might sprout—deadly or healing—in years to come. She is seven years old, and an artist. Already her pictures are thoughtful and detailed and she's not afraid of taking risks: cats shaped like hearts, people with feathers for hair, roses made entirely of concentric arcs. Does the man on the ceiling have anything to do with this?

I imagine him crawling into bed with my youngest son, whispering things into my son's ear, and suddenly my son's sweet character has changed forever.

I imagine him climbing the attic stairs and passing through the door to my teenage daughter's bedroom without making a sound, slipping over her sleeping form so gradually it's as if a car's headlights had passed and the shadows in the room had shifted and now the man from the ceiling is kissing my daughter and infecting her with a yearning she'll never be rid of.

I imagine him flying out of the house altogether, leaving behind a shadow of his shadow who is no less dangerous than he is, flying away from our house to find our troubled oldest son, filling his head with thoughts he won't be able to control, filling his brain with hallucinations he won't have to induce, imprisoning him forever where he is now imprisoned.

I imagine the young man who is not quite our son and is far more than our friend, who lives much of the time in some other reality, who wants so desperately to believe himself alien, chosen, destined to change the world by sheer virtue of the fact that he is so lonely. He hears voices—I wonder if the voices in his head help him ignore his man on the ceiling, or if they are the voices of the man on the ceiling.

Every night since that first night the man on the ceiling climbed down, I have followed him all evening like this: in my dreams, or sitting up in bed, or resting in a chair, or poised in front of a computer screen typing obsessively, waiting for him to reveal himself through my words.

Our teenage daughter has night terrors. I suspect she always has. When she came to us a tiny and terrified seven-year-old, I think the terrors were everywhere, day and night.

Now she's sixteen, and she's still afraid of many things. Her strength, her wisdom beyond her years, is in going toward what frightens her. I watch her do that, and I am amazed. She worries, for instance, about serial killers, and so she's read and re-read everything she could find about Ted Bundy, Jeffrey Daumer, John Wayne Gacy. She's afraid of death, partly because it's seductive, and so she wants to be a mortician or a forensic photographer—get inside death, see what makes a dead body dead, record the evidence. Go as close to the fear as you can. Go as close to the monster. Know it. Claim it. Name it. Take it in.

She's afraid of love, and so she falls in love often and deeply.

Her night terrors now most often take the form of a faceless lady in white who stands by her bed with a knife and intends to kill her, tries to steal her breath the way they used to say cats would do if you let them near the crib. The lady doesn't disappear even when our daughter wakes herself up, sits up in bed, and turns on the light.

Our daughter wanted something alive to sleep with. The cats betrayed her, wouldn't be confined to her room. So we got her a dog. Ezra was abandoned, too, or lost and never found, and he's far more worried than she is, which I don't think she thought possible. He sleeps with her. He sleeps under her covers. He would sleep on her pillow, covering her face, if she'd let him, and she would let him if she could breathe. She says the lady hasn't come once since Ezra has been here.

I don't know if Ezra will keep the night terrors away forever. But, if she trusts him, he'll let her know whether the lady is real. That's no small gift.

Our daughter is afraid of many things, and saddened by many things. She accepts pain better than most people, takes in pain. I think that now her challenge, her adventure, is to learn to accept happiness. That's scary.

So maybe the lady at the end of her bed doesn't intend to kill her after all. Maybe she intends to teach her how to take in happiness.

Which is, I guess, a kind of death.

I know that the lady beside my daughter's bed is real, but this is not something I have yet chosen to share with my daughter. I have seen this lady in my own night terrors when I was a teenager, just as I saw the devil in my bedroom one night in the form of a giant goat, six feet tall at the shoulder. I sat up in my bed and watched as the goat's body disappeared slowly, one layer of hair and skin at a time, leaving giant, bloodshot, humanoid eyes, the eyes of the devil, suspended in midair where they remained for several minutes while I gasped for a scream that would not come.

I had night terrors for years until I began experimenting with dream control and learned to extend myself directly into a dream where I could rearrange its pieces and have things happen the way I wanted them to happen. Sometimes when I write now it's as if I'm in the midst of this extended night terror and I'm frantically using powers of the imagination I'm not even sure belong to me to arrange the pieces and make everything turn out the way it should, or at least the way I think it was meant to be.

If the man on the ceiling were just another night terror, I should have the necessary tools to stop him in his tracks, or at least to divert him. But I've followed the man on the ceiling night after night. I've seen what he does to my wife and children. And he's already carried one of our children away.

Remember what I said in the beginning. Everything we're telling you here is true.

I follow the man on the ceiling around the attic of our house, my flashlight burning off pieces of his body which grow back as soon as he moves beyond the beam. I chase him down three flights of stairs into our basement where he hides in the laundry. My hands turn into frantic paddles which scatter the clothes and I'm already thinking about how I'm going to explain the mess to Melanie in the morning when he slips like a pool of oil under my feet and out to other corners of the basement where my children keep their toys. I imagine the edge of his cheek in an oversized doll, his amazingly sharp fingers under the hoods of my son's Matchbox cars.

But the man on the ceiling is a story and I know something about stories. One day I will figure out just what this man on the ceiling is "about." He's a character in the dream of our lives and he can be changed or killed.

It always makes me cranky to be asked what a story is "about," or who my characters "are." If I could tell you, I wouldn't have to write them.

Often I write about people I don't understand, ways of being in the world that baffle me. I want to know how people make sense of things, what they say to themselves, how they live. How they name themselves to themselves.

Because life is hard. Even when it's wonderful, even when it's beautiful—which it is a lot of the time—it's hard. Sometimes I don't know how any of us makes it through the day. Or the night.

The world has in it: Children hurt or killed by their parents, who would say they do it out of love. Children whose beloved fathers, uncles, brothers, cousins, mothers love them, too, fall in love with them, say anything we do to each other's bodies is okay because we love each other, but don't tell anybody because then I'll go to jail and then I won't love you anymore.

Perverted love.

The world also has in it: Children whose only chance to grow up is in

THE MAN ON THE CEILING

prison, because they're afraid to trust love on the outside. Children who die, no matter how much you love them.

Impotent love.

And the world also has in it: Werewolves, whose unclaimed rage transforms them into something not human but also not inhuman (modern psychiatry sometimes finds the bestial "alter" in the multiple personality). Vampires, whose unbridled need to experience leads them to suck other people dry and are still not satisfied. Zombies, the chronically insulated, people who will not feel anything because they will not feel pain. Ghosts.

I write in order to understand these things. I write dark fantasy because it helps me see how to live in a world with monsters.

But one day last week, transferring at a crowded and cold downtown bus stop, late as usual, I was searching irritably in my purse for my bus pass, which was not there, and then for no reason and certainly without conscious intent my gaze abruptly lifted and followed the upswept lines of the pearly glass building across the street, up, up, into the Colorado-blue sky, and it was beautiful.

It was transcendently beautiful. An epiphany. A momentary breakthrough into the dimension of the divine.

That's why I write, too. To stay available for breakthroughs into the dimension of the divine. Which happen in this world all the time.

I think I always write about love.

I married Melanie because she uses words like "divine" and "transcendent" in everyday conversation. I love that about her. It scares me, and it embarrasses me sometimes, but still I love that about her. I was a secretive and frightened male, perhaps like most males, when I met her. And now sometimes even I will use a word like "transcendent." I'm still working on "divine."

And sometimes I write about love. Certainly I love all my characters, miserable lot though they may be. (Another writer once asked me why I wrote about "nebbishes." I told him I wanted to write about "the common man.") Sometimes I even love the man on the ceiling, as much as I hate him, because of all the things he enables me to see. Each evening, carrying my flashlight, I follow him through all the dark rooms of my life. He doesn't need a light because he has learned these rooms so well and because he carries his own light; if you'll look at him carefully you'll notice that his grin glows in the night. I follow him because I need to understand him. I follow him because he always has something new to show me.

One night I followed him into a far corner of our attic. Apparently this was where he slept when he wasn't clinging to our ceiling or prowling our children's rooms. He had made himself a nest out of old photos chewed up and their emulsions spat out into a paste to hold together bits of outgrown clothing and the gutted stuffings of our children's discarded dolls and teddy bears. He lay curled up, his great dark sides heaving.

I flashed the light on him. And then I saw his wings.

They were patchwork affairs, the separate sections molded out of burnt newspaper, ancient lingerie, metal road signs, and fish nets, stitched together with shoelaces and Bubble Yum, glued and veined with tears, soot, and ash. The man on the ceiling turned his obsidian head and blew me a kiss of smoke.

I stood perfectly still with the light in my hand growing dimmer as he drained away its brightness. So the man on the ceiling was in fact an angel, a messenger between our worldly selves and—yes, I'll say it—the divine. And it bothered me that I hadn't recognized his angelic nature before. I should have known, because aren't ghosts nothing more than angels with wings of memory, and vampires angels with wings of blood?

Everything we're trying to tell you here is true.

And there are all kinds of truths to tell. There's the true story about how the man, the angel, on the ceiling killed my mother, and what I did with her body. There's the story about how my teenage daughter fell in love with the man on the ceiling and ran away with him and we didn't see her for weeks. There's the story about how I tried to become the man on the ceiling in order to understand him and ended up terrorizing my own children.

There are so many true stories to tell. So many possibilities.

There are so many stories to tell. I could tell this story:

Melanie smiled at the toddler standing up backwards in the seat in front of her. He wasn't holding on to anything, and his mouth rested dangerously on the metal bar across the back of the seat. His mother couldn't have been much more than seventeen, from what Melanie could see of her pug-nosed, rouged and sparkly-eye-shadowed, elaborately poufed profile; Melanie was hoping it was his big sister until she heard him call her "Mama."

"Mama," he kept saying. "Mama. Mama." The girl ignored him. His prattle became increasingly louder and more shrill until everyone on the bus was looking at him, except his mother, who had her head turned as far away from him as she could. She was cracking her gum.

The sunset was lovely, peach and purple and gray, made more lovely by the streaks of dirt on the bus windows and by the contrasting bright white dots of headlights and bright red dots of taillights moving everywhere under it. When they passed slowly over the Valley Highway, Melanie saw that the lights were exquisite, and hardly moving at all.

"Mama! Mama! Mama!" The child swiveled clumsily toward his mother and reached out both hands for her just as the driver hit the brakes. The little boy toppled sideways and hit his mouth on the metal bar. A small spot of blood appeared on his lower lip. There was a moment of stunned silence from the child; his mother—still staring off away from him, earphones over her ears, still popping her gum rhythmically—obviously hadn't noticed what had happened.

Then he shrieked. At last disturbed, she whirled on him furiously, an epithet halfway out of her child-vamp mouth, but when she saw the blood on her son's face she collapsed into near-hysteria. Although she did hold him and wipe at his face with her long-nailed fingertips, it was clear she didn't know what to do.

Melanie considered handing her a tissue, lecturing her about child safety, even—ridiculously—calling social services. But here was her stop. Fuming, she followed the lady with the shoulder-length white hair down the steps and out into the evening, which was tinted peach and purple and gray from the sunset of however dubious origin and, no less prettily, red and white from the Safeway sign.

The man on the ceiling laughs at me as he remains always just out of the reach of my understanding, floating above me on his layered wings, telling me about how, someday, everyone I love is going to die and how, after I die, no one is going to remember me no matter how much I write, how much I shamelessly reveal, brushing his sharp fingers against the wallpaper and leaving deep gouges in the walls. He rakes back the curtains and shows me the sky: peach and purple and gray like the colors of his eyes when he opens them, like the colors of his mouth, the colors of his tongue when he laughs even more loudly and heads for the open door of one of my children's rooms.

The white-haired woman was always on this bus. Always wore the same ankle-length red coat when it was cold enough to wear any coat at all. Grim-faced and always frowning, but with that crystalline hair falling softly over her shoulders.

They always got off at the same stop, waited at the intersection for the light to change, walked together a block and a half until the lady turned into the Spanish-style stucco apartment building that had once been a church—it still had "Jesus Is the Light of the World" inscribed in an arc over one doorway and a pretty enclosed courtyard overlooked by tall windows shaped as if to hold stained glass. At that point, Melanie's house was still two blocks away, and she always just kept walking. She and the white-haired lady had never exchanged a word. Maybe someday she'd think how to start a conversation. Not tonight.

Tonight, like most nights, she just wanted to be home. Safe and patently loved in the hubbub of her family. Often, disbelieving, she would count to herself the number of discrete living creatures whose lives she shared, and she loved the changing totals: tonight it was Steve, and five kids, four cats, three dogs, even twenty-three plants. Exhausted from work, she could almost always count on being revitalized when she went home.

The man on the ceiling turns and screams at me until I feel my flesh beginning to shred. The man on the ceiling puts his razor-sharp fingers into my joints and twists, and I clench my fists and bite the insides of my lips trying not to scream. The man on the ceiling grins and grins and grins. He sticks both hands into my belly and pulls out my organs and offers to tell me how long I have to live.

I tell him I don't want to know, and then he offers to tell me how long Melanie is going to live, how long each of my children is going to live.

The man on the ceiling crawls into my belly through the hole he has made and curls up inside himself to become a cancer resting against my spinal column. I can no longer walk and I fall to the ground.

The man on the ceiling rises into my throat and I can no longer speak. The man on the ceiling floats into my skull and I can no longer dream.

The man on the ceiling crawls out of my head, his sharp black heels piercing my tongue as he steps out of my mouth.

The man on the ceiling starts devouring our furniture a piece at a time, beating his great conglomerate wings in orgasmic frenzy, releasing tiny gifts of decay into the air.

How might I explain why supposedly good people could imagine such things? How might I explain how I could feel such passion for my wife and children, or for the simplest acts of living, when such creatures travel in packs through my dreams?

It is because the man on the ceiling is a true story that I find life infinitely interesting. It is because of such dark, transcendent angels in each of our houses that we are able to love. Because we must. Because it is all there is.

Daffodils were blooming around the porch of the little yellow house set down away from the sidewalk. Melanie stopped, amazed. They had not been there yesterday. Their scent lasted all the way to the corner.

One year Steve had given her a five-foot-long, three-foot-high Valentine showing a huge flock of penguins, all of them alike, and out of the crowd two of them with pink hearts above their heads, and the caption: "I'm so glad we found each other." It was, of course, a miracle.

She crossed the street and entered her own block. The sunset was paling now, and the light was silvery down the street. A trick of the light made it look as though the hill on which her house sat was flattened. Melanie smiled and wondered what Matilda McCollum, who'd had the house built in 1898 and had the hill constructed so it would be grander than her sister's otherwise identical house across the way, would say to that. A huge, solid, sprawling, red-brick Victorian rooted in Engelmann ivy so expansive as to be just this side of overgrown, the house was majestic on its hill. Grand. Unshakable. Matilda had been right.

The man on the ceiling opens his mouth and begins eating the wall by the staircase. First he has to taste it. He rests the dark holes that have been drilled into his face for nostrils against the brittle flocked wallpaper and sniffs out decades' worth of noise, conversation, and prayers. Then he slips his teeth over the edges and pulls it away from the wall, shoveling the crackling paper into his dark maw with fingers curved into claws. Tiny trains of silverfish drift down the exposed wall before the man on the ceiling devours them as well, then his abrasive tongue scoops out the crumbling plaster from the wooden lath and minutes later he has started on the framing itself.

Powerless to stop him, I watch as he sups on the dream of my life. Suddenly I am sixteen again and this life I have written for myself is all ahead of me, and impossibly out of reach.

Melanie was looking left at the catalpa tree between the sidewalk and the street, worrying as she did every spring that this time it really would never leaf out and she would discover it was dead, had died over the winter and she hadn't known, had in fact always been secretly dead, when she turned right to go up the steps to her house. Stumbled. Almost fell. There were no steps. There was no hill.

She looked up. There was no house.

And she knew there never had been.

There never had been a family. She had never had children.

She had somehow made up: sweet troubled Christopher, Mark who heard voices and saw the molecules dancing in tree trunks and most of the time was glad, Veronica of the magnificent chestnut hair and heart bursting painfully with love, Anthony whose laughter had been like seashells, Joe for whom the world was an endless adventure, Gabriella who knew how to go inside herself and knew to tell you what she was doing there: "I be calm."

She'd made up the golden cat Cinnabar, who would come to purr on her chest and ease the pain away. She'd made up the hoya plant that sent out improbable white flowers off a leafless woody stem too far into the dining room. She'd made up the rainbows on the kitchen walls from the prisms she hung in the south window.

She'd made up Steve.

There had never been love.

There had never been a miracle.

Angels. Our lives are filled with angels.

The man on the ceiling smiles in the midst of the emptiness, his wings beating heavily against the clouds, his teeth the color of the cold I am feeling now. Melanie used to worry so much when I went out late at night for milk, or ice cream for the both of us, that I'd need to call her from a phone booth if I thought I'd be longer than the forty-five minutes it took for her anxiety and her fantasies about all that can happen to people to kick in. Sometimes she fantasized about the police showing up at the door to let her know about the terrible accident I'd had, or sometimes I just didn't come back—I got the milk or the ice cream and I just kept on going.

I can't say that I was always helpful. Sometimes I'd tell her I had to come home because the ice cream would melt if I didn't get it into the freezer right away. I'm not sure that was very reassuring.

What I tried not to think about was what if I never could find my way home, what if things weren't as I'd left them. What if everything had changed? One night I got lost along the southern edge of the city after a late night movie and wandered for an hour or so convinced that my worst fantasies had come true.

The man on the ceiling smiles and begins devouring my dream of the sky.

A wise man asks me, when I've told him this story of my vanishing home again, "And then what?"

I glare at him. He's supposed to understand me. "What do you mean?"

"And then what happens? After you discover that your house and your family have disappeared?"

"Not disappeared," I point out irritably. "Have never existed."

"Yes. Have never existed. And then what happens?"

I've never thought of that. The never-having-existed seems final enough, awful enough. I can't think of anything to say, so I don't say anything, hoping he will. But he's wise, and he knows how to use silence. He just sits there, being calm, until finally I say, "I don't know."

"Maybe it would be interesting to find out," he suggests.

So we try. He eases me into a light trance; I'm eager and highly suggestible, and I trust this man, so my consciousness alters easily. He guides me through the fantasy again and again, using my own words and some of his own. But every time I stop at the point where I come home and there isn't any home. The point where I look up and my life, my love, isn't there. Has never existed.

I don't know what happens next. I can't imagine what happens next. Do I die? Does the man on the ceiling take me into his house? Does he fly away with me into an endless sky? Does he help me create another life, another miracle?

That's why I write. To find out what happens next.

So what happens next? This might happen:

After the man on the ceiling devours my life I imagine it back again: I fill in the walls, the doorways, the empty rooms with colors and furnishings different from, but similar to, the ones I imagine to have been there before. Our lives are full of angels of all kinds. So I call on some of those other angels to get my life back.

I write myself a life, and it is very different from the one I had before, and yet very much the same. I make mistakes different from the ones I made with my children before. I love Melanie the same way I did before. Different wonderful things happen. The same sad, wonderful events recur.

The man on the ceiling just smiles at me and makes of these new imaginings his dessert. So what happens next? In a different kind of story I might take out a machete and chop him into little bits of shadow. Or I might blast him into daylight with a machine gun. I might douse him with lighter fluid and set him on fire.

But I don't write those kinds of stories.

And besides, the man on the ceiling is a necessary angel.

There are so many truths to tell. There are so many different lives I could dream for myself.

What happens next?

There are so many stories to tell. I could tell this story:

The man from the ceiling was waiting for Melanie behind the fence (an ugly, bare, chain-link and chicken wire fence, not the black wrought iron fence plaited with rosebushes that she'd made up), where her home had never existed. He beckoned to her. He called her by name, his own special name for her, a name she never got used to no matter how often he said it, which was often. He reached for her, trying to touch her but not quite touching.

She could have turned and run away from him. He wouldn't have chased her down. His arms wouldn't have telescoped long and impossibly jointed to capture her at the end of the block. His teeth wouldn't have pushed themselves out of his mouth in gigantic segmented fangs to cut her off at the knees, to bite her head off. He wouldn't have sucked her blood.

But he'd have kept calling her, using his special name for her. And he'd have scaled her windows, dropped from her roof, crawled across her ceiling again that night, and every night for the rest of her life.

So Melanie went toward him. Held out her arms.

There are so many different dreams. That one was Melanie's. This one is mine:

I sit down at the kitchen table. The man on the ceiling lies on my plate, collapsed and folded up neatly in the center. I slice him into hundreds of oily little pieces which I put into my mouth one morsel at a time. I bite through his patchwork wings. I gnaw on his inky heart. I chew his long, narrow fingers well. I make of him my daily meal of darkness.

There are so many stories to tell.

And all of the stories are true.

⊹ ⊹

We wait for whatever happens next.

We stay available.

We name it to make it real.

It was hard for us to write this piece.

For one thing, we write differently. My stories tend more toward magical realism, Steve's more toward surrealism. Realism, in both cases, but we argued over form: "This isn't a story! It doesn't have a plot!"

"What do you want from a plot? Important things happen, and it does move from A to B."

In our fiction, Melanie's monsters usually are ultimately either vanquished or accepted, while at the end of my stories you often find out that the darkness in one form or another lives on and on. There's no escaping it, and I question whether you should try to escape it in the first place.

Since words can only approximate both the monsters and the vanquishment, we wrote each other worried notes in the margins of this story.

"I don't know if we can really use the word 'divine.' "

"If someone looked inside your dreams, would they really see only darkness?"

It was hard for us to write this piece.

"This upsets me," Melanie would say.

Steve would nod. "Maybe we can't do this."

"Oh, we have to," I'd insist. "We've gone too far to stop now. I want to see what happens."

This piece is about writing and horror and fear and about love. We're utterly separate from each other, of course, yet there's a country we share, a rich and wonderful place, a divine place, and we create it by naming all of its parts, all of the angels and all of the demons who live there with us.

What happens next?

There are so many stories to tell.

We could tell

another story:

The Great God Pan

M. John Harrison

But is there really something far more horrible than ever could resolve itself into reality, and is it that something which terrifies me so?
—Katherine Mansfield
Journals, March 1914

nn took drugs to manage her epilepsy. They often made her depressed and difficult to deal with; and Lucas, who was nervous himself, never knew what to do. After their divorce he relied increasingly on me as a go-between. "I don't like the sound of her voice," he would tell me. "You try her." The drugs gave her a screaming, false-sounding laugh that went on and on. Though he had remained sympathetic over the years, Lucas was always embarrassed and upset by it. I think it frightened him. "See if you can get any sense out of her." It was guilt, I think, that encouraged him to see me as a steadying influence: not his own guilt so much as the guilt he felt all three of us shared. "See what she says."

On this occasion what she said was:

"Look, if you bring on one of my turns, bloody Lucas Fisher will regret it. What business is it of his how I feel, anyway?"

I was used to her, so I said carefully, "It was just that you wouldn't talk to him. He was worried that something was happening. Is there something wrong, Ann?" She didn't answer, but I had hardly expected her to. "If you don't want to see me," I suggested, "couldn't you tell me now?"

I thought she was going to hang up, but in the end there was only a kind of paroxysm of silence. I was phoning her from a call box in the middle of Huddersfield. The shopping precinct outside was full of pale bright sunshine, but windy and cold; sleet was forecast for later in the day. Two or three teenagers went past, talking and laughing. I heard one of them say, "What acid rain's got to do with my career, I don't know. But that's what they asked me: 'What do you know about acid rain?' " When they had gone, I could hear Ann breathing raggedly.

"Hello?" I said.

Suddenly she shouted, "Are you mad? I'm not talking on the phone. Before you know it, the whole thing's public property!"

Sometimes she was more dependent on medication than usual; you knew when, because she tended to use that phrase over and over again. One of the first things I ever heard her say was, "It looks so easy, doesn't it? But before you know it, the bloody thing's just slipped straight out of your hands," as she bent down nervously to pick up the bits of a broken glass. How old were we then? Twenty? Lucas believed she was reflecting in language some experience either of the drugs or the disease itself, but I'm not sure he was right. Another thing she often said was, "I mean, you have to be careful, don't you?" drawing out in a wondering, childlike way both *care* and *don't,* so that you saw immediately it was a mannerism learned in adolescence.

"You must be mad if you think I'm talking on the phone!"

I said quickly, "Okay, then, Ann. I'll come over this evening."

"You might as well come now and get it over with. I don't feel well."

Epilepsy since the age of twelve or thirteen, as regular as clockwork; and then, later, a classic migraine to fill in the gaps, a complication which, rightly or wrongly, she had always associated with our experiments at Cambridge in the late sixties. She must never get angry or excited. "I reserve my adrenaline," she would explain, looking down at herself with a comical distaste. "It's a physical thing. I can't let it go at the time." Afterward, though, the reservoir would burst, and it would all be released at once by some minor stimulus—a lost shoe, a missed bus, rain—to cause her hallucinations, vomiting, loss of bowel control. "Oh, and then euphoria. It's wonderfully relaxing," she would say bitterly. "Just like sex."

"Okay, Ann, I'll be there soon. Don't worry."

"Piss off. Things are coming to bits here. I can already see the little floating lights."

As soon as she put the receiver down, I telephoned Lucas.

"I'm not doing this again," I said. "Lucas, she isn't well. I thought she was going to have an attack there and then."

"She'll see you, though? The thing is, she just kept putting the phone down on me. She'll see you today?"

"You knew she would."

"Good."

I hung up.

"Lucas, you're a bastard," I told the shopping precinct.

The bus from Huddersfield wound its way for thirty minutes through exhausted mill villages given over to hairdressing, dog breeding, and an undercapitalized tourist trade. I got off the bus at three o'clock in the afternoon. It seemed much later. The church clock was already lit, and a mysterious yellow light was slanting across the window of the nave—someone was inside with only a forty-watt bulb for illumination. Cars went past endlessly as I waited to cross the road, their exhaust steaming in the dark air. For a village it was quite noisy: tires hissing on the wet road, the bang and clink of soft-drink bottles being unloaded from a lorry, some children I couldn't see, chanting one word over and over again. Suddenly, above all this, I heard the pure musical note of a thrush and stepped out into the road.

"You're sure no one got off the bus behind you?"

Ann kept me on the doorstep while she looked anxiously up and down the street, but once I was inside, she seemed glad to have someone to talk to.

"You'd better take your coat off. Sit down. I'll make you some coffee.

No, here, just push the cat off the chair. He knows he's not supposed to be there."

It was an old cat, black and white, with dull, dry fur, and when I picked it up, it was just a lot of bones and heat that weighed nothing. I set it down carefully on the carpet, but it jumped back onto my knee again immediately and began to dribble on my pullover. Another, younger animal was crouching on the windowsill, shifting its feet uncomfortably among the little intricate baskets of paper flowers as it stared out into the falling sleet, the empty garden. "Get down off there!" Ann shouted suddenly. It ignored her. She shrugged. "They act as if they own the place." It smelled as if they did. "They were strays," she said. "I don't know why I encouraged them." Then, as though she were still talking about the cats:

"How's Lucas?"

"He's surprisingly well," I said. "You ought to keep in touch with him, you know."

"I know." She smiled briefly. "And how are you? I never see you."

"Not bad. Feeling my age."

"You don't know the half of it yet," she said. She was standing in the kitchen doorway holding a tea towel in one hand and a cup in the other. "None of us do." It was a familiar complaint. When she saw I was too preoccupied to listen, she went and banged things about in the sink. I heard water rushing into the kettle. While it filled up, she said something she knew I wouldn't catch; then, turning off the tap:

"Something's going on in the Pleroma. Something new. I can feel it."

"Ann," I said, "all that was over and done with twenty years ago."

The fact is that even at the time I wasn't at all sure what we *had* done. This will seem odd to you, I suppose; but it was 1968 or 1969, and all I remember now is a June evening drenched with the half-confectionary, half-corrupt smell of hawthorn blossoms. It was so thick, we seemed to swim through it, through that and the hot evening light that poured between the hedgerows like transparent gold. I remember Sprake because you don't forget him. What the four of us did escapes me, as does its significance. There was, undoubtedly, a loss; but whether you described what was lost as "innocence" was very much up to you—anyway, that was how it appeared to me. Lucas and Ann made a lot more of it from the very start. They took it to heart. Afterward—perhaps two or three months afterward, when it was plain that something had gone wrong, when things first started to pull out of shape—it was Ann and Lucas who convinced me to go and talk to Sprake, whom we had promised never to contact again. They wanted to see if what we had done could somehow be reversed or annulled; if what we'd lost could be bought back again.

"I don't think it works that way," I warned them; but I could see they weren't listening.

"He'll have to help us," Lucas said.

"Why did we ever do it?" Ann asked me.

Though he hated the British Museum, Sprake had always lived one way or another in its shadow. I met him at the Tivoli Espresso Bar, where I knew he would be every afternoon. He was wearing a thick, old-fashioned black overcoat—the weather that October was raw and damp—but from the way his wrists stuck out of the sleeves, long and fragile-looking and dirty, covered with sore grazes as though he had been fighting with some small animal, I suspected he wore no shirt or jacket underneath it. For some reason he had bought a copy of the *Church Times*. The top half of his body curled painfully around it; along with his stoop and his gray-stubbled lower jaw, the newspaper gave him the appearance of a disappointed verger. It was folded carefully to display part of a headline, but I never saw him open it.

At the Tivoli in those days, they always had the radio on. Their coffee was watery and, like most espresso, too hot to taste of anything. Sprake and I sat on stools by the window. We rested our elbows on a narrow counter littered with dirty cups and half-eaten sandwiches and watched the pedestrians in Museum Street. After ten minutes, a woman's voice said clearly from behind us:

"The fact is, the children just won't try."

Sprake jumped and glanced round haggardly, as if he expected to have to answer this.

"It's the radio," I reassured him.

He stared at me the way you would stare at someone who was mad, and it was some time before he went on with what he had been saying.

"You knew what you were doing. You got what you wanted, and you weren't tricked in any way."

"No," I admitted tiredly.

My eyes ached, even though I had slept on the journey down, waking—just as the train from Cambridge crawled the last mile into London—to see sheets of newspaper fluttering round the upper floors of an office block like butterflies courting a flower.

"I can see that," I said. "That isn't at issue. But I'd like to be able to reassure them in some way...."

Sprake wasn't listening. It had come on to rain quite hard, driving visitors—mainly Germans and Americans who were touring the Museum—in from the street. They all seemed to be wearing brand-new clothes. The Tivoli filled with steam from the espresso machine, and the air was heavy with the smell of wet coats. People trying to find seats constantly brushed our backs, murmuring, "Excuse me, please. Excuse me." Sprake soon became irritated, though I think their politeness affected him more than the disturbance itself. "Dog muck," he said loudly in a matter-of-fact voice; and then, as a whole family pushed past him one by one, "Three generations of rabbits." None of them seemed to take offense, though they must have heard him. A drenched-looking woman in a purple coat came in, looked anxiously for an empty seat, and, when she couldn't see one, hurried out again. "Mad bitch!" Sprake called after her. "Get yourself reamed out." He stared challengingly at the other customers.

"I think it would be better if we talked in private," I said. "What about your flat?"

For twenty years he had lived in the same single room above the Atlantis Bookshop. He was reluctant to take me there, I could see, though it was only next door, and I had been there before. At first he tried to pretend it would be difficult to get in. "The shop's closed," he said. "We'd have to use the other door." Then he admitted:

"I can't go back there for an hour or two. I did something last night that means it may not be safe."

He grinned.

"You know the sort of thing I mean," he said.

I couldn't get him to explain further. The cuts on his wrists made me remember how panicky Ann and Lucas had been when I last spoke to them. All at once I was determined to see inside the room.

"If you don't want to go back there for a bit," I suggested, "we could always talk in the Museum."

Researching in the manuscript collection one afternoon a year before, he had turned a page of Jean de Wavrin's *Chroniques d'Angleterre*—that oblique history no complete version of which is known—and come upon a miniature depicting in strange, unreal greens and blues the coronation procession of Richard Coeur de Lion. Part of it had moved; which part, he would never say. "Why, if it is a coronation," he had written almost plaintively to me at the time, "are these four men carrying a coffin? And who is walking there under the awning—with the bishops not with them?" After that he had avoided the building as much as possible, though he could always see its tall iron railings at the end of the street. He had begun, he told me, to doubt the authenticity of some of the items in the medieval collection. In fact, he was frightened of them.

"It would be quieter there," I insisted.

He didn't respond but sat hunched over the *Church Times*, staring into the street with his hands clamped violently together in front of him. I could see him thinking.

"That fucking pile of shit!" he said eventually.

He got to his feet.

"Come on, then. It's probably cleared out by now, anyway."

Rain dripped from the blue-and-gold front of the Atlantis. There was a faded notice, CLOSED FOR COMPLETE REFURBISHMENT. The window display had been taken down, but they had left a few books on a shelf for the look of things. I could make out, through the condensation on the plate glass, de Vries's classic *Dictionary of Symbols & Imagery*. When I pointed it out to Sprake, he only stared at me contemptuously. He fumbled with his key. Inside, the shop smelled of cut timber, new plaster, paint, but this gave way on the stairs to an odor of cooking. Sprake's bed-sitter, which was quite large and on the top floor, had uncurtained sash windows on opposing walls. Nevertheless, it didn't seem well lit.

From one window you could see the sodden facades of Museum Street, bright green deposits on the ledges, stucco scrolls and garlands gray with pigeon dung; out of the other, part of the blackened clock tower of St. George's Bloomsbury, a reproduction of the tomb of Mausoleus lowering up against the racing clouds.

"I once heard that clock strike twenty-one," said Sprake.

"I can believe that," I said, though I didn't. "Do you think I could have some tea?"

He was silent for a minute. Then he laughed.

"I'm not going to help them," he said. "You know that. I wouldn't be allowed to. What you do in the Pleroma is irretrievable."

"All that was over and done with twenty years ago, Ann."

"I know. I know that. But—"

She stopped suddenly, and then went on in a muffled voice, "Will you just come here a minute? Just for a minute?"

The house, like many in the Pennines, had been built right into the side of the valley. A near vertical bank of earth, cut to accommodate it, was held back by a dry-stone revetment twenty or thirty feet high, black with damp even in the middle of July, dusted with lichen and tufted with fern like a cliff. In December, the water streamed down the revetment day after day and, collecting in a stone trough underneath, made a sound like a tap left running in the night. Along the back of the house ran a passage hardly two feet wide, full of broken roof slates and other rubbish. It was a dismal place.

"You're all right," I told Ann, who was staring, puzzled, into the gathering dark, her head on one side and the tea towel held up to her mouth as if she thought she might be sick.

"It knows who we are," she whispered. "Despite the precautions, it always remembers us."

She shuddered, pulled herself away from the window, and began pouring water so clumsily into the coffee filter that I put my arm around her shoulders and said, "Look, you'd better go and sit down before you scald yourself. I'll finish this, and then you can tell me what's the matter."

She hesitated.

"Come on," I said. "All right?"

"All right."

She went into the living room and sat down heavily. One of the cats ran into the kitchen and looked up at me. "Don't give them milk," she called. "They had it this morning."

"How are you feeling?" I asked. "In yourself, I mean?"

"About how you'd expect." She had taken some propranolol, she said, but it never seemed to help much. "It shortens the headaches, I suppose." As a side effect, though, it made her feel so tired. "It slows my heartbeat down. I can feel it slow right down." She watched the steam rising from her coffee cup, first slowly, and then with a rapid, plaiting motion as it was caught by some tiny draft. Eddies form and break to the same rhythm on the surface of a deep, smooth river. A slow coil, a sudden whirl. What was tranquil is revealed as a mass of complications that can be resolved only as motion.

I remembered when I had first met her: she was twenty then, a small, excitable, attractive girl who wore moss-colored jersey dresses to show off her waist and hips. Later, fear coarsened her. With the divorce a few gray streaks appeared in her blond bell of hair, and she chopped it raggedly off and dyed it black. She drew in on herself. Her body broadened into a kind of dogged, muscular heaviness. Even her hands and feet seemed to become bigger.

"You're old before you know it," she would say. "Before you know it." Separated from Lucas, she was easily chafed by her surroundings; moved every six months or so, although never very far, and always to the same sort of dilapidated, drearily furnished cottage, though you suspected that she was looking for precisely the things that made her nervous and ill; and tried to keep down to fifty cigarettes a day.

"Why did Sprake never help us?" she asked me. "You must know."

Sprake fished two cups out of a plastic washing-up bowl and put tea bags in them.

"Don't tell me you're frightened too!" he said. "I expected more from you."

I shook my head. I wasn't sure whether I was afraid or not. I'm not sure today. The tea, when it came, had a distinctly greasy aftertaste, as if somehow he had fried it. I made myself drink half while Sprake watched me cynically.

"You ought to sit down," he said. "You're worn-out." When I refused, he shrugged and went on as if we were still at the Tivoli. "Nobody tricked them, or tried to pretend it would be easy. If you get anything out of an experiment like that, it's by keeping your head and taking your chance. If you try to move cautiously, you may never be allowed to move at all."

He looked thoughtful.

"I've seen what happens to people who lose their nerve."

"I'm sure," I said.

"They were hardly recognizable, some of them."

I put the teacup down.

"I don't want to know," I said.

"I bet you don't."

He smiled to himself.

"Oh, they were still alive," he said softly, "if that's what you're worried about."

"You talked us into this," I reminded him.

"You talked yourselves into it."

Most of the light from the street was absorbed as soon as it entered the room, by the dull green wallpaper and sticky-looking yellow veneer of the furniture. The rest leaked eventually into the litter on the floor, pages of crumpled and partly burned typescript, hair clippings, broken chalks that had been used the night before to draw something on the flaking lino: among this stuff, it died. Though I knew Sprake was playing some sort of game with me, I couldn't see what it was; I couldn't make the effort. In the end, he had to make it for me.

When I said from the door, "You'll get sick of all this mess one day," he only grinned, nodded, and advised me:

"Come back when you know what you want. Get rid of Lucas Fisher, he's an amateur. Bring the girl if you must."

"Fuck off, Sprake."

He let me find my own way back down to the street.

That night I had to tell Lucas, "We aren't going to be hearing from Sprake again."

"Christ," he said, and for a second I thought he was going to cry. "Ann feels so ill," he whispered. "What did he say?"

"Forget him. He could never have helped us."

"Ann and I are getting married," Lucas said in a rush.

What could I have done? I knew as well as he did that they were doing it only out of a need for comfort. Nothing would be gained by making them admit it. Besides, I was so tired by then, I could hardly stand. Some kind of visual fault, a neon zigzag like a bright little flight of stairs, kept showing up in my left eye. So I congratulated Lucas and, as soon as I could, began thinking about something else.

"Sprake's terrified of the British Museum," I said. "In a way, I sympathize with him."

As a child I had hated it too. All the conversations, every echo of a voice or a footstep or a rustle of clothes, gathered up in its high ceilings in a kind of undifferentiated rumble and sigh—the blurred and melted remains of meaning—which made you feel as if you had been abandoned in a derelict swimming bath. Later, when I was a teenager, it was the vast, shapeless heads in Room 25 that frightened me, the vagueness of the inscriptions. I saw clearly what was there—"Red sandstone head of a king"... "Red granite head from a colossal figure of a king"—but what was I looking at? The faceless wooden figure of Ramses emerged perpetually from an alcove near the lavatory door, a Ramses who had to support himself with a stick—split, syphilitic, worm-eaten by his passage through the world, but still condemned to struggle helplessly on.

"We want to go and live up north," Lucas said. "Away from all this."

As the afternoon wore on, Ann became steadily more disturbed. "Listen," she would ask me, "*is* that someone in the passage? You can always tell me the truth." After she had promised several times in a vague way—"I can't send you out without anything to eat. I'll cook us something in a minute, if you'll make some more coffee"—I realized she was frightened to go back into the kitchen. "No matter how much coffee I drink," she explained, "my throat is dry. It's all that smoking." She returned often to the theme of age. She had always hated to feel old. "You comb your hair in the mornings and it's just another ten years gone, every loose hair, every bit of dandruff, like a lot of old snapshots showering down." She shook her head and said, as if the connection would be quite clear to me:

"We moved around a lot after university. It wasn't that I couldn't settle, more that I had to leave something behind every so often, as a sort of sacrifice. If I liked a job I was in, I would always give it up. Poor old Lucas!"

She laughed.

"Do you ever feel like that?" She made a face. "I don't suppose you do," she said. "I remember the first house we lived in, over near Dunford Bridge. It was huge, and falling apart inside. It was always on the market until we bought it. Everyone who'd had it before us had tried some new way of dividing it up to make it livable. They put in a new staircase or knocked two rooms together. They'd abandoned parts of it because they couldn't afford to heat it all. Then they'd buggered off before anything was finished and left it to the next one—"

She broke off suddenly.

"I could never keep it tidy," she said.

"Lucas always loved it."

"Does he say that? You don't want to pay too much attention to him," she warned me. "The garden was so full of builders' rubbish, we could never grow anything. And the winters!" She shuddered. "Well, you know what it's like out there. The rooms reeked of Calor gas; before he'd been there a week, Lucas had every kind of portable heater you could think of. I hated the cold, but never as much as he did."

With an amused tenderness she chided him—"Lucas, Lucas, Lucas"— as if he were in the room there with us. "How you hated it, and how untidy you were!"

By now it was dark outside, but the younger cat was still staring out into the grayish, sleety well of the garden, beyond which you could just make out—as a swelling line of shadow with low clouds racing over it— the edge of the moor. Ann kept asking the cat what it could see. "There are children buried all over the moor," she told the cat. Eventually she got up with a sigh and pushed it onto the floor. "That's where cats belong. Cats belong on the floor." Some paper flowers were knocked down; stooping to gather them up, she said, "If there is a God, a real one, He gave up long ago. He isn't so much bitter as apathetic." She winced, held her hands up to her eyes.

"You don't mind if I turn the main light off?" And then: "He's filtered away into everything, so that now there's only this infinitely thin, stretched *thing*, presenting itself in every atom, so tired it can't go on, so haggard you can only feel sorry for it and its mistakes. That's the real God. What we saw is something that's taken its place."

"What did we see, Ann?"

She stared at me.

"You know, I was never sure what Lucas thought he wanted from me." The dull yellow light of a table lamp fell across the left side of her face. She was lighting cigarettes almost constantly, stubbing them out, half smoked, into the nest of old ends that had accumulated in the saucer of her cup. "Can you imagine? In all those years I never knew what he wanted from me."

She seemed to consider this for a moment or two. She looked at me, puzzled, and said, "I don't feel he ever loved me." She buried her face in her hands. I got up, with some idea of comforting her. Without warning, she lurched out of her chair and in a groping, desperately confused manner took a few steps toward me. There, in the middle of the room, she stumbled into a low fretwork table someone had brought back from a visit to Kashmir twenty years before. Two or three paperback books and a vase of anemones went flying. The anemones were blowsy, past their best. She looked down at *The Last of Cheri* and *Mrs. Palfrey at the Claremont,* strewn with great blue and red petals like dirty tissue paper; she touched them thoughtfully with her toe. The smell of the fetid flower water made her retch.

"Oh, dear," she murmured. "Whatever shall we do, Lucas?"

"I'm not Lucas," I said gently. "Go and sit down, Ann."

While I was gathering the books and wiping their covers, she must have overcome her fear of the kitchen—or, I thought later, simply forgotten it—because I heard her rummaging about for the dustpan and brush she kept under the sink. By now, I imagined, she could hardly see for the migraine; I called impatiently, "Let me do that, Ann. Be sensible." There was a gasp, a clatter, my name repeated twice. "Ann, are you all right?"

No one answered.

"Hello? Ann?"

I found her by the sink. She had let go of the brush and pan and was twisting a damp floor cloth so tightly in her hands that the muscles of her short forearms stood out like a carpenter's. Water had dribbled out of it and down her skirt.

"Ann?"

She was looking out of the window into the narrow passage where, clearly illuminated by the fluorescent tube in the kitchen ceiling, something big and white hung in the air, turning to and fro like a chrysalis in a privet hedge.

"Christ!" I said.

It wriggled and was still, as though whatever it contained was tired of the effort to get out. After a moment it curled up from its tapered base, seemed to split, welded itself together again. All at once I saw that these movements were actually those of two organisms, two human figures hanging in the air, unsupported, quite naked, writhing and embracing and parting and writhing together again, never presenting the same angle twice, so that now you viewed the man from the back, now the woman, now both of them from one side or the other. When I first saw them, the woman's mouth was fastened on the man's. Her eyes were closed; later she rested her head on his shoulder. Later still, they both turned their attention to Ann. They had very pale skin, with the curious bloom of white chocolate; but that might have been an effect of the light. Sleet blew between us and them in eddies, but never obscured them.

"What are they, Ann?"

"There's no limit to suffering," she said. Her voice was slurred and thick. "They follow me wherever I go."

I found it hard to look away from them.

"Is this why you move so often?" It was all I could think of to say.

"No."

The two figures were locked together in something that—had their eyes been fastened on each other rather than on Ann—might have been described as love. They swung and turned slowly against the black, wet wall like fish in a tank. They were smiling. Ann groaned and began vomiting noisily into the sink. I held her shoulders. "Get them away," she said indistinctly. "Why do they always look at me?" She coughed, wiped her mouth, ran the cold tap. She had begun to shiver, in powerful, disconnected spasms. "Get them away."

Though I knew quite well they were there, it was my mistake that I never believed them to be real. I thought she might calm down if she couldn't see them. But she wouldn't let me turn the light out or close the curtains; and when I tried to encourage her to let go of the edge of the sink and come into the living room with me, she only shook her head and retched miserably. "No, leave me," she said. "I don't want you now." Her body had gone rigid, as awkward as a child's. She was very strong. "Just try to come away, Ann, please." She looked at me helplessly and said, "I've got nothing to wipe my nose with." I pulled at her angrily, and we fell down. My shoulder was on the dustpan, my mouth full of her hair, which smelled of cigarette ashes. I felt her hands move over me.

"Ann! Ann!" I shouted.

I dragged myself from under her—she had begun to groan and vomit again—and, staring back over my shoulder at the smiling creatures in the passage, ran out of the kitchen and out of the house. I could hear myself sobbing with panic—"I'm phoning Lucas, I can't stand this, I'm going to phone Lucas"—as if I were still talking to her. I blundered about the village until I found the telephone box opposite the church.

I remember Sprake—though it seems too well-put to have been him—once saying, "It's no triumph to feel you've given life the slip." We were talking about Lucas Fisher. "You can't live intensely except at the cost of the self. In the end, Lucas's reluctance to give himself wholeheartedly will make him shabby and unreal. He'll end up walking the streets at night staring into lighted shop windows." At the time I thought this harsh. I still believed that with Lucas it was a matter of energy rather than will, of the lows and undependable zones of a cyclic personality rather than any deliberate reservation of powers.

When I told Lucas, "Something's gone badly wrong here," he was silent. After a moment or two I prompted him. "Lucas?"

I thought I heard him say:

"For God's sake, put that down and leave me alone."

"This line must be bad," I said. "You sound a long way off. Is there someone with you?"

He was silent again—"Lucas? Can you hear me?"—and then he asked, "How is Ann? I mean, in herself?"

"Not well," I said. "She's having some sort of attack. You don't know how relieved I am to talk to someone. Lucas, there are two completely hallucinatory figures in that passage outside her kitchen. What they're doing to one another is . . . look, they're a kind of dead white color, and they're smiling at her all the time. It's the most appalling thing—"

He said, "Wait a minute. Do you mean that you can see them too?"

"That's what I'm trying to say. The thing is that I don't know how to help her. Lucas?"

The line had gone dead. I put the receiver down and dialed his number again. The engaged signal went on and on. Afterward I would tell Ann, "Someone else must have called him," but I knew he had simply taken his phone off the hook. I stood there for some time, anyway, shivering in the wind that blustered down off the moor, in the hope that he would change his mind. In the end, I got so cold, I had to give up and go back. Sleet blew into my face all the way through the village. The church clock said half past six, but everything was dark and untenanted. All I could hear was the wind rustling the black plastic bags of rubbish piled around the dustbins.

"Fuck you, Lucas," I whispered. "Fuck you, then."

Ann's house was as silent as the rest. I went into the front garden and pressed my face up to the window, in case I could see into the kitchen through the open living room door; but from that angle, the only thing visible was a wall calendar with a color photograph of a Persian cat: *October.* I couldn't see Ann. I stood in the flower bed and the sleet turned to snow.

The kitchen was filled less with the smell of vomit than a sourness you felt somewhere in the back of your throat. Outside, the passage lay deserted under the bright suicidal wash of fluorescent light. It was hard to imagine anything had happened out there. At the same time, nothing looked comfortable, not the disposition of the old roof slates, or the clumps of fern growing out of the revetment, or even the way the snow was settling in the gaps between the flagstones. I found that I didn't want to turn my back on the window. If I closed my eyes and tried to visualize the white couple, all I could remember was the way they had smiled. A still, cold air seeped in above the sink, and the cats came up to rub against my legs and get underfoot; the taps were still running.

In her confusion Ann had opened all the kitchen cupboards and strewn their contents on the floor. Saucepans, cutlery, and packets of dried food had been mixed up with a polythene bucket and some yellow J-cloths; she had upset a bottle of household detergent among several tins of cat food, some of which had been half opened, some merely pierced, before she dropped them or forgot where she had put the opener. It was hard to see what she had been trying to do. I picked it all up and put it away. To make them leave me alone, I fed the cats. Once or twice I heard her moving about on the floor above.

She was in the bathroom, slumped on the old-fashioned pink lino by the sink, trying to get her clothes off. "For God's sake, go away," she said. "I can do it."

"Oh, Ann."

"Put some disinfectant in the blue bucket, then."

"Who are they, Ann?" I asked.

That was later, when I had gotten her to bed. She answered:

"Once it starts, you never get free."

I was annoyed.

"Free from what, Ann?"

"You know," she said. "Lucas said you had hallucinations for weeks afterward."

"Lucas had no right to say that!"

This sounded absurd, so I added as lightly as I could, "It was a long time ago. I'm not sure anymore."

The migraine had left her exhausted, though much more relaxed. She had washed her hair, and between us we had found her a fresh nightdress to wear. Sitting up in the cheerful little bedroom with its cheap ornaments and modern wallpaper, she looked vague and young; she kept apologizing for the design on her Continental quilt, some bold diagrammatic flowers in black and red, the intertwined stems of which she traced with the index finger of her right hand across a clean white background. "Do you like this? I don't really know why I bought it. Things look so bright and energetic in the shops," she said wistfully, "but as soon as you get them home, they just seem crude." The older cat had jumped up onto the bed; whenever Ann spoke, it purred loudly. "He shouldn't be in here, and he knows it." She wouldn't eat or drink, but I had persuaded her to take some more propranolol, and so far she had kept it down.

"Once it starts, you never get free," she repeated. Her finger followed the pattern across the quilt. Inadvertently she touched the cat's dry, graying fur, stared suddenly at her own hand as if it had misled her. "It was some sort of smell that followed you about, Lucas seemed to think."

"Some sort," I agreed.

"You won't get rid of it by ignoring it. We both tried that to begin with. A scent of roses, Lucas said." She laughed and took my hand. "Very romantic! I've no sense of smell—I lost it years ago, luckily."

This reminded her of something else.

"The first time I had a fit," she said, "I kept it from my mother because I saw a vision with it. I was only a child, really. The vision was very clear: a seashore, steep and with no sand, and men and women lying on some rocks in the sunshine like lizards, staring quite blankly at the spray as it exploded up in front of them; huge waves that might have been on a cinema screen for all the notice they took of them."

She narrowed her eyes, puzzled. "You wondered why they had so little common sense."

She tried to push the cat off her bed, but it only bent its body in a rubbery way and avoided her hand. She yawned suddenly.

"At the same time," she went on after a pause, "I could see that some spiders had made their webs between the rocks, just a foot or two above the tide line." Though they trembled and were sometimes filled with spray-like dewdrops so that they glittered in the sun, the webs remained unbroken. She couldn't describe, she said, the sense of anxiety with which this filled her. "So close to all that violence. You wondered why they had so little common sense," she repeated. "The last thing I heard was someone saying, 'On your own, you really can hear voices in the tide. . . .' "

Before she fell asleep, she clutched my hand harder and said:

"I'm so glad you got something out of it. Lucas and I never did. Roses! It was worth it for that."

I thought of us as we had been twenty years before. I spent the night in the living room and awoke quite early in the morning. I didn't know where I was until I walked in a drugged way to the window and saw the street full of snow.

For a long time after that last meeting with Sprake, I had a recurrent dream of him. His hands were clasped tightly across his chest, the left hand holding the wrist of the right, and he was going quickly from room to room of the British Museum. Whenever he came to a corner or a junction of corridors, he stopped abruptly and stared at the wall in front of him for thirty seconds before turning very precisely to face in the right direction before he moved on. He did this with the air of a man who has for some reason taught himself to walk with his eyes closed through a perfectly familiar building; but there was also, in the way he stared at the walls—and particularly in the way he held himself so upright and rigid—a profoundly hierarchal air, an air of premeditation and ritual. His shoes, and the bottoms of his faded corduroy trousers, were soaking wet, just as they had been the morning after the rite, when the four of us had walked back through the damp fields in the bright sunshine. He wore no socks.

In the dream I was always hurrying to catch up with him. I was stopping every so often to write something in a notebook, hoping he wouldn't see me. He strode purposefully through the Museum, from cabinet to cabinet of twelfth-century illuminated manuscripts. Suddenly he stopped, looked back at me, and said:

"There are sperm in this picture. You can see them quite plainly. What are sperm doing in a religious picture?"

He smiled, opened his eyes very wide.

Pointing to the side of his own head with one finger, he began to shout and laugh incoherently.

When he had gone, I saw that he had been examining a New Testament miniature from Queen Melisande's Psalter, depicting "The Women at the Sepulchre." In it an angel was drawing Mary Magdalene's attention to some strange luminous shapes that hovered in the air in front of her. They did, in fact, look something like the spermatozoa that often border the tormented Paris paintings of Edvard Munch.

I would wake up abruptly from this dream, to find that it was morning and that I had been crying.

Ann was still asleep when I left the house, with the expression people have on their faces when they can't believe what they remember about themselves. "On your own, you really can hear voices in the tide, cries for help or attention," she had said. "I started to menstruate the same day. For years I was convinced that my fits began then too."

That was the last time I saw her.

A warm front had moved in from the southwest during the night; the snow had already begun to melt, the Pennine stations looked like leaky downspouts, the moors were locked beneath gray clouds. Two little boys sat opposite me on the train until Stalybridge, holding their Day Rover tickets thoughtfully in their laps. They might have been eight or nine years old. They were dressed in tiny, perfect workman's jackets, tight trousers, Dr. Marten's boots. Close up, their shaven skulls were bluish and vulnerable, perfectly shaped. They looked like acolytes in a Buddhist temple: calm, wide-eyed, compliant. By the time I got to Manchester, a fine rain was falling. It was blowing the full length of Market Street and through the door of the Kardomah Café, where I had arranged to meet Lucas Fisher.

The first thing he said was, "Look at these pies! They aren't plastic, you know, like a modern pie. These are from the plaster era of café pies, the earthenware era. Terra-cotta pies, realistically painted, glazed in places to have exactly the cracks and imperfections any real pie would have! Aren't they wonderful? I'm going to eat one."

I sat down next to him.

"What happened to you last night, Lucas? It was a bloody nightmare."

He looked away. "How is Ann?" he asked. I could feel him trembling.

"Fuck off, Lucas."

He smiled over at a toddler in an appalling yellow suit. The child stared back vacantly, upset, knowing full well they were from competing species. A woman near us said, "I hear you're going to your grandma's for dinner on Sunday. Something special, I expect?" Lucas glared at her, as if she had been speaking to him. She added: "If you're going to buy toys this afternoon, remember to look at them where they are, so that no one can accuse you of stealing. Don't take them off the shelf." From somewhere near the kitchens came a noise like a tray of crockery falling down a short flight of stairs; Lucas seemed to hate this. He shuddered.

"Let's get out!" he said. He looked savage and ill. "I feel it as badly as Ann," he said. He accused me: "You never think of that." He looked over at the toddler again. "Spend long enough in places like this and your spirit will heave itself inside out."

"Come on, Lucas, don't be spoiled. I thought you liked the pies here."

All afternoon he walked urgently about the streets, as if he were on his own. I could hardly keep up with him. The city centre was full of wheelchairs, old women slumped in them with impatient, collapsed faces, partially bald, done up in crisp white raincoats. Lucas had turned up the collar of his gray cashmere jacket against the rain but left the jacket itself hanging open, its sleeves rolled untidily back above his bare wrists. He left me breathless. He was forty years old, but he still had the ravenous face of an adolescent. Eventually he stopped and said, "I'm sorry." It was halfway through the afternoon, but the neon signs were on and the lower windows of the office blocks were already lit up. Near Piccadilly Station, an arm of the canal appears suddenly from under the road; he stopped and gazed down at its rain-pocked surface, dim and oily, scattered with lumps of floating Styrofoam like seagulls in the fading light.

"You often see fires on the bank down there," he said. "They live a whole life down there, people with nowhere else to go. You can hear them singing and shouting on the old towpath."

He looked at me with wonder.

"We aren't much different, are we? We never came to anything, either."

I couldn't think of what to say.

"It's not so much that Sprake encouraged us to ruin something in ourselves," he said, "as that we never got anything in return for it. Have you ever seen Joan of Arc kneel down to pray in the Kardomah Café? And then a small boy comes in leading something that looks like a goat, and it gets on her there and then and fucks her in a ray of sunlight?"

"Look, Lucas," I explained, "I'm never doing this again. I was frightened last night."

"I'm sorry."

"Lucas, you always are."

"It isn't one of my better days today."

"For God's sake, fasten your coat."

"I can't seem to get cold."

He gazed dreamily down at the water—it had darkened into a bottomless, opal-colored trench between the buildings—perhaps seeing goats, fires, people who had nowhere to go. " 'We worked but we were not paid,' " he quoted. Something forced him to ask shyly:

"You haven't heard from Sprake?"

I felt sick with patience. I seemed to be filled up with it.

"I haven't seen Sprake for twenty years, Lucas. You know that. I haven't seen him for twenty years."

"I understand. It's just that I can't bear to think of Ann on her own in a place like that. I wouldn't have mentioned it otherwise. We said we'd always stick together, but—"

"Go home, Lucas. Go home now."

He turned away miserably and walked off. I meant to leave him to that maze of unredeemed streets between Piccadilly and Victoria, the failing pornography and pet shops, the weed-grown car parks that lie in the shadow of the yellowish-tiled hulk of the Arndale Centre. In the end, I couldn't. He had gotten as far as the Tib Street fruit market when a small figure came out of a side street and began to follow him closely along the pavement, imitating his typical walk, head thrust forward, hands in pockets. When he stopped to button his jacket, it stopped too. Its own coat was so long, it trailed in the gutter. I started running to catch up with them, and it paused under a street lamp to stare back at me. In the sodium light I saw that it was neither a child nor a dwarf but something of both, with the eyes and gait of a large monkey. Its eyes were quite blank, stupid and implacable in a pink face. Lucas became aware of it suddenly and jumped with surprise; he ran a few aimless steps, shouting, then dodged around a corner, but it only followed him hurriedly. I thought I heard him pleading, "Why don't you leave me alone?" and in answer came a voice at once tinny and muffled, barely audible but strained, as if it were shouting. Then there was a terrific clatter and I saw some large object like an old zinc dustbin fly out and go rolling about in the middle of the road.

"Lucas!" I called.

When I rounded the corner, the street was full of smashed fruit boxes and crates; rotten vegetables were scattered everywhere; a barrow lay as if it had been thrown along the pavement. There was such a sense of violence and disorder and idiocy that I couldn't express it to myself. But neither Lucas nor his persecutor was there; and though I walked about for an hour afterward, looking into doorways, I saw nobody at all.

A few months later Lucas wrote to tell me that Ann had died.

"A scent of roses," I remembered her saying. "How lucky you were!"

"It was a wonderful summer for roses, anyway," I had answered. "I never knew a year like it." All June, the hedgerows were full of dog roses, with their elusive, fragile odor. I hadn't seen them since I was a boy. The gardens were bursting with Gallicas, great blowsy things whose fragrance was like a drug. "How can we ever say that Sprake had anything to do with that, Ann?"

But I sent roses to her funeral, anyway, though I didn't go myself.

What did we do, Ann and Lucas and I, in the fields of June, such a long time ago?

"It is easy to misinterpret the Great God," writes de Vries. "If He represents the long slow panic in us which never quite surfaces, if He signifies our perception of the animal, the uncontrollable in us, He must also stand for that direct sensual perception of the world that we have lost by ageing—perhaps even by becoming human in the first place."

Shortly after Ann's death, I experienced a sudden, inexplicable resurgence of my sense of smell. Common smells became so distinct and detailed, I felt like a child again, every new impression astonishing and clear, my conscious self not yet the sore lump encysted in my own skull, as clenched and useless as a fist, impossible to modify or evict, as it was later to become. This was not quite what you should call memory; all I recollected in the smell of orange peel or ground coffee or rowan blossom was that I once had been able to experience things so powerfully. It was as if, before I could recover one particular impression, I had to rediscover the language of all impressions. But nothing further happened. I was left with an embarrassment, a ghost, a hyperesthesia of middle age. It was cruel and undependable; it made me feel like a fool. I was troubled by it for a year or two, and then it went away.

The Voice of
the Beach

Ramsey Campbell

I

I met Neal at the station.

Of course I can describe it, I have only to go up the road and look, but there is no need. That isn't what I have to get out of me. It isn't me, it's out there, it can be described. I need all my energy for that, all my concentration, but perhaps it will help if I can remember before that, when everything looked manageable, expressible, familiar enough—when I could bear to look out of the window.

Neal was standing alone on the small platform, and now I see that I dare not go up the road after all, or out of the house. It doesn't matter, my memories are clear, they will help me hold on. Neal must have rebuffed the station-master, who was happy to chat to anyone. He was gazing at the bare tracks, sharpened by June light, as they cut their way through the forest—gazing at them as a suicide might gaze at a razor. He saw me and swept his hair back from his face, over his shoulders. Suffering had pared his face down, stretched the skin tighter and paler over the skull. I can re-member exactly how he looked before. "I thought I'd missed the station," he said, though surely the station's name was visible enough, despite the flowers that scaled the board. If only he had! "I had to make so many changes. Never mind. Christ, it's good to see you. You look marvellous. I expect you can thank the sea for that." His eyes had brightened, and he sounded so full of life that it was spilling out of him in a tumble of words, but his handshake felt like cold bone. I hurried him along the road that led home and to the   He was beginning to screw up his eyes at the sun-light, and I thought I should get him inside; presumably headaches were among his symptoms. At first the road is gravel, fragments of which always succeed in working their way into your shoes. Where the trees fade out as though stifled by sand, a concrete path turns aside. Sand sifts over the gravel; you can hear the gritty conflict underfoot, and the musing of the sea. Beyond the path stands this crescent of bungalows. Surely all this is still true. But I remember now that the bungalows looked unreal against the burning blue sky and the dunes like embryo hills; they looked like a dream set down in the piercing light of June.

"You must be doing well to afford this." Neal sounded listless, envious only because he felt it was expected. If only he had stayed that way! But once inside the bungalow he seemed pleased by everything—the view, my books on show in the living-room bookcase, my typewriter displaying a to-ken page that bore a token phrase, the Breughel prints that used to remind me of humanity. Abruptly, with a moody eagerness that I hardly remarked at the time, he said, "Shall we have a look at the beach?"

There, I've written the word. I can describe the beach, I must describe it, it is all that's in my head. I have my notebook which I took with me that day. Neal led the way along the gravel path. Beyond the concrete turn-off to the bungalows the gravel was engulfed almost at once by sand, despite the thick ranks of low bushes that had been planted to keep back the sand. We squeezed between the bushes, which were determined to close their ranks across the gravel.

Once through, we felt the breeze, whose waves passed through the marram grass that spiked the dunes. Neal's hair streamed back, pale as the grass. The trudged dunes were slowing him down, eager as he was. We slithered down to the beach, and the sound of the unfurling sea leapt closer, as though we'd awakened it from dreaming. The wind fluttered, trapped in my ears, leafed through my notebook as I scribbled the image of wakening and thought with an appalling innocence: perhaps I can use that image. Now we were walled off from the rest of the world by the dunes, faceless mounds with unkempt green wigs, mounds almost as white as the sun.

Even then I felt that the beach was somehow separate from its surroundings: introverted, I remember thinking. I put it down to the shifting haze which hovered above the sea, the haze which I could never focus, whose distance I could never quite judge. From the self-contained stage of the beach the bungalows looked absurdly intrusive, anachronisms rejected by the geo-morphological time of sand and sea. Even the skeletal car and the other debris, half engulfed by the beach near the coast road, looked less alien. These are my memories, the most stable things left to me, and I must go on. I found today that I cannot go back any further.

Neal was staring, eyes narrowed against the glare, along the waste of beach that stretched in the opposite direction from the coast road and curved out of sight. "Doesn't anyone come down here? There's no pollution, is there?"

"It depends on who you believe." Often the beach seemed to give me a headache, even when there was no glare—and then there was the way the beach looked at night. "Still, I think most folk go up the coast to the resorts. That's the only reason I can think of."

We were walking. Beside us the edge of the glittering sea moved in several directions simultaneously. Moist sand, sleek as satin, displayed shells which appeared to flash patterns, faster than my mind could grasp. Pinpoint mirrors of sand gleamed, rapid as Morse. My notes say this is how it seemed.

"Don't your neighbors ever come down?"

Neal's voice made me start. I had been engrossed in the designs of shell and sand. Momentarily I was unable to judge the width of the beach: a few paces, or miles? I grasped my sense of perspective, but a headache was starting, a dull impalpable grip that encircled my cranium. Now I know what all this meant, but I want to remember how I felt before I knew.

"Very seldom," I said. "Some of them think there's quicksand." One old lady, sitting in her garden to glare at the dunes like Canute versus sand, had told me that warning notices kept sinking. I'd never encountered quicksand, but I always brought my stick to help me trudge.

"So I'll have the beach to myself."

I took that to be a hint. At least he would leave me alone if I wanted to work. "The bungalow people are mostly retired," I said. "Those who aren't in wheelchairs go driving. I imagine they've had enough of sand, even if they aren't past walking on it." Once, further up the beach, I'd encountered nudists censoring themselves with towels or straw hats as they ventured down to the sea, but Neal could find out about them for himself. I wonder now if I ever saw them at all, or simply felt that I should.

Was he listening? His head was cocked, but not toward me. He'd slowed, and was staring at the ridges and furrows of the beach, at which the sea was lapping. All at once the ridges reminded me of convolutions of the brain, and I took out my notebook as the grip on my skull tightened. The beach as a subconscious, my notes say: the horizon as the imagination— sunlight set a ship ablaze on the edge of the world, an image that impressed me as vividly yet indefinably symbolic—the debris as memories, half-buried, half-comprehensible. But then what were the bungalows, perched above the dunes like boxes carved of dazzling bone?

I glanced up. A cloud had leaned toward me. No, it had been more as though the cloud were rushing at the beach from the horizon, dauntingly fast. Had it been a cloud? It had seemed more massive than a ship. The sky was empty now, and I told myself that it had been an effect of the haze— the magnified shadow of a gull, perhaps.

My start had enlivened Neal, who began to chatter like a television wakened by a kick. "It'll be good for me to be alone here, to get used to being alone. Mary and the children found themselves another home, you see. He earns more money than I'll ever see, if that's what they want. He's the head of the house type, if that's what they want. I couldn't be that now if I tried, not with the way my nerves are now." I can still hear everything he said, and I suppose that I knew what had been wrong with him. Now they are just words.

"That's why I'm talking so much," he said, and picked up a spiral shell, I thought to quiet himself.

"That's much too small. You'll never hear anything in that."

Minutes passed before he took it away from his ear and handed it to me. "No?" he said.

I put it to my ear and wasn't sure what I was hearing. No, I didn't throw the shell away, I didn't crush it underfoot; in any case, how could I have done that to the rest of the beach? I was straining to hear, straining to make out how the sound differed from the usual whisper of a shell. Was that it seemed to have a rhythm that I couldn't define, or that it sounded shrunken by distance rather than cramped by the shell? I felt expectant, entranced—precisely the feeling I'd tried so often to communicate in my fiction, I believe. Something stooped toward me from the horizon. I jerked, and dropped the shell.

There was nothing but the dazzle of sunlight that leapt at me from the waves. The haze above the sea had darkened, staining the light, and I told myself that was what I'd seen. But when Neal picked up another shell I felt uneasy. The grip on my skull was very tight now. As I regarded the vistas of empty sea and sky and beach my expectancy grew oppressive, too imminent, no longer enjoyable.

"I think I'll head back now. Maybe you should as well," I said, rummaging for an uncontrived reason, "just in case there is quicksand."

"All right. It's in all of them," he said, displaying an even smaller shell to which he'd just listened. I remember thinking that his observation was so self-evident as to be meaningless.

As I turned toward the bungalows the glitter of the sea clung to my eyes. After-images crowded among the debris. They were moving; I strained to make out their shape. What did they resemble? Symbols—hieroglyphs? Limbs writhing rapidly, as if in a ritual dance? They made the debris appear to shift, to crumble. The herd of faceless dunes seemed to edge forward; an image leaned toward me out of the sky. I closed my eyes, to calm their antics, and wondered if I should take the warnings of pollution more seriously.

We walked toward the confusion of footprints that climbed the dunes. Neal glanced about at the sparkling of sand. Never before had the beach so impressed me as a complex of patterns, and perhaps that means it was already too late. Spotlighted by the sun, it looked so artificial that I came close to doubting how it felt underfoot.

The bungalows looked unconvincing too. Still, when we'd slumped in our chairs for a while, letting the relative dimness soothe our eyes while our bodies guzzled every hint of coolness, I forgot about the beach. We shared two liters of wine and talked about my work, about his lack of any since graduating.

Later I prepared melon, salads, water ices. Neal watched, obviously embarrassed that he couldn't help. He seemed lost without Mary. One more reason not to marry, I thought, congratulating myself.

As we ate he kept staring out at the beach. A ship was caught in the amber sunset: a dream of escape. I felt the image less deeply than I'd experienced the metaphors of the beach; it was less oppressive. The band around my head had faded.

When it grew dark Neal pressed close to the pane. "What's that?" he demanded.

I switched out the light so that he could see. Beyond the dim humps of the dunes the beach was glowing, a dull pallor like moonlight stifled by fog. Do all beaches glow at night? "That's what makes people say there's pollution," I said.

"Not the light," he said impatiently. "The other things. What's moving?"

I squinted through the pane. For minutes I could see nothing but the muffled glow. At last, when my eyes were smarting, I began to see forms thin and stiff as scarecrows, jerking into various contorted poses. Gazing for so long was bound to produce something of the kind, and I took them to be after-images of the tangle, barely visible, of bushes.

"I think I'll go and see."

"I shouldn't go down there at night," I said, having realized that I'd never gone to the beach at night and that I felt a definite, though irrational, aversion to doing so.

Eventually he went to bed. Despite all his travelling, he'd needed to drink to make himself sleepy. I heard him open his bedroom window, which overlooked the beach. There is so much still to write, so much to struggle through, and what good can it do me now?

II

I had taken the bungalow, one of the few entries in my diary says, to give myself the chance to write without being distracted by city life—the cries of the telephone, the tolling of the doorbell, the omnipresent clamor—only to discover, once I'd left it behind, that city life was my theme. But I was a compulsive writer: if I failed to write for more than a few days I became depressed. Writing was the way I overcame the depression of not writing.

Now writing seems to be my only way of hanging on to what remains of myself, of delaying the end.

The day after Neal arrived, I typed a few lines of a sample chapter. It wasn't a technique I enjoyed—tearing a chapter out of the context of a novel that didn't yet exist. In any case, I was distracted by the beach, compelled to scribble notes about it, trying to define the images it suggested. I hoped these notes might build into a story. I was picking at the notes in search of their story when Neal said, "Maybe I can lose myself for a bit in the countryside."

"Mm," I said curtly, not looking up.

"Didn't you say there was a deserted village?"

By the time I directed him I would have lost the thread of my thoughts. The thread had been frayed and tangled, anyway. As long as I was compelled to think about the beach I might just as well be down there. I can still write as if I don't know the end, it helps me not to think of "I'll come with you," I said.

The weather was nervous. Archipelagos of cloud floated low on the hazy sky, above the sea; great Rorschach blots rose from behind the slate hills, like dissolved stone. As we squeezed through the bushes, a shadow came hunching over the dunes to meet us. When my foot touched the beach a moist, shadowy chill seized me, as though the sand disguised a lurking marsh. Then sunlight spilled over the beach, which leapt into clarity.

I strode, though Neal appeared to want to dawdle. I wasn't anxious to linger; after all, I told myself, it might rain. Glinting mosaics of grains of sand changed restlessly around me, never quite achieving a pattern. Patches of sand, flat shapeless elongated ghosts, glided over the beach and faltered, waiting for another breeze. Neal kept peering at them as though to make out their shapes.

Half a mile along the beach the dunes began to sag, to level out. The slate hills were closing in. Were they the source of the insidious chill? Perhaps I was feeling the damp; a penumbra of moisture welled up around each of my footprints. The large wet shapes seemed quite unrelated to my prints, an effect which I found unnerving. When I glanced back, it looked as though something enormous was imitating my walk.

The humidity was almost suffocating. My head felt clamped by tension. Wind blundered booming in my ears, even when I could feel no breeze. Its jerky rhythm was distracting because indefinable. Gray cloud had flooded the sky; together with the hills and the thickening haze above the sea, it caged the beach. At the edge of my eye the convolutions of the beach seemed to writhe, to struggle to form patterns. The insistent sparkling nagged at my mind.

I'd begun to wonder whether I had been blaming imagined pollution for the effects of heat and humidity—I was debating whether to turn back before I grew dizzy or nauseous—when Neal said, "Is that it?"

I peered ahead, trying to squint the dazzle of waves from my eyes. A quarter of a mile away the hills ousted the dunes completely. Beneath the spiky slate a few uprights of rock protruded from the beach like standing stones. They glowed sullenly as copper through the haze; they were encrusted with sand. Surely that wasn't the village.

"Yes, that's it," Neal said, and strode forward.

I followed him, because the village must be further on. The veil of haze drew back, the vertical rocks gleamed unobscured, and I halted bewildered. The rocks weren't encrusted at all; they were slate, gray as the table of rock on which they stood above the beach. Though the slate was jagged, some of its gaps were regular: windows, doorways. Here and there walls still formed corners. How could the haze have distorted my view so spectacularly?

Neal was climbing rough steps carved out of the slate table. Without warning, as I stood confused by my misperception, I felt utterly alone. A bowl of dull haze trapped me on the bare sand. Slate, or something more massive and vague, loomed over me. The kaleidoscope of shells was about to shift; the beach was ready to squirm, to reveal its pattern, shake off its artificiality. The massive looming would reach down, and

My start felt like a convulsive awakening. The table was deserted except for the fragments of buildings. I could hear only the wind, baying as though its mouth was vast and uncontrollable. "Neal," I called. Dismayed by the smallness of my voice, I shouted, "Neal."

I heard what sounded like scales of armor chafing together—slate, of course. The gray walls shone lifelessly, cavitied as skulls; gaping windows displayed an absence of faces, of rooms. Then Neal's head poked out of half a wall. "Yes, come on," he said. "It's strange."

As I climbed the steps, sand gritted underfoot like sugar. Low drifts of sand were piled against the walls; patches glinted on the small plateau.

Could that sand have made the whole place look encrusted and half-buried? I told myself that it had been an effect of the heat.

Broken walls surrounded me. They glared like storm-clouds in lightning. They formed a maze whose center was desertion. That image stirred another, too deep in my mind to be definable. The place was—not a maze, but a puzzle whose solution would clarify a pattern, a larger mystery. I realized that then; why couldn't I have fled?

I suppose I was held by the enigma of the village. I knew there were quarries in the hills above, but I'd never learned why the village had been abandoned. Perhaps its meagerness had killed it—I saw traces of less than a dozen buildings. It seemed further dwarfed by the beach; the sole visible trace of humanity, it dwindled beneath the gnawing of sand and the elements. I found it enervating, its lifelessness infectious. Should I stay with Neal, or risk leaving him there? Before I could decide, I heard him say amid a rattle of slate, "This is interesting."

In what way? He was clambering about an exposed cellar, among shards of slate. Whatever the building had been, it had stood furthest from the sea. "I don't mean the cellar," Neal said. "I mean that."

Reluctantly I peered where he was pointing. In the cellar wall furthest from the beach, a rough alcove had been chipped out of the slate. It was perhaps a yard deep, but barely high enough to accommodate a huddled man. Neal was already crawling in. I heard slate crack beneath him; his feet protruded from the darkness. Of course they weren't about to jerk convulsively—but my nervousness made me back away when his muffled voice said, "What's this?"

He backed out like a terrier with his prize. It was an old notebook, its pages stuck together in a moist wad. "Someone covered it up with slate," he said, as though that should tempt my interest.

Before I could prevent him he was sitting at the edge of the beach and peeling the pages gingerly apart. Not that I was worried that he might be destroying a fragment of history—I simply wasn't sure that I wanted to read whatever had been hidden in the cellar. Why couldn't I have followed my instincts?

He disengaged the first page carefully, then frowned. "This begins in the middle of something. There must be another book."

Handing me the notebook, he stalked away to scrabble in the cellar. I sat on the edge of the slate table, and glanced at the page. It is before me now on my desk. The pages have crumbled since then—the yellowing paper looks more and more like sand—but the large writing is still legible, unsteady capitals in a hand that might once have been literate before it grew senile. No punctuation separates the words, though blotches sometimes do. Beneath the relentless light at the deserted village the faded ink looked unreal, scarcely present at all.

FROM THE BEACH EVERYONE GONE NOW BUT ME ITS NOT SO BAD IN DAYTIME EXCEPT I CANT GO BUT AT NIGHT I CAN HEAR IT REACHING FOR (a blot of fungus had consumed a word here) AND THE VOICES ITS VOICE AND THE GLOWING AT LEAST IT HELPS ME SEE DOWN HERE WHEN IT COMES

I left it at that; my suddenly unsteady fingers might have torn the page. I wish to God they had, I was on edge with the struggle between humidity and the chill of slate and beach; I felt feverish. As I stared at the words they touched impressions, half-memories. If I looked up, would the beach have changed?

I heard Neal slithering on slate, turning over fragments. In my experience, stones were best not turned over. Eventually he returned. I was dully fascinated by the shimmering of the beach; my fingers pinched the notebook shut.

"I can't find anything," he said. "I'll have to come back." He took the notebook from me and began to read, muttering "What? Jesus!" Gently he separated the next page from the wad. "This gets stranger," he murmured. "What kind of guy was this? Imagine what it must have been like to live inside his head."

How did he know it had been a man? I stared at the pages, to prevent Neal from reading them aloud. At least it saved me from having to watch the antics of the beach, which moved like slow flames, but the introverted meandering of words made me nervous.

IT CANT REACH DOWN HERE NOT YET BUT OUTSIDE IS CHANGING OUTSIDES PART OF THE PATTERN I READ THE PATTERN THATS WHY I CANT GO SAW THEM DANCING THE PATTERN IT WANTS ME TO DANCE ITS ALIVE BUT ITS ONLY THE IMAGE BEING PUT TOGETHER

Neal was wide-eyed, fascinated. Feverish disorientation gripped my skull; I felt too unwell to move. The heat-haze must be closing in: at the edge of my vision, everything was shifting.

WHEN THE PATTERNS DONE IT CAN COME BACK AND GROW ITS HUNGRY TO BE EVERYTHING I KNOW HOW IT WORKS THE SAND MOVES AT NIGHT AND SUCKS YOU DOWN OR MAKES YOU GO WHERE IT WANTS TO MAKE (a blotch had eaten several words) WHEN THEY BUILT LEWIS THERE WERE OLD STONES THAT THEY MOVED MAYBE THE STONES KEPT IT SMALL NOW ITS THE BEACH AT LEAST

On the next page the letters are much larger, and wavery. Had the light begun to fail, or had the writer been retreating from the light—from the entrance to the cellar? I didn't know which alternative I disliked more.

GOT TO WRITE HANDS SHAKY FROM CHIPPING TUNNEL AND NO FOOD THEYRE SINGING NOW HELPING IT REACH CHANTING WITH NO MOUTHS THEY SING AND DANCE THE PATTERN FOR IT TO REACH THROUGH

Now there are very few words to the page. The letters are jagged, as though the writer's hand kept twitching violently.

GLOW COMING ITS OUT THERE NOW ITS LOOKING IN AT ME IT CANT GET HOLD IF I KEEP WRITING THEY WANT ME TO DANCE SO ITLL GROW WANT ME TO BE

There it ends. "Ah, the influence of Joyce," I commented sourly. The remaining pages are blank except for fungus. I managed to stand up; my head felt like a balloon pumped full of gas. "I'd like to go back now. I think I've a touch of sunstroke."

A hundred yards away I glanced back at the remnants of the village— Lewis, I assumed it had been called. The stone remains wavered as though striving to achieve a new shape; the haze made them look coppery, fat with a crust of sand. I was desperate to get out of the heat.

Closer to the sea I felt slightly less oppressed—but the whispering of sand, the liquid murmur of the waves, the bumbling of the wind, all chanted together insistently. Everywhere on the beach were patterns, demanding to be read.

Neal clutched the notebook under his arm. "What do you make of it?" he said eagerly.

His indifference to my health annoyed me, and hence so did the question. "He was mad," I said. "Living here—is it any wonder? Maybe he moved there after the place was abandoned. The beach must glow there too. That must have finished him. You saw how he tried to dig himself a refuge. That's all there is to it."

"Do you think so? I wonder," Neal said, and picked up a shell.

As he held the shell to his ear, his expression became so withdrawn and unreadable that I felt a pang of dismay. Was I seeing a symptom of his nervous trouble? He stood like a fragment of the village—as though the shell was holding him, rather than the reverse.

Eventually he mumbled, "That's it, that's what he meant. Chanting with no mouths."

I took the shell only very reluctantly; my head was pounding. I pressed the shell to my ear, though I was deafened by the storm of my blood. If the shell was muttering, I couldn't bear the jaggedness of its rhythm. I seemed less to hear it than to feel it deep in my skull.

"Nothing like it," I said, almost snarling, and thrust the shell at him.

Now that I'd had to strain to hear it, I couldn't rid myself of the muttering; it seemed to underlie the sounds of wind and sea. I trudged onward, eyes half shut. Moisture sprang up around my feet; the glistening shapes around my prints looked larger and more definite. I had to cling to my sense of my own size and shape.

When we neared home I couldn't see the bungalows. There appeared to be only the beach, grown huge and blinding. At last Neal heard a car leaving the crescent, and led me up the path of collapsed footprints.

In the bungalow I lay willing the lights and patterns to fade from my closed eyes. Neal's presence didn't soothe me, even though he was only poring over the notebook. He'd brought a handful of shells indoors. Occasionally he held one to his ear, muttering, "It's still there, you know. It does sound like chanting." At least, I thought peevishly, *I* knew when something was a symptom of illness—but the trouble was that in my delirium I was tempted to agree with him. I felt I had almost heard what the sound was trying to be.

III

Next day Neal returned to the deserted village. He was gone for so long that even amid the clamor of my disordered senses, I grew anxious. I couldn't watch for him; whenever I tried, the white-hot beach began to judder, to quake, and set me shivering.

At last he returned, having failed to find another notebook. I hoped that would be the end of it, but his failure had simply frustrated him. His irritability chafed against mine. He managed to prepare a bedraggled salad, of which I ate little. As the tide of twilight rolled in from the horizon he sat by the window, gazing alternately at the beach and at the notebook.

Without warning he said, "I'm going for a stroll. Can I borrow your stick?"

I guessed that he meant to go to the beach. Should he be trapped by darkness and sea, I was in no condition to go to his aid. "I'd rather you didn't," I said feebly.

"Don't worry, I won't lose it."

My lassitude suffocated my arguments. I lolled in my chair and through the open window heard him padding away, his footsteps muffled by sand. Soon there was only the vague slack rumble of the sea, blundering back and forth, and the faint hiss of sand in the bushes.

After half an hour I made myself stand up, though the ache in my head surged and surged, and gaze out at the whitish beach. The whole expanse appeared to flicker like hints of lightning. I strained my eyes. The beach looked crowded with debris, all of which danced to the flickering. I had to peer at every movement, but there was no sign of Neal.

I went out and stood between the bushes. The closer I approached the beach, the more crowded with obscure activity it seemed to be—but I suspected that much, if not all, of this could be blamed on my condition, for within five minutes my head felt so tight and unbalanced that I had to retreat indoors, away from the heat.

Though I'd meant to stay awake, I was dozing when Neal returned. I woke to find him gazing from the window. As I opened my eyes the beach lurched forward, shining. It didn't look crowded now, presumably because my eyes had had a rest. What could Neal see to preoccupy him so? "Enjoy your stroll?" I said sleepily.

He turned, and I felt a twinge of disquiet. His face looked stiff with doubt; his eyes were uneasy, a frown dug its ruts in his forehead. "It doesn't glow," he said.

Assuming I knew what he was talking about, I could only wonder how badly his nerves were affecting his perceptions. If anything, the beach looked brighter. "How do you mean?"

"The beach down by the village—it doesn't glow. Not anymore."

"Oh, I see."

He looked offended, almost contemptuous, though I couldn't understand why he'd expected me to be less indifferent. He withdrew into a scrutiny of the notebook. He might have been trying to solve an urgent problem.

Perhaps if I hadn't been ill I would have been able to divert Neal from his obsession, but I could hardly venture outside without growing dizzy; I could only wait in the bungalow for my state to improve. Neither Neal nor I had had sunstroke before, but he seemed to know how to treat it. "Keep drinking water. Cover yourself if you start shivering." He didn't mind my staying in—he seemed almost too eager to go out alone. Did that matter? Next day he was bound only for the library.

My state was crippling my thoughts, yet even if I'd been healthy I couldn't have imagined how he would look when he returned: excited, conspiratorial, smug. "I've got a story for you," he said at once.

Most such offers proved to be prolonged and dull. "Oh yes?" I said warily.

He sat forward as though to infect me with suspense. "That village we went to—it isn't called Lewis. It's called Strand."

Was he pausing to give me a chance to gasp or applaud? "Oh yes," I said without enthusiasm.

"Lewis was another village, further up the coast. It's deserted too."

That seemed to be his punch line. The antics of patterns within my eyelids had made me irritable. "It doesn't seem much of a story," I complained.

"Well, that's only the beginning." When his pause had forced me to open my eyes, he said, "I read a book about your local unexplained mysteries."

"Why?"

"Look, if you don't want to hear—"

"Go on, go on, now you've started." Not to know might be even more nerve-racking.

"There wasn't much about Lewis," he said eventually, perhaps to give himself more time to improvise.

"Was there much at all?"

"Yes, certainly. It may not sound like much. Nobody knows why Lewis was abandoned, but then nobody knows that about Strand either." My impatience must have showed, for he added hastily, "What I mean is, the people who left Strand wouldn't say why."

"Someone asked them?"

"The woman who wrote the book. She managed to track some of them down. They'd moved as far inland as they could, that was one thing she noticed. And they always had some kind of nervous disorder. Talking about Strand always made them more nervous, as though they felt that talking might make something happen, or something might hear."

"That's what the author said."

"Right."

"What was her name?"

Could he hear my suspicion? "Jesus *Christ,*" he snarled, "I don't know. What does it matter?"

In fact it didn't, not to me. His story had made me feel worse. The noose had tightened round my skull, the twilit beach was swarming and vibrating. I closed my eyes. Shut up, I roared at him. Go away.

"There was one thing," he persisted. "One man said that kids kept going on the beach at night. Their parents tried all ways to stop them. Some of them questioned their kids, but it was as though the kids couldn't stop themselves. Why was that, do you think?" When I refused to answer he said irrelevantly, "All this was in the 1930s."

I couldn't stand hearing children called kids. The recurring word had made me squirm: drips of slang, like water torture. And I'd never heard such a feeble punch line. His clumsiness as a storyteller enraged me; he couldn't even organize his material. I was sure he hadn't read any such book.

After a while I peered out from beneath my eyelids, hoping he'd decided that I was asleep. He was poring over the notebook again, and looked rapt. I only wished that people and reviewers would read my books as carefully. He kept rubbing his forehead, as though to enliven his brain.

I dozed. When I opened my eyes he was waiting for me. He shoved the notebook at me to demonstrate something. "Look, I'm sorry," I said without much effort to sound so. "I'm not in the mood."

He stalked into his room, emerging without the book but with my stick. "I'm going for a walk," he announced sulkily, like a spouse after a quarrel.

I dozed gratefully, for I felt more delirious; my head felt packed with grains of sand that gritted together. In fact, the whole of me was made of sand. Of course it was true that I was composed of particles, and I thought my delirium had found a metaphor for that. But the grains that floated through my inner vision were neither sand nor atoms. A member, dark and vague, was reaching for them. I struggled to awaken; I didn't want to distinguish its shape, and still less did I want to learn what it meant to do with the grains—for as the member sucked them into itself, engulfing them in a way that I refused to perceive, I saw that the grains were worlds and stars.

I woke shivering. My body felt uncontrollable and unfamiliar. I let it shake itself to rest—not that I had a choice, but I was concentrating on the problem of why I'd woken head raised, like a watchdog. What had I heard?

Perhaps only wind and sea: both seemed louder, more intense. My thoughts became entangled in their rhythm. I felt there had been another sound. The bushes threshed, sounding parched with sand. Had I heard Neal returning? I stumbled into his room. It was empty.

As I stood by his open window, straining my ears, I thought I heard his voice, blurred by the dull tumult of waves. I peered out. Beyond the low heads of the bushes, the glow of the beach shuddered toward me. I had to close my eyes, for I couldn't tell whether the restless scrawny shapes were crowding my eyeballs or the beach; it felt, somehow, like both. When I looked again, I seemed to see Neal.

Or was it Neal? The unsteady stifled glow aggravated the distortions of my vision. Was the object just a new piece of debris? I found its shape bewildering; my mind kept apprehending it as a symbol printed on the whitish expanse. The luminosity made it seem to shift, tentatively and jerkily, as though it was learning to pose. The light, or my eyes, surrounded it with dancing.

Had my sense of perspective left me? I was misjudging size, either of the beach or of the figure. Yes, it was a figure, however large it seemed. It was moving its arms like a limp puppet. And it was half-buried in the sand.

I staggered outside, shouting to Neal, and then I recoiled. The sky must be thick with a storm cloud; it felt suffocatingly massive, solid as rock, and close enough to crush me. I forced myself toward the bushes, though my head was pounding, squeezed into a lump of pain.

Almost at once I heard plodding on the dunes. My blood half deafened me; the footsteps sounded vague and immense. I peered along the dim path. At the edge of my vision the beach flickered repetitively. Immense darkness hovered over me. Unnervingly close to me, swollen by the glow, a head rose into view. For a moment my tension seemed likely to crack my skull. Then Neal spoke. His words were incomprehensible amid the wind, but it was his voice.

As we trudged back toward the lights the threat of a storm seemed to withdraw, and I blamed it on my tension. "Of course I'm all right," he muttered irritably. "I fell and that made me shout, that's all." Once we were inside I saw the evidence of his fall; his trousers were covered with sand up to the knees.

IV

Next day he hardly spoke to me. He went down early to the beach, and stayed there. I didn't know if he was obsessed or displaying pique. Perhaps he couldn't bear to be near me; invalids can find each other unbearable.

Often I glimpsed him, wandering beyond the dunes. He walked as though in an elaborate maze and scrutinized the beach. Was he searching for the key to the notebook? Was he looking for pollution? By the time he found it, I thought sourly, it would have infected him.

I felt too enervated to intervene. As I watched, Neal appeared to vanish intermittently; if I looked away, I couldn't locate him again for minutes. The beach blazed like bone, and was never still. I couldn't blame the aberrations of my vision solely on heat and haze.

When Neal returned, late that afternoon, I asked him to phone for a doctor. He looked taken aback, but eventually said, "There's a box by the station, isn't there?"

"One of the neighbours would let you phone."

"No, I'll walk down. They're probably all wondering why you've let some long-haired freak squat in your house, as it is."

He went out, rubbing his forehead gingerly. He often did that now. That, and his preoccupation with the demented notebook, were additional reasons why I wanted a doctor: I felt Neal needed examining too.

By the time he returned, it was dusk. On the horizon, embers dulled in the sea. The glow of the beach was already stirring; it seemed to have intensified during the last few days. I told myself I had grown hypersensitive.

"Dr. Lewis. He's coming tomorrow." Neal hesitated, then went on, "I think I'll just have a stroll on the beach. Want to come?"

"Good God no. I'm ill, can't you see?"

"I know that." His impatience was barely controlled. "A stroll might do you good. There isn't any sunlight now."

"I'll stay in until I've seen the doctor."

He looked disposed to argue, but his restlessness overcame him. As he left, his bearing seemed to curse me. Was his illness making him intolerant of mine, or did he feel that I'd rebuffed a gesture of reconciliation?

I felt too ill to watch him from the window. When I looked I could seldom distinguish him or make out which movements were his. He appeared to be walking slowly, poking at the beach with my stick. I wondered if he'd found quicksand. Again his path made me think of a maze.

I dozed, far longer than I'd intended. The doctor loomed over me. Peering into my eyes, he reached down. I began to struggle, as best I could: I'd glimpsed the depths of his eye-sockets, empty and dry as interstellar space. I didn't need his treatment, I would be fine if he left me alone, just let me go. But he had reached deep into me. As though I was a bladder that had burst, I felt myself flood into him; I felt vast emptiness absorb my substance and my self. Dimly I understood that it was nothing like emptiness—that my mind refused to perceive what it was, so alien and frightful was its teeming.

It was dawn. The muffled light teemed. The beach glowed fitfully. I gasped: someone was down on the beach, so huddled that he looked shapeless. He rose, levering himself up with my stick, and began to pace haphazardly. I knew at once that he'd spent the night on the beach.

After that I stayed awake. I couldn't imagine the state of his mind, and I was a little afraid of being asleep when he returned. But when, hours later, he came in to raid the kitchen for a piece of cheese, he seemed hardly to see me. He was muttering repetitively under his breath. His eyes looked dazzled by the beach, sunk in his obsession.

"When did the doctor say he was coming?"

"Later," he mumbled, and hurried down to the beach.

I hoped he would stay there until the doctor came. Occasionally I glimpsed him at his intricate pacing. Ripples of heat deformed him; his blurred flesh looked unstable. Whenever I glanced at the beach it leapt forward, dauntingly vivid. Cracks of light appeared in the sea. Clumps of grass seemed to rise twitching, as though the dunes were craning to watch Neal. Five minutes' vigil at the window was as much as I could bear.

The afternoon consumed time. It felt lethargic and enervating as four in the morning. There was no sign of the doctor. I kept gazing from the front door. Nothing moved on the crescent except wind-borne hints of the beach.

Eventually I tried to phone. Though I could feel the heat of the pavement through the soles of my shoes, the day seemed bearable; only threats of pain plucked at my skull. But nobody was at home. The bungalows stood smugly in the evening light. When I attempted to walk to the phone box, the noose closed on my skull at once.

In my hall I halted startled, for Neal had thrown open the living-room door as I entered the house. He looked flushed and angry. "Where were you?" he demanded.

"I'm not a hospital case yet, you know. I was trying to phone the doctor."

Unfathomably, he looked relieved. "I'll go down now and call him."

While he was away I watched the beach sink into twilight. At the moment, this seemed to be the only time of day I could endure watching— the time at which shapes become obscure, most capable of metamorphosis. Perhaps this made the antics of the shore acceptable, more apparently natural. Now the beach resembled clouds in front of the moon; it drifted slowly and variously. If I gazed for long it looked nervous with lightning. The immense bulk of the night edged up from the horizon.

I didn't hear Neal return; I must have been fascinated by the view. I turned to find him watching me. Again he looked relieved—because I was still here? "He's coming soon," he said.

"Tonight, do you mean?"

"Yes, tonight. Why not?"

I didn't know many doctors who would come out at night to treat what was, however unpleasant for me, a relatively minor illness. Perhaps attitudes were different here in the country. Neal was heading for the back door, for the beach. "Do you think you could wait until he comes?" I said, groping for an excuse to detain him. "Just in case I feel worse."

"Yes, you're right." His gaze was opaque. "I'd better stay with you."

We waited. The dark mass closed over beach and bungalows. The nocturnal glow fluttered at the edge of my vision. When I glanced at the beach, the dim shapes were hectic. I seemed to be paying for my earlier fascination, for now the walls of the room looked active with faint patterns.

Where was the doctor? Neal seemed impatient too. The only sounds were the repetitive ticking of his footsteps and the irregular chant of the sea. He kept staring at me as if he wanted to speak; occasionally his mouth twitched. He resembled a child both eager to confess and afraid to do so.

Though he made me uneasy I tried to look encouraging, interested in whatever he might have to say. His pacing took him closer and closer to the beach door. Yes, I nodded, tell me, talk to me.

His eyes narrowed. Behind his eyelids he was pondering. Abruptly he sat opposite me. A kind of smile, tweaked awry, plucked at his lips. "I've got another story for you," he said.

"Really?" I sounded as intrigued as I could.

He picked up the notebook. "I worked it out from this."

So we'd returned to his obsession. As he twitched pages over, his feet shifted constantly. His lips moved as though whispering the text. I heard the vast mumbling of the sea.

"Suppose this," he said all at once. "I only said suppose, mind you. This guy was living all alone in Strand. It must have affected his mind, you said that yourself—having to watch the beach every night. But just suppose it didn't send him mad? Suppose it affected his mind so that he saw things more clearly?"

I hid my impatience. "What things?"

"The beach." His tone reminded me of something—a particular kind of simplicity I couldn't quite place. "Of course we're only supposing. But from things you've read, don't you feel there are places that are closer to another sort of reality, another plane or dimension or whatever?"

"You mean the beach at Strand was like that?" I suggested, to encourage him.

"That's right. Did you feel it too?"

His eagerness startled me. "I felt ill, that's all. I still do."

"Sure. Yes, of course. I mean, we were only supposing. But look at what he says." He seemed glad to retreat into the notebook. "It started at Lewis where the old stones were, then it moved on up the coast to Strand. Doesn't that prove that what he was talking about is unlike anything we know?"

His mouth hung open, awaiting my agreement; it looked empty, robbed of sense. I glanced away, distracted by the fluttering glow beyond him. "I don't know what you mean."

"That's because you haven't read this properly." His impatience had turned harsh. "Look here," he demanded, poking his fingers at a group of words as if they were a Bible's oracle.

WHEN THE PATTERNS READY IT CAN COME BACK. "So what is that supposed to mean?"

"I'll tell you what I think it means—what he meant." His low voice seemed to stumble among the rhythms of the beach. "You see how he keeps mentioning patterns. Suppose this other reality was once all there was? Then ours came into being and occupied some of its space. We didn't destroy it—it can't be destroyed. Maybe it withdrew a little, to bide its time. But it left a kind of imprint of itself, a kind of coded image of itself in our reality. And yet that image is itself in embryo, growing. You see, he says it's alive but it's only the image being put together. Things become part of its image, and that's how it grows. I'm sure that's what he meant."

I felt mentally exhausted and dismayed by all this. How much in need of a doctor was he? I couldn't help sounding a little derisive. "I don't see how you could have put all that together from that book."

"Who says I did?"

His vehemence was shocking. I had to break the tension, for the glare in his eyes looked as unnatural and nervous as the glow of the beach. I went to gaze from the front window, but there was no sign of the doctor.

"Don't worry," Neal said. "He's coming."

I stood staring out at the lightless road until he said fretfully, "Don't you want to hear the rest?"

He waited until I sat down. His tension was oppressive as the hovering sky. He gazed at me for what seemed minutes; the noose dug into my skull. At last he said, "Does this beach feel like anywhere else to you?"

"It feels like a beach."

He shrugged that aside. "You see, he worked out that whatever came from the old stones kept moving toward the inhabited areas. That's how it added to itself. That's why it moved on from Lewis and then Strand."

"All nonsense, of course. Ravings."

"No. It isn't." There was no mistaking the fury that lurked, barely restrained, beneath his low voice. That fury seemed loose in the roaring night, in the wind and violent sea and looming sky. The beach trembled wakefully. "The next place it would move to would be here," he muttered. "It has to be."

"If you accepted the idea in the first place."

A hint of a grimace twitched his cheek; my comment might have been an annoying fly—certainly as trivial. "You can read the pattern out there if you try," he mumbled. "It takes all day. You begin to get a sense of what might be there. It's alive, though nothing like life as we recognize it."

I could only say whatever came into my head, to detain him until the doctor arrived. "Then how do you?"

He avoided the question, but only to betray the depths of his obsession. "Would an insect recognize us as a kind of life?"

Suddenly I realized that he intoned "the beach" as a priest might name his god. We must get away from the beach. Never mind the doctor now. "Look, Neal, I think we'd better—"

He interrupted me, eyes glaring spasmodically. "It's strongest at night. I think it soaks up energy during the day. Remember, he said that the quicksands only come out at night. They move, you know—they make you follow the pattern. And the sea is different at night. Things come out of it. They're like symbols and yet they're alive. I think the sea creates them. They help make the pattern live."

Appalled, I could only return to the front window and search for the lights of the doctor's car—for any lights at all.

"Yes, yes," Neal said, sounding less impatient than soothing. "He's coming." But as he spoke I glimpsed, reflected in the window, his secret triumphant grin.

Eventually I managed to say to his reflection, "You didn't call a doctor, did you?"

"No." A smile made his lips tremble like quicksand. "But he's coming."

My stomach had begun to churn slowly; so had my head, and the room. Now I was afraid to stand with my back to Neal, but when I turned I was more afraid to ask the question. "Who?"

For a moment I thought he disdained to answer; he turned his back on me and gazed toward the beach—but I can't write any longer as if I have doubts, as if I don't know the end. The beach was his answer, its awesome transformation was, even if I wasn't sure what I was seeing. Was the beach swollen, puffed up as if by the irregular gasping of the sea? Was it swarming with indistinct shapes, parasites that scuttled dancing over it, sank into it, floated writhing to its surface? Did it quiver along the whole of its length like luminous gelatin? I tried to believe that all this was an effect of the brooding dark—but the dark had closed down so thickly that there might have been no light in the world outside except the fitful glow.

He craned his head back over his shoulder. The gleam in his eyes looked very like the glimmering outside. A web of saliva stretched between his bared teeth. He grinned with a frightful generosity; he'd decided to answer my question more directly. His lips moved as they had when he was reading. At last I heard what I'd tried not to suspect. He was making the sound that I'd tried not to hear in the shells.

Was it meant to be an invocation, or the name I'd asked for? I knew only that the sound, so liquid and inhuman that I could almost think it was shapeless, nauseated me, so much so that I couldn't separate it from the huge loose voices of wind and sea. It seemed to fill the room. The pounding of my skull tried to imitate its rhythm, which I found impossible to grasp, unbearable. I began to sidle along the wall toward the front door.

His body turned jerkily, as if dangling from his neck. His head laughed, if a sound like struggles in mud is laughter. "You're not going to try to get away?" he cried. "It was getting hold of you before I came, he was. You haven't a chance now, not since we brought him into the house," and he picked up a shell.

As he leveled the mouth of the shell at me my dizziness flooded my skull, hurling me forward. The walls seemed to glare and shake and break out in swarms; I thought that a dark bulk loomed at the window, filling it.

Neal's mouth was working, but the nauseating sound might have been roaring deep in a cavern, or a shell. It sounded distant and huge, but coming closer and growing more definite—the voice of something vast and liquid that was gradually taking shape. Perhaps that was because I was listening, but I had no choice.

All at once Neal's free hand clamped his forehead. It looked like a pincer desperate to tear something out of his skull. "It's growing," he cried, somewhere between sobbing and ecstasy. As he spoke, the liquid chant seemed to abate not at all. Before I knew what he meant to do, he'd wrenched open the back door and was gone. In a nightmarish way, his nervous elaborate movements resembled dancing.

As the door crashed open, the roar of the night rushed in. Its leap in volume sounded eager, voracious. I stood paralyzed, listening, and couldn't tell how like his chant it sounded. I heard his footsteps, soft and loose, running unevenly over the dunes. Minutes later I thought I heard a faint cry, which sounded immediately engulfed.

I slumped against a chair. I felt relieved, drained, uncaring. The sounds had returned to the beach, where they ought to be; the room looked stable now. Then I grew disgusted with myself. Suppose Neal was injured, or caught in quicksand? I'd allowed his hysteria to gain a temporary hold on my sick perceptions, I told myself—was I going to use that as an excuse not to try to save him?

At last I forced myself outside. All the bungalows were dark. The beach was glimmering, but not violently. I could see nothing wrong with the sky. Only my dizziness, and the throbbing of my head, threatened to distort my perceptions.

I made myself edge between the bushes, which hissed like snakes, mouths full of sand. The tangle of footprints made me stumble frequently. Sand rattled the spikes of marram grass. At the edge of the dunes, the path felt ready to slide me down to the beach.

The beach was crowded. I had to squint at many of the vague pieces of debris. My eyes grew used to the dimness, but I could see no sign of Neal. Then I peered closer. Was that a pair of sandals, half buried? Before my giddiness could hurl me to the beach, I slithered down.

Yes, they were Neal's, and a path of bare footprints led away toward the crowd of debris. I poked gingerly at the sandals, and wished I had my stick to test for quicksand—but the sand in which they were partially engulfed was quite solid. Why had he tried to bury them?

I followed his prints, my eyes still adjusting. I refused to imitate his path, for it looped back on itself in intricate patterns which made me dizzy and wouldn't fade from my mind. His paces were irregular, a cripple's dance. He must be a puppet of his nerves, I thought. I was a little afraid to confront him, but I felt a duty to try.

His twistings led me among the debris. Low obscure shapes surrounded me: a jagged stump bristling with metal tendrils that groped in the air as I came near; half a car so rusty and misshapen that it looked like a child's fuzzy sketch; the hood of a pram within which glimmered a bald lump of sand. I was glad to emerge from that maze, for the dim objects seemed to shift; I'd even thought the bald lump was opening a crumbling mouth.

But on the open beach there were other distractions. The ripples and patterns of sand were clearer, and appeared to vibrate restlessly. I kept glancing toward the sea, not because its chant was troubling me—though, with its insistent loose rhythm, it was—but because I had a persistent impression that the waves were slowing, sluggish as treacle.

I stumbled, and had to turn back to see what had tripped me. The glow of the beach showed me Neal's shirt, the little of it that was left unburied. There was no mistaking it; I recognized its pattern. The glow made the nylon seem luminous, lit from within.

His prints danced back among the debris. Even then, God help me, I wondered if he was playing a sick joke—if he was waiting somewhere to leap out, to scare me into admitting I'd been impressed. I trudged angrily into the midst of the debris, and wished at once that I hadn't. All the objects were luminous, without shadows.

There was no question now: the glow of the beach was increasing. It made Neal's tracks look larger: their outlines shifted as I squinted at them. I stumbled hastily toward the deserted stretch of beach, and brushed against the half-engulfed car.

That was the moment at which the nightmare became real. I might have told myself that rust had eaten away the car until it was thin as a shell, but I was past deluding myself. All at once I knew that nothing on this beach was as it seemed, for as my hand collided with the car roof, which should have been painfully solid, I felt the roof crumble—and the entire structure flopped on the sand, from which it was at once indistinguishable.

I fled toward the open beach. But there was no relief, for the entire beach was glowing luridly, like mud struggling to suffocate a moon. Among the debris I glimpsed the rest of Neal's clothes, half absorbed by the beach. As I staggered into the open, I saw his tracks ahead—saw how they appeared to grow, to alter until they became unrecognizable, and then to peter out at a large dark shapeless patch on the sand.

I glared about, terrified. I couldn't see the bungalows. After minutes I succeeded in glimpsing the path, the mess of footprints cluttering the dune. I began to pace toward it, very slowly and quietly, so as not to be noticed by the beach and the looming sky.

But the dunes were receding. I think I began to scream then, scream almost in a whisper, for the faster I hurried, the further the dunes withdrew. The nightmare had overtaken perspective. Now I was running wildly, though I felt I was standing still. I'd run only a few steps when I had to recoil from sand that seized my feet so eagerly I almost heard it smack its lips. Minutes ago there had been no quicksand, for I could see my earlier prints embedded in that patch. I stood trapped, shivering uncontrollably, as the glow intensified and the lightless sky seemed to descend—and I felt the beach change.

Simultaneously I experienced something which, in a sense, was worse: I felt myself change. My dizziness whirled out of me. I felt light-headed but stable. At last I realized that I had never had sunstroke. Perhaps it had been my inner conflict—being forced to stay yet at the same time not daring to venture onto the beach, because of what my subconscious knew would happen.

And now it was happening. The beach had won. Perhaps Neal had given it the strength. Though I dared not look, I knew that the sea had stopped. Stranded objects, elaborate symbols composed of something like flesh, writhed on its paralyzed margin. The clamor which surrounded me, chanting and gurgling, was not that of the sea: it was far too articulate, however repetitive. It was underfoot too—the voice of the beach, a whisper pronounced by so many sources that it was deafening.

I felt ridges of sand squirm beneath me. They were firm enough to bear my weight, but they felt nothing like sand. They were forcing me to shift my balance. In a moment I would have to dance, to imitate the jerking shapes that had ceased to pretend they were only debris, to join in the ritual of the objects that swarmed up from the congealed sea. Everything glistened in the quivering glow. I thought my flesh had begun to glow too.

Then, with a lurch of vertigo worse than any I'd experienced, I found myself momentarily detached from the nightmare. I seemed to be observing myself, a figure tiny and trivial as an insect, making a timid hysterical attempt to join in the dance of the teeming beach. The moment was brief, yet felt like eternity. Then I was back in my clumsy flesh, struggling to prance on the beach.

At once I was cold with terror. I shook like a victim of electricity, for I knew what viewpoint I'd shared. It was still watching me, indifferent as outer space—and it filled the sky. If I looked up I would see its eyes, or eye, if it had anything that I would recognize as such. My neck shivered as I held my head down. But I would have to look up in a moment, for I could feel the face, or whatever was up there, leaning closer—reaching down for me.

If I hadn't broken through my suffocating panic I would have been crushed to nothing. But my teeth tore my lip, and allowed me to scream. Released, I ran desperately, heedless of quicksand. The dunes crept back from me, the squirming beach glowed, the light flickered in the rhythm of the chanting. I was spared being engulfed—but when at last I reached the dunes, or was allowed to reach them, the dark massive presence still hovered overhead.

I clambered scrabbling up the path. My sobbing gasps filled my mouth with sand. My wild flight was from nothing that I'd seen. I was fleeing the knowledge, deep-rooted and undeniable, that what I perceived blotting out the sky was nothing but an acceptable metaphor. Appalling though the presence was, it was only my mind's version of what was there—a way of letting me glimpse it without going mad at once.

V

I have not seen Neal since—at least, not in a form that anyone else would recognize.

Next day, after a night during which I drank all the liquor I could find to douse my appalled thoughts and insights, I discovered that I couldn't leave. I pretended to myself that I was going to the beach to search for Neal. But the movements began at once; the patterns stirred. As I gazed, dully entranced, I felt something grow less dormant in my head, as though my skull had turned into a shell.

Perhaps I stood engrossed by the beach for hours. Movement distracted me: the skimming of a windblown patch of sand. As I glanced at it I saw that it resembled a giant mask, its features ragged and crumbling. Though its eyes and mouth couldn't keep their shape, it kept trying to resemble Neal's face. As it slithered whispering toward me I fled toward the path, moaning.

That night he came into the bungalow. I hadn't dared go to bed; I dozed in a chair, and frequently woke trembling. Was I awake when I saw his huge face squirming and transforming as it crawled out of the wall? Certainly I could hear his words, though his voice was the inhuman chorus I'd experienced on the beach. Worse, when I opened my eyes to glimpse what might have been only a shadow, not a large unstable form fading back into the substance of the wall, for a few seconds I could still hear that voice.

Each night, once the face had sunk back into the wall as into quicksand, the voice remained longer—and each night, struggling to break loose from the prison of my chair, I understood more of its revelations. I tried to believe all this was my imagination, and so, in a sense, it was. The glimpses of Neal were nothing more than acceptable metaphors for what Neal had become, and what I was becoming. My mind refused to perceive the truth more directly, yet I was possessed by a temptation, vertiginous and sickening, to learn what that truth might be.

For a while I struggled. I couldn't leave, but perhaps I could write. When I found that however bitterly I fought I could think of nothing but the beach, I wrote this. I hoped that writing about it might release me, but of course the more one thinks of the beach, the stronger its hold becomes.

Now I spend most of my time on the beach. It has taken me months to write this. Sometimes I see people staring at me from the bungalows. Do they wonder what I'm doing? They will find out when their time comes—everyone will. Neal must have satisfied it for a while; for the moment it is slower. But that means little. Its time is not like ours.

Each day the pattern is clearer. My pacing helps. Once you have glimpsed the pattern you must go back to read it, over and over. I can feel it growing in my mind. The sense of expectancy is overwhelming. Of course that sense was never mine. It was the hunger of the beach.

My time is near. The large moist prints that surround mine are more pronounced—the prints of what I am becoming. Its substance is everywhere, stealthy and insidious. Today, as I looked at the bungalows, I saw them change; they grew like fossils of themselves. They looked like dreams of the beach, and that is what they will become.

The voice is always with me now. Sometimes the congealing haze seems to mouth at me. At twilight the dunes edge forward to guard the beach. When the beach is dimmest I see other figures pacing out the pattern. Only those whom the beach has touched would see them; their outlines are unstable—some look more like coral than flesh. The quicksands make us trace the pattern, and he stoops from the depths beyond the sky to watch. The sea feeds me.

Often now I have what may be a dream. I glimpse what Neal has become, and how that is merely a fragment of the imprint which it will use to return to our world. Each time I come closer to recalling the insight when I wake. As my mind changes, it tries to prepare me for the end. Soon I shall be what Neal is. I tremble uncontrollably, I feel deathly sick, my mind struggles desperately not to know. Yet in a way I am resigned. After all, even if I managed to flee the beach, I could never escape the growth. I have understood enough to know that it would absorb me in time, when it becomes the world.

Body

Brian Evenson

I. BODY

I have been privately removed to St. Sebastian's Correctional Facility and Haven for the Wayward, where they are fitting me for a new mind, and body too. Most of my distress, they believe, results from having a wayward body and no knowledge of how to manage it. As mine is a body which does not sit easy with the world, they have chosen to begin again from scratch.

The body, says Brother Johanssen, *is not simple flesh staunching blood and slung over bones, but a way of slipping and spilling through the world.* While others slip like water through the world, I am always bottling the world up. The only way I can come unbottled is to crack the world apart. *One cannot refashion flesh and blood,* Brother Johanssen tells me, *but one can refashion the paths that flesh and blood take through the world.*

In a way you can remake the flesh and blood too, whispers Skarmus, *or unmake it, as you know, dear boy.* It is late one midnight, and I lie bound to the slab. I have no answer to this. His fingers are pushing through my hair. In the dark, I hear the grim smile in his voice. *That you hear what others see,* Brother Johanssen tells me, *is but further index of your illness.*

It is true, as Skarmus says, that I have acquired a certain skill at un-making flesh and blood, dividing it and sectioning it into new creatures and forms as a means of transforming the distress of my wayward body into pleasure. Put into the brothers' terms, the only commerce I can stomach is with the dead. In a little time, I know to work away my distress by transforming another into a stripped- and lopped-off dark lump of flies. They do not know all of this, though they surely suspect. For what they do know, I am conscripted in St. Sebastian's, subject to all things as I prepare to take up another, purer body.

Four buildings, four stations, four doors. Before I may enter any station, I am required to salute the door frame of the remaining three. First lintel, then post, then lintel again, addressed in such fashion first with my right mitt, then with my left, then my body must spin sharply and stride to the next door.

Skarmus is with me as my private demon, tasked by the brothers to ensure I meet all proscription regarding motion, that I salute door frames in proper order and fashion, that I locomote as they would have me do. I am to be impeded and interrupted by him. All is an effort and the brothers' belief is that my mind in the face of that effort must opt for the construction of another body.

There must, for reasons never explained to me, be an interval of five seconds between each gesture, no more, no less. I must regulate seconds as Skarmus challenges me with hands and voice. When my movements are irregular, the intervals inexact, I am forced to begin again. If I fail a second time, Skarmus is allowed to tighten the flap over my mouth until I can barely respire and slowly lose consciousness.

I cannot know if at night Skarmus whispers his own opinions or if his words are part of the brothers' larger plan for me. I attempt not to respond to his whispers or actions, attempt as far as possible to ignore Skarmus and coax him off guard. I have twice, despite the padded restraints engaging my hands and feet, despite the system wiring my jaw closed, beaten Skarmus senseless. Indeed, I would have beaten him dead and attempted, despite my restraints, commerce with what was left of him, had not the brothers rapidly intervened.

✝ ✝

Four stations, then, as follows: the Living, the Instruction, the Restriction, the Resurrection. I have entered all stations save the Resurrection. Here, Brother Johanssen believes, I am not yet prepared to go.

The Living: I am strapped flat around chest, wrists, ankles, throat. The mask is undone and set aside, the lights extinguished. I am allowed to sleep if I can so manage with Skarmus mumbling over me.

At some point, lights flash on. A tube is forced between the wires encasing my mouth and I am fed.

Brother Johanssen arrives, the jawscrews are loosened, I am allowed a moment of untrammeled expression.

"How are you, brother?" Brother Johanssen asks. "Are you uncovering a new body within your skin?"

"I have a new body," I tell him. "I am utterly changed. I have given up evil and become a purely normal fellow."

He shakes his head, smiling thinly. "You believe me so credible?" he asks. He makes a gesture and the jawscrews are tightened down, the mask re-initiated.

You must learn to deceive him, whispers Skarmus. *You must master better the art of the lie.*

Then we are up and outside and walking. The weights and baffles and mitts, always varied slightly from one day to the next. The restrictions, Skarmus's constant tug and thrust as I walk. My body remains aching and sore, unsure on its feet.

Skarmus is beside me, a half pace behind. Brother Johanssen is somewhere behind, out of sight, the other brothers as well. I am at the center of a world whose sole purpose is to circle about me.

The Instruction: I am made to listen to Brother Johanssen, Skarmus still whispering in my ear. *That which is wayward must be angled forward, the body surrendered for another,* Brother Johanssen preaches. I have, I am told, been wandering all the years of my life in the darkness of my imperfect body. Only the brothers can bring me into light.

You cannot be brought into the so-called light, whispers Skarmus. *You shall never survive it. For you there is no so-called light but only so-called darkness.*

I fail to understand the role of Skarmus. He seems intent on undoing all that Brother Johanssen attempts. Together, it is as if they are trying to tear me apart.

The beauty of the world, Brother Johanssen is saying, *objective, impersonal. For a body such as that which you still persist in wearing, an affront. Affreux. You must acquire a body which will live with beauty rather than against it.*

There is only against, states Skarmus.

The Restriction: when I am inattentive, when I resist, when I follow Skarmus's advice rather than that of the good brother, when I fail in my tasks and motions. The mask is tightened almost to suffocation, the flaps zipped down to block my ears, eyes, nose, the hands chained and dragged up above the head. The back of the rubber suit is loosened, parted, a range of sensations scattered over it or into it by devices I cannot perceive. At some point sweat begins to crease my back, or perhaps welts and blood.

It all revolves around not knowing. I cannot say if it is pain or pleasure I feel, the line between the two so easily traversable in the artificial distance from my own flesh. The dull thud coming distanced through my blocked ears, the flash of sensation flung across the skull at first and then barely perceptible, the damp smell within the leather mask.

"How are you, brother?" Brother Johanssen asks. "Have you found your new body?"

"I have a new body now, dear brother," I say. I strain against the straps. "I am a changed man."

He shakes his finger back and forth over me slowly. "I see you take me for a fool," he says.

A brief flash through the stations, a day in the space of a moment, my mind at some distance from my body and the light goes off. I feel fingers in my hair. *You cannot believe any of this,* Skarmus says. *You must not allow them to take away what you are.*

Lintel, post, lintel with right. Lintel, post, lintel with left. The muffled blows the mitt offers with each strike.

A slow turn, the foot coming up. Stumbling to the next door, Skarmus clinging to one of my legs.

"You are not prepared for the Resurrection," says Brother Johanssen, leaning benevolently over me.

You'll never be ready, Skarmus whispers.

The chains tighten. I feel my back stripped bare. In the darkness inside my mask, I see streaks of light.

I open my mouth to speak. They are already screwing my jaw down.

A remembered ruin of bodies and myself panting among them, yet with no complete memory of having taken them apart.

I am different from anyone else in the world.

He is smiling, waiting for me to speak. I close my eyes. He pries them open, waits, waits. Finally lets them go, tightens the jawscrews down until my teeth ache and grate.

Skarmus falls slightly ahead of me and for a moment I feel myself and my body clearly my own again. He stumbles and I have my mitts on either side of his head and am holding his head still as I strike through it with my own masked head, as I lift him up to bring the side of his skull down against my muffled knee. Were I not so restrained and softened by padding he would be dead. As it is, it is a sort of awkward game.

I try to snap his head to one side and break his neck, but the mitts give slightly and the neck groans but refuses to snap. There is a flurry of bodies and Skarmus is dragged away and other hands are holding me down, pulling the mask off, holding my own head down. I see the brief glint of the long needle, feel it pricked into my skull, just above the rim of my eye.

"An inch more," says Brother Johanssen. "A simple rotation of the wrist, brother, and you shall have little relation to any body at all. Is that what you choose?"

I move my eyes no, feel the pressure of the needle.

"Are you telling me that all our time has been wasted?" He looks at me long, without expression, the needle an everpresent pressure, a red blot now drawing itself into my vision. "It is too late for a full cure," says Brother Johanssen. "Your body is too stubborn in its ways. We can redirect it but slightly."

Brother Johanssen gestures and I feel the needle slick back out, see it fluxed and dripping blood, moving away. There lies Skarmus, his jaw blistered black and blue. He is silent for once.

"The Resurrection then," says Brother Johanssen as blood curls over my eye. "This is all we can do. May God forgive us."

II. SHOE

In the polished ceiling of the Living, in the few moments I have free of the mask, I see the flesh above my eye gone dark and turgid, swelling like a second eye. Below it the original eye wavers and falls dim. In a few awakenings its vision is altogether gone, the enormous fist of death beginning to open in its place.

They sedate me and scrape the eye from the socket and drain the ichor from it and scald the socket clean. Skarmus speaks muffled, morphined, his jaw wrapped, his voice mumbled.

I was right, he means to say. *I was right all along.*

His gestures of impediment have subsided, seem half-hearted at best. I am allowed to touch each door frame largely unimpeded, move in my wires and chains into the Resurrection at last.

It is a simple station, a single room, a low light in the center of it. Brother Johanssen is already there, waiting, at attention, his simple garments exchanged for brighter brocaded robes.

I am made to sit. I am then strapped in place and into a head-brace locked so I am forced to regard him.

"These are the initial terms of the Resurrection," he says:

Top Lift

Eyelet

Aglet

Grommet

Vamp

He holds it up, cupped in his hand. He displays it in the light.

"Do you see the curve here?" asks Brother Johanssen a few sessions later, tracing along the side. "Employ your imagination. What does it conjure up?"

They are trying to change you, whispers Skarmus.

"On a woman's body, brother. What does it recall?"

He brings it close, traces the curves, holds it close to my face, describes the minor shadings and traces. When I close my eyes, Brother Johanssen commands Skarmus to hold them open, both of them, the missing and the whole. He is touching the shoe, caressing it, speaking still in a way that makes the shoe steam and glimmer, glister in the odd light as if threatening to become something else.

Quarter, he says.

Cuff.

Counter.

Heel.

When I wake he is there, leaning over me, my jaw already screwed open. "Do you accept the fruits of your new faith?" he asks.

"What?" I say.

"What?" he says. He stands and begins to weave away. "What?" he repeats, "What?"

Throat, someone says behind me.

Tongue, someone says.

He dims the central light, disappears himself somewhere behind me. A square of light as big as myself appears, flashes onto the wall before me.

You are in it, says Skarmus. *Too late to step back now.*

The square of light goes dark, is exchanged for the image of the forepart of a woman's shoe, the dip between the first and second toe captured in the low cleft of the vamp. It flashes away and is replaced by pallid white flesh, the dip of a dress, the slow curve and fall of the woman's body.

There may be a resemblance, says Skarmus. *Yet it is entirely superficial.*

The images are flashed back and forth, one replacing the other soon with such speed it becomes difficult to know where one image stops, the other begins.

Breast, someone says.

Cleave.

Box.

I hear the clatter behind me, the square of light pulsing and then a shoe fading up and angling in and transforming into a woman. Then the shoe again and a difference place, followed by a section of the woman. The clatter, swirling motes of dust bright in the beam of light.

It is her breast, its breast, her feet, its foot, her neck and shoulder, its neck and shoulder, cleave, cleave, thigh, thigh, box, box, counter, counter, welt, welt, looping to begin all over again.

Skarmus is speaking filth into my ear.

The film is sped double time, looped over and over. In my good eye I am seeing the parsed shoe, in my missing eye the parsed woman. At some point there stops being a difference.

Sole.

I feel his hands through my hair. I test my bonds, find them tight.

Every shoe was once a woman, he says. *A shoe is a woman in a new body. There is, for your purpose, no distinction.*

Welt, he whispers. *Box.*

When I open my eye there is a flash of gold, pendulant, turning back and forth above me. I try to lift my head but cannot lift it. I do not feel the pressure of the jawscrew, yet my jaw will not move.

There is the steady sweep of Brother Johanssen's voice, speaking slowly and calmly and with authority, his body invisible except, above the flush of gold, a pale and disembodied hand. Skarmus is nowhere to be seen or heard.

His cadence changes, his words coming slower, matching the rhythm of the swinging gold. "One," he intones. "Two. Thr—"

I have lately been experiencing some uncertainty as to who I am and where and when. I am becoming strange to myself, caught somehow outside my own skin.

I hear a noise like the snap of a bone.

I am in the Resurrection, not knowing how I have come to be here. The padding and restrictions have been removed from my arms and instead I hold in my hands the subject of all my time in the Resurrection.

I stand still, holding it, observing it. I begin to stroke softly, my heart beating harder, until I feel my arms overwhelmed by other hands and the object is falling out of my hands, and I am crying out into the closed surface of a mask.

The mouth flap is tightened, and I feel the breath slowly leaving me. The baffles are fitted over my hands. Brother Johanssen moves until I can see him through the eyelets of the mask. He is smiling. He has picked the subject up, holds it suspended from a single finger, swaying, near my face.

"Dear brother," he says, leaning forward as my air gives out. "Welcome to the fold."

⊹ ⊹

They hold me down and in place and strip all the apparati from me piece by piece until I am bare and shivering and in a heap on the ground, lost without the sweat and smell of baffles and rubber and leather and wire. They carry me by the arms and legs, toss me. There is the moment of collision with the floor, a sensation more naked and complete than anything I have felt in some time.

As I am getting up, stumbling in my body, I hear the sound of the door snapping to.

I can barely walk, the ground wavering under my feet.

I am, I know, in the Resurrection. In the cast light, centered, a woman of red leather, sleek and low cut, satined inside, without eyelets, aglets, grommets, perhaps twelve inches from heel to toe box. She is lovely, her shank perfectly curved, needle heeled, her vamp v-shaped and elongated.

I am moving forward. I reach and pick her up in my hand, touch her against my long encased skin.

After that I cannot explain what happens. There is a rush of dizziness and when I awake she is destroyed, strips of leather and thin wood and metal are scattered about, her heel broken off and free. There is, as always, tremendous regret and shame.

I turn to see Brother Johanssen and Skarmus together, complicitous in the doorway. I lift my shoulders, try to think of something to say. Then the door opens and all the brothers are upon me in a rush, ladening me down, binding me again.

Each day I am stripped to my skin, left alone with her. I may, Brother Johanssen tells me, remain with her as long as I do not destroy her.

I do what I can to resist. I make conversation. I resist, for a time, touching her. When I do touch her it is merely slightly, turning her, attempting to perceive, briefly, a new aspect. I let things build slowly, but in the end am always lying spent, strips and fragments of her scattered about me.

Yet each day she is there again, the same, velvet on the outside, silken innards. I can destroy her, but she keeps returning. It is, after all, the Resurrection.

+ +

That's right, says Skarmus. *Keep destroying it.*
It? I wonder.

The film gets stuck. I watch the image darken, bloom black and dissolve into light. I am not the only one who destroys.
There is some confusion in me about who I am, what I desire.

I keep destroying her. I am not changed, my body just as wayward as ever. Yet they are happier with me. I understand none of it.

Then I am stripped and thrown in again, as if to the lions. Yet this time there is no woman, only an odd and curious creature, the same size as myself, much like myself, only not a man. It grimaces, brushes back its hair. It is all familiar somehow.
"This is your body's test," says Brother Johanssen. "Do not fail us."
I do not know what is expected of me. I approach slowly. It makes no move, seems at ease, relaxed. It begins to mumble words that I can't quite string together.
Breast, throat, quarter. Suddenly I can see the woman hidden in it, luminous, the leather and satin cached just beneath hair and teeth and skin.
Through her skin I brush her vamp, finger the damp welt. They cannot conceal her from me in such a carapace. In a minute, I know, I will have shucked the carapace and she will be strips of leather, her box torn apart and open, her throat undone, all of her gone.

Louise's Ghost

Kelly Link

Two women and a small child meet in a restaurant. The restaurant is nice—there are windows everywhere. The women have been here before. It's all that light that makes the food good. The small child—a girl dressed all in green, hairy green sweater, green T-shirt, green corduroys, and dirty sneakers with green-black laces—sniffs. She's a small child but she has a big nose. She might be smelling the food that people are eating. She might be smelling the warm light that lies on top of everything.

None of her greens match except of course they are all green.

"Louise," one woman says to the other.

"Louise," the other woman says.

They kiss.

The maitre d' comes up to them. He says to the first woman, "Louise, how nice to see you. And look at Anna! You're so big. Last time I saw you, you were so small. This small." He holds his index finger and his thumb together as if pinching salt. He looks at the other woman.

Louise says, "This is my friend, Louise. My best friend. Since Girl Scout camp. Louise."

The maitre d' smiles. "Yes, Louise. Of course. How could I forget?"

-¦ ¦-

Louise sits across from Louise. Anna sits between them. She has a note-book full of green paper, and a green crayon. She's drawing something, only it's difficult to see what, exactly. Maybe it's a house.

Louise says, "Sorry about you know who. Teacher's day. The sitter can-celed at the last minute. And I had such a lot to tell you, too! About you know, number eight. Oh boy, I think I'm in love. Well, not in love."

She is sitting opposite a window, and all that rich soft light falls on her. She looks creamy with happiness, as if she's carved out of butter. The light loves Louise, the other Louise thinks. Of course it loves Louise. Who doesn't?

This is one thing about Louise. She doesn't like to sleep alone. She says that her bed is too big. There's too much space. She needs someone to roll up against, or she just rolls around all night. Some mornings she wakes up on the floor. Mostly she wakes up with other people.

When Anna was younger, she slept in the same bed as Louise. But now she has her own room, her own bed. Her walls are painted green. Her sheets are green. Green sheets of paper with green drawings are hung up on the wall. There's a green teddy bear on the green bed and a green duck. She has a green light in a green shade. Louise has been in that room. She helped Louise paint it. She wore sunglasses while she painted. This passion for greenness, Louise thinks, this longing for everything to be a variation on a theme, it might be hereditary.

This is the second thing about Louise. Louise likes cellists. For about four years, she has been sleeping with a cellist. Not the same cellist. Dif-ferent cellists. Not all at once, of course. Consecutive cellists. Number eight is Louise's newest cellist. Numbers one through seven were cellists as well, although Anna's father was not. That was before the cellists. BC. In any case, according to Louise, cellists generally have low sperm counts.

Louise meets Louise for lunch every week. They go to nice restaurants. Louise knows all the maitre d's. Louise tells Louise about the cellists. Cel-lists are mysterious. Louise hasn't figured them out yet. It's something about the way they sit, with their legs open and their arms curled around, all hunched over their cellos. She says they look solid but inviting. Like a door. It opens and you walk in.

Doors are sexy. Wood is sexy, and bows strung with real hair. Also cellos don't have spit valves. Louise says that spit valves aren't sexy.

Louise is in public relations. She's a fundraiser for the symphony—she's good at what she does. It's hard to say no to Louise. She takes rich people out to dinner. She knows what kinds of wine they like to drink. She plans charity auctions and masquerades. She brings sponsors to the symphony to sit on stage and watch rehearsals. She takes the cellists home afterward.

Louise looks a little bit like a cello herself. She's brown and curvy and tall. She has a long neck and her shiny hair stays pinned up during the day. Louise thinks that the cellists must take it down at night—Louise's hair—slowly, happily, gently.

At camp Louise used to brush Louise's hair.

Louise isn't perfect. Louise would never claim that her friend was perfect. Louise is a bit bowlegged and she has tiny little feet. She wears long, tight silky skirts. Never pants, never anything floral. She has a way of turning her head to look at you, very slowly. It doesn't matter that she's bowlegged.

The cellists want to sleep with Louise because she wants them to. The cellists don't fall in love with her, because Louise doesn't want them to fall in love with her. Louise always gets what she wants.

Louise doesn't know what she wants. Louise doesn't want to want things.

Louise and Louise have been friends since Girl Scout camp. How old were they? Too young to be away from home for so long. They were so small that some of their teeth weren't there yet. They were so young they wet the bed out of homesickness. Loneliness. Louise slept in the bunk bed above Louise. Girl Scout camp smelled like pee. Summer camp is how Louise knows Louise is bowlegged. At summer camp they wore each other's clothes.

Here is something else about Louise, a secret. Louise is the only one who knows. Not even the cellists know. Not even Anna.

Louise is tone deaf. Louise likes to watch Louise at concerts. She has this way of looking at the musicians. Her eyes get wide and she doesn't blink. There's this smile on her face as if she's being introduced to someone whose name she didn't quite catch. Louise thinks that's really why

Louise ends up sleeping with them, with the cellists. It's because she doesn't know what else they're good for. Louise hates for things to go to waste.

A woman comes to their table to take their order. Louise orders the grilled chicken and a house salad and Louise orders salmon with lemon butter. The woman asks Anna what she would like. Anna looks at her mother.

Louise says, "She'll eat anything as long as it's green. Broccoli is good. Peas, lima beans, iceberg lettuce. Lime sherbet. Bread rolls. Mashed potatoes."

The woman looks down at Anna. "I'll see what we can do," she says.

Anna says, "Potatoes aren't green."

Louise says, "Wait and see."

Louise says, "If I had a kid—"

Louise says, "But you don't have a kid." She doesn't say this meanly. Louise is never mean, although sometimes she is not kind.

Louise and Anna glare at each other. They've never liked each other. They are polite in front of Louise. It is humiliating, Louise thinks, to hate someone so much younger. The child of a friend. I should feel sorry for her instead. She doesn't have a father. And soon enough, she'll grow up. Breasts. Zits. Boys. She'll see old pictures of herself and be embarrassed. She's short and she dresses like a Keebler Elf. She can't even read yet!

Louise says, "In any case, it's easier than the last thing. When she only ate dog food."

Anna says, "When I was a dog—"

Louise says, hating herself, "You were never a dog."

Anna says, "How do you know?"

Louise says, "I was there when you were born. When your mother was pregnant. I've known you since you were this big." She pinches her fingers together, the way the maitre d' pinched his, only harder.

Anna says, "It was before that. When I was a dog."

Louise says, "Stop fighting, you two. Louise, when Anna was a dog, that was when you were away. In Paris. Remember?"

"Right," Louise says. "When Anna was a dog, I was in Paris."

Louise is a travel agent. She organizes package tours for senior citizens. Trips for old women. To Las Vegas, Rome, Belize, cruises to the Caribbean.

She travels frequently herself and stays in three-star hotels. She tries to imagine herself as an old woman. What she would want.

Most of these women's husbands are in care or dead or living with younger women. The old women sleep two to a room. They like hotels with buffet lunches and saunas, clean pillows that smell good, chocolates on the pillows, firm mattresses. Louise can see herself wanting these things. Sometimes Louise imagines being old, waking up in the mornings, in unfamiliar countries, strange weather, foreign beds. Louise asleep in the bed beside her.

Last night Louise woke up. It was three in the morning. There was a man lying on the floor beside the bed. He was naked. He lay on his back, staring up at the ceiling, his eyes open, his mouth open, nothing coming out. He was bald. He had no eyelashes, no hair on his arms or legs. He was large, not fat but solid. Yes, he was solid. It was hard to tell how old he was. It was dark, but Louise doesn't think he was circumcised. "What are you doing here?" she said loudly.

The man wasn't there anymore. She turned on the lights. She looked under the bed. She found him in her bathroom, above the bathtub, flattened up against the ceiling, staring down, his hands and feet pressed along the ceiling, his penis drooping down, apparently the only part of him that obeyed the laws of gravity. He seemed smaller now. Deflated. She wasn't frightened. She was angry.

"What are you doing?" she said. He didn't answer. Fine, she thought. She went to the kitchen to get a broom. When she came back, he was gone. She looked under the bed again, but he was really gone this time. She looked in every room, checked to make sure that the front door was locked. It was.

Her arms creeped. She was freezing. She filled up her hot water bottle and got in bed. She left the light on and fell asleep sitting up. When she woke up in the morning, it might have been a dream, except she was holding the broom.

The woman brings their food. Anna gets a little dish of peas, brussels sprouts, and collard greens. Mashed potatoes and bread. The plate is green. Louise takes a vial of green food coloring out of her purse. She adds three drops to the mashed potatoes. "Stir it," she tells Anna.

Anna stirs the mashed potatoes until they are a waxy green. Louise mixes more green food coloring into a pat of butter and spreads it on the dinner roll.

"When I was a dog," Anna says, "I lived in a house with a swimming pool. And there was a tree in the living room. It grew right through the ceiling. I slept in the tree. But I wasn't allowed to swim in the pool. I was too hairy."

"I have a ghost," Louise says. She wasn't sure that she was going to say this. But if Anna can reminisce about her former life as a dog, then surely she, Louise, is allowed to mention her ghost. "I think it's a ghost. It was in my bedroom."

Anna says, "When I was a dog I bit ghosts."

Louise says, "Anna, be quiet for a minute. Eat your green food before it gets cold. Louise, what do you mean? I thought you had ladybugs."

"That was a while ago," Louise says. Last month she woke up because people were whispering in the corners of her room. Dead leaves were crawling on her face. The walls of her bedroom were alive. They heaved and dripped red. "What?" she said, and a ladybug walked into her mouth, bitter like soap. The floor crackled when she walked on it, like red cellophane. She opened up her windows. She swept ladybugs out with her broom. She vacuumed them up. More flew in the windows, down the chimney. She moved out for three days. When she came back, the ladybugs were gone—mostly gone—she still finds them tucked into her shoes, in the folds of her underwear, in her cereal bowls and her wine glasses and between the pages of her books.

Before that it was moths. Before the moths, an opossum. It shat on her bed and hissed at her when she cornered it in the pantry. She called an animal shelter and a man wearing a denim jacket and heavy gloves came and shot it with a tranquilizer dart. The opossum sneezed and shut its eyes. The man picked it up by the tail. He posed like that for a moment. Maybe she was supposed to take a picture. Man with opossum. She sniffed. He wasn't married. All she smelled was opossum.

"How did it get in here?" Louise said.

"How long have you been living here?" the man asked. Boxes of Louise's dishes and books were still stacked up against the walls of the rooms downstairs. She still hadn't put the legs on her mother's dining room table. It lay flat on its back on the floor, amputated.

"Two months," Louise said.

"Well, he's probably been living here longer than that," the man from the shelter said. He cradled the opossum like a baby. "In the walls or the attic. Maybe in the chimney. Santa claws. Huh." He laughed at his own joke. "Get it?"

"Get that thing out of my house," Louise said.

"Your house!" the man said. He held out the opossum to her, as if she might want to reconsider. "You know what he thought? He thought this was his house."

"It's my house now," Louise said.

Louise says, "A ghost? Louise, it is someone you know? Is your mother okay?"

"My mother?" Louise says. "It wasn't my mother. It was a naked man. I'd never seen him before in my life."

"How naked?" Anna says. "A little naked or a lot?"

"None of your beeswax," Louise says.

"Was it green?" Anna says.

"Maybe it was someone that you went out with in high school," Louise says. "An old lover. Maybe they just killed themselves, or were in a horrible car accident. Was he covered in blood? Did he say anything? Maybe he wants to warn you about something."

"He didn't say anything," Louise says. "And then he vanished. First he got smaller and then he vanished."

Louise shivers and then so does Louise. For the first time she feels frightened. The ghost of a naked man was levitating in her bathtub. He could be anywhere. Maybe while she was sleeping, he was floating above her bed. Right above her nose, watching her sleep. She'll have to sleep with the broom from now on.

"Maybe he won't come back," Louise says, and Louise nods. What if he does? Who can she call? The rude man with the heavy gloves?

The woman comes to their table again. "Any dessert?" she wants to know. "Coffee?"

"If you had a ghost," Louise says, "how would you get rid of it?"

Louise kicks Louise under the table.

The woman thinks for a minute. "I'd go see a psychiatrist," she says. "Get some kind of prescription. Coffee?"

But Anna has to go to her tumble class. She's learning how to stand on her head. How to fall down and not be hurt. Louise gets the woman to put the leftover mashed green potatoes in a container, and she wraps up the dinner rolls in a napkin and bundles them into her purse along with a few packets of sugar.

They walk out of the restaurant together, Louise first. Behind her, Anna whispers something to Louise. "Louise?" Louise says.

"What?" Louise says, turning back.

"You need to walk behind me," Anna says. "You can't be first."

"Come back and talk to me," Louise says, patting the air. "Say thank you, Anna."

Anna doesn't say anything. She walks before them, slowly so that they have to walk slowly as well.

"So what should I do?" Louise says.

"About the ghost? I don't know. Is he cute? Maybe he'll creep in bed with you. Maybe he's your demon lover."

"Oh please," Louise says. "Yuck."

Louise says, "Sorry. You should call your mother."

"When I had the problem with the ladybugs," Louise says, "she said they would go away if I sang them that nursery rhyme. Ladybug, ladybug, fly away home."

"Well," Louise says, "they did go away, didn't they?"

"Not until I went away first," Louise says.

"Maybe it's someone who used to live in the house before you moved in. Maybe he's buried under the floor of your bedroom or in the wall or something."

"Just like the opossum," Louise says. "Maybe it's Santa Claus."

Louise's mother lives in a retirement community two states away. Louise cleaned out her mother's basement and garage, put her mother's furniture in storage, sold her mother's house. Her mother wanted this. She gave Louise the money from the sale of the house so that Louise could buy her own house. But she won't come visit Louise in her new house. She won't let Louise send her on a package vacation. Sometimes she pretends not to recognize Louise when Louise calls. Or maybe she really doesn't recognize her. Maybe this is why Louise's clients travel. Settle down in one place and you get lazy. You don't bother to remember things like taking baths, or your daughter's name.

When you travel, everything's always new. If you don't speak the language, it isn't a big deal. Nobody expects you to understand everything they say. You can wear the same clothes every day and the other travelers will be impressed with your careful packing. When you wake up and you're not sure where you are. There's a perfectly good reason for that.

"Hello, Mom," Louise says when her mother picks up the phone.

"Who is this?" her mother says.

"Louise," Louise says.

"Oh yes," her mother says. "Louise, how nice to speak to you."

There is an awkward pause and then her mother says, "If you're calling because it's your birthday, I'm sorry. I forgot."

"It isn't my birthday," Louise says. "Mom, remember the ladybugs?"

"Oh yes," her mother says. "You sent pictures. They were lovely."

"I have a ghost," Louise says, "and I was hoping that you would know how to get rid of it."

"A ghost!" her mother says. "It isn't your father, is it?"

"No!" Louise says. "This ghost doesn't have any clothes on, Mom. It's naked and I saw it for a minute and then it disappeared and then I saw it again in my bathtub. Well, sort of."

"Are you sure it's a ghost?" her mother says.

"Yes, positive," Louise says.

"And it isn't your father?"

"No, it's not Dad. It doesn't look like anyone I've ever seen before."

Her mother says, "Lucy—you don't know her—Mrs. Peterson's husband died two nights ago. Is it a short fat man with an ugly moustache? Dark-complected?"

"It isn't Mr. Peterson," Louise says.

"Have you asked what it wants?"

"Mom, I don't care what it wants," Louise says. "I just want it to go away."

"Well," her mother says. "Try hot water and salt. Scrub all the floors. You should polish them with lemon oil afterward so they don't get streaky. Wash the windows, too. Wash all the bed linens and beat all the rugs. And put the sheets back on the bed inside out. And turn all your clothes on the hangers inside out. Clean the bathroom."

"Inside out," Louise says.

"Inside out," her mother says. "Confuses them."

"I think it's pretty confused already. About clothes, anyway. Are you sure this works?"

"Positive," her mother says. "We're always having supernatural infestations around here. Sometimes it gets hard to tell who's alive and who's dead. If cleaning the house doesn't work, try hanging garlic up on strings. Ghosts hate garlic. Or they like it. It's either one or the other, love it, hate it. So what else is happening? When are you coming to visit?"

"I had lunch today with Louise," Louise says.

"Aren't you too old to have an imaginary friend?" her mother says.

"Mom, you know Louise. Remember? Girl Scouts? College? She has the little girl, Anna? Louise?"

"Of course I remember Louise," her mother says. "My own daughter. You're a very rude person." She hangs up.

Salt, Louise thinks. Salt and hot water. She should write these things down. Maybe she could send her mother a tape recorder. She sits down on the kitchen floor and cries. That's one kind of salt water. Then she scrubs floors, beats rugs, washes her sheets and her blankets. She washes her clothes and hangs them back up, inside out. While she works, the ghost lies half under the bed, feet and genitalia pointed at her accusingly. She scrubs around it. Him. It.

She is being squeamish, Louise thinks. Afraid to touch it. And that makes her angry, so she picks up her broom. Pokes at the fleshy thighs, and the ghost hisses under the bed like an angry cat. She jumps back and then it isn't there anymore. But she sleeps on the living room sofa. She keeps all the lights on in all the rooms of the house.

"Well?" Louise says.

"It isn't gone," Louise says. She's just come home from work. "I just don't know *where* it is. Maybe it's up in the attic. It might be standing behind me, for all I know, while I'm talking to you on the phone and every time I turn around, it vanishes. Jumps back in the mirror or wherever it is that it goes. You may hear me scream. By the time you get here, it will be too late."

"Sweetie," Louise says, "I'm sure it can't hurt you."

"It hissed at me," Louise says.

"Did it just hiss, or did you do something first?" Louise says. "Kettles hiss. It just means the water's boiling."

"What about snakes?" Louise says. "I'm thinking it's more like a snake than a pot of tea."

"You could ask a priest to exorcise it. If you were Catholic. Or you could go to the library. They might have a book. Exorcism for dummies. Can you come to the symphony tonight? I have extra tickets."

"You've always got extra tickets," Louise says.

"Yes, but it will be good for you," Louise says. "Besides I haven't seen you for two days."

"Can't do it tonight," Louise says. "What about tomorrow night?"

"Well, okay," Louise says. "Have you tried reading the Bible to it?"

"What part of the Bible would I read?"

"How about the begetting part? That's official sounding," Louise says.

"What if it thinks I'm flirting? The guy at the gas station today said I should spit on the floor when I see it and say, 'In the name of God, what do you want?' "

"Have you tried that?"

"I don't know about spitting on the floor," Louise says. "I just cleaned it. What if it wants something gross, like my eyes? What if it wants me to kill someone?"

"Well," Louise says, "that would depend on who it wanted you to kill."

Louise goes to dinner with her married lover. After dinner, they will go to a motel and fuck. Then he'll take a shower and go home, and she'll spend the night at the motel. This is a *Louise*-style economy. It makes Louise feel slightly more virtuous. The ghost will have the house to himself.

Louise doesn't talk to Louise about her lover. He belongs to her, and to his wife, of course. There isn't enough left over to share. She met him at work. Before him she had another lover, another married man. She would like to believe that this is a charming quirk, like being bowlegged or sleeping with cellists. But perhaps it's a character defect instead, like being tone deaf or refusing to eat food that isn't green.

Here is what Louise would tell Louise, if she told her. I'm just borrowing him—I don't want him to leave his wife. I'm glad he's married. Let someone else take care of him. It's the way he smells—the way married men smell. I can smell when a happily married man comes into a room, and they can smell me too, I think. So can the wives—that's why he has to take a shower when he leaves me.

But Louise doesn't tell Louise about her lovers. She doesn't want to sound as if she's competing with the cellists.

"What are you thinking about?" her lover says. The wine has made his teeth red.

It's the guiltiness that cracks them wide open. The guilt makes them taste so sweet, Louise thinks. "Do you believe in ghosts?" she says.

Her lover laughs. "Of course not."

If he were her husband, they would sleep in the same bed every night. And if she woke up and saw the ghost, she would wake up her husband. They would both see the ghost. They would share responsibility. It would be a piece of their marriage, part of the things they don't have (can't have) now, like breakfast or ski vacations or fights about toothpaste. Or maybe he would blame her. If she tells him now that she saw a naked man in her bedroom, he might say that it's her fault.

"Neither do I," Louise says. "But if you did believe in ghosts. Because you saw one. What would you do? How would you get rid of it?"

Her lover thinks for a minute. "I wouldn't get rid of it," he says. "I'd charge admission. I'd become famous. I'd be on *Oprah*. They would make a movie. Everyone wants to see a ghost."

"But what if there's a problem," Louise says. "Such as: What if the ghost is naked?"

Her lover says, "Well, that would be a problem. Unless you were the ghost. Then I would want you to be naked all the time."

But Louise can't fall asleep in the motel room. Her lover has gone home to his home which isn't haunted, to his wife who doesn't know about Louise. Louise is as unreal to her as a ghost. Louise lies awake and thinks about her ghost. The dark is not dark, she thinks, and there is something in the motel room with her. Something her lover has left behind. Something touches her face. There's something bitter in her mouth. In the room next door someone is walking up and down. A baby is crying somewhere, or a cat.

She gets dressed and drives home. She needs to know if the ghost is still there or if her mother's recipe worked. She wishes she'd tried to take a picture.

She looks all over the house. She takes her clothes off the hangers in the closet and hangs them back right-side out. The ghost isn't anywhere. She can't find him. She even sticks her face up the chimney.

She finds the ghost curled up in her underwear drawer. He lies face down, hands open and loose. He's naked and downy all over like a baby monkey.

Louise spits on the floor, feeling relieved. "In God's name," she says, "what do you want?"

The ghost doesn't say anything. He lies there, small and hairy and forlorn, facedown in her underwear. Maybe he doesn't know what he wants any more than she does. "Clothes?" Louise says. "Do you want me to get you some clothes? It would be easier if you stayed the same size."

The ghost doesn't say anything. "Well," Louise says. "You think about it. Let me know." She closes the drawer.

Anna is in her green bed. The green light is on. Louise and the baby-sitter sit in the living room while Louise and Anna talk. "When I was a dog," Anna says, "I ate roses and raw meat and borscht. I wore silk dresses."

"When you were a dog," Louise hears Louise say, "you had big silky ears and four big feet and a long silky tail and you wore a collar made out of silk and a silk dress with a hole cut in it for your tail."

"A green dress," Anna says. "I could see in the dark."

"Good night, my green girl," Louise says, "good night, good night."

Louise comes into the living room. "Doesn't Louise look beautiful," she says, leaning against Louise's chair and looking in the mirror. "The two of us. Louise and Louise and Louise and Louise. All four of us."

"Mirror, mirror on the wall," the babysitter says, "who is the fairest Louise of all?" Patrick the babysitter doesn't let Louise pay him. He takes symphony tickets instead. He plays classical guitar and composes music himself. Louise and Louise would like to hear his compositions, but he's too shy to play for them. He brings his guitar sometimes, to play for Anna. He's teaching her the simple chords.

"How is your ghost?" Louise says. "Louise has a ghost," she tells Patrick.

"Smaller," Louise says. "Hairier." Louise doesn't really like Patrick. He's in love with Louise for one thing. It embarrasses Louise, the hopeless way he looks at Louise. He probably writes love songs for her. He's friendly with Anna. As if that will get him anywhere.

"You tried garlic?" Louise says. "Spitting? Holy water? The library?"

"Yes," Louise says, lying.

"How about country music?" Patrick says. "Johnny Cash, Patsy Cline, Hank Williams?"

"Country music?" Louise says. "Is that like holy water?"

"I read something about it," Patrick says. "In *New Scientist*, or *Guitar* magazine, or maybe it was *Martha Stewart Living*. It was something about the pitch, the frequencies. Yodeling is supposed to be effective. Makes sense when you think about it."

"I was thinking about summer camp," Louise says to Louise. "Remember how the counselors used to tell us ghost stories?"

"Yeah," Louise says. "They did that thing with the flashlight. You made me go to the bathroom with you in the middle of the night. You were afraid to go by yourself."

"I wasn't afraid," Louise says. "You were afraid."

At the symphony, Louise watches the cellists and Louise watches Louise. The cellists watch the conductor and every now and then they look past him, over at Louise. Louise can feel them staring at Louise. Music goes everywhere, like light and, like light, music loves Louise. Louise doesn't know how she knows this—she can just feel the music, wrapping itself around Louise, insinuating itself into her beautiful ears, between her lips, collecting in her hair and in the little scoop between her legs. And what good does it do Louise, Louise thinks? The cellists might as well be playing jackhammers and spoons.

Well, maybe that isn't entirely true. Louise may be tone deaf, but she's explained to Louise that it doesn't mean she doesn't like music. She feels it in her bones and back behind her jaw. It scratches itches. It's like a crossword puzzle. Louise is trying to figure it out, and right next to her, Louise is trying to figure out Louise.

The music stops and starts and stops again. Louise and Louise clap at the intermission and then the lights come up and Louise says, "I've been thinking a lot. About something. I want another baby."

"What do you mean?" Louise says, stunned. "You mean like Anna?"

"I don't know," Louise says. "Just another one. You should have a baby, too. We could go to Lamaze classes together. You could name yours Louise after me and I could name mine Louise after you. Wouldn't that be funny?"

"Anna would be jealous," Louise says.

"I think it would make me happy," Louise says. "I was so happy when Anna was a baby. Everything just tasted good, even the air. I even liked being pregnant."

Louise says, "Aren't you happy now?"

Louise says, "Of course I'm happy. But don't you know what I mean? Being happy like that?"

"Kind of," Louise says. "Like when we were kids. You mean like Girl Scout camp."

"Yeah," Louise says. "Like that. You would have to get rid of your ghost first. I don't think ghosts are very hygienic. I could introduce you to a very nice man. A cellist. Maybe not the highest sperm count, but very nice."

"Which number is he?" Louise says.

"I don't want to prejudice you," Louise says. "You haven't met him. I'm not sure you should think of him as a number. I'll point him out. Oh, and number eight, too. You have to meet my beautiful boy, number eight. We have to go out to lunch so I can tell you about him. He's smitten. I've smited him."

Louise goes to the bathroom and Louise stays in her seat. She thinks of her ghost. Why can't she have a ghost and a baby? Why is she always supposed to give up something? Why can't other people share?

Why does Louise want to have another baby anyway? What if this new baby hates Louise as much as Anna does? What if it used to be a dog? What if her own baby hates Louise?

When the musicians are back on stage, Louise leans over and whispers to Louise, "There he is. The one with big hands, over on the right."

It isn't clear to Louise which cellist Louise means. They all have big hands. And which cellist is she supposed to be looking for? The nice cellist she shouldn't be thinking of as a number? Number eight? She takes a closer look. All of the cellists are handsome from where Louise is sitting. How fragile they look, she thinks, in their serious black clothes, letting the music run down their strings like that and pour through their open fingers. It's careless of them. You have to hold on to things.

There are six cellists on stage. Perhaps Louise has slept with all of them. Louise thinks, If I went to bed with them, with any of them, I would recognize the way they tasted, the things they liked, and the ways they liked them. I would know which number they were. But they wouldn't know me.

The ghost is bigger again. He's prickly all over. He bristles with hair. The hair is reddish brown and sharp looking. Louise doesn't think it would be a good idea to touch the ghost now. All night he moves back and forth in front of her bed, sliding on his belly like a snake. His fingers dig into the floorboards, and he pushes himself forward with his toes. His mouth stays open as if he's eating air.

Louise goes to the kitchen. She opens a can of beans, a can of pears, hearts of palm. She puts the different things on a plate and places the plate in front of the ghost. He moves around it. Maybe he's like Anna—picky. Louise doesn't know what he wants. Louise refuses to sleep in the living room again. It's her bedroom after all. She lies awake and listens to the ghost press himself against her clean floor, moving backward and forward before the foot of the bed all night long.

In the morning the ghost is in the closet, upside down against the wall. Enough, she thinks, and she goes to the mall and buys a stack of CDs. Patsy Cline, Emmylou Harris, Hank Williams, Johnny Cash, Lyle Lovett. She asks the clerk if he can recommend anything with yodeling on it, but he's young and not very helpful.

"Never mind," she says. "I'll just take these."

While he's running her credit card, she says, "Wait. Have you ever seen a ghost?"

"None of your business, lady," he says. "But if I had, I'd make it show me where it buried its treasure. And then I'd dig up the treasure and I'd be rich and then I wouldn't be selling you this stupid country shit. Unless the treasure had a curse on it."

"What if there wasn't any treasure?" Louise says.

"Then I'd stick the ghost in a bottle and sell it to a museum," the kid says. "A real live ghost. That's got to be worth something. I'd buy a hog and ride it to California. I'd go make my own music, and there wouldn't be any fucking yodeling."

-I- -I-

The ghost seems to like Patsy Cline. It isn't that he says anything. But he doesn't disappear. He comes out of the closet. He lies on the floor so that Louise has to walk around him. He's thicker now, more solid. Maybe he was a Patsy Cline fan when he was alive. The hair stands up all over his body, and it moves gently, as if a breeze is blowing through it.

They both like Johnny Cash. Louise is pleased—they have something in common now.

"I'm onto Jackson," Louise sings. "You big talken man."

The phone rings in the middle of the night. Louise sits straight up in bed. "What?" she says. "Did you say something?" Is she in a hotel room? She orients herself quickly. The ghost is under the bed again, one hand sticking out as if flagging down a bedroom taxi. Louise picks up the phone.

"Number eight just told me the strangest thing," Louise says. "Did you try the country music?"

"Yes," Louise says. "But it didn't work. I think he liked it."

"That's a relief," Louise says. "What are you doing on Friday?"

"Working," Louise says. "And then I don't know. I was going to rent a video or something. Want to come over and see the ghost?"

"I'd like to bring over a few people," Louise says. "After rehearsal. The cellists want to see the ghost, too. They want to play for it, actually. It's kind of complicated. Maybe you could fix dinner. Spaghetti's fine. Maybe some salad, some garlic bread. I'll bring wine."

"How many cellists?" Louise says.

"Eight," Louise says. "And Patrick's busy. I might have to bring Anna. It could be educational. Is the ghost still naked?"

"Yes," Louise says. "But it's okay. He got furry. You can tell her he's a dog. So what's going to happen?"

"That depends on the ghost," Louise says. "If he likes the cellists, he might leave with one of them. You know, go into one of the cellos. Apparently it's very good for the music. And it's good for the ghost, too. Sort of like those little fish that live on the big fishes. Remoras. Number eight is explaining it to me. He said that haunted instruments aren't just instruments. It's like they have a soul. The musician doesn't play the instrument anymore. He or she plays the ghost."

"I don't know if he'd fit," Louise says. "He's largish. At least part of the time."

Louise says, "Apparently cellos are a lot bigger on the inside than they look on the outside. Besides, it's not like you're using him for anything."

"I guess not," Louise says.

"If word gets out, you'll have musicians knocking on your door day and night, night and day," Louise says. "Trying to steal him. Don't tell anyone."

Gloria and Mary come to see Louise at work. They leave with a group in a week for Greece. They're going to all the islands. They've been working with Louise to organize the hotels, the tours, the passports, and the buses. They're fond of Louise. They tell her about their sons, show her pictures. They think she should get married and have a baby.

Louise says, "Have either of you ever seen a ghost?"

Gloria shakes her head. Mary says, "Oh honey, all the time when I was growing up. It runs in families sometimes, ghosts and stuff like that. Not as much now, of course. My eyesight isn't so good now."

"What do you do with them?" Louise says.

"Not much," Mary says. "You can't eat them and you can't talk to most of them and they aren't worth much."

"I played with a Ouija board once," Gloria says. "With some other girls. We asked it who we would marry, and it told us some names. I forget. I don't recall that it was accurate. Then we got scared. We asked it who we were talking to, and it spelled out Z-E-U-S. Then it was just a bunch of letters. Gibberish."

"What about music?" Louise says.

"I like music," Gloria says. "It makes me cry sometimes when I hear a pretty song. I saw Frank Sinatra sing once. He wasn't so special."

"It will bother a ghost," Mary says. "Some kinds of music will stir it up. Some kinds of music will lay a ghost. We used to catch ghosts in my brother's fiddle. Like fishing, or catching fireflies in a jar. But my mother always said to leave them be."

"I have a ghost," Louise confesses.

"Would you ask it something?" Gloria says. "Ask it what it's like being dead. I like to know about a place before I get there. I don't mind going someplace new, but I like to know what it's going to be like. I like to have some idea."

Louise asks the ghost, but he doesn't say anything. Maybe he can't remember what it was like to be alive. Maybe he's forgotten the language. He just lies on the bedroom floor, flat on his back, legs open, looking up at her like she's something special. Or maybe he's thinking of England.

Louise makes spaghetti. Louise is on the phone talking to caterers. "So you don't think we have enough champagne," she says. "I know it's a gala, but I don't want them falling over. Just happy. Happy signs checks. Falling over doesn't do me any good. How much more do you think we need?"

Anna sits on the kitchen floor and watches Louise cutting up tomatoes. "You'll have to make me something green," she says.

"Why don't you just eat your crayon," Louise says. "Your mother isn't going to have time to make you green food when she has another baby. You'll have to eat plain food like everybody else, or else eat grass like cows do."

"I'll make my own green food," Anna says.

"You're going to have a little brother or a little sister," Louise says. "You'll have to behave. You'll have to be responsible. You'll have to share your room and your toys—not just the regular ones, the green ones, too."

"I'm not going to have a sister," Anna says. "I'm going to have a dog."

"You know how it works, right?" Louise says, pushing the drippy tomatoes into the saucepan. "A man and a woman fall in love and they kiss and then the woman has a baby. First she gets fat and then she goes to the hospital. She comes home with a baby."

"You're lying," Anna says. "The man and the woman go to the pound. They pick out a dog. They bring the dog home and they feed it baby food. And then one day all the dog's hair falls out and it's pink. And it learns how to talk, and it has to wear clothes. And they give it a new name, not a dog name. They give it a baby name and it has to give the dog name back."

"Whatever," Louise says. "I'm going to have a baby, too. And it will have the same name as your mother and the same name as me. Louise. Louise will be the name of your mother's baby, too. The only person named Anna will be you."

"My dog name was Louise," Anna says. "But you're not allowed to call me that."

Louise comes in the kitchen. "So much for the caterers," she says. "So where is it?"

"Where's what?" Louise says.

"The you know what," Louise says, "you know."

"I haven't seen it today," Louise says. "Maybe this won't work. Maybe it would rather live here." All day long she's had the radio turned on, tuned to the country station. Maybe the ghost will take the hint and hide out somewhere until everyone leaves.

The cellists arrive. Seven men and a woman. Louise doesn't bother to remember their names. The woman is tall and thin. She has long arms and a long nose. She eats three plates of spaghetti. The cellists talk to each other. They don't talk about the ghost. They talk about music. They complain about acoustics. They tell Louise that her spaghetti is delicious. Louise just smiles. She stares at the woman cellist, sees Louise watching her. Louise shrugs, nods. She holds up five fingers.

Louise and the cellists seem comfortable. They tease each other. They tell stories. Do they know? Do they talk about Louise? Do they brag? Compare notes? How could they know Louise better than Louise knows her? Suddenly Louise feels as if this isn't her house after all. It belongs to Louise and the cellists. It's their ghost, not hers. They live here. After dinner they'll stay and she'll leave.

Number five is the one who likes foreign films, Louise remembers. The one with the goldfish. Louise said number five had a great sense of humor.

Louise gets up and goes to the kitchen to get more wine, leaving Louise alone with the cellists. The one sitting next to Louise says, "You have the prettiest eyes. Have I seen you in the audience sometimes?"

"It's possible," Louise says.

"Louise talks about you all the time," the cellist says. He's young, maybe twenty-four or twenty-five. Louise wonders if he's the one with the big hands. He has pretty eyes, too. She tells him that.

"Louise doesn't know everything about me," she says, flirting.

Anna is hiding under the table. She growls and pretends to bite the cellists. The cellists know Anna. They're used to her. They probably think she's cute. They pass her bits of broccoli, lettuce.

The living room is full of cellos in black cases the cellists brought in, like sarcophaguses on little wheels. Sarcophabuses. Dead baby carriages. After dinner the cellists take their chairs into the living room. They take out their cellos and tune them. Anna insinuates herself between cellos, hanging on the backs of chairs. The house is full of sound.

Louise and Louise sit on chairs in the hall and look in. They can't talk. It's too loud. Louise reaches into her purse, pulls out a packet of earplugs. She gives two to Anna, two to Louise, keeps two for herself. Louise puts her earplugs in. Now the cellists sound as if they are underground, down in some underground lake, or in a cave. Louise fidgets.

The cellists play for almost an hour. When they take a break Louise feels tender, as if the cellists have been throwing things at her. Tiny lumps of sound. She almost expects to see bruises on her arms.

The cellists go outside to smoke cigarettes. Louise takes Louise aside. "You should tell me now if there isn't a ghost," she says. "I'll tell them to go home. I promise I won't be angry."

"There is a ghost," Louise says. "Really." But she doesn't try to sound too convincing. What she doesn't tell Louise is that she's stuck a Walkman in her closet. She's got the Patsy Cline CD on repeat with the volume turned way down.

Louise says, "So he was talking to you during dinner. What do you think?"

"Who?" Louise says. "Him? He was pretty nice."

Louise sighs. "Yeah. I think he's pretty nice, too."

The cellists come back inside. The young cellist with the glasses and the big hands looks over at both of them and smiles a big blissed smile. Maybe it wasn't cigarettes that they were smoking.

Anna has fallen asleep inside a cello case, like a fat green pea in a coffin.

Louise tries to imagine the cellists without their clothes. She tries to picture them naked and fucking Louise. No, fucking *Louise*, fucking her instead. Which one is number four? The one with the beard? Number four, she remembers, likes Louise to sit on top and bounce up and down. She does all the work while he waves his hand. He conducts her. Louise thinks it's funny.

Louise pictures all of the cellists, naked and in the same bed. She's in the bed. The one with the beard first. Lie on your back, she tells him. Close your eyes. Don't move. I'm in charge. I'm conducting this affair. The one with the skinny legs and the poochy stomach. The young one with curly black hair, bent over his cello as if he might fall in. Who was flirting with her. Do this, she tells a cellist. Do this, she tells another one. She can't figure out what to do with the woman. Number five. She can't even figure out how to take off number five's clothes. Number five sits on the edge of the bed, hands tucked under her buttocks. She's still in her bra and underwear.

Louise thinks about the underwear for a minute. It has little flowers on it. Periwinkles. Number five waits for Louise to tell her what to do. But Louise is having a hard enough time figuring out where everyone else goes. A mouth has fastened itself on her breast. Someone is tugging at her hair. She is holding on to someone's penis with both hands, someone else's penis is rubbing against her cunt. There are penises everywhere. Wait your turn, Louise thinks. Be patient.

Number five has pulled a cello out of her underwear. She's playing a sad little tune on it. It's distracting. It's not sexy at all. Another cellist stands up on the bed, jumps up and down. Soon they're all doing it. The bed creaks and groans, and the woman plays faster and faster on her fiddle. Stop it, Louise thinks, you'll wake the ghost.

"Shit!" Louise says—she's yanked Louise's earplug out, drops it in Louise's lap. "There he is under your chair. Look. Louise, you really do have a ghost."

The cellists don't look. Butter wouldn't melt in their mouths. They are fucking their cellos with their fingers, stroking music out, promising the ghost yodels and Patsy Cline and funeral marches and whole cities of music and music to eat and music to drink and music to put on and wear like clothes. It isn't music Louise has ever heard before. It sounds like a lullaby, and then it sounds like a pack of wolves, and then it sounds like a slaughterhouse, and then it sounds like a motel room and a married man saying I love you and the shower is running at the same time. It makes her teeth ache and her heart rattle.

It sounds like the color green. Anna wakes up. She's sitting in the cello case, hands over her ears.

This is too loud, Louise thinks. The neighbors will complain. She bends over and sees the ghost, small and unobjectionable as a lapdog, lying under her chair. Oh, my poor baby, she thinks. Don't be fooled. Don't fall for the song. They don't mean it.

But something is happening to the ghost. He shivers and twists and gapes. He comes out from under the chair. He leaves all his fur behind, under the chair in a neat little pile. He drags himself along the floor with his strong beautiful hands, scissoring with his legs along the floor like a swimmer. He's planning to change, to leave her and go away. Louise pulls out her other earplug. She's going to give them to the ghost. "Stay here," she says out loud, "stay here with me and the real Patsy Cline. Don't go." She can't hear herself speak. The cellos roar like lions in cages and licks of fire. Louise opens her mouth to say it louder, but the ghost is going. Fine, okay, go comb your hair. See if I care.

Louise and Louise and Anna watch as the ghost climbs into a cello. He pulls himself up, shakes the air off like drops of water. He gets smaller. He gets fainter. He melts into the cello like spilled milk. All the other cellists pause. The cellist who has caught Louise's ghost plays a scale. "Well," he says. It doesn't sound any different to Louise but all the other cellists sigh.

It's the bearded cellist who's caught the ghost. He holds on to his cello as if it might grow legs and run away if he lets go. He looks like he's discovered America. He plays something else. Something old-fashioned, Louise thinks, a pretty old-fashioned tune, and she wants to cry. She puts her earplugs back in again. The cellist looks up at Louise as he plays and he smiles. You owe me, she thinks.

But it's the youngest cellist, the one who thinks Louise has pretty eyes, who stays. Louise isn't sure how this happens. She isn't sure that she has the right cellist. She isn't sure that the ghost went into the right cello. But the cellists pack up their cellos and they thank her and they drive away, leaving the dishes piled in the sink for Louise to wash.

The youngest cellist is still sitting in her living room. "I thought I had it," he says. "I thought for sure I could play that ghost."

"I'm leaving," Louise says. But she doesn't leave.

"Good night," Louise says.

"Do you want a ride?" Louise says to the cellist.

He says, "I thought I might hang around. See if there's another ghost in here. If that's okay with Louise."

Louise shrugs. "Good night," she says to Louise.

"Well," Louise says, "good night." She picks up Anna, who has fallen asleep on the couch. Anna was not impressed with the ghost. He wasn't a dog and he wasn't green.

"Good night," the cellist says, and the door slams shut behind Louise and Anna.

Louise inhales. He's not married, it isn't that smell. But it reminds her of something.

"What's your name?" she says, but before he can answer her, she puts her earplugs back in again. They fuck in the closet and then in the bathtub and then he lies down on the bedroom floor and Louise sits on top of him. To exorcise the ghost, she thinks. Hotter in a chilly sprout.

The cellist's mouth moves when he comes. It looks like he's saying, "Louise, Louise," but she gives him the benefit of the doubt. He might be saying her name.

She nods encouragingly. "That's right," she says. "Louise."

The cellist falls asleep on the floor. Louise throws a blanket over him. She watches him breathe. It's been a while since she's watched a man sleep. She takes a shower and she does the dishes. She puts the chairs in the living room away. She gets an envelope and she picks up a handful of the ghost's hair. She puts it in the envelope and she sweeps the rest away. She takes her earplugs out but she doesn't throw them away.

In the morning, the cellist makes her pancakes. He sits down at the table and she stands up. She walks over and sniffs his neck. She recognizes that smell now. He smells like Louise. Burnt sugar and orange juice and talcum powder. She realizes that she's made a horrible mistake.

Louise is furious. Louise didn't know Louise knew how to be angry. Louise hangs up when Louise calls. Louise drives over to Louise's house and no one comes to the door. But Louise can see Anna looking out the window.

Louise writes a letter to Louise. "I'm so sorry," she writes. "I should have known. Why didn't you tell me? He doesn't love me. He was just drunk. Maybe he got confused. Please, please forgive me. You don't have to forgive me immediately. Tell me what I should do."

At the bottom she writes, "P.S. I'm not pregnant."

Three weeks later, Louise is walking a group of symphony patrons across the stage. They've all just eaten lunch. They drank wine. She is pointing out architectural details, rows of expensive spotlights. She is standing with her back to the theater. She is talking, she points up, she takes a step back into air. She falls off the stage.

A man—a lawyer—calls Louise at work. At first she thinks it must be her mother who has fallen. The lawyer explains. Louise is the one who is dead. She broke her neck.

While Louise is busy understanding this, the lawyer, Mr. Bostick, says something else. Louise is Anna's guardian now.

"Wait, wait," Louise says. "What do you mean? Louise is in the hospital? I have to take care of Anna for a while?"

No, Mr. Bostick says. Louise is dead.

"In the event of her death, Louise wanted you to adopt her daughter, Anna Geary. I had assumed that my client, Louise Geary, had discussed this with you. She has no living family. Louise told me that you were her family."

"But I slept with her cellist," Louise said. "I didn't mean to. I didn't realize which number he was. I didn't know his name. I still don't. Louise is so angry with me."

But Louise isn't angry with Louise anymore. Or maybe now she will always be angry with Louise.

Louise picks Anna up at school. Anna is sitting on a chair in the school office. She doesn't look up when Louise opens the door. Louise goes and stands in front of her. She looks down at Anna and thinks, this is all that's left of Louise. This is all I've got now. A little girl who only likes things that are green, who used to be a dog. "Come on, Anna," Louise says. "You're going to come live with me."

Louise and Anna live together for a week. Louise avoids her married lover at work. She doesn't know how to explain things. First a ghost and now a little girl. That's the end of the motel rooms.

Louise and Anna go to Louise's funeral and throw dirt at Louise's coffin. Anna throws her dirt hard, like she's aiming for something. Louise holds on to her handful too tightly. When she lets go, there's dirt under her fingernails. She sticks a finger in her mouth.

All the cellists are there. They look amputated without their cellos, smaller, childlike. Anna, in her funereal green, looks older than they do. She holds Louise's hand grudgingly. Louise has promised that Anna can have a dog. No more motels for sure. She'll have to buy a bigger house, Louise thinks, with a yard. She'll sell her house and Louise's house and put the money in trust for Anna. She did this for her mother—this is what you have to do for family.

While the minister is still speaking, number eight lies down on the ground beside the grave. The cellists on either side each take an arm and pull him back up again. Louise sees that his nose is running. He doesn't look at her, and he doesn't wipe his nose, either. When the two cellists walk him away, there's grave dirt on the seat of his pants.

Patrick is there. His eyes are red. He waves his fingers at Anna, but he stays where he is. Loss is contagious—he's keeping a safe distance.

The woman cellist, number five, comes up to Louise after the funeral. She embraces Louise, Anna. She tells them that a special memorial concert has been arranged. Funds will be raised. One of the smaller concert halls will be named the Louise Geary Memorial Hall. Louise agrees that Louise would have been pleased. She and Anna leave before the other cellists can tell them how sorry they are, how much they will miss Louise.

In the evening Louise calls her mother and tells her that Louise is dead.

"Oh sweetie," her mother says. "I'm so sorry. She was such a pretty girl. I always liked to hear her laugh."

"She was angry with me," Louise says. "Her daughter, Anna, is staying with me now."

"What about Anna's father?" her mother says. "Did you get rid of that ghost? I'm not sure it's a good idea having a ghost in the same house as a small girl."

"The ghost is gone," Louise says.

There is a click on the line. "Someone's listening in," her mother says. "Don't say anything—they might be recording us. Call me back from a different phone."

Anna has come into the room. She stands behind Louise. She says, "I want to go live with my father."

"It's time to go to sleep," Louise says. She wants to take off her funeral clothes and go to bed. "We can talk about this in the morning."

Anna brushes her teeth and puts on her green pajamas. She does not want Louise to read to her. She does not want a glass of water. Louise says, "When I was a dog . . ."

Anna says, "You were never a dog—" and pulls the blanket, which is not green, up over her head and will not say anything else.

Mr. Bostick knows who Anna's father is. "He doesn't know about Anna," he tells Louise. "His name is George Candle and he lives in Oregon. He's married and has two kids. He has his own company—something to do with organic produce, I think, or maybe it was construction."

"I think it would be better for Anna if she were to live with a real parent," Louise says. "Easier. Someone who knows something about kids. I'm not cut out for this."

Mr. Bostick agrees to contact Anna's father. "He may not even admit he knew Louise," he says. "He may not be okay about this."

"Tell him she's a fantastic kid," Louise says. "Tell him she looks just like Louise."

In the end George Candle comes and collects Anna. Louise arranges his airline tickets and his hotel room. She books two return tickets out to Portland for Anna and her father and makes sure Anna has a window seat. "You'll like Oregon," she tells Anna. "It's green."

"You think you're smarter than me," Anna says. "You think you know all about me. When I was a dog, I was ten times smarter than you. I knew who my friends were because of how they smelled. I know things you don't."

But she doesn't say what they are. Louise doesn't ask.

George Candle cries when he meets his daughter. He's almost as hairy as the ghost. Louise can smell his marriage. She wonders what Anna smells.

"I loved your mother very much," George Candle says to Anna. "She was a very special person. She had a beautiful soul."

They go to see Louise's gravestone. The grass on her grave is greener than the other grass. You can see where it's been tipped in, like a bookplate. Louise briefly fantasizes her own funeral, her own gravestone, her own married lover standing beside her gravestone. She knows he would go straight home after the funeral to take a shower. If he went to the funeral.

The house without Anna is emptier than Louise is used to. Louise didn't expect to miss Anna. Now she has no best friend, no ghost, no adopted former dog. Her lover is home with his wife, sulking, and now George Candle is flying home to his wife. What will she think of Anna? Maybe Anna will miss Louise just a little.

That night Louise dreams of Louise endlessly falling off the stage. She falls and falls and falls. As Louise falls she slowly comes apart. Little bits of her fly away. She is made up of ladybugs.

Anna comes and sits on Louise's bed. She is a lot furrier than she was when she lived with Louise. "You're not a dog," Louise says.

Anna grins her possum teeth at Louise. She's holding a piece of okra. "The supernatural world has certain characteristics," Anna says. "You can recognize it by its color, which is green, and by its texture, which is hirsute. Those are its outside qualities. Inside the supernatural world things get sticky but you never get inside things, Louise. Did you know that George Candle is a werewolf? Look out for hairy men, Louise. Or do I mean married men? The other aspects of the green world include music and smell."

Anna pulls her pants down and squats. She pees on the bed, a long acrid stream that makes Louise's eyes water.

Louise wakes up sobbing. "Louise," Louise whispers. "Please come and lie on my floor. Please come haunt me. I'll play Patsy Cline for you and comb your hair. Please don't go away."

She keeps a vigil for three nights. She plays Patsy Cline. She sits by the phone because maybe Louise could call. Louise has never not called, not for so long. If Louise doesn't forgive her, then she can come and be an angry ghost. She can make dishes break or make blood come out of the faucets. She can give Louise bad dreams. Louise will be grateful for broken things and blood and bad dreams. All of Louise's clothes are up on their hangers, hung right-side out. Louise puts little dishes of flowers out, plates with candles and candy. She calls her mother to ask how to make a ghost appear but her mother refuses to tell her. The line may be tapped. Louise will have to come down, she says, and she'll explain in person.

Louise wears the same dress she wore to the funeral. She sits up in the balcony. There are enormous pictures of Louise up on the stage. Influential people go up on the stage and tell funny stories about Louise. Members of the orchestra speak about Louise. Her charm, her beauty, her love of music. Louise looks through her opera glasses at the cellists. There is the young one, number eight, who caused all the trouble. There is the bearded cellist who caught the ghost. She stares through her glasses at his cello. Her ghost runs up and down the neck of his cello, frisky. It coils around the strings, hangs upside down from a peg.

She examines number five's face for a long time. Why you, Louise thinks. If she wanted to sleep with a woman, why did she sleep with you? Did you tell her funny jokes? Did you go shopping together for clothes? When you saw her naked, did you see that she was bowlegged? Did you think that she was beautiful?

The cellist next to number five is holding his cello very carefully. He runs his fingers down the strings as if they were tangled and he were combing them. Louise stares through her opera glasses. There is something in his cello. Something small and bleached is looking back at her through the strings. Louise looks at Louise and then she slips back through the f hole, like a fish.

They are in the woods. The fire is low. It's night. All the little girls are in their sleeping bags. They've brushed their teeth and spit, they've washed their faces with water from the kettle, they've zipped up the zippers of their sleeping bags.

A counselor named Charlie is saying, "I am the ghost with the one black eye, I am the ghost with the one black eye."

Charlie holds her flashlight under her chin. Her eyes are two black holes in her face. Her mouth yawns open, the light shining through her teeth. Her shadow eats up the trunk of the tree she sits under.

During the daytime Charlie teaches horseback riding. She isn't much older than Louise or Louise. She's pretty and she lets them ride the horses bareback sometimes. But that's daytime Charlie. Nighttime Charlie is the one sitting next to the fire. Nighttime Charlie is the one who tells stories.

"Are you afraid?" Louise says.

"No," Louise says.

They hold hands. They don't look at each other. They keep their eyes on Charlie.

Louise says, "Are *you* afraid?"

"No," Louise says. "Not as long as you're here."

The Sadness of Detail

Jonathan Carroll

I used to spend a lot of time at the Café Bremen. The coffee there is bitter and delicious, and the teal-blue velvet seats are as comfortable as old friends. The large windows greet the morning light like Herr Ritter, the waiter, greets anyone who comes in. You don't have to order much: a cup of tea or a glass of wine. The croissants come from the bakery next door and are delivered twice a day. Late in the evening, the café bakes its own specialty for the night-owl customers—"heavies," a kind of sugar doughnut the size of a pocket watch. A wonderful treat is to go in there late on a winter night and have a warm plate full of them.

The Bremen is open nineteen hours a day. December twenty-fourth is the only day of the year it's closed, but on Christmas it opens again, wearing green and red tablecloths, full of people in bright new sweaters or singles looking a little less lonely on a day when people should be home.

There are small, real pleasures in life—the latest issue of our favorite magazine, a fresh pack of cigarettes, the smell of things baking. You can have all of them in that café; you can be happy there without any of them.

I often went in to sit, look out the window, and hum. A secret vice. My husband sneaks candy bars, my mother reads movie magazines, I hum. Give me a free hour with nothing to do and a good window to stare out of and I'll gladly hum you all of Mahler's Fifth or any song off the Beatles' White Album.

I'm the first to admit I'm not very good at it, but humming is only meant for an audience of one, yourself, and anyone who eavesdrops does it at their own peril.

This happened on a late November afternoon when the whole town seemed one liquid glaze of reflected light and rain. A day when the rain is colder than snow and everything feels meaner, harder edged. A day to stay inside and read a book, drink soup out of a thick white cup.

I'd decided to treat myself to the Bremen because I was beat. Arguing with the children, a trip to the dentist, then endless shopping for invisible things—toilet paper, glue, salt. Things no one ever knows are there until they're gone and are then needed desperately. An invisible day where you exhaust yourself running around, doing thankless errands that are necessary but meaningless: the housewife's oxymoron.

Walking in, wet and loaded down with bags, I think I groaned with joy when I saw my favorite table was empty. I flew to it like a tired robin to its nest.

Herr Ritter came right over, looking elegant and very nineteenth century in his black suit and bow tie, a white towel as always draped carefully over his arm.

"You look very tired. A hard day?"

"A nothing day, Herr Ritter."

He suggested a piece of cream cake, damn the calories, but I ordered a glass of red wine instead. There was an hour before the kids would be home. An hour to let the knots inside slowly untie themselves while I looked out the window and watched the now-romantic rain. How long could it have been, two minutes? Three? Almost without knowing it, I'd begun to hum, but then from the booth behind, someone gave a loud, long "Sssh!"

Embarrassed, I turned and saw an old man with a very pink face glaring at me.

"Not everyone likes Neil Diamond, you know!"

The perfect end to a perfect day: now I was on trial for humming "Holly Holy."

I made an "excuse me" face and was about to turn around again when, out of the corner of my eye, I noticed a number of photographs he had spread out on the table in front of him. Most of the pictures were of my family and me.

"Where did you get those?"

He reached behind him and, picking one up, handed it to me. Not looking at it, he said, "That is your son in nine years. He's wearing a patch because he lost that eye in an automobile accident. He wanted to be a pilot, as you know, but one needs good eyesight for that, so he paints houses instead and drinks a lot. The girl in the picture is the one he lives with. She takes heroin."

My son, Adam, is nine and the only thing that matters to him in the world is airplanes. We call his room the hangar because he's covered every wall with pictures of the Blue Angels, the British Red Arrows, and the Italian Frecce Tricolori precision flying teams. There are models and magazines and so many different airplane things in his room that it's a little overwhelming. Recently he spent a week writing to all of the major airlines (including Air Maroc and Tarom, the national airline of Romania), asking what one has to do to qualify as a pilot for their company. My husband and I have always been both charmed and proud of Adam's obsession and have never thought of him as anything but a future pilot. In the picture I held, our little boy with a crew cut and smart green eyes looked like a haggard eighteen-year-old panhandler. The expression on his face was a bad combination of boredom, bitterness, and no hope. It was obviously Adam in a few years, but a young man far past the end of his line, someone you'd sneer at or move to avoid if you saw him approaching on the street.

And the eye patch! Imagining the mutilation of one of our children is as wrenching as the thought of them dead. None of that is . . . allowed. It cannot *be*. And if, tragically, it does happen, then it is always our fault, no matter their age or the circumstances. As parents, our wings must always be large enough to cover and protect them from hurt or pain. It is in our contract with God when we take on the responsibility of their lives. I remember so well the character in *Macbeth* who, upon learning of the deaths of all his children, starts calling them "chicks." "Where are all my little chicks?" The sight of my son wearing an eye patch gave me the taste of blood in my mouth.

"Who are you?"

"Here's one of your husband after the divorce. He thinks that new mustache is becoming. I think it's a little silly."

Willy has tried on and off for years to grow a mustache. Each one looked worse than the last. Once in the middle of a very nasty fight, I said he always began one at the same time as he began an affair. That stopped them.

In the picture, besides the mustache, he was wearing one of those typically silly heavy-metal fan T-shirts (covered with flames and lightning) announcing a group called Braindead. What was ominous about that was Adam had recently brought home an album *by* Braindead and said they were "awesome."

"My name is Thursday, Frau Becker."

"Today is Thursday."

"That's right. If we'd met yesterday, I'd be Wednesday—"

"Who are you? What's this about? What are these pictures?"

"They're your future. Or rather, one of them. Futures are unstable, tricky things. They depend on different factors.

"The way you're going now, the way you handle your life and those around you, this is what will happen." He pointed to the picture I held and then opened both hands in a gesture that said, "What can you do? That's the way it is."

"I don't believe it. Get away from me!" I moved to turn, but he touched my shoulder.

"Your favorite smell is burning wood. You always lie when you say the first person you ever slept with was Joe Newman. The first was really your parents' handyman, Leon Bell."

No one knew that. Not my husband, my sister, no one. Leon Bell! I thought of him so rarely. He was kind and gentle but it still hurt, and I was so scared someone would come home and find us in my bed. "What do you want?" I asked.

He took the photograph out of my hand and put it back on the table with the others.

"Futures can change. They're like the lines on our hands. Fate is a negotiable thing. I'm here to negotiate with you."

"What do I have that you want?"

"Your talent. Remember the drawing you did the other night of the child under the tree? I want it. Bring me the picture and your son'll be saved."

"That's all? It was only a sketch! It took ten minutes. I did it while watching television!"

"Bring it to me here tomorrow at exactly this time."

"How can I believe you?"

He picked up a photograph that had been covered by the others. He held it in front of my eyes: my old bedroom. Leon Bell and me.

"I don't even know you. Why are you doing this to me?"

He slid the pictures together as if they were cards he was about to shuffle. "Go home and find that drawing."

I was pretty good once. Went to art school on a full scholarship and some of my teachers said I had the makings to be a real painter. But you know how I reacted to that? Got scared. I painted because I liked it. When people started looking carefully at my work and with their hands on their checkbooks, I ran away and got married. Marriage (and its responsibilities) is a perfect rock to hide behind when an enemy (parents, maturity, success) is out gunning for you. Squeeze down into a ball behind it and virtually nothing can touch you. For me, being happy didn't mean being a successful artist. I saw success as stress and demands I'd never be able to fulfill, thus disappointing people who thought I was better than I really was.

Just recently, now that the children were old enough to get their own snacks, I'd bought some expensive English oil paints and two stretched canvases. But I've been almost too embarrassed to bring them out because the only "art" I've done in the last years has been funny sketches for the kids or a little scribble at the bottom of a letter to a good friend.

Plus the sketchbook, my oldest friend. I'd always wanted to keep a diary but never had the kind of persistence that's needed to save something in writing about every day you live. My sketchbook is different because the day I began it, when I was seventeen, I promised myself to make drawings in there only when I wanted or when an event was so important (the birth of the kids, the day I discovered Willy was having an affair) that I had to "say" something about it. As an old woman I'd give it to my children and say, "These are things you didn't know. They aren't important now except to tell you more about me, if that interests you." Or maybe I'll only look at it, then sigh and throw it away.

I go through the book sometimes, but it generally depresses me, even the good parts, the nice memories. Because there is so much sadness in the details. How current and glamorous I thought I was, wearing striped bell-bottom pants to a big party just after we were married. Or one of Willy at his desk, smoking a cigar, so happy to be finishing the article on Fischer von Erlach that he had thought would make his career but which was never even published. I drew these things carefully and in great detail, but all I see now are the silly pants or the spread of his excited fingers on the typewriter. But if it depresses me, why do I continue drawing in the book? Because it is the only life I have and I am not pretentious enough to think I know answers now that might come to me when I'm older. I keep hoping thirty or forty years from now when I look at those drawings, I'll have some kind of revelation that will make parts of my life clearer to me.

I couldn't find the drawing he wanted. I went through everything: wastebaskets, drawers, the kids' old homework papers. How brutally panic can build when you can't find something needed! Whatever you are looking for becomes the most important object in the world, however trivial—a suitcase key, a year-old receipt from the gas company. Your apartment becomes an enemy—hiding the thing you need, indifferent to your pleas. It wasn't in my sketchbook, on the telephone table, stuck in a coat pocket. Neither the gray prairies under the beds nor the false pine and chemical smells in the kitchen closet offered anything. Would my son really lose his eye if I couldn't find one stupid little drawing? Yes, that's what the old man said. I believed him after seeing the picture of Leon and me together.

It was a terrible night, trying to be good old normal "Mom" to the family, while madly exploring every corner of our place for the picture. At dinner I casually asked if anyone had seen it in their travels. No one had. They were used to my drawings and doodles around the house. Now and then someone liked one and took it to their room but no luck with this one.

Throughout the evening I kept glancing at Adam, which gave me further reason to search. He had plain eyes but they were smart and welcoming. He looked straight at you in a conversation, gave you his full attention.

At midnight there were no further places to look. The drawing was gone. Sitting at the kitchen table with a glass of orange juice, I knew that there were only two things I could do when I met Thursday at the Bremen the next afternoon: Tell the truth or try and re-create from memory the drawing he demanded. It was such a simple sketch that I didn't think there would be much trouble drawing something that looked similar, but *exactly* the same? Not possible.

I went into the living room and got my clipboard. At least the paper would be the same. Willy bought the stuff by the ream because it was cheap and sturdy and we both liked using it. You didn't feel guilty crumpling up a piece if you'd made a mistake. I could easily see myself crumpling up that damned drawing and not thinking about it again. A child standing under a tree. A little girl in jeans. A chestnut tree. What was special about it?

It took five minutes to do, five minutes to be sure it was as I remembered, five more minutes with it in my lap knowing it was hopeless. Fifteen minutes from start to finish.

The next afternoon before I'd even sat down, Thursday was tapping an insistent finger on the marble table. "Did you find it? Do you have it?"

"Yes. It is in my bag."

Everything about him relaxed. His face went slack, the finger lay down with the rest of his palm on the table, he leaned back against the velvet seat. "That's great. Give it to me, please."

He was feeling better, but I wasn't. As coolly as I could, I pulled the wrinkled piece of paper out of my purse.

Before leaving the apartment I'd crumpled up the drawing into a tight ball to perhaps fool him a little. If he didn't look too closely, maybe I'd be safe. Maybe I wouldn't. There wasn't much chance of being lucky, but at that point what else could I hope for?

Yet watching how carefully he flattened out the paper and pored over it as if it were some unique and priceless document, I knew he'd notice the difference any moment and everything would go to hell from there. I took off my coat and slid into the booth.

He looked up from the picture. "You can hum if you'd like. I'll just be a minute."

I liked this café so much, but today it had been changed by this man into an unpleasant, menacing place where all I wanted to do was finish our business and leave. Even the sight of Herr Ritter standing there at the counter reading the newspaper was irritating. How could life go on so normally when the worst kind of magic was in the air, thick as cigar smoke?

"You have a good memory."

"What do you mean?"

He reached into his breast pocket and took out a piece of paper. Unfolding it, he held up the original drawing of the little girl under the tree I'd done.

"You had it!"

He nodded. "Both of us played tricks. I said you had it; you were trying to give me a copy and saying it was the original. Who was more dishonest?"

"But I couldn't find it because you had it! Why did you do that?"

"Because we had to see how well you remember things. It's very important."

"What about my son?" I asked. "Will he be all right?"

"I guarantee he will. I can show you a photograph of him then, but it might be better just knowing he'll be fine and will live a very contented life. Because of what you did for him here." He pointed to the second drawing. "Do you want to see the photograph of him?"

I was tempted but finally said no. "Just tell me if he'll be a pilot."

Thursday crossed his arms. "He'll be captain of a Concorde flying the Paris-to-Caracas route. One day his plane will be hijacked, but your Adam will do something so clever and heroic that he single-handedly will save the plane and the passengers. A genuinely heroic act. There'll even be a cover story about him in *Time* magazine titled 'Maybe There Are Still Heroes.' He held up the drawing. "Your son. Because of this."

"What about my getting divorced?"

"Do you really want to know?"

"Yes, I do."

He took another piece of folded paper out of his pocket along with the nub of a pencil. "Draw a pear."

"A pear?"

"Yes. Draw a picture of a pear, then I can tell you."

I took the pencil and smoothed the paper on the table. "I don't understand any of this, Mr. Thursday."

A pear. A fat bottom and a half-so-fat top. A stem. A little cross-hatching to give it shadow and depth. One pear.

I handed it to him and he barely gave it a glance before folding it and putting it in another pocket.

"There will be a divorce because you will leave your husband, not vice versa, as you fear."

"But why would I do that?"

"Because Frank Elkin is coming for you."

I think if I had married Frank Elkin I would have been all right. I certainly loved him enough. But besides loving me, too, he also loved parachuting. One day he jumped, pulled his rip cord, but nothing happened. How long ago was that, twenty years? Twenty-four?

"Frank Elkin is dead."

"He is, but you can change that."

The apartment was empty when we got back. Thursday said he would keep it empty until we finished what we had to do. In the bedroom I took my sketchbook out of the table beside the bed. That familiar gray and red cover. I remembered the day I'd bought it and paid for it with new coins. Somehow every coin I handed the salesgirl was gleaming like gold and silver. I was romantic enough to take that as a good omen.

In the living room again, I handed my book to Mr. Thursday, who took it from me without comment.

"Sit down."

"What will happen to the children?"

"If you want, the court will award them to you. You can prove your husband is an alcoholic and incapable of caring for them."

"But Willy doesn't drink!"

"You can change that."

"How? How can I change all these things? What do you mean?"

He opened the sketchbook and whipped quickly through it, not stopping or slowing anywhere. When he'd finished, he looked at me. "Somewhere in this book you've drawn pictures of God. I can't tell you which ones they are, but I just checked and they're here. Some people have this talent. Some have been able to write God, others can compose Him in music. I'm not talking about people like Tolstoy or Beethoven, either. They were only great artists.

"You know the sadness of detail, using your phrase. That is what makes you capable of transcendence.

"For the rest of your life, if you choose, I will come sometimes and ask you to do a drawing. Like the pear today. I'll ask for things like that, as well as copies of certain of the works in your sketchbook. I *can* say that your book is full of astounding work, Mrs. Becker. There are at least three different important drawings of God, one I've never even seen. Other things,

too. We need this book and we need you, but unfortunately I cannot tell you more than that. Even if I were to show you which of your work is...
transcendent, you wouldn't understand what I was talking about.

"You can do things we can't and vice versa. For us, bringing Frank Elkin back from the dead is no problem. Or saving your son." He held up my book with both hands. "But we can't do this, and that is why we need you."

"What if I were to say no?"

"We keep our word. Your son will still become a pilot, but you will sink deeper into your meager life until you will realize even more than now you've been suffocating in it for years."

"And if I give you the book and do your drawings?"

"You can have Frank Elkin and whatever else you want."

"Are you from heaven?"

Mr. Thursday smiled for the first time. "I can't honestly answer that because I don't know. That is why we need your drawings, Mrs. Becker. Because even God doesn't know or remember anymore. It is as if He has a kind of progressive amnesia. He forgets things, to put it simply. The only way we can get Him to remember is to show Him pictures like yours of Himself or play certain music, read passages from books. Only then does He remember and tell us the things we need to know. We are recording everything He says, but there are fewer and fewer periods of clarity. You see, the saddest thing of all is even He has begun to forget the details. And as He forgets, things change and go away. Right now they're small things—certain smells, forgetting to give this child arms, that man his freedom when he deserves it. Some of us who work for God don't know where we come from or if we are even doing the right thing. All we do know is His condition is becoming worse and something must be done quickly. When He sees your pictures, He is reminded of things, and sometimes He even becomes His old self again. We can work with Him then. But without your work, when we can't show Him pictures of Himself, images He once created, or words He spoke, He is only an old man with a failing memory. When His memory is gone, there will be nothing left."

I don't go to the Café Bremen anymore. A few days after I last met with Thursday I had a strange experience there that soured me on the place. I was in my favorite seat drawing the pig, the Rock of Gibraltar, and the ancient Spanish coin he had requested. Having just finished the coin, I looked up and saw Herr Ritter watching me closely from his place behind the counter. Too closely. I have to be careful about who I let see my drawings. Thursday said there are a great many around who would like nothing more than for a certain memory to disappear forever.

Leda

M. Rickert

I cannot crack an egg without thinking of her. How could she do this to me, beautiful Leda, how could you do this to me? I begin each day with a three-egg omelet. I hold each fragile orb and think of the swell of her vulva. Then I hit it against the bowl. It breaks. A few shell pieces fall in with the sticky egg white and I chase them around with the tines of a fork and they always seem out of grasp and I think, just like her. But not really. Not ever-graspable Leda.

How do you love a beautiful woman? I thought I knew. I thought my love was enough. My devotion. I remember, when she went through that dragonfly stage and wore dragonfly earrings and we had dragonfly sheets and dragonfly lampshades and dragonfly pajamas, and I was just about sick of dragonflies, did I tell her? Did I say, Leda, I am just about sick of these goddamn dragonflies. No. I said nothing. In fact, I sent away for dragonfly eggs. Eggs, imagine how that mocks me now! I followed the directions carefully and kept them a secret from her, oh it pains my heart to think of what she learned from my gift, I was like a dragonfly mother for Christ's sake. I kept them in pond water. I kept them warm. At last they hatched, or uncocooned, however you'd call it, and still I tended them, secretly, until almost a thousand were born and these I presented to her in a box and when she opened it (quickly or the results might have changed) they flew out, blue and silver, yellow green purple. A thousand dragonflies for her and she looked at me with those violet eyes, and she looked at them as they flit about and then she said, and I'll never forget this, she said, "They look different from the ones on our pajamas."

Oh Leda! My Leda in the garden bent over the summer roses, in her silk kimono with the dragonflies on it, and nothing underneath, and I come upon her like that, a vision, my wife, and she looks up just then and sees me watching and knows what she is doing when she unties the robe and lets it fall to the ground and then turns, and bends over, to prune the roses! Ha! In the dirt, in the sun, in the night. Always Leda. Always. Except for this.

She comes into the kitchen. Her eyes, black ringed, her feet bare and swollen, her belly juts out before her. She stands for a moment, just watching me crack eggs and then she coughs and shuffles over to the coffee-maker and pours herself a cup into which she starts spooning heaps of sugar and I try to resist the impulse but I cannot stop myself, after all, didn't I once love her, and I say, "S'not decaf."

I can tell she looks at me with those tired violet eyes but I refuse to return the courtesy and with proper wrist action (oh what Leda knew about proper wrist action!) whisk the eggs to a froth.

"How many times do I got a tell you," she says, "it ain't that kind a birth."

I shrug. Well, what would I know about it? A swan, she says. An egg.

Yeah, he did that thing with the dragonflies and I ain't never heard the end of it. "Don't you know how I love you?" he goes. "Don't you remember all them dragonflies?"

Yeah, I remember. I remember dragonflies in the sugar bowl, dragonflies in the honey. I remember dragonflies trapped in the window screens and dragonflies in my hair and on my bare skin with their tiny sticky legs creeping me out.

What I remember most about the dragonflies is how he didn't get it. He always thinks he has to, you know, improve on me. That's how he loves me. I know that and I've known it for a long time and it didn't matter because he was good in bed, and in the dirt, and on the kitchen table and I thought we was friends, so what if he didn't really understand? A nice pair of dragonfly earrings, a necklace, that would have been enough. If I wanted bugs I wouldn't of been wearing them. Anyway, that's how I always felt and I didn't care that he's kind a stupid but now I do.

He cracks those eggs like it means something. I'm too tired to try to understand. I pour myself a coffee and he makes a big point of not looking at me and mumbling about how it ain't decaf and I want a pour the coffee right over his head but I resist the impulse and go sit in the living room in the green recliner that I got cozied up with piles of blankets like a nest and I drink my coffee and watch the birds. My whole body aches. I should leave him. He's failed me so completely. I sip the coffee. I try not to remember. Wings, oh impossible wings. The smell of feathers. The sharp beak. The cry. The pulsing beat. I press my hands against my belly. I should call someone but, after that first night, and that first phone call, I don't have the energy. I've entered a different life. I am no longer beautiful and loved. I am strange and lonely.

Rape hotline.

I...I...

OK, take a deep breath.

He...he...

Yes?

He...

Yes?

Raped.

OK. OK. I am so sorry. It's good you called. We're here to help you. Is he gone?

Yes.

Are you safe?

What?

Is anyone with you?

My husband but...

Your husband is with you now?

Yes, but...

If you give me your address I can send someone over.

I...

OK, are you crying?

He...

Yes?

Raped me.

Your husband?

No, no. He don't believe ...

I'm sorry, I'm really sorry.

It happened.

I know. I know. OK, can you give me your address?

A swan.

What?

Horrible.

Did you say swan?

I always thought they was so beautiful.

Swans?

Yes.

What do swans, I mean—

I was just taking a walk in our yard, you know, the moon was so pretty tonight and then he flew at me.

The swan?

Oh ... god ... yes. It was horrible.

Ma'am, are you saying you were raped by a swan?

Yes. I think I could recognize him in a lineup.

Could, could you put your husband on the phone?

He don't believe me.

I would really like to speak to him.

I showed him the feathers, the claw marks. I got red welts all over my skin, and bites, and he, do you know what he thinks?

Ma'am—

He thinks I cheated on him. He thinks I just made this up.

Ma'am, I think you've called the wrong number. There are other help lines.

You don't believe me either.

I believe you've suffered some kind of trauma.

You don't believe a swan raped me, do you?

Ma'am, there are people who can help you.

No, I don't think so. I think everyone loves birds too much. Maybe not crows or blue jays 'cause everyone knows they steal eggs and peck out the brains of little birds but swans, everyone loves swans, right?

Please, let me give you a different number to call.

No. I don't think so.

Yes, I remember that particular phone call. It's always bothered me. What really happened to her? Or was it a joke? We do get prank calls, you know, though I can't imagine how confused someone must be to think calling a rape hotline could be entertaining. I mean, after all, if I'm talking to someone who isn't even serious, I'm not available for somebody who might really need my help.

What? Well, no, it wasn't a busy night at all. This isn't New York, for God's sake; we average, maybe, two, three rapes a year.

Well she said she was raped by a swan. How believable is that? Not very, I can tell you. But I don't know . . . ever since then I've thought I could have handled that call better, you know? I'm a psych major and so I wonder, what really happened? What did the swan symbolize? I mean it's a classically beautiful bird, associated with fairy tales and innocence. Sometimes I wonder, was she really raped?

What? No. Of course I don't mean by a bird. I said a psych major, not a fairy-tale believer. I mean, I know what's real and imagined. That's my area of expertise. Women are not raped by birds. But they are raped. Sometimes I wonder if that's what happened, you know, she was raped and it was all so horrible that she lost her mind and grasped this winged symbol of innocence, a swan. I mean let's not be too graphic here, but after all, how big is a swan's penis?

Excuse me? Well no, of course I don't mean to suggest that the horror of rape is measured by the size of the instrument used. What newspaper did you say you're from again? I think I've answered enough questions anyway, what can you tell me about this girl, I mean, woman?

WOMAN LAYS EGG!

Emergency room physicians were shocked and surprised at the delivery of a twenty-pound egg laid by a woman brought to the hospital by her husband Thursday night.

"She just look pregnant," said H. O. Mckille, an orderly at the hospital.

"She didn't look no different from any other pregnant lady except maybe a little more hysterical 'cause she was shouting about the egg coming but nobody paid no attention really. Ladies, when they is in labor say all sorts a things. But then I heard Dr. Stephens saying, call Dr. Hogan, and he says, he's a veterinarian in town and that's when I walked over and got a good look and sure enough, ain't no baby coming out of that lady. It's a egg, for sure. But then Nurse Hiet pulls the curtain shut and I'm just standing there next to the husband and so I says, 'You can go in there, that Nurse Hiet just trying to keep me out. You're the husband, right?' He looked kind of in shock, poor guy, I mean who can blame him, it ain't every day your wife lays a twenty pound egg."

Hospital officials refuse to comment on rumors that the woman is still a patient in a private room in the hospital, where she sits on her egg except for small periods of time when her husband relieves her.

An anonymous source reports, "None of us are supposed to be talking about it. I could lose my job. But, yeah, she's in there, trying to hatch the thing, and let me tell you something else, she's not too happy of a lady and she wants to go home to do this there but she's getting a lot of attention from the doctors and I'm not sure it's because they care about her. You know what I mean? I mean, remember that sheep that got cloned? Well, this is way more exciting than that, a woman who lays eggs. You ask me, there'll be some pressure for her to do it again. It ain't right really. She's a woman. She's gonna be a mama. She ain't some pet in the zoo. Don't use my name, OK, I need this job."

Sometimes she falls asleep on the egg. My Leda, who used to be so beautiful. Why did this happen to her? Why did it happen to us? I lift her up. She's light again since she's laid that thing. I lay her down on the bed. Her violet eyes flutter open. "My egg," she says, and struggles against me, "my baby."

"Shh," I say, "go to sleep. I'll sit on it," and I do. I sit on this egg, which is still warm from Leda's upside-down-heart-shaped ass that I used to cup in my hands and call my favorite valentine, and I think how life seems so strange to me now, all the things I used to know are confused.

Leda sleeps, gently snoring. I readjust my weight. It's rather uncomfortable on the egg. Even in sleep she looks exhausted. I can see the blue of her veins, new lines in her face. I never believed she was raped. By a swan. And now there's this, this impossible thing. Does it mean the whole story was true? If so, I have really failed her. How will I ever make it up to her? If not, if she cuckolded me, an old-fashioned word that seems so appropriate here, then she is making me into a laughingstock. You should hear the guys at work. The women just look at me and don't say anything at all.

I dream of a gun I do not own. I point it in different directions. Sometimes I am a hunter in red and black, stalking swans. Sometimes I bring the gun to work and spray the office with bullets. Sometimes I point it at a mirror. Sometimes it is Leda's violet eyes I see. She doesn't scream. She doesn't really care about anything now. Except this egg.

He lifts me off the egg and carries me to the bed. "My egg. My baby." I'll sit on it, he says, and he does. I sink into sleep. I dream of feathers falling like snow. The sweep of wings across the sky. The pale white moon. My garden roses closed in the night. The sound of wings. A great white bird. White. I dream white. Silence and emptiness. The inside of an egg. A perfect world.

When I wake up he is still sitting on the egg. "Are you crying?" I say.

"Yes," he says, like it's something noble.

"Get off," I go, "I'll sit on it now."

"Don't you want a know why I'm crying?" he says.

"Get off. I don't want you making the baby sad with all your sad energy, it's had a hard enough beginning already."

"Leda, I'm sorry," he goes.

"Get off!" I shout. "Get off! Get off!"

He stands up.

A bunch of hospital people run into the room.

"Leave us alone!" I shout.

He turns to the hospital people, those tears still on his face but drying up some, and he goes, "We need to be alone."

"No!" I shout. "You go too. Leave me and my baby alone." Then I pick up the egg.

They all gasp.

The egg is very heavy. I hold it close to my chest. "Forget it. I'll leave," I say.

That Nurse Hiet steps toward me but Dr. Hogan, the veterinarian, puts up his hand like a school crossing guard and she stops. "We don't want her to hurt the egg," he says.

Which shows how they don't understand. Hurt the egg? Why would I hurt the egg? My baby. It's not my baby's fault what the father did.

They all take a step back. Even my husband, which just proves how whatever he was loving it ain't about me. It was someone he imagined. Someone mean enough to crush my baby just to make a point. I hold the egg real close. I am leaving the hospital. I was not prepared for the photographers.

CHICKEN WOMEN ESCAPES HOSPITAL WITH EGG! EXCLUSIVE PHOTOS

Well, I thought they were artists or something like that. I was very surprised to learn that he is an insurance salesman. There's not much I can really tell you for certain. Their house is set back, off the road a bit, and for most of the year it's well hidden by the foliage. During the winter months I've seen it, from a distance. It looks cute, bungalowish. I have a friend who knows somebody who once went to a party there, before they owned it, and she said it was very charming. The only personal experience I have had with either of them was a couple of springs ago when I was at Flormine's Garden Shop and she was there looking at rose bushes. I remember this so vividly because she was one of the most beautiful women I have ever seen. She had purple eyes, quite striking really, pale skin, blond hair, a striking figure. Everyone noticed her. When I look at these photographs, I have a hard time believing this is the same person. What happened to her? She looks quite frightened, doesn't she? I can't comment on the egg. I mean it's pretty obvious, isn't it? I don't know how she fooled the doctors but of course she didn't lay that egg. She's an ordinary woman. And by all appearances she needs help. I wish everyone would forget this nonsense and just get her the help she needs.

When he came home I had to let him in because sometimes I would get so tired I'd fall asleep and then when I woke up, I was kind of only half on the egg and half off and so I let him in if he promised to sit on it and he goes, "Leda, I love you" but I've heard that before and it don't mean nothing anymore from him. "Leda, please forgive me," he goes. I say, sit on the egg. I ain't got the strength to begin forgiving and I don't know if I ever will. I go upstairs and stare out the window at the garden which is all overgrowed now and I think how sorry just ain't enough.

We just made love, me and him and he fell asleep like he does, and I thought it would be nice to walk near my roses underneath that pale full moon and I put on my dragonfly kimono, it's silk and it feels so nice against my skin and it was a beautiful night just a little bit smelling of roses and I thought I was happy and then that swan comes swooping down and for just a moment I thought it was a sign, like of a good thing happening to me 'cause I ain't never seen a swan in my garden and I ain't never seen one flying and then it was on top of me. It was much heavier than I ever thought and when it flew into me I fell to the ground and I couldn't imagine, it was all feathers and wings and claws and beak and I was hitting it and trying to get away and also, at the same time feeling like why would a bird attack me and I didn't want a hurt it I just wanted out and then, my god, I felt it, you know, and my mind could not, I couldn't . . . a swan doing this to me. I hit at it and clawed at it and it bit me and scratched me and the whole time those wings was flapping and . . . So now people are making jokes about it, about me. I ain't stupid. I know that. Don't tell me about some lady I never met who feels sorry for me because she don't really believe it happened. I don't give a shit.

And when my husband keeps saying, sorry, sorry what am I supposed to do with that? This happened to me and it was horrible and when I needed him most he was making three-egg omelets and trying to figure out who I cheated on him with. So, he's sorry? Well, what's he gonna do about that? I can't take care of him. It's all I can do to take care of myself and my baby.

Also, one more thing. Since it's truth time. It did occur to me once or twice to break the egg, I mean in the beginning. What will I do if I hatch a swan? Thanksgiving, I guess. Yeah, sometimes I think like that and don't gasp and look away from me. I ain't evil. I'm just a regular woman that something really bad happened to and when it did I learned some things about the world and myself that maybe I'd rather not know. But that don't change it. I stand at the bedroom window and watch my garden dying. What do I believe in now? I don't know.

-‡ ‡-

I don't know what to do for her. I sit on the egg and remember the good times. Leda laughing. Leda in the garden. Leda dancing. Leda naked. Beautiful, beautiful Leda. Beneath me I feel a movement, hear a sound. I sit very still, listen very carefully. There it is again. "Leda!" I shout. "Leda!" She comes running down the stairs. Where'd she get that robe? I didn't even know she owned such a thing. Blue terry cloth, stained with coffee. She stares at me with those dark-rimmed eyes, wide with fright. "What?" she says.

"Baby's coming," I whisper and slide off the egg.

We stand side by side watching the egg shake. I can hardly breathe. A chip of eggshell falls on the quilt. I find myself praying. Just a general sort of plea. Please.

Please let my baby not be a swan.

He takes my hand. I let him. It is the first human touch other than the doctors and I don't feel like they count, since the night when it happened. It feels strange to be touched. I can feel his pulse, his heat. It feels good and strange. Not bad. I just ain't sure how long I will let it continue.

We watch the egg tremble and crack and I feel like I am standing at the edge of something big, like the white in my dreams. Everything is here now. All my life. All my love. What comes out of that egg will make me either drown in the white or fly out of it. I want a fly out of it but I ain't got the strength to do anything about it.

That's when I see a tiny fist.

I pull my hand away from him and cover my mouth. No wings, I pray, please.

A violet eye!

I am standing so still in case if I move we fall into a different reality.

No beak, I think, and just then, like the world was made of what we want, I see the mouth and I start to laugh but I stop because some more eggshell falls off and a second mouth appears right beside the first one and I don't know what that's all about.

Please, I think, please.

-‡ ‡-

I didn't know what to think. I've been pretty ambivalent about the whole egg thing to be honest. I mean, I only sat on it for her. But as soon as it started hatching I felt excited and then kind of nervous. Like, what's happening here? Are we going to have a baby bird? How do I feel about that? I didn't even think about it when I reached over and took her hand. I just did it like we hadn't been having all this trouble and then I realized we were holding hands and I was so happy about that, it distracted me from the egg for a minute.

I think we were both relieved to see the little fist. Of course, I knew we weren't in the clear yet. I mean it was very possible that we were hatching some kind of feathered human, or some such combination.

Could I love the baby? Yes, this thought occurred to me. Could I love this baby from this horrible act? To be honest, I didn't know if I could.

She pulled her hand away. I ached for her immediately. We saw an eye, violet, just like hers, and I thought I could definitely love the baby if it looked like her and then we saw the mouth, and after a moment, another mouth and I thought FREAK. I know I shouldn't have thought it, but I did. I thought, we are going to have this freak for a child.

All these images flashed through my mind of me carrying around this two-mouthed baby, of it growing feathers during puberty, long talks about inner beauty. I had it all figured out. That's when I knew. Even if it had two mouths and feathers, I could love this kid.

I looked at Leda. It was like something momentous had happened to me and she didn't even realize it. She stood there in that old blue terry cloth robe, with the coffee stains down the front, her hair all a tangle, her violet eyes circled in fright, her face creased with lines, her hands in fists near her mouth and I wanted to tell her, "Sh, don't worry. Everything's going to be all right. It doesn't matter how it looks." But I didn't say anything because I also finally realized I wasn't going to teach her anything about love. Not Leda, who carried this thing, and laid it, and took it away from all those cold and curious doctors and brought it home and sat on it and let her own beauty go untended so she could tend to it. I have nothing to teach her. I have much to learn.

Then I knowed what was happening. When the egg really started to fall apart. Two mouths. Four fists. Four legs. Two heads. And, thank god, two

separate beautiful perfect little girl bodies. Two babies, exhausted and crying. I walked over to them and kneel down beside them and then I just
brushed the eggshell off and that gooey stuff and one of them had violet
eyes, and the other looks like my husband, I realized that on that night I
got pregnant twice. Once by my husband and once by that swan and both
babies are beautiful in their own way though I got a admit the one that
looks kind of like me, from before this all happened, will probably grow to
be the greater beauty, and for this reason I hold her a little tighter, 'cause I
know how hard it can be to be beautiful.

My husband bends over and helps brush the eggshell and gooey stuff
off and we carry the babies to the couch and I lay down with them and untie my robe and I can hear my husband gasp, whether for pleasure or sorrow I don't know. My body has changed so much. I lay there, one baby at
each breast sucking.

Oh Leda, will you ever forgive me? Will you trust me with our girls? Will
I fail them too? Is this what love means? The horrible burden of the damage we do to each other? If only I could have loved you perfectly. Like a
god, instead of a human. Forgive me. Let me love you and the children.
Please.

She smiles for the first time in months, yawns and closes those beautiful eyes, then opens them wide, a frightened expression on her face. She
looks at me, but I'm not sure she sees me and she says, "swan" or was it
"swine"? I can't be sure. I am only certain that I love her, that I will always
love her. Leda. Always, always Leda. In your terry cloth robe with coffee
stains, while the girls nap and you do too, the sun bright on the lines of
your face; as you walk to the garden, careful and unsure; as you weed
around the roses, Leda, I will always love you, Leda in the dirt, Leda in the
sun, Leda shading her eyes and looking up at the horrible memory of what
was done to you, always Leda, always.

In Praise of Folly

Thomas Tessier

FOR GWYN HEADLEY AND YVONNE SEELEY

*H*e drove north in air-conditioned comfort, a road map on the seat beside him, Satie's piano music rippling pleasantly from the stereo speakers. Thank God for the little things that make human life bearable when summer's on your neck.

It was August. The stagnant heat and humidity were so heavy they no longer seemed like atmospheric phenomena, but had assumed a suffocating gelatinous density. People moved slowly if at all, dazed creatures in the depths of a fungal deliquescence.

It had to be better up in the Adirondacks, cooler and drier. But Roland Turner was not just another vacationer seeking escape. He was on a mission of discovery, he hoped, a one-man expedition in search of a serious folly.

Roland was one of the very few American members of the Folly Fellowship, an organization based in London that was dedicated to "preserve and promote the enjoyment and awareness of follies . . . to protect lonely and unloved buildings of little purpose . . . unusual, intriguing or simply bizarre structures and sites." Roland first learned about the group two years earlier, when he came across an issue of their quarterly magazine in a Connecticut bookshop. The photographs were fascinating, the text charming and witty.

A typical English eccentricity, Roland thought at the time, the sort of thing that lasts for a year or two and then dies away as enthusiasm and funds decline. He wrote a letter to ask if the Fellowship was still going, and was surprised to get a reply from the president and editor himself, one Gwyn Headley. Not only was the Fellowship still active, it was thriving, with more than five hundred members worldwide (most of them, naturally, residents of the United Kingdom).

Roland immediately mailed off a bank draft to cover the cost of membership, a set of back issues of the magazine, a folder of color postcards, and a copy of Headley's definitive work, *Follies: A National Trust Guide* (Cape, 1986).

There was something romantic and mysterious about monuments, castles, and old ruins that had always appealed to Roland. He saw the past in them, and he loved to imagine what life had been like so long ago. Perhaps it was because his own day-to-day existence was placid and humdrum. Roland owned a printing company, a small outfit that produced trade newsletters and supermarket fliers for the Westchester County market. Over the years he had worked long and hard to build up a reliable trade, and now he presided over a solid, secure business operation. On the negative side, Roland's personal life was somewhat threadbare.

He'd been through a number of brief intimate encounters, but none of them even came close to marriage. Now in his middle age, Roland could take it or leave it. He enjoyed a good book, mainly history or historical fiction, as well as classical music, and he had a special fondness for follies.

A genuine folly was a building, garden, grotto, or other such architectural construct that had been designed with a deliberate disregard for the normal rules. A folly was something literally "to gasp at," as Headley put it in his massive tome. Roland had not yet been able to travel to Britain, due to pressure of work, but he had managed to track down a few American follies, such as Holy Land in Waterbury and the Watts Towers in Los Angeles. He'd also visited a fully functional house that had been built out of beer bottles in Virginia, a four-acre Sahara located in the Maine woods, and a home designed as Noah's ark in the Tennessee hills. American follies tended to lack the air of lost grandeur that was the hallmark of classic

British follies, but they often displayed a kind of heroic zaniness that was utterly endearing.

Roland could only look forward to the time in his life when he would at last be free to spend two or three months journeying around England, Scotland, and Wales, leisurely inspecting some of the remarkable things he could only read about now—such as the rocket ship in Aysgarth, the "house in the clouds" at Thorpeness, Clavell's Tower, and Portmeirion, not to mention all the splendid follies that could still be found in and around the great city of London itself.

Follies are the dizzy, demented lacework on the edge of the vast human tapestry, Roland had written in a letter that for some unknown reason Mr. Headley had not yet seen fit to publish in the magazine of the Follies Fellowship. In his spare hours, Roland continued to hone his thoughts and write up notes on the American follies he came across.

Then, two weeks ago, the message had arrived from London. A "rather spectacular" folly was rumored to exist on the grounds of the old Jorgenson summer cottage in Glen Allen, New York. Would Mr. Turner be able to check it out and report back? If it proved to be a worthwhile site, photographs and notes would be welcome. Roland immediately faxed his answer: "Absolutely."

It took a while to find Glen Allen on the map. Apparently a rural village, it was some two hundred miles away, a little north of Big Moose Lake in the Adirondacks. Definitely a weekend trek.

Get up there and find a rustic inn Friday evening, spend Saturday investigating the Jorgenson property, and then drive back down to Rye on Sunday. Roland fled the office at noon, and a few minutes later hit the turnpike.

As far as anyone knew he was enjoying a short getaway in the countryside. Roland had mentioned his interest in follies to one other person, Patty Brennan, a robust divorcée who had worked for him briefly last year. Roland thought he fancied Patty, but they never got beyond the talking stage.

"You mean like Coney Island, or Grant's Tomb," had been her reaction when he told her about follies.

"Well, no, not exactly . . ."

Perhaps Roland had explained it badly. He decided then and there to keep the world of follies to himself, his little secret. Patty soon fell in love with the man who cleaned the heads of her VCR, and quit to take a position in his business. It was all for the best, Roland convinced himself. When you share something you treasure with another person, it's no longer quite so special; it inevitably loses a little of its magic aura.

Roland made fairly good time, but the actual journey clocked in at closer to three hundred miles, so it was a little after six in the evening when he reached Glen Allen. He passed by the Glen Motel on his way into town but found no other accommodation, and eventually circled back to it. A satellite dish, a room full of vending machines, three other cars parked in the lot. Nothing at all like a rustic inn, but it would have to do. Roland went into the office and paid for a room.

The middle-aged woman on duty took his cash, gave him a key and some brochures about the boating and fishing opportunities in the vicinity.

"Where's the best place to eat in town?" Roland asked.

"Bill's Friendly Grille, right on Main," the woman replied. "By the way, there's an electrical storm supposed to come through tonight. If the power goes out, you'll find some candles in your closet."

"Thanks. I was thinking of taking a look at the Jorgenson estate tomorrow. Is it hard to find?"

"The Jorgenson estate," she repeated carefully, as if giving the matter some thought. She was a large woman with bland, empty features. "No, it's not hard to find but it might be hard to get to. It's just a couple of miles up the glen, but nobody's lived there in about thirty years, so the private road's all overgrown. You'd have to hike some." Then added, "From what I heard there's nothing much left to see."

"Oh."

"Are you in real estate?"

"No, no, I represent the—well, it's a British fellowship, you see, and we're interested in neglected sites of architectural distinction."

He was upset with himself for hesitating and then failing to utter the word "folly," but there was no point in trying to explain it to this woman. As it was, she made a vague sound and appeared to have no interest whatsoever.

"Well, I could be wrong but I don't think you'll find there is any architecture up there."

"None at all?" Roland asked in disbelief. Until now he hadn't even considered the possibility that he might have come all this way on a wild goose chase. "There's nothing left?"

The woman shrugged blithely, seeming to take pleasure in his distress. "Place burned down ages ago." She picked up the book she had been reading—a paperback account of some lurid murders in Texas—and found her place.

"Ah. Well . . ."

His room was adequate, just. There was mildew on the shower curtain, and the air had a damp musty smell that some city people regard as the authentic flavor of the countryside, but the sheets were clean and the air conditioner worked. Outside, the heat and humidity were nearly as oppressive as they'd been in Rye.

Roland decided not to linger in his room. He was hungry and a storm was coming. He left his overnight bag, still packed, on a rock maple armchair, left his camera locked in the trunk of his car, and set off to find Bill's Friendly Grille.

Glen Allen, what there was of it, had the peeling, outdated look of a town still stuck in the forties or fifties. It was not unpleasant—the weathered clapboards, the old Flying Red Horse gas pumps, the rusty cars and battered pickups, the general store with a group of kids hanging around out front—a curious mix of what was genuinely quaint and what was merely Tobacco Road.

But it wasn't what was there, Roland realized as he parked. It was what wasn't there—no trendy boutiques, no video stores, no T-shirt joints, no fast-food chains, no blaring boom boxes, not even one odorific Chinese takeaway—that was somehow pleasing. The present had not yet arrived in Glen Allen, at least not with the full force of all its tawdry enterprise.

Roland sat at the bar and had the cheeseburger deluxe, which was suitably greasy and rather good. The fries were on the soggy side, but the coleslaw was tangy and delicious. Roland washed it all down with a large mug of cold beer—the first of several he would enjoy that evening.

There were a handful of other customers, regulars it seemed, who clutched their glasses, kept an eye on the Yankee game on the TV at the far end of the bar, and chatted easily with each other. None of them showed any particular interest in Roland, which was fine with him. Most of them were young and probably knew nothing firsthand about the Jorgensons.

But Roland did eventually manage to learn something from Bill, the elderly owner of the place, who also presided over the bar.

"Old man Jorgenson made it big in steel, right up there with Carnegie. Lot of money. My father worked on the house when they built it, back in the twenties. Oh, it was beautiful. Wood from South America, marble from Italy, you name it. French furniture, big paintings on the walls. No expense spared. They lived there about two months a year, every summer. They called it a cottage, you know, because it only had about twenty rooms."

Roland nodded, smiling. Bill had a way of saying something and slapping his hand lightly on the bar as if to signal that he was finished. He would turn and drift away, tending to his other customers, but sooner or later he would wander back to Roland and continue, gradually filling in the rest of the story.

The Jorgenson clan came and went year after year. They kept pretty much to themselves. Nothing memorable happened until the winter of 1959, when the house burned down mysteriously. It was gutted, a complete loss. The only people there at the time were the caretaker and his wife, both of whom died in the blaze. Some people thought it was an accident, others that local vandals were responsible—the rich are always resented. There was a lengthy investigation, but no final verdict.

The place was abandoned, the Jorgensons never came back. It wasn't until a few years ago that the estate was in the news once more. A new generation of Jorgensons had seen fit, no doubt with tax considerations in mind, to deed the hundred-plus acres to the state of New York. The surrounding Adirondack forest had already reclaimed it, and now it was a legal fact.

"Weren't there any other buildings, besides the main house?" Roland asked anxiously. "Any other structures?"

"Oh, sure," Bill said. "There was a big garage, a gazebo, a few sheds, and an icehouse. And, uh, Little Italy."

"What?" Roland's hopes soared. "Little Italy?"

"Yeah, my kids used to play there when they were growing up back in the sixties. Crazy thing."

It was a folly, no question. It seemed that the old man had been in love with Italy, so much so that he decided to create a garden that featured miniature replicas of famous Italian sights: the Trevi fountain, Vesuvius and Pompei, the Blue Grotto at Capri, and the Colosseum, among others.

Jorgenson had added to it every summer for nearly three decades, and by the time of the fire the Italian garden was said to cover nearly four acres.

Roland was both encouraged and depressed. Yes, there was an authentic folly, but it had been rotting away since 1959, exposed to hot summers, freezing winters, and the random violence of local kids. Whatever still survived was no doubt crumbling in the grip of the forest. It was sad, and Roland thought he would be lucky to get one halfway decent photograph. But it was certainly worth writing up—and publishing—it would be Roland Turner's first appearance in the pages of the Fellowship magazine.

It was well past ten when he finally left the bar. The heat had eased considerably and a breeze blew through town. The storm was closer. Roland could only hope it would be long gone when he went looking for the Jorgenson place in the morning. He caught a glimpse of lightning in the sky, but it seemed far away and there was no following rumble of thunder.

Main Street was now deserted, and Roland thought it looked a bit like an abandoned movie set. Signs swayed, windows rattled, leaves and dust swirled about, and everything was cast in the dim yellow glow of a few widely spaced streetlamps. The bright neon Genesee sign at Bill's stood out in welcome contrast.

Roland was about to get into his car when he first heard the sound, and he stopped to listen to it. Choir practice? No, this was not musical in the sense that it followed any pattern; it was not even human. Roland slowly turned his head, trying to figure out which direction it came from, but it was too diffuse, and the wind in the trees frequently overwhelmed it.

Back at the motel, Roland heard the sound again as soon as he stepped out of his car. It was stronger and clearer, yet just as hard to define as it had been in town. An Aeolian chorus that sang in the night, rising and fading, shrilling and moaning. The wind was part of it, but there had to be more, some unusual local feature that produced this effect. Roland actually liked it. He was reminded of certain ethereal passages from Debussy and Vaughan Williams. In his room, he turned off the air conditioner, opened a window, and listened to it awhile longer.

The storm passed by a few miles to the north, crackling and thundering in the distance like a transient war, and the village of Glen Allen took an intense strafing of rain. But it was gone in a quarter of an hour, and its aftermath was a humid, dripping stillness.

In the morning, as he was about to set off for the Jorgenson place, Roland spotted the woman who ran the motel. She came out of the vending machine room with a full garbage sack in one hand. Roland crossed the parking lot and asked her about the sounds he had heard the previous night.

"That's the wind coming down the glen," she told him. "When it blows a certain direction, you get that."

"Yes, but what exactly causes it?"

"The wind coming down the glen," she repeated, as if he were dense. "You don't notice it so much in the winter."

"Ah."

He stopped at Colbert's Store, a few doors up from Bill's on Main Street, to buy a grinder and a carton of juice for lunch. A few minutes later he nearly drove past what had been the entrance to the Jorgenson summer estate. As Bill had explained, it wasn't hard to find: about two miles up North Street, which was the only road north out of town, and look for it on your left. There were two stone columns flanking a single-lane driveway. Roland backed up and studied the scene for a moment.

The stone columns bore the dead pastel blue and green stains of lichen, and their caps were severely chipped and cracked. The wrought iron gate was long gone—only a pair of deeply corroded hinges remained. Then Roland realized that Jorgenson had planted a wall of arborvitae along the road in both directions. It could still be seen, but barely. It must have reached twenty or thirty feet high, but now it was a skeletal ruin, shot through with tall weeds, young maples, choke cherries, wild grapes, and other vines and parasites. The entryway itself was so thick with brush that Roland couldn't even park in it; he had to go another fifty yards before he found a grassy spot on the right. He slung his camera around his neck, took his lunch cooler, locked the car, and walked back down the road.

The original dirt road to the house was thoroughly overgrown with weeds and field grass, but it wasn't hard to follow. Roland wandered off it twice and immediately noticed the change from the firm gravel base to a more yielding soil underfoot.

He passed through a tunnel of trees, a landscape effect that may well have been quite lovely once; now it was ragged, dark, and gloomy, devastated by secondary growth. He came out of it on the edge of a large clearing, and sensed that he was now close to the site of the house. It was no longer "cleared" at all, of course, but the perimeter was unmistakably marked by the much taller pine trees of the surrounding forest.

Roland's pants were soaked. The sky was overcast, so all of the plants he waded through were still wet from the rain. But he preferred it that way to a blazing hot sun. He followed the road as it climbed a very gradual rise and then leveled off. Yes, he thought excitedly, this has to be it. Where else would you build a house? The three or four acres of flat high ground he stood on provided a gorgeous southern view.

Roland gazed down across the old clearance, looking for any human traces. There was a small lake—perhaps Jorgenson had it created for him— and the stumpy remnants of a wooden pier. The lake was nearly dead now, choked with algae, reeds, and silt, but it must have been beautiful once.

Roland found it easy to visualize the Jorgenson children out on the lake canoeing, or jumping from the pier and swimming. The family might well have had picnic lunches in the shade of the big sugar maple that still stood by itself not far from the water. A view of the past. The lives, the dreams, so much effort to build a little world within the world. Were the Jorgensons haughty and unbearable, or decent and worthy of what they had? But it didn't matter, because what they had here was gone and so were they.

Roland turned and snagged his toe on a rock. It was part of the foundation of the house. He walked it, leaving his own trail in the tall grass and wildflowers. The fire, and the years, had left nothing but a rectangle of stones that barely protruded from the earth. The outbuildings had vanished as well; maybe some of the locals had dismantled them for the lumber and fittings.

Roland took a photograph of the ground on which the house had stood, and then another of the broad clearance, including the lake. He ate his lunch quickly, eyes scanning the landscape for a sign, a clue. If the Italian folly was hidden somewhere in the forest, he could spend a week looking for it. There was only one other possibility—somewhere up behind the house. Beyond a low ridge only a hundred yards away, the land seemed to hollow out as steep walls formed on either side. That was north. That was the beginning of the glen, or the end of it.

Roland trudged up the rise, and gaped. There it was, Little Italy, Jorgenson's folly. He was so excited he nearly broke into a run, but then he steadied himself and clicked off several shots of the whole panorama.

There were all kinds of houses—country villas, farmhouses, squat urban blocks—scattered in clumps and clusters. There were statues, many statues, fountains, archways, piazzas, towers, churches, stables, barns, and much more. It went on into the glen as far as Roland could see.

The land on which most of the folly had been built was low, but it was marked by any number of little hillocks that enhanced the visual effect. In addition, the walls of the glen had a way of jutting out and cutting back that created niches, defiles, and recesses of varying size and depth. Every wacky detail somehow worked, and it all came together to create a remarkable illusion at first sight.

In fact, it looked its best at a distance. When Roland came down the slope to it and began to make his way through the narrow passages, the decay was all too obvious. Most of the structures had been built with cinder blocks, or plaster on chicken wire, and then coated with paint or whitewash. Tin roofs had been painted a reddish-brown to suggest tile. Cheap stuff for a rich guy, and it showed the effects of age, neglect, and intermittent vandalism. Whole walls had been knocked down or worn away. Much of the tin was corroded, the paint blistered and peeling—what there still was of it. Statues were missing hands or heads, sometimes both. Everything was severely chipped or cracked.

Brambles and vines proliferated, often making it difficult for Roland to move about. But in that respect the folly had been spared worse damage. The ground was rocky and the soil thin, so not much else managed to grow there.

Roland advanced slowly, taking pictures as he went. He knew little about Italy but he recognized most of the famous landmarks Jorgenson had chosen to replicate. He was particularly impressed by a fifty-foot section of the aqueduct high enough to walk under without ducking his head. It was broken only in three places and actually dripped a tiny residue of last night's rain. Roland had to smile when he noticed that the plaster aqueduct was lined with cast iron half-pipe.

What really made the whole thing work was the dizzy range of scale— or rather, the complete lack of scale. A two-foot house stood next to a three-foot statue of a dog. Mt. Etna was somehow smaller than the Duomo, while the Spanish Steps were larger than all of Venice. Nothing matched anything.

That, and sheer quirkiness. Working only two months a year, Jorgenson obviously felt compelled to add a number of ready-made items to his dream world. The statues, for instance. And Roland especially liked the birdbath—a common garden birdbath—that utterly dominated St. Peter's Square. There were other birdbaths to be seen, as well as birdhouses that could be purchased in any garden shop or nursery even today; perhaps in the extreme reaches of his obsession Jorgenson saw an ideal Italy popu-lated solely by birds. Roland grinned a few moments later when he came across a statue of Saint Francis of Assisi, surrounded by birdhouses that were mounted on sections of lead pipe—with the entire tableau situated between a trattoria and a bizarre little maze apparently meant to suggest the catacombs.

Roland came into a small clearing with a stone bench. Maybe this was where old man Jorgenson sat, pondering his extraordinary creation and dreaming up more additions to it. Roland rested his feet for a moment and changed the film in his camera.

It was easy to lose track of the size of the folly. Many of the structures were only three feet high, but quite a few were as tall as men, and with the gently undulating flow of the ground it was impossible to see ahead to the point where the folly displays finally came to an end. But it was also im-possible to get lost, since the walls of the glen were always visible.

Roland had to keep moving. The sky seemed to be darker now, not from the lateness of the hour but from the appearance of more storm clouds. He hadn't thought to check the weather report, and he had no idea whether a new storm was due or it was the same one circling back. Roland didn't like the idea of having to hike all the way back to the car in a down-pour, but it might come to that. He wasn't going to leave until he had seen and photographed every part of the folly.

Jorgenson had saved his most astounding flight of fancy for the last. Roland stepped through a gap in a wall, and he thought that he was stand-ing in a courtyard. A stretch of ground roughly one hundred feet square had been covered with large paving stones that had subsequently buckled and heaved. Now the whole area was shot through with tufts of dull green weeds, laced with some kind of wild ground ivy.

There was a line of columns along the left edge and another on the right. They were ten or twelve feet high and some of them had fallen over, but they created a sudden impression that still had power. Roland found himself thinking of the Pantheon, but he had no clear mental image of the original to compare.

All this, however, was peripheral to the set piece straight ahead. Where the paving stones ended, the ground rose up slightly before it leveled off, creating a rough natural platform. It was as wide as the courtyard, and it was full of statues. There were dozens of them. Roland stumbled forward.

Several interesting features, he thought in a daze. All the statues were positioned to face the center of the glen. They all had their arms raised and their faces uplifted, as if acclaiming the gods or seeking their merciful help. None of them had hands. They had open mouths but otherwise there were no facial features, not a nose or an eye or an ear in the entire assembly. They had no feet, unless they were buried in the ground, for the legs rose up out of the soil, converging in thick, trunklike torsos. The statues were crude and stark, and yet they seemed to be possessed of a terrible poignancy.

They weren't presented as Romans in togas and robes. There were no gods or creatures of myth, not even a Venetian gondolier. They were like golems, clad in stone. Roland climbed the rise to inspect them close up. The surface was brownish in color, rough but firm in texture—like partly annealed sand. Perhaps there was an underlayer of plaster or cement. Roland had seen nothing else like it in Jorgenson's Little Italy. It was an improvement; these statues showed very little evidence of erosion.

But what madness!

Roland was in the middle of his final roll of film, snapping medium shots of the amazing statuary, when the first hand grabbed him by the belt in the small of his back. Then there were others on his body, pulling him down from behind. Something banged him along the side of the head, stunning him briefly.

How much time had passed? Roland's vision was blurred, and would not correct. His head throbbed painfully. It was dark and the air was somehow different. Maybe he was in a cave. He could just make out flickering firelight, and the busy movements of his captors. Roland couldn't move. They held him to the ground, his arms outstretched.

They were like kids—not yet fully grown, voices unformed. He thought there were about a half dozen of them. He had no idea what was going on, he couldn't understand anything. An unnatural silence alarmed him.

Roland tried to speak to them, but they sat on his chest and legs, pinned his head in place, and stuffed foul rags in his mouth. Then he saw the dull glint of an axe blade as it began its downward descent to the spot where his left hand was firmly held. Same thing on the right a few seconds later, but by then Roland was already unconscious.

Searing pain revived him; that, and perhaps a lingering will to struggle and save his life. He was alone for the moment, but he could hear them— their squeaky murmurs, and a disturbing wet scraping noise.

Demented teenagers. Maybe some weird sect or cult. Or they could be a brain-stunted, inbred rural clan that preyed on anyone who was foolish enough to stray into their territory. How could this happen? Was the whole town in on it? What could they want? Perhaps in exploring and photo-graphing Jorgenson's Italian folly, he had somehow violated their sacred ground. But it seemed most likely that they were insane, pure and simple.

Roland still couldn't move. His wrist-stumps were bandaged. The bas-tards had actually chopped his hands off. The realization nearly knocked him out again but Roland fought off total panic. He had to think clearly, or he was surely lost. The rest of his body from the neck down seemed to be wrapped in some kind of wire mesh. His mouth was still clogged with the hideous rags, and he had to breathe through his nose. He tried to lever his tongue to push the rags out, or to one side, so he could speak, but at that moment they came back for him.

They dragged him, and it became clear to Roland that some of the monstrous pain he felt was coming from where his two feet had been. They threw him down in a torch-lit clearing. They spread his legs, held his arms out, and began to smear some thick, gooey substance on him. Roland flipped and squirmed like a fish on the floor of a boat until they clubbed him again.

Fresh air, dusk light.

The same day? Couldn't be. But overcast, the wind whipping loudly— and that choral sound Roland had heard his first night in town. They car-ried him out of the cave, and the wailing noise seemed to fill his brain. He was in the center of it, and it was unbearable.

Only his head was exposed—the rest of his body now stone. It came up to his neck in a rigid collar and forced his head back at a painful angle. Roland caught sight of them as they propped him in his place on the third rank of the statuary. They weren't kids, they didn't even look human—

pinched little faces, stubby fingers, a manic bustle to their movements, and the insect jabber that was all but lost in the boiling wind.

Like caricature scientists, they turned him one way and then another, tilting, nudging, and adjusting. They finally yanked the rags out of his mouth. Roland tried to croak out a few words but his tongue was too dry. Then the final mystery was solved as his captors thrust a curious device into his mouth. He saw it for an instant—a wire cage that contained several loose wooden balls. They were of varying sizes, and Roland thought he saw grooves and holes cut in them. It fit so well that his tongue was pressed to the floor of his mouth. A couple of strands of rawhide were tied around his head, securing the device even more tightly.

A last corrective nudge, and then the wind took hold and the wooden balls danced and bounced. Another voice joined the choir. Satisfied, they went on to complete their work, covering the rest of his head with the sticky cement and then applying the exterior finish. Only his open mouth was left untouched.

Roland thought of insects nesting there. He pictured a warm mist billowing out on cool mornings as he rotted inside. And he wondered how long it would take to die. They must do repair work later, to keep the cages in place after the flesh disappeared. A strangely comforting thought in the giddy swirl of despair.

The wind came gusting down the glen. Empty arms raised, his anonymous face lifted to the unseeing sky, he sang.

Plot Twist

David J. Schow

On the morning of the fifth day, Donny announced that he'd figured it all out. It wasn't the first time.

"Okay," he said. "Millions of years ago, these aliens come to Earth and find all this slowly evolving microspodia. Maybe they're, like, college students working on their thesis project. And they seed the planet with germs that eventually evolve into human society—our culture is literally a *culture*, right? Except that we're not what was intended. It was an impure formula or something. And they come back after millennia, which is like summer vacation to them, and they see their science experiment has spoiled in the dish. We're the *worst* thing that could have happened. We've blown their control baseline, their work is down the toilet, and they have to declare us a cull, flush the first experiment, and start over. But they take a look at us and decide, hey, maybe there's something here worth saving. Something they can use to, you know, rescue their asses from flunking. So they take this teeny sample, like one cell, and decide to test it to see if it does anything interesting. And that's why we're here."

Vira said, "That's above and beyond your previous bullshit, and I think I've hit my patience ceiling."

Zach didn't say anything because he was staring forlornly at their remaining food supply—one energy bar, destined for a three-way split, one tin of Vienna sausage (eight count), and a pint of bottled water that had already been hit hard.

"I'm waiting for *your* brilliant explanation," Donny said sourly. His real name was Demetrius, but he hated it. Vira's real name was Ellen, but she'd legally changed it. Zach was born "Kevyn"; same general deal.

"I'm out," said Vira, tired of the game. "Tapped. Done. I give up." She looked up at the reddening sunrise sky and shouted. "Hey! Hear me? I quit. Fuck you. If there's aliens up there toying with us, then they can kiss my anal squint!"

Donny startled, as though he actually thought outer space men might materialize to punish them. At least that would have brought some sort of closure.

"Don't yell," said Zach, nailing her, still playing leader. "That'll dry you up. Who got to the water while I was sleeping?"

Donny and Vira both denied it; the usual stalemate. Zach expected this, and let it slide because he already knew he'd stolen that bonus sip himself.

"Sun's coming up," said Donny unnecessarily. "The only constant seems to be this man-against-nature thing."

"You said that yesterday, too, sexist asshole," said Vira.

"Look around you," said Zach, pointing to each extreme of the compass. "Desert. Road. Desert. More road. More desert. And so on. Do you see, for example, a crashed plane that we could rebuild into a cleverly composited escape vehicle? No. A glint on the horizon that would indicate a breath of civilization? No way. A social dynamic among us, two men and one woman, that will lead to some sort of revelation that can save us? Uh-uh, negative." He pointed again. "Road. Desert. Let's get moving."

"Why?" said Vira, watching her little patch of shade dwindle.

"Because when we moved the first time, and didn't stay put, we found the food, didn't we?"

"That's the only reason?"

"We might find something else."

She colored with anger, or perhaps it was just the odd, vividly tilted light of dawn. "So we can just keep going, keep doing this?"

"We last another day, we might figure something out."

"Like the 'why'?" Donny said. "As in 'why us'?"

"No, all I meant was we might get back to normal, and we certainly won't do that sitting on our butts and staying in one place waiting for the supplies to run out."

Vira snorted at the all-encompassing grandeur of the word "supplies" pertaining to their edibles, which did not even total to a snack.

"I want an answer," said Donny. "I want to know why."

"That's your biggest problem, Don-O." Zach extended his open hand to Vira, who rose tropistically, like a plant turning automatically to meet the light. "Come on, sweetie, let's go."

They turned their backs on the sun and began their march, in the same direction they'd been tracking since, well, forever.

Most of the fourth day had been wasted on equally stupid theories.

"I've got it," Donny said, which caused Vira to roll her eyes. It was becoming her comedic double-take reaction to anything Donny proposed. Donny was an endlessly hopeful idiot.

"Okay, like, we're characters in this movie, or a novel or something. And we can't figure out where we are or how we got here, and shit keeps happening, and we keep on keeping on, but our memories and characters keep altering when we're not looking. It's because we're fictional characters, right, except we don't know we are. And the movie studio guys keep asking for changes, or the editors at the publishing house keep saying, 'what's their arc?' or 'how do they grow from their experience?' And we don't know because we were just *made up* by some writer, who has no idea we're cognizant and suffering."

"I wish there was a big, shiny-new toilet, right here in the middle of the scrub," said Vira.

"Why?" said Donny, tired of performing his body functions in the wild.

"Because I don't know what I'd do first," said Vira. "Drink some water from the tank, or jam your head into the bowl and flush."

"Children, children," said Zach. "Come on. We hit a spot of luck yesterday, didn't we? The food."

"Yeah," Donny chimed in. "Plot twist, see? Nobody'd ever expect that we'd just find food when we needed it. In stories, everything has to be explained; everything has to pay off."

"Your definition of *food* and mine differ radically," said Vira. "I want a quart of goddamn seltzer, and then a bacon cheeseburger and a goddamn fucking chocolate malt, with a goddamn fucking cherry, and fuck you and your latest fucking lame-ass, bullshit story."

"Yeah, great, terrific," said Donny. "Thanks for your boundlessly vast contribution to the resolution of our predicament. You're not helping."

"I'm the chaos factor," said Vira. "I'm here precisely to fuck up all your neat little explanations."

"And I'm the third wheel," said Donny. "You guys will kill me first, because you've already got a, you know, relationship."

"Yeah, that'll get us far," said Zach, trying for drollery and failing. It was just too hot to screw around.

They kept their bearings on the sun and tried not to deviate from the straight line inscribed on the sand by their passage. Yesterday's footprints had blown away as soon as they were out of sight. The desert was harshly Saharan—dunes tessellated by wind, with vegetation so sporadic it appeared to be an afterthought, or really sub-par set dressing. They were amazed by the appearance of a paddle cactus, just one, and even more amazed when Zach demonstrated how it could provide drinkable moisture.

"Perfect example," Donny said. "How did you know that?"

"I don't know," said Zach. "I've always known it."

"Read it in a manual? See it on a nature documentary? Or maybe you came wired with that specific information for a reason."

"There is no reason," said Zach, trying to work up spit and failing at that, too. His throat was arid. His brain was frying. "I just knew it."

"It doesn't work," Donny said, shaking his head, sniffing at denial. "There's gotta be a reason."

"Reason for *what*?!" Vira apparently had plenty of spit left. "We had an accident! You are so full of shit."

"Maybe it wasn't an accident," said Donny. He was trying for an ominous tone, but neither Zach nor Vira cared to appreciate his dramatic sense.

By the middle of the third day, they were all sunburnt, peeling, and dehydrated. They resembled lost Foreign Legionnaires, dusted to a desert tan, with wildly white Lawrence of Arabia eyes, long sleeves and makeshift burnooses keeping the solar peril from most of their desperately thirsty flesh.

"If you mention God to me one more time, I'm going to knock a few of your teeth out, and you can drink your own blood," warned Zach.

"My only point is that this strongly resembles some sort of biblical test," said Donny, chastened. "This kind of stuff happens all the time in the Bible, the Koran, Taoist philosophy, native superstitions—they're all moral parables. Guys are always undergoing extreme physical hardship, and at the end there's a revelation. That's what a vision quest is."

"A vision quest is when you starve yourself until you see hallucinations," said Vira. "We've been there and done that. I don't feel particularly revelated."

"We haven't gone far enough, is all."

"Then explain why we haven't seen a smidge of traffic on this goddamn road since we started walking. We should have seen a thousand cars by now, all headed to and from Vegas. We should have passed a dozen convenience marts and gas stations with nice, air-conditioned restrooms. And all we've got since we lost sight of our own car, which was alone on the road, is hot, hot, more hot, and about a bazillion highway stripes, all cooking on this goddamn fucking roadway that leads to fucking nowhere!"

"Alternate dimension," said Donny.

Zach actually stopped walking to crank around and peer at Donny with disgust. "*What?*"

"Alternate dimension, co-existing simultaneously with our own reality. We got knocked out of sync. And now we're trapped in a place that's sort of like where we were—the world we came from—except there's nothing around, and nobody, and we've got to find a rift or convergence and wait for the planes to re-synchronize, and plop, we're back to normal."

"Do you want to strangle him, or should I?" said Vira.

"I liked the God explanation better," said Zach. He was joking, but no one appreciated it just now.

"Aren't we grown-ups?" said Vira. "Aren't we rational adults? Can we please leave all that goddamn God shit and the fucking Bible and all that outmoded tripe and corrupt thinking behind in the twentieth century, where it belongs? Shit, it was useless and stupid a couple of whole cen-

turies earlier than that—enslaving people, giving sheep a butcher to can-
onize. Giving morons false hope. Pie in the sky by and by when you die.
It's such exhausted, wheezy, rote crap."

"Aren't we operating on false hope?" said Donny.

"No, Donny," said Zach. "We're operating on the tightrope between
slim, pathetic hope and none at all. Free your mind. You're too strictured
and trapped by your need to organize everything so it has a nice, neat ending—a little snap in the tail to make idiots go *woooo*. You want to know
reasons, and there ain't no reasons, and you want to know something real?
I'll tell you this one for free: Real freedom is the complete loss of hope."

"That's deep," said Donny, not getting it.

Vira shielded her eyes and tried to see into the future. "Forget cars and
stop-marts," she said. "We haven't seen any animals. Desert animals lie low
in the daytime, but we haven't seen any. Not a single bird. Not a vulture,
even."

"It's not life, but it's a living," joked Zach.

"The sun is cooking me," said Vira. "Pretty soon we'll all be deep-fried
to a golden-black." She shielded her eyes to indict the glowering sphere
above, which was slow-cooking them like a laggard comet. The sky was
cloudless.

"If it is the sun," said Donny.

Zach and Vira could not complain anymore. They merely stopped,
turned in unison, and sighed at Donny, who would not stop. Donny, naturally, took this as a cue to elaborate.

"I mean, this east-to-west trajectory could be just an assumption on
our part. We could be walking north for all we really know. What if it's not
the sun? What if it's just some errant fireball, messing with us?"

"Then we just spent another day walking in the wrong direction," said
Zach.

"What if it's not a 'day'?" said Donny. He dug his wristwatch out of his
pocket. He'd stowed it yesterday when the heat had begun to brand his
wrist with convection. Now he noticed, for the first time, that his watch
had stopped.

"Five thirty-five," he said. "Weird."

Zach and Vira turned slowly (conserving energy), did not speak (conserving moisture), and glowered at Donny with an expression Donny had

come to class as The Look. When people gave you The Look, they were awaiting a punch line they were sure they would dislike.

"It's when the car shut down yesterday," he said. "I remember because I made a mental note of it."

"That's it?" said Vira. "No dumb theory about how we're all slip-slid into the spaces between ticks of the clock?"

"Donny, when was the last time you looked at your watch before yesterday? Isn't it possible that your crappy watch just doesn't work, and has been dead all this time, and you just thought it was 5:35 when you glanced at it yesterday?" Somehow, while Donny wasn't looking, Zach had become the leader of their little expedition.

"You guys aren't listening to me," Donny said, feeling somewhat whipped. "The watch shut down the same time the car did."

Vira was strapping on attitude, full-bore: "And that's got to *mean something*, right? Spare us."

What Donny spared them was the hurt reaction that had almost made it past his lips: *I thought you guys were my friends.* He just stared, blankly, as though channeling alien radio.

"Hey." Zach had found something. Topic closed.

A black nylon loop was sticking out of the sand off the right shoulder of the road. When Zach pulled, he freed a small backpack that looked identical to the one Vira was already toting. They both waited, almost fatalistically, for Donny to make a point of this.

He held both hands palm-out in a placating gesture. "I'm not saying a word, if that makes you happy."

Inside the backpack they found two malt-flavored energy bars, two pint bottles of water, two tins of Vienna sausage, and two bags of salty chips, and everything was nearly too hot to touch.

"That's just plain scary," said Vira, examining the rucksack. "It *is* like mine."

"Oh, shit," said Donny. "Maybe we've done this already."

Vira caught herself short of showing Donny a little mercy. "Here we go," she said in a vast sigh, hotly expelling air she couldn't afford to lose.

"We're trapped inside of some kind of Möbius strip, endlessly repeating our previous actions. Has to be. Look at the backpack. It doesn't look like Vira's—it *is* Vira's. From the last time we were here. And we don't remember because whatever purpose is behind all this hasn't been achieved. Whatever happened, last time, we blew it. And if we blow it again, we'll find another backpack just like this one."

"Do you want a third of this or do you want to continue the lecture?" Zach had drawn his Swiss Army knife to divide one of the energy bars, but the protein goo was already so warm it practically poured apart.

"No, look at it." Donny was flushed with fear and anger now. "Two of everything. Only two. Why only two? Who's the odd guy out, here? Me. What the fuck happens to me?!"

"Shut up, Donny!" said Vira. "Look at the damned thing—it doesn't have my wallet, my I.D., my hairbrush, tampons, or any of the other stuff in *my* backpack. It's a fucking coincidence!"

"No. Something happens. Something changes. One of us gets gone."

"Donny, you're gonna pop a blood vessel, man." Zach cracked one of the tins and took a ginger sip of the water packing the mini-wieners.

"And I'm not hungry," Donny continued. "I see that stuff, food, and I should be starving, but I'm not. We walked all day yesterday and all today and we should be ready to hog a whole buffet . . . but all I feel is that *edge* of hunger, of thirst. Just enough to keep me crazy."

"I wholeheartedly agree about the 'crazy' part," said Vira.

"Eat anyway," said Zach. "Save your energy for your next explanation of what the hell has happened to us."

"Yeah, we'll be laughing about this tomorrow," said Vira, methodically swallowing capfuls from the sports bottle of water, knowing enough not to chug, not to waste, to take it extraordinarily slow and easy.

"Anybody care for an alternate point of view?" said Zach, relishing the salt in the chips even though they made him thirsty. "The backpack is a marker. Someone else has made this trip. And they left this stuff behind because they got out, got rescued, or didn't need it anymore."

"Yeah, maybe because they died." Donny was still sour, and not meeting their eyes. Privately he thought Zach's proposal was too upbeat to be real, and was full of holes besides. Maybe he was just playing optimist to cheer Vira up. In a book or a TV show or a movie, it just would not track because it begged too much backstory.

"If somebody just dropped this and died, we'd've seen a body," said Vira. She was always on Zach's side.

"Not if the sand blew over it," said Donny.

"Jesus fuck, there's just no winning with you," she said. "You just *have* to be right all the time."

That caused more long minutes to elapse in silence as they picked through their paltry booty. Donny looked out, away ... anywhere but at his two increasingly annoying friends. Vira and Zach huddled, murmuring things he could not overhear, and neither of them acknowledged his presence until he jerked them back to the real world.

"Look at that," he said.

"What?" Zach rose to squint downroad.

Donny pointed. "I think I see something. That way."

"Then it's time to burn a little energy, I guess. We get lucky, we can leave the backpack in the sand for the next sucker. Sweetie?"

Vira dusted her jeans and stood up. "Yeah. Ten-hut, let's march." She tried to think of a sarcasm about the Yellow Brick Road and Dorothy, or the Wild Bunch, minus one, but it was just too goddamned hot.

Donny led them, appearing to scent-track. Normally he liked to walk two paces behind Zach and Vira, because he enjoyed watching Vira's ass move. Perhaps if he walked with his partners to the rear, they would just disappear at some point. Plucked away. It could happen. It happened in stories, in movies.

They walked toward it, but it turned out to be nothing.

They had wasted most of the second day waiting around the car under the arc of the sun. Waiting for rescue. Waiting for answers, for trespassers, for anything outside themselves. That was when Donny had begun ticking off his handy theories.

"Okay, we're all drunk," he said, knowing they weren't. "We're stoned. This is really a dream. See the car? We actually crashed it and we're all dead, and this is Hell or something. Purgatory. Limbo."

"I love that concept," said Zach. "Hell-or-something."

"Water jug's empty," said Vira. They'd stashed a gallon container in the backseat prior to departing on their road trip. One day of busy hydration had killed it. Her careful makeup had smudged, melted, run down her face, and evaporated.

Zach tied a T-shirt around his head to save his scalp from getting fried.

"We just sit tight and try not to perspire," he joked. "Someone'll come along. *We* came along."

"Las Vegas used to be the greatest psychological temptation in the country," said Donny. "Going there to gamble was an act of will, requiring a pilgrim to penetrate a sterile cordon of desert. You can't go to Vegas accidentally; you have to make the decision and then travel across a wasteland to get there. It's not like you're at a mall and think, *oh, I'll do a little gambling while I'm here, too.* And once you do the forced march, you're there and there's only one thing to do, really—what you came for. That's more strategically subtle than most ordinary people can handle. Nobody thinks about that."

"And your point," said Vira, "is . . . what?"

"Just that it's interesting, don't you think?"

"I think it's fucking *hot* and I wish I wasn't here." She fanned herself and Donny won an unexpected flash of sweat-beaded nipple, perfect as a liquor ad.

"We can't drink the water out of the radiator," said Zach, returning from beneath the hood and wiping oil from his hands.

"Why are you even thinking like that?" said Vira. "We're not stranded. We're on a main highway, even if it is in the middle of buttfuck-nowhere. Some hillbilly in a pickup truck will come along. What about all the other people driving to Vegas? We didn't just wander off the map, or get lost on some country switchback. We're not going to have to wait here long enough to think about drinking the water from the radiator, or eating the goddamn car."

"Guy did that in New Hampshire," said Donny. "Cut a Chevy up into little cubes and ate it. Ingested it, passed it. Guy ate a car."

"*Shut up,* Donny!" Vira had been making a point, and resented derailment at the mercy of Donny's internal almanac. Donny was chock-full of trivia like this. He thought he was urbane. He was passably-interesting at parties and good for scut errands since he always volunteered. Now Vira guessed that Donny's canine openness and availability was just a cruel trick, a dodge intended to keep him around people who could at least pretend to be interested in all the useless shit that spilled from his mouth.

Ever the mediator, Zach tried to defuse her. "What are you getting at, Vira?"

"You guys talk as if we just drove off the edge of the Earth or something. The car just stopped, period. We're not going to have to dig a god-damn well to find drinking water because the car just stopped, and it just stopped a couple of hours ago, and other people will come along, and we'll be inconvenienced and probably have to rent another car, or stay overnight in some shithole like Barstow, but it's an inconvenience, and Donny is running his face-hole like we've been abducted to another planet."

"I'm not saying anything," said Donny. "But have you seen any more cars, for, what, five-six hours we've been here?"

"Children, children," said Zach. "Stop fighting or I'll turn this car right around." That made Vira laugh. If only. Then Zach ambled toward the sprawl of flat-paddle cactus they'd pressed into service as a restroom privacy shield.

"Maybe you should piss in the empty water jug," said Donny. "We might have to boil our own urine and drink it."

"I'd rather die," said Vira. "Hey, there's an idea—we can kill you and eat you for the moisture in your body, if you don't shut up."

When Zach had buttoned up and returned, he had resumed his air of command and decision. "So I guess it's down to this: Do we stay, or do we start walking?"

"Stay," said Vira. "At least we've got the car for shade. Who knows how cold it gets at night? This is the desert, after all, and we didn't bring a lot of blankets."

"We march," said Donny. "Vegas could be just over the next rise and we've been sitting here all day like the victims of some cosmic joke."

"Sun's going down," said Zach. "I'm inclined to spend the night walking. We've got two flashlights, matches, a melted candy bar, and half a bottle of flat soda I found under the passenger seat. We take extra clothes to cover our skin in case we get stuck another day. And we stay on the road, in case somebody comes along—that'll do us as much good as sticking by the car, hoping someone spots it."

"It also wears us out faster," said Vira. "I'm not built for this nature shit. *Nature* is what you go through to get from the limo to the hotel lobby."

"Come on, Vira," Donny said. "Where's your sense of adventure?"

"The only adventure I want to have right now is in a Jacuzzi, with room service."

"Ahh," said Donny. "Cable porn and pizza and cold, cold beer."

"Three A.M. blackjack action and free cocktails," said Zach. "Hot showers and cool sheets. Jesus, I have to stop; I'm getting a hard-on."

"Yeah, Donny, you start walking and Zach and I will stay here and try to conserve moisture." Vira smiled wickedly. At least they were bantering now, grabbing back toward something normal. But she collected her backpack from the seat, as though resigned to a hike, hoping it would turn out to be brief but worthwhile.

They walked away the hours absorbed by dusk, until the sun was gone. The road stayed flat and straight except for regular hummocks that kept the distance maddeningly out of view, diffused in heat shimmer. At the crest of each rise waited another long stretch of road, and another rise in the distance.

"Human walking speed is four to six miles per hour at a brisk and steady pace," said Donny. His voice tended to lapse into a statistical drone. "Figure half that, the way we're clumping along."

"Conserving moisture," Vira reminded him.

"The arc of the sun says we've been doing this for about four hours. That would put us between twelve and fifteen miles from the car. And I still don't see anything."

"That's because it's dark," said Zach. He knew what Donny was intimating. At night you could see the glow of Vegas against the sky from a hundred miles out. There was no glow.

"Yeah, and if it's dark for eight hours, say, and the sun comes up over *there*, we've got another twenty-odd miles."

"I am *not* walking twenty miles," said Vira. "I've got to sit down and cool off."

"Good idea," said Zach. "When it gets cold, we can walk to stay warm."

Vira flumped heavily down in the sand, trying to kink out her legs. "You guys notice something else?"

They both looked at her, wrestling off her athletic shoes.

"All the time we've been walking and walking? Since we started there hasn't been a single highway sign."

The trip had been Vira's idea, another of her just-jump-in-the-car-and-go notions. Spontaneity permitted her the pretense of no encumbrances or responsibilities, which in turn allowed her the fantasy that she was still under thirty, still abrim with potential with no room for regret.

Zach grumpily acceded, mostly because he liked to gamble. A two-day pass to Vegas would allow him to flush his brain and sort out his life, which was in danger of becoming stale from too much easy despair, the snake of self-deconstruction gobbling its own tail.

Taking off on an adventure gave them the illusion of control over their lives. They weren't dead yet, nor off the map. Most of their friends, however, begged off with the usual smorgasbord of excuses—jobs, babies, commitments, obligations, all couched in placating language that broadcast its intention not to offend. It was a good method of sifting one's so-called allies: Hit them with a wild-card proposition and see who bites.

"What about Donny?" said Vira.

"He'll be farting around his apartment, waiting for his phone to ring," said Zach. "He can spell the driving, and you know he'll volunteer half the gas, just to get out and see different scenery."

"Remind me why he's our friend?" Vira was nude, mistrusting her vanity mirror, working search-and-destroy on perceived flaws. No tan lines. They had a variety of acquaintances, each good for one isolated conversational topic, to be accessed as needed. Donny's status held at mid-list.

Zach shook his head, feeling superior to the shortcomings of his friends. None of *them* were about to get laid right now. "Because we both know that Donny doesn't really have anybody else. He's our holiday orphan, our warm body. Spear carrier. Cannon fodder. Come on, he's not so bad. We get stranded in the desert, we can stand back-to-back and defend your honor."

She had turned sidesaddle in the chair before the vanity, and gathered his tumescing cock into her grasp to speak to it. "Are you suggesting the Sandwich of Love? Hm? One below and one above? You're the buns and I'm the meat?"

"No," he said between clenched teeth, sucking a breath, coming up rock-hard.

"Good." She stroked the beast in her hand. "Donny's not my type, anyway."

He showed up so fast that Zach and Vira barely had time to jump out of the shower, the aura of sex still clinging to them. Vira just made it into abbreviated cutoffs and a knotted top while Zach struggled wet legs into unyielding jeans. Vira felt Donny's eyes take inventory, up-down, from her still-damp cascade of black hair, the full length of both slender legs, to her big feet. Her breasts were nicely scooped, with hard nubs declaring themselves too prominently as they blotted through the sheer material of her top. She caught Donny cutting his gaze away when she looked up. Not her type.

Donny was well-groomed but brittle, as though his look had been not so much preserved as shellacked. He had always lived moment-to-moment, hand to mouth, check to check; not so charming, when one began to add on years without progress. He had duly logged his time as a depressed philosopher, overstaying college, scooping up handy opportunities, staying slightly out of step but thereby remaining available for any lark or diversion.

Zach emerged from the bedroom, toweling his hair and pretending like he hadn't just had sex. He was at least ten years older than Vira; what the hell was *that* about, wondered Donny. What really worried him was that he might be no further along than Zach, given another decade. A better apartment, a cleaner car, steady sex, and ... what else? Zach had two degrees and worked for an airline company doing god knew what. He had Vira. He seemed to understand how the world worked, as though he could perceive things just out of reach by Donny's sensory apparatus. But was that progress? Donny always teased himself with the possibilities, should he finally catch up to his paternal pal; pass him, maybe. All Donny needed was the right opportunity. He had spent his entire life training to be ready when it knocked.

Their friendship was convenient, if nothing else.

"Okay, now we're far enough gone that you have to catch me up on the important stuff," bellowed Zach from the pilot bucket of his muscle car. Air, industrial-dryer hot, blasted through the open cabin and tried to sterilize them. "No chitchat. The good stuff. Like, are you seeing anybody?"

"Nope." Donny tried to make it sound offhand, like *not today,* but it came out like *not ever, and you know it.*

Vira craned around, one arm over the seat, mischief in her eyes. "Don't even *try* to convince me that nobody's looking."

"I'm just not in a big hurry, that's all," Donny said from the backseat.

He watched the knowing glance flicker between his two amigos. Zach had laid out the argument many times before, convinced that Donny set girlfriend standards so high that any candidate was already sabotaged. Donny would counter that his last serious relationship had wrecked him. Then Vira would swoop in a flanking maneuver, accusing him of inventing the former mystery girlfriend (whom Zach and Vira had neither seen nor met) in order to simplify his existence by virtue of a romantic catastrophe. Donny's perfect love was so perfect she could not be real, Vira would say. Or: so perfect that she would never have had anything to do with him in the first place. It was nothing aberrant; lots of people lived their lives exactly this way.

Zach and Vira would claim they just wanted to see their friend happy. Happier.

Donny deflected the whole topic, thinking himself humble and respectful, a gentleman. In his mind, he dared them to feel sorry for him.

They chugged supercaffeinated soda and ate up miles and listened to music. They were alone on the road when Zach smelled the gaskets burning.

None of them knew how much they would miss the car, how much they would long for it, days later.

"We have to do something unpredictable," said Donny.

"Is this another theory?" Vira was in no mood.

The day was shading into night. They had been walking at least a week, by rough estimate and a sunrise-sunset count.

"If we were supposed to just keeping doing this, ad infinitum, then we would have tripped over some more food," said Donny. "What has to happen now is we need to shake up the system. Do something deterministic. Declare ourselves in a way that has nothing to do with patterns."

"Well, I declare I'm gonna collapse here and try to sleep," said Zach, sitting down heavily in the sand.

"You've just contradicted every other argument you've made," said Vira, more weary than surprised.

"No, Vira," said Zach. "I can see it. No explanation works. Therefore, logic isn't a way out. It's the kind of answer you get to by working through all the other answers. Right, Donny?"

He shrugged. "Except I can't suggest what to try."

"We could walk back to the car," said Vira. They glared at her. "Joke," she said, putting up her hands, surrendering. She shielded her eyes and plopped backward onto the sand as though her spine had been extracted.

Zach encamped nearby—not cuddle-close, but near enough to look possessive—like an infantryman who has learned how to drop and sleep in full gear. Soon he was snoring softly, the sound obscured by the light wind that always seemed to kick up at sunset. Just enough to stir the sand into a genuine annoyance. Zach rolled over, cushioning his forehead on his arms, forming a little box of deeper darkness. Burying his head in the sand, thought Donny, who remained irritated that his friends had accepted the routine of their bizarre situation so readily, and without question.

Donny pulled off his boots, one-two. There was nothing else to look at except the skyline, the sand, an occasional weed, and the two sleepers. He was not tired. His heart was racing.

He weighed one boot in his hand. It was scuffed and dusty, and radiated stored heat like fresh bread from an oven. One-two.

One: Holding the toe of the boot, Donny clocked Zach smartly in his occipital ditch, right where the backbone met the brain stem. Zach went limp and Vira did not stir. They were exhausted; fled to another place, chasing dreams. Donny sat on Zach's head, mashing it down into the sand until Zach stopped breathing.

Now Donny felt the surge. He had it all—correctitude, the energizing thud of his heart, dilated pupils, an erection, and the exhilarative adrenaline spike of knowing he was on the right track. He was *doing* something, taking declarative action.

After all, what were friends for?

Two: There were no fist-sized rocks or round stones, so Donny used his other boot to hit Vira in the back of the head, so he would not have to look at fresh blood while he raped her. By the second time, she was bloody anyway. She might have orgasmed once, through sheer autonomic reflex. Donny pinched her nose shut and clamped her mouth until she, too, stopped breathing. As she cooled, he did her once more. It really had been a while since he'd gotten laid. He woke up still on top of her, neck cricked from the odd position in which he'd dozed. His weight had pushed her partially into the sand, half-interring her, but she was in no position to complain, or criticize, or judge him anymore. Or feel sorry for him.

POE'S CHILDREN

Their water bottle was down to condensation. Night was better for walking in a desert. And Donny had taken action.

He left his companions behind and soldiered onward, alone, until his boot heels wore away to nothing. If he ever found civilization, he'd feel sorry later.

The Two Sams

Glen Hirshberg

FOR BOTH OF YOU

What wakes me isn't a sound. At first, I have no idea what it is: an earthquake, maybe; a vibration in the ground; a two A.M. truck shuddering along the switchback road that snakes up from the beach, past the ruins of the Baths, past the Cliff House and the automatons and coin-machines chattering in the Musee Mechanique, past our apartment building until it reaches the flatter stretch of the Great Highway, which will return it to the saner neighborhoods of San Francisco. I lie still, holding my breath without knowing why. With the moon gone, the watery light rippling over the chipping bas-relief curlicues on our wall and the scuffed, tilted hardwood floor makes the room seem insubstantial, a projected reflection from the camera obscura perched on the cliffs a quarter mile away.

Then I feel it again, and I realize it's in the bed, not the ground. Right beside me. Instantly, I'm smiling. I can't help it. *You're playing on your own, aren't you?* That's what I'm thinking. Our first game. He sticks up a tiny fist, a twitching foot, a butt cheek, pressing against the soft roof and walls of his world, and I lay my palm against him, and he shoots off across the womb, curls in a far corner, waits. Sticks out a foot again.

The game terrified me at first. I kept thinking about signs in aquariums warning against tapping on glass, giving fish heart attacks. But he kept playing. And tonight, the thrum of his life is like magic fingers in the mattress, shooting straight up my spine into my shoulders, settling me, squeezing the terror out. Shifting the sheets softly, wanting Lizzie to sleep, I lean closer, and know, all at once, that this isn't what woke me.

For a split second, I'm frozen. I want to whip my arms around my head, ward them off like mosquitoes or bees, but I can't hear anything, not this time. There's just that creeping damp, the heaviness in the air, like a fogbank forming. Abruptly, I dive forward, drop my head against the hot, round dome of Lizzie's stomach. Maybe I'm wrong, I think. I could be wrong. I press my ear against her skin, hold my breath, and for one horrible moment, I hear nothing at all, just the sea of silent, amniotic fluid. I'm thinking about that couple, the Super Jews from our Bradley class who started coming when they were already seven months along. They came five straight weeks, and the woman would reach out, sometimes, tug her husband's prayer-curls, and we all smiled, imagining their daughter doing that, and then they weren't there anymore. The woman woke up one day and felt strange, empty, she walked around for hours that way and finally just got in her car and drove to the hospital and had her child, knowing it was dead.

But under my ear, something is moving now. I can hear it inside my wife. Faint, unconcerned, unmistakable. Beat. Beat.

" 'Get out Tom's old records ...' " I sing, so softly, into Lizzie's skin. It isn't the song I used to use. Before, I mean. It's a new song. We do everything new, now. " 'And he'll come dancing 'round.' " It occurs to me that this song might not be the best choice, either. There are lines in it that could come back to haunt me, just the way the others have, the ones I never want to hear again, never even used to notice when I sang that song. They come creeping into my ears now, as though they're playing very quietly in a neighbor's room. " 'I dreamed I held you. In my arms. When I awoke, dear. I was mistaken. And so I hung my head and I cried.' " But then, I've found, that's the first great lesson of pregnancy: it all comes back to haunt you.

I haven't thought of this song, though, since the last time, I realize. Maybe they bring it with them.

Amidst the riot of thoughts in my head, a new one spins to the surface.

Was it there the very first time? Did I feel the damp then? Hear the song? Because if I did, and I'm wrong...

I can't remember. I remember Lizzie screaming. The bathtub, and Lizzie screaming.

Sliding slowly back, I ease away toward my edge of the bed, then sit up, holding my breath. Lizzie doesn't stir, just lies there like the gutshot creature she is, arms wrapped tight and low around her stomach, as though she could hold this one in, hold herself in, just a few days more. Her chin is tucked tight to her chest, dark hair wild on the pillow, bloated legs clamped around the giant, blue cushion between them. Tip her upright, I think, and she'd look like a little girl on a Hoppity Horse. Then her kindergarten students would laugh at her again, clap and laugh when they saw her, the way they used to. Before.

For the thousandth time in the past few weeks, I have to quash an urge to lift her black-framed, square glasses from around her ears. She has insisted on sleeping with them since March, since the day the life inside her became—in the words of Dr. Seger, the woman Lizzie believes will save us—"viable," and the ridge in her nose is red and deep, now, and her eyes, always strangely small, seem to have slipped back in their sockets, as though cringing away from the unaccustomed closeness of the world, its unblurred edges. "The second I'm awake," Lizzie tells me, savagely, the way she says everything these days, "I want to see."

"Sleep," I mouth, and it comes out a prayer.

Gingerly, I put my bare feet on the cold ground and stand. Always, it takes just a moment to adjust to the room. Because of the tilt of the floor—caused by the earthquake in '89—and the play of light over the walls and the sound of the surf and, sometimes, the seals out on Seal Rock and the litter of wood scraps and sawdust and half-built toys and menorahs and disemboweled clocks on every tabletop, walking through our apartment at night is like floating through a shipwreck.

Where are you? I think to the room, the shadows, turning in multiple directions as though my thoughts were a lighthouse beam. If they are, I need to switch them off. The last thing I want to provide, at this moment, for them, is a lure. Sweat breaks out on my back, my legs, as though I've been wrung. I don't want to breathe, don't want this infected air in my lungs, but I force myself. I'm ready. I have prepared, this time. I'll do what I must, if it's not too late and I get the chance.

"Where are you?" I whisper aloud, and something happens in the hall, in the doorway. Not movement. Not anything I can explain. But I start over there, fast. It's much better if they're out there. "I'm coming," I say, and I'm out of the bedroom, pulling the door closed behind me as if that will help, and when I reach the living room, I consider snapping on the light but don't.

On the wall over the square, dark couch—we bought it dark, we were anticipating stains—the Pinocchio clock, first one I ever built, at age four-teen, makes its steady, hollow tock. It's all nose, that clock, which seems like such a bad idea, in retrospect. What was I saying, and to whom? *The hour is a lie. The room is a lie. Time is a lie.* "Gepetto," Lizzie used to call me be-fore we were married, then after we were married, for a while, back when I used to show up outside her classroom door to watch her weaving be-tween desks, balancing hamsters and construction paper and graham crackers and half-pint milk cartons in her arms while kindergartners nipped between and around her legs like ducklings.

Gepetto. Who tried so hard to make a living boy.

Tock.

"Stop," I snap to myself, to the leaning walls. There is less damp here. They're somewhere else.

The first tremble comes as I return to the hall. I clench my knees, my shoulders, willing myself still. As always, the worst thing about the trem-bling and the sweating is the confusion that causes them. I can never de-cide if I'm terrified or elated. Even before I realized what was happening, there was a kind of elation.

Five steps down the hall, I stop at the door to what was once our work-shop, housing my building area and Lizzie's cut-and-paste table for class-room decorations. It has not been a workshop for almost four years, now. For four years, it has been nothing at all. The knob is just a little wet when I slide my hand around it, the hinges silent as I push open the door.

"Okay," I half-think, half-say, trembling, sliding into the room and shut-ting the door behind me. "It's okay." Tears leap out of my lashes as though they've been hiding there. It doesn't feel like I actually cried them. I sit down on the bare floor, breathe, and stare around the walls, also bare. One week more. Two weeks, tops. Then, just maybe, the crib, fully assembled, will burst from the closet, the dog-cat carpet will unroll itself like a Torah scroll over the hardwood, and the mobiles Lizzie and I made together will spring from the ceiling like streamers. *Surprise!*

The tears feel cold on my face, uncomfortable, but I don't wipe them. What would be the point? I try to smile. There's a part of me, a small, sad part, that feels like smiling. "Should I tell you a bedtime story?"

I could tell about the possum. We'd lost just the one, then, and more than a year had gone by, and Lizzie still had moments, seizures, almost, where she ripped her glasses off her face in the middle of dinner and hurled them across the apartment and jammed herself into the kitchen corner behind the stacked washer-dryer unit. I'd stand over her and say, "Lizzie, no," and try to fight what I was feeling, because I didn't like that I was feeling it. But the more often this happened, and it happened a lot, the angrier I got. Which made me feel like such a shit.

"Come on," I'd say, extra-gentle, to compensate, but of course I didn't fool her. That's the thing about Lizzie. I knew it when I married her, even loved it in her: she recognizes the worst in people. She can't help it. And she's never wrong about it.

"You don't even care," she'd hiss, her hands snarled in her twisting brown hair as though she were going to rip it out like weeds.

"Fuck you, of course I care."

"It doesn't mean anything to you."

"It means what it means. It means we tried, and it didn't work, and it's awful, and the doctors say it happens all the time, and we need to try again. It's awful but we have to deal with it, we have no choice if we want—"

"It means we lost a child. It means our child died. You asshole."

Once—one time—I handled that moment right. I looked down at my wife, my playmate since junior high, the perpetually sad person I make happy, sometimes, and who makes everyone around her happy even though she's sad, and I saw her hands twist harder in her hair, and I saw her shoulders cave in toward her knees, and I just blurted it out.

"You look like a lint ball," I told her.

Her face flew off her chest, and she glared at me. Then she threw her arms out, not smiling, not free of anything, but wanting me with her. Down I came. We were lint balls together.

Every single other time, I blew it. I stalked away. Or I started to cry. Or I fought back.

"Let's say that's true," I'd say. "We lost a child. I'll admit it, I can see how one could choose to see it that way. But I don't feel that. By the grace of God, it doesn't quite feel like that to me."

"That's because it wasn't inside you."

"That's such . . ." I'd start, then stop, because I didn't really think it was. And it wasn't what I was trying to say, anyway. "Lizzie. God. I'm just . . . I'm trying to do this well. I'm trying to get us to the place where we can try again. Where we can have a child. One that lives. Because that's the point, isn't it? That's the ultimate goal?"

"Honey, this one just wasn't meant to be," Lizzie would sneer, imitating her mom, or maybe my mom, or any one of a dozen people we knew. "Is that what you want to say next?"

"You know it isn't."

"How about, *The body knows. Something just wasn't right. These things do happen for a reason.*"

"Lizzie, stop."

"Or, *Years from now, you'll look at your child, your living, breathing, beautiful child, and you'll realize that you wouldn't have had him or her if the first one had survived. There'd be a completely different creature there.* How about that one?"

"Lizzie, Goddamnit. Just shut up. I'm saying none of those things, and you know it. I'm saying I wish this had never happened. And now that it has happened, I want it to be something that happened in the past. Because I still want to have a baby with you."

Usually, most nights, she'd sit up, then. I'd hand her her glasses, and she'd fix them on her face and blink as the world rushed forward. Then she'd look at me, not unkindly. More than once, I'd thought she was going to touch my face or my hand.

Instead, what she said was, "Jake. You have to understand." Looking through her lenses at those moments was like peering through a storm window, something I would never again get open, and through it I could see the shadows of everything Lizzie carried with her and could not bury and didn't seem to want to. "Of all the things that have happened to me. All of them. You're probably the best. And this is the worst."

Then she'd get up, step around me, and go to bed. And I'd go out to walk, past the Cliff House, past the Musee, sometimes all the way down to the ruins of the Baths, where I'd stroll along the crumbling concrete walls which once had framed the largest public bathing pool in the United States and now framed nothing but marsh grass and drain-water and echo. Sometimes, the fog would roll over me, a long, gray ghost-tide, and I'd float off on it, in it, just another trail of living vapor combing the earth in search of a world we'd all gotten the idea was here somewhere. Where, I wonder, had that idea come from, and how did so many of us get it?

"But that isn't what you want to hear," I say suddenly to the not-quite-empty workroom, the cribless floor. "Is it?" For a second, I panic, fight down the urge to leap for my feet and race for Lizzie. If they've gone back in there, then I'm too late anyway. And if they haven't, my leaping about just might scare them in that direction. In my head, I'm casting around for something to say that will hold them while I swing my gaze back and forth, up to the ceiling and down again.

"I was going to tell you about the possum, right? One night, maybe eight months or so after you were ..." The word curls on my tongue like a dead caterpillar. I say it anyway. "Born." Nothing screams in my face or flies at me, and my voice doesn't break. And I think something might have fluttered across the room from me, something other than the curtains. I have to believe it did. And the damp is still in here.

"It was pretty amazing," I say fast, staring at where the flutter was, as though I could pin it there. "Lizzie kicked me and woke me up. 'You hear that?' she asked. And of course, I did. Fast, hard scrabbling, click-click-click, from right in here. We came running and saw a tail disappear behind the dresser. There was a dresser, then, I made it myself. The drawers came out sideways and the handles formed kind of a pumpkin-face, just for fun, you know? Anyway, I got down on my hands and knees and found this huge, white possum staring right at me. I didn't even know there were possums here. This one took a single look at me and keeled over with its feet in the air. Playing dead."

I throw myself on the ground with my feet in the air. It's like a memory, a dream, a memory of a dream, but I half-believe I feel a weight on the soles of my feet, as though something has climbed onto them, for a ride, maybe.

"I got a broom. Your ... Lizzie got a trash can. And for the next, I don't know, three hours, probably, we chased this thing around and around the room. We had the windows wide open. All it had to do was hop up and out. Instead, it hid behind the dresser, playing dead, until I poked it with the broom, and then it would race along the baseboard or into the middle of the room and flip on its back again, as if to say, okay, now I'm really dead, and we couldn't get it to go up and out. We couldn't get it to do anything but die. Over and over and over. And . . ."

I stop, lower my legs abruptly, sit up. I don't say the rest. How, at 3:45 in the morning, Lizzie dropped the trash can to the floor, looked at me, and burst out crying. Threw her glasses at the wall and broke one of the lenses and wept while I stood there, so tired, with this possum belly-up at my feet and the sea air flooding the room. I'd loved the laughing. I could hardly stand up for exhaustion, and I'd loved laughing with Lizzie so goddamn much.

"Lizzie," I'd said. "I mean, fuck. Not everything has to relate to that. Does it? Does everything we ever think or do, for the rest of our lives . . ." But of course, it does. I think I even knew that then. And that was after only one.

"Would you like to go for a walk?" I say carefully, clearly. Because this is it. The only thing I can think of, and therefore the only chance we have. How does one get a child to listen, really? I wouldn't know. "We'll go for a stroll, okay? Get nice and sleepy?" I still can't see anything. Most of the other times, I've caught half a glimpse, at some point, a trail of shadow. Turning, leaving the door cracked open behind me, I head for the living room. I slide my trench coat over my boxers and Green Apple T-shirt, slip my tennis shoes onto my bare feet. My ankles will be freezing. In the pocket of my coat, I feel the matchbook I left there, the single, tiny, silver key. It has been two months, at least, since the last time they came, or at least since they let me know it. But I have stayed ready.

As I step onto our stoop, wait a few seconds, and pull the door closed, I am flooded with sensory memory—it's like being dunked—of the day I first became aware. Over two years ago, now. Over a year after the first one. Halfway to dreaming, all but asleep, I was overcome by an overwhelming urge to put my ear to Lizzie's womb and sing to the new tenant in there. Almost six weeks old, at that point. I imagined seeing through my wife's skin, watching toe and finger shapes forming in the red, waving wetness like lines on an Etch A Sketch.

"*You are my sun*—" I started, and knew, just like that, that something else was with me. There was the damp, for one thing, and an extra sound-

lessness in the room, right beside me. I can't explain it. The sound of someone else listening.

I reacted on instinct, shot upright and accidentally yanked all the blankets off Lizzie and shoved out my arms at where the presence seemed to
be, and Lizzie blinked awake and narrowed her spectacle-less eyes at the
shape of me, the covers twisted on the bed.

"There's something here," I babbled, pushing with both hands at the
empty air.

Lizzie just squinted, coolly. Finally, after a few seconds, she snatched
one of my waving hands out of the air and dropped it against her belly. Her
skin felt smooth, warm. My forefinger slipped into her bellybutton, felt the
familiar knot of it, and I found myself aroused. Terrified, confused, ridiculous, and aroused.

"It's just Sam," she said, stunning me. It seemed impossible that she
was going to let me win that fight. Then she smiled, pressing my hand to
the second creature we had created together. "You and me and Sam." She
pushed harder on my hand, slid it down her belly toward the center of her.

We made love, held each other, sang to her stomach. Not until long after Lizzie had fallen asleep, just as I was dropping off at last, did it occur
to me that she could have been more right than she knew. Maybe it was
just us, and Sam. The first Sam—the one we'd lost—returning to greet his
successor with us.

Of course, he hadn't come just to listen, or to watch. But how could I
have known that, then? And how did I know that that was what the presence was, anyway? I didn't. And when it came back late the next night, with
Lizzie this time sound asleep and me less startled, I slid aside to make
room for it so we could both hear. Both whisper.

Are both of you with me now, I wonder? I'm standing on my stoop and
listening, feeling, as hard as I can. Please, God, let them be with me. Not
with Lizzie. Not with the new one. That's the only name we have allowed
ourselves this time. The new one.

"Come on," I say to my own front door, to the filigrees of fog that float
forever on the air of Sutro Heights, as though the atmosphere itself has developed bas-relief and gone art deco. "Please. I'll tell you a story about the
day you were born."

I start down the warped, wooden steps toward our garage. Inside my pocket, the little silver key darts between my fingers, slippery and cool as a minnow. In my mouth, I taste the fog and the perpetual garlic smell from the latest building to perch at the jut of the cliffs and call itself the Cliff House—the preceding three all collapsed or burned to the ground—and something else, too. I realize, finally, what it is, and the tears come flooding back.

What I'm remembering, this time, is Washington, D.C., the grass brown and dying in the blazing August sun as we raced down the Mall from museum to museum in a desperate, headlong hunt for cheese. We were in the ninth day of the ten-day tetracycline program Dr. Seger had prescribed, and Lizzie just seemed tired, but I swear I could feel the walls of my intestines, raw and sharp and scraped clean, the way teeth feel after a particularly vicious visit to the dentist. I craved milk, and got nauseous just thinking about it. Drained of its germs, its soft, comforting skin of use, my body felt skeletal, a shell without me in it.

That was the point, as Dr. Seger explained it to us. We'd done our Tay-Sachs, tested for lead, endured endless blood screenings to check on things like prolactin, lupus anticoagulant, TSH. We would have done more tests, but the doctors didn't recommend them, and our insurance wouldn't pay. "A couple of miscarriages, it's really not worth intensive investigation." Three different doctors told us that. "If it happens a couple more times, we'll know something's really wrong."

Dr. Seger had a theory, at least, involving old bacteria lingering in the body for years, decades, tucked up in the fallopian tubes or hidden in the testicles or just adrift in the blood, riding the heart-current in an endless, mindless, circle. "The mechanism of creation is so delicate," she told us. "So efficiently, masterfully created. If anything gets in there that shouldn't be, well, it's like a bird in a jet engine. Everything just explodes."

How comforting, I thought but didn't say at that first consultation, because when I glanced at Lizzie, she looked more than comforted. She looked hungry, perched on the edge of her chair with her head half over Dr. Seger's desk, so pale, thin, and hard, like a starved pigeon being teased with crumbs. I wanted to grab her hand. I wanted to weep.

As it turns out, Dr. Seger may have been right. Or maybe we got lucky this time. Because that's the thing about miscarriage: three thousand years of human medical science, and no one knows any fucking thing at all. It just happens, people say, like a bruise, or a cold. And it does, I suppose. Just happen, I mean. But not like a cold. Like dying. Because that's what it is.

So for ten days, Dr. Seger had us drop tetracycline tablets down our throats like depth charges, blasting everything living inside us out. And on that day in DC—we were visiting my cousin, the first time I'd managed to coax Lizzie anywhere near extended family since all this started—we'd gone to the Holocaust Museum, searching for anything strong enough to take our minds off our hunger, our desperate hope that we were scoured, healthy, clean. But it didn't work. So we went to the Smithsonian. And three people from the front of the ticket line, Lizzie suddenly grabbed my hand, and I looked at her, and it was the old Lizzie, or the ghost of her, eyes flashing under their black rims, smile instantaneous, shockingly bright.

"Dairy," she said. "Right this second."

It took me a breath to adjust. I hadn't seen my wife this way in a long, long while, and as I stared, the smile slipped on her face. With a visible effort, she pinned it back in place. "Jake. Come on."

None of the museum cafés had what we wanted. We went racing past sculptures and animal dioramas and parchment documents to the cafés, where we stared at yogurt in plastic containers—but we didn't dare eat yogurt—and cups of tapioca that winked, in our fevered state, like the iced-over surfaces of Canadian lakes. But none of it would have served. We needed a cheddar wheel, a lasagna we could scrape free of pasta and tomatoes so we could drape our tongues in strings of crusted mozzarella. What we settled for, finally, was four giant bags of generic cheese puffs from a 7-Eleven. We sat together on the edge of a fountain and stuffed each other's mouths like babies, like lovers.

It wasn't enough. The hunger didn't abate in either of us. Sometimes I think it hasn't since.

God, it was glorious, though. Lizzie's lips around my orange-stained fingers, that soft, gorgeous crunch as each individual puff popped apart in our mouths, dusting our teeth and throats while spray from the fountain brushed our faces and we dreamed separate, still-hopeful dreams of children.

And that, in the end, is why I have to, you see. My two Sams. My lost, loved ones. Because maybe it's true. It doesn't seem like it could be, but maybe it is. Maybe, mostly, it just happens. And then, for most couples, it just stops happening one day. And afterward—if only because there isn't time—you start to forget. Not what happened. Not what was lost. But what the loss meant, or at least what it felt like. I've come to believe that time alone won't swallow grief or heal a marriage. But perhaps filled time...

In my pocket, my fingers close over the silver key, and I take a deep breath of the damp in the air, which is mostly just Sutro Heights damp now that we're outside. We have always loved it here, Lizzie and I. In spite of everything, we can't bring ourselves to flee. "Let me show you," I say, try-ing not to plead. I've taken too long, I think. They've gotten bored. They'll go back in the house. I lift the ancient, rusted padlock on our garage door, tilt it so I can see the slot in the moonlight, and slide the key home.

It has been months since I've been out here—we use the garage for storage, not for our old Nova—and I've forgotten how heavy the salt-saturated wooden door is. It comes up with a creak, slides over my head, and rocks unsteadily in its runners. How, I'm thinking, did I first realize that the presence in my room was my first, unborn child? The smell, I guess, like an unripe lemon, fresh and sour all at once. Lizzie's smell. Or maybe it was the song springing unbidden, over and over, to my lips. *"When I awoke dear. I was mistaken."* Those things, and the fact that now, these last times, they both seem to be there.

The first thing I see once my eyes adjust is my grandfather glaring out of his portrait at me, his hair thread-thin and wild on his head like a spi-derweb swinging free, his lips flat, crushed together, his ridiculous lumpy potato of a body under his perpetually half-zipped judges' robes. And there are his eyes, one blue, one green, which he once told me allowed him to see 3-D, before I knew that everyone could. A children's rights activist be-fore there was a name for such things, a three-time candidate for a state bench seat and three-time loser, he'd made an enemy of his daughter, my mother, by wanting a son so badly. And he'd made a disciple out of me by saving Lizzie's life. Turning her father in to the cops, then making sure that he got thrown in jail, then forcing both him and his whole family into counseling, getting him work when he got out, checking in on him every single night, no matter what, for six years, until Lizzie was away and free. Until eight months ago, on the day Dr. Seger confirmed that we were preg-nant for the third time, his portrait hung beside the Pinocchio clock on the living room wall. Now it lives here. One more casualty.

"Your namesake," I say to the air, my two ghosts. But I can't take my eyes off my grandfather. Tonight is the end for him, too, I realize. The real end, where the ripples his life created in the world glide silently to stillness. Could you have seen them, I want to ask, with those 3-D eyes that saw so much? Could you have saved them? Could you have thought of another, better way? Because mine is going to hurt. "His name was Nathan, really. But he called us 'Sam.' Your mother and me, we were both 'Sam.' That's why . . ."

That's why Lizzie let me win that argument, I realize. Not because she'd let go of the idea that the first one had to have a name, was a specific, living creature, a child of ours. But because she'd rationalized. Sam was to be the name, male or female. So whatever the first child had been, the second would be the other. Would have been. You see, Lizzie, I think to the air, wanting to punch the walls of the garage, scream to the cliffs, break down in tears. *You think I don't know. But I do.*

If we survive this night, and our baby is still with us in the morning, and we get to meet him someday soon, he will not be named Sam. He won't be Nathan, either. My grandfather would have wanted Sam.

"Goodbye, Grandpa," I whisper, and force myself toward the back of the garage. There's no point in drawing this out, surely. Nothing to be gained. But at the door to the meat freezer, where the game hunter who rented our place before us used to store waxed-paper packets of venison and elk, I suddenly stop.

I can feel them. They're still here. They have not gone back to Lizzie. They are not hunched near her navel, whispering their terrible, soundless whispers. That's how I imagine it happening, only it doesn't feel like imagining. And it isn't all terrible. I swear I heard it happen to the second Sam. The first Sam would wait, watching me, hovering near the new life in Lizzie like a hummingbird near nectar, then darting forward when I was through singing, or in between breaths, and singing a different sort of song, of a whole other world, parallel to ours, free of terrors or at least this terror, the one that just plain living breeds in everything alive. Maybe that world we're all born dreaming really does exist, but the only way to it is through a trapdoor in the womb. Maybe it's better where my children are. God, I want it to be better.

"You're by the notebooks," I say, and I almost smile, and my hand slides volitionlessly from the handle of the freezer door and I stagger toward the boxes stacked up, haphazard, along the back wall. The top one on the nearest stack is open slightly, its cardboard damp and reeking when I peel the flaps all the way back.

There they are. The plain, perfect-bound school-composition notebooks Lizzie bought as diaries, to chronicle the lives of her first two children in the 280 or so days before we were to know them. "I can't look in those," I say aloud, but I can't help myself. I lift the top one from the box, place it on my lap, and sit down. It's my imagination, surely, that weight on my knees, as though something else has just slid down against me. Like a child, to look at a photo album. *Tell me, Daddy, about the world without me in it.* Suddenly, I'm embarrassed. I want to explain. That first notebook, the other one, is almost half my writing, not just Lizzie's. But this one... I was away, Sam, on a selling trip, for almost a month. And when I came back... I couldn't. Not right away. I couldn't even watch your mom doing it. And two weeks later...

"The day you were born," I murmur, as if it were a lullaby, "we went to the redwoods, with the Giraffes." Whatever it is, that weight on me, shifts a little. Settles. "That isn't really their name, Sam. Their name is Girard. Giraffe is what you would have called them, though. They would have made you. They're so tall. So funny. They would have put you on their shoulders to touch EXIT signs and ceiling tiles. They would have dropped you upside down from way up high and made you scream.

"This was December, freezing cold, but the sun was out. We stopped at a gas station on our way to the woods, and I went to get Bugles, because that's what Giraffes eat. The ones we know, anyway. Your mom went to the restroom. She was in there a long time. And when she came out, she just looked at me. And I knew."

My fingers have pushed open the notebook, pulled apart the pages. They're damp, too. Half of them are ruined, the words in multicolored inks like pressed flowers on the pages, smeared out of shape, though their meaning remains clear.

"I waited. I stared at your mother. She stared at me. Joseph—Mr. Giraffe—came in to see what was taking so long. Your mom just kept on staring. So I said, 'Couldn't find the Bugles.' Then I grabbed two bags of them, turned away, and paid. And your mom got in the van beside me, and the Giraffes put on their bouncy, happy, Giraffe music, and we kept going.

"When we got to the woods, we found them practically empty, and there was this smell, even though the trees were dead. It wasn't like spring. You couldn't smell pollen or see buds, there was just the sunlight and bare branches and this mist floating up, catching in the trees and forming shapes like the ghosts of leaves. I tried to hold your mother's hand, and she let me at first. And then she didn't. She disappeared into the mist. The Giraffes had to go find her in the end, when it was time to go home. It was almost dark as we got in the van, and none of us were speaking. I was the last one in. And all I could think, as I took my last breath of that air, was, *Can you see this? Did you see the trees, my sweet son, daughter or son, on your way out of the world?*

Helpless, now, I drop my head, bury it in the wet air as though there were a child's hair there, and my mouth is moving, chanting the words in the notebook on my lap. I only read them once, on the night Lizzie wrote them, when she finally rolled over, with no tantrum, no more tears, nothing left, closed the book against her chest, and went to sleep. But I remember them, still. There's a sketch, first, what looks like an acorn with a dent in the top. Next to it Lizzie has scrawled, *"You. Little rice-bean."* On the day before it died. Then there's the list, like a rosary: *"I'm so sorry. I'm so sorry I don't get to know you. I'm so sorry for wishing this was over, now, for wanting the bleeding to stop. I'm so sorry that I will never have the chance to be your mother. I'm so sorry you will never have the chance to be in our family. I'm so sorry that you are gone."*

I recite the next page, too, without even turning to it. The *I-don't-wants:* *"a D & C; a phone call from someone who doesn't know, to ask how I'm feeling; a phone call from someone who does, to ask how I am; to forget this, ever; to forget you."*

And then, at the bottom of the page: *"I love fog. I love seals. I love the ghosts of Sutro Heights. I love my mother, even though. I love Jake. I love having known you. I love having known you. I love having known you."*

With one, long shuddering breath, as though I'm trying to slip out from under a sleeping cat, I straighten my legs, lay the notebook to sleep in its box, tuck the flaps around it, and stand. It's time. Not past time, just time. I return to the freezer, flip the heavy white lid.

The thing is, even after I looked in here, the same day I brought my grandfather out and wound up poking around the garage, lifting box tops, touching old, unused bicycles and cross-country skis, I would never have realized. If she'd done the wrapping in waxed paper, laid it in the bottom of the freezer, I would have assumed it was meat, and I would have left it there. But Lizzie is Lizzie, and instead of waxed paper, she'd used red and blue construction paper from her classroom, folded the paper into perfect squares with perfect corners, and put a single star on each of them. So I lifted them out, just as I'm doing now.

They're so cold cradled against me. The red package. The blue one. So light. The most astounding thing about the wrapping, really, is that she managed it all. How do you get paper and tape around nothing and get it to hold its shape? From another nearby box, I lift a gold and green blanket. I had it on my bottom bunk when I was a kid. The first time Lizzie lay on my bed—without me in it, she was just lying there—she wrapped herself in this. I spread it now on the cold, cement floor, and gently lay the packages down.

In Hebrew, the word for miscarriage translates, literally, as *something dropped*. It's no more accurate a term than any of the others humans have generated for the whole, apparently incomprehensible process of reproduction, right down to *conception*. Is that what we do? Conceive? Do we literally dream our children? Is it possible that miscarriage, finally, is just waking up to the reality of the world a few months too soon?

Gently, with the tip of my thumbnail, I slit the top of the red package, fold it open. It comes apart like origami, so perfect, arching back against the blanket. I slit the blue package, pull back its flaps, widening the opening. One last parody of birth.

How did she do it, I wonder? The first time, we were home, she was in the bathroom. She had me bring Ziploc baggies and ice. *For testing,* she'd said. *They'll need it for testing.* But they'd taken it for testing. How had she gotten it back? And the second one had happened—finished happening—in a gas-station bathroom somewhere between the Golden Gate Bridge and the Muir Woods. And she'd said nothing, asked for nothing.

"Where did she keep you?" I murmur, staring down at the formless red and gray spatters, the bunched-up tissue that might have been tendon one day, skin one day. Sam, one day. In the red package, there is more, a hump of frozen something with strings of red spiraling out from it, sticking to the paper, like the rays of an imploding sun. In the blue package, there are some red dots, a few strands of filament. Virtually nothing.

The song comes, and the tears with them. *You'll never know. Dear. How much I love you. Please don't take. Please don't take.* I think of my wife upstairs in our life, sleeping with her arms around her child. The one that won't be Sam, but just might live.

The matches slide from my pocket. Pulling one out of the little book is like ripping a blade of grass from the ground. I scrape it to life, and its tiny light warms my hand, floods the room, flickering as it sucks the oxygen out of the damp. Will this work? How do I know? For all I know, I am imagining it all. The miscarriages were bad luck, hormone deficiencies, a virus in the blood, and the grief that got in me was at least as awful as what got in Lizzie, it just lay dormant longer. And now it has made me crazy.

But if it is better where you are, my Sams. And if you're here to tell the new one about it, to call him away...

"The other night, dear," I find myself saying, and then I'm singing it, like a Shabbat blessing, a Hanukkah song, something you offer to the emptiness of a darkened house to keep the dark and emptiness back one more week, one more day. *"As I lay sleeping. I dreamed I held you. In my arms."*

I lower the match to the red paper, then the blue, and as my children melt, become dream once more, I swear I hear them sing to me.

Notes on the Writing of Horror: A Story

Thomas Ligotti

or much too long I have been promising to formulate my views on the writing of supernatural horror tales. Until now I just haven't had the time. Why not? I was too busy churning out the leetle darlings. But many people, for whatever reasons, would like to be writers of horror tales, I know this. Fortunately, the present moment is a convenient one for me to share my knowledge and experience regarding this special literary vocation. Well, I guess I'm ready as I'll ever be. Let's get it over with.

The way I plan to proceed is quite simple. First, I'm going to sketch out the basic plot, characters, and various other features of a short horror story. Next, I will offer suggestions on how these raw elements may be treated in a few of the major styles which horror writers have exploited over the years. Each style is different and has its own little tricks. This approach will serve as an aid in deciding which style is the right one and for whom. And if all goes well, the novitiate teller of terror tales will be saved much time and agony discovering such things for himself. We'll pause at certain spots along the way to examine specific details, make highly biased evaluations, submit general commentary on the philosophy of horror fiction, and so forth.

At this point it's only fair to state that the following sample story, or rather its rough outline form, is not one that appears in the published works of Gerald K. Riggers, nor will it ever appear. Frankly, for reasons we'll explore a little later, I just couldn't find a way to tell this one that really satisfied me. Such things happen. (Perhaps farther down the line we'll analyze these extreme cases of irreparable failure, perhaps not.) Nevertheless the unfinished state of this story does not preclude using it as a perfectly fit display model to demonstrate how horror writers do what they do. Good. Here it is, then, as told in my own words. A couple-three paragraphs, at most.

THE STORY

A thirtyish but still quite youthful man, let's name him Nathan, has a date with a girl whom he deeply wishes to impress. Toward this end, a minor role is to be played by an impressive new pair of trousers he intends to find and purchase. A few obstacles materialize along the way, petty but frustrating bad luck, before he finally manages to secure the exact trousers he needs and at an extremely fair price. They are exceptional in their tailoring, this is quite plain. So far, so good. Profoundly good, to be sure, since Nathan intensely believes that one's personal possessions should themselves possess a certain substance, a certain quality. For example, Nathan's winter overcoat is the same one his father wore for thirty winters; Nathan's wristwatch is the same one his grandfather wore going on four decades, in all seasons. For Nathan, peculiar essences inhere in certain items of apparel, not to mention certain other articles small and large, certain happenings in time and space, certain people, and certain notions. In Nathan's view, yes, every facet of one's life should shine with these essences which alone make things really real. What are they? Nathan, over a period of time, has narrowed the essential elements down to three: something magic, something timeless, something profound. Though the world around him is for the most part lacking in these special ingredients, he perceives his own life to contain them in fluctuating but usually acceptable quantities. His new trousers certainly do; and Nathan hopes, for the first time in his life, that a future romance—to be conducted with one Lorna McFickel—will too.

So far, so good. Luckwise. Until the night of Nathan's first date. Miss McFickel resides in a respectable suburb but, in relation to where Nathan lives, she is clear across one of the most dangerous sectors of the city. No problem: Nathan's ten-year-old car is in mint condition, top form. If he just keeps the doors locked and the windows rolled up, everything will be fine. Worst luck, broken bottles on a broken street, and a flat tire. Nathan curbs the car. He takes off his grandfather's watch and locks it in the glove compartment; he takes off his father's overcoat, folds it up neatly, and snuggles it into the shadows beneath the dashboard. As far as the trousers are concerned, he would simply have to exercise great care while attempting to change his flat tire in record time, and in a part of town known as Hope's Back Door. With any luck, the trousers would retain their triple traits of magicality, timelessness, and profundity. Now, all the while Nathan is fixing the tire, his legs feel stranger and stranger. He could have attributed this to the physical labor he was performing in a pair of trousers not exactly designed for such abuse, but he would have just been fooling himself. For Nathan remembers his legs feeling strange, though less noticeably so, when he first tried on the trousers at home. Strange how? Strange as in a little stiff, and even then some. A little funny. Nonsense, he's just nervous about his date with lovely Lorna McFickel.

To make matters worse, two kids are now standing by and watching Nathan change the tire, two kids who look like they recently popped up from a bottomless ash pit. Nathan tries to ignore them, but he succeeds a little too well in this. Unseen by him, one of the kids edges toward the car and opens the front door. Worst luck, Nathan forgot to lock it. The kid lays his hands on Nathan's father's coat, and then both kids disappear into a rundown apartment house.

Very quickly now, Nathan chases the kids into what turns out to be a condemned building, and he falls down the stairs leading to a lightless basement. It's not that the stairs were rotten, no. It *is* that Nathan's legs have finally given out; they just won't work anymore. They are very stiff and feel funnier than ever. And not only his legs, but his entire body below the waist... except, for some reason, his ankles and feet. They're fine. For the problem is not with Nathan himself. It's with those pants of his. The following is why. A few days before Nathan purchased the pants, they were returned to the store for a cash refund. The woman returning them claimed that her husband didn't like the way they felt. She lied. Actually, her husband couldn't have cared less how the pants felt, since he'd collapsed from a long-standing heart ailment not long after trying them on. And with no one home to offer him aid, he died. It was only after he had lain several hours dead in those beautiful trousers that his unloving wife came home and, trying to salvage what she could from the tragedy, put her husband into a pair of old dungarees before making another move. Poor Nathan, of course, was not informed of his pants' sordid past. And when the kids see that he is lying helpless in the dust of that basement, they decide to take advantage of the situation and strip this man of his valuables... starting with those expensive-looking slacks and whatever treasures they may contain. But after they relieve a protesting, though paralyzed Nathan of his pants, they do not pursue their pillagery any further. Not after they see Nathan's legs, which are the putrid members of a man many days dead. With the lower half of Nathan rapidly rotting away, the upper must also die among the countless shadows of that condemned building. And mingled with the pain and madness of his untimely demise, Nathan abhors and grieves over the thought that, for a while anyway, Miss McFickel will think he has stood her up on the first date of what was supposed to be a long line of dates destined to evolve into a magic and timeless and profound affair of two hearts....

Incidentally, this story was originally intended for publication under my perennial pen name, G. K. Riggers, and entitled: "Romance of a Dead Man."

THE STYLES

There is more than one way to write a horror story, so much one expects to be told at this point. And such a statement, true or false, is easily demonstrated. In this section we will examine what may be termed three primary techniques of terror. They are: The *realistic* technique, the *traditional Gothic* technique, and the *experimental* technique. Each serves its user in different ways and realizes different ends, there's no question about that. After a little soul-searching, the prospective horror writer may awaken to exactly what his ends are and arrive at the most efficient technique for handling them. Thus . . .

The realistic technique. Since the cracking dawn of consciousness, restless tongues have asked: is the world, and are its people, real? Yes, answers realistic fiction, but only when it is, and they are, normal. The supernatural, and all it represents, is profoundly abnormal, and therefore unreal. Few would argue with these conclusions. Fine. Now the highest aim of the realistic horror writer is to prove, in realistic terms, that the unreal is real. The question is, can this be done? The answer is, of course not: one would look silly attempting such a thing. Consequently the realistic horror writer, wielding the hollow proofs and premises of his art, must settle for merely *seeming* to smooth out the ultimate paradox. In order to achieve this effect, the supernatural realist must really know the normal world, and deeply take for granted its reality. (It helps if he himself is normal and real.) Only then can the unreal, the abnormal, the supernatural be smuggled in as a plain brown package marked Hope, Love, or Fortune Cookies, and postmarked: the Edge of the Unknown. And of the dear reader's seat. Ultimately, of course, the supernatural explanation of a given story depends entirely on some irrational principle which in the real, normal world looks as awkward and stupid as a rosy-cheeked farm lad in a den of reeking degenerates. (Amend this, possibly, to rosy-cheeked degenerate . . . reeking farm lads.) Nevertheless, the hoax can be pulled off with varying degrees of success, that much is obvious. Just remember to assure the reader, at certain points in the tale and by way of certain signals, that it's now all right to believe the unbelievable. Here's how Nathan's story might be told using the realistic technique. Fast forward.

Nathan is a normal and real character, sure. Perhaps not as normal and real as he would like to be, but he does have his sights set on just this goal. He might even be a little too intent on it, though without passing beyond the limits of the normal and the real. His fetish for things "magic, timeless, and profound" may be somewhat unusual, but certainly not abnormal, not unreal. (And to make him a bit more real, one could supply his coat, his car, and grandfather's wristwatch with specific brand names, perhaps autobiographically borrowed from one's own closet, garage, and wrist.) The triple epithet which haunts Nathan's life—similar to the Latinical slogans on family coats-of-arms—also haunts the text of the tale like a song's refrain, possibly in italics as the submerged chanting of Nathan's undermind, possibly not. (Try not to be too artificial, one recalls this is realism.) Nathan wants his romance with Lorna McFickel, along with everything else he considers of value in existence, to be magic, timeless, and the other thing. For, to Nathan, these are attributes that are really normal and really real in an existence ever threatening to go abnormal and unreal on one, anyone, not just him.

Okay. Now Lorna McFickel represents all the virtues of normalcy and reality. She could be played up in the realistic version of the story as much more normal and real than Nathan. Maybe Nathan is just a little neurotic, maybe he needs normal and real things too much, I don't know. Whatever, Nathan wants to win a normal, real love, but he doesn't. He loses, even before he has a chance to play. He loses badly. Why? For the answer we can appeal to a very prominent theme in the story: Luck. Nathan is just unlucky. He had the misfortune to brush up against certain outside supernatural forces and they devastated him body and soul. But *how* did they devastate him, this is really what a supernatural horror story, even a realistic one, is all about.

Just how, amid all the realism of Nathan's life, does the supernatural sneak past Inspectors Normal and Real standing guard at the gate? Well, sometimes it goes in disguise. In realistic stories it is often seen impersonating two inseparable figures of impeccable reputation. I'm talking about Dr. Cause and Prof. Effect. Imitating the habits and mannerisms of these two, not to mention taking advantage of their past record of reliability, the supernatural can be accepted in the best of places, be unsuspiciously abandoned on almost any doorstep—not the bastard child of reality but its legitimized heir. Now in Nathan's story the source of the supernatural is somewhere inside those mysterious trousers. They are woven of some fabric which Nathan has never seen the like of; they have no labels to indicate their maker; there is something indefinably alluring in their makeup. When Nathan asks the salesman about them, we introduce our *first cause*: the trousers were made in a foreign land—South America, Eastern Europe, Southeast Asia—which fact clarifies many mysteries, while also making them even more mysterious. The realistic horror writer may also allude to well-worn instances of sartorial magic (enchanted slippers, invisible-making jackets), though one probably doesn't want the details of this tale to be overly explicit. Don't risk insulting your gentle reader.

At this point the alert student may ask: but even if the trousers are acknowledged as magic, why do they have the particular effect they eventually have, causing Nathan to rot away below the waist? To answer this question we need to introduce our *second cause*: the trousers were worn, for several hours, by a dead man. But these "facts" explain nothing, right? Of course they don't. However, they may seem to explain everything if they are revealed in the right manner. All one has to do is link up the first and second causes (there may even be more) within the scheme of a realistic narrative. For example, Nathan might find something in the trousers leading him to deduce that he is not their original owner. Perhaps he finds a winning lottery ticket of significant, though not too tempting, amount. (This also fits in nicely with the theme of luck.) Being a normally honest type of person, Nathan calls the clothes store, explains the situation, and they give him the name and phone number of the gentleman who originally put those pants on his charge account and, afterward, returned them. Nathan puts in the phone call and finds out that the pants were returned not by a man, but by a woman. The very same woman who explains to Nathan that since her husband has passed on, rest his soul, she could really use the modest winnings from that lottery ticket. By now Nathan's mind, and the reader's, is no longer on the lottery ticket at all, but on the revealed fact that Nathan is the owner and future wearer of a pair of pants once owned (and worn? it is interrogatively hinted) by a *dead man*. After a momentary bout with superstitious repellence, Nathan forgets all about the irregular background of his beautiful, almost new trousers. The reader, however, doesn't forget. And so when almost-real, almost-normal Nathan loses all hope of achieving full normalcy and reality, the reader knows why, and in more ways than one.

The *realistic* technique.

It's easy. Now try it yourself.

The *traditional Gothic technique*. Certain kinds of people, and a fortiori certain kinds of writers, have always experienced the world around them in the Gothic manner, I'm almost positive. Perhaps there was even some little stump of an ape-man who witnessed prehistoric lightning as it parried with prehistoric blackness in a night without rain, and felt his soul rise and fall at the same time to behold this cosmic conflict. Perhaps such displays provided inspiration for those very first imaginings that were not born of the daily life of crude survival, who knows? Could this be why all our primal mythologies are Gothic? I only pose the question, you see. Perhaps the labyrinthine events of triple-volumed shockers passed, in abstract, through the brains of hairy, waddling things as they moved around in moon-trimmed shadows during their angular migrations across lunar landscapes of craggy rock or skeletal wastelands of jagged ice. These ones needed no convincing, for nothing needed to *seem* real to their little minds as long as it *felt* real to their blood. A gullible bunch of creatures, these. And to this day the fantastic, the unbelievable, remains potent and unchallenged by logic when it walks amid the gloom and grandeur of a Gothic world. So much goes without saying, really.

Therefore, the advantages of the *traditional Gothic* technique, even for the contemporary writer, are two. One, isolated supernatural incidents don't look as silly in a Gothic tale as they do in a realistic one, since the latter obeys the hard-knocking school of reality while the former recognizes only the University of Dreams. (Of course the entire Gothic tale itself may look silly to a given reader, but this is a matter of temperament, not technical execution.) Two, a Gothic tale gets under a reader's skin and stays there far more insistently than other kinds of stories. Of course it has to be done right, whatever you take the words *done right* to mean. Do they mean that Nathan has to function within the massive incarceration of a castle in the mysterious fifteenth century? No, but he may function within the massive incarceration of a castlelike skyscraper in the just-as-mysterious twentieth. Do they mean that Nathan must be a brooding Gothic hero and Miss McFickel an ethereal Gothic heroine? No, but it may mean an extra dose of obsessiveness in Nathan's psychology, and Miss McFickel may seem to him less the ideal of normalcy and reality than the pure Ideal itself. Contrary to the realistic story's allegiance to the normal and the real, the world of the Gothic tale is fundamentally unreal and abnormal, harboring essences which are magic, timeless, and profound in a way the realistic Nathan never dreamed. So, to rightly do a Gothic tale requires, let's be frank, that the author be a bit of a lunatic, at least while he's authoring, if not at all times. Hence, the well-known inflated rhetoric of the Gothic tale can be understood as more than an inflatable raft on which the imagination floats at its leisure upon the waves of bombast. It is actually the sails of the Gothic artist's soul filling up with the winds of ecstatic hysteria. And these winds just won't blow in a soul whose climate is controlled by central air-conditioning. So it's hard to tell someone how to write the Gothic tale, since one really has to be born to the task. Too bad. The most one can do is offer a pertinent example: a Gothic scene from "Romance of a Dead Man," translated from the original Italian of Geraldo Riggenni. This chapter is entitled "The Last Death of Nathan."

Through a partially shattered window, its surface streaked with a blue film of dust and age, the diluted glow of twilight seeped down onto the basement floor where Nathan lay without hope of mobility. In the dark you're not anywhere, he had thought as a child at each and every bedtime; and, in the bluish semiluminescence of that stone cellar, Nathan was truly not anywhere. He raised himself up on one elbow, squinting through tears of confusion into the filthy azure dimness. His grotesque posture resembled the half-anesthetized efforts of a patient who has been left alone for a moment while awaiting surgery, anxiously looking around to see if he's simply been forgotten on that frigid operating table. If only his legs would move, if only that paralyzing pain would suddenly become cured. Where were those wretched doctors, he asked himself dreamily. Oh, there they were, standing behind the turquoise haze of the surgery lamps. "He's out of it, man," said one of them to his colleague. "We can take everything he's got on him." But after they removed Nathan's trousers, the operation was abruptly terminated and the patient abandoned in the blue shadows of silence. "Jesus, look at his legs, look," they had screamed. Oh, if only he could now scream like that, Nathan thought among all the fatal chaos of his other thoughts. If only he could scream loud enough to be heard by that girl, by way of apologizing for his permanent absence from their magic, timeless, and profound future, which was in fact as defunct as the two legs that now seemed to be glowing glaucous with putrefaction before his eyes. Couldn't he now emit such a scream, now that the tingling agony of his liquefying legs was beginning to spread upward throughout his whole body and being? But no. It was impossible— to scream that loudly—though he did manage, in no time at all, to scream himself straight to death.

The *traditional Gothic* technique.

It's easy. Now try it yourself.

The *experimental technique.* Every story, even a true one, wants to be told in only one single way by its writer, yes? So, really, there's no such thing as experimentalism in its trial-and-error sense. A story is not an experiment, an experiment is an experiment. True. The "experimental" writer, then, is simply following the story's commands to the best of his human ability. The writer is not the story, the story is the story. See? Sometimes this is very hard to accept, and sometimes too easy. On the one hand, there's the writer who can't face his fate: that the telling of a story has nothing at all to do with him; on the other hand, there's the one who faces it too well: that the telling of the story has nothing at all to do with him. Either way, literary experimentalism is simply the writer's imagination, or lack of it, and feeling, or absence of same, thrashing their chains around in the escape-proof dungeon of the words of the story. One writer is trying to get the whole breathing world into the two dimensions of his airless cell, while the other is adding layers of bricks to keep that world the hell out. But despite the most sincere efforts of each prisoner, the sentence remains the same: to stay exactly where they are, which is where the story is. It's a condition not unlike the world itself, except it doesn't hurt. It doesn't help either, but who cares?

The question we now must ask is: is Nathan's the kind of horror story that demands treatment outside the conventional realistic or Gothic techniques? Well, it may be, depending on whom this story occurred to. Since it occurred to me (and not too many days ago), and since I've pretty much given up on it, I guess there's no harm in giving this narrative screw another turn, even if it's in the wrong direction. Here's the way mad Dr. Riggers would experiment, blasphemously, with his man-made Nathanstein. The secret of life, my ugly Igors, is time ... time ... time.

The experimental version of this story could actually be told as two stories happening "simultaneously," each narrated in alternating sections which take place in parallel chronologies. One section begins with the death of Nathan and moves backward in time, while its counterpart story begins with the death of the original owner of the magic pants and moves forward. Needless to say, the facts in the case of Nathan must be juggled around so as to be comprehensible from the beginning, that is to say from the end. (Don't risk confusing your worthy readers.) The stories converge at the crossroads of the final section where the destinies of their characters also converge, this being the clothes store where Nathan purchases the fateful trousers. On his way into the store he bumps into a woman who is preoccupied with counting a handful of cash, this being the woman who has just returned the trousers.

"Excuse me," says Nathan.

"Look where you're going," says the woman at the same instant.

Of course at this point we have already seen where Nathan is going and, in a way too spooky to explain right now, so has he.

The experimental technique. It's easy, now try it yourself.

ANOTHER STYLE

All the styles we have just examined have been simplified for the purposes of instruction, haven't they? Each is a purified example of its kind, let's not kid ourselves. In the real world of horror fiction, however, the above three techniques often get entangled with one another in hopelessly mysterious ways, almost to the point where all previous talk about them is useless for all practical purposes. But an ulterior purpose, which I'm saving for later, may thus be better served. Before we get there, though, I'd like, briefly, to propose still another style.

The story of Nathan is one very close to my heart and I hope, in its basic trauma, to the hearts of many others. I wanted to write this horror tale in such a fashion that its readers would be distressed not by the personal, individual catastrophe of Nathan but by his very existence in a world, even a fictional one, where a catastrophe of this type and magnitude is possible. I wanted to employ a style that would conjure all the primordial powers of the universe independent of the conventional realities of the Individual, Society, or Art. I aspired toward nothing less than a pure style without style, a style having nothing whatever to do with the normal or abnormal, a style magic, timeless, and profound . . . and one of great horror, the horror of a god. The characters of the story would be Death himself in the flesh, Desire in a new pair of pants, the pretty eyes of Desiderata and the hideous orbs of Loss. And linked hand-in-hand with these terrible powers would be the more terrible ones of Luck, Fate, and all the miscellaneous minions of Doom.

I couldn't do it, my friends. It's not easy, and I don't suggest that you try it yourself.

THE FINAL STYLE

Dear horror writers of the future, I ask you: what is the style of horror? What is its tone, its *voice*? Is it that of an old storyteller, keeping eyes wide around the tribal campfire; is it that of a documentarian of current or historical happenings, reporting events heard-about and conversations overheard; is it even that of a yarn-spinning god who can see the unseeable and reveal, from viewpoint omniscient, the horrific hearts of man and monster? I have to say that it's none of these, sorry if it's taken so long.

To tell you the truth, I'm not sure myself what the voice of horror really is. But throughout my career of eavesdropping on the dead and the damned, I know I've heard it; and Gerry Riggers, you remember him, has tried to put it on paper. Most often it sounds to me very simply like a voice calling out in the middle of the night, a single voice with no particular qualities. Sometimes it's muffled, like the voice of a tiny insect crying for help from inside a sealed coffin; and other times the coffin shatters, like a brittle exoskeleton, and from within rises a piercing, crystal shriek that lacerates the midnight blackness. These are approximations, of course, but highly useful in pinning down the sound of the voice of horror, if one still wants to.

In other words, the proper style of horror is really that of the *personal confession,* and nothing but: manuscripts found in lonely places. While some may consider this the height of cornball melodrama, and I grant that it is, it is also the rawhead and bloody bones of true blue grue. It's especially true when the confessing narrator has something he must urgently get off his chest and labors beneath its nightmarish weight all the while he is telling the tale. Nothing could be more obvious, except perhaps that the tale teller, ideally, should himself be a writer of horror fiction by trade. That really is more obvious. Better. But how can the *confessional* technique be applied to the story we've been working with? Its hero isn't a horror writer, at least not that I can see. Clearly some adjustments have to be made.

As the reader may have noticed, Nathan's character can be altered to suit a variety of literary styles. He can lean toward the normal in one and the abnormal in another. He can be transformed from fully fleshed person to disembodied fictional abstraction. He can play any number of basic human and nonhuman roles, representing just about anything a writer could want. Mostly, though, I wanted Nathan, when I first conceived him and his ordeal, to represent none other than my real life self. For behind my pseudonymic mask of Gerald Karloff Riggers, I am no one if not Nathan Jeremy Stein.

So it's not too far-fetched that in his story Nathan should be a horror writer, at least an aspiring one. Perhaps he dreams of achieving Gothic glory by writing tales that are nothing less than magic, timeless, and you know what. Perhaps he would sell his soul in order to accomplish this fear, I mean *feat*. But Nathan was not born to be a seller of his soul or anything else, that's why he became a horror writer rather than going into Dad's (and Granddad's) business. Nathan is, however, a buyer: a haunter of spectral marketplaces, a visitant of discount houses of unreality, a bargain hunter in the deepest basement of the unknown. And in some mysterious way, he comes to procure his dream of horror without even realizing what it is he's bought or with what he has bought it. Like the other Nathan, *this* Nathan eventually finds that what he's bought is not quite what he bargained for—a pig in a poke rather that a nice pair of pants. What? I'll explain.

In the confessional version of Nathan's horror story, the main character must be provided with something horrible to confess, something fitting to his persona as a die-hard horrorist. The solution is quite obvious, which doesn't prevent its also being freakish to the core. Nathan will confess that he's gone too far into FEAR. He's always had a predilection for this particular discipline, but now it's gotten out of hand, out of control, and out of this world.

The turning point in Nathan's biography of horror-seeking is, as in previous accounts, an aborted fling with Lorna McFickel. In the other versions of the story, the character known by this name is a personage of shifting significance, representing at turns the ultra-real or the super-ideal to her would-be romancer. The confessional version of "Romance of a Dead Man," however, gives her a new identity, namely that of Lorna McFickel herself, who lives across the hall from me in a Gothic castle of high-rise apartments, twin-towered and honeycombed with newly carpeted passageways. But otherwise there's not much difference between the female lead in the fictional story and her counterpart in the factual one. While the storybook Lorna will remember Nathan as the creep who spoiled her evening, who disappointed her—Real Lorna, Normal Lorna feels exactly the same way, or rather felt, since I doubt she even thinks about the one she called, and not without good reason, *the most disgusting creature on the face of the earth.* And although this patent exaggeration was spoken in the heat of a very hot moment, I believe her attitude was basically sincere. Even so, I will never reveal the motivation for this outburst of hers, not even under the throbbing treat of torture. (I meant, of course, to write *threat.* Only a tricky trickle of the pen's ink, nothing more.) Such things as motivation are not important to this horror story anyway, not nearly as important as what happens to Nathan following Lorna's revelatory rejection.

For he now knows, as he never knew before, how weird he really is, how unlike everyone else, how abnormal and unreal fate has made him. He knows that supernatural influences have been governing his life all along, that he is subject only to the rule of demonic forces, which now want this expatriate from the red void back in their bony arms. In brief, Nathan should never have been born a human being, a truth he must accept. Hard. (The most painful words are "never again," or just plain "never!") And he knows that someday the demons will come for him.

The height of the crisis comes one evening when the horror writer's ego is at low ebb, possibly to ebb all the way back to the abyss. He has attempted to express his supernatural tragedy in a short horror story, his last, but he just can't reach a climax of suitable intensity and imagination, one that would do justice to the cosmic scale of his pain. He has failed to embody in words his semi-autobiographical sorrow, and all these games with protective names have only made it more painful. It hurts to hide his heart within pseudonyms of pseudonyms. Finally, the horror writer sits down at his desk and begins whining like a brat all over the manuscript of his unfinished story. This goes on for quite some time, until Nathan's sole desire is to seek a human oblivion in a human bed. Whatever its drawbacks, grief is a great sleeping draught to drug oneself into a noiseless, lightless paradise far from an agonizing universe. This is so.

Later on there comes a knocking at the door, an impatient rapping, really. Who is it? One must open it to find out.

"Here, you forgot these," a pretty girl said to me, flinging a woolly bundle into my arms. Just as she was about to walk away, she turned and scanned the features of my face a little more scrupulously. I have sometimes pretended to be other people, the odd Norman and even a Nathan or two, but I knew I couldn't get away with it anymore. Never again! "I'm sorry," she said. "I thought you were Norman. This is his apartment, right across and one down the hall from mine." She pointed to show me. "Who're you?"

"I'm a friend of Norman's," I answered.

"Oh, I guess I'm sorry then. Well, those're his pants I threw at you."

"Were you mending them or something?" I asked innocently, checking them as if looking for the scars of repair.

"No, he just didn't have time to put them back on the other night when I threw him out, you know what I mean? I'm moving out of this creepy dump just to get away from him, and you can tell him those words."

"Please come in from that drafty hallway and you can tell him yourself."

I smiled my smile and she, not unresponsively, smiled hers. I closed the door behind her.

"So, do you have a name?" she asked.

"Penzance," I replied. "Call me Pete."

"Well, at least you're not Harold Wackers, or whatever the name is on those lousy books of Norman's."

"I believe it's *Wickers*, H. J. Wickers."

"Anyway, you don't seem at all like Norman, or even someone who'd be a friend of his."

"I'm sure that was intended as a compliment, from what I've gathered about you and Norm. Actually, though, I too write books not unlike those of H. J. Wickers. My apartment across town is being painted, and Norman was kind enough to take me in, even loan me his desk for a while." I manually indicated the cluttered, weeped-upon object of my last remark. "In fact, Norman and I sometimes collaborate under a common pen-name, and right now we're working together on a manuscript." That was an eternity ago, but somehow it seems like the seconds and minutes of those days are still nipping at our heels. What tricks human clocks can play, even on us who are no longer subject to them! But it's a sort of reverse magic, I suppose, to enshackle the timeless with Granddaddy's wrist-grips of time, just as it is the most negative of miracles to smother unburdened spirits with the burdensome overcoat of matter.

"That's nice, I'm sure," she replied to what I said a few statements back. "By the way. I'm Laura—"

"O'Finney," I finished. "Norman's spoken quite highly of you." I didn't mention that he had also spoken quite lowly of her too.

"Where is the creep, anyway?" she inquired.

"He's sleeping," I answered, lifting a vague finger toward the rear section of the apartment, where a shadowy indention led to bathrooms and bedrooms. "He's had a hard night of writing."

The girl's face assumed a disgusted expression.

"Forget it," she said, heading for the door. Then she turned and very slowly walked a little ways back toward me. "Maybe we'll see each other again."

"Anything is possible," I assured her.

"Just do me a favor and keep Norman away from me, if you don't mind."

"I think I can do that very easily. But you have to do something for me."

"What?"

I leaned toward her very confidentially.

"Please die, Desiderata," I whispered in her ear, while gripping her neck with both hands, cutting short a scream along with her life. Then I really went to work.

"Wake up, Norman," I shouted a little later. I was standing at the foot of his bed, my hands positioned behind my back. "You were really dead to the world, you know that?"

A little drama took place on Norman's face in which surprise overcame sleepiness and both were vanquished by anxiety. He had been through a lot the past couple nights, struggling with our "Notes" and other things, and really needed his sleep. I hated to wake him up.

"Who? What do you want?" he said, quickly sitting up in bed.

"Never mind what I want. Right now we are concerned with what *you* want, you know what I mean? Remember what you told that girl the other night, remember what you wanted her to do that got her so upset?"

"If you don't get the hell out of here—"

"That's what *she* said too, remember? And then she said she wished she had *never met you*. And that was the line, wasn't it, that gave you the inspiration for our fictionalized adventure. Poor Nathan never had the chance you had. Oh yes, very fancy rigmarole with the enchanted trousers. Blame it all on some old bitch and her dead husband. Very realistic, I'm sure. When the real reason—"

"Get out of here!" he yelled. But he calmed down somewhat when he saw that ferocity in itself had no effect on me.

"What did you expect from that girl. You did tell her that you wanted to embrace, what was it? Oh yes, a headless woman. A headless woman, for heaven's sake, that's asking a lot. And you did want her to make herself look like one, at least for a little while. Well, I've got the answer to your prayers. How's this for headless?" I said, holding up the head from behind my back.

He didn't make a sound, though his two eyes screamed a thousand times louder than any single mouth. I tossed the long-haired and bloody noggin in his lap, but he threw the bedcovers over it and frantically pushed the whole business onto the floor with his feet.

"The rest of her is in the bathtub. Go see, if you want. I'll wait."

He didn't make a move or say a word for quite a few moments. But when he finally did speak, each syllable came out so calm and smooth, so free of the vibrations of fear, that I have to say it shook me up a bit.

"Whooo are you?" he asked as if he already knew.

"Do you really need to have a name, and would it even do any good? Should we call that disengaged head down there Laura or Lorna, or just plain Desiderata? And what, in heaven's name, should I call you—Norman or Nathan, Harold or Gerald?"

"I thought so," he said disgustedly. Then he began to speak in an eerily rational voice, but very rapidly. He did not even seem to be talking to anyone in particular. "Since the thing to which I am speaking," he said, "since this thing knows what only I could know, and since it tells me what only I could tell myself, I must therefore be completely alone in this room, or perhaps even dreaming. Yes, dreaming. Otherwise the diagnosis is insanity. Very true. Profoundly certain. Go away now, Mr. Madness. Go away, Dr. Dream. You made your point, now let me sleep. I'm through with you." Then he lay his head down on the pillow and closed his eyes.

"Norman," I said. "Do you always go to bed with your trousers on?"

He opened his eyes and now noticed what he had been too deranged to notice before. He sat up again.

"Very good, Mr. Madness. These look like the real thing. But that's not possible since Laura still has them, sorry about that. Funny, they won't come off. The imaginary zipper must be stuck. Gee, I guess I'm in trouble now. I'm a dead man if there ever was one, hoo. Always make sure you know what you're buying, that's what I say. Heaven help me, please. You never know what you might be getting into. Come off, damn you! Oh, what grief. Well, so when do I start to rot, Mr. Madness? Are you still there? What happened to the lights?"

The lights had gone out in the room and everything glowed with a bluish luminescence. Lightning began flashing outside the bedroom window, and thunder resounded through a rainless night. The moon shone through an opening in the clouds, a blood-red moon only the damned and the dead can see.

"Rot your way back to us, you freak of creation. Rot your way out of this world. Come home to a pain so great that it is bliss itself. You were born to be bones not flesh. Rot your way free of that skin of mere skin."

"Is this really happening to me? I mean, I'm doing my best, sir. It isn't easy, not at all. Horrible electricity down there. Horrible. Am I bathed in magic acid or something? Oh, it hurts, my love. Ah, ah, ah. It hurts so much. Never let it end. If I have to be like this, then never let me wake up, Dr. Dream. Can you do that, at least?"

I could feel my bony wings rising out of my back and saw them spread gloriously in the blue mirror before me. My eyes were now jewels, hard and radiant. My jaws were a cavern of dripping silver and through my veins ran rivers of putrescent gold. He was writhing on the bed like a wounded insect, making sounds like nothing in human memory. I swept him up and wrapped my sticky arms again and again around his trembling body. He was laughing like a child, the child of another world. And a great wrong was about to be rectified.

I signaled the windows to open onto the night, and, very slowly, they did. His infant's laughter had now turned to tears, but they would soon run dry, I knew this. At last we would be free of the earth. The windows opened wide over the city below and the profound blackness above welcomed us.

I had never tried this before. But when the time came, I found it all so easy.

Unearthed

Benjamin Percy

Denis began acting strangely soon after he dug up the dead Indian. This happened in Christmas Valley, in Eastern Oregon, among the sand dunes and sage flats and rimrock canyons where he and his son, Elwood, often spent their weekends. They called themselves rock hounds, fossil hunters, archaeologists, and they carried on their backs shovels and picks and trowels and paintbrushes to whisk away the dust and calcite. When they hiked through the high desert, their eyes studied the soil for the sparkle of a quartzite vein, the scattered depressions of a long-rotted Paiute village, some hint of treasure, some sign they might point to and say, "There!"

They dug up thunder eggs, opals, petrified wood, fist-sized agates that seemed to emit a foggy light, like tiny suns breaking through a cloud. In a grotto with a small spring bubbling from it, they discovered a deer skull encased in rose quartz. And in the Mt. Mazama ash—as hard-packed as kiln-cooked clay—they found fossils of all sorts, of leaves and clams and ferns. After they filled their Bronco and drove the hundred miles back to Redmond, they cleaned their treasures and labeled them and put them on display so that their house resembled a museum.

In the center of their dining room table sat the rose-quartz skull, glowing pink, like a crystallized ham. Their bookcases and tables overflowed with precious stones, and their walls were crowded with velvet-lined display cases holding chert and obsidian projectile points—"*Not* arrowheads," Denis would say. "Arrowhead is an all-encompassing hack term that should *not* be used with reference to carving tools or spear and atlatal points." He talked like that, like a textbook—using words like prismatic and tetrahedron, occipital, Macedonian—and Elwood listened to him with the same polite disinterest he gave his tenth-grade teachers.

Which was not far off the mark. His father worked as an anthropology lecturer at Central Oregon Community College—though at first glance you would guess him a construction worker or a truck driver, not a scholar. Years ago he had played catcher for the Oregon State Beavers, and he looked like a catcher, at once too short and too wide for most clothes. When he got excited, he would repeatedly pound his hand into his palm as if it were the peach basket of a mitt.

Elwood loved and half-loved many things about him, but more than anything, he felt sorry for him. How else can you feel about a man who randomly bursts into tears—at the grocery store, the movies, the buffet at the Golden Corral—mourning his dead wife? What else can you do except follow him into the desert, where there were no enclosures, where everything seemed to draw a free breath, and where the two of them regularly escaped the present in a quest to dig up the past?

Elwood remembered his mother, Misty. He remembered her hair, a deep brown, almost black. He remembered how she always wore tank tops and how the bones came out of her shoulders like angel wings. He remembered his father constantly telling him how sick she was, how very sick. He remembered the medications—the Prozac, the Lithium, the green-and-white pills meant to tame the yo-yo effect of her bipolar condition—and how they sometimes made her act drunk, made her dizzy, made her slur her words. She would stroke his cheek and look at him with her eyes half-lidded, like a set of collapsing moons, and say, "My Elwood. Thank God for my Elwood." He remembered her laughing one instant, sobbing the next—one time lurching up from the dinner table with sudden tears on her cheeks, sweeping the turkey off its platter, onto the floor, because his father said it tasted "a bit dry, but good."

And he remembered, finally, the night she shook him awake and said, "You know I love you, right?" Somewhere between waking and dreaming, he saw her hovering above him in the dark and he said, "Yeah, Mom. Love you, too." She left him then and he lay there, still tangled in his dreams' cobwebs, realizing too late—after he tossed away the covers, after he hurried down the hall, down the stairs, after he heard the snap of the rifle—that something was wrong.

She left him a red carnation of brain matter on the wall, and on the kitchen table she left him a letter, its handwriting so sharp and hurried it reminded him of barbed wire. "I'm so sorry," it read. "And I know that doesn't mean anything. I know that's just a bunch of shitty words. But I'm really truly sorry."

It didn't make any sense. *She* didn't make any sense. He tore the letter up and let its pieces flutter into the toilet, but six months later the words remained imprinted on his brain like the patterns of a long-dead leaf, fossilized by the intense pressure of the moment.

Summers in Eastern Oregon, the wind blows in heated gusts, like the breath of a big animal. The July day Elwood and Denis discovered the dead Indian, to keep the seething grit from their eyes and lungs, they wore sunglasses and tied wet bandanas around their faces as bandits would.

They were hiking through a shallow canyon when they noticed among its basalt pillars a six-foot notch with a cool wind blowing from it, indicating depth. This wind brought with it a low drone, like someone blowing across the mouth of an open bottle. They clicked on their flashlights and ducked inside, and the notch opened up into a cave over a hundred-feet deep and thirty-feet wide.

They took off their sunglasses and bandanas in a hurry. Here, breathing was like drinking from a cellar floor puddle, a taste both cool and mineraly and tinged with mold. Their flashlights spotlighted the many suns and rattlesnakes and antelope and men with gigantic penises that covered the walls. Some were pictographs—colored blends of ocher and blood and berry juices—and some were petroglyphs, crudely chipped into the stone. Above all this hung many bats, chirping softly in their upside-down sleep, their brown bodies tangled together and moving so that the cave seemed a living thing.

"Man," Elwood said, and Denis said, "Wow."

Denis took out some butcher paper and held it against a petroglyph and rubbed it lightly with a crayon. The image of a pig or a bear or a dog—something—transferred onto the paper, and he rolled it up and put it in a plastic tube.

It wasn't long before they prostrated their bodies and began to dig. Their fingers had darkened and thickened from so much time in the desert, and they used them now, along with their trowels, to claw away the soil.

For the next several hours they filled their backpacks with the cave soil—so cool and black with guano—and carried it outside, dumping it in a pile that grew larger as the cave grew deeper. They discovered a seed cache, a thick layer of charcoal, obsidian chips, and a collection of bones, so broken they no longer had names. Then Elwood's trowel scraped across something smooth and brown.

"Dad," he said. "I think I've got something here."

The Indian had been buried upright, in a fetal position. A soft cocoon of dust and papery skin surrounded its brown bones. Elwood and Denis whisked away the soil, revealing first the skull's round crown—erratically haired—and then the hollows of its eyes, and then its shriveled nose, its teeth showing in an eternal snarl.

The more they unearthed, the more agitated Denis became. He pounded his fist into his palm, his cheeks glowing a painful red, his breath coming in big gusts as if some desert storm brewed within him. From the look on his face, Elwood could not tell if his father was blissfully happy or simply afraid.

"Dad?" he said. "You okay?"

Denis ran a hand across his face, leaving dirt there, and said, "Are you kidding? This is unbelievable. I'm in Paleolithic heaven, buddy." Despite his apparent enthusiasm, his voice struck Elwood as robotic, insincere, as a gray thing that swallowed emotion and gave nothing back.

Buried with the Indian were a pipe, a knife, an atlatal, a pair of moccasins, and a decayed leather robe braided with elk teeth. Denis and Elwood took everything.

They never thought about the legality or the *rightness* of what they did. They only knew that it brought them pleasure, somehow—taking these things, these hidden treasures, and making them their own.

It was nearly night when they left and a massive flapping followed them as hundreds of bats escaped the cave, like ashes blown from a chimney, riding the hot gusts into the purpling sky until they were lost from sight.

Their house was an ordinary house—a tan two-story box with plastic siding—except that it was full of dead things. Bones and fossils, tools from long-dead tribes, and now, a mummified Paiute Indian. Denis carried the body across the threshold as you would a bride, proudly, staring down at the thing in his arms as if it held great promise.

He could not decide where he would put the Indian. On the end table in the corner of the living room? Perched on top of the television, the refrigerator? Or how about... Denis removed the rose-quartz deer skull from the dining room table and replaced it with the corpse... how about here?

Elwood watched all this with a vague sense of disgust, and when his father asked him what he thought, he said, "I don't really like it anywhere. I don't really want it in the house at all."

Denis gave him a look, like: why on earth not?

Because of the dresses hanging in your closet, the perfume in the bathroom, the photographs staring at me from the mantel, the spackled section of wall where the bullet lodged itself like a seed. Because this house is full of too much death already, is what Elwood wanted to say, but didn't.

"It's a dead body, Dad. It's creepy."

"Hmm," Denis said and looked at the Indian as if for the first time. It sat on the table, its bones shining dully beneath the chandelier, like some spirit summoned by séance. "Maybe you've got a point." He scooped up the Indian—it was quite small, weighing ten, fifteen pounds at most—and sort of rocked it in his arms, peering around, seeking a place for it.

"I tell you what," he said. "If it bothers you that much, I'll keep it in my bedroom. Locked up tight. Okay? Don't you think that's a good place for it?"

From where he stood, some five feet away, Elwood could smell the Indian. It smelled like mothballs and old fruit. One of its eyes was pinched tightly closed—the overlying skin a greenish black color, like that of a diurnal bird—while the other eye was a gaping black hole. From this Elwood felt he was being watched.

-|- |-

Ten days after Misty died—the middle of February—Denis demanded Elwood come outside and play catch. "But it's freezing," Elwood said, and
Denis said, "So put on a fucking coat." Elwood had never heard his father
swear: he did as he was told.

Snow fell when they faced each other across the front lawn, the grass
frozen and crunching beneath their feet. They began to lightly toss the ball
back and forth, and then their muscles limbered and their aim improved
and the speed of the ball increased, until they were hurling it at each other,
throwing as hard as they could, as if their lives depended on it. They would
seek out the ball with their mitts, zapping it from the air, pocketing its
speed, and then—with a full windup, a big windmill motion—they would
whip it back in the direction it came from. The snow grew thicker, the air
colder, and before long, their hands went numb, and they could hardly see
the ball as it sizzled through all that whiteness. Cars slowed to watch them,
the drivers no doubt smiling at first, and then gasping, saying, "My word,"
when they realized they were not witnessing a snowball fight but something else entirely.

Then Elwood got struck in the forehead with such force his sinuses
bled out his nose and an immediate lump rose between his eyebrows.
Denis said, "I'm sorry. Jesus, am I sorry," and carried Elwood inside and
cleaned his face with a cold washcloth and helped him to bed and placed
an ice pack over his eyes.

Since her suicide, they had not talked about Misty, but now they did.
There was something about hurting his son that made Denis feel so guilty,
he wanted, he *needed* to bring out a hurt of his own. "Elwood?" he said.
"You want to hear something terrible?"

Elwood did not. Every sound, every bit of light, seemed to intensify the
red throbbing behind his eyes. But he listened, and his father finally said,
"I more than once wished she was dead." He laughed quietly, wretchedly.
"You know how it is, you get in a fight, you see some beautiful woman on
the street, and you think terrible things? You think: *Man,* how great would
it be if tomorrow the wife died of brain cancer or whatever. You don't really
mean it, but you think it." He blew a sigh out his nose. "It's awful, I know."

There followed a long silence, and then Elwood took off the ice pack
and locked eyes with his father before reaching out and taking his hand
and asking if he, too, felt weighed down by like, say, fifty pounds of grief?

"Yeah," his father said, his eyes stained yellow as if exposed to something toxic. "More like a hundred-forty."

This was the last they spoke of Misty, except to occasionally say, "Jeez, do I miss her." There was an understanding between them. They had both lost the love of their lives, and a bond like that makes words more often than not unnecessary. She was always there, between them, like an awkward silence Denis sought to fill, first with baseball, then boxing, hunting, fishing, Chuck Norris movies, and finally, the desert. Here they would peel away the soil and smash open rocks and loot the dead for as long as it took them to answer the question: What next?

The Monday after they returned from Christmas Valley, Elwood thought he heard voices coming from his parents' room. He peeked inside and saw his father sitting on the edge of his bed, and next to him, like some primordial stuffed animal, the Indian.

Without Misty, the garden had gone wild. Dandelions and crabgrass took over the sod, weeds choked away all the flowers except the sunflowers, and morning glory and kudzu vines groped their way up the house, to the roof, tangling their way across the second-story window Denis stared out of now.

The leafy vines shaded the room, and when the breeze blew, a flashing green and yellow light shuddered across Denis and the Indian, and he stared at the window as if it were a television, his mouth agape, as if he were hypnotized by it.

"Dad?"

Denis snapped shut his mouth and looked at Elwood as if he didn't recognize him. "I didn't hear you," he said in the too-loud voice he sometimes used on the telephone. "You spooked me." He protectively put his arm around the Indian and drew it a little closer to him. Some blackness remained where it had sat before.

"Dad, I thought you taught class on Mondays?"

His forehead creased. "That's correct," he said. "I do." He lifted his arm and examined his wristwatch, and then his arm continued its journey up so that he could squeeze the bridge of his nose. "Dang."

Sometimes his father looked emotional enough to kiss Elwood on the mouth. Other times—such as right now—his eyes seemed unfocused, his words distant, as if he were someplace else entirely. This had been happening more and more often—until his standard state of mind was elsewhere and nowhere.

Missing the occasional class was par for the course. No big deal, Elwood thought. Nothing to worry about.

Then Denis began to paint. He bought a crate of salmonberries at the farmers' market and with a mortar and pestle he mashed them, filling a big bowl. He added to this blood—brought out of his thumb by a tack—and then carpenter's glue, which thickened the mix into a bright red paste. He applied it to the living room walls with his fingers and with a stick whose end he hammered and chewed into a bristly brush, painting animals and hunters and suns and strange geometric patterns. Above the couch, over the spackled section of wall, he painted a crude rendering of Misty, so red she seemed on fire.

He did all this with the Indian seated on the La-Z-Boy recliner, supervising, and when Elwood came home from baseball practice and saw his father's hands gloved in blood, when he saw the murals swirling around him, he could only say, "Dad?"

Pizza Hut was where Elwood worked part-time over the summer—in the back, since he didn't like dealing with customers. Here, the conveyer-belt oven blasted heat, a heat so tremendous Elwood imagined it as the source of the Eastern Oregon winds. With temperatures hovering around one hundred degrees, he would sweat through his clothes and season pans with cornmeal and flour, garlic and salt, and he would stretch the refrigerated dough balls, at first caressing them—sometimes imagining them into boobs—and then squeezing, kneading, tossing them with an artful flick of his wrist—up—fitting each pie perfectly into its pan, and then painting it with sauce and cheese and meats and vegetables.

He liked it. He got lost in the heat and the repetitive motions.

His daze broke when from the front register came a shout: "Elwood! Hey, Elwood!" His manager, Joanne, an overweight grandmother with a cigarette voice, was motioning to him with one hand and to his father with the other.

His father stood across the counter, waving, his face painted with what Elwood recognized as baseball grease. Six black stripes started at his eyes and ended at his hairline like tall eyelashes or backward tear trails. His chin and cheeks were patterned with swirling designs, the kind a cartoonist would use to indicate wind.

Elwood wiped the sweat off his face with his forearm and went to him. "What are you doing here, Dad?"

"I always come here." Which was true. He often dropped by during Elwood's shift. "Just saying hello."

Elwood noticed some people in the buffet line staring. "But what are you *doing* here . . . like *that!* Like it's Halloween."

"Pretty cool, huh?" He smiled and touched his face lightly and checked his fingers for paint. "I'll do you later, if you want."

"I don't think so, Dad."

"Okay." They stood there a moment, just looking at each other, and then Denis said, "Hey, I just wanted to let you know I'm going to a bar tonight. I won't be home when you get home."

"You? A bar?" Elwood would not have been more surprised if his father said the world was flat and cows came from outer space.

"I know this may come as a shock to you, Elwood, but I need to have fun. I need to intermingle with people. People of the opposite sex. It's part of the healing process."

"Whatever. I don't care." Which was not entirely true, but Elwood felt more stunned than upset. "But you can't go like *that*. You'll get beat up."

"It's Cowboys and Indians Night down at the Wounded Soldier Tavern. I'm just adhering to dress code." Here he winked, and Elwood noticed the Atlanta Braves shirt, the fringed buckskin pants, and the moccasin bedroom slippers his father wore. "I'll see you later, bucko." With that he patted his mouth with his hand and made a woo-woo noise and rain-danced his way down the aisle and out the door.

Later that night Denis came home with a woman.

From his bed, propped up on his elbow, Elwood heard them laughing in the kitchen and then whispering in the hallway as they tiptoed past him and clicked closed the bedroom door.

There followed a great deal of moaning. Elwood felt simultaneously aroused and disgusted. The bedsprings began to chirp, the headboard began to thud against the wall—and in her final excited release, the woman made these *yee-yee-yee* noises that reminded Elwood of coyotes barking.

His mind was still hazy from sleep when he shuffled downstairs for breakfast and saw his mother in the kitchen, doing dishes, bending her knees and singing quietly, a sort of undersong to the bluegrass playing on the radio.

She was lovely to look at, her dark rolling hair and soft brown eyes.

Hello, Mom—Elwood thought—Did you know I just can't seem to get you out of my head? Everywhere I look *there you are*—at the grocery store where they sell mangoes, your favorite fruit, and in the woods where I see the columbine you might have stuck in vases. And now you have returned to your kitchen, miraculously reincarnated, making me think that night with the rifle was nothing more than an elaborate joke, a dummy covered in ketchup.

One year later and here is the punch line: Dad and I can't get along without you.

His mother turned to grab a dishcloth. When she turned she turned into an Indian woman who dried a coffee cup. Last night flashed through his mind—he could hardly believe what had happened *happened*—and she blew on a dirty spot, her lips pursing into kissable goodness, and Elwood wished more than anything he were that cup.

She noticed him standing there and clicked off the radio. "Morning," she said, and he said, "Hi."

Her hair was long and black and her face was round and brown. She was pretty, Elwood thought, but a different sort of pretty. Not as pretty as his mother, but close.

She wore blue jeans and an untucked white blouse, wrinkled across its bottom from being tucked in. She wiped her hand off on her thigh and held it out. He took it and she shook like a man would—like: let's see who can squeeze harder.

She said her name was Kim White Owl, from the Warm Springs Reservation. "You guys are messy, huh? Hardly a clean dish in the house."

Elwood looked at the counter, where fruit flies swarmed around the pile of dirty dishes. Mostly he and his father ate off paper plates or over the sink, so they wouldn't have to wash anything.

"What's with your house?" she said. "What's with all this stuff?" She poured coffee into her cup—the sunflower cup his mother always drank from—and sort of toasted it at the walls, where the projectile points hung in fanlike displays, and then at the adjacent living room, where blood-red murals crowded every corner of wall, where beaded moccasins and a mortar-and-pestle and an atlatal and a dozen other artifacts covered the bookshelves and end tables.

"Is my dad here?"

"He went to get cinnamon rolls. He said you liked cinnamon rolls." She had this husky quality to her—a uniform layer of fat beneath which muscles moved—that to Elwood made her seem equally suited for hard labor or tender sex. "So tell me, where'd you guys get all this stuff?"

"How long ago did my dad leave?"

"I don't know. Twenty, thirty minutes. Long enough for me to get dressed and make coffee and poke around." She slurped her coffee and sat down at the table and scooted a chair toward him with her bare foot. "Sit down, why don't you. Take a load off. You drink coffee?" He shook his head, no, and sat next to her. He could feel her eyes on him, but couldn't meet them. He concentrated instead on the rose-quartz deer skull, the way it sparkled under the sun shining through the window. "You're a handsome kid. You look a lot like your old man."

When she didn't say anything else, he said, "Thanks."

From the garage came the noise of the door rumbling up and the Bronco pulling in, and Kim said, "Speak of the devil."

They both stared at the far end of the kitchen, waiting for the door there to open, and when it did, Denis hurried in with a brown grocery bag clutched to his chest. "Hey," he said, his eyes jogging between them, settling on Elwood. "You're up."

An uncomfortable silence filled the kitchen, along with the smells of cinnamon and butter warming in the microwave, as Denis prepared their plates and poured orange juice and coffee. His war paint had faded and smeared so that his face looked bruised, shadowy.

He dropped a rolled-up newspaper on the table and Kim took the rubber band off it and spread it between her thumb and forefinger. She then let her head fall between her knees and whipped it back, grabbing her hair into a ponytail. This made her face appear even rounder.

She wants us to see her, Elwood thought. She wants us to see her clenched jaw and narrowed eyes, to know we're in trouble.

The microwave beeped and Denis pulled from it a steaming paper plate with three rolls on it. When he set one on Elwood's plate, and then on Kim's, she said, "You know what I'd like to know?" Denis didn't answer, but kept his eyes on her. He knew something was coming—and then it came. "I'd like to know how two white boys ended up owning a bunch of museum-quality redskin shit they don't have any right owning." She said this softly, calmly, which made her seem all the more threatening, somehow.

Denis took a step away from her and said, "I don't know how to answer that." There were weird pauses in his speaking, as if he was out of breath.

She pointed a thick brown finger at him, and her face twisted into a grotesque scowl. "You better learn how to answer. You better learn." She began to punctuate every few words by stabbing her finger into the table. "Come tomorrow, I'm thinking you might have some elders and some tribal police asking some pretty serious fucking questions you better learn how to answer."

Elwood watched his father's hands ball into fists, and he wondered, would he strike her? But he only lowered his head, concentrating on his shoes.

Kim continued, the anger mounting in her voice. "I mean, what were you thinking? Bringing *me* here?" Elwood wondered the very same thing. "You *want* to get caught or something? Or you just so dumb and horny you hoped I wouldn't notice?" Here she put her hands to either side of her head, incredulous. "*Or* you think I'm going to be all, like, wow and shit. Like happy to see your little museum?" She snorted like a horse after a hot run. "You gotta be kidding me." She jumped from her chair with such force it fell backward. "Where's my shoes? Where's my jacket?"

She walked in an aimless circle and then went to the closet next to the staircase. She jerked it open and screamed. Sitting among the coats and boots was the dead Indian, snarling at them, monkeylike in its huddled brown shape.

She put a hand between her breasts, over her heart, as if to calm it. She seemed to spit at them when she spoke. "You dug up a grave?" She faced the closet again and stared at the thing. "What's wrong with you?" She examined the corpse another moment and then all of a sudden scooped it up and more ran than walked to the front door.

Denis hurried after her. "No! Leave that alone! Misty!"

She yanked open the front door and the house grew a little brighter. Stepping outside, she yelled over her shoulder, "Who you calling Misty? What the hell is wrong with you?"

Denis followed her outside, and Elwood followed him. The sky was cloudless, the air so bright everything seemed flat and bleached of color. A hot wind blew and ruffled their lawn's long grass, bending it flat, swirling it in ever-changing directions. Kim cut through it, moving toward her beater Ford pickup parked in the driveway.

"Give me the body," Denis said, his voice cracking with emotion. He grabbed the back of her shirt but she kept moving, even when it tore a little. "Please. *Please.*" He was begging her, and right then Elwood felt more than sorry for his father: he felt disgusted and embarrassed by him. "I'll give you money. As much as you want."

Kim reached the pickup and turned, a red flush burning through her brown skin, and at that moment, Elwood thought, if you sort of closed your eyes and made everything blurry, she looked so much like his mother it was creepy. "You're sick," she said. "You gotta let the dead rest."

Denis lunged at her and they began to wrestle with the corpse, their hands clasping it, tugging, and then—with a soft crack, like a popped knuckle—it broke in half. Chunks of skin and bone and the dust of decayed organs littered the driveway and they all gathered around staring at the mess, as it moved this way and that, blown by the wind, whirling and changing across the concrete so that it looked like some strange text, some hidden message left by the corpse they would never understand.

Gardener of Heart

Bradford Morrow

I know that I have to die like everyone else, and that displeases me, and I know every human born so far has died except for those now living, and that distresses me and makes most distinctions . . . look false or absurd.

—Harold Brodkey

espite the grief I felt as my train chased up the coast toward home, I had to confess that after many years of self-imposed exile it might be strangely comforting to see the old town again, walk the streets where she and I grew up. Imagining the neighborhood absent its finest flower, its single best soul, was unthinkable. Yet it seemed that my visiting our various childhood haunts and willing Julie's spirit—whatever *that* is—a prolonged residence in each of these places would be salutary for her. And cathartic for me. We had made a pact when we were young that whoever died first would try to stay alive in essence, palpably alive, in order to wait for the other. Death was somehow to be held in abeyance until both halves of our twins' soul had succumbed. Sure, we were kids, given to crazy fantasies.

But the covenant still held, no matter how unspiritual, how skeptical I had become in the interim. Indeed, I had only the vaguest idea of what to do. Just go. Walk, look, breathe, since she could not.

For some reason, I could envision the mortuary home in radiant detail. A breathtaking late-eighteenth-century neoclassical edifice of hewn stone, two imposing stories surmounted by a slate roof and boasting a porch with fluted marble Doric columns. Huge oaks and horse chestnuts surrounded it where it perched on one of the highest hills in town which, aside from the steeples of local Presbyterian and Catholic churches that rose to almost similar heights, dwarfed everything if not everyone in their vicinity. To think that Julie and I, who grew up several doors down the block from this mysterious temple of death, used to love to climb those trees, play kickball on its velvet lawns, or hide in the carefully groomed hedges, peeping in the windows to giggle at the whimpering adults inside. What did we know? Crying was for babies and the unbrave, Julie and I agreed. We laughed ourselves sick and pissing in the greenery, and now, as I imagined, she was lying embalmed, a formal lace dress her winding sheet, in the very wainscoted chapel whose many mourners gave us so much perverse pleasure to observe over the years of our youth.

Mother would be present at the service, and our father with his third wife, Maureen. Probably a crowd of Julie's friends would be there, few of whom, actually none of whom, I had ever met. Parents aside, I doubted I'd be recognized, so much time having passed since I bared my émigré's face in the unrocking cradle of noncivilization, as I deemed home. If only I could attend her rites invisibly, I thought, as the Acela flew by ocean-edge marshes punctuated by osprey stilt nests and anomalous junkyards where sumac grew through the windshields of gutted trucks. As Jul's only brother, her best childhood friend, I knew what my sibling responsibilities were, even though a part of me presumed she'd find it apt, no, downright hilarious, if I chose to mourn her from our cherished outpost in shrubbery beneath the casement windows.

When I left home three decades ago, I left with collar up and feet pointed in one direction only: away. By some ineffable irony, Julie's staying made my great escape possible. Being the younger twin—she was delivered a few minutes before I breached forth—it was as if some part of me safely stayed behind with her in Middle Falls, even as a wayward spark in her soul came along with me to New York and far beyond. Julie wasn't the wandering type, though, and after college and a mandatory trip to Europe, she returned home with the idea of seeing our mom through a tough divorce (where's an easy one? I asked her) then simply stayed, as if reattaching roots severed temporarily by some careless shovel. For my part, when I left, I was gone. There were many reasons for this, an awful lot of them now irrelevant thanks to, among so much else, scathing but unscathed time.

By informal agreement my father and I rarely spoke, and my mother and I only talked on holidays or during family crises—which are essentially one and the same, by my lights—so when she called on a nondescript day that celebrated nothing, I knew, even before she gave me the news, that something was badly amiss. Her voice, raspy as a mandolin dragged across macadam, hoarse from years of passionate cigarette smoking, made her words nearly impossible to understand. If I hadn't known she wasn't a drinker I could have sworn she was totally polluted.

Your ... dead, she's ... you're, your sister's ...

I tried to slow her down, but she was weeping hysterically. Soon enough, I who had always scoffed at weepers became one, too. As tears swamped my eyes, I stared hard out my dirty office window across the rooftops and water towers of the city. A cloud shaped like a Chagall fiddler snatched up from his task of serenading blue farmwives and purple goats, and thrust unexpectedly into the blackening sky, moved slowly over the Hudson toward Jersey. My Julie was dead, my other half. I told my mother I'd be up on the morning train and as abruptly as our conversation, call it that, began, it ended.

Middle Falls lies midway between Rehoboth and Segreganset, east of East Providence, Rhode Island. A place steeped, like they say, in history. One of the diabolical questions that perplexed me and Julie when we were kids was that if there was a *middle* falls, where were the falls on either side? We knew that Pawtucket means Great Falls, and Pawtuxet means Little Falls. Yet while our narrow, timid waterfall did dribble near the main street of the village, where the stream paralleled a row of old brick-facade shops quaintly known as downtown, even in the wettest season it hardly deserved its designation as a waterfall. Nor, again, were there any neighboring falls. Be that as it may, Julie and I on many a summer afternoon took our fishing poles down there (never caught so much as a minnow), or paddleboats made with chunks of wood and rubber bands, and had a grand

time of it by the cold thin water. One of our little jokes was that Middle
Falls meant if you're caught in the middle you fall. Our nickname for the
place was Muddlefuls.

Julie, much like myself, was neither unusually attractive nor unattractive. We were plain, with faces one wouldn't pick out in a crowd. Both of
us had brown hair and eyes, with fair skin. We were each slender and tall,
given to gawkiness. Since her hair was sensibly short and mine a little long,
I suppose that in a low-lit room it would have been possible to mistake one
of us for the other. Like me, my twin sister had the thinnest legs in the
world, bless her heart, with gnarly knees to boot. She hated hers—wish-
bones, she figured them, or scarecrow sticks—and as a result never went
along with friends to sunbathe on the Vineyard or out on Nantucket. Mine
were always a matter of indifference to me, and I never bothered with the
seashore, anyway. Two modest people with even temperaments and in
good health, entering early middle age, sailing forward with steady dispo-
sitions, one a homebody, the other an inveterate expatriate, neither of us
ever married. Never even came close. Some of our aversion to the holy
state of matrimony undoubtedly was a function of our response to our father's fickle philandering and the train wreck of a wife he left behind with
her lookalike rug rats. At least for Julie all such concerns, from skinny legs
to a broken family, had come to an end. Given the chance, how I'd have
loved to take the old man aside after the funeral and let him know, just for
once, how very much Jul and I always resented his failure to father us. As
the train pulled into the Providence station, I found myself hoping that the
embalmer was instructed to go light on the makeup. Julie never wore lipstick or eyeliner or rouge when she was alive. What a travesty it would be
for her to enter eternity painted up like some Yoruba death mask.

The autumn leaves were at peak, and those that had let go of their
branches drifted like lifeless butterflies across the road in the coolwarm
breeze. I made the drive from Providence—bright, rejuvenated capital of
the Ocean State—to Middle Falls, and as I reached the outskirts of town
I was seized by an intuition of something both unexpected and yet longed
for, weirdly anticipated. It was as if I were driving from the hermetic present into the wily certainty of the past. Providence, with its sparkling glass
office towers and fashionable storefronts, was transfigured from the seedy
backwater whose very name held it in contempt when I was a boy, while
the scape around Middle Falls appeared unchanged. There were no other

cars on the road so I could slow down a little, take in the rolling vistas of our childhood, Jul's and mine, and luxuriate in this New England fall day. A flock of noisy Canada geese cleaved the otherwise unarticulated deep blue sky. Look there, Bob Trager's pumpkin patch, Trager's where we used to pick our own this time of year to carve into jack-o'-lanterns. Sentimental as the thought was, not to mention foolish, I wished we could walk here again just once, scouting plump ones that most looked like human heads. And, feeling a little silly in fact, I pulled over and rambled into the field among the pumpkins attached to the sallow green umbilicals of their dying stalks, and might even have bought a couple, had anybody been manning the farm stand.

I called out, *Anyone here?*

A dog barked, unseen in a nearby copse of silver birches whose flittering leaves were golden wafers, barked incessantly, madly, in response. Unnerved, I traipsed back to where the rental was parked beside the road. In a moment that felt dreamlike as déjà vu, as I stepped into the car I mistook my foot for Julie's—by that, I mean, her shoe was on my foot. No question but my grief, which I had been holding closer to my vest than I imagined, was weighing on me. On second glance the hallucination passed.

Hers was one of those deaths that leave the living in a state of questioning shock. How could this happen to someone so healthy? Yesterday she was alive, vibrant, bright. Today she's mute, still, dead. Gone in a literal heartbeat. Before my mother and I hung up, I did manage to extract from her the cause of death. Brain aneurysm. Like a blood adder born inside a rose, a fleshy pink rose, or one of those peculiar coxcomb flowers, a lethal serpent which when suddenly awakened understood that in order to live and breathe it must gnaw its way to freedom. How long this aneurysm had been lying dormant in Julie's cerebrum none of us will ever know. Her death, the doctor assured our mother, was almost instantaneous. That my sister didn't suffer a protracted demise is some consolation, though one wonders what happens in a person's mind during the irrevocable instant that constitutes the *almost* instantaneous. It's the *almost* that is appalling in its endless possibilities.

Images from days long past continued to accrue beyond the windshield, like those on some inchoate memory jug, and I knew that while they were exhilarating as an unanticipated archaeological find, they were also a clear manifestation of mourning. Although I was anxious to get home—I'd be staying in my sister's room, since my bedroom had long ago been converted into a solarium in which Julie tended her heirloom orchids—I was compelled to drive even more slowly, in order to take in every detail of what I had so studiously dismissed over half my life.

A canary yellow and emerald kite in the shape of a widemouthed carp, or Ming dragon, ascended as if on cue above the turning trees, and while I couldn't see the kid at the other end of its silvery string, I easily pictured myself and Julie behind the leaves, pulling and letting out more line. After all, we had a kite that looked a lot like it, way back when. I drove across a stone bridge, a fabled one when we were young, beneath which hunchbacks and trolls loitered in the dank shadows. (Several women accused of witchcraft were hung there in the middle of the century before last, in good old Commonwealth of Massachusetts style.) My sister and I, left so often to our own devices, and admitted addicts of anything frightening or macabre, would egg each other on to wander down here in the twilight and throw taunting stones at the shadow people who lived beneath the bridge. Once, to our surprise, we interrupted a man under the embankment who chased us—yelping, his pants caught around his ankles—halfway home under the snickering stars. Here was a telephone pole we had once tied a boy to, whom we'd caught shooting at crows, our favorite bird, behind an abandoned canning factory. I could still hear his indignant, pleading screams in the wind that whistled at the car window.

Now I saw the church spires above the sea of trees, then one by one the charming clapboard houses of our childhood, and above all that mortuary roof, gun-barrel gray against the jay-blue sky. There were the glorious smells of leaves burning; a garden of dying asters whose yellow centers were catafalques for exhausted wasps in their final throes; the blood-red cardinal acrobating about in his holly bush. Julie and I loved these things, and today felt no different than decades ago. If I didn't know better, I'd have sworn that time had somehow collapsed and, as a result, the many places my work as an archaeologist had taken me—from Zimbabwe to Bonampak, Palenque to the Dordogne—were as unreal as my campus office cluttered with a lifetime of artifacts and books, my affection for film noir and vintage Shiraz, and everything else I had presumed was specifically a part of my existence. My whole adult life, in other words, was an arc of fabrication. Oddly fraudulent was how I felt, unfledged, and in the midst of all this, also abruptly—how else to put it?—liberated. Liberated from what precisely, I couldn't say. But the feeling was strong. I reemerged from this small reverie to find myself staring at Julie's pale and slender hands where they lay like wax replicas on the steering wheel. The magnitude of my loss had plainly gotten the better of me. Breathe, I thought. Pull yourself together. And again the world returned to me, or I to it. I pressed forward toward the turnoff that would take me uphill, up the block where our mother awaited me.

Julie did have a boyfriend once. Peter was his name. Peter Rhodes. He was our runaround friend since forever, lived across the street from our house, was all but family. Peter was more or less expected, by everyone who knew him and Julie, to become my sister's husband. Had it happened, it would have been one of those sandbox to cemetery relationships that are inconceivable these days. Julie and I had the curbs in on Peter Rhodes from the beginning, however, and in my heart I understood they were never meant to be. Still, we did love to work the Ouija board in the basement, by candlelight, little punks goading the universe to cough up its intimate secrets that lay just there beneath our fingertips. Not to mention overnights, when we camped out in a makeshift carnival tent of Hudson Bays and ladder-back chairs. We played hide and seek, freeze tag, Simon Says, all those games that children love. We learned how to ride bikes together, and together we slogged through adolescence. Peter took Julie to the prom when we graduated from Middle Falls High, and I, in my powder blue tuxedo and dun brown shoes, went with Priscilla Chao, a sweet, shy girl who was as happy to be asked as I was relieved that she, or anyone, would bother to accompany me; not that I wanted to go in the first place. We four stood at the back of the gymnasium, far away from the rock band, watching classmates flailing like fools beneath oscillating lights, as our teachers stood nodding by the long sheeted tables set with punch bowls and chips and cheese wheels. In retrospect, I realize how normal—for unassimilateds—Jul and I must have seemed to anyone who bothered to watch. Throughout those years we subtly kept poor Peter at a near-far distance, especially when it came to some of our more transgressive ventures—indeed, he never knew about our passion for the mortuary home, its mourners, hearse driver, gun-for-hire pallbearers, and all the rest. Doubtless, he would have thought us not a little odd if he had any idea about our graveyard rambles under the full moon, headstones sparkling naughtily under their berets of fresh-fallen snow. But then no one truly knew Julie and me. A bond formed in the womb was, it seemed, as impossible for others to fathom as to break. I believe Peter married a nice woman he met during his stint as a Peace Corps volunteer, having fled Middle Falls in the wake of Julie's rejection of his marriage proposal. To this day, I never wished Peter Rhodes ill. I know Julie didn't, either.

Like she, I went to college. A scholarship to Columbia saved me from having to lean on my father for tuition money—I'd sooner have committed myself to an assembly line in a clothes-hanger plant. After dabbling in history and the arts, I settled into the sciences and knew early on that archaeology was my calling. Just as Audubon made his sketches from *nature morte,* I believed the best portrait of a person, or civilization, was only accomplishable after the death knell tolled. Schliemann and Layard were like gods to me, just as Troy and Nineveh were secular heavens. Conze at Samothrace; Andrae in Assyria. Grad work at Oxford was floated on more scholarships, and I'd truly discovered my métier, I felt. A first excursion to Africa, and I was all but over the moon.

As with most disciplines, archaeology is fundamentally the art of attempting to understand ourselves through understanding others. All cultures eventually connect. Language, myth, variant customs, mores, bones, are like cultural continental drifts. Put them on a reverse-time trajectory and they relink. They become a single supercontinent called Pangea. My inability, my stubborn refusal to admit to having a true familial home, an ancestral hearth from which I set forth on my specialized journeying, I'd always considered a hidden asset. I had a knack for entering others' homes, that is to say ruins and burial sites, and quickly understand, sometimes even master, the essential *idiom* of a locale and its inhabitants. Middle Falls I simply never understood. With Julie gone, if I wanted to comprehend this place of personal origin, I might be forever locked out. All the more reason to honor our covenant. Perhaps, through my twin as medium, I might come to some understanding of who I'd been and was no more.

The house was empty. I assumed our mother had gone out somewhere to finalize arrangements. The front door was unlocked, a practice poor Mom inaugurated after the divorce, saying there wasn't anything left to steal here (morose absurdity, but whatever), so I let myself in. Odd, she'd obviously been baking cookies, Julie's beloved peanut butter and pecans, as the whole house was redolent with the warm scent. Maybe she planned to host a small gathering of mourners at the house after the rites. Upstairs in my old room, I saw Julie's private garden of potted orchids and exotic herbs was as opulent as she'd described it in letters and during our monthly phone conversations (it didn't matter how distant I was, I never failed to call her). The scent, it struck me, was precisely what heaven should smell like, were there such a place. Fluid, rich, evocative, somehow soft. I closed my eyes and breathed this sensual air, and as I did, a wave of deep tranquillity washed through me. This tranquillity even had a color, a dense matte cream, into which I rose, or sank, it was hard to tell the difference. I believed I was crying, though the cognitive disconnect, however brief, wouldn't quite allow me to know this with certainty. The episode, like some epileptic seizure of the psyche, finally passed but not before delivering me another of the hallucinations I had been experiencing. As I turned to leave—flee, rather—the room, I caught sight of a vertiginous Julie, alive in the mirror on the wall behind a sinuously arched blooming orchid, her dark eyes as filled with hysteria as mine must have been. Then she was gone, replaced, as before, by myself—and yes, my eyes displayed a scouring dread, not without a tinge of sad disbelief. Nothing like this had ever happened to me, and if they weren't so eminently *real*, I'd have insisted to myself that these petit mals were strictly the effects of melancholy. But something else was in play about which I had no clear insight. Some incipient voice inside me suggested that the covenant Julie and I had made as children bore more authority than she and I'd imagined possible. Placing my overnight bag on her bed, I asked myself, Could she have managed to pull it off, to linger, to keep our childhood pact?

Voices downstairs brought me to my senses. I was about to shout to my mother that I'd arrived, when I realized I was hearing my father and Maureen, the last people on earth I needed to see just now. Like so many houses from the Victorian era, this one had a set of narrow back steps leading down to a pantry off the kitchen. Julie and I never tired of playing in this claustrophobic corridor, which was lit by octagonal stained-glass windows, and often used it, to our mother's exasperation, as an escape route when we happened to be hightailing it from some chore or punishment. Its usefulness in this regard was as valued now as then—having to confront my father at that moment would have qualified as both a chore and punishment—so I slipped quietly downstairs, and out the pantry door into the backyard.

Some clouds had intruded on the earlier pure blue above, and the temperature definitely had dropped since morning. I wished I could run back inside and grab the windbreaker I'd shoved into my bag in the city, but figured it wasn't worth the risk. Rolling down the sleeves of my shirt, I headed quickly across the lawn (needed mowing) and along a row of pin oaks whose leaves were ruddy red, like dyed leather. Other than the drone of distant machinery—a road crew clearing a fallen branch with a wood chipper, I guessed—the air was dead silent. Someone was burning a pile of brush nearby; a skein of transparent brownish gray floated across the middle air. Two girls, from out of nowhere, came running past me laughing wildly, paying no attention to me, nearly knocking me down in their great rush. It smelled a little like it might rain.

Once I was out of sight of the house, walking the next block over, I slackened my pace and contemplated, as best I could manage given the crosscurrents of what had been happening, what to do. Not that I needed to deliberate for long. My feet instinctively knew it was imperative to go to Middle Falls cemetery. The graveyard was in a meadow on the far side of the town's pathetic waterfall, and it involved crossing down past the main street where, I expected—rightly, it turned out—no one would notice me, John Tillman, Julie Tillman's brother who defected a lifetime ago. The soda shop we'd loved to frequent was, amazingly, still there. Katzman's, run by one of the few Jews in this largely Christian enclave, made the best egg creams north of Coney Island. Ancient but still alive, there behind the counter stood, I swore, Katzman himself, who had concocted for Julie every Saturday afternoon a superb monstrosity made with pistachio ice cream, green maraschino cherries, sprinkles, whipped cream, and salted peanuts. The thought of it still makes my spine tingle, but she loved it, and good old Katzman, too. I walked on, my head crowded with memories. There was the grocery market. There the post office. There was the combined barbershop and shoe store (its owner, Mr. Fry was his name, boasted of *head to toe service under one roof,* as I recollect). There was the package store whose proprietor was always lobbying, without success, for a repeal of the blue laws. And there was the florist where I'd stop on my way back to pick up a dozen calla lilies. It wasn't hard to picture my sister walking in and out of any of these places and, yes, I had to admit there was a misty comfort in village life. God knows, I'd seen trace evidence of such systemized culture clusters in my own fieldwork, and admired—from an objective distance of hundreds, or sometimes thousands, of years—the purity and practicality of intimate social configuration. In many ways it was a shame misty comfort never agreed with me, I thought, as I crossed the footbridge that led through another neighborhood and, finally, to the cemetery where Julie was to be buried. But one cannot change intrinsic self-truths, I didn't believe.

What did we love about this boneyard? For one, all the carved white stones, the cherubic faces of angels and upward-soaring doves, the bas-relief gargoyles, not to mention the glorious names and antique dates. The trees here were especially old and seemed to us repositories of special knowledge; Frazer knew all about this. Here was a place our minds could run as wild as the spirits of the dead. This was how we thought, two pale skinny children with no better friends than each other. I saw, quite soon, half a hundred yards away, the pile of freshly dug dirt I'd come looking for without really knowing it. I strode between grave markers to the earthen cavity into which my Julie would be lowered to begin the longest part of any human existence: eternal repose. I peered in, curious and frankly as un-inhibited as anyone who'd spent his time excavating artifacts of the long dead, and the desiccated, frozen, or bog-preserved remains of men whose hands had fashioned those very tools and trinkets. One always forgot how deep a contemporary North American grave is. My guess is that in our memories we fill them in a little, make them shallower, as if we might undo a bit the terminal ruination that is mortality. Against my archaeological in-stincts I kicked some soil back into the hole. Some queer corner of my soul concocted the idea that I ought to climb down into her sepulcher myself and spend a few speculative moments on my back, looking upward at the now fully overcast sky, try to commune with Julie in her future resting place while there was still the chance.

I didn't. Instead, I walked back to town, forgetting, in my sudden rush to climb the hill to the mortuary and view the corpse of my dear twin, to purchase the dozen lilies I'd wanted to lay at the foot of her coffin gurney, her penultimate berth. It seemed I was moving swiftly and slowly at the same time, thoughts streaming like an ironic spring melt under a harvest moon.

She and I were in a play together in high school once. *Love's Labour's Lost*. Julie was the Princess of France, and I, who coveted the role of King Ferdinand of Navarre, wasn't much of a thespian and wound up playing Costard, the clown. I can only remember one of her lines, which went, *To the death we will not move a foot,* which I naturally misinterpreted at the time to mean that, like Julie and myself, the princess had no intention of giving in to mortality. Later, I realized Shakespeare's message was quite different. All Julie's princess was trying to say was, well, *never.* As for my poor Costard, I can't remember a single word I worked so hard to memorize for the production. What made me think of this? Impossible to know, since the high school was located on the southeast edge of town and my walk from the cemetery in no way converged with it. I felt that my mind, which unlike my body wasn't used to wandering, was out of sync with itself.

Reentering the house by the pantry door, I found myself alone, the hollow ticking of the kitchen clock the only sound in the place. On the table lay a note, a memo in my mother's gracefully dated round handwriting, with the words *We've gone ahead up the hill, will meet you there, dear.* What had I been thinking? Here it was already half past four, and in my daydreamy meandering I had managed to miss the beginning of Julie's funeral. No time to change clothes. Informed by many summers' trampings up to the mortuary grounds, my feet intimately knew the path. As I made my way, I noticed the edges of my vision were blurred, causing me to believe I'd begun to weep again, just as I had back in the city when I first learned the news of my sister's death. But when I touched my eyes to brush away the tears, I found them dry. Though this was not the first intimation that something might be wrong with me, that I somehow seemed to have lost a crucial equilibrium without which consciousness makes little or no sense, it was the first of my hallucinations I could not ignore.

I climbed the hill with a quicker step, yet it was as if I approached my destination ever more unhurriedly. What was before me oddly receded. It felt like I was walking backward. All the while, my tearless weeping—or whatever caused my sight to smear—continued unabated, worsened actually, the neighborhood elms and oaks melting into watery pools of ocher, hazel, and every sort of red. I believe I blinked hard, several times, hoping to will away this tunneling vision. The great Victorian houses on either side of the block, dressed in their cheery gingerbread, were like shimmery globules of undifferentiated mass rising up toward the now gray ceiling of sky overhead. By sheer volition I managed to reach the top of the hill, where I left the sidewalk and made my way across the lawn toward the mortuary.

In the mid-eighties, I was invited to participate in a dig on the southern coast of Cyprus. The Greco-Roman port city of Kourian, which had been partially excavated in the thirties, but had since been untouched by grave robbers and classical archaeologists alike, was to be our site. Early on the morning of July 21st, in 365 AD, a massive earthquake leveled every structure in this seaside town even as it snuffed out the lives of its inhabitants in a matter of minutes. What few people may have survived the falling rubble were drowned in the monster tidal waves that followed. While we dug from room to room through the hive of attached stone houses, the discoveries made by the team were nothing shy of miraculous. The skeleton of a little girl, whom we named Camelia, was found next to the remains of a mule—her workmate, we presumed—in a stable adjacent to her bedroom. Coins littered the sandy floor, as well as glass from the jar that once held them. Here was a wrought copper volute lamp; here were amphorae. As we unearthed the physical record of this disaster, a tender intimacy developed between the members of our team and the victims of the quake. On our final day we made a discovery that was, for me at least, the most moving of any I'd ever witnessed. A baby cradled in its mother's arms, the woman in turn being embraced by a man who was clearly trying to shelter them both with his body. Such love and natural courage were present in these spooning bones. I could hardly wait to get Julie on a transatlantic line to tell her what we had found.

For reasons that will now never be wholly clear to me, I did decide, as I approached the mortuary with its imposing, if very fake, Doric columns, to attend my sister's funeral from the vantage of our old secret hiding place. Maybe I felt, deep down, I simply couldn't face my father. Perhaps I feared sitting next to my mother whose tears, no doubt, would be as real as they were copious. I don't know; it hardly matters. My vision, in any case, had only further disintegrated during the moments of my memory of the dig at Cyprus, and I had to wonder if I could manage to make myself presentable in front of others inside the funeral home. Pushing aside the hawthorn leaves, my hands splaying the shrubbery just as they might if I were wading into an ocean, I peeked through the window and saw, with what sight was left to me, the mourners within. A smaller group than I might have expected, since Julie had always been the more gregarious of the two of us. It was as if I could hear her voice whispering in my ear, just then, when I remembered my sister's response to that call I made telling her about the family in Kourian.

Over the years from time to time, she'd referred to me as a gardener of stones, but that day she told me she thought I was a gardener of heart. I liked that. It was the nicest thing anyone ever said to me, before or since. As the first drops of rain began to fall, and the crumbling margins of my vision grew inward toward the center of all that I could see, I felt a strong communion with the community of the many dead, and with my sister, too. My sister, Julie, who turned from where she sat in the front row nearest the casket and gazed at her shocked and vanishing brother in the window, her brother who offered her, as best he could, a smile of farewell.

Little Red's Tango

Peter Straub

LITTLE RED PERCEIVED AS A MYSTERY

What a mystery is Little Red! How he sustains himself, how he lives, how he gets through his days, what passes through his mind as he endures that extraordinary journey.... Is not mystery precisely that which does not yield, does not give access?

LITTLE RED, HIS WIFE, HIS PARENTS, HIS BROTHERS

Little is known of the woman he married. Little Red seldom speaks of her, except now and then to say, "My wife was half-Sicilian" or "All you have to know about my wife is that she was half-Sicilian." Some have speculated, though not in the presence of Little Red, that the long-vanished wife was no more than a fictional or mythic character created to lend solidity to his otherwise amorphous history. Years have been lost. Decades have been lost. (In a sense, an entire life has been lost, some might say Little Red's.)

The existence of a wife, even an anonymous one, does lend a semblance of structure to the lost years.

Half of her was Sicilian; the other half may have been Irish. "People like that you don't mess with," says Little Red. "Even when you mess with them, you don't *mess* with them, know what I mean?"

The parents are likewise anonymous, though no one has ever speculated that they may have been fictional or mythic. Even anonymous parents must be of flesh and blood. Since Little Red has mentioned, in his flat, dry Long Island accent, a term in the Uniondale High School jazz ensemble, we can assume that for a substantial period his family resided in Uniondale, Long Island. There were, apparently, two brothers, both older. The three boys grew up in circumstances modest but otherwise unspecified. A lunch counter, a diner, a small mom and pop grocery may have been in the picture. Some connection with food, with nourishment.

Little Red's long years spent waiting on tables, his decades as a "waiter," continue this nourishment theme, which eventually becomes inseparable from the very conception of Little Red's existence. In at least one important way, *nourishment* lies at the heart of the mystery. Most good mysteries are rooted in the question of nourishment. As concepts, nourishment and sacrifice walk hand in hand, like old friends everywhere. Think of Judy Garland. The wedding at Cana. Think of the fish grilled at night on the Galilean shore. A fire, the fish in the simple pan, the flickeringly illuminated men.

The brothers have not passed through the record entirely unremarked, nor are they anonymous. In the blurry comet-trail of Little Red's history, the brothers exist as sparks, embers, brief coruscations. Blind, unknowing, they shared his early life, the life of Uniondale. They were, categorically, brothers, intent on their bellies, their toys, their cars, and their neuroses, all of that, and attuned not at all to the little red-haired boy who stumbled wide-eyed in their wake. Kyle, the recluse; Ernie, the hopeless. These are the names spoken by Little Red. After graduation from high school, the recluse lived one town over with a much older woman until his aging parents bought a trailer and relocated to rural Georgia, whereupon he moved into a smaller trailer on the same lot. When his father died, Kyle sold the little trailer and settled in with his mother. The hopeless brother, Ernie, followed Kyle and parents to Georgia within six weeks of their departure from Nassau County. He soon found both a custodial position in a local middle school and a girlfriend, whom he married before the year was out. Ernie's weight, 285 pounds on his wedding day, ballooned to 350 soon after. No longer capable of fulfilling his custodial duties, he went on welfare. Kyle, though potentially a talented musician, experienced nausea and an abrupt surge in blood pressure at the thought of performing in public, so that source of income was forever closed to him. Fortunately, his only other talent, that of putting elderly women at their ease, served him well—his mother's will left him her trailer and the sum of $40,000, twice the amount bequested to her other two sons.

We should note that, before Kyle's windfall, Little Red periodically mailed him small sums of money—money he could ill-afford to give away—and that he did the same for brother Ernie, although Ernie's most useful talent was that of attracting precisely the amount of money he needed at exactly the moment he needed it. While temporarily separated from his spouse, between subsistence-level jobs and cruelly hungry, Ernie waddled a-slouching past an abandoned warehouse, was tempted by the presence of a paper sack placed on the black leather passenger seat of an aubergine Lincoln Town Car, tested the door, found it open, snatched up the sack, and rushed Ernie-style into the cobweb-strewn shelter of the warehouse. An initial search of the bag revealed two foil-wrapped cheese-burgers, still warm. A deeper investigation uncovered an eight-ounce bottle of Poland Spring water and a green cling-film-covered brick comprised of $2,300 in new fifties and twenties.

Although Ernie described this coup in great detail to his youngest brother, he never considered, not for a moment, sharing the booty.

These people are his immediate family. Witnesses to the trials, joys, despairs, and breakthroughs of his childhood, they noticed nothing. Of the actualities of his life, they knew less than nothing, for what they imagined they knew was either peripheral or inaccurate. Kyle and Ernie mistook the tip for the iceberg. And deep within herself, their mother had chosen, when most she might have considered her youngest son's life, to avert her eyes.

Little Red carries these people in his heart. He grieves for them; he forgives them everything.

WHAT HE HAS BEEN

Over many years and in several cities, a waiter and a bartender; a bass player, briefly; a husband, a son, a nephew; a dweller in caves; an adept of certain magisterial substances; a friend most willing and devoted; a reader, chiefly of crime, horror, and science fiction; an investor and day trader; a dedicated watcher of cable television, especially the History, Discovery, and Sci-Fi channels; an intimate of nightclubs, joints, dives, and after-hour she-beens, also of restaurants, cafés, and diners; a purveyor of secret knowl-edge; a photographer; a wavering candle-flame; a voice of conundrums; a figure of steadfast loyalty; an intermittent beacon; a path beaten through the undergrowth.

THE BEATITUDES OF LITTLE RED, I

Whatsoever can be repaid, should be repaid with kindness.

Whatsoever can be borrowed, should be borrowed modestly.

Tip extravagantly, for they need the money more than you do.

You can never go wrong by thinking of God as Louis Armstrong.

Those who swing, should swing some more.

Something always comes along. It really does.

Cleanliness is fine, as far as it goes.

Remember—even when you are alone, you're in the middle of a party.

The blues ain't nothin' but a feeling, but *what* a feeling.

What goes up sometimes just keeps right on going.

Try to eat solid food at least once a day.

There is absolutely nothing wrong with television.

Anybody who thinks he sees everything around him isn't looking.

When you get your crib the way you like it, stay there.

Order can be created in even the smallest things, but that doesn't mean you have to create it.

Clothes are for sleeping in, too. The same goes for chairs.

Everyone makes mistakes, including deities and higher powers.

Avoid the powerful, for they will undoubtedly try to hurt you.

Doing one right thing in the course of a day is good enough.

Stick to beer, mainly.

Pay attention to musicians.

Accept your imperfections, for they can bring you to Paradise.

No one should ever feel guilty about fantasies, no matter how shameful they may be, for a thought is not a deed.

Sooner or later, jazz music will tell you everything you need to know.

There is no significant difference between night and day.

Immediately after death, human beings become so beautiful you can hardly bear to look at them.

To one extent or another, all children are telepathic.

If you want to sleep, sleep. Simple as that.

Do your absolute best to avoid saying bad things about people, especially those you dislike.

In the long run, grasshoppers and ants all wind up in the same place.

LITTLE RED, HIS APPEARANCE

When you meet Little Red for the first time, what do you see?

He will be standing in the doorway of his ground-floor apartment on West 55th Street, glancing to one side and backing away to give you entry. The atmosphere, the tone created by these gestures, will be welcoming and gracious in an old-fashioned, even almost rural, manner.

He will be wearing jeans and an old T-shirt, or a worn gray bathrobe, or a chain-store woolen sweater and black trousers. Black, rubber-soled Chinese slippers purchased from a sidewalk vendor will cover his narrow feet. Very slightly, his high, pale forehead will bulge forward beneath his long red hair, which will have been pulled back from his face and fastened into a ragged ponytail by means of a twisted rubber band. An untrimmed beard, curled at the bottom like a giant ruff, will cover much of his face. When he speaks, the small, discolored pegs of his teeth will flicker beneath the fringe of his mustache.

Little Red will strike you as gaunt, in fact nearly haggard. He will seem detached from the world beyond the entrance of his apartment building. West 55th Street and the rest of Manhattan will fade from consciousness as you step through the door and move past your host, who, still gazing to one side, will be gesturing toward the empty chair separated from his re-cliner by a small, round, marble-topped table or nightstand heaped with paperback books, pads of paper, ballpoint pens upright in a cup.

When first you enter Little Red's domain, and every subsequent time thereafter, he will suggest dignity, solicitude, and pleasure in the fact of your company. Little Red admits only those from whom he can be assured of at least some degree of acknowledgment of that which they will receive from him. People who have proven themselves indifferent to the rewards of Little Red's hospitality are forbidden return, no matter how many times they press his buzzer or rap a quarter against his big, dusty front window. He can tell them by their buzzes, their rings, their raps: He knows the identities of most of his callers well before he glances down the corridor to find them standing before his building's glass entrance. (Of course, nearly all of Little Red's visitors take the precaution of telephoning him before they venture to West 55th Street, both for the customary reason of confirming his availability and for one other reason, which shall be disclosed in good time.)

Shortly after your entrance into his domain, his den, his consulting room, his confessional, Little Red will tender the offer of a bottle of Beck's beer from the Stygian depths of his kitchen. On the few occasions when his refrigerator is empty of Beck's beer, he will have requested that you purchase a six-pack on your way, and will reimburse you for the purchase upon your arrival.

His hands will be slim, artistic, and often in motion.

He will sometimes appear to stoop, yet at other times, especially when displeased, will adopt an almost military posture. A mild rash, consisting of a scattering of welts a tad redder than his hair and beard will now and then constellate the visible areas of his face. From time to time, he will display the symptoms of pain, of an affliction or afflictions not readily diagnosed. These symptoms may endure for weeks. Such is his humanity, Little Red will often depress his buzzer (should the buzzer be operational) and admit his guests, his supplicants, when in great physical discomfort.

He will not remind you of anyone you know. Little Red is not a *type*.

The closest you will come to thinking that someone has reminded you of Little Red will occur in the midst of a movie seen late in a summer afternoon on which you have decided to use a darkened theater to walk away from your troubles for a couple of hours. As you sit surrounded by empty seats in the pleasant murk, watching a scene depicting a lavish party or a crowded restaurant, an unnamed extra will move through the door and depart, and at first you will feel no more than a mild tingle of recognition all the more compelling for having no obvious referent. *Someone is going, someone has gone,* that is all you will know. Then the tilt of the departing head or the negligent gesture of a hand will return to you a quality more closely akin to the emotional context of memory than to memory itself,

and with the image of Little Red rising into your mind, you will find yourself pierced by an unexpected sense of loss, longing, and sweetness, as if
someone had just spoken the name of a long-vanished, once-dear childhood friend.

LITTLE RED, HIS DWELLING-PLACE

He came to West 55th Street in his early thirties, just at the final cusp of
his youth, after the years of wandering. From Long Island he had moved
into Manhattan, no one now knows where—Little Red himself may have
forgotten the address, so little had he come into his adult estate. To earn
his keep, he "waited." Kyle's small collection of jazz records, also Kyle's enthusiasm for Count Basie, Maynard Ferguson, and Ella Fitzgerald, had
given direction to his younger brother's yearnings, and it was during this
period that Little Red made his initial forays into the world of which he
would later become so central an element.

Photographs were taken, and he kept them. Should you be privileged
to enter Little Red's inmost circle of acquaintances, he will one night fetch
from its hidey-hole an old album of cross-grained fabric and display its
treasures: snapshots of the boyish, impossibly youthful, impossibly fresh,
Little Red, his hair short and healthy, his face shining, his spirit fragrant, in
the company of legendary heroes. The album contains no photographs of
other kinds. Its centerpiece is a three-by-five, taken outside a sun-drenched
tent during a mid-sixties Newport Jazz Festival, of a dewy Little Red leaning forward and smiling at the camera as Louis Armstrong, horn tucked beneath his elbow, imparts a never-to-be-forgotten bit of wisdom. On
Armstrong's other side, grinning broadly, hovers a bearded man in his mid-
forties. This is John Elder, who has been called "the first Little Red." Little
Red was sixteen, already on his way.

From New York he wandered, "waiting," from city to city. A hidden de-
sign guided his feet, represented by an elderly, dung-colored Volkswagen
Beetle with a retractable sunroof and a minimum of trunk space. Directed
by the design, the VW brought him to New Orleans, birthplace of Mighty
Pops, and there he began his true instruction in certain sacred mysteries.
New Orleans was *instructive*, New Orleans *left a mark*. And his journey

through the kitchens and dining rooms of great restaurants, his tutelage under their pitiless taskmasters, ensured that henceforth he would never have to go long without remunerative employment.

It was in New Orleans that small groups of people, almost always male, began to visit Little Red at all hours of day or night. Some stayed half an hour; others lingered for days, participating in the simple, modest life of the apartment. John Elder is said to have visited the young couple. In those days, John Elder crisscrossed the country, staying with friends, turning up in jazz clubs to be embraced between sets by the musicians. Sometimes late at night, he spoke in a low voice to those seated on the floor around his chair. During these gatherings, John Elder oft-times mentioned Little Red, referring to him as his *son*.

Did John Elder precede Little Red to Aspen, Colorado? Although we have no documentation, the evidence suggests he did. An acquaintance of both men can recall Zoot Sims, the late tenor saxophonist, mentioning strolling into the kitchen of the Red Onion, Aspen's best jazz club, late on an afternoon in the spring of 1972 and finding John Elder deep in conversation with the owner over giant bowls of pasta. If this memory is accurate, John Elder was *preparing the way*—six months later, Little Red began working at the Red Onion.

He lived above a garage in a one-bedroom apartment accessible only by an exterior wooden staircase. As in New Orleans, individuals and small groups of men called upon him, in nearly every case having telephoned beforehand, to share his company for an hour or a span of days. Up the staircase they mounted, in all sorts of weather, to press the buzzer and await admittance. Little Red entertained his visitors with records and television programs; he invited them to partake of the Italian meals prepared by his wife, who always made herself scarce on these occasions. He produced bottles of Beck's beer from the refrigerator. Late at night, he spoke softly and without notes for an hour or two, no more. It was enough.

And too much for his wife, however, for she vanished from his life midway through his residency in Aspen. Single once more, pulling behind the VW a small U-Haul trailer filled with records, Little Red returned to Manhattan in the summer of 1973 and proceeded directly to the apartment on West 55th Street then occupied by his old friend and mentor, John Elder, who unquestioningly turned over to his new guest the large front room of his long, railroad-style apartment.

-⊦ ⊦-

The dwelling-place Little Red has inhabited alone since 1976, when John Elder retired into luxurious seclusion, parses itself as three good-sized rooms laid end-to-end. Between the front room with its big shielded window and the sitting room lies a semi-warren of two small chambers separated by a door.

These chambers, the first containing a sink and shower stall, the second a toilet, exist in a condition of perpetual chiaroscuro, perhaps to conceal the stains encrusted on the fittings, especially the shower stall and curtain. Those visitors to Little Red's realm who have been compelled to wash their hands after the ritual of defecation generally glance at the shower arrangement, which in the ambient darkness at first tends to resemble a hulking stranger more than it does a structure designed for bodily cleansing, shudder at what they think, what they fear they may have seen there, then execute a one-quarter turn of the entire body before groping for the limp, threadbare towels drooping from a pair of hooks.

Beyond the sitting room and reached via a doorless opening in the wall is the kitchen.

Oh the kitchen, oh me oh my.

The kitchen has devolved into a progressive squalor. Empty bottles of Beck's in six-pack configurations piled chest-high dominate something like three-fourths of the grubby floor. Towers of filthy dishes and smeared glasses loom above the sink. The dirty dishes and beer bottles appear organic, as if they have grown untouched here in the gloom over the decades of Little Red's occupancy, producing bottle after bottle and plate after plate of the same ancient substance.

Heavy shades, the dusty tan of nicotine, conceal the kitchen's two windows, and a single forty-watt bulb dangles from a fraying cord over the landscape of stacked empties.

In the sitting room, a second low-wattage bulb of great antiquity oversees the long shelves, the two chairs, and the accumulation of goods before them. Not the only source of light in this barely illuminated chamber, the bulb has been in place, off and on but for several years mostly off, during the entire term of Little Red's occupancy of the apartment. "John Elder was using that lightbulb when I moved in," he says. "When you get that old, you'll need a lot of rest, too." Two ornate table lamps, one beside the command post and the other immediately to the visitor's right, shed a ghost-like yellow pall. Little Red has no intrinsic need of bright light, including that of the sun. Shadow and relative darkness ease the eyes, calm the soul. The images on the rectangular screen burn more sharply in low light, and the low, moving banner charting the moment-by-moment activity of the stock market marches along with perfect clarity, every encoded symbol crisp as a snap bean.

A giant shelving arrangement blankets the wall facing the two chairs, and Little Red's beloved television set occupies one of its open cabinets. Another black shelf, located just to the right of the television, holds his au-dio equipment—a CD player, a tape recorder, a tuner, a turntable, an am-plifier, as well as the machines they have superseded, which are stacked beneath them, as if beneath headstones. A squat black speaker stands at ei-ther end of the topmost shelf. A cabinet located beneath the right-hand speaker houses several multivolume discographies, some so worn with use they are held together with rubber bands. All the remaining shelves sup-port ranks of long-playing records. Records also fill the lower half of the freestanding bookshelf in front of the narrow wall leading from the small foyer area into the sitting room. Little Red must strain to reach the LPs lo-cated on the highest shelf; cardboard boxes of yet more jazz records stand before the ground-level shelves, their awkwardness and weight blocking ac-cess to the LPs arrayed behind them. Sometimes Little Red will wish to play a record hidden behind one of the boxes, then pause to consider the problems involved—the bending, the shoving, the risk to his lower back, the high concentration of dust likely to be disturbed—and will decide to feature another artist, one situated in a more convenient portion of the al-phabet.

The records were alphabetized long ago. Two or three years after the accomplishment of the stupendous task, Little Red further refined the sys-tem by placing the records in alpha-chronological order, so that they stood not only in relation to the artists' placement in the alphabet, but also by date of recording, running from earliest to latest, oldest to newest, in each individual case. This process took him nearly a year to complete and oc-cupied most of his free time—the time not given to his callers—during that period. For the callers kept coming, so they did, in numbers unceasing.

Actually, the alpha-chronologicalization process has not yet reached total completion, nor will it, nor can it, for reasons to be divulged in the next section of this account. Alpha-chronologicalization is an endless labor.

What occupies the territory between the chairs and the bookshelves constitutes the grave, grave problem of this room. The territory in question makes up the central portion of Little Red's sitting room, which under optimum conditions would provide a companionable open space for passage to and from the kitchen, to and from the bathroom and the front door, modest exercise, pacing, and for those so disposed, floor-sitting. Such a space would grant Little Red unimpeded access to the thousands of records packed onto the heavily-laden shelves (in some cases so tightly that the withdrawal of a single LP involves pulling out an extra three or four on either side).

Once, a table of eccentric design was installed in the middle of the sitting room. At the time, it would have been a considerable amenity, with its broad, flat top for the temporary disposal of the inner and outer sleeves of the record being played, perhaps as well the sleeves containing those records to be played after that one. A large, square table it was, roughly the size of two steamer trunks placed side by side, and trunklike in its solidity from top to bottom, for its flanks contained a clever nest of drawers for the disposition of magazines, gewgaws, and knickknacks. It is believed that Little Red found this useful object on the street, the source of a good deal of his household furnishings, but it is possible that John Elder found it on the street, and that the table was already in place when Little Red was welcomed within.

Large as it was, the table offered no obstacle to a gaunt, red-haired individual moving from the command post to the records, or from any particular shelf of records to the cabinet-like space housing the turntable and other sound equipment. The table *cooperated,* it must have done. At one time—shortly after Little Red or John Elder managed to get the unwieldy thing off the sidewalk and into the sitting room—the table must have functioned properly, that is as a literal support system. The table undoubtedly performed this useful function for many months. After that . . . entropy took over, and the literal support system began to disappear beneath the mass and quantity of material it was required literally to support. In time, the table *vanished,* as an old car abandoned in a field gradually vanishes beneath and into the mound of weeds that overtakes it, or as the genial scientist who became ferocious Swamp Thing vanished beneath and into the vegetation that had surrounded, supported, nourished his wounded body. Little Red's is the Swamp Thing of the table family.

From the command post and the guest's chair, the center of the sitting room can be seen to be dominated by a large, unstable mound rising from the floor to a height of something like three and a half feet and comprised in part of old catalogs from Levenger, Sharper Image, and Herrington; copies of *Downbeat, Jazz Times,* and *Biblical Archaeology Review;* record sleeves and CD jewel boxes; take-out menus; flyers distributed on behalf of drug stores; copies of *Life* magazine containing particularly eloquent photographs of Louis Armstrong or Ella Fitzgerald; books about crop circles and alien visitations; books about miracles; concert programs of considerable sentimental value; sheets of notepaper scribbled over with cryptic messages (What in the world does *mogrom* mean? Or *rambichure?*); the innards of old newspapers; photographs of jazz musicians purchased from a man on the corner of West 57th Street and 8th Avenue; posters awaiting reassignment to the walls; and other suchlike objects submerged too deeply to be identified. Like the dishes in the sink, the mound seems to be increasing in size through a version of parthenogenesis.

Leaning against the irregular sides of Swamp Thing are yet more records, perhaps as few as fifty, perhaps as many as a hundred, already alphabetized; and around the listing, accordion-shaped constructions formed by propped-up records sit a varying number of cardboard boxes filled with still *more* records, these newly acquired from a specialist dealer or at a vintage record show. (John Elder, who in his luxurious seclusion possesses eighty to ninety thousand records stored on industrial metal shelves, annually attends a record fair in Newark, New Jersey, where he allows Little Red a corner at his lavish table.)

Long-playing records may be acquired virtually anywhere: in little shops tucked into obscure byways; from remote bins in vast retail outlets; from boxes carelessly arranged on the counters of small-town Woolworth's stores; within the outer circles of urban flea markets located in elementary-school playgrounds; from boxes, marked $1 EACH, displayed by unofficial sidewalk vendors who with their hangers-on lounge behind their wares on lawn furniture, smoking cigars and muffled up against the cold.

So Little Red gets and he spends, but when it comes to records he gets a lot more than he spends. His friends and followers occasionally give him CDs, and Little Red enjoys the convenience of compact discs; however, as long as they do not skip, he much prefers the sound of LPs, even scratchy ones. They are warmer and more resonant: the atmosphere of *distant places, distant times* inhabits long-playing vinyl records, whereas CDs are always in the here and now.

And what Little Red gets must in time be accommodated within his vast system, and a new old Duke Ellington record will eventually have to find its correct alpha-chronological position.

The word Little Red uses for this placement process is "filing." "Filing" records has become his daily task, his joy, his curse, his primary occupation.

LITTLE RED, HIS FILING

Should you telephone Little Red and should he answer, you, like numerous others, might ask, with a hopeful lilt in your voice, what he has been up to lately.

"Nothing much," Little Red will answer. "Doing a lot of filing."

"Ah," you say.

"Got started yesterday afternoon around three, right after S— and G— G— left. They were here since about ten o'clock the night before—we played some cards. Between three and six I filed at least two hundred records. Something like that, anyhow. Then I was thinking about going out and having dinner somewhere, but R— was coming over at eight, and I looked at the boxes on the floor, and I just kept on filing. R— left an hour ago, and I went right back into it. Got a lot of work done, man. The next time you come over, you'll see a big difference."

This assertion means only that *Little Red* sees a great difference. Nine times out of ten, you won't have a prayer. Swamp Thing will seem no less massive than on your previous visit; the boxes of records and accordion-shapes will appear untouched.

Of course, time-lapse photography would prove you wrong, for Little Red's collection, filed and unfiled, is in constant motion. Occasionally, as in the case of the Japanese Gentleman, or during one of Little Red's visits to the record fair, albums are sold, leaving gaps on the shelves. These gaps are soon filled with the new old records from the accordions, which have already been alphabetized, and from the boxes, which have not. The customary progress of an album is from box to accordion, then finally to the shelf, after a consultation of the discographical record has pinned down its chronological moment. (Those discographies are in constant use, and their contents heavily annotated, underlined, and highlighted in a variety of cheerful colors.)

The quantity of rearrangement necessitated by the box-accordion-shelf progression would be daunting, exhausting, unbearable to anyone but Little Red. The insertion onto the proper shelf of four recently-acquired Roy Eldridge LPs could easily involve redistributing two or three hundred records over four long shelves, so that a three-inch gap at the beginning of the Monk section might be transferred laterally and up to the midst of the Roys. The transferal of this gap requires twenty minutes of shifting and moving, not counting the time previously spent in chronologizing the new acquisitions with the aid of the (sometimes warring) discographies. It's surprisingly dirty work, too. After ten or twelve hours of unbroken filing, Little Red resembles a coal miner at shift's end, grubby from head to foot, with grime concentrated on his face and hands, bleary-eyed, his hair in wisps and tangles.

At the end of your conversation, Little Red will say, "You can come over tonight, if you feel like it. It doesn't matter how late it is. I'll be up."

None of Little Red's friends, followers, or acquaintances has ever seen him in the act of filing his records. He files only when alone.

MIRACLES ATTRIBUTED TO LITTLE RED

1. The Miracle of the Japanese Gentleman
The Japanese people include a surprising number of record collectors, a good half of whom specialize in jazz. Japanese collectors are famous for the purity of their standards, also for their willingness to expend great sums in pursuit of the prizes they desire. One of these gentlemen, a Kyoto businessman named Mr. Yoshi, learned of Little Red's collection from John Elder, with whom he had done business for many years. By this time, Mr. Yoshi's collection nearly equaled John Elder's in size, though only in the numbers of LP, EP, and 78 records it contained. In memorabilia, Mr. Yoshi

lagged far behind his friend: when it comes to items like plaster or ceramic effigies of Louis Armstrong, signed photos of Louis Armstrong, and over-sized white handkerchiefs once unfurled onstage by Louis Armstrong, John Elder is and always will be in a class by himself.

Little Red knew that the Japanese Gentleman had a particular interest in Blue Note and Riverside recordings from the 1950s, especially those by Sonny Clark and Kenny Dorham. Mr. Yoshi would accept only records in or near mint condition and in their original state—original cover art and record label, as if they had been issued yesterday and were essentially un-played.

Little Red's monthly rent payment of $980 was coming due, and his bank balance stood at a dismal $205.65. The sale of two mint-condition records to Mr. Yoshi could yield the amount needed, but Little Red faced the insurmountable problem of not owning any mint-condition Sonny Clark or Kenny Dorham records on the Blue Note or Riverside labels. He had, it is true, a dim memory of once seeing *The Sonny Clark Trio*, the pi-anist's first recording as a leader for Blue Note and an object greatly cov-eted by Japanese collectors, pass through his hands, but that was the entire content of the memory: the record's shiny sleeve passing into and then out of his hands. He had not been conscious of its value on the collector's mar-ket; Sonny Clark had never been one of his favorites. However, he *knew* that he had once purchased a nice copy of Kenny Dorham's *Una Mas*, maybe not in mint condition but Excellent, at least Very Good anyhow, A to A-, worth perhaps $150 to $200 to a fanatical Japanese collector who did not already own one.

Little Red scanned the spines of his Kenny Dorham records without finding a single original 1963 copy of *Una Mas*. He had a Japanese reis-sue, but imagine offering a Japanese reissue to a Japanese collector!

Yet if he had neither of the most desired records, he did have a good number of consolation prizes, Blue Notes and Riversides maybe not ex-actly unplayed but certainly eminently playable and with sleeves in Fine to Very Fine condition. These twenty records he coaxed from the shelves and stacked on a folding chair for immediate viewing. With luck, he imagined, they could go for $30 to $40 apiece—he had seen them listed at that price in the catalogs. If he sold them all, he would make about $700, leaving him only a few dollars short of his rent.

Mr. Yoshi appeared at precisely the designated hour and wasted no time before examining the records set aside for him. Five-seven, with a se-vere face and iron-gray hair, he wore a beautiful dark blue pinstriped suit and gleaming black loafers. His English was rudimentary, but his tact was sublime. He had to pick his way around Swamp Thing to reach the folding chair, but the Japanese Gentleman acknowledged its monstrous presence by not as much as a raised eyebrow. For him, Swamp Thing did not exist. All that existed, all that deserved notice, was the stack of records passed to him, two at a time, by Little Red.

"No good," he said. "Not for me."

"That's a shame," said his host, hiding his disappointment. "I hope your trip hasn't been wasted."

Mr. Yoshi ignored this remark and turned to face the crowded shelves. "Many records," he said. "Many, many." Little Red understood it was a show of politeness, and he appreciated the gesture.

"For sale?"

"Some, I guess," said Little Red. "Take a look."

The Japanese Gentleman cautiously made his way around the accor-dions and through the boxes on Swamp Thing's perimeter. When he stood before the shelves, he clasped his hands behind his back. "You have Blue Note?"

"Sure," said Little Red. "All through there. Riverside, too."

"You have Sonny Clark, Kenny Dorham?"

"Some Kenny, yeah," said Little Red, pointing to a shelf. "Right there."

"Aha," said Mr. Yoshi, moving closer. "I have funny feeling. . . ."

Little Red clasped his own hands behind his back, and the Japanese Gentleman began to brush the tip of his index finger against the spines of the Dorham records. "Here is reason for funny feeling," he said, and ex-tracted a single record. "*Una Mas.* Blue Note, 1963. Excellent condition."

"Yeah, well," said Little Red.

But the record in Mr. Yoshi's right hand was not the Japanese reissue. The Japanese Gentleman was holding, in a state akin to reverence, exactly what he had said it was, the original Blue Note issue from 1963, in im-maculate condition.

"Huh!" said Little Red.

"Must look," said Mr. Yoshi, and slid the record from its sleeve. No less than his shoes, the grooved black vinyl shone.

"You try to keep this one for yourself," Mr. Yoshi teased. "Suppose I give you $500, would you sell?"

"Uh, sure," said Little Red.

"What else you hiding here?" asked Mr. Yoshi, more to the intoxicating shelves than to Little Red. He picked his way along, flicking his fingers on the spines. "Uh-huh. Uh-huh. Not bad. Uh-oh, very bad. Poor, poor condition. Should throw out, no good anymore to listen."

Little Red said he would think about it.

"I have funny feeling again." Mr. Yoshi stiffened his spine and glared at the spines of the records. "Oh yes, *very* funny feeling."

Little Red came closer.

"Something here."

The Japanese Gentleman leaned forward and pushed two B- Kenny Clarke Trio records on Savoy as far apart as they would go, about a quarter of an inch. A collector's instincts are not those of an ordinary man. He twitched out the Kenny Clarke Trio records and passed them to Little Red without turning his head. His hand slid into the widened gap, his head moved nearer. "Aha."

Very gently, Mr. Yoshi pulled out his arm from between the records. A fine layer of dust darkened his white, elegant cuff. When his hand cleared the shelf, it brought into view two LPs which had been shoved into an opening once occupied by John Elder's long-departed reel-to-reel tape recorder. On the albums' identical covers, staggered red, blue, green, and yellow bars formed keyboard patterns. *The Sonny Clark Trio*, Blue Note, 1957, still in their plastic wrappers.

"You hide, I find," said the Japanese Gentleman. "This the Sonny Clark mother lode!"

"Sure looks like it," said dumbfounded Little Red.

"All three records, I give $2,000. Right now. In cash."

"Talked me into it," said Little Red, and the Japanese Gentleman counted out two months' rent in new, sequentially numbered hundred-dollar bills and pressed them into his host's waiting hand. Little Red threw in a plastic LP carrier that looked a bit like a briefcase, and Mr. Yoshi left beaming.

After the departure of the Japanese Gentleman, Little Red remembered the wad of bills remaining in his guest's wallet after the removal of twenty hundreds and realized that he could have asked for and received another ten.

Don't be greedy, he told himself. *Be grateful.*

2. The Miracle of the Weeping Child

Late on a winter night, Little Red emerged from stuporous slumber and observed that he was fully dressed and seated at his command post in the freezing semidarkness. Across the room, the twinkling screen displayed in black and white a flylike Louis Jourdan scaling down the facade of a hideous castle. (He had thought to enjoy the BBC's '70s *Dracula* as a reward for long hours of filing.) By the dim lamplight he saw that the time was 3:25. He had been asleep for about an hour and a half. His arms ached from the evening's labor; the emptiness in his stomach reminded him that he had failed to eat anything during the course of the busy day. Little Red's hands and feet were painfully cold. He reached down for the plaid blanket strewn at the left-hand side of his recliner. Even in his state of mild befuddlement, Little Red wondered what had pulled him so urgently into wakefulness.

How many days had passed without the refreshment of sleep? Two? Three? When deprived so long of sleep, the rebelling body and mind yield to phantoms. Elements of the invisible world take on untrustworthy form and weight, and their shapes speak in profoundly ambiguous voices. Little Red had been in this condition many times before; now he wished only to return to the realm from which he had been torn.

A push on the lever tilted the back of the chair to an angle conducive to slumber. Little Red draped the blanket over his legs and drew its upper portion high upon his chest.

Faintly but clearly, from somewhere in his apartment came the sound of a child weeping in either pain or despair. As soon as Little Red heard the sound, he knew that this was what had awakened him: a dream had rippled and broken beneath its pressure. He had been pulled upward, drawn *up* into the cold.

It came again, this time it seemed from the kitchen: a hiccup of tears, a muffled sob.

"Anybody there?" asked Little Red in a blurry voice. Wearily, he turned his head toward the kitchen and peered at the nothing he had expected to see. Of course no distraught child sat weeping in his kitchen. Little Red supposed that it had been two or three years since he had even *seen* a child.

He dropped his head back into the pillowy comfort of the recliner and heard it again—the cry of a child in misery. This time it seemed not to come from the kitchen but from the opposite end of his apartment, either the bathroom or the front room that served as storage shed and bedroom. Although Little Red understood that the sound was a hallucination and the child did not exist, that the sound should seem to emanate from the bedroom disturbed him greatly. He kept his bedroom to himself. Only in extreme cases had he allowed a visitor entrance to this most private of his chambers.

He closed his eyes, but the sound continued. False, false perception! He refused to be persuaded. There was no child; the misery was his own, and it derived from exhaustion. Little Red nearly arose from his command post to unplug his telephone, but his body declined to cooperate.

The child fell silent. Relieved, Little Red again closed his eyes and folded his hands beneath the rough warmth of the woolen blanket. A delightful rubbery sensation overtook the length of his body, and his mind lurched toward a dream. A series of sharp cries burst like tracers within his skull, startling him back into wakefulness.

Little Red cursed and raised his head. He heard another flaring outcry, then another, and the sound subsided back into pathetic weeping. "Go to sleep!" he yelled, and at that moment realized what had happened: a woman, not a child, was standing distressed on the sidewalk outside his big front window, crying loudly enough to be audible deep within. A woman sobbing on West 55th Street at 3:30 in the morning, no remedy existed for a situation like that. He could do nothing but wait for her to leave. An offer of assistance or support would earn only rebuff, vituperation, insults, and the threat of criminal charges. Nothing could be done, Little Red advised himself. Leave well enough alone, stay out. He shut his eyes and waited for quiet. At least he had identified the problem, and sooner or later the problem would take care of itself. Tired as he was, he thought he might fall asleep before the poor creature moved on. He might, yes, for he felt the gravity of approaching unconsciousness slip into his body's empty spaces despite the piteous noises floating through his window.

Then he opened his eyes again and swung his legs from beneath the blanket's embrace and out of the chair, for he was Little Red and could not do otherwise. The woman's misery was intolerable, how could he pretend not to hear it? Thinking to peek around the side of the front window's shade, Little Red pushed himself out of the command center and marched stiff-legged into the toilet.

As if the woman had heard his footsteps, the noise cut off. He paused, took a slow step forward. *Just let me get a look at you,* he thought. *If you don't look completely crazy, I'll give you whatever help you can accept.* In a moment he had passed through the bathroom and was opening the door to his bedroom, the only section of the apartment we have not as yet seen.

The weeping settled into a low, steady, fearful wail. The woman must have heard him, he thought, but was too frightened to leave the window. "Can't be as bad as that," he said, making his slow way down the side of the bed toward the far wall, where an upright piano covered half of the big window. Now the wailing seemed very close at hand. Little Red imagined the woman huddled against his building, her head bent to his window. Her mechanical cries pierced his heart. He almost felt like going outside immediately.

Little Red reached the right edge of the window and touched the stiff, dark material of the shade. Unraised for nearly forty years, it smelled like a sick animal. A pulse of high-pitched keening filled his ears, and a dark shape that huddled beside the piano moved nearer the wall. Little Red dropped his hand from the shade and stepped back, fearing that he had come upon a monstrous rat. His heart pounded, and his breath caught in his throat. Even the most ambitious rat could not grow so large; Little Red quieted his impulse to run from the room and looked down at the being crouching beside the piano.

A small dark head bent over upraised knees tucked under a white stretched-out T-shirt. Two small feet shone pale in the darkness. Little Red stared at the creature before him, which appeared to tighten down into itself, as if trying to disappear. A choked sound of combined misery and terror came from the little being. It was a child after all: he had been right the first time.

"How did you get in here?" Little Red asked.

The child hugged its knees and buried its face. The sound it made went up in pitch and became a fast, repeated *ih ih ih.*

Little Red lowered himself to the floor beside the child. "You don't have to be so afraid," he said. "I'm not going to hurt you."

A single eye peeked at him, then dropped back to the T-shirt and the bent knees. The boy was about five or six, with short brown hair and thin arms and legs. He shivered from the cold. Little Red patted him lightly on the back and was surprised by the relief aroused in him by the solidity of what he touched.

"Do you have a name?"

The boy shook his head.

"No?"

"No." It was the smallest whisper.

"That's too bad. I bet you have a name, really."

No response, except that the shivering child had stopped whimpering *ih ih ih.*

"Can you tell me what you're doing here?"

"I'm *cold*," the boy whispered.

"Well, sure you are," said Little Red. "Here we are in the middle of winter, and all you have on is a T-shirt. Hold on, I'm going to get you a blanket."

Little Red pushed himself to his feet and went quickly to the sitting room, fearing that the child might vanish before his return. *But why do I want him to stay?* he asked himself, and had no answer.

When he came back, the child was still huddled alongside the piano. Little Red draped the blanket over his shoulders and once again sat beside him.

"Better?"

"A little." His teeth made tiny clicking noises.

Little Red rubbed a hand on the boy's blanket-covered arms and back.

"I want to lie down," the child said.

"Will you tell me your name now?"

"I don't have a name."

"Do you know where you are?"

"Where I am? I'm here."

"Where do you live? What's your address? Or how about your phone number? You're old enough to know your phone number."

"I want to lie down," the boy said. "Put me on the bed. Please." He nodded at Little Red's bed, in the darkness seemingly buried beneath the rounded bodies of many sleeping animals. These were the mounds of T-shirts, underpants, socks, sweatshirts, and jeans Little Red had taken, the previous night, to the 24-hour Laundromat on the corner of 55th Street and 9th Avenue. He had filled five washers, then five dryers, with his semi-annual wash, taken the refreshed clothing home in black garbage bags, and sorted it all on his bed, where it was likely to remain for the entirety of the coming month, if not longer.

"Whatever you say," said Little Red, and lifted the child in his arms and carried him to the bed. The boy seemed to weigh no more than a handful of kitchen matches. He leaned over the bed and nestled the child between a pile of balled socks and a heap of folded jazz festival T-shirts. "You can't stay here, you know, little boy," he said.

The child said, "I'm not going to stay here. This is just where I *am.*"

"You don't have to be scared anymore."

"I thought you were going to hurt me." For a second his eyes narrowed, and his skin seemed to shrink over his skull. He was actually a very unattractive little boy, thought Little Red. The child looked devious and greedy, like an urchin who had lived too long by its wits. In some ways, he had the face of a sour, bad-tempered old man. Little Red felt as though he had surrendered his bed to a beast like a weasel, a coyote.

But he's only a little boy, Little Red told Little Red, who did not believe him. This was not a child—this was something that had come in from the freezing night. "Do you think you can go to sleep now?"

But the child—the being—had slipped into unconsciousness before Little Red asked the question.

What to *do* with him? The ugly little thing asleep in the midst of Little Red's laundry was never going to produce an address or a telephone number, that was certain. Probably it was telling the truth about not having a name.

But that was crazy—he had gone too long without sleep, and his mind could no longer work right. A wave of deep weariness rolled through him, bringing with it the recognition that his mind could no longer work at all, at least not rationally. If he did not lie down, he was going to fall asleep standing up. So Little Red got his knees up on the mattress, pushed aside some heaps of clothing, stretched out, and watched his eyes close by themselves.

Asleep, he inhaled the scent of clean laundry, which seemed the most beautiful odor in the world. Clean laundry smelled like sunshine, fresh air, and good health. This lovely smell contained a hint of the celestial, of the better world that heaven is said to be. It would be presumptuous to speak of angels, but if angels wore robes, those robes would smell like the clean, fluffy socks and underwear surrounding Little Red and his nameless guest. The guest's own odor now and then came to Little Red. Mingled with the metallic odor of steam vented from underground regions, the sharp, gamy tang of fox sometimes cut through the fragrance of the laundry, for in his sleep Little Red had shifted nearer to the child.

To sleeping Little Red, the two scents twisted together and became a single thing, an odor of architectural complexity filled with wide plazas and long colonnades, also with certain cramped, secret dens and cells. And from the hidden dens and cells a creature came in pursuit of him, whether for good or ill he did not know. But in pursuit it came: Little Red felt the displacement of the air as it rushed down long corridors, and there were times when he spun around a corner an instant before his pursuer would have caught sight of him. And though he continued to run as if for his life, Little Red still did not know if the creature meant him well or meant to do him harm.

He twisted and squirmed in imitation of the motions of his dream-body, and it so fell out that eventually he had folded his body around that of his little guest, and the animal smell became paramount.

During what happened next, Little Red could not make out whether he was asleep and dreaming of being half-awake, or half-awake and still dreaming of being asleep. He seemed to pass back and forth between two states of being with no registration of their boundaries. His hand had fallen on the child's chest—he remembered that, for instantly he had thought to snatch it back from this accidental contact. Yet in pulling back his hand he had somehow succeeded in pulling the child with it, though his hand was empty and his fingers open. The child, the child-*thing*, floated up from the rumpled blanket and the disarranged piles of laundry, clinging to Little Red's hand as metal clings to a magnet. That was how it seemed to Little Red: the boy *adhered* to his raised hand, the boy *followed* the hand to his side, and when the boy-thing came to rest beside him, the boy-thing smiled a wicked smile and bit him in the neck.

The gamy stink of fox streamed into his nostrils, and he cried out in pain and terror...and in a moment the child-thing was stroking his head and telling him he had nothing to fear, and the next moment he dropped through the floor of sleep into darkness and knew nothing.

Little Red awakened in late afternoon of the following day. He felt wonderfully rested and restored. A decade might have been subtracted from his age, and he became a lad of forty once again. Two separate mental events took place at virtually the same moment, which came as he sat up and stretched out his arms in a tremendous yawn. He remembered the weeping child he had placed in this bed; and he noticed that one of his arms was spattered with drying blood.

He gasped and looked down at his chest, his waist, his legs. Bloodstains covered his clothes like thrown paint. The blanket and the folded clothing littered across the bed were drenched in blood. There were feathery splashes of blood on the dusty floor. Spattered bloodstains mounted the colorless wall.

For a moment, Little Red's heart stopped moving. His breathing was harsh and shallow. Gingerly, he swung his legs to the floor and got out of bed. First he looked at the blanket, which would have to be thrown out, then, still in shock, down at his own body. Red blotches bloomed on his shirt. The bottom of his shirt and the top of his jeans were sodden, too soaked in blood to have dried.

Little Red peeled the shirt off over his head and dropped it to the floor. His chest was irregularly stained with blood but otherwise undamaged. He saw no wounds on his arms. His fingers unbuckled his belt and undid his zipper, and he pushed his jeans down to his ankles. The Chinese slippers fell off his feet when he stepped out of the wet jeans. From mid-thigh to feet, he was unmarked; from navel to mid-thigh he was solid red.

Yet he felt no pain. The blood could not be his. Had something terrible happened to the child? Moaning, Little Red scattered the clothing across the bed, looked in the corners of the room, and went as far as the entrance to the sitting room, but saw no trace of his guest. Neither did he see further bloodstains. The child, the *thing*, had disappeared.

When Little Red stood before his bathroom mirror, he remembered the dream, if it had been a dream, and leaned forward to inspect the side of his neck. The skin was pale and unbroken. So it had been a dream, all of it.

Then he remembered the sounds of weeping that had awakened him at his command post, and *ih ih ih,* and he remembered the weight of the child in his arms and his foxy smell. Little Red turned on his shower and stepped into the stall. Blood sluiced down his body, his groin, his legs to the drain. He remembered the blissful fragrance of his clean laundry. That magnificent odor, containing room upon room. Thinking to aid a distressed woman, he had discovered a terrified child, or something that looked like a child, and had given it a night's shelter and a bed of socks and underwear. Standing in the warm spray of the shower, Little Red said, "In faith, a miracle."

3. The Miracle of C— M— and Vic Dickenson

Late one summer afternoon, C— M—, a young trombonist of growing reputation, sat in Little Red's guest chair listening to *Very Saxy* and bemoaning the state of his talent.

"I feel stuck," he said. "I'm playing pretty well...."

"You're playing great," said Little Red.

"Thanks, but I feel like there's some direction I ought to go, but I can't figure out what it is. I keep doing the same things over and over. It's like, I don't know, like I have to wash my ears before I'll be able to make any progress."

"Ah," said Little Red. "Let me play something for you." He rose from his chair.

"What?"

"Just listen."

"I don't need this jive bullshit, Little Red."

"I said, just *listen.*"

"Okay, but if you were a musician, you'd know this isn't how it works."

"Fine," said Little Red, and placed on the turntable a record by the Vic Dickenson Trio—trombone, bass, and guitar—made in 1949. "I'm going to my bedroom for a few minutes," he said. "Something screwy happened to my laundry a while ago, and I have to throw about half of it away."

C— M— leaned forward to rest his forearms on his knees, the posture in which he listened most carefully.

Little Red disappeared through the door to the toilet and went to his bedroom. Whatever he did there occupied him for approximately twenty minutes, after which he returned to the sitting room.

His face wet with tears, C— M— was leaning far back in his chair, looking as though he had just been dropped from a considerable height. "God bless you," he said. "God bless you, Little Red!"

4. The Miracle of the Blind Beggar-Man

He had been seeing the man for the better part of the year, seated on a wooden box next to the flowers outside the Korean deli on the corner of 55th Street and 8th Avenue, shaking a white paper cup salted with coins. Tall, heavy, dressed always in a double-breasted dark blue pinstriped suit of wondrous age, his skin a rich chocolate brown, the man was at his post four days every week from about nine in the morning to well past midnight. Whatever the weather, he covered his head with an ancient brown fedora, and he always wore dark glasses with lenses the size of quarters.

He was present on days when it rained and days when it snowed. On sweltering days, he never removed his hat to wipe his forehead, and on days when the temperature dropped into the teens he wore neither gloves nor overcoat. Once he had registered the man's presence, Little Red soon observed that he took in much more money than the other panhandlers who worked Hell's Kitchen. The reason for his success, Little Red surmised, was that his demeanor was as unvarying as his wardrobe.

He was a beggar who did not beg. Instead, he allowed you to give him money. Enthroned on his box, elbows planted on his knees, cup upright in his hand, he offered a steady stream of greetings, compliments, and benedictions to those who walked by.

You're sure looking fine today, miss . . . God bless you, son . . . You make sure to have a good day today, sir . . . God bless you, ma'am . . . Honey, you make me happy every time you come by . . . God bless you . . . God bless . . . God bless . . .

And so it happened that one day Little Red dropped a dollar bill into the waiting cup.

"God bless," the man said.

On the following day, Little Red gave him another dollar.

"Thank you and God bless you, son," the man said.

The next day, Little Red put two dollars in the cup.

"Thank you, Little Red, God bless you," said the man.

"How did you learn my name?" asked Little Red. "And how did you know it was me?"

"I hear they come to you, the peoples," the man said. "Night and day, they come. Ain't that the righteous truth? Night *and* day."

"They come, each in his own way," said Little Red. "But how do you know my name?"

"I always knew who you were," said the man. "And now I know what you are."

Little Red placed another dollar in his cup.

"Maybe I come see you myself, one day."

"Maybe you will," said Little Red.

5. The Miracle of the Greedy Demon (from Book I, Little Red, His Trials)

The greedy demons were everywhere. He saw them in the patrons' eyes— the demons, glaring out, saying *more, more*. While Little Red dressed to go to work, while he laced up his sturdy shoes, while taking the crosstown bus, as he opened the door to the bar and the headwaiter's desk, his stomach tightened at the thought of the waiting demons. Where demons reign, all joy is hollow, all happiness is pain in disguise, all pleasure merely the product of gratified envy. Daily, as he padded to the back of the restaurant to don his bow tie and white jacket, he feared he would be driven away by the flat, toxic stench of evil.

This occurred in the waning days of Little Red's youth, when he had not as yet entered fully into his adult estate.

The demons gathered here because they enjoyed each other's company. Demons can always recognize other demons, but the human beings they inhabit are ignorant of their possession and don't have a clue what is going on. They suppose they simply enjoy going to certain restaurants, or, say, a particular restaurant, because the food is decent and the atmosphere pleasant. The human beings possessed by demons fail to notice that while the prices have gone up a bit, the food has slipped and the atmosphere grown leaden, sour, stale. The headwaiter notices only that a strange languor has taken hold of the service staff, but he feels too languid himself to get excited about it. Ninety-nine percent of the waiters fail to notice that they seldom wish to look their patrons in the eye and record only that the place seems rather dimmer than it once was. Only Little Red sees the frantic demons jigging in the eyes of the torpid diners; only Little Red understands, and what he understands sickens him.

There came a day when a once-handsome gentleman in a blue blazer as taut as a sausage casing waved Little Red to his table and ordered a second 16-oz. rib eye steak, rare, and a second order of onion rings, and oh yeah, might as well throw in a second bottle of that Napa Valley cabernet.

"I won't do that," said Little Red.

"Kid, you gotta be shitting me," said the patron. His face shone a hectic pink. "I ordered another rib eye, more onion rings, and a fresh bottle of wine."

"You don't want any more food," said Little Red. He bent down and gazed into the man's eyes. "Something inside you wants it, but you don't."

The man gripped his wrist and moved his huge head alongside Little Red's. "You act that way with me, kid, and one cold night you could wake up and find me in your room, wearing nothing but a T-shirt."

"Then let it be so," said Little Red.

6. The Miracle of the Murdered Cat

Years after he had come into his adult estate, Little Red one day left his apartment to replenish his stock of Beck's beer. It was just before 6:00 A.M. on a Saturday morning in early June. Two trumpet players and a petty thief who had dropped in late Thursday night were scattered around the sitting room, basically doing nothing but waiting for him to come back with their breakfasts.

The Koreans who owned the deli on the corner of 55th and 8th lately had been communicating some kind of weirdness, so he turned the corner, intending to walk past the front of their shop and continue north to the deli on the corner of 56th Street, where the Koreans were still sane. The blind beggar startled him by stepping out of the entrance and saying, "My man, Little Red Man! Good morning to you, son. Seems to me you ought to be thinkin' about getting more sleep one of these days."

"Morning to you, too," said Little Red. "Early for you to be getting to work, isn't it?"

"Somethin' big's gonna happen today," said the beggar-man. "Wanted to make sure I didn't miss out." He set down his box, placed himself on it, and opened the 12-oz. bottle of Dr Pepper he had just purchased.

Only a few taxicabs moved up wide 8th Avenue, and no one else was on the sidewalk on either side. Iron shutters protected the windows of most of the shops.

As he moved up the block, Little Red looked across the street and saw a small shape leave the shelter of a rank of garbage cans and dart into the avenue. It was a little orange cat, bony with starvation.

The cat had raced to within fifteen feet of the western curb when a taxi rocketing north toward Columbus Circle swerved toward it. The cat froze, eyed the taxi, then gathered itself into a ball and streaked forward.

Little Red stood open-mouthed on the sidewalk. "You worthless little son of a bitch," he said. "Get moving!"

As the cat came nearly within leaping distance of the curb, the cab picked up speed and struck it. Little Red heard a muffled sound, then saw the cat roll across the surface of the road and come to rest in the gutter.

"Damn," he said, and glanced back at the beggar-man. He sat on his box, gripping his bottle of Dr Pepper and staring straight ahead at nothing. Little Red came up to the lifeless cat and lowered himself to the sidewalk. "You just get on now," he said. "Get going, little cat."

The lump of fur in the gutter twitched, twitched again, and struggled to its feet. It turned its head to Little Red and regarded him with opaque, suspicious eyes.

"Git," said Little Red.

The cat wobbled up onto the sidewalk, sat to drag its tongue over an oily patch of fur, and limped off into the shelter of a doorway.

Little Red stood up and glanced back down the street. The blind man cupped his hands around his mouth and called out something. Little Red could not quite make out his words, but they sounded approving.

7. The Miracle of the Kitchen Mouse

On a warm night last year, Little Red awakened in his command center to a silent apartment. His television set was turned off, and a single red light burned in the control panel of his CD player, which, having come to the end of *The Count on the Coast, Vol. II,* awaited further instructions.

Little Red rubbed his hands over his face and sat up, trying to decide whether or not to put on a new CD before falling back asleep. Before he could make up his mind, a small gray mouse slipped from between two six-packs of Beck's empties and hesitated at the edge of the sitting room. The mouse appeared to be looking at him.

"You go your way, and I'll go mine," said Little Red.

"God bless you, Little Red," said the mouse. Its voice was surprisingly deep.

"Thank you," said Little Red, and lapsed back into easy-breathing slumber.

THE BEATITUDES OF LITTLE RED, II

Over the long run, staying on good terms with your dentist really pays off.

Bargain up, not down.

When you're thinking about sex, the only person you have to please is yourself.

At least once a day, think about the greatest performance you ever heard.

Every now and then, remember Marilyn Monroe.

Put your garbage in the bin.

When spring comes, *notice* it.

Taste what you eat, dummy.

God pities demons, but He does not love them.

No matter how poor you are, put a little art up on your walls.

Let other people talk first. Your turn will come.

Wealth is measured in books and records.

All leases run out, sorry.

Every human being is beautiful, especially the ugly ones.

Resolution and restitution exist only in fantasy.

Learn to live *broken*. It's the only way.

Dirty dishes are just as sacred as clean ones.

In the midst of death, we are in life.

If some miserable bastard tries to cheat you, you might as well let the sorry piece of shit get away with it.

As soon as possible, move away from home.

Don't buy shoes that hurt your feet.

We are all walking through fire, so keep walking.

Never tell other people how to raise their children.

The truth not only hurts, it's unbearable. You have to live with it anyway.

Don't reject what you don't understand.

Simplicity works.

Only idiots boast, and only fools believe in "bragging rights."

You are *not* better than anyone else.

Cherish the dents in your armor.

Always look for the *source*.

Rhythm is repetition, repetition, repetition.

Snobbery is a disease of the imagination.

Happiness is primarily for children.

When it's time to go, that's what time it is.

LITTLE RED, HIS HOBBIES AND AMUSEMENTS

Apart from music, books, and television, he has no hobbies or amusements.

EPISTLE OF C— M— to R— B—, CONCERNING LITTLE RED

Dear R—,

Have you heard of the man, *if he is a man,* called Little Red? Has the word reached you? Okay, I know how that sounds, but don't start getting worried about me, because I haven't flipped out or lost my mind or anything, and I'm not trying to *convert* you to anything. I just want to describe something to you, that's all. You can make up your own mind about it afterward. Whatever you think will be okay with me. I guess I'm still trying to make up my own mind—probably that's one reason why I'm writing you this letter.

I told you that before I left Chicago the last time, I took some lessons from C— F—, right? What a great player that cat is. Well, you know. The year we got out of high school, we must have listened to *Live in Las Vegas* at least a thousand times. Man, he really opened our eyes, didn't he? And not just about the trombone, as amazing as that was, but about music in general, remember? So he was playing in town, and I went every night and stayed for every set, and before long he noticed I was there all the time, and on the third night I bought him a drink, and we got talking, and he found out I played trombone, and when and where and all that, and he asked me if I would sit in during the second set the next night. So I brought my horn and I sat in, and he was amazing. I guess I did okay, because he said, "That was nice, kid." Which made me feel very, very good, as you can imagine. I asked could he give me some lessons while he was in town. Know what he told me? "I can probably show you some things, sure."

We met four times in his hotel room, besides spending an hour or two together after the gig, most nights. Mainly, he worked on my breathing and lip exercises, but apart from that the real education was just listening to him talk, man. Crazy shit that happened on the road with Kenton and Woody Herman, stories about the guys who could really cut it and the guys who couldn't but got over anyhow, all kinds of great stories. And one day he says to me, When you get to New York, kid, you should look up this guy Little Red, and tell him I said you were okay.

"What is he," I asked, "a trombone player?"

Nah, he said, just a guy he thought I should know. Maybe he could do me some good. "Little Red, he's hard to describe if you haven't met him," he said. "Being with the guy is sort of like doing the tango." Then he laughed.

"The tango?" I asked.

"Yeah," he said. "You might wind up with your head up your ass, but you know you had a hell of a time anyway."

So when I got to New York I asked around about this Little Red, and plenty of people knew him, it turned out, musicians especially, but nobody could tell me exactly what the guy did, or what made him so special. It was like—if you *know*, then there's no point in talking about it, and if you don't, you can't talk about it at all, you can't even begin. Because I met a couple of guys like that, when Little Red's name came up they just shrugged their shoulders and shook their heads. One guy even walked out of the room we were in!

Eventually I decided I had to see for myself, and I called him up. He acted sort of cagey. How did I hear about him, who did I know? "C— F— said to tell you I was okay," I said. All right, he said, come on over later, around 10, when he'd be free.

About 10:30, I got to his building—55th off 8th, an easy walk from my room on 44th and 9th. I buzz his apartment, he buzzes me in. And here he is, opening the door to his apartment, this skinny guy with a red beard and long red hair tied back in a ponytail. His face looks sad, and he looks pretty tired, but he gives me a beer right away and sits me down in his incredibly messy room, stuff piled up in front of a wall of about a million records, and asks me what I'd like to hear. I dunno, I say, I'm a trombone player, is it possible he has some good stuff I maybe don't know about? And we're off! The guy has *hundreds* of great things I'd never heard before, some I never heard of at all, and before I know it five or six hours have gone by and I have to get back to my room before I pass out in his chair. He says he'll make me a tape of the best stuff we heard, and I go home. In all that time, I realized, Little Red said maybe a dozen words altogether. I felt like something tremendously important had happened to me, but I couldn't have told you what it was.

The third time I went back to Little Red's, I started complaining about feeling stuck in my playing, and he put on an old Vic Dickenson record that made my head spin around on my shoulders. It was exactly what I needed, and he knew it! He *understood*.

After that, I started spending more and more time at his place. Winter had ended, but spring hadn't come yet. When I walked up 9th Avenue, the air was bright and cold. Little Red seemed not to notice how frigid his apartment was, and after a while, I forgot all about it. The sunlight burned around the edges of the shades in his kitchen and his living room, and as the time went by it faded away and turned to utter darkness, and sometimes I thought of all the stars filling the sky over 55th Street, even though we wouldn't be able to see them if we went outside.

Usually, we were alone. He talked to me—he *spoke*. There were times when other people came in, said a few things, then left us alone again.

Often, he let his words drift away into silence, brought some fresh bread in from his kitchen, and shared it with me. That bread had a wonderful, wonderful taste. I've never managed to find that taste again.

A couple of times he poured out wine for me instead of beer, and that wine seemed extraordinary. It tasted like sunshine, like sunshine on rich farmland.

Once, he asked me if I knew anything about a woman named something like Simone Vey. When I said I'd never heard of her, he said that was all right, he was just asking. Later he wrote out her name for me, and it was spelled W-E-I-L, not V-E-Y. Who is this woman? What did she do? I can't find out anything about her.

After a couple of weeks, I got out of the habit of going home when it was time to sleep, and I just stretched out on the floor and slept until I woke up again. Little Red almost always went to sleep in his chair, and when I woke up I would see him, tilted back, his eyes closed, looking like the most peaceful man in the world.

He talked to me, but it wasn't as though he was *teaching* me anything, exactly. We talked back and forth, off and on, during the days and nights, in the way friends do, and to me everything seemed comfortable, familiar, as it should be.

One morning he told me that I had to go, it was time. "You're kidding," I said. "This is perfect. I don't really have to leave, do I?"

"You must go," he said. I wanted to fall to the floor and beg, I wanted to clutch the cuffs of his trousers and hang on until he changed his mind.

He shoved me out into the hallway and locked the door behind me. I had no choice but to leave. I stumbled down the hall and wandered into the streets, remembering a night when I'd seen a mouse creep out of his kitchen, bless him by name, and receive his blessing in return. When I had staggered three or four blocks south on 8th Avenue, I realized that I could never again go back.

It was a mistake that I had been there in the first place—he had taken me in by mistake, and my place was not in that crowded apartment. My place might be anywhere, a jail cell, a suburban bedroom with tacky paintings on the wall, a bench in a subway station, anywhere but in that apartment.

I often try to remember the things he said to me. My heart thickens, my throat constricts, a few words come back, but how can I know if they are the right words? He can never tell me if they are.

I think: some kind of love did pass between us. But how could Little Red have loved me? He could not, it is impossible. And yet, R—, a fearful, awkward bit of being, a particle hidden deep within myself, has no choice but to think that maybe, just maybe, in spite of everything, he does after all love me.

So tell me, old friend, have you ever heard of Little Red?

Yours,

C—

The Ballad of the
Flexible Bullet

Stephen King

*J*he barbecue was over. It had been a good one; drinks, char-coaled T-bones, rare, a green salad, and Meg's special dressing. They had started at five. Now it was eight-thirty and almost dusk—the time when a big party is just starting to get rowdy. But they weren't a big party. There were just the five of them: the agent and his wife, the celebrated young writer and *his* wife, and the magazine editor, who was in his early sixties and looked older. The editor stuck to Fresca. The agent had told the young writer before the editor arrived that there had once been a drinking problem there. It was gone now, and so was the editor's wife...which was why they were five instead of six.

Instead of getting rowdy, an introspective mood fell over them as it started to get dark in the young writer's backyard, which fronted the lake. The young writer's first novel had been well reviewed and had sold a lot of copies. He was a lucky young man, and to his credit he knew it.

The conversation had turned with playful gruesomeness from the young writer's early success to other writers who had made their marks early and had then committed suicide. Ross Lockridge was touched upon, and Tom Hagen. The agent's wife mentioned Sylvia Plath and Anne Sexton, and the young writer said that he didn't think Plath qualified as a successful writer. She had not committed suicide because of success, he said; she had gained success because she had committed suicide. The agent smiled.

"Please, couldn't we talk about something else?" the young writer's wife asked, a little nervously.

Ignoring her, the agent said, "And madness. There have been those who have gone mad because of success." The agent had the mild but nonetheless rolling tones of an actor offstage.

The writer's wife was about to protest again—she knew that her husband not only liked to talk about these things so he could joke about them, and he wanted to joke about them because he thought about them too much—when the magazine editor spoke up. What he said was so odd she forgot to protest.

"Madness is a flexible bullet."

The agent's wife looked startled. The young writer leaned forward quizzically. He said, "That sounds familiar—"

"Sure," the editor said. "That phrase, the image, 'flexible bullet,' is Marianne Moore's. She used it to describe some car or other. I've always thought it described the condition of madness very well. Madness is a kind of mental suicide. Don't the doctors say now that the only way to truly measure death is by the death of the mind? Madness is a kind of flexible bullet to the brain."

The young writer's wife hopped up. "Anybody want another drink?" She had no takers.

"Well, I do, if we're going to talk about this," she said, and went off to make herself one.

The editor said: "I had a story submitted to me once, when I was working over at *Logan's*. Of course it's gone the way of *Collier's* and *The Saturday Evening Post* now, but we outlasted both of them." He said this with a trace of pride. "We published thirty-six short stories a year, or more, and every year four or five of them would be in somebody's collection of the year's best. And people read them. Anyway, the name of this story was 'The Ballad of the Flexible Bullet,' and it was written by a man named Reg Thorpe. A young man about this young man's age, and about as successful."

"He wrote *Underworld Figures,* didn't he?" the agent's wife asked.

"Yes. Amazing track record for a first novel. Great reviews, lovely sales in hardcover and paperback, Literary Guild, everything. Even the movie was pretty good, although not as good as the book. Nowhere near."

"I loved that book," the author's wife said, lured back into the conversation against her better judgment. She had the surprised, pleased look of someone who has just recalled something which has been out of mind for too long. "Has he written anything since then? I read *Underworld Figures* back in college and that was . . . well, too long ago to think about."

"You haven't aged a day since then," the agent's wife said warmly, although privately she thought the young writer's wife was wearing a too-small halter and a too-tight pair of shorts.

"No, he hasn't written anything since then," the editor said. "Except for this one short story I was telling you about. He killed himself. Went crazy and killed himself."

"Oh," the young writer's wife said limply. Back to *that.*

"Was the short story published?" the young writer asked.

"No, but not because the author went crazy and killed himself. It never got into print because the *editor* went crazy and *almost* killed himself."

The agent suddenly got up to freshen his own drink, which hardly need freshening. He knew that the editor had had a nervous breakdown in the summer of 1969, not long before *Logan's* had drowned in a sea of red ink.

"I was the editor," the editor informed the rest of them. "In a sense we went crazy together, Reg Thorpe and I, even though I was in New York, he was out in Omaha, and we never even met. His book had been out about six months and he had moved out there 'to get his head together,' as the phrase was then. And I happen to know this side of the story because I see his wife occasionally when she's in New York. She paints, and quite well. She's a lucky girl. He almost took her with him."

The agent came back and sat down. "I'm starting to remember some of this now," he said. "It wasn't just his wife, was it? He shot a couple of other people, one of them a kid."

"That's right," the editor said. "It was the kid that finally set him off."

"The *kid* set him off?" the agent's wife asked. "What do you mean?"

But the editor's face said he would not be drawn; he would talk, but not be questioned.

"I know my side of the story because I lived it," the magazine editor said. "I'm lucky, too. Damned lucky. It's an interesting thing about those who try to kill themselves by pointing a gun at their heads and pulling the trigger. You'd think it would be the foolproof method, better than pills or slashing the wrists, but it isn't. When you shoot yourself in the head, you just can't tell what's going to happen. The slug may ricochet off the skull and kill someone else. It may follow the skull's curve all the way around and come out on the other side. It may lodge in the brain and blind you and leave you alive. One man may shoot himself in the forehead with a .38 and wake up in the hospital. Another may shoot himself in the forehead with a .22 and wake up in hell... if there is such a place. I tend to believe it's here on earth, possibly in New Jersey."

The writer's wife laughed rather shrilly.

"The only foolproof suicide method is to step off a very high building, and that's a way out that only the extraordinarily dedicated ever take. So damned messy, isn't it?

"But my point is simply this: When you shoot yourself with a flexible bullet, you really don't know what the outcome is going to be. In my case, I went off a bridge and woke up on a trash-littered embankment with a trucker whapping me on the back and pumping my arms up and down like he had only twenty-four hours to get in shape and he had mistaken me for a rowing machine. For Reg, the bullet was lethal. He... But I'm telling you a story I have no idea if you want to hear."

He looked around at them questioningly in the gathering gloom. The agent and the agent's wife glanced at each other uncertainly, and the writer's wife was about to say she thought they'd had enough gloomy talk when her husband said, "I'd like to hear it. If you don't mind telling it for personal reasons, I mean."

"I never have told it," the editor said, "but not for personal reasons. Perhaps I never had the correct listeners."

"Then tell away," the writer said.

"Paul—" His wife put her hand on his shoulder. "Don't you think—"

"Not now, Meg."

The editor said:

"The story came in over the transom, and at that time *Logan's* no longer read unsolicited scripts. When they came in, a girl would just put them into return envelopes with a note that said 'Due to increasing costs and the increasing inability of the editorial staff to cope with a steadily increasing number of submissions, *Logan's* no longer reads unsolicited manuscripts. We wish you the best of luck in placing your work elsewhere.' Isn't that a lovely bunch of gobbledygook? It's not easy to use the word 'increasing' three times in one sentence, but they did it."

"And if there was no return postage, the story went into the wastebasket," the writer said. "Right?"

"Oh, absolutely. No pity in the naked city."

An odd expression of unease flitted across the writer's face. It was the expression of a man who is in a tiger pit where dozens of better men have been clawed to pieces. So far this man hasn't seen a single tiger. But he has a feeling that they are there, and that their claws are still sharp.

"Anyway," the editor said, taking out his cigarette case, "this story came in, and the girl in the mailroom took it out, paper-clipped the form rejection to the first page, and was getting ready to put it in the return envelope when she glanced at the author's name. Well, she had read *Underworld Figures*. That fall, everybody had read it, or was reading it, or was on the library waiting list, or checking the drugstore racks for the paperback."

The writer's wife, who had seen the momentary unease on her husband's face, took his hand. He smiled at her. The editor snapped a gold Ronson to his cigarette, and in the growing dark they could all see how haggard his face was—the loose, crocodile-skinned pouches under the eyes, the runneled cheeks, the old man's jut of chin emerging out of that late-middle-aged face like the prow of a ship. That ship, the writer thought, is called old age. No one particularly wants to cruise on it, but the staterooms are full. The gangholds too, for that matter.

The lighter winked out, and the editor puffed his cigarette meditatively.

"The girl in the mailroom who read that story and passed it on instead of sending it back is now a full editor at G. P. Putnam's Sons. Her name doesn't matter; what matters is that on the great graph of life, this girl's vector crossed Reg Thorpe's in the mailroom of *Logan's* magazine. Hers was going up and his was going down. She sent the story to her boss and her boss sent it to me. I read it and loved it. It was really too long, but I could see where he could pare five hundred words off it with no sweat. And that would be plenty."

"What was it about?" the writer asked.

"You shouldn't even have to ask," the editor said. "It fits so beautifully into the total context."

"About going crazy?"

"Yes, indeed. What's the first thing they teach you in your first college creative-writing course? Write about what you know. Reg Thorpe knew about going crazy, because he was engaged in going there. The story probably appealed to me because I was also going there. Now you could say— if you were an editor—that the one thing the American reading public doesn't need foisted on them is another story about Going Mad Stylishly in America, subtopic A, Nobody Talks to Each Other Anymore. A popular theme in twentieth-century literature. All the greats have taken a hack at it and all the hacks have taken an ax to it. But this story was funny. I mean, it was really hilarious.

"I hadn't read anything like it before and I haven't since. The closest would be some of F. Scott Fitzgerald's stories . . . and *Gatsby*. The fellow in Thorpe's story was going crazy, but he was doing it in a very funny way. You kept grinning, and there were a couple of places in this story—the place where the hero dumps the lime Jell-O on the fat girl's head is the best— where you laugh right out loud. But they're jittery laughs, you know. You laugh and then you want to look over your shoulder to see what heard you. The opposing lines of tension in that story were really extraordinary. The more you laughed, the more nervous you got. And the more nervous you got, the more you laughed . . . right up to the point where the hero goes home from the party given in his honor and kills his wife and baby daughter."

"What's the plot?" the agent asked.

"No," the editor said, "that doesn't matter. It was just a story about a young man gradually losing his struggle to cope with success. It's better left vague. A detailed plot synopsis would only be boring. They always are.

"Anyway, I wrote him a letter. It said this: 'Dear Reg Thorpe, I've just read "The Ballad of the Flexible Bullet" and I think it's great. I'd like to publish it in *Logan's* early next year, if that fits. Does $800 sound okay? Payment on acceptance. More or less.' New paragraph."

The editor indented the evening air with his cigarette.

"'The story runs a little long, and I'd like you to shorten it by about five hundred words, if you could. I would settle for a two-hundred-word cut, if it comes to that. We can always drop a cartoon.' Paragraph. 'Call, if you want.' My signature. And off the letter went, to Omaha."

"And you remember it, word for word like that?" the writer's wife asked.

"I kept all the correspondence in a special file," the editor said. "His letters, carbons of mine back. There was quite a stack of it by the end, including three or four pieces of correspondence from Jane Thorpe, his wife. I've read the file over quite often. No good, of course. Trying to understand the flexible bullet is like trying to understand how a Möbius strip can have only one side. That's just the way things are in this best-of-all-possible worlds. Yes, I know it all word for word, or almost. Some people have the Declaration of Independence by heart."

"Bet he called you the next day," the agent said, grinning. "Collect."

"No, he didn't call. Shortly after *Underworld Figures*, Thorpe stopped using the telephone altogether. His wife told me that. When they moved to Omaha from New York, they didn't even have a phone put in the new house. He had decided, you see, that the telephone system didn't really run on electricity but on radium. He thought it was one of the two or three best-kept secrets in the history of the modern world. He claimed—to his wife—that all the radium was responsible for the growing cancer rate, not cigarettes or automobile emissions or industrial pollution. Each telephone had a small radium crystal in the handset, and every time you used the phone, you shot your head full of radiation."

"Yuh, he was crazy," the writer said, and they all laughed.

"He wrote instead," the editor said, flicking his cigarette in the direction of the lake. "His letter said this: 'Dear Henry Wilson (or just Henry, if I may), Your letter was both exciting and gratifying. My wife was, if anything, more pleased than I. The money is fine ... although in all honesty I must say that the idea of being published in *Logan's* at all seems like more than adequate compensation (but I'll take it, I'll take it). I've looked over your cuts, and they seem fine. I think they'll improve the story as well as clear space for those cartoons. All best wishes, Reg Thorpe.'

"Under his signature was a funny little drawing ... more like a doodle. An eye in a pyramid, like the one on the back of the dollar bill. But instead of Novus Ordo Seclorum on the banner beneath there were these words: Fornit Some Fornus."

"Either Latin or Groucho Marx," the agent's wife said.

"Just part of Reg Thorpe's growing eccentricity," the editor said. "His wife told me that Reg had come to believe in 'little people,' sort of like elves or fairies. The Fornits. They were luck-elves, and he thought one of them lived in his typewriter."

"Oh my Lord," the writer's wife said.

"According to Thorpe, each Fornit has a small device, like a flit-gun, full of . . . good-luck dust, I guess you'd call it. And the good-luck dust—"

"—is called fornus," the writer finished. He was grinning broadly.

"Yes. And his wife thought it quite funny, too. At first. In fact, she thought at first—Thorpe had conceived the Fornits two years before, while he was drafting *Underworld Figures*—that it was just Reg, having her on. And maybe at first he was. It seems to have progressed from a whimsy to a superstition to an outright belief. It was . . . a flexible fantasy. But hard in the end. Very hard."

They were all silent. The grins had faded.

"The Fornits had their funny side," the editor said. "Thorpe's typewriter started going to the shop a lot near the end of their stay in New York, and it was even a more frequent thing when they moved to Omaha. He had a loaner while it was being fixed for the first time out there. The dealership manager called a few days after Reg got his own machine back to tell him he was going to send a bill for cleaning the loaner as well as Thorpe's own machine."

"What was the trouble?" the agent's wife asked.

"I think I know," the writer's wife said.

"It was full of food," the editor said. "Tiny bits of cake and cookies. There was peanut butter smeared on the platens of the keys themselves. Reg was feeding the Fornit in his typewriter. He also 'fed' the loaner, on the off chance that the Fornit had made the switch."

"Boy," the writer said.

"I knew none of these things then, you understand. For the nonce, I wrote back to him and told him how pleased I was. My secretary typed the letter and brought it in for my signature, and then she had to go out for something. I signed it and she wasn't back. And then—for no real reason at all—I put the same doodle below my name. Pyramid. Eye. And 'Fornit Some Fornus.' Crazy. The secretary saw it and asked me if I wanted it sent out that way. I shrugged and told her to go ahead.

"Two days later Jane Thorpe called me. She told me that my letter had

excited Reg a great deal. Reg thought he had found a kindred soul...
someone else who knew about the Fornits. You see what a crazy situation
it was getting to be? As far as I knew at that point, a Fornit could have been
anything from a left-handed monkey wrench to a Polish steak knife. Ditto
fornus. I explained to Jane that I had merely copied Reg's own design. She
wanted to know why. I slipped the question, although the answer would
have been because I was very drunk when I signed the letter."

He paused, and an uncomfortable silence fell on the back lawn area.
People looked at the sky, the lake, the trees, although they were no more
interesting now than they had been a minute or two before.   .

"I had been drinking all my adult life, and it's impossible for me to say
when it began to get out of control. In the professional sense I was on top
of the bottle until nearly the very end. I would begin drinking at lunch and
come back to the office el blotto. I functioned perfectly well there, however.
It was the drinks after work—first on the train, then at home—that pushed
me over the functional point.

"My wife and I had been having problems that were unrelated to the
drinking, but the drinking made the other problems worse. For a long time
she had been preparing to leave, and a week before the Reg Thorpe story
came in, she did it.

"I was trying to deal with that when the Thorpe story came in. I was
drinking too much. And to top it all off, I was having—well, I guess now
it's fashionable to call it a midlife crisis. All I knew at the time was that I
was as depressed about my professional life as I was about my personal
one. I was coming to grips—or trying to—with a growing feeling that ed-
iting mass-market stories that would end up being read by nervous dental
patients, housewives at lunchtime, and an occasional bored college student
was not exactly a noble occupation. I was coming to grips—again, trying
to, all of us at Logan's were at that time—with the idea that in another six
months, or ten, or fourteen, there might not be any Logan's.

"Into this dull autumnal landscape of middle-aged angst comes a very
good story by a very good writer, a funny, energetic look at the mechanics
of going crazy. It was like a bright ray of sun. I know it sounds strange to
say that about a story that ends with the protagonist killing his wife and
infant child, but you ask any editor what real joy is, and he'll tell you it's
the great story or novel you didn't expect, landing on your desk like a big
Christmas present. Look, you all know that Shirley Jackson story 'The Lot-

tery.' It ends on one of the most downbeat notes you can imagine. I mean, they take a nice lady out and stone her to death. Her son and daughter participate in her murder, for Christ's sake. But it was a great piece of storytelling...and I bet the editor at *The New Yorker* who read the story first went home that night whistling.

"What I'm trying to say is the Thorpe story was the best thing in my life right then. The one good thing. And from what his wife told me on the phone that day, my acceptance of that story was the one good thing that had happened to him lately. The author-editor relationship is always mutual parasitism, but in the case of Reg and me, that parasitism was heightened to an unnatural degree."

"Let's go back to Jane Thorpe," the writer's wife said.

"Yes, I did sort of leave her on a sidetrack, didn't I? She was angry about the Fornit business. At first. I told her I had simply doodled that eye-and-pyramid symbol under my signature, with no knowledge of what it might be, and apologized for whatever I'd done.

"She got over her anger and spilled everything to me. She'd been getting more and more anxious, and she had no one at all to talk to. Her folks were dead, and all her friends were back in New York. Reg wouldn't allow anyone at all in the house. They were tax people, he said, or FBI, or CIA. Not long after they moved to Omaha, a little girl came to the door selling Girl Scout cookies. Reg yelled at her, told her to get the hell out, he knew why she was there, and so on. Jane tried to reason with him. She pointed out that the girl had only been ten years old. Reg told her that the tax people had no souls, no consciences. And besides, he said, the little girl might have been an android. Androids wouldn't be subject to the child-labor laws. He wouldn't put it past the tax people to send an android Girl Scout full of radium crystals to find out if he was keeping any secrets...and to shoot him full of cancer rays in the meantime."

"Good Lord," the agent's wife said.

"She'd been waiting for a friendly voice and mine was the first. I got the Girl Scout story, I found out about the care and feeding of Fornits, about fornus, about how Reg refused to use a telephone. She was talking to me from a pay booth in a drugstore five blocks over. She told me that she was afraid it wasn't really tax men or FBI or CIA Reg was worried about. She thought he was really afraid that *They*—some hulking, anonymous group that hated Reg, was jealous of Reg, would stop at nothing to get Reg—had found out about his Fornit and wanted to kill it. If the Fornit was dead, there would be no more novels, no more short stories, nothing. You see? The essence of insanity. *They* were out to get him. In the end, not even the IRS, which had given him the very devil of a time over the income *Underworld Figures* generated, would serve as the boogeyman. In the end it was just *They*. The perfect paranoid fantasy. *They* wanted to kill his Fornit."

"My God, what did you say to her?" the agent asked.

"I tried to reassure her," the editor said. "There I was, freshly returned from a five-martini lunch, talking to this terrified woman who was standing in a drugstore phone booth in Omaha, trying to tell her it was all right, not to worry that her husband believed that the phones were full of radium crystals, that a bunch of anonymous people were sending android Girl Scouts to get the goods on him, not to worry that her husband had disconnected his talent from his mentality to such a degree that he could believe there was an elf living in his typewriter.

"I don't believe I was very convincing.

"She asked me—no, begged me—to work with Reg on his story, to see that it got published. She did everything but come out and say that 'The Flexible Bullet' was Reg's last contact to what we laughingly call reality.

"I asked her what I should do if Reg mentioned Fornits again. 'Humor him,' she said. Her exact words—humor him. And then she hung up.

"There was a letter in the mail from Reg the next day—five pages, typed, single-spaced. The first paragraph was about the story. The second draft was getting on well, he said. He thought he would be able to shave seven hundred words from the original ten thousand five hundred, bringing the final down to a tight nine thousand eight.

"The rest of the letter was about Fornits and fornus. His own observations, and questions . . . dozens of questions."

"Observations?" The writer leaned forward. "He was actually seeing them, then?"

"No," the editor said. "Not seeing them in an actual sense, but in another way . . . I suppose he was. You know, astronomers knew Pluto was there long before they had a telescope powerful enough to see it. They knew all about it by studying the planet Neptune's orbit. Reg was observing the Fornits in that way. They liked to eat at night, he said, had I noticed that? He fed them at all hours of the day, but he noticed that most of it disappeared after eight P.M."

"Hallucination?" the writer asked.

"No," the editor said. "His wife simply cleared as much of the food out of the typewriter as she could when Reg went out for his evening walk. And he went out every evening at nine o'clock."

"I'd say she had quite a nerve getting after you," the agent grunted. He shifted his large bulk in the lawn chair. "She was feeding the man's fantasy herself."

"You don't understand why she called and why she was so upset," the editor said quietly. He looked at the writer's wife. "But I'll bet you do, Meg."

"Maybe," she said, and gave her husband an uncomfortable sideways look. "She wasn't mad because you were feeding his fantasy. She was afraid you might upset it."

"Bravo." The editor lit a fresh cigarette. "And she removed the food for the same reason. If the food continued to accumulate in the typewriter, Reg would make the logical assumption, proceeding directly from his own decidedly illogical premise. Namely, that his Fornit had either died or left. Hence, no more fornus. Hence, no more writing. Hence . . ."

The editor let the word drift away on cigarette smoke and then resumed:

"He thought that Fornits were probably nocturnal. They didn't like loud noises—he had noticed that he hadn't been able to write on mornings after noisy parties—they hated the TV, they hated free electricity, they hated radium. Reg had sold their TV to Goodwill for twenty dollars, he said, and his wristwatch with the radium dial was long gone. Then the questions. How did I know about Fornits? Was it possible that I had one in residence? If so, what did I think about this, this, and that? I don't need to be more specific, I think. If you've ever gotten a dog of a particular breed and can recollect the questions you asked about its care and feeding, you'll know most of the questions Reg asked me. One little doodle below my signature was all it took to open Pandora's box."

"What did you write back?" the agent asked.

The editor said slowly, "That's where the trouble really began. For both of us. Jane had said, 'Humor him,' so that's what I did. Unfortunately, I rather overdid it. I answered his letter at home, and I was very drunk. The apartment seemed much too empty. It had a stale smell—cigarette smoke, not enough airing. Things were going to seed with Sandra gone. The drop cloth on the couch all wrinkled. Dirty dishes in the sink, that sort of thing. The middle-aged man unprepared for domesticity.

"I sat there with a sheet of my personal stationery rolled into the type-writer and I thought: *I need a Fornit. In fact, I need a dozen of them to dust this damn lonely house with fornus from end to end.* In that instant I was drunk enough to envy Reg Thorpe his delusion.

"I said I had a Fornit, of course. I told Reg that mine was remarkably similar to his in its characteristics. Nocturnal. Hated loud noises, but seemed to enjoy Bach and Brahms...I often did my best work after an evening of listening to them, I said. I had found my Fornit had a decided taste for Kirschner's bologna...had Reg ever tried it? I simply left little scraps of it near the Scripto I always carried—my editorial blue pencil, if you like—and it was almost always gone in the morning. Unless, as Reg said, it had been noisy the night before. I told him I was glad to know about radium, even though I didn't have a glow-in-the-dark wristwatch. I told him my Fornit had been with me since college. I got so carried away with my own invention that I wrote nearly six pages. At the end I added a paragraph about the story, a very perfunctory thing, and signed it."

"And below your signature—?" the agent's wife asked.

"Sure. *Fornit Some Fornus.*" He paused. "You can't see it in the dark, but I'm blushing. I was so goddammed drunk, so goddammed *smug*...I might have had second thoughts in the cold light of dawn, but by then it was too late."

"You'd mailed it the night before?" the writer murmured.

"So I did. And then, for a week and a half, I held my breath and waited. One day the manuscript came in, addressed to me, no covering letter. The cuts were as we had discussed them, and I thought that the story was letter-perfect, but the manuscript was...well, I put it in my briefcase, took it home, and retyped it myself. It was covered with weird yellow stains. I thought..."

"Urine?" the agent's wife asked.

"Yes, that's what I thought. But it wasn't. And when I got home, there was a letter in my mailbox from Reg. Ten pages this time. In the course of the letter the yellow stains were accounted for. He hadn't been able to find Kirschner's bologna, so had tried Jordan's.

"He said they loved it. Especially with mustard.

"I had been quite sober that day. But his letter combined with those pitiful mustard stains ground right into the pages of his manuscript sent me directly to the liquor cabinet. Do not pass go, do not collect two hundred dollars. Go directly to drunk."

"What else did the letter say?" the agent's wife asked. She had grown more and more fascinated with the tale, and was now leaning over her not inconsiderable belly in a posture that reminded the writer's wife of Snoopy standing on his doghouse and pretending to be a vulture.

"Only two lines about the story this time. All credit thrown to the Fornit . . . and to me. The bologna had really been a fantastic idea. Rackne loved it, and as a consequence—"

"Rackne?" the author asked.

"That was the Fornit's name," the editor said. "Rackne. As a consequence of the bologna, Rackne had really gotten behind in the rewrite. The rest of the letter was a paranoid chant. You have never seen such stuff in your life."

"Reg and Rackne . . . a marriage made in heaven," the writer's wife said, and giggled nervously.

"Oh, not at all," the editor said. "Theirs was a working relationship. And Rackne was male."

"Well, tell us about the letter."

"That's one I don't have by heart. It's just as well for you that I don't. Even abnormality grows tiresome after a while. The mailman was CIA. The paperboy was FBI; Reg had seen a silenced revolver in his sack of papers. The people next door were spies of some sort; they had surveillance equipment in their van. He no longer dared to go down to the corner store for supplies because the proprietor was an android. He had suspected it before, he said, but now he was sure. He had seen the wires crisscrossing under the man's scalp, where he was beginning to go bald. And the radium count in his house was way up; at night he could see a dull, greenish glow in the rooms.

"His letter finished this way: 'I hope you'll write back and apprise me of your own situation (and that of your Fornit) as regards *enemies*, Henry. I believe that reaching you has been an occurrence that transcends coincidence. I would call it a life-ring from (God? Providence? Fate? supply your own term) at the last possible instant.

" 'It is not possible for a man to stand alone for long against a thousand *enemies*. And to discover, at last, that one is *not* alone...is it too much to say that the commonality of our experience stands between myself and total destruction? Perhaps not. I must know: Are the *enemies* after your Fornit as they are after Rackne? If so, how are you coping? If not, do you have any idea *why not*? I repeat, *I must know.'*

"The letter was signed with the Fornit Some Fornus doodle beneath, and then a P.S. Just one sentence. But lethal. The P.S. said: 'Sometimes I wonder about my wife.'

"I read the letter through three times. In the process, I killed an entire bottle of Black Velvet. I began to consider options on how to answer his letter. It was a cry for help from a drowning man, that was pretty obvious. The story had held him together for a while, but now the story was done. Now he was depending on me to hold him together. Which was perfectly reasonable, since I'd brought the whole thing on myself.

"I walked up and down the house, through all the empty rooms. And I started to unplug things. I was very drunk, remember, and heavy drinking opens unexpected avenues of suggestibility. Which is why editors and lawyers are willing to spring for three drinks before talking contract at lunch."

The agent brayed laughter, but the mood remained tight and tense and uncomfortable.

"And please keep in mind that Reg Thorpe was one hell of a writer. He was absolutely convinced of the things he was saying. FBI. CIA. IRS. *They. The enemies.* Some writers possess a very rare gift for cooling their prose the more passionately they feel their subject. Steinbeck had it, so did Hemingway, and Reg Thorpe had that same talent. When you entered his world, everything began to seem very logical. You began to think it very likely, once you accepted the basic Fornit premise, that the paperboy *did* have a silenced .38 in his bag of papers. That the college kids next door with the van might indeed be KGB agents with death-capsules in wax molars, on a do-or-die mission to kill or capture Rackne.

"Of course, I didn't accept the basic premise. But it seemed so hard to think. And I unplugged things. First the color TV, because everybody knows that they really do give off radiation. At *Logan's* we had published an article by a perfectly reputable scientist suggesting that the radiation given off by the household color television was interrupting human brain-waves just enough to alter them minutely but permanently. This scientist suggested that it might be the reason for declining college-board scores, literacy tests, and grammar-school development of arithmetical skills. After all, who sits closer to the TV than a little kid?

"So I unplugged the TV, and it really did seem to clarify my thoughts. In fact, it made it so much better that I unplugged the radio, the toaster, the washing machine, the dryer. Then I remembered the microwave oven, and I unplugged that. I felt a real sense of relief when that fucking thing's teeth were pulled. It was one of the early ones, about the size of a house, and it probably really was dangerous. Shielding on them's better these days.

"It occurred to me just how many things we have in any ordinary middle-class house that plug into the wall. An image occurred to me of this nasty electrical octopus, its tentacles consisting of electrical cables, all snaking into the walls, all connected with wires outside, and all the wires leading to power stations run by the government.

"There was a curious doubling in my mind as I did those things," the editor went on, after pausing for a sip of his Fresca. "Essentially, I was responding to a superstitious impulse. There are plenty of people who won't walk under ladders or open an umbrella in the house. There are basketball players who cross themselves before taking foul shots and baseball players who change their socks when they're in a slump. I think it's the rational mind playing a bad stereo accompaniment with the irrational subconscious. Forced to define 'irrational subconscious,' I would say that it is a small padded room inside all of us, where the only furnishing is a small card table, and the only thing on the card table is a revolver loaded with flexible bullets.

"When you change course on the sidewalk to avoid the ladder or step out of your apartment into the rain with your furled umbrella, part of your integrated self peels off and steps into that room and picks the gun up off the table. You may be aware of two conflicting thoughts: *Walking under a ladder is harmless*, and *Not walking under a ladder is also harmless*. But as soon as the ladder is behind you—or as soon as the umbrella is open—you're back together again."

The writer said, "That's very interesting. Take it a step further for me, if you don't mind. When does that irrational part actually stop fooling with the gun and put it up to its temple?"

The editor said, "When the person in question starts writing letters to the op-ed page of the paper demanding that all the ladders be taken down because walking under them is dangerous."

There was a laugh.

"Having taken it that far, I suppose we ought to finish. The irrational self has actually fired the flexible bullet into the brain when the person begins tearing around town, knocking ladders over and maybe injuring the people that were working on them. It is not certifiable behavior to walk around ladders rather than under them. It is not certifiable behavior to write letters to the paper saying that New York City went broke because of all the people callously walking under workmen's ladders. But it is certifiable to start knocking over ladders."

"Because it's overt," the writer muttered.

The agent said, "You know, you've got something there, Henry. I've got this thing about not lighting three cigarettes on a match. I don't know how I got it, but I did. Then I read somewhere that it came from the trench warfare in World War I. It seems that the German sharpshooters would wait for the Tommies to start lighting each other's cigarettes. On the first light, you got the range. On the second one, you got the windage. And on the third one, you blew the guy's head off. But knowing all that didn't make any difference. I still can't light three on a match. One part of me says it doesn't matter if I light a dozen cigarettes on one match. But the other part—this very ominous voice, like an interior Boris Karloff—says *'Ohhhh, if you dooo...'* "

"But all madness isn't superstitious, is it?" the writer's wife asked timidly.

"Isn't it?" the editor replied. "Jeanne d'Arc heard voices from heaven. Some people think they are possessed by demons. Others see gremlins ... or devils ... or Fornits. The terms we use for madness suggest superstition in some form or other. Mania ... abnormality ... irrationality ... lunacy ... insanity. For the mad person, reality has skewed. The whole person begins to reintegrate in that small room where the pistol is.

"But the rational part of me was still very much there. Bloody, bruised, indignant, and rather frightened, but still on the job. Saying: 'Oh, that's all right. Tomorrow when you sober up, you can plug everything back in, thank God. Play your games if you have to. But no more than this. No further than this.'

"That rational voice was right to be frightened. There's something in us that is very much attracted to madness. Everyone who looks off the edge of a tall building has felt at least a faint, morbid urge to jump. And anyone who has ever put a loaded pistol up to his head..."

"Ugh, don't," the writer's wife said. "Please."

"All right," the editor said. "My point is just this: even the most well-adjusted person is holding on to his or her sanity by a greased rope. I really believe that. The rationality circuits are shoddily built into the human animal.

"With the plugs pulled, I went into my study, wrote Reg Thorpe a letter, put it in an envelope, stamped it, took it out and mailed it. I don't actually remember doing any of these things. I was too drunk. But I deduce that I did them because when I got up the next morning, the carbon was still by my typewriter, along with the stamps and the box of envelopes. The letter was about what you'd expect from a drunk. What it boiled down to was this: the enemies were drawn by electricity as well as by the Fornits themselves. Get rid of the electricity and you got rid of the enemies. At the bottom I had written, 'The electricity is fucking up your thinking about these things, Reg. Interference with brainwaves. Does your wife have a blender?' "

"In effect, you had started writing letters to the paper," the writer said.

"Yes. I wrote that letter on a Friday night. On Saturday morning I got up around eleven, hung over and only blurrily aware of what sort of mischief I'd been up to the night before. Great pangs of shame as I plugged everything back in. Greater pangs of shame—and fear—when I saw what I'd written to Reg. I looked all over the house for the original to that letter, hoping like hell I hadn't mailed it. But I had. And the way I got through that day was by making a resolution to take my lumps like a man and go on the wagon. Sure I was.

"The following Wednesday there was a letter from Reg. One page, handwritten. Fornit Some Fornus doodles all over it. In the center, just this: 'You were right. Thank you, thank you, thank you. Reg. You were right. Everything is fine now. Reg. Thanks a lot. Reg. Fornit is fine. Reg. Thanks. Reg.' "

"Oh, my," the writer's wife said.

"Bet his wife was mad," the agent's wife said.

"But she wasn't. Because it worked."

"Worked?" the agent said.

"He got my letter in the Monday-morning post. Monday afternoon he went down to the local power-company office and told them to cut his power off. Jane Thorpe, of course, was hysterical. Her range ran on electricity, she did indeed have a blender, a sewing machine, a washer-dryer combination ... well, you understand. On Monday evening I'm sure she was ready to have my head on a plate.

"But it was Reg's behavior that made her decide I was a miracle worker instead of a lunatic. He sat her down in the living room and talked to her quite rationally. He said that he knew he'd been acting in a peculiar fashion. He knew that she'd been worried. He told her that he felt much better with the power off, and that he would be glad to help her through any inconvenience that it caused. And then he suggested that they go next door and say hello."

"Not to the KGB agents with the radium in their van?" the writer asked.

"Yes, to them. Jane was totally floored. She agreed to go over with him but she told me that she was girding herself up for a really nasty scene. Accusations, threats, hysteria. She had begun to consider leaving Reg if he wouldn't get help for his problem. She told me that Wednesday morning on the phone that she had made herself a promise: the power was the next-to-the-last straw. One more thing, and she was going to leave for New York. She was becoming afraid, you see. The thing had worsened by such degrees as to be nearly imperceptible, and she loved him, but even for her it had gotten as far it could go. She had decided that if Reg said one strange word to the students next door, she was going to break up housekeeping. I found out much later that she had already asked some very circumspect questions about the procedure in Nebraska to effect an involuntary committal."

"The poor woman," the writer's wife murmured.

"But the evening was a smashing success," the editor said. "Reg was at his most charming ... and according to Jane, that was very charming indeed. She hadn't seen him so much on in three years. The sullenness, the secretiveness, they were gone. The nervous tics. The involuntary jump and look over his shoulder whenever a door opened. He had a beer and talked about all the topics that were current back in those dim dead days: the war, the possibilities of a volunteer army, the riots in the cities, the pot laws.

"The fact that he had written *Underworld Figures* came up, and they were . . . 'author-struck' was the way Jane put it. Three of the four had read it, and you can bet the odd one wasn't going to linger any on his way to the library."

The writer laughed and nodded. He knew about that bit.

"So," the editor said, "we leave Reg Thorpe and his wife for just a little while, without electrical power but happier than they've been in a good long time—"

"Good thing he didn't have an IBM typewriter," the agent said.

"—and return to Ye Editor. Two weeks have gone by. Summer is ending. Ye Editor has, of course, fallen off the wagon any number of times, but has managed on the whole to remain pretty respectable. The days have gone their appointed rounds. At Cape Kennedy, they are getting ready to put a man on the moon. The new issue of *Logan's*, with John Lindsay on the cover, is out on the stands, and selling miserably, as usual. I had put in a purchase order for a short story called 'The Ballad of the Flexible Bullet,' by Reg Thorpe, first serial rights, proposed publication January 1970, proposed purchase price $800, which was standard then for a *Logan's* lead story.

"I got a buzz from my superior, Jim Dohegan. Could I come up and see him? I trotted into his office at ten in the morning, looking and feeling my very best. It didn't occur to me until later that Janey Morrison, his secretary, looked like a wake in progress.

"I sat down and asked Jim what I could do for him, or vice versa. I won't say the Reg Thorpe name hadn't entered my mind; having the story was a tremendous coup for *Logan's*, and I suspected a few congratulations were in order. So you can imagine how dumbfounded I was when he slid two purchase orders across the desk at me. The Thorpe story, and a John Updike novella we had scheduled as the February fiction lead. RETURN stamped across both.

"I looked at the revoked purchase orders. I looked at Jimmy. I couldn't make any of it out. I really couldn't get my brains to work over what it meant. There was a block in there. I looked around and I saw his hot plate. Janey brought it in for him every morning when she came to work and plugged it in so he could have fresh coffee when he wanted it. That had been the drill at *Logan's* for three years or more. And that morning all I could think of was, *if that thing was unplugged, I could think. I know if that thing was unplugged, I could put this together.*

"I said, 'What is this, Jim?'

"'I'm sorry as hell to have to be the one to tell you this, Henry,' he said. '*Logan's* isn't going to be publishing any more fiction as of January 1970.' "

The editor paused to get a cigarette, but his pack was empty. "Does anyone have a cigarette?"

The writer's wife gave him a Salem.

"Thank you, Meg."

He lit it, shook out the match, and dragged deep. The coal glowed mellowly in the dark.

"Well," he said, "I'm sure Jim thought I was crazy. I said, 'Do you mind?' and leaned over and pulled the plug on his hot plate.

"His mouth dropped open and he said, 'What the hell, Henry?'

" 'It's hard for me to think with things like that going,' I said. 'Interference.' And it really seemed to be true, because with the plug pulled, I was able to see the situation a great deal more clearly. 'Does this mean I'm pinked?' I asked him.

" 'I don't know,' he said. 'That's up to Sam and the board. I just don't know, Henry.'

"There were a lot of things I could have said. I guess what Jimmy was expecting was a passionate plea for my job. You know that saying, 'He had his ass out to the wind'? . . . I maintain that you don't understand the meaning of that phrase until you're the head of a suddenly nonexistent department.

"But I didn't plead my cause or the cause of fiction at *Logan's*. I pleaded for Reg Thorpe's story. First I said that we could move it up over the deadline—put it in the December issue.

"Jimmy said, 'Come on, Henry, the December ish is locked up. You know that. And we're talking ten thousand words here.'

" 'Nine-thousand-eight,' I said.

" 'And a full-page illo,' he said. 'Forget it.'

" 'Well, we'll scrap the art,' I said. 'Listen, Jimmy, it's a great story, maybe the best fiction we've had in the last five years.'

"Jimmy said, 'I read it, Henry. I know it's a great story. But we just can't do it. Not in December. It's Christmas, for God's sake, and you want to put a story about a guy who kills his wife and kid under the Christmas trees of America? You must be—' He stopped right there, but I saw him glance over at his hot plate. He might as well have said it out loud, you know?"

The writer nodded slowly, his eyes never leaving the dark shadow that was the editor's face.

"I started to get a headache. A very small headache at first. It was getting hard to think again. I remembered that Janey Morrison had an electric pencil sharpener on her desk. There were all those fluorescents in Jim's office. The heaters. The vending machines in the concession down the hall. When you stopped to think of it, the whole fucking building ran on electricity; it was a wonder that anyone could get anything done. That was when the idea began to creep in, I think. The idea that *Logan's* was going broke because no one could think straight. And the reason no one could think straight was because we were all cooped up in this high-rise building that ran on electricity. Our brainwaves were completely messed up. I remember thinking that if you could have gotten a doctor in there with one of those EEG machines, they'd get some awfully weird graphs. Full of those big, spiky alpha waves that characterize malignant tumors in the forebrain.

"Just thinking about those things made my headache worse. But I gave it one more try. I asked him if he would at least ask Sam Vadar, the editor-in-chief, to let the story stand in the January issue. As *Logan's* fiction valedictory, if necessary. The final *Logan's* short story.

"Jimmy was fiddling with a pencil and nodding. He said, 'I'll bring it up, but you know it's not going to fly. We've got a story by a one-shot novelist and we've got a story by John Updike that's just as good . . . maybe better . . . and—'

" *'The Updike story is not better!'* I said.

" 'Well, Jesus, Henry, you don't have to shout—'

" *'I am not shouting!'* I shouted.

"He looked at me for a long time. My headache was quite bad by then. I could hear the fluorescents buzzing away. They sounded like a bunch of flies caught in a bottle. It was a really hateful sound. And I thought I could hear Janey running her electric pencil sharpener. *They're doing it on purpose,* I thought. *They want to mess me up. They know I can't think of the right things to say while those things are running, so . . . so . . .*

"Jim was saying something about bringing it up at the next editorial meeting, suggesting that instead of an arbitrary cutoff date they publish all the stories which I had verbally contracted for . . . although . . .

"I got up, went across the room, and shut off the lights.

" 'What did you do that for?' Jimmy asked.

" 'You know why I did it,' I said. 'You ought to get out of here, Jimmy, before there's nothing left of you.'

"He got up and came over to me. 'I think you ought to take the rest of the day off, Henry,' he said. 'Go home. Rest. I know you've been under a strain lately. I want you to know I'll do the best I can on this. I feel as strongly as you do . . . well, almost as strongly. But you ought to just go home and put your feet up and watch some TV.'

" 'TV,' I said, and laughed. It was the funniest thing I'd ever heard. 'Jimmy,' I said. 'You tell Sam Vadar something else for me.'

" 'What's that, Henry?'

" 'Tell him he needs a Fornit. This whole outfit. One Fornit? A dozen of them.'

" 'A Fornit,' he said, nodding. 'Okay, Henry. I'll be sure to tell him that.'

"My headache was very bad. I could hardly even see. Somewhere in the back of my mind I was already wondering how I was going to tell Reg and wondering how Reg was going to take it.

" 'I'll put in the purchase order myself, if I can find out who to send it to,' I said. 'Reg might have some ideas. A dozen Fornits. Get them to dust this place with fornus from end to end. Shut off the fucking power, all of it.' I was walking around his office and Jimmy was staring at me with his mouth open. 'Shut off all the power, Jimmy, you tell them that. Tell Sam that. No one can think with all that electrical interference, am I right?'

" 'You're right, Henry, one hundred percent. You just go on home and get some rest, okay? Take a nap or something.'

" 'And Fornits. They don't like all that interference. Radium, electricity, it's all the same thing. Feed them bologna. Cake. Peanut butter. Can we get requisitions for that stuff?' My headache was this black ball of pain behind my eyes. I was seeing two of Jimmy, two of everything. All of a sudden I needed a drink. If there was no fornus, and the rational side of my mind assured me there was not, then a drink was the only thing in the world that would get me right.

" 'Sure, we can get the requisitions,' he said.

" 'You don't believe any of this, do you, Jimmy?' I asked.

" 'Sure I do. It's okay. You just want to go home and rest a little while.'

" 'You don't believe it now,' I said, 'but maybe you will when this rag goes into bankruptcy. How in the name of God can you believe you're making rational decisions when you're sitting less than fifteen yards from a bunch of Coke machines and candy machines and sandwich machines?' Then I really had a terrible thought. '*And a microwave oven!*' I screamed at him. *'They got a microwave oven to heat the sandwiches up in!'*

"He started to say something, but I didn't pay any attention. I ran out. Thinking of that microwave oven explained everything. I had to get away from it. That was what made the headache so bad. I remember seeing Janey and Kate Younger from the ad department and Mert Strong from publicity in the outer office, all of them staring at me. They must have heard me shouting.

"My office was on the floor just below. I took the stairs. I went into my office, turned off all the lights, and got my briefcase. I took the elevator down to the lobby, but I put my briefcase between my feet and poked my fingers in my ears. I also remember the other three or four people in the elevator looking at me rather strangely." The editor uttered a dry chuckle. "They were scared. So to speak. Cooped up in a little moving box with an obvious madman, you would have been scared, too."

"Oh, surely, *that's* a little strong," the agent's wife said.

"Not at all. Madness has to start *somewhere*. If this story's about anything—if events in one's own life can ever be said to be about anything—then this is a story about the genesis of insanity. Madness has to start somewhere, and it has to go somewhere. Like a road. Or a bullet from the barrel of a gun. I was still miles behind Reg Thorpe, but I was over the line. You bet.

"I had to go somewhere, so I went to Four Fathers, a bar on Forty-ninth. I remember picking that bar specifically because there was no juke and no color TV and not many lights. I remember ordering the first drink. After that I don't remember anything until I woke up the next day in my bed at home. There was puke on the floor and a very large cigarette burn in the sheet over me. In my stupor I had apparently escaped dying in one of two extremely nasty ways—choking or burning. Not that I probably would have felt either."

"Jesus," the agent said, almost respectfully.

"It was a blackout," the editor said. "The first real bona fide blackout of my life—but they're always a sign of the end, and you never have very many. One way or the other, you never have very many. But any alcoholic will tell you that a blackout isn't the same as *passing* out. It would save a lot of trouble if it was. No, when an alky blacks out, he keeps *doing* things. An alky in a blackout is a busy little devil. Sort of like a malign Fornit. He'll call up his ex-wife and abuse her over the phone, or drive his car the wrong way on the turnpike and wipe out a carload of kids. He'll quit his job, rob a market, give away his wedding ring. Busy little devils.

"What *I* had done, apparently, was to come home and write a letter. Only this one wasn't to Reg. It was to me. And *I* didn't write it—at least, according to the *letter* I didn't."

"Who did?" the writer's wife asked.

"Bellis."

"Who's Bellis?"

"His Fornit," the writer said almost absently. His eyes were shadowy and faraway.

"Yes, that's right," the editor said, not looking a bit surprised. He made the letter in the sweet night air for them again, indenting at the proper points with his finger.

" 'Hello from Bellis. I am sorry for your problems, my friend, but would like to point out at the start that you are not the only one with problems. This is no easy job for me. I can dust your damned machine with fornus from now unto forever, but moving the KEYS is supposed to be your job. That's what God made big people FOR. So I sympathize, but that's all of the sympathy you get.

" 'I understand your worry about Reg Thorpe. I worry not about Thorpe but my brother, Rackne. Thorpe worries about what will happen to him if Rackne leaves, but only because he is selfish. The curse of serving writers is that they are *all* selfish. He worries not about what will happen to Rackne if THORPE leaves. Or goes *el bonzo seco*. Those things have apparently never crossed his oh-so-sensitive mind. But, luckily for us, all our unfortunate problems have the same short-term solution, and so I strain my arms and my tiny body to give it to you, my drunken friend. YOU may wonder about long-term solutions; I assure you there are none. All wounds are mortal. Take what's given. You sometimes get a little slack in the rope but the rope always has an end. So what. Bless the slack and don't waste breath cursing the drop. A grateful heart knows that in the end we all swing.

" 'You must pay him for the story yourself. But not with a personal check. Thorpe's mental problems are severe and perhaps dangerous but this in no way indicates stupiddity.'" The editor stopped here and spelled: S-t-u-p-i-d-d-i-t-y. Then he went on. "'If you give him a personal check he'll crack wise in about nine seconds.

" 'Withdraw eight hundred and some few-odd dollars from your personal account and have your bank open a new account for you in the name Arvin Publishing, Inc. Make sure they understand you want checks that look businesslike—nothing with cute dogs or canyon vistas on them. Find a friend, someone you can trust, and list him as co-drawer. When the checks arrive, make one for eight hundred dollars and have the co-drawer sign the check. Send the check to Reg Thorpe. That will cover your ass for the time being.

" 'Over and out.' It was signed 'Bellis.' Not in holograph. In type."

"Whew," the writer said again.

"When I got up the first thing I noticed was the typewriter. It looked like somebody had made it up as a ghost-typewriter in a cheap movie. The day before it was an old black office Underwood. When I got up—with a head that felt about the size of North Dakota—it was a sort of gray. The last few sentences of the letter were clumped up and faded. I took one look and figured my faithful old Underwood was probably finished. I took a taste and went out into the kitchen. There was an open bag of confectioner's sugar on the counter with a scoop in it. There was confectioner's sugar everywhere between the kitchen and the little den where I did my work in those days."

"Feeding your Fornit," the writer said. "Bellis had a sweet tooth. You thought so, anyway."

"Yes. But even as sick and hung over as I was, I knew perfectly well who the Fornit was."

He ticked off the points on his fingers.

"First, Bellis was my mother's maiden name.

"Second, that phrase *el bonzo seco*. It was a private phrase my brother and I used to use to mean crazy. Back when we were kids.

"Third, and in a way most damning, was that spelling of the word 'stupidity.' It's one of those words I habitually misspell. I had an almost screamingly literate writer once who used to spell 'refrigerator' with a d—'refridgerator'—no matter how many times the copy editors blooped it. And for this guy, who had a doctoral degree from Princeton, 'ugly' was always going to be 'ughly.'"

The writer's wife uttered a sudden laugh—it was both embarrassed and cheerful. "I do that."

"All I'm saying is that a man's misspellings—or a woman's—are his literary fingerprints. Ask any copy editor who has done the same writer a few times.

"No, Bellis was me and I was Bellis. Yet the advice was damned good advice. In fact, I thought it was *great* advice. But here's something else—the subconscious leaves its fingerprints, but there's a stranger down there, too. A hell of a weird guy who knows a hell of a lot. I'd never seen that word 'co-drawer' in my life, to the best of my knowledge ... but there it was, and it was a good one, and I found out some time later that banks actually use it.

"I picked up the phone to call a friend of mine, and this bolt of pain—incredible!—went through my head. I thought of Reg Thorpe and his radium and put the phone down in a hurry. I went to see the friend in person after I'd taken a shower and gotten a shave and had checked myself about nine times in the mirror to make sure my appearance approximated how a rational human being is supposed to look. Even so, he asked me a lot of questions and looked me over pretty closely. So I guess there must have been a few signs that a shower, a shave, and a good dose of Listerine couldn't hide. He wasn't in the biz, and that was a help. News has a way of traveling, you know. In the biz. So to speak. Also, if he'd been in the biz, he would have known Arvin Publishing, Inc., was responsible for *Logan's* and would have wondered just what sort of scam I was trying to pull. But he wasn't, he didn't, and I was able to tell him it was a self-publishing venture I was interested in since *Logan's* had apparently decided to eighty-six the fiction department."

"Did he ask you why you were calling it Arvin Publishing?" the writer asked.

"Yes."

"What did you tell him?"

"I told him," the editor said, smiling a wintry smile, "that Arvin was my mother's maiden name."

There was a little pause, and then the editor resumed; he spoke almost uninterrupted to the end.

"So I began waiting for the printed checks, of which I wanted exactly one. I exercised to pass the time. You know—pick up the glass, flex the elbow, empty the glass, flex the elbow again. Until all that exercise wears you out and you just sort of fall forward with your head on the table. Other things happened, but those were the ones that really occupied my mind—the waiting and the flexing. As I remember. I have to reiterate that, because I was drunk a lot of the time, and for every single thing I remember, there are probably fifty or sixty I don't.

"I quit my job—that caused a sigh of relief all around, I'm sure. From them because they didn't have to perform the existential task of firing me for craziness from a department that was no longer in existence, me because I didn't think I could ever face that building again—the elevator, the fluorescents, the phones, the thought of all that waiting electricity.

"I wrote Reg Thorpe and his wife a couple of letters each during that three-week period. I remember doing hers, but not his—like the letter from Bellis, I wrote those letters in blackout periods. But I hewed to my old work habits when I was blotto, just as I hewed to my old misspellings. I never failed to use a carbon...and when I came to the next morning, the carbons were lying around. It was like reading letters from a stranger.

"Not that the letters were crazy. Not at all. The one where I finished up with the P.S. about the blender was a lot worse. These letters seemed... almost reasonable."

He stopped and shook his head, slowly and wearily.

"Poor Jane Thorpe. Not that things *appeared* to be all that bad at their end. It must have seemed to her that her husband's editor was doing a very skillful—and humane—job of humoring him out of his deepening depression. The question of whether or not it's a good idea to humor a person who has been entertaining all sorts of paranoid fantasies—fantasies which almost led in one case to an actual assault on a little girl—probably occurred to her; if so, she chose to ignore the negative aspects, because she was humoring him, too. Nor have I ever blamed her for it—he wasn't just a meal ticket, some nag that was to be worked and humored, humored and worked until he was ready for the knacker's shop; she loved the guy. In her own special way, Jane Thorpe was a great lady. And after living with Reg from the Early Times to the High Times and finally to the Crazy Times, I think she would have agreed with Bellis about blessing the slack and not wasting your breath cursing the drop. Of course, the more slack you get, the harder you snap when you finally fetch up at the end . . . but even that quick snap can be a blessing, I reckon—who wants to strangle?

"I had return letters from both of them in that short period—remarkably sunny letters . . . although there was a strange, almost final quality to that sunlight. It seemed as if . . . well, never mind the cheap philosophy. If I can think of what I mean, I'll say it. Let it go for now.

"He was playing hearts with the kids next door every night, and by the time the leaves started to fall, they thought Reg Thorpe was just about God come down to earth. When they weren't playing cards or tossing a Frisbee they were talking literature, with Reg gently rallying them through their paces. He'd gotten a puppy from the local animal shelter and walked it every morning and night, meeting other people on the block the way you do when you walk your mutt. People who'd decided the Thorpes were really very peculiar people now began to change their minds. When Jane suggested that, without electrical appliances, she could really use a little house help, Reg agreed at once. She was flabbergasted by his cheery acceptance of the idea. It wasn't a question of money—after *Underworld Figures* they were rolling in dough—it was a question, Jane figured, of *they*. *They* were everywhere, that was Reg's scripture, and what better agent for *they* than a cleaning woman that went everywhere in your house, looked under beds and in closets and probably in desk drawers as well, if they weren't locked and then nailed shut for good measure.

"But he told her to go right ahead, told her he felt like an insensitive clod not to've thought of it earlier, even though—she made a point of telling me this—he was doing most of the heavy chores, such as the handwashing, himself. He only made one small request: that the woman not be allowed to come into his study.

"Best of all, most encouraging of all from Jane's standpoint, was the fact that Reg had gone back to work, this time on a new novel. She had read the first three chapters and thought they were marvelous. All of this, she said, had begun when I had accepted 'The Ballad of the Flexible Bullet' for *Logan's*—the period before that had been dead low ebb. And she blessed me for it.

"I am sure she really meant that last, but her blessing seemed to have no great warmth, and the sunniness of her letter was marred somehow—

here we are, back to that. The sunshine in her letter was like sunshine on a day when you see those mackerel-scale clouds that mean it's going to rain like hell soon.

"All this good news—hearts and dog and cleaning woman and new novel—and yet she was too intelligent to really believe he was getting well again . . . or so I believed, even in my own fog. Reg had been exhibiting symptoms of psychosis. Psychosis is like lung cancer in one way—neither one of them clears up on its own, although both cancer patients and lunatics may have their good days.

"May I borrow another cigarette, dear?"

The writer's wife gave him one.

"After all," he resumed, bringing out the Ronson, "the signs of his *idée fixe* were all around her. No phone; no electricity. He'd put Reynolds Wrap over all of the switch plates. He was putting food in his typewriter as regularly as he put it into the new puppy's dish. The students next door thought he was a great guy, but the students next door didn't see Reg putting on rubber gloves to pick up the newspaper off the front stoop in the morning because of his radiation fears. They didn't hear him moaning in his sleep, or have to soothe him when he woke up screaming with dreadful nightmares he couldn't remember.

"You, my dear"—he turned toward the writer's wife—"have been wondering why she stuck with him. Although you haven't said as much, it's been on your mind. Am I right?"

She nodded.

"Yes. And I'm not going to offer a long motivational thesis—the convenient thing about stories that are true is that you only need to say *this is what happened* and let people worry for themselves about the why. Generally, nobody ever knows why things happen anyway . . . particularly the ones who say they do.

"But in terms of Jane Thorpe's own selective perception, things *had* gotten one hell of a lot better. She interviewed a middle-aged black woman about the cleaning job, and brought herself to speak as frankly as she could about her husband's idiosyncrasies. The woman, Gertrude Rulin by name, laughed and said she'd done for people who were a whole lot stranger. Jane spent the first week of the Rulin woman's employ pretty much the way she'd spent that first visit with the young people next door—waiting for some crazy outburst. But Reg charmed her as completely as he'd charmed the kids, talking to her about her church work, her husband, and her youngest son, Jimmy, who, according to Gertrude, made Dennis the Menace look like the biggest bore in the first grade. She'd had eleven children in all, but there was a nine-year gap between Jimmy and his next oldest sib. He made things hard on her.

"Reg seemed to be getting well . . . at least, if you looked at things a certain way he did. But he was just as crazy as ever, of course, and so was I. Madness may well be a sort of flexible bullet, but any ballistics expert worth his salt will tell you no two bullets are exactly the same. Reg's one letter to me talked a little bit about his new novel, and then passed directly to Fornits. Fornits in general, Rackne in particular. He speculated on whether *they* actually wanted to kill Fornits, or—he thought this more likely—capture them alive and study them. He closed by saying, 'Both my appetite and my outlook on life have improved immeasurably since we began our correspondence, Henry. Appreciate it all. Affectionately yours, Reg.' And a P.S. below inquiring casually if an illustrator had been assigned to do his story. That caused a guilty pang or two and a quick trip to the liquor cabinet on my part.

"Reg was into Fornits; I was into wires.

"My answering letter mentioned Fornits only in passing—by then I really was humoring the man, at least on that subject; an elf with my mother's maiden name and my own bad spelling habits didn't interest me a whole hell of a lot.

"What had come to interest me more and more was the subject of electricity, and microwaves, and RF waves, and RF interference from small appliances, and low-level radiation, and Christ knows what else. I went to the library and took out books on the subject; I bought books on the subject. There was a lot of scary stuff in them . . . and of course that was just the sort of stuff I was looking for.

"I had my phone taken out and my electricity turned off. It helped for a while, but one night when I was staggering in the door drunk with a bottle of Black Velvet in my hand and another one in my topcoat pocket, I saw this little red eye peeping down at me from the ceiling. God, for a minute I thought I was going to have a heart attack. It looked like a bug up there at first . . . a great big dark bug with one glowing eye.

"I had a Coleman gas lantern and I lit it. Saw what it was at once. Only instead of relieving me, it made me feel worse. As soon as I got a good look at it, it seemed I could feel large, clear bursts of pain going through my head—like radio waves. For a moment it was as if my eyes had rotated in their sockets and I could look into my own brain and see cells in there smoking, going black, dying. It was a smoke detector—a gadget which was even newer than microwave ovens back in 1969.

"I bolted out of the apartment and went downstairs—I was on the fifth floor but by then I was always taking the stairs—and hammered on the super's door. I told him I wanted that thing out of there, wanted it out of there *right away*, wanted it out of there *tonight*, wanted it out of there *within the hour*. He looked at me as though I had gone completely—you should pardon the expression—*bonzo seco*, and I can understand that now. That smoke detector was supposed to make me feel *good*, it was supposed to make me *safe*. Now, of course, they're the law, but back then it was a Great Leap Forward, paid for by the building tenants' association.

"He removed it—it didn't take long—but the look in his eyes was not lost upon me, and I could, in some limited way, understand his feelings. I needed a shave, I stank of whiskey, my hair was sticking up all over my head, my topcoat was dirty. He would know I no longer went to work; that I'd had my television taken away; that my phone and electrical service had been voluntarily interrupted. He thought I was crazy.

"I may have been crazy but—like Reg—I was not stupid. I turned on the charm. Editors have got to have a certain amount, you know. And I greased the skids with a ten-dollar bill. Finally I was able to smooth things over, but I knew from the way people were looking at me in the next couple of weeks—my last two weeks in the building, as things turned out—that the story had traveled. The fact that no members of the tenants' association approached me to make wounded noises about my ingratitude was particularly telling. I suppose they thought I might take after them with a steak knife.

"All of that was very secondary in my thoughts that evening, however. I sat in the glow of the Coleman lantern, the only light in the three rooms except for all the electricity in Manhattan that came through the windows. I sat with a bottle in one hand, a cigarette in the other, looking at the plate in the ceiling where the smoke detector with its single red eye—an eye which was so unobtrusive in the daytime that I had never even noticed it—had been. I thought of the undeniable fact that, although I'd had all the electricity turned off in my place, there had been that one live item...and where there was one, there might be more.

"Even if there wasn't, the whole building was rotten with wires—it was filled with wires the way a man dying of cancer is filled with evil cells and rotting organs. Closing my eyes I could see all those wires in the darkness of their conduits, glowing with a sort of green nether light. And beyond them, the entire city. One wire, almost harmless in itself, running to a switch plate...the wire behind the switch plate a little thicker, leading down through a conduit to the basement where it joined a still thicker wire... that one leading down under the street to a whole *bundle* of wires, only those wires so thick that they were really cables.

"When I got Jane Thorpe's letter mentioning the tinfoil, part of my mind recognized that she saw it as a sign of Reg's craziness, and that part knew I would have to respond as if my *whole* mind thought she was right. The other part of my mind—by far the largest part now—thought: 'What a marvelous idea!' and I covered my own switch plates in identical fashion the very next day. I was the man, remember, that was supposed to be helping Reg Thorpe. In a desperate sort of way it's actually quite funny.

"I determined that night to leave Manhattan. There was an old family place in the Adirondacks I could go to, and that sounded fine to me. The one thing keeping me in the city was Reg Thorpe's story. If 'The Ballad of the Flexible Bullet' was Reg's life-ring in a sea of madness, it was mine, too—I wanted to place it in a good magazine. With that done, I could get the hell out.

"So that's where the not-so-famous Wilson-Thorpe correspondence stood just before the shit hit the fan. We were like a couple of dying drug addicts comparing the relative merits of heroin and ludes. Reg had Fornits in his typewriter, I had Fornits in the walls, and both of us had Fornits in our heads.

"And there was *they*. Don't forget *they*. I hadn't been flogging the story around for long before deciding *they* included every magazine fiction editor in New York—not that there were many by the fall of 1969. If you'd grouped them together, you could have killed the whole bunch of them with one shotgun shell, and before long I started to feel that was a damned good idea.

"It took about five years before I could see it from their perspective. I'd upset the super, and he was just a guy who saw me when the heat was screwed up and when it was time for his Christmas tip. These other guys . . . well, the irony was just that a lot of them really *were* my friends. Jared Baker was the assistant fiction editor at *Esquire* in those days, and Jared and I were in the same rifle company during World War II, for instance. These guys weren't just uneasy after sampling the new improved Henry Wilson. They were appalled. If I'd just sent the story around with a pleasant covering letter explaining the situation—my version of it, anyway—I probably would have sold the Thorpe story almost right away. But oh no, that wasn't good enough. Not for this story. I was going to see that this story got the *personal treatment*. So I went from door to door with it, a stinking, grizzled ex-editor with shaking hands and red eyes and a big old bruise on his left cheekbone from where he ran into the bathroom door on the way to the can in the dark two nights before. I might as well have been wearing a sign reading BELLEVUE-BOUND.

"Nor did I want to talk to these guys in their offices. In fact, I could not. The time had long since passed when I could get into an elevator and ride it up forty floors. So I met them like pushers meet junkies—in parks, on steps, or in the case of Jared Baker, in a Burger Heaven on Forty-ninth Street. Jared at least would have been delighted to buy me a decent meal, but the time had passed, you understand, when any self-respecting *maître d'* would have let me in a restaurant where they serve business people."

The agent winced.

"I got perfunctory promises to read the story, followed by concerned questions about how I was, how much I was drinking. I remember—hazily—trying to tell a couple of them about how electricity and radiation leaks were fucking up everyone's thinking, and when Andy Rivers, who edited fiction for *American Crossings*, suggested I ought to get some help, I told him *he* was the one who ought to get some help.

" 'You see those people out there on the street?' I said. We were standing in Washington Square Park. 'Half of them, maybe even three-quarters of them, have got brain tumors. I wouldn't sell you Thorpe's story on a bet, Andy. Hell, you couldn't understand it in this city. Your brain's in the electric chair and you don't even know it.'

"I had a copy of the story in my hand, rolled up like a newspaper. I whacked him on the nose with it, the way you'd whack a dog for piddling in the corner. Then I walked off. I remember him yelling for me to come back, something about having a cup of coffee and talking it over some more, and then I passed a discount record store with loudspeakers blasting heavy metal onto the sidewalk and banks of snowy-cold fluorescent lights inside, and I lost his voice in a kind of deep buzzing sound inside my head. I remember thinking two things—I had to get out of the city soon, very soon, or I would be nursing a brain tumor of my own, and I had to get a drink right away.

"That night when I got back to my apartment I found a note under the door. It said: 'We want you out of here, you crazy-bird.' I threw it away without so much as a second thought. We veteran crazy-birds have more important things to worry about than anonymous notes from fellow tenants.

"I was thinking over what I'd said to Andy Rivers about Reg's story. The more I thought about it—and the more drinks I had—the more sense it made. 'Flexible Bullet' was funny, and on the surface it was easy to follow . . . but below that surface level it was surprisingly complex. Did I really think another editor in the city could grasp the story on all levels? Maybe once, but did I still think so now that my eyes had been opened? Did I really think there was room for appreciation and understanding in a place that was wired up like a terrorist's bomb? God, loose volts were leaking out everywhere.

"I read the paper while there was still enough daylight to do so, trying to forget the whole wretched business for a while, and there on page one of the *Times* there was a story about how radioactive material from nuclear-power plants kept disappearing—the article went on to theorize that enough of that stuff in the right hands could quite easily be used to make a very dirty nuclear weapon.

"I sat there at the kitchen table as the sun went down, and in my mind's eye I could see *them* panning for plutonium dust like 1849 miners panning for gold. Only *they* didn't want to blow up the city with it, oh no. *They* just wanted to sprinkle it around and fuck up everyone's minds. They were the bad Fornits, and all that radioactive dust was bad-luck fornus. The worst bad-luck fornus of all time.

"I decided I didn't want to sell Reg's story after all—at least, not in New York. I'd get out of the city just as soon as the checks I'd ordered arrived. When I was upstate, I could start sending it around to the out-of-town literary magazines. *Sewanee Review* would be a good place to start, I reckoned, or maybe *Iowa Review*. I could explain to Reg later. Reg would understand. That seemed to solve the whole problem, so I took a drink to celebrate. And then the drink took a drink. And then the drink took the man. So to speak. I blacked out. I only had one more blackout left in me, as it happened.

"The next day my Arvin Company checks came. I typed one of them up and went to see my friend, the 'co-drawer.' There was another one of those tiresome cross-examinations, but this time I kept my temper. I wanted that signature. Finally, I got it. I went to a business supply store and had them make up an Arvin Company letter-stamp while I waited. I stamped a return address on a business envelope, typed Reg's address (the confectioner's sugar was out of my machine but the keys still had a tendency to stick), and added a brief personal note, saying that no check to an author had ever given me more personal pleasure . . . and that was true. Still is. It was almost an hour before I could bring myself to mail it—I just couldn't get over how *official* it looked. You never would have known that a smelly drunk who hadn't changed his underwear in about ten days had put *that* one together."

He paused, crushed out his cigarette, looked at his watch. Then, oddly like a conductor announcing a train's arrival in some city of importance, he said, "We have reached the inexplicable.

"This is the point in my story which most interested the two psychiatrists and various mental caseworkers with whom I was associated over the next thirty months of my life. It was the only part of it they really wanted me to recant, as a sign that I was getting well again. As one of them put it, 'This is the only part of your story which cannot be explicated as faulty induction . . . once, that is, your sense of logic has been mended.' Finally I *did* recant, because I knew—even if they didn't—that I *was* getting well, and I was damned anxious to get out of the sanitarium. I thought if I didn't get out fairly soon, I'd go crazy all over again. So I recanted—Galileo did, too, when they held his feet to the fire—but I have never recanted in my own mind. I don't say that what I'm about to tell you really happened; I only say I still *believe* it happened. That's a small qualification, but to me it's crucial.

"So, my friends, the inexplicable:

"I spent the next two days preparing to move upstate. The idea of driving the car didn't disturb me at all, by the way. I had read as a kid that the inside of a car is one of the safest places to be during an electrical storm, because the rubber tires serve as near-perfect insulators. I was actually looking forward to getting in my old Chevrolet, cranking up all the windows, and driving out of the city, which I had begun to see as a sink of lightning. Nevertheless, part of my preparations included removing the bulb in the dome light, taping over the socket, and turning the headlight knob all the way to the left to kill the dash lights.

"When I came in on the last night I meant to spend in the apartment, the place was empty except for the kitchen table, the bed, and my typewriter in the den. The typewriter was sitting on the floor. I had no intention of taking it with me—it had too many bad associations, and besides, the keys were going to stick forever. Let the next tenant have it, I thought—it, and Bellis, too.

"It was just sunset, and the place was a funny color. I was pretty drunk, and I had another bottle in my topcoat pocket against the watches of the night. I started across the den, meaning to go into the bedroom, I suppose. There I would sit on the bed and think about wires and electricity and free radiation and drink until I was drunk enough to go to sleep.

"What I called the den was really the living room. I made it my workplace because it had the nicest light in the whole apartment—a big westward-facing window that looked all the way to the horizon. That's something close to the Miracle of the Loaves and Fishes in a fifth-floor Manhattan apartment, but the line of sight was there. I didn't question it; I just enjoyed it. That room was filled with a clear, lovely light even on rainy days.

"But the quality of the light that evening was eerie. The sunset had filled the room with a red glow. Furnace light. Empty, the room seemed too big. My heels made flat echoes on the hardwood floor.

"The typewriter sat in the middle of the floor, and I was just going around it when I saw there was a ragged scrap of paper stuck under the roller—that gave me a start, because I knew there had been no paper in the machine when I went out for the last time to get the fresh bottle.

"I looked around, wondering if there was someone—some intruder—in the place with me. Except it wasn't really intruders, or burglars, or junkies, I was thinking of . . . it was ghosts.

"I saw a ragged blank place on the wall to the left of the bedroom door.

I at least understood where the paper in the typewriter had come from. Someone had simply torn off a ragged piece of the old wallpaper.

"I was still looking at this when I heard a single small clear noise—*clack!*—from behind me. I jumped and whirled around with my heart knocking in my throat. I was terrified, but I knew what that sound was just the same—there was no question at all. You work with words all your life and you know the sound of a typewriter platen hitting paper, even in a deserted room at dusk, where there is no one to strike the key."

They looked at him in the dark, their faces blurred white circles, saying nothing, slightly huddled together now. The writer's wife was holding one of the writer's hands tightly in both of her own.

"I felt . . . outside myself. Unreal. Perhaps this is always the way one feels when one arrives at the point of the inexplicable. I walked slowly over to the typewriter. My heart was pounding madly up there in my throat, but I felt mentally calm . . . icy, even.

"*Clack!* Another platen popped up. I saw it this time—the key was in the third row from the top, on the left.

"I got down on my knees very slowly, and then all the muscles in my legs seemed to go slack and I half-swooned the rest of the way down until I was sitting there in front of the typewriter with my dirty London Fog topcoat spread around me like the skirt of a girl who has made her very deepest curtsy. The typewriter clacked twice more, fast, paused, then clacked again. Each *clack* made the same kind of flat echo my footfalls had made on the floor.

"The wallpaper had been rolled into the machine so that the side with the dried glue on it was facing out. The letters were ripply and bumpy, but I could read them: *rackn,* it said. Then it clacked again and the word was *rackne.*

"Then—" He cleared his throat and grinned a little. "Even all these years later this is hard to tell . . . to just say right out. Okay. The simple fact, with no icing on it, is this. I saw a hand come out of the typewriter. An incredibly tiny hand. It came out from between the keys B and N in the bottom row, curled itself into a fist, and hammered down on the space bar. The machine jumped a space—very fast, like a hiccough—and the hand drew back down inside."

The agent's wife giggled shrilly.

"Can it, Marsha," the agent said softly, and she did.

"The clacks began to come a little faster," the editor went on, "and after a while I fancied I could hear the creature that was shoving the key arms up gasping, the way anyone will gasp when he is working hard, coming closer and closer to his physical limit. After a while the machine was hardly printing at all, and most of the keys were filled with that old gluey stuff, but I could read the impressions. It got out *rackne is d* and then the *y* key stuck to the glue. I looked at it for a moment and then I reached out one finger and freed it. I don't know if it—Bellis—could have freed it himself. I think not. But I didn't want to see it . . . him . . . try. Just the fist was enough to have me tottering on the brink. If I saw the elf entire, so to speak, I think I really would have gone crazy. And there was no question of getting up to run. All the strength had gone out of my legs.

"*Clack-clack-clack*, those tiny grunts and sobs of effort, and after every word that pallid ink- and dirt-streaked fist would come out between the B and the N and hammer down on the space bar. I don't know exactly how long it went on. Seven minutes, maybe. Maybe ten. Or maybe forever.

"Finally the clacks stopped, and I realized I couldn't hear him breathing anymore. Maybe he fainted . . . maybe he just gave up and went away . . . or maybe he died. Had a heart attack or something. All I really know for sure is that the message was not finished. It read, completely in lowercase: *rackne is dying its the little boy jimmy thorpe doesn't know tell thorpe rackne is dying the little boy jimmy is killing rackne bel . . .* and that was all.

"I found the strength to get to my feet then, and I left the room. I walked in great big tippy-toe steps, as if I thought it had gone to sleep and if I made any of those flat echoey noises on the bare wood it would wake up and the typing would start again . . . and I thought if it did, the first clack would start me screaming. And then I would just go on until my heart or my head burst.

"My Chevy was in the parking lot down the street, all gassed and loaded and ready to go. I got in behind the wheel and remembered the bottle in my topcoat pocket. My hands were shaking so badly that I dropped it, but it landed on the seat and didn't break.

"I remembered the blackouts, and, my friends, right then a blackout was exactly what I wanted, and exactly what I got. I remember taking the first drink from the neck of the bottle, and the second. I remember turning the key over to accessory and getting Frank Sinatra on the radio singing

'That Old Black Magic,' which seemed fitting enough. Under the circumstances. So to speak. I remember singing along, and having a few more drinks. I was in the back row of the lot, and I could see the traffic light on the corner going through its paces. I kept thinking of those flat clacking sounds in the empty room, and the fading red light in the den. I kept thinking of those puffing sounds, as if some body-building elf had hung fishing sinkers on the ends of a Q-Tip and was doing bench presses inside my old typewriter. I kept seeing the pebbly surface on the back side of that torn scrap of wallpaper. My mind kept wanting to examine what must have gone on before I came back to the apartment . . . kept wanting to see it— him—Bellis—jumping up, grabbing the loose edge of the wallpaper by the door to the bedroom because it was the only thing left in the room approximating paper—hanging on—finally tearing it loose and carrying it back to the typewriter on its—on *his*—head like the leaf of a nipa palm. I kept trying to imagine how he—it—could ever have run it into the typewriter. And none of that was blacking out so I kept drinking and Frank Sinatra stopped and there was an ad for Crazy Eddie's and then Sarah Vaughan came on singing 'I'm Gonna Sit Right Down and Write Myself a Letter' and that was something *else* I could relate to since I'd done just that recently or at least I'd *thought* I had up until tonight when something happened to give me cause to rethink my position on that matter so to speak and I sang along with good old Sarah Soul and right about then I must have achieved escape velocity because in the middle of the second chorus with no lag at all I was puking my guts out while somebody first thumped my back with his palms and then lifted my elbows behind me and put them down and then thumped my back with his palms again. That was the trucker. Every time he thumped I'd feel a great clot of liquid rise up in my throat and get ready to go back down except then he'd lift my elbows and every time he lifted my elbows I'd puke again, and most of it wasn't even Black Velvet but river water. When I was able to lift my head enough to look around it was six o'clock in the evening three days later and I was lying on the bank of the Jackson River in western Pennsylvania, about sixty miles north of Pittsburgh. My Chevy was sticking out of the river, rear end up. I could still read the McCarthy sticker on the bumper.

"Is there another Fresca, love? My throat's dry as hell."

The writer's wife fetched him one silently, and when she handed it to him she impulsively bent and kissed his wrinkled, alligator-hide cheek. He smiled, and his eyes sparkled in the dim light. She was, however, a good and kindly woman, and the sparkle did not in any way fool her. It was never merriness which made eyes sparkle that way.

"Thank you, Meg."

He drank deeply, coughed, waved away the offer of a cigarette.

"I've had enough of those for the evening. I'm going to quit them entirely. In my next incarnation. So to speak.

"The rest of my own tale really needs no telling. It would have against it the only sin that any tale can ever really be guilty of—it's predictable. They fished something like forty bottles of Black Velvet out of my car, a good many of them empty. I was babbling about elves, and electricity, and Fornits, and plutonium miners, and fornus, and I seemed utterly insane to them, and that of course is exactly what I was.

"Now here's what happened in Omaha while I was driving around—according to the gas credit slips in the Chevy's glove compartment—five northeastern states. All of this, you understand, was information I obtained from Jane Thorpe over a long and painful period of correspondence, which culminated in a face-to-face meeting in New Haven, where she now lives, shortly after I was dismissed from the sanitarium as a reward for finally recanting. At the end of that meeting we wept in each other's arms, and that was when I began to believe that there could be a real life for me—perhaps even happiness—again.

"That day, around three o'clock in the afternoon, there was a knock at the door of the Thorpe home. It was a telegraph boy. The telegram was from me—the last item of our unfortunate correspondence. It read:

REG HAVE RELIABLE INFORMATION THAT RACKNE IS DYING IT'S
THE LITTLE BOY ACCORDING TO BELLIS BELLIS SAYS THE BOY'S
NAME IS JIMMY FORNIT SOME FORNUS HENRY.

"In case that marvelous Howard Baker question of *What did he know and when did he know it?* has gone through your mind, I can tell you that I knew Jane had hired a cleaning woman; I didn't know—except through Bellis—that she had a li'l-devil son named Jimmy. I suppose you'll have to take my word for that, although in all fairness I have to add that the shrinks who worked on my case over the next two and a half years never did.

"When the telegram came, Jane was at the grocery store. She found it, after Reg was dead, in one of his back pockets. The time of transmission and delivery were both noted on it, along with the added line *No telephone/Deliver original.* Jane said that although the telegram was only a day old, it had been so much handled that it looked as if he'd had it for a month.

"In a way, that telegram, those twenty-six words, was the real flexible bullet, and I fired it directly into Reg Thorpe's brain all the way from Paterson, New Jersey, and I was so fucking drunk I don't even remember doing it.

"During the last two weeks of his life, Reg had fallen into a pattern that seemed normality itself. He got up at six, made breakfast for himself and his wife, then wrote for an hour. Around eight o'clock he would lock his study and take the dog for a long, leisurely walk around the neighborhood. He was very forthcoming on these walks, stopping to chat with anyone who wanted to chat with him, tying the pooch outside a nearby café to have a midmorning cup of coffee, then rambling on again. He rarely got back to the house before noon. On many days it was twelve-thirty or one o'clock. Part of this was an effort to escape the garrulous Gertrude Rulin, Jane believed, because his pattern hadn't really begun to solidify until a couple of days after she started working for them.

"He would eat a light lunch, lie down for an hour or so, then get up and write for two or three hours. In the evenings he would sometimes go next door to visit with the young people, either with Jane or alone; sometimes he and Jane took in a movie, or just sat in the living room and read. They turned in early, Reg usually a while before Jane. She wrote there was very little sex, and what there was of it was unsuccessful for both of them. 'But sex isn't as important for most women,' she said, 'and Reg was working full-out again, and that was a reasonable substitute for him. I would say that, under the circumstances, those last two weeks were the happiest in the last five years.' I damn near cried when I read that.

"I didn't know anything about Jimmy, but Reg did. Reg knew everything except for the most important fact—that Jimmy had started coming to work with his mother.

"How furious he must have been when he got my telegram and began to realize! Here *they* were, after all. And apparently his own wife was one of *them,* because *she* was in the house when Gertrude and Jimmy were there, and she had never said a thing to Reg about Jimmy. What was it he had written to me in that earlier letter? 'Sometimes I wonder about my wife.'

"When she arrived home on that day the telegram came, she found Reg gone. There was a note on the kitchen table which said, 'Love—I've gone down to the bookstore. Back by suppertime.' This seemed perfectly fine to Jane ... but if Jane had known about my telegram, the very normal-ity of that note would have scared the hell out of her, I think. She would have understood that Reg believed she had changed sides.

"Reg didn't go near any bookstore. He went to Littlejohn's Gun Em-porium downtown. He bought a .45 automatic and two thousand rounds of ammunition. He would have bought an AK-70 if Littlejohn's had been allowed to sell them. He meant to protect his Fornit, you see. From Jimmy, from Gertrude, from Jane. From *them.*

"Everything went according to established routine the next morning. She remembered thinking he was wearing an awfully heavy sweater for such a warm fall day, but that was all. The sweater, of course, was because of the gun. He went out to walk the dog with the .45 stuffed into the waist-band of his chinos.

"Except the restaurant where he usually got his morning coffee was as far as he went, and he went directly there, with no lingering or conversa-tion along the way. He took the pup around to the loading area, tied its leash to a railing, and then went back toward his house by way of back-yards.

"He knew the schedule of the young people next door very well; knew they would all be out. He knew where they kept their spare key. He let him-self in, went upstairs, and watched his own house.

"At eight-forty he saw Gertrude Rulin arrive. And Gertrude wasn't alone. There was indeed a small boy with her. Jimmy Rulin's boisterous first-grade behavior convinced the teacher and the school guidance coun-selor almost at once that everyone (except maybe Jimmy's mother, who could have used a rest from Jimmy) would be better off if he waited an-other year. Jimmy was stuck with repeating kindergarten, and he had after-noon sessions for the first half of the year. The two day-care centers in her area were full, and she couldn't change to afternoons for the Thorpes because she had another cleaning job on the other side of town from two to four.

"The upshot of everything was Jane's reluctant agreement that Gertrude could bring Jimmy with her until she was able to make other arrangements. Or until Reg found out, as he was sure to do.

"She thought Reg *might* not mind—he had been so sweetly reasonable about everything lately. On the other hand, he might have a fit. If that happened, other arrangements would *have* to be made. Gertrude said she understood. And for heaven's sake, Jane added, the boy was not to touch any of Reg's things. Gertrude said for sure not; the mister's study door was locked and would stay locked.

"Thorpe must have crossed between the two yards like a sniper crossing no-man's-land. He saw Gertrude and Jane washing bed linen in the kitchen. He didn't see the boy. He moved along the side of the house. No one in the dining room. No one in the bedroom. And then, in the study, where Reg had morbidly expected to see him, there Jimmy was. The kid's face was hot with excitement, and Reg surely must have believed that here was a bona fide agent of *they* at last.

"The boy was holding some sort of death-ray in his hand, it was pointed at the desk... and from inside his typewriter, Reg could hear Rackne screaming.

"You may think I'm attributing subjective data to a man who's now dead—or, to be more blunt, making stuff up. But I'm not. In the kitchen, both Jane and Gertrude heard the distinctive warbling sound of Jimmy's plastic space blaster... he'd been shooting it around the house ever since he started coming with his mother, and Jane hoped daily that its batteries would go dead. There was no mistaking the sound. No mistaking the place it was coming from, either—Reg's study.

"The kid really *was* Dennis the Menace material, you know—if there was a room in the house where he wasn't supposed to go, that was the one place he *had* to go, or die of curiosity. It didn't take him long to discover that Jane kept a key to Reg's study on the dining-room mantel, either. Had he been in there before? I think so. Jane said she remembered giving the boy an orange three or four days before, and later, when she was clearing out the house, she found orange peels under the little studio sofa in that room. Reg didn't eat oranges—claimed he was allergic to them.

"Jane dropped the sheet she was washing back into the sink and rushed into the bedroom. She heard the loud *wah-wah-wah* of the space blaster, and she heard Jimmy, yelling: *'I'll getcha! You can't run! I can seeya through the GLASS!'* And . . . she said . . . she said that she heard something screaming. A high, despairing sound, she said, so full of pain it was almost insupportable.

" 'When I heard that,' she said, 'I knew that I would have to leave Reg no matter *what* happened, because all the old wives' tales were true . . . madness was catching. Because it was Rackne I was hearing; somehow that rotten little kid was shooting Rackne, killing it with a two-dollar space-gun from Kresge's.

" 'The study door was standing open, the key in it. Later on that day I saw one of the dining-room chairs standing by the mantel, with Jimmy's sneaker prints all over the seat. He was bent over Reg's typewriter table. He—Reg—had an old office model with glass inserts in the sides. Jimmy had the muzzle of his blaster pressed against one of those and was shooting it into the typewriter. *Wah-wah-wah-wah*, and purple pulses of light shooting out of the typewriter, and suddenly I could understand everything Reg had ever said about electricity, because although that thing ran on nothing more than harmless old C or D cells, it really did feel as if there were waves of poison coming out of that gun and rolling through my head and frying my brains.

" ' "I seeya in there!" Jimmy was screaming, and his face was filled with a small boy's glee—it was both beautiful and somehow gruesome. *"You can't run away from Captain Future! You're dead, alien!"* And that screaming . . . getting weaker . . . smaller . . .

" ' "Jimmy, you stop it!" I yelled.

" 'He jumped. I'd startled him. He turned around . . . looked at me . . . stuck out his tongue . . . and then pushed the blaster against the glass panel and started shooting again. *Wah-wah-wah*, and that rotten purple light.

" 'Gertrude was coming down the hall, yelling for him to stop, to get out of there, that he was going to get the whipping of his life . . . and then the front door burst open and Reg came up the hall, bellowing. I got one good look at him and understood that he was insane. The gun was in his hand.

" ' "Don't you shoot my baby!" Gertrude screamed when she saw him, and reached out to grapple with him. Reg simply clubbed her aside.

" 'Jimmy didn't even seem to realize any of this was going on—he just went on shooting the space blaster into the typewriter. I could see that purple light pulsing in the blackness between the keys, and it looked like one of those electrical arcs they tell you not to look at without a pair of special goggles because otherwise it might boil your retinas and make you blind.

" 'Reg came in, shoving past me, knocking me over.

" ' "RACKNE!" he screamed. "YOU'RE KILLING RACKNE!"

" 'And even as Reg was rushing across the room, apparently planning to kill that child,' Jane told me, 'I had time to wonder just how many times he *had* been in that room, shooting that gun into the typewriter when his mother and I were maybe upstairs changing beds or in the backyard hanging clothes where we couldn't hear the *wah-wah-wah* . . . where we couldn't hear that thing . . . the Fornit . . . inside, screaming.

" 'Jimmy didn't stop even when Reg came bursting in—just kept shooting into the typewriter as if he knew it was his last chance, and since then I have wondered if perhaps Reg wasn't right about *they,* too—only maybe *they* just sort of float around, and every now and then they dive into a person's head like someone doing a double-gainer into a swimming pool and *they* get that somebody to do the dirty work and then check out again, and the guy *they* were in says, "Huh? Me? Did *what?*"

" 'And in the second before Reg got there, the screaming from inside the typewriter turned into a brief, drilling shriek—and I saw blood splatter all over the inside of that glass insert, as if whatever was in there had finally just exploded, the way they say a live animal will explode if you put it in a microwave oven. I know how crazy it sounds, but I *saw* that blood—it hit the glass in a blot and then started to run.

" ' "Got it," Jimmy said, highly satisfied. "Got—"

" 'Then Reg threw him all the way across the room. He hit the wall. The gun was jarred out of his hand, hit the floor, and broke. It was nothing but plastic and Eveready batteries, of course.

" 'Reg looked into the typewriter, and he screamed. Not a scream of pain or fury, although there was fury in it—mostly it was a scream of grief. He turned toward the boy then. Jimmy had fallen to the floor, and whatever he *had* been—if he ever *was* anything more than just a mischievous little boy—now he was just a six-year-old in terror. Reg pointed the gun at him, and that's all I remember.' "

The editor finished his soda and put the can carefully aside.

"Gertrude Rulin and Jimmy Rulin remember enough to make up for the lack," he said. "Jane called out, '*Reg, NO!*' and when he looked around at her, she got to her feet and grappled with him. He shot her, shattering her left elbow, but she didn't let go. As she continued to grapple with him, Gertrude called to her son, and Jimmy ran to her.

"Reg pushed Jane away and shot her again. This bullet tore along the left side of her skull. Even an eighth of an inch to the right and he would have killed her. There is little doubt of that, and none at all that, if not for Jane Thorpe's intervention, he would have surely killed Jimmy Rulin and quite possibly the boy's mother as well.

"He *did* shoot the boy—as Jimmy ran into his mother's arms just outside the door. The bullet entered Jimmy's left buttock on a downward course. It exited from his upper-left thigh, missing the bone, and passed through Gertrude Rulin's shin. There was a lot of blood, but no major damage done to either.

"Gertrude slammed the study door and carried her screaming, bleeding son down the hallway and out the front door."

The editor paused again, thoughtfully.

"Jane was either unconscious by that time or she has deliberately chosen to forget what happened next. Reg sat down in his office chair and put the muzzle of the .45 against the center of his forehead. He pulled the trigger. The bullet did not pass through his brain and leave him a living vegetable, nor did it travel in a semicircle around his skull and exit harmlessly on the far side. The fantasy was flexible, but the final bullet was as hard as it could be. He fell forward across the typewriter, dead.

"When the police broke in, they found him that way; Jane was sitting in a far corner, semiconscious.

"The typewriter was covered with blood, presumably filled with blood as well; head wounds are very, very messy.

"All of the blood was Type O.

"Reg Thorpe's type.

"And that, ladies and gentlemen, is my story; I can tell no more." Indeed, the editor's voice had been reduced to little more than a husky whisper.

There was none of the usual post-party chatter, or even the awkwardly bright conversation people sometimes use to cover a cocktail-party indiscretion of some moment, or to at least disguise the fact that things had at some point become much more serious than a dinner-party situation usually warranted.

But as the writer saw the editor to his car, he was unable to forbear one final question. "The story," he said. "What happened to the story?"

"You mean Reg's—"

" 'The Ballad of the Flexible Bullet,' that's right. The story that caused it all. *That* was the real flexible bullet—for you, if not for him. What in the hell happened to this story that was so goddamn great?"

The editor opened the door of his car; it was a small blue Chevette with a sticker on the back bumper which read FRIENDS DON'T LET FRIENDS DRIVE DRUNK. "No, it was never published. If Reg had a carbon copy, he destroyed it following my receipt and acceptance of the tale—considering his paranoid feelings about *they,* that would have been very much in character.

"I had his original plus three photocopies with me when I went into the Jackson River. All four in a cardboard carton. If I'd put that carton in the trunk, I would have the story now, because the rear end of my car never went under—even if it had, the pages could have been dried out. But I wanted it close to me, so I put it in the front, on the driver's side. The windows were open when I went into the water. The pages . . . I assume they just floated away and were carried out to sea. I'd rather believe that than believe they rotted along with the rest of the trash at the bottom of that river, or were eaten by catfish, or something even less aesthetically pleasing. To believe they were carried out to sea is more romantic, and slightly more unlikely, but in matters of what I choose to believe, I find I can still be flexible."

"So to speak."

The editor got into his small car and drove away. The writer stood and watched until the taillights had winked out, and then turned around. Meg was there, standing at the head of their walk in the darkness, smiling a little tentatively at him. Her arms were crossed tightly across her bosom, although the night was warm.

"We're the last two," she said. "Want to go in?"

"Sure."

Halfway up the walk she stopped and said: "There are no Fornits in your typewriter, are there, Paul?"

And the writer, who had sometimes—often—wondered exactly where the words *did* come from, said bravely: "Absolutely not."

They went inside arm in arm and closed the door against the night.

20th Century Ghost

Joe Hill

he best time to see her is when the place is almost full.

There is the well-known story of the man who wanders in for a late show, and finds the vast six-hundred-seat theater almost deserted. Halfway through the movie, he glances around and discovers her sitting next to him, in a chair that only moments before had been empty. Her witness stares at her. She turns her head and stares back. She has a nosebleed. Her eyes are wide, stricken. My head hurts, *she whispers.* I have to step out for a moment. Will you tell me what I miss? *It is in this instant that the person looking at her realizes she is as insubstantial as the shifting blue ray of light cast by the projector. It is possible to see the next seat over through her body. As she rises from her chair she fades away.*

Then there is the story about the group of friends who go in to the Rosebud together on a Thursday night. One of the bunch sits down next to a woman by herself, a woman in blue. When the movie doesn't start right away, the person who sat down beside her decides to make conversation. What's playing tomorrow? *he asks her.* The theater is dark tomorrow, *she whispers.* This is the last show. *Shortly after the movie begins she vanishes. On the drive home, the man who spoke to her is killed in a car accident.*

These, and many of the other best-known legends of the Rosebud, are false ... the ghost stories of people who have seen too many horror movies and who think they know exactly how a ghost story should be.

Alec Sheldon, who was one of the first to see Imogene Gilchrist, owns the Rosebud, and at seventy-three still operates the projector most nights. He can always tell, after talking to someone for just a few moments, whether or not they really saw her, but what he knows he keeps to himself, and he never publicly discredits anyone's story ... that would be bad for business.

He knows, though, that anyone who says they could see right through her didn't see her at all. Some of the put-on artists talk about blood pouring from her nose, her ears, her eyes; they say she gave them a pleading look, and asked for them to find somebody, to bring help. But she doesn't bleed that way, and when she wants to talk it isn't to tell someone to bring a doctor. A lot of the pretenders begin their stories by saying, you'll never believe what I just saw. *They're right. He won't, although he will listen to all that they have to say, with a patient, even encouraging smile.*

The ones who have seen her don't come looking for Alec to tell him about it. More often than not he finds **them**, *comes across them wandering the lobby on unsteady legs; they've had a bad shock, they don't feel well. They need to sit down awhile. They don't ever say,* you won't believe what I just saw. *The experience is still too immediate. The idea that they might not be believed doesn't occur to them until later. Often they are in a state that might be described as subdued, even submissive. When he thinks about the effect she has on those who encounter her, he thinks of Steven Greenberg coming out of* The Birds *one cool Sunday afternoon in 1963. Steven was just twelve then, and it would be another twelve years before he went and got so famous; he was at that time not a golden boy, but just a boy.*

Alec was in the alley behind the Rosebud, having a smoke, when he heard the fire door into the theater clang open behind him. He turned to see a lanky kid leaning in the doorway—just leaning there, not going in or out. The boy squinted into the harsh white sunshine, with the confused, wondering look of a small child who has just been shaken out of a deep sleep. Alec could see past him into a darkness filled with the shrill sounds of thousands of squeaking sparrows. Beneath that, he could hear a few in the audience stirring restlessly, beginning to complain.

Hey kid, in or out? *Alec said.* You're lettin' the light in.

The kid—Alec didn't know his name then—turned his head and stared back into the theater for a long, searching moment. Then he stepped out and the door settled shut behind him, closing gently on its pneumatic hinge. And still he didn't go anywhere, didn't say anything. The Rosebud had been show-ing The Birds *for two weeks, and although Alec had seen others walk out be-fore it was over, none of the early exits had been twelve-year-old boys. It was the sort of film most boys of that age waited all year to see, but who knew? Maybe the kid had a weak stomach.*

I left my Coke in the theater, *the kid said, his voice distant, almost tone-less.* I still had a lot of it left.

You want to go back in and look for it?

And the kid lifted his eyes and gave Alec a bright look of alarm, and then Alec knew. No.

Alec finished his cigarette, pitched it.

I sat with the dead lady, *the kid blurted.*

Alec nodded.

She talked to me.

What did she say?

He looked at the kid again, and found him staring back with eyes that were now wide and round with disbelief.

I need someone to talk to she said. When I get excited about a movie I need to talk.

Alec knows when she talks to someone she always wants to talk about the movies. She usually addresses herself to men, although sometimes she will sit and talk with a woman—Lois Weisel most notably. Alec has been work-ing on a theory of what it is that causes her to show herself. He has been keeping notes in a yellow legal pad. He has a list of who she appeared to and in what movie and when (Leland King, Harold and Maude, *'72; Joel Har-lowe,* Eraserhead, *'76; Hal Lash,* Blood Simple, *'84; and all the others). He has, over the years, developed clear ideas about what conditions are most likely to produce her, although the specifics of his theory are constantly being revised.*

As a young man, thoughts of her were always on his mind, or simmer-ing just beneath the surface; she was his first and most strongly felt obses-sion. Then for a while he was better—when the theater was a success, and he was an important businessman in the community, chamber of commerce, town planning board. In those days he could go weeks without thinking about her; and then someone would see her, or pretend to have seen her, and stir the whole thing up again.

But following his divorce—she kept the house, he moved into the one-bedroom under the theater—and not long after the eight-screen Cineplex opened just outside of town, he began to obsess again, less about her than about the theater itself (is there any difference, though? Not really, he supposes, thoughts of one always circling around to thoughts of the other). He never imagined he would be so old and owe so much money. He has a hard time sleeping, his head is so full of ideas—wild, desperate ideas—about how to keep the theater from failing. He keeps himself awake thinking about income, staff, salable assets. And when he can't think about money anymore, he tries to picture where he will go if the theater closes. He envisions an old folks' home, mattresses that reek of Ben-Gay, hunched geezers with their dentures out, sitting in a musty common room watching daytime sitcoms; he sees a place where he will passively fade away, like wallpaper that gets too much sunlight and slowly loses its color.

This is bad. What is more terrible is when he tries to imagine what will happen to her if the Rosebud closes. He sees the theater stripped of its seats, an echoing empty space, drifts of dust in the corners, petrified wads of gum stuck fast to the cement. Local teens have broken in to drink and screw; he sees scattered liquor bottles, ignorant graffiti on the walls, a single, grotesque, used condom on the floor in front of the stage. He sees the lonely and violated place where she will fade away.

Or won't fade . . . the worst thought of all.

Alec saw her—spoke to her—for the first time when he was fifteen, six days after he learned his older brother had been killed in the South Pacific. President Truman had sent a letter expressing his condolences. It was a form letter, but the signature on the bottom—that was really his. Alec hadn't cried yet. He knew, years later, that he spent that week in a state of shock, that he had lost the person he loved most in the world and it had badly traumatized him. But in 1945 no one used the word "trauma" to talk about emotions, and the only kind of shock anyone discussed was "shell."

He told his mother he was going to school in the mornings. He wasn't going to school. He was shuffling around downtown looking for trouble. He shoplifted candy bars from the American Luncheonette and ate them out at the empty shoe factory—the place closed down, all the men off in

France, or the Pacific. With sugar zipping in his blood, he launched rocks through the windows, trying out his fastball.

He wandered through the alley behind the Rosebud and looked at the door into the theater and saw that it wasn't firmly shut. The side facing the alley was a smooth metal surface, no door handle, but he was able to pry it open with his fingernails. He came in on the 3:30 P.M. show, the place crowded, mostly kids under the age of ten and their mothers. The fire door was halfway up the theater, recessed into the wall, set in shadow. No one saw him come in. He slouched up the aisle and found a seat in the back.

"Jimmy Stewart went to the Pacific," his brother had told him while he was home on leave, before he shipped out. They were throwing the ball around out back. "Mr. Smith is probably carpet-bombing the red fuck out of Tokyo right this instant. How's that for a crazy thought?" Alec's brother, Ray, was a self-described film freak. He and Alec went to every single movie that opened during his month-long leave: *Bataan*, *The Fighting Seabees*, *Going My Way*.

Alec waited through an episode of a serial concerning the latest adventures of a singing cowboy with long eyelashes and a mouth so dark his lips were black. It failed to interest him. He picked his nose and wondered how to get a Coke with no money. The feature started.

At first Alec couldn't figure out what the hell kind of movie it was, although right off he had the sinking feeling it was going to be a musical. First the members of an orchestra filed onto a stage against a bland blue backdrop. Then a starched shirt came out and started telling the audience all about the brand-new kind of entertainment they were about to see. When he started blithering about Walt Disney and his artists, Alec began to slide downwards in his seat, his head sinking between his shoulders. The orchestra surged into big dramatic blasts of strings and horns. In another moment his worst fears were realized. It wasn't just a musical; it was also a *cartoon*. Of course it was a cartoon, he should have known—the place crammed with little kids and their mothers—a 3:30 show in the middle of the week that led off with an episode of *The Lipstick Kid*, singing sissy of the high plains.

After a while he lifted his head and peeked at the screen through his fingers, watched some abstract animation for a while: silver raindrops falling against a background of roiling smoke, rays of molten light shimmering

across an ashen sky. Eventually he straightened up to watch in a more comfortable position. He was not quite sure what he was feeling. He was bored,
but interested too, almost a little mesmerized. It would have been hard not
to watch. The visuals came at him in a steady hypnotic assault: ribs of red
light, whirling stars, kingdoms of cloud glowing in the crimson light of a
setting sun.

The little kids were shifting around in their seats. He heard a little girl
whisper loudly, "Mom, when is there going to be *Mickey?*" For the kids it
was like being in school. But by the time the movie hit the next segment,
the orchestra shifting from Bach to Tchaikovsky, he was sitting all the way
up, even leaning forward slightly, his forearms resting on his knees. He
watched fairies flitting through a dark forest, touching flowers and spider-
webs with enchanted wands and spreading sheets of glittering, incandes-
cent dew. He felt a kind of baffled wonder watching them fly around, a
curious feeling of yearning. He had the sudden idea he could sit there and
watch forever.

"I could sit in this theater forever," whispered someone beside him. It
was a girl's voice. "Just sit here and watch and never leave."

He didn't know there was someone sitting beside him, and jumped to
hear a voice so close. He thought—no, he knew—that when he sat down
the seats on either side of him were empty. He turned his head.

She was only a few years older than him, couldn't have been more than
twenty, and his first thought was that she was very close to being a fox; his
heart beat a little faster to have such a girl speaking to him. He was already
thinking *don't blow it.* She wasn't looking at him. She was staring up at the
movie, and smiling in a way that seemed to express both admiration and a
child's dazed wonder. He wanted desperately to say something smooth, but
his voice was trapped in his throat.

She leaned towards him without glancing away from the screen, her
left hand just touching the side of his arm on the armrest.

"I'm sorry to bother you," she whispered. "When I get excited about a
movie I want to talk. I can't help it."

In the next moment he became aware of two things, more or less simultaneously. The first was that her hand against his arm was cold. He
could feel the deadly chill of it through his sweater, a cold so palpable it
startled him a little. The second thing he noticed was a single teardrop of
blood on her upper lip, under her left nostril.

"You have a nosebleed," he said, in a voice that was too loud. He immediately wished he hadn't said it. You only had one opportunity to impress a fox like this. He should have found something for her to wipe her nose with, and handed it to her, murmured something real Sinatra: *you're bleeding, here.* He pushed his hands into his pockets, feeling for something she could wipe her nose with. He didn't have anything.

But she didn't seem to have heard him, didn't seem the slightest bit aware he had spoken. She absent-mindedly brushed the back of one hand under her nose, and left a dark smear of blood over her upper lip . . . and Alec froze with his hands in his pockets, staring at her. It was the first he knew there was something wrong about the girl sitting next to him, something slightly *off* about the scene playing out between them. He instinctively drew himself up and slightly away from her without even knowing he was doing it.

She laughed at something in the movie, her voice soft, breathless. Then she leaned towards him and whispered, "This is all wrong for kids. Harry Parcells loves this theater but he plays all the wrong movies, Harry Parcells who runs the place?"

There was a fresh runner of blood leaking from her left nostril and blood on her lips, but by then Alec's attention had turned to something else. They were sitting directly under the projector beam, and there were moths and other insects whirring through the blue column of light above. A white moth had landed on her face. It was crawling up her cheek. She didn't notice, and Alec didn't mention it to her. There wasn't enough air in his chest to speak.

She whispered, "He thinks just because it's a cartoon they'll like it. It's funny he could be so crazy for movies and know so little about them. He won't run the place much longer."

She glanced at him and smiled. She had blood staining her teeth. Alec couldn't get up. A second moth, ivory white, landed just inside the delicate cup of her ear.

"Your brother Ray would have loved this," she said.

"Get away," Alec whispered hoarsely.

"You belong here, Alec," she said. "You belong here with me."

He moved at last, shoved himself up out of his seat. The first moth was crawling into her hair. He thought he heard himself moan, just faintly. He started to move away from her. She was staring at him. He backed a few feet down the aisle and bumped into some kid's legs, and the kid yelped. He glanced away from her for an instant, down at a fattish boy in a striped T-shirt who was glaring back at him, *watch where you're going meathead.*

Alec looked at her again and now she was slumped very low in her seat. Her head rested on her left shoulder. Her legs hung lewdly open. There were thick strings of blood, dried and crusted, running from her nostrils, bracketing her thin-lipped mouth. Her eyes were rolled back in her head. In her lap was an overturned carton of popcorn.

Alec thought he was going to scream. He didn't scream. She was perfectly motionless. He looked from her to the kid he had almost tripped over. The fat kid glanced casually in the direction of the dead girl, showed no reaction. He turned his gaze back to Alec, his eyes questioning, one corner of his mouth turned up in a derisive sneer.

"Sir," said a woman, the fat kid's mother. "Can you move, *please?* We're trying to watch the movie."

Alec threw another look towards the dead girl, only the chair where she had been was empty, the seat folded up. He started to retreat, bumping into knees, almost falling over once, grabbing someone for support. Then suddenly the room erupted into cheers, applause. His heart throbbed. He cried out, looked wildly around. It was Mickey, up there on the screen in droopy red robes—Mickey had arrived at last.

He backed up the aisle, swatted through the padded leather doors into the lobby. He flinched at the late-afternoon brightness, narrowed his eyes to squints. He felt dangerously sick. Then someone was holding his shoulder, turning him, walking him across the room, over to the staircase up to balcony-level. Alec sat down on the bottom step, sat down hard.

"Take a minute," someone said. "Don't get up. Catch your breath. Do you think you're going to throw up?"

Alec shook his head.

"Because if you think you're going to throw up, hold on till I can get you a bag. It isn't so easy to get stains out of this carpet. Also when people smell vomit they don't want popcorn."

Whoever it was lingered beside him for another moment, then without a word turned and shuffled away. He returned maybe a minute later.

"Here. On the house. Drink it slow. The fizz will help with your stomach."

Alec took a wax cup sweating beads of cold water, found the straw with his mouth, sipped icy cola bubbly with carbonation. He looked up. The man standing over him was tall and slope-shouldered, with a sagging roll around the middle. His hair was cropped to a dark bristle and his eyes, behind his absurdly thick glasses, were small and pale and uneasy. He wore his slacks too high, the waistband up around his navel.

Alec said, "There's a dead girl in there." He didn't recognize his own voice.

The color drained out of the big man's face and he cast an unhappy glance back at the doors into the theater. "She's never been in a matinee before. I thought only night shows, I thought—for God's sake, it's a kid's movie. What's she trying to do to me?"

Alec opened his mouth, didn't even know what he was going to say, something about the dead girl, but what came out instead was: "It's not really a kid's film."

The big man shot him a look of mild annoyance. "Sure it is. It's Walt Disney."

Alec stared at him for a long moment, then said, "You must be Harry Parcells."

"Yeah. How'd you know?"

"Lucky guesser," Alec said. "Thanks for the Coke."

Alec followed Harry Parcells behind the concessions counter, through a door, and out onto a landing at the bottom of some stairs. Harry opened a door to the right and let them into a small, cluttered office. The floor was crowded with steel film cans. Fading film posters covered the walls, overlapping in places: Boys Town, David Copperfield, Gone With the Wind.

"Sorry she scared you," Harry said, collapsing into the office chair behind his desk. "You sure you're all right? You look kind of peaked."

"Who is she?"

"Something blew out in her brain," he said, and pointed a finger at his left temple, as if pretending to hold a gun to his head. "Four years ago. During The Wizard of Oz. The very first show. It was the most terrible thing. She used to come in all the time. She was my steadiest customer. We used to talk, kid around with each other—" his voice wandered off, confused and distraught. He squeezed his plump hands together on the desktop in front of him, said finally, "Now she's trying to bankrupt me."

"You've seen her." It wasn't a question.

Harry nodded. "A few months after she passed away. She told me I don't belong here. I don't know why she wants to scare me away when we used to get along so great. Did she tell you to go away?"

"Why is she here?" Alec said. His voice was still hoarse, and it was a strange kind of question to ask. For a while, Harry just peered at him through his thick glasses with what seemed to be total incomprehension.

Then he shook his head and said, "She's unhappy. She died before the end of *The Wizard* and she's still miserable about it. I understand. That was a good movie. I'd feel robbed too."

"Hello?" someone shouted from the lobby. "Anyone there?"

"Just a minute," Harry called out. He gave Alec a pained look. "My concession stand girl told me she was quitting yesterday. No notice or anything."

"Was it the ghost?"

"Heck no. One of her paste-on nails fell into someone's food so I told her not to wear them anymore. No one wants to get a fingernail in a mouthful of popcorn. She told me a lot of boys she knows come in here, and if she can't wear her nails she wasn't going to work for me no more so now I got to do everything myself." He said this as he was coming around the desk. He had something in one hand, a newspaper clipping. "This will tell you about her." And then he gave Alec a look—it wasn't a glare exactly, but there was at least a measure of dull warning in it—and he added: "Don't run off on me. We still have to talk."

He went out, Alec staring after him, wondering what that last funny look was about. He glanced down at the clipping. It was an obituary—her obituary. The paper was creased, the edges worn, the ink faded; it looked as if it had been handled often. Her name was Imogene Gilchrist, she had died at nineteen, she worked at Water Street Stationery. She was survived by her parents, Colm and Mary. Friends and family spoke of her pretty laugh, her infectious sense of humor. They talked about how she loved the movies. She saw all the movies, saw them on opening day, first show. She could recite the entire cast from almost any picture you cared to name, it was like a party trick—she even knew the names of actors who had had just one line. She was president of the drama club in high school, acted in all the plays, built sets, arranged lighting. "I always thought she'd be a movie star," said her drama professor. "She had those looks and that laugh.

All she needed was someone to point a camera at her and she would have been famous."

When Alec finished reading he looked around. The office was still empty. He looked back down at the obituary, rubbing the corner of the clipping between thumb and forefinger. He felt sick at the unfairness of it, and for a moment there was a pressure at the back of his eyeballs, a tingling, and he had the ridiculous idea he might start crying. He felt ill to live in a world where a nineteen-year-old girl full of laughter and life could be struck down like that, for no reason. The intensity of what he was feeling didn't really make sense, considering he had never known her when she was alive; didn't make sense until he thought about Ray, thought about Harry Truman's letter to his mom, the words *died with bravery, defending freedom, America is proud of him.* He thought about how Ray had taken him to *The Fighting Seabees,* right here in this theater, and they sat together with their feet up on the seats in front of them, their shoulders touching. "Look at John Wayne," Ray said. "They oughta have one bomber to carry him, and another one to carry his balls." The stinging in his eyes was so intense he couldn't stand it, and it hurt to breathe. He rubbed at his wet nose, and focused intently on crying as soundlessly as possible.

He wiped his face with the tail of his shirt, put the obituary on Harry Parcells's desk, looked around. He glanced at the posters, and the stacks of steel cans. There was a curl of film in the corner of the room, just eight or so frames—he wondered where it had come from—and he picked it up for a closer look. He saw a girl closing her eyes and lifting her face, in a series of little increments, to kiss the man holding her in a tight embrace; giving herself to him. Alec wanted to be kissed that way sometime. It gave him a curious thrill to be holding an actual piece of a movie. On impulse he stuck it into his pocket.

He wandered out of the office and back onto the landing at the bottom of the stairwell. He peered into the lobby. He expected to see Harry behind the concession stand, serving a customer, but there was no one there. Alec hesitated, wondering where he might have gone. While he was thinking it over, he became aware of a gentle whirring sound coming from the top of the stairs. He looked up them, and it clicked—the projector. Harry was changing reels.

Alec climbed the steps and entered the projection room, a dark compartment with a low ceiling. A pair of square windows looked into the theater below. The projector itself was pointed through one of them, a big machine made of brushed stainless steel, with the words VITAPHONE stamped on the case. Harry stood on the far side of it, leaning forward, peering out the same window through which the projector was casting its beam. He heard Alec at the door, shot him a brief look. Alec expected to be ordered away, but Harry said nothing, only nodded and returned to his silent watch over the theater.

Alec made his way to the VITAPHONE, picking his way carefully through the dark. There was a window to the left of the projector that looked down into the theater. Alec stared at it for a long moment, not sure if he dared, and then put his face close to the glass and peered into the darkened room beneath.

The theater was lit a deep midnight blue by the image on the screen: the conductor again, the orchestra in silhouette. The announcer was introducing the next piece. Alec lowered his gaze and scanned the rows of seats. It wasn't much trouble to find where he had been sitting, an empty cluster of seats close to the back, on the right. He half-expected to see her there, slid down in her chair, face tilted up towards the ceiling and blood all down it—her eyes turned perhaps to stare up at *him*. The thought of seeing her filled him with both dread and a strange nervous exhilaration, and when he realized she wasn't there, he was a little surprised by his own disappointment.

Music began: at first the wavering skirl of violins, rising and falling in swoops, and then a series of menacing bursts from the brass section, sounds of an almost military nature. Alec's gaze rose once more to the screen—rose and held there. He felt a chill race through him. His forearms prickled with gooseflesh. On the screen the dead were rising from their graves, an army of white and watery specters pouring out of the ground and into the night above. A square-shouldered demon, squatting on a mountain-top, beckoned them. They came to him, their ripped white shrouds fluttering around their gaunt bodies, their faces anguished, sorrowing. Alec caught his breath and held it, watched with a feeling rising in him of mingled shock and wonder.

The demon split a crack in the mountain, opened Hell. Fires leaped, the Damned jumped and danced, and Alec knew what he was seeing was about the war. It was about his brother dead for no reason in the South Pacific, *America is proud of him,* it was about bodies damaged beyond repair, bodies sloshing this way and that while they rolled in the surf at the edge of a beach somewhere in the far east, getting soggy, bloating. It was about Imogene Gilchrist, who loved the movies and died with her legs spread open and her brain swelled full of blood and she was nineteen, her parents were Colm and Mary. It was about young people, young healthy bodies, punched full of holes and the life pouring out in arterial gouts, not a single dream realized, not a single ambition achieved. It was about young people who loved and were loved in return, going away, and not coming back, and the pathetic little remembrances that marked their departure, *my prayers are with you today, Harry Truman,* and *I always thought she'd be a movie star.*

A church bell rang somewhere, a long way off. Alec looked up. It was part of the film. The dead were fading away. The churlish and square-shouldered demon covered himself with his vast black wings, hiding his face from the coming of dawn. A line of robed men moved across the land below, carrying softly glowing torches. The music moved in gentle pulses. The sky was a cold, shimmering blue, light rising in it, the glow of sunrise spreading through the branches of birch trees and northern pine. Alec watched with a feeling in him like religious awe until it was over.

"I liked *Dumbo* better," Harry said.

He flipped a switch on the wall, and a bare light bulb came on, filling the projection room with harsh white light. The last of the film squiggled through the VITAPHONE and came out at the other end, where it was being collected on one of the reels. The trailing end whirled around and around and went *slap, slap, slap.* Harry turned the projector off, looked at Alec over the top of the machine.

"You look better. You got your color back."

"What did you want to talk about?" Alec remembered the vague look of warning Harry gave him when he told him not to go anywhere, and the thought occurred to him now that maybe Harry knew he had slipped in without buying a ticket, that maybe they were about to have a problem.

But Harry said, "I'm prepared to offer you a refund or two free passes to the show of your choice. Best I can do."

Alec stared. It was a long time before he could reply.

"For what?"

"For what? To shut up about it. You know what it would do to this place if it got out about her? I got reasons to think people don't want to pay money to sit in the dark with a chatty dead girl."

Alec shook his head. It surprised him that Harry thought it would keep people away, if it got out that the Rosebud was haunted. Alec had an idea it would have the opposite effect. People were happy to pay for the opportunity to experience a little terror in the dark—if they weren't there wouldn't be any business in horror pictures. And then he remembered what Imogene Gilchrist had said to him about Harry Parcells: *he won't run the place much longer.*

"So what do you want?" Harry asked. "You want passes?"

Alec shook his head.

"Refund then."

"No."

Harry froze with his hand on his wallet, flashed Alec a surprised, hostile look. "What do you want then?"

"How about a job? You need someone to sell popcorn. I promise not to wear my paste-on nails to work."

Harry stared at him for a long moment without any reply, then slowly removed his hand from his back pocket.

"Can you work weekends?" he asked.

In October, Alec hears that Steven Greenberg is back in New Hampshire, shooting exteriors for his new movie on the grounds of Phillips Exeter Academy—something with Tom Hanks and Haley Joel Osment, a misunderstood teacher inspiring troubled kid-geniuses. Alec doesn't need to know any more than that to know it smells like Steven might be on his way to winning another Oscar. Alec, though, preferred the earlier work, Steven's fantasies and suspense thrillers.

He considers driving down to have a look, wonders if he could talk his way onto the set—Oh yes, I knew Steven when he was a boy—wonders if he might even be allowed to speak with Steven himself. But he soon dismisses the idea. There must be hundreds of people in this part of New England who could claim to have known Steven back in the day, and it isn't as if they were ever close. They only really had that one conversation, the day Steven saw her. Nothing before; nothing much after.

So it is a surprise when one Friday afternoon close to the end of the month Alec takes a call from Steven's personal assistant, a cheerful, efficient-sounding woman named Marcia. She wants Alec to know that Steven was hoping to see him, and if he can drop in—is Sunday morning all right?—there will be a set pass waiting for him at Main Building, on the grounds of the Academy. They'll expect to see him around 10:00 A.M., she says in her bright chirp of a voice, before ringing off. It is not until well after the conversation has ended, that Alec realizes he has received not an invitation, but a summons.

A goateed P.A. meets Alec at Main and walks him out to where they're filming. Alec stands with thirty or so others, and watches from a distance, while Hanks and Osment stroll together across a green quad littered with fallen leaves, Hanks nodding pensively while Osment talks and gestures. In front of them is a dolly, with two men and their camera equipment sitting on it, and two men pulling it. Steven and a small group of others stand off to the side, Steven observing the shot on a video monitor. Alec has never been on a movie set before, and he watches the work of professional make-believe with great pleasure.

After he has what he wants, and has talked with Hanks for a few minutes about the shot, Steven starts over towards the crowd where Alec is standing. There is a shy, searching look on his face. Then he sees Alec and opens his mouth in a gap-toothed grin, lifts one hand in a wave, looks for a moment very much the lanky boy again. He asks Alec if he wants to walk to craft services with him, for a chili dog and a soda.

On the walk Steven seems anxious, jiggling the change in his pockets and shooting sideways looks at Alec. Alec knows he wants to talk about Imogene, but can't figure how to broach the subject. When at last he begins to talk, it's about his memories of the Rosebud. He talks about how he loved the place, talks about all the great pictures he saw for the first time there. Alec smiles and nods, but is secretly a little astounded at the depths of Steven's self-deception. Steven never went back after The Birds. He didn't see any of the movies he says he saw there.

At last, Steven stammers, What's going to happen to the place after you retire? Not that you should retire! I just mean—do you think you'll run the place much longer?

Not much longer, Alec replies—it's the truth—but says no more. He is concerned not to degrade himself asking for a handout—although the *thought is in him that this is in fact why he came. That ever since receiving Steven's invitation to visit the set he had been fantasizing that they would talk about the Rosebud, and that Steven, who is so wealthy, and who loves movies so much, might be persuaded to throw Alec a life preserver.*

The old movie houses are national treasures, *Steven says.* I own a couple, believe it or not. I run them as revival joints. I'd love to do something like that with the Rosebud someday. That's a dream of mine, you know.

Here is his chance, the opportunity Alec was not willing to admit he was hoping for. But instead of telling him that the Rosebud is in desperate straits, sure to close, Alec changes the subject ... ultimately lacks the stomach to do what must be done.

What's your next project? *Alec asks.*

After this? I was considering a remake, *Steven says, and gives him another of those shifty sideways looks from the corners of his eyes.* You'd never guess what. *Then, suddenly, he reaches out, touches Alec's arm.* Being back in New Hampshire has really stirred some things up for me. I had a dream about our old friend, would you believe it?

Our old—*Alec starts, then realizes who he means.*

I had a dream the place was closed. There was a chain on the front door, and boards in the windows. I dreamed I heard a girl crying inside, *Steven says, and grins nervously.* Isn't that the funniest thing?

Alec drives home with a cool sweat on his face, ill at ease. He doesn't know why he didn't say anything, why he couldn't say anything; Greenberg was practically begging to give him some money. Alec thinks bitterly that he has become a very foolish and useless old man.

At the theater there are nine messages on Alec's machine. The first is from Lois Weisel, who Alec has not heard from in years. Her voice is brittle. She says, Hi Alec, Lois Weisel at B.U. *As if he could have forgotten her. Lois saw Imogene in* Midnight Cowboy. *Now she teaches documentary film-making to graduate students. Alec knows these two things are not unconnected, just as it is no accident Steven Greenberg became what he became.* Will you give me a call? I wanted to talk to you about—I just—will you call me? *Then she laughs, a strange, frightened kind of laugh, and says,* This is crazy. *She exhales heavily.* I just wanted to find out if something was happening to the Rosebud. Something bad. So—call me.

The next message is from Dana Lewellyn who saw her in The Wild

Bunch. *The message after that is from Shane Leonard, who saw Imogene in American Graffiti. Darren Campbell, who saw her in* Reservoir Dogs. *Some of them talk about the dream, a dream identical to the one Steven Greenberg described, boarded-over windows, chain on the door, girl crying. Some only say they want to talk. By the time the answering machine tape has played its way to the end, Alec is sitting on the floor of his office, his hands balled into fists—an old man weeping helplessly.*

Perhaps twenty people have seen Imogene in the last twenty-five years, and nearly half of them have left messages for Alec to call. The other half will get in touch with him over the next few days, to ask about the Rosebud, to talk about their dream. Alec will speak with almost everyone living who has ever seen her, all of those Imogene felt compelled to speak to: a drama professor, the manager of a video rental store, a retired financier who in his youth wrote angry, comical film reviews for The Lansdowne Record, *and others. A whole congregation of people who flocked to the Rosebud instead of church on Sundays, those whose prayers were written by Paddy Chayefsky and whose hymnals were composed by John Williams and whose intensity of faith is a call Imogene is helpless to resist. Alec himself.*

Steven's accountant handles the fine details of the fund-raiser to save the Rosebud. The place is closed for three weeks to refurbish. New seats, state-of-the-art sound. A dozen artisans put up scaffolding and work with little paintbrushes to restore the crumbling plaster molding on the ceiling. Steven adds personnel to run the day-to-day operations. He has bought a controlling interest, and the place is really his now, although Alec has agreed to stay on to manage things for a little while.

Lois Weisel drives up three times a week to film a documentary about the renovation, using her grad students in various capacities, as electricians, sound people, grunts. Steven wants a gala reopening to celebrate the Rosebud's past. When Alec hears what he wants to show first—a double feature of The Wizard of Oz *and* The Birds—*his forearms prickle with gooseflesh; but he makes no argument.*

On reopening night, the place is crowded like it hasn't been since Titanic. *The local news is there to film people walking inside in their best suits. Of course, Steven is there, which is why all the excitement ... although Alec thinks he would have a sell-out even without Steven, that people would have come just to see the results of the renovation. Alec and Steven pose for pho-*

tographs, the two of them standing under the marquee in their tuxedoes, shaking hands. Steven's tuxedo is Armani, bought for the occasion. Alec got married in his.

Steven leans into him, pressing a shoulder against his chest. What are you going to do with yourself?

Before Steven's money, Alec would have sat behind the counter handing out tickets, and then gone up himself to start the projector. But Steven hired someone to sell tickets and run the projector. Alec says, Guess I'm going to sit and watch the movie.

Save me a seat, *Steven says.* I might not get in until *The Birds,* though. I have some more press to do out here.

Lois Weisel has a camera set up at the front of the theater, turned to point at the audience, and loaded with high-speed film for shooting in the dark. She films the crowd at different times, recording their reactions to The Wizard of Oz. *This was to be the conclusion of her documentary—a packed house enjoying a twentieth-century classic in this lovingly restored old movie palace—but her movie wasn't going to end like she thought it would.*

In the first shots on Lois's reel it is possible to see Alec sitting in the back left of the theater, his face turned up towards the screen, his glasses flashing blue in the darkness. The seat to the left of him, on the aisle, is empty, the only empty seat in the house. Sometimes he can be seen eating popcorn. Other times he is just sitting there watching, his mouth open slightly, an almost worshipful look on his face.

Then in one shot he has turned sideways to face the seat to his left. He has been joined by a woman in blue. He is leaning over her. They are un-mistakably kissing. No one around them pays them any mind. The Wizard of Oz is ending. We know this because we can hear Judy Garland, reciting the same five words over and over in a soft, yearning voice, saying—well, you know what she is saying. They are only the loveliest five words ever said in all of film.

In the shot immediately following this one, the house lights are up, and there is a crowd of people gathered around Alec's body, slumped heavily in his seat. Steven Greenberg is in the aisle, yelping hysterically for someone to bring a doctor. A child is crying. The rest of the crowd generates a low rustling buzz of excited conversation. But never mind this shot. The footage that came just before it is much more interesting.

It is only a few seconds long, this shot of Alec and his unidentified com-

panion—*a few hundred frames of film*—but it is the shot that will make Lois Weisel's reputation, not to mention a large sum of money. It will appear on television shows about unexplained phenomena, it will be watched and re-watched at gatherings of those fascinated with the supernatural. It will be studied, written about, debunked, confirmed, and celebrated. Let's see it again.

He leans over her. She turns her face up to his and closes her eyes and she is very young and she is giving herself to him completely. Alec has removed his glasses. He is touching her lightly at the waist. This is the way people dream of being kissed, a movie star kiss. Watching them, one almost wishes the moment would never end. And over all this, Dorothy's small, brave voice fills the darkened theater. She is saying something about home. She is saying something everyone knows.

The Green Glass Sea

Ellen Klages

*I*n the summer of 1945, Dr. Gordon was gone for the first two weeks in July. Dewey Kerrigan noticed that a lot of the usual faces were missing from the dining hall at the Los Alamos Lodge, and everyone seemed tense, even more tense than usual.

Dewey and her father had come to the Hill two years before, when she was eight. When he was sent to Washington, she came to live with the Gordons. They were both scientists, like Papa, and their daughter, Suze, was about the same age as Dewey. Dewey's mom hadn't been around since she was a baby.

One Sunday night Mrs. Gordon had shooed the girls to bed early, then woke them before dawn for a hike with some of the other wives, many of whom also had jobs and titles other than Mrs. They carried blankets and sandwiches and thermoses of coffee out to a place on the edge of the mesa where they had a clear view of the southern horizon and sat in the still early darkness, smoking and waiting.

Right before sunrise there was a bright light. Dewey thought it might be the sun coming up, except it came from the wrong direction. It lit up the sky for a moment, then disappeared, like the fireworks they'd had in May when the war in Europe ended. There was silence for a minute after the light faded, then Mrs. Gordon and the other women started hugging each other, smiling and talking. They hugged Dewey and Suze too, but Dewey wasn't sure why.

She figured it must have something to do with the gadget. Everything on the Hill had something to do with the gadget. She just wished she knew what the gadget *was*.

That evening, around dinnertime, a caravan of cars full of men returned to the Hill. They looked tired and hot and dusty and were greeted with cheers. Dr. Gordon walked into the apartment about 7:30. He had deep circles under his eyes and he hadn't shaved.

"Well, we did it," he said as he hugged Mrs. Gordon. He hugged Suze next, and ruffled his hand through Dewey's curls. He didn't say what "it" was. He just ate a ham sandwich, drank two shots of whiskey, and slept until the next afternoon.

On the fourth of August, Dr. Gordon came into the apartment late in the afternoon. He was whistling, his hat tipped back on his head, carrying a pink box from the bakery down in Santa Fe.

He put the box down on the table and opened a bottle of beer. "Got a birthday surprise for you," he said to Suze.

She stopped coloring in Dorothy's dress with her blue crayon and looked up. "Can I open it now, Daddy?"

"Nope. Your birthday's not until the sixth. Besides, it isn't something you can unwrap. It's a trip, a little vacation. I've gotten special passes."

"Where are we going?"

"Well now, that's the surprise."

"Farther than Santa Fe?"

He smiled. "Just a bit." He took a deep swig of beer. "Why don't you go and pack up a few things before supper. You won't need much. Just a change of clothes and your toothbrush. Your mom left a paper sack for you to put them in."

Suze threw her coloring book onto the table with a thump and ran into the bedroom, her shoes clattering loudly on the linoleum.

Dewey sat on the couch reading a book about Faraday. She ducked her head behind the page and didn't say anything. She was used to people leaving. It was better to stay quiet. She pushed her glasses up on her nose and concentrated on the orderly rows of black type.

"Aren't you going to get your things ready?" asked Dr. Gordon. He had picked up the newspaper and was looking at it without really reading.

Dewey was startled. "Am I coming *with* you?"

He chuckled. "Of course. What did you think? The whole family's going."

From the bedroom there was a loud sigh, then a snap! as Suze unfolded the paper bag.

"Oh," Dewey said slowly. "Family." The Gordons weren't her family, really. Nobody was, not since she'd gotten the Army telegram about Papa and the accident. But they were nice. Mrs. Gordon even tucked her in, some nights, if she wasn't working late at her lab.

"Don't you want to go on an adventure?" Dr. Gordon asked.

"I guess so." Dewey wasn't sure. She liked being on the Hill. She knew where everything was, and when dinner was served at the Lodge. There weren't any surprises. She'd had enough surprises.

But Dr. Gordon seemed to be waiting for an answer. Dewey carefully replaced her bookmark and closed the book. "I'll go pack my things," she said.

The next morning Mrs. Gordon was up early, making stacks of ham and cheese sandwiches that she wrapped in waxed paper. She put the picnic basket and their paper sacks into the big black Ford, and just after eleven they showed their passes to the guard at the East Gate and set off down the long, twisting road that led to the highway several thousand feet below. The temperature climbed as they descended.

Dewey and Suze sat in the backseat, a foot or so of black serge between them. Suze had the road map spread out across her lap. Los Alamos wasn't on the map, of course, but a thin blue line trickled down from the mesa through Pojoaque. When it became a fatter red line, Highway 285, in Santa Fe, Dr. Gordon turned right and they headed south.

Dewey stared out the window. She had never been anywhere in New Mexico except the Hill, not since she and Papa had arrived two years before, and then it had been night. She'd imagined that everything looked like the mesa, just more of it. But now outside the window the land was flat and endless, bounded by craggy brown mountain canyons on one side and distant dusky blue ridges on the far horizons.

Close up, everything that went by the window was brown. Brown dirt, brown fences, brown tumbleweeds, brown adobe houses. But all the distances were blue. Crystal blue, huge sky that covered everything for as far as she could see until the earth curved. Faraway slate blue, hazy blue mountains and mesas, ledges of blue land stretching away from the road, blurring into the sky at the edges. Blue land. She had never seen anything like that before.

Dr. Gordon had gas coupons from the Army, and he filled up the tank when they crossed Route 66. They stopped for a late lunch on the banks of a trickle of river a few miles farther south, eating their sandwiches and drinking Orange Nehi in the shade of a piñon pine. The summer sun was bright and the air smelled like dust and resin.

"How much farther are we going?" Suze asked, putting the bottle caps in her pocket.

"Another three, maybe four hours. We'll spend the night in a little town called Carrizozo," Dr. Gordon said.

Dewey watched as Suze bent over the map and her finger found Carrizozo. It was a very small dot, and other than being a place where two roads crossed, there didn't seem to be anything interesting nearby.

Suze looked puzzled. "Why are we going *there*?"

"We're not. It's just the closest place to spend the night, unless you want to sleep in the car. I certainly don't." He lit his pipe, leaned back against the tree, and closed his eyes, smiling.

It was the most relaxed Dewey had ever seen him.

After lunch, the land stayed very flat and the mountains stayed far away. There was nothing much to see. Beyond the asphalt the land was parched brown by the heat, and there were no trees, just stubby greasewood bushes and low grass, with an occasional spiky yucca or flat cactus.

Dewey's eyes closed and she slept, almost, just aware enough to hear the noise of the car wheels and the wind. When the car slowed and bumped over a set of railroad tracks, she opened her eyes again. They were in Carrizozo, and it was twilight. The distant blues had turned to purples and the sky was pale and looked as if it had been smeared with bright orange sherbet. Dr. Gordon pulled off onto the gravel of the Crossroads Motor Court.

They walked a few blocks into town for dinner. Carrizozo was not much more than the place where the north-south highway heading toward El Paso crossed the east-west road that led to Roswell. There was a bar called the White Sands, a Texaco station, and some scattered stores and houses between the railroad tracks and the one main street.

Through the blue-checked curtains of the café Dewey could see mountains to the east. "Are we going into the mountains in the morning?"

"Nope," said Dr. Gordon, spearing a piece of meatloaf. "The other direction."

Dewey frowned. She had spent most of the day looking over Suze's shoulder at the map. There wasn't anything in the other direction. It was an almost perfectly blank place on the map. White Sands was a little bit west, but almost a hundred miles to the south. If they'd been going there, Dewey thought, it would have made more sense to stay in Alamogordo.

"But...," Dewey said, and Mrs. Gordon smiled. "You're confused, my little geographer. That's because where we're going isn't *on* the map. Not yet, anyway."

That didn't make a lot of sense either. But when Mrs. Gordon smiled at her with warm eyes, Dewey felt like everything would be okay, even if she didn't understand.

It was barely light when Mrs. Gordon woke them the next morning. Dr. Gordon had gotten two cups of coffee in paper cups from the café, and Cokes for the girls, even though it was breakfast. The air was still and already warm, and everything was very quiet.

They drove south, and then west for about an hour, the rising sun making a long dark shadow in front of the car. There was nothing much to see out the window or on the map. At an unmarked dirt road, Dr. Gordon turned left.

Thin wire ran from wooden fence posts, separating the pale brown of the road from the pale beige of the desert. A few straggly yucca plants, spiky gray-green balls with stalks of yellow flowers, were the only color forever. The car raised plumes of dust so thick that Dewey could see where they were going, but no longer where they'd been.

After half an hour, they came to a gate with an Army MP. He seemed to be guarding more empty desert. The Gordons both showed their passes and their Los Alamos badges. The guard nodded and waved the car through, then closed the gate behind them.

Dr. Gordon pulled the car off to the side of the road a mile later and turned off the engine. It ticked slowly in the hot, still air.

"Daddy? Where *are* we?" Suze asked after a minute.

They didn't seem to be anywhere. Except for a small range of low mountains to the west, where they'd stopped was the middle of a flat, featureless desert, scattered with construction debris—pieces of wooden crates, lengths of wire and cable, flattened sheets of metal.

Dr. Gordon took her hand. "It's called Trinity," he said. "It's where I was working last month. Let's walk."

They started across the dirt. There were no plants, not even grass or yucca. Just reddish-beige, sandy dirt. Every few yards there was a charred greasewood bush. Each bush was twisted at the same odd angle, like a little black skeleton that had been pushed aside by a big wind.

They kept walking. The skeletons disappeared and then there was nothing at all. It was the emptiest place Dewey had ever seen.

After about five minutes, Dewey looked down and saw burned spots that looked like little animals, like a bird or a desert mouse had been stenciled black against the hard flat ground. She looked over at Mrs. Gordon. Mrs. Gordon had stopped walking.

She stood a few yards back from the others, her lips pressed tight together, staring down at one of the black spots. "Christ," she said to the spot. "What *have* we done?" She lit a Chesterfield and stood there for almost a minute, then looked up at Dr. Gordon. He walked back to her.

"Phillip? How safe is this?" She looked around, holding her arms tight across her chest, as if she were cold, although the temperature was already in the eighties.

He shrugged. "Ground zero's still pretty hot. But Oppie said the rest is okay, as long as we don't stay out too long. Fifteen minutes. We'll be fine."

Dewey didn't know what he was talking about. Maybe sunburn. There wasn't any shade. There wasn't any anything.

Mrs. Gordon nodded without smiling. A few minutes later she reached down and took Suze's hand and held it tight.

They kept walking through the empty place.

And then, just ahead of them, the ground sloped gently downward into a huge green sea. Dewey took a few more steps and saw that it wasn't water. It was glass. Shiny jade-green glass, everywhere, coloring the bare, empty desert as far ahead as she could see. It wasn't smooth, like a Pyrex bowl, or sharp like a broken bottle, but more like a giant candle had dripped and splattered green wax everywhere.

Dr. Gordon reached down and broke off a piece about as big as his hand. It looked like a green, twisted root. He gave it to Suze.

"Happy birthday, kiddo," he said. "I really wanted you to see this. The boys are calling it trinitite."

Suze turned the glass over and over in her hand. It was shiny on the top, with some little bubbles in places, like a piece of dark green peanut brittle. The bottom was pitted and rough and dirty where it had been lying in the sand. "Is it very, very old?" she asked.

He shook his head. "Very, very new. Three weeks today. It's the first new mineral created on this planet in millions of years." He sounded very pleased.

Dewey counted back in her head. Today was August 6th. Three weeks ago was when they got up early and saw the bright light. "Did the gadget make this?" Dewey asked.

Dr. Gordon looked surprised. He tipped his hat back on his head and thought for a minute. "I suppose it's all right to tell you girls now," he said. "Yes, the gadget did this. It was so hot that it melted the ground. Over a hundred million degrees. Hotter than the sun itself. It fused seventy-five acres of this desert sand into glass."

"How is that going to win the war?" Dewey asked. It was strange to finally be talking about secret stuff out loud.

"It'll melt all the Japs!" Suze said. "Right, Daddy?"

Mrs. Gordon winced. "Well, if cooler heads prevail," she said, "we'll never have to find out, will we, Phillip?" She gave Dr. Gordon a look, then took a few steps away and stared out toward the mountains.

"You girls go on, take a walk around," he said. "But when I call, you scamper back pronto, okay?"

Dewey and Suze agreed and stepped out onto the green glass sea. The strange twisted surface crunched and crackled beneath their feet as if they were walking on braided ice. They walked in from the edge until all they could see was green: splattered at their feet, merging into solid color at the edges of their vision.

"I didn't know war stuff could make anything pretty," Suze said. "It looks like we're on the planet Oz, doesn't it?"

Dewey was as amazed by the question as by the landscape. Suze usually acted like she didn't exist. "I guess so," she nodded.

"This is probably what they made the Emerald City out of." Suze reached down and picked up a long flat piece. "I am the Wicked Witch of the West. Bow down before my powerful magic." She waved her green glass wand in the air, and a piece of it broke off, landing a few feet away. She giggled.

"I'm going to take some pieces of Oz home," she said. She pulled the bottom of her seersucker blouse out to make a pouch and dropped in the rest of the piece she was holding.

Suze began to fill up her shirt. Dewey walked a few feet away with her head down, looking for one perfect piece to take back with her. The glassy surface was only about half an inch thick, and many of the pieces Dewey picked up were so brittle they crumbled and cracked apart in her hands. She picked up one odd, rounded lump and the thin glass casing on the outside shattered under her fingers like an eggshell, revealing a lump of plain dirt inside. She finally kept one flat piece bigger than her hand, spread out. Suze had her shirttails completely filled.

Dewey was looking carefully at a big piece with streaks of reddish brown when Dr. Gordon whistled. "Come on back. Now," he called.

She looked at Suze, and the other girl smiled, just a little. They walked slowly back until they could see brown dirt ahead of them again. At the edge, Dewey turned back for a minute, trying to fold the image into her memory. Then she stepped back onto the bare, scorched dirt.

They walked back to the car in silence, holding their new, fragile treasure.

Dr. Gordon opened the trunk and pulled out a black box with a round lens like a camera. He squatted back on his heels. "Okay, now hand me each of the pieces you picked up, one by one," he said.

Suze pulled a flat piece of pebbled glass out of her shirt pouch. When Dr. Gordon put it in front of the black box, a needle moved over a bit, and the box made a few clicking sounds. He put that piece down by his foot and reached for the next one. It was one of the round eggshell ones, and it made the needle go all the way over. The box clicked like a cicada.

He put it down by his other foot. "That one's too hot to take home," he said.

Suze pulled out her next piece. "This one's not hot," she said, laying her hand flat on top of it.

Her mother patted Suze's head. "It's not temperature, sweetie. It's radiation. That's a Geiger counter."

"Oh. Okay." Suze handed the piece to her father.

Dewey knew what a Geiger counter was. Most of the older kids on the Hill did. She wasn't quite sure what it measured, but it was gadget stuff, so it was important.

"Did Papa help make this?" she asked, handing her piece over to Dr. Gordon.

Mrs. Gordon made a soft sound in her throat and put her arm around Dewey's shoulders. "He certainly did. None of this would have been possible without brave men like Jimmy—, like your papa."

Dewey leaned into Mrs. Gordon and nodded silently.

Dr. Gordon made Suze leave behind two eggshell pieces. He wrapped the rest in newspaper and put them into a shoebox, padded with some more newspaper crumpled up, then put out his hand for Dewey's.

Dewey shook her head. "Can I just hold mine?" She didn't want it to get mixed up with Suze's. After a glance at his wife, Dr. Gordon shrugged and tied the shoebox shut with string and put it in the trunk. They took off their shoes and socks and brushed all the dust off before they got into the car.

"Thanks, Daddy," Suze said. She kissed him on the cheek and climbed into the backseat. "I bet this is the best birthday party I'll ever, ever have."

Dewey thought that was probably true. It was the most wonderful place *she* had ever been. As they drove east, she pressed her face to the window, smiling out at the desert. She closed her eyes and felt the comforting weight of the treasure held tight against her chest. One last present from Papa, a piece of the beautiful green glass sea.

The Kiss

Tia V. Travis

'Twas on the Isle of Capri that I found her
Beneath the shade of an old walnut tree
I can still see the flow'rs blooming round her
Where we met on the Isle of Capri

—"The Isle of Capri,"
Jimmy Kennedy, 1934

*T*he angel's heart was torn from its chest.

The stained-glass box that once held it was smashed; ruby tears scattered the fountain. The ruins of the valentine lay amidst splinters of red glass and oak leaves mottled with rot. Soaked through, it had been half-devoured by birds. I didn't know whether it had been ripped away strip by ragged strip or swallowed mouthful by mouthful, a bloody delicacy fought over by many. Either way, it came as no shock that there was nothing left but a few anemic tatters. This was a cemetery, after all, and in the land of the dead the birds were reigning lords.

They perched everywhere: on the crypts, on the cypress and oak, on the eaves troughs where the rain ran rivers into the sodden earth. At the funeral forty years ago their ancestors screamed obscenities from the trees as the preacher droned on about love and eternity. Furious screeches and feathered rage. I clutched Sister Constance-Evangeline's habit in a hailstorm of birds and terror, covering my ears until all I could hear was the rushing of blood . . . the beating of wings.

But the birds didn't frighten me now as they did then. I slogged through the mud toward the fountain.

The heart was in ruins but a sinewy strand still twisted around the rusted wire frame. Bleached by sun and leeched by rain, the crepe was white as aged scar tissue. When I touched it, it collapsed into fibers. The last damp mouthful of air trapped within the empty chamber expired on a breath of wind. Gently, I replaced what was left of the heart in the fountain bowl. Stained amber with the sap of cypress needles it seemed more like a Canopic jar, and my heart, my heart lay dead within.

I tried to remember the day when they buried my mother, but I felt as empty as that paper husk. Forty years will do that to you. It wasn't that I didn't understand the pain; I just couldn't feel it anymore.

For stone angels and dead whores there is no pain, I reminded myself. A crepe heart does not beat. A lifeless body does not suffer the ravages of nature's savage little ways, nor does it endure the gut wrenching of scavengers as they tear it to shreds. For the dead there are no haunting regrets, no aching remorse, no dreams to torment deep into the night. There is no laughter, no music, no dancing. No dream of an Isle of Capri . . .

Mixed blessings.

The blessings of heartless angels.

The workings of the human heart have always been a mystery to me.

The heart of my mother, Lana Lake, has been the greatest mystery of all. Nothing remains of that heart now but a dry chamber, a mummified fist wrapped around a hardened clot where once had been caged a wild and fiercely beating thing, scarlet and raw as ripped silk.

In the autumn of 1958 when I was eleven years old, my mother, Lana Lake, was bombed out of her mind in the back garden on a bed of crushed birds-of-paradise. She shouted to the sky that spun overhead like a top that I could mix an Angel's Kiss so coo-coo crazy Frank Sinatra himself would have married me on the spot for one sip of that utterly endsville elixir.

He was between mistresses, Lana said with a wicked wink that blushed me down to my toes. At the wedding, she storied her enraptured audience of one, Francis Albert would stare into my eyes with his cause-for-swooning baby blues. He would hold me tenderly and croon "The Isle of Capri" until it was my bedtime and Mrs. Sinatra arrived to take him home.

I laughed in sheer delight at the possibilities, licking fingers sticky with pomegranate juice. Crimson fingerprints decorated the front of my virgin-white Catholic school blouse. The woolen stockings and sensible shoes had long since been kicked off in favor of squirming bare toes.

It had been Daddy's idea for me to attend Our Lady of Perpetual Sorrow Convent School for girls. I hated his surprisingly stubborn old world ways, making me go just because his mother had, God rest her soul. I couldn't wait to run home to my own sinning mother, who would light-heartedly endure my tortured catechisms while she painted my toenails an unrepentant shade of Mary Magdalene red.

"So, should I call him?" Lana said in her leading way.

"Frank *Sinatra?*"

She snatched my pomegranate and sucked the bitten part. *"Call the one who loves you only, I can be so warm and tender..."*

"No no *no!*" I rolled on the grass, shrieking with laughter.

"He owes me a favor," Lana added in a low, theatrical voice.

I sat up in a tumble of fallen leaves. "He does?"

"What do you think?" On the tip of her tongue, a jewel glittered. Pomegranate seed, like the one she wore in her navel when she did her routine. It disappeared into her mouth, a ruby on that dancing tongue. *"Call me, don't be afraid, you can caaalll me, baby it's late..."*

Skip and a jump. That's what my heart did. Mother really *had* met Frank Sinatra, and every night after that I practically expected The Man With the Golden Charm to appear magically on my doorstep in a tuxedo, with a handkerchief as orange as birds-of-paradise tucked sharp-as-you-please in the breast pocket.

Now that was style, Lana said. Ring-a-ding-ding.

For an aperitif I would serve him an Angel's Kiss: equal parts white crème de cacao, crème de violette, prunelle, and sweet cream.

That was the Angel's Kiss.

Too candy-sweet for anyone else, Mother downed them like after-dinner mints after dancing all night at the Cocoa Club.

The Cocoa Club: there was a swinging spot. Peter Lawford, one of Sinatra's fellow rat-packers, had bought the prohibition clip joint for a song in 1952 and fixed it up. Pink neon martini glasses and palm trees with beckoning fronds out front. It was the place where you went to see and be seen if you were *anybody at all* in the San Francisco Bay area. Tuxedos were de rigueur for the men; the women wore strapless evening dresses and shoulder-length gloves and jewelry from exclusive shops. Every table had little deco lights that lit up the room like diamonds. The waiters with their pencil-thin mustachios swept the tables over their heads like party hats as they glided down the grand staircase to the backlit stage. Best seat in the house, when you slipped them a little something extra. *Duke 'em good!* in Sinatra's slang book, but he was way too slick to flaunt a bill.

Daddy pounded the pads at the Cocoa Club every night. *Ba da da!* The hottest drummer in town, Joe Caiola would dish it up any way you liked it: slow and swinging or fast and hopping. He'd learned to bang the bongos from the master, Chano Pozo himself, when he and Daddy palled around with Dizzy Gillespie.

Sometimes for a few extra bucks he'd fly down to Los Angeles or to New York or Chicago and sit in with Sam Butera or Artie Shaw's band or some other swingers who were hip to the beat. Or maybe Sinatra would hire him for a private party in The Tonga Room at the Fairmont and then word would get out about this real gone cat who could really lick those skins, and then everyone else would want him for their parties, too.

Bongos were big back then, and Daddy would get top dollar for those gigs. Sometimes he'd even team up with Tito Contreros or Jack Costanza and then the money would roll in on a cloud of fine Cuban cigar smoke because Sinatra and his pallies were outrageous tippers who partied every night when they were in town. But as hot as Daddy was, my mother was the star attraction.

Lana Lake was a "class act," Daddy said, even when she stripped down to bare canvas. She was a work of art, a living painting with a beating heart and eyes outlined in fiery yellow like the tropical flowers she loved.

Once when they were doing the bossa nova and thought I was asleep on a stack of records, I saw her slip her tongue into the heart of a bird-of-paradise and I thought I'd die. They danced like they were built for each other, Mother and Daddy: not just the bossa nova but the mambo, the samba, the tango. Lana cocked her hips for Perez Prado and swung to

Count Basie and jumped to Louis Prima. There was Sinatra, of course, the Ultimate Big Spender. "Isle of Capri" was Lana's favorite, though she liked others: "Three Coins in the Fountain" and "Love is the Tender Trap," and the melancholy "Don't Cry, Joe" that was like a dance hall after closing.

Daddy would hold Mother close, his dark head buried in her shoulder. *"Amorino, amorino..."* he whispered over and over, like a man lost at sea and found.

Don't cry, Joe
Let her go, let her go, let her go

Lana's voice warm and dark as espresso at midnight.

You've gotta realize this is the windup
Things will be much better when you make your mind up...

Dancing slow and easy, her hands wrapped in his hair, pulling, pulling...

Daddy could sing, too. But mostly he liked to play the drums, with a subtle, expert flick of his wrists. A true musician, Joe Caiola lost himself in the rhythm, a ghost of a cigarette in the ashtray, a cylinder of burned ash.

Sometimes it would be jazz drumming with lots of metal brushes, with his eyes half-closed like window shades. The fringe of the brushes was like the fringe of his eyelashes sweeping his cheekbone. It was an angular face with too many planes and corners. It sliced shadows in the lamplight and made a chiaroscuro of his features.

"A face you could get cut on," I'd heard my mother say more than once.

"Or a face you could cut," Daddy teased back with a swat of brushes.

Tino laughed, ice clinking in his glass with a little *cha cha cha.* Jack Daniel's and ice. That's how he liked it. "Maybe a face *Cassie* could cut, eh, Joe?"

Daddy ice-picked a look at him while Mother, poured into a jade silk sheath, slipped out from behind the Chinese screen. The needle swung across Martin Denny's *Exotica* on the hi-fi. Screeching birds with jeweled plumes, grinning monkeys, and purring leopards, growling things on the prowl in the heart of the jungle where claws cut to the quick.

"You hear what I said, Lana?" Tino lazily tipped back his J.D.

"Don't tempt me, Tino," Lana said, waving a finger at him. Polished fingernails the shade of dragonfly wings. "Don't..."

She smiled at them both with a curve of lips, and most times it would be fine, but sometimes there'd be something behind that smile, a sheet-lightning flash that raised the hairs on my neck.

Sometimes Daddy called Mother his Scarlet Tornado. Sometimes, his Red Flame.

White ice melting red flame, burning the glass, the two as one.

I was alone in the cemetery. The air was wet with late-winter rain that had already soaked me and my shredded heart through the skin. A brisk wind shook a wash of icy drops from the shadow-dark cypresses. It rattled the twisted branches of the live oaks that grew behind the crypt and shed their leaves in the angel's fountain. All around me stormed a cyclone of needles, of torn black leaves. They whipped around the worn crevices of the head-stones with leafy tongues. They clung like leeches to my shivering body. God, I was cold.

I stared at the birds lined up in the trees like snipers. They watched my every movement. Talons raked straight to the heart, deep enough to draw blood. What was I doing here?

Chasing the ghost of a song.

My hands started to shake but I couldn't leave.

"I *can't* leave," I whispered. To the birds, to myself, I wasn't sure. The wind carried my voice through the branches of the black oaks, rustled the wings of the birds whose eyes had never left me, not once in forty years. I had to hear that song again. I had to know.

In the early 1940s, before I was born, my mother had some throwaway parts in crime movies. She was invariably cast as the siren for whom they dragged the rivers while the opening credits ran: *Murder on the Rocks. The Sweet Kill. Venus Under Glass. Sonata for a Night Angel.* No big studios, no contracts, no options. It was all strictly B-league. Still, Lana's not inconsiderable on-screen charms had attracted her share of attention, almost all of it male. And while Lana Lake might have been a minor starlet in the Tinseltown constellation, she shone bright as Polaris in her hometown of Martinez after she decided that dancing and drinking, not moviemaking, were more in tune with her nocturnal rhythms.

Location turned out to be everything of course. Martinez, a shot-glass toss away from San Francisco's infamous Cocoa Club, was home not only to Lana Lake, but to the equally infamous martini. Mother's drink of choice was, naturally, Dean Martin's choice. *The Flame of Love: swirl three drops expensive sherry in an iced stem glass, then pour out. Squeeze one strip of orange peel into the glass and flambé. Throw away the peel. Fill the glass with ice to chill it. Toss out ice. Add very expensive vodka, then flambé another strip of orange peel around the rim. Throw away the peel. Stir very gently.*

"*I like a new Lincoln with all of its class,*" Mother sang to Daddy while sitting in his lap. "*I like a martini and burn on the glass!*"

That was Lana Lake: burn on the glass all the way.

Myself, I'd never experienced the forbidden and fermented fruits of the Cocoa Club. And liberal as Lana was, she still couldn't slip me under the velvet ropes and into the backdoor of the smoky nightspot.

To make up for it, she rehearsed her act for us in the living room, for Daddy and me, and maybe some of the boys in the band who always seemed to be lounging around there, smoking and joking, or tinkling "Street Scene '58" on the piano, because sooner or later, everyone ended up at our house.

Including Daddy.

Lana's little trick started like this: first she would disappear behind the Chinese screen—*Chinoise, en français,* she explained in her crazy put-on accent, not quite French, not quite anything. Then she would slink out from behind the screen with a wink of an emerald eye.

And then she would dance.

The lights played with the curves of her silhouette on rice paper as satiny-smooth as the head of Daddy's snare drum. He kept time with the jive of her hips. His shirtsleeves would be rolled up, the collar unbuttoned, his tanned skin dark against his white undershirt. Cigarette half-forgotten in the corner of his mouth as he stared at her. As we all stared at her.

Luis Ramirez whistled. "Now that's what I call a sweet little cookie," he said, shaking his head.

"A *fortune* cookie. All wrapped up in Chinese silk," Daddy said with a proud swish of cymbals. He wasn't the only one who loved Mother. They all loved her: the boys in the band, and Daddy...and me. Burn on the glass, all the way.

Lana had hundreds of costumes jammed in her closet like piñatas: Spanish bullfighter bolero jacket and a snorting bull painted above her breast. Caravan gypsy with bright scarves and an evil silver blade licking the tip of her rouged nipple. Queen of the Nile in a sleek leopard pelt and a painted python with an amber eye that wound around her narrow waist.

Daddy's wife, Cassandra (she liked to be called Mrs. Joe Caiola), had called Mother a common whore. Right to her face once, when we ran into her in town. With all those people standing there like a church choir. Nervous titters and uneasy glances all around. Lana Lake was Lana Lake, after all, and there was no telling what she'd do for a slight like that. To everyone's amazement Mother only smiled, and we kept walking. Still, there was a tightness to her steps. Red dress. Red high heels. Red hair bouncing down her back, burning like her cheeks.

I never understood, then, how it was possible to hate something so unabashedly beautiful. I was transfixed by unrestrained female beauty in a way that only a girl of eleven, uninitiated to the mysteries that awaited the thrust into adulthood, could be. God, how I wanted that life for myself: a hundred handsome boyfriends to drive me anywhere I wanted in a shiny limousine. And a private jet to fly me to the Isle of Capri.

They should burn that damn club down, Mrs. Caiola said. She was arguing with Daddy in the house next door. It was a scorching summer morning; all the windows were open. You couldn't help but hear her.

Burn it down...

My nostrils singed with blazing palm fronds, scorched maître d's, bandstands showering sparks, highball glasses exploding like a string of firecrackers behind the bar. I envisioned incinerated skeletons locked in charred embraces, teeth clattering on the dance floor like smoky pearls. Would they really burn it down?

But the Cocoa Club remained open despite Cassandra Caiola. A glorification of all things sinful: a palace of pleasure, a den of desire.

Sometimes Lana wore a g-string of tiny pagodas and the spangled pasties of Imperial China. On those formal occasions Mother, with an artist's steady hand and a little silver mirror, would paint an oriental dragon that began at her left breast and licked the nape of her neck with a forked tongue. When Lana breathed, the dragon breathed, and my heart pounded with excitement. When she danced ... it was like watching the unfolding of an origami bird. The Emperor's Nightingale with nipples like ripe raspberries. Her arms moved like vines, slim as the necks of Ming vases. The dragon sank its claws into her creamy skin, wrapped its serpentine body around her breasts, and swayed with every gyration, swayed with us all....

Other times Mother slipped into a sky-blue dress of chiffon that concealed nothing. Then she painted an angel on her breast, plucking a harp of pure gold. Daddy said that when she danced with the angel, she danced with God, and the chiffon floated around her like a cloud.

When he told me that, I wished, how I wished, that Sister Constance-Evangeline would take me to the Cocoa Club to see Mother dance, just once. I knew she'd never do it, though her rosary had even fewer beads than Lana's g-string, and the g-string was strung with heavenly blue glass instead of dead brown seeds that grew nothing at all.

In the cemetery.

Beyond the angel to the crypt itself.

Passing years and the wash of vintage wine-country rains in the Northern California valley had smoothed its curvilinear lines to a winding shell that seemed to curl in upon itself. Glistening beneath a sheen of rain, it had a dreamlike, almost translucent quality. In graceful script:

LANA LAKE

December 24, 1926—October 4, 1958

An unknown admirer—some gossiped about a movie star carrying a torch or a lovedrunk Mafioso with money to burn—had laid out the green for Lana's lavish but astonishingly tasteful crypt and the guardian angel with its wings outstretched to the heavens. Mountains of fresh flowers had, for years, been delivered weekly. Lana's favorite birds-of-paradise, with petals shading from the palest saffron to the burnt orange of twilight over a bottomless lake.

More than a few had disapproved of this extravagance, hardly befitting an ex-starlet and second-rate nightclub performer. Especially one who'd expressed her passions in such an explicit way. But such was the mystique of a dead exotic dancer, the kind whose name is inevitably more notorious in death than in life.

I thought about that life as I leaned my cheek against the angel's cool base. I clasped a pale ankle, traced the angel's serene expression with the back of my hand. The stone was crumbling, braceleted with Medusa-green moss. As I breathed, vapors swirled in the chill air. They reminded me of the frescoed clouds on the ceiling of the chapel where God created Man, in the country where my father, too, had been created. But whether it was my breaths, or God's, or those of the stone angel that formed those curlicues, I could not tell. In the fading light the angel's lips seemed to move, to form pearls of condensation with every exhalation, to whisper words in a language almost too perfect, too divine, to be heard.

> She whispered softly, "It's best not to linger,"
> Then as I kissed her hand I could see . . .

God, how I wanted to see. To sing. To remember. There was so much life here, so much unfinished. The stones, the earth, the oaks sang with it. I couldn't leave. Not now. Chasing the ghost of a song. So many songs . . .

In 1958 my hair was the bane of my existence. There was nothing coo-coo crazy about it. It was fine and straight and utterly *Clyde*. Lana insisted it was as fine as bone china, but who wanted hair like a tea party when you could have hair like a Bloody Mary? Lana's was dark and rich, a sinuous red fire. When she danced she coiled it on her head to accentuate her long and erotic neck.

I, however, was profoundly dissatisfied with my looks. Summing up all the pre-adolescent fervor I could muster I announced: "I HATE my hair. I want YOUR hair."

Loving me too much to laugh, Mother still couldn't prevent her lips from playing with a smile. Her hands moved like silk, in sweeping brush-strokes. "Well, your hair isn't exactly like mine, but that makes it no less beautiful, barefoot contessa." She was wearing a chemise that skimmed the tops of her thighs. In the day she lived in chemises.

"What's a contessa?" I asked. I was still disconsolate with my lot in life.

Lana French-inhaled her cigarette. I couldn't tell what she was thinking. "A contessa is ... a beautiful rich lady who lives in a castle."

I straightened suddenly. "On the Isle of Capri?"

Lana let out an explosive little laugh. Smoke jetted through her nostrils. "Yes, yes, yes, on the Isle of Capri."

I settled back, satisfied, sinking into her hypnotic brushstrokes. "Daddy wants to take us to the Isle of Capri someday," I reminded her. Daddy had been to Capri. He'd told us he'd take us there lots of times.

"Mmmhmm...."

I dreamed awhile. Idly, I supposed: "Would Daddy marry you if you were a contessa?"

Mother stopped brushing, just for an instant. The hairbrush tightened in her hand. A crackle of static. In my daydream I hardly noticed.

"Daddy can't have two wives," Mother said. She set the hairbrush on the vanity with a finality that was lost on me.

I thought about Daddy's wife, Cassandra, the crazy lady who lived next door. The one who called Mother a whore and who was always watching us from behind the curtain. Cassandra was rich and *almost* as beautiful as Mother, and the glossy white house she and Daddy lived in could *almost* have been a castle. But I was pretty sure she'd never been to the Isle of Capri.

A thought struck me. "Do you think Frank Sinatra would marry me if I were a contessa?"

Lana, distracted, suddenly looked at me. She laughed unexpectedly and wrapped her arms around me from behind. "Why not? You're Sicilian *and* Catholic. You could make an Angel's Kiss to knock his socks off." She smiled at me in the mirror. "He'd go wild for you. Coo-coo crazy."

"I'm only *half* Sicilian," I corrected her. My tone was reproachful and smacked of Sister Constance-Evangeline's elocution class.

"But you are a full Catholic, *and to show my devotion to thee, I consecrate to thee my eyes, my ears, my mouth, my heart, my entire self.* Shake with it, sugar, shake with it."

Shake with it, I did not. I hated convent school. I hated the dour nuns at Our Lady of Perpetual Sorrow who refused to let me run barefoot through the arched courtyard where the pear trees burst with juice and there was cool black soil I was dying to sink my toes into. The pears, I was warned sternly, were not to be eaten. They were full of worms.

Mother's breasts were like the heavy flesh of ripe pears. After she and Daddy were dead and buried I'd sit beneath those trees for hours, sucking the golden skins and thinking of nothing, nothing at all, until there was nothing but a pile of rotting cores.

Kicking my heels at Lana's vanity table I complained that Sister Constance-Evangeline was always after me to get to confession.

"A little confession is good for the soul," Mother said, painting my lips with a little stiff brush. She had never attended convent school. She said it was too late for her; that she'd been on God's shit list for years.

I surmised I probably had been, too.

"Oh, no, honey. Not you. Make like you're going to kiss someone," Lana instructed. "Like this—"

I exaggerated a movie-star pout. I had never kissed anyone. Not for *real*. Sometimes the girls practiced with movie magazines they hid under their pillows. But kissing boring old pieces of paper with ads for underarm deodorant on the backs wasn't like it would be in real life. Was it?

"Perfect!" Mother dabbed with the brush. "You look like Frida Kahlo. Or Carmen. Tell Daddy to buy the opera for you, you crazy chick!"

Later Daddy came in with some of the boys, Sam and Luis, and Chuy Hernando, and Tino Alvarez and Domingo. Daddy laughed and said, "Hey Tino, she looks more like Carmen *Miranda!*" Then he swirled me up in the air with my glitzy red lips and glitzy red toenails the color of the wax cherries on the Chiquita's famous turban. He swung me around just like Lana said Frank Sinatra would at our wedding, and the boys clapped a quick Latin rhythm and Lana did a little swing of her hips against Domingo's, and I could not, at that moment, have been happier.

A little confession . . .

Mother died before she could confess. I wondered what Sister Constance-Evangeline would have made of that. The murder/suicide was a wet-dream for the tabloids, who'd pronounced it "an act of passion." *Amorrazo.* Joe Caiola wouldn't leave his wife for the temperamental showgirl. Ergo, the temperamental showgirl shot him, then shot herself, straight through the heart.

Ring-a-ding-ding. One, two, three.

Thoroughly drenched in Mother's perfume, I whispered scented Hail Marys for her in church. After I'd finished Sister Constance-Evangeline scoured my neck, my wrists, the backs of my knees, all the secret places, until the skin bled pomegranate-red under the faucet. Watching the red wash down the sink, I wondered: did dead whores go to heaven?

I gripped the marble angel's ankles, tighter now. I was dreaming of a girl who ran through the damp earth in the garden like a barefoot contessa, hair a wildfire, copper leaves falling around her like pennies in the autumn wind. I tried to remember the song that whistled through her painted red lips as she pounded up the porch steps trailing birds-of-paradise in both fists, her tongue clicking against her teeth like a castanet. I remembered the girl, innocent then and unafraid, as she clattered open the screen door and ran, barefoot, into the heart of a nightmare. But after forty years, the song had stuck in my throat.

My eyes ached from the blinding white marble, the blinding white sky. I stared at the heart in the fountain. It was drained and pale. But it became for me another heart: my mother's heart, pumping wet and red and hard through the splinters of a ribcage that gleamed white as the wings of the angel gracing her left breast.

The angel had bled a halo of red.

The red was everywhere, a flutter of smears on Mother's hands and face like the frantic sweep of butterfly wings. The red was on Daddy's face, too. Mother was bent over him on the floor in a widening pool of blood, her mouth pressed tightly to the third finger of his left hand in the rich, wet kiss of one who loves deeply. It was not her own wedding ring she kissed.

She looked up at me as I banged through the screen door. A bubble of blood escaped her lips.

And it burst, like the world, around us all.

Mother and Daddy and Cassandra and me.

The four of us, together. As we always would be.

Red flame and thieving birds, the two burned into one. Blood and ashes.

My shoulders heaved as I held the statue. I wanted to cry, but no tears came.

"What's a whore?" I asked Mother the afternoon Mrs. Caiola had called her that in the street. Instantly, I chewed my tongue in regret. Mother's lips twitched. Without a word she drew me into arms as cool as a Tom Collins. The breeze rustled musically through the leaves of the eucalyptus trees in the backyard. The sound of a thousand chopsticks, swish swish. . . .

We listened, Mother and I. I closed my eyes and leaned back in her arms. After a moment she started to hum softly. Snapped her fingers. Staring across the garden at the picket fence next door, she sang in a low voice: *"She gets too hungry for dinner at eight—"*

The bedroom window was open. The pane refracted a dazzle of light. Someone stirred behind the muslin curtain, ever so slightly.

Singing louder, now: *"She loves the theater, but never comes late!"* Mother tumbled me to my feet. Eucalyptus shells sprayed from my skirt as she swept me across the garden.

I grinned at Mother, but she wasn't looking at me. Not at me.

"Sing it with me, baby!" she cried. *"She loves the theater, but never comes late!"*

Thoughts of mysterious whores vanished. I sang the only words I could remember, sang them off-key, at the top of my lungs: *"SHE'D NEVER BOTHER WITH PEOPLE SHE'D HATE!"*

Lana wasn't dancing now. A smile twisted her lips as she stared straight at the window.

Big finale, now, lots of brass. I did a cartwheel and belted it out: *"THAT'S WHY THE LADY IS A TRAMP!"*

The curtains in the house next door snapped shut.

Mother blew a kiss.

I collapsed in the grass, sweaty and breathless and gassed to be alive.

In the Whispering Pines Cemetery, the wind stole the kiss I blew and carried it back to the curtain of trees, the spying eyes in the branches. Hair lashed my eyes and I turned away. I gazed up at the stone angel, at the gaping cavity in its chest where its life had gushed, and the wings that hooked a silver awning of sky. In the corner of one eye balanced a single teardrop: spider. A delicate leg caught in a shred of web quivered in the wind like an eyelash. Eternally poised, I knew the arachnid teardrop would never fall. The spider was long-dead, and its hollow shell had, over time, become a crust of sleep in the angel's eye.

The angel's dry eye.

God weeps no tears for whores.

A roosting magpie, thief of hearts, cawed from the cypress with bony branch-wings dark as dusk. Soon night would roll in on the back of a rumbling thunderhead. I grit my teeth hard, my knuckles whitening on the marble ankles.

Why had she done it? I didn't know—how could I? All I knew was that the angel's heart had not been torn out, then. Not yet. The heart still beat, if only for a few moments more. It felt everything. Knew everything. Told everything. It whispered a single word: a wet red kiss blown to me from across a kitchen floor, from the lips of the dying to the heart of the living.

One kiss, one word.

> *Summertime was nearly over*
> *Blue Italian sky above*

One kiss, one word.

> *I said, "Lady, I'm a rover*
> *Can you spare a sweet word of love?"*

One word was enough. I never forgot what Mother had whispered while she lay on the floor, her life seeping away from her, from me, in the burnished brass light of that autumn afternoon. But I'd misunderstood what she meant by it.

Until this moment. Maybe, until this moment.

It was this remembering that had carried me back to the angel's arms.

Remembering and time, and dreams and hearts, and forgotten songs and dying angels. The kiss of angels, painted and real and dancing and drunk, with lips wide open and hearts torn out, as sweet as crème de cacao.

Mrs. Caiola never did leave Daddy. She'd threatened to a thousand times but there was no way in hell she'd give him his freedom so he could be with *her*. That's how Daddy told it, when he and Mother stayed up talking and I caught snatches of their heated discussions in the other room.

Then there were the accusations and counteraccusations pitched back and forth through the night like hardballs from the house next door. Begging on both sides. *Cassandra, this is crazy. You know it isn't any good. Why don't you let me go? Not on your life, Joe. Not on your GODDAMNED life.*

Then she'd turn on the waterworks. That's what Mother called them, with a snort.

I knew about waterworks.

"What does the water in the convent fountain taste like, Capri?" she asked me once, squeezing my hands. "Jesus' tears?"

"Crème de cacao," I answered, giggling.

An angel's kiss....

Sunday afternoons, after the Cocoa Club shakedown, I poured and mixed the Angel's Kisses carefully. I set them on a tray inlaid with opal dragons that wound round it like the painted twin on Lana's neck. Then I took them on tiptoe to her boudoir. Stolen sips of Angel's Kisses. I used to think in sweet rapture: she's like that. An Angel's Kiss, as pure as bliss....

Mother, lying in bed with a sleeping mask strewn on the sheets like a leftover from a masquerade, sipped her drink. "Mmm. Just the thing for that Mood Indigo," she confided.

"The mood indigo?"

Shadow of a smile. "Mood Indigo, baby."

Through Mother's bedroom window I watched Cassandra Caiola *click-click-click* down the front walk in high heels and a Christian Dior suit. Her hair was pulled tightly back from her made-up face, not a strand out of place. She paused, frowning, fastening the little buttons on her gloves. I'd never seen her go anywhere without those gloves. Perfect and pristine and white as ice. She called Daddy's name sharply as she unlocked the door to her Cadillac, so shiny you could see your reflection in it. White, just like her gloves.

White ice melting red flame, burning the glass, the two as one.

Mother and Cassandra: fire and ice.

I watched Daddy amble out of the house and toss his cigarette on the sidewalk. Slouch his hat forward. *Slam.*

"You know that wasn't our arrangement, Joe." Backing out. "*You* said you wanted the brat. And far be it for *me* to stand in your way, especially since you'd already knocked her up. Though God only knows what *that*

one will turn—" squeal of rubber "—with a mother like—" Frosted lips in
a rearview mirror.

Daddy not looking at her. Tapping a rhythm on the dash.

"You *know* what an understanding woman I am, Joe. You *know* I am.
But I've had just about enough of living right next door to that—that—"

Sigh. "Why don't you just let me go, then, Cassandra."

We never heard the reply as the Cadillac peeled down the driveway.

Lana lay languidly in bed. She lifted her glass. "To sweethearts and
wives," she said wryly. "May they never meet."

The Angel's Kiss.

Full on the lips.

It was time that carried me to Whispering Pines and the place where my
mother lay wrapped in her past like a skein of stars. It was time, chased by
that ghost of a song I couldn't quite remember, and couldn't quite forget.
And now I stood with the iron door swinging wide behind me.

The wet northern California wind blew at my back, bringing with it a
smattering of soaked oak leaves. Inside the crypt it was dim, but there was
still a little dying light. I knew I'd be able to see what I needed to see.

I had to see Mother's rich red lips while Sinatra sang the word and
Lana spoke it with that terrible hurt, that desperate pleading in her eyes.
One word.

One sweet word of love

For a moment I wasn't sure if the suitcase record player I'd left for her
would still be there. Somehow, I'd always imagined otherworldly hands
spiriting it and Lana away, at last, to that elusive Mediterranean isle. But
there it was, as it had waited in the vault the last four decades. Beside it,
beneath a thick layer of dust, lay the laminated cover of Frank Sinatra's
Come Fly with Me. Old Blue Eyes, now dust himself, his voice echoing in
a tomb.

I picked up the record. It smelled of damp, of decay, of shut-in places.
But in my mind, a song rang out that was gay and swinging, a song that
was really going somewhere. A song brimming with sparkling vino and
Italian palazzos and illicit romance. It was the song that once carried me

away to a villa on the Isle of Capri, an isle of tangerine sunsets and whispered words of love.

I stood with my eyes closed, swaying to a song I heard only in memory. And, swaying, I remembered at last the song I had forgotten.

The weeklies sizzled with stories of Mother tossing full glasses of champagne in men's faces. Stories of stinging slaps that rang through the room. Her fits of temper were legendary, as was her childish pouting, her brooding silences and black depressions when she'd scratch the needle across "The Isle of Capri" again and again. Sometimes Daddy would walk in whistling some tune kicking around in his head, all unsuspecting with hands in his pockets, and she'd spring like a cobra. Back him into a corner. He'd grin at her and throw up his hands in surrender, and she'd spit out, "Joe, you really are a sonofabitch." Then she'd kiss him hard and bite his lip until it bled.

It was a savage dance, that give and take of love they had, stronger and wilder than any act the Cocoa Club had ever witnessed. No one was particularly surprised when Lana Lake and Joe Caiola turned up dead in a pool of red on her kitchen floor. A man between two houses, between two worlds—ice-cold wife in one, red-hot mistress and child in the other. Maybe *Mrs.* Joe Caiola could put up with an "arrangement" like that, but not a wildcat like Lana Lake. People like Lana, their passions boiled over like a pot of sauce on the stove.

I remember everything about that moment: Lana's chili-pepper-red toreador pants...the smell of Daddy's favorite Napoli spaghetti sauce bubbling like Mount Vesuvius before a blast...the pungent odor of garlic and garden oregano and Roma tomatoes the color of arterial blood...the gun on the floor by Lana's bare feet. Red lacquer, chipped on the pinkie.

I remember the pain and horror in Mother's eyes, the silent pleading, the grasping fingers, the choking sound she made as she tried to speak....

I tried to picture that kitchen now: blood that had pooled and seeped into linoleum now badly discolored. Knife on a butcher block where decades-old onions had shriveled up like blackened flies. An apron stained with sauce the color of blood, and an icebox filled with dried-out spaghetti. A forty-year-old menu that never changed.

Old Blue Eyes hit it on the head: *She wore a lovely meatball on her finger.*

It turned out Daddy had been shot through the heart with a bullet from the same .22 automatic Tino Alvarez gave Lana to protect herself from the nuts who were always hitting on her at the club. She'd even used it once, shot a man in the crotch without an ounce of remorse. Clutching the bloody mess in his pants he'd stumbled to the bar on the corner where he soused what was left of his manhood in a glass of scotch because a guy there told him he'd heard somewhere it made a pretty good disinfectant. The screams were heard clear to the next county.

So the story ran, anyhow. . . . The tabloids had a parade with it. Mother was acquitted and after that, everyone in town knew about the .22 locked in the nightstand. Everyone. And men knew better than to tangle with Lana Lake.

Everyone also knew how Mother wanted Joe Caiola all to herself for years, and how things would never, ever be the way she wanted them, not while Cassandra was kicking up her little white pumps in protest. It was the standard story: one too many nights, one too many fights. And it wasn't too hard for people to picture Lana storming off to the bedroom in tears, banging open the nightstand, fumbling around for the gun. . . .

Maybe she'd even meant to go after Cassandra, but it never got as far as that. Somehow the gun went off. Lana herself was probably as surprised as hell. And what was left now with Joe lying dead on the floor? Snake eyes, no matter which way you rolled it, and nothing left to do but squeeze the trigger one more time.

> *Don't cry, Joe.*
> *Let her go, let her go, let her go . . .*

God, let him go.
What do you say, baby . . . you and me on the Isle of Capri. . . .
Don't joke, Joe.

I thought a lot about that gun. About Mrs. Joe Caiola. About how Cassandra had bought our house the day after the funerals. It stood there for the next forty years. Boarded up, falling into disrepair, a sprawling bungalow choked in a stranglehold of climbing vines as thick as a dragon's body. The vines bled green in the rain, and the rain seeped into the ground.

Over the years I'd often wondered how the sunlight would look as it filtered through the windowpanes in the house where, once upon a time, I'd danced in a dream. Heavy, still green light that made everything look as though you were seeing it through a glass-bottomed boat, a sleepy lagoon.

It was a haunted house in every sense, wrapped in its secrets, and its faded Chinese screens, and its un-drunk bottles of crème de cacao, now crystallized sugar. All those unmixed Angel's Kisses.

Sweetcream dreams, sour-curdled by time.

I don't know how long I stood like that in the tomb, but when I opened my eyes it was almost dark and Sinatra's smile was a flicker in the moonlight. I put the record down. Touched the casket wrapped in its sensuous cloak of dust. I held my breath as I lifted the lid—carefully, carefully—and the dust fell from it in sparkles, the spent lanterns of weary fireflies.

There were those who said that Lana Lake was buried naked in the sapphire-blue mink stole Joe Caiola had once draped over her milk-white shoulders. *Confession* magazine reported, with more than a hint of morality, that they had buried her in her g-string.

I tried to imagine that g-string, swinging across the cavern of my mother's caved-in pelvis, a glittering rope bridge over a sea of peacock feathers now powdered to iridescent dust.

I didn't know for certain what I would find in that box.

But my breath caught in my throat when I saw her hair. Still red as blood. Dried blood. I thought of the heart I had made all those years ago, that childish cathedral of paper and wire, now rusted away. My eyes drifted down to the bird-of-paradise I'd twisted between her fingers, entwined swan necks. A ghost of fragrance still lingered in the withered blooms. I blinked back the tears that balanced on my lashes.

God weeps no tears for dead whores, Capri.

I made myself look.

Down.

There, there.

I couldn't help it: my eyes misted as I stared at the beaded vertebrae that shone like a strand of luminescent pearls, pearl upon shimmering pearl. Concentric layers of secrets. God in heaven, she was so beautiful, even now.

> *She whispered softly, "It's best not to linger,"*
> *Then as I kissed her hand I could see*

And now I *did* see. Trembling, I slipped my hand beneath the delicate spinal column.

> *She wore a plain golden ring on her finger*
> *'Twas goodbye on the Isle of Capri*

There. On the satin lining.

A plain golden ring, sucked off the hand of a dead man and trapped for forty years in the throat of the woman who loved him.

A plain golden ring.

It was the last verse of the song. The verse I couldn't remember.

Until now.

And now I remembered everything. The pain and horror in Mother's eyes, the pleading, the grasping fingers, the choking sound she made as she tried to speak. . . .

It wasn't horror in her eyes, but fear. Fear that even her own daughter would misunderstand the deaths that had come too soon. And now I knew what my mother had been trying to tell me that copper autumn afternoon so long ago. One word:

"Capri," she had said. *Capri.* . . .

But it wasn't my *name* she whispered with those lush red lips. Not a beg for forgiveness, a plea for understanding. It was the name of the song: "The Isle of Capri."

And then, standing there at my mother's casket, I knew what it was she'd tried to tell me but couldn't. Couldn't—because a wedding ring engraved with the name of a murderess had lodged in her windpipe like a piece of candy and stolen her voice.

Forever Cassandra.

And that plain golden ring had never been found.

The police, and the courts, and the press, and the people, had all believed Mrs. Caiola. And why shouldn't they? She was beautiful, an ice god-dess sitting there in the witness stand in her black Christian Dior and veiled hat, wringing her gloved hands, with just the appropriate touch of widow's wetness in her eyes.

Not the same set of gloves she'd had on when she shot first her hus-band, then his mistress, before spinning smartly on her high heels and *click-click-clicking* out of the kitchen. Always the perfect lady, that particu-lar pair of gloves had been neatly disposed of. One, two, three. As easy as that. Ring-a-ding-ding.

Except the mistress hadn't died quite so quickly as the husband. The mistress had time for one last kiss, a kiss that would name her murderess.

Forty years later.

Dabbing her eyes, careful not to smudge her mascara, Cassandra ex-plained to the court that she and Joe had reconciled, that he'd gone to Lana Lake's to tell her once and for all he wanted nothing more to do with her, that he was suing for custody of his daughter on the grounds that Lana was an unfit mother, and that Cassandra, awaiting his return, had heard the gunshots all the way across the garden. It was Cassandra who had called the police.

Everyone pitied the little girl sitting there in her black woolen uniform beside Sister Constance-Evangeline of Our Lady of Perpetual Sorrow. Capri Lake, the daughter of the whore, with her downcast eyes and burn-ing cheeks and hands locked on her lap like a heart without a key.

And what a kind and generous woman was Cassandra Caiola to wel-come into her own home, with open arms, the illegitimate child of her hus-band's mistress.

It was how Joe would have wanted it, Mrs. Caiola explained. She had never been able to have children of her own. He would have wanted her to raise the child as her own flesh and blood to be a respectable and decent young lady. And everyone's heads nodded in sympathetic agreement, and Cassandra smiled to herself, and in that moment, the course of my life changed forever.

Forever Cassandra.

A hand clad in an ice-white glove that smelled of Chanel No. 5 closed around a wrist braceleted with ruby tears. I was led numbly down the courtroom steps through a mill of people and reporters and photographers with flashbulbs. There was a controlled yet agonizing wrench of my arm socket as I ducked my head into the shining white Cadillac, and Cassandra Caiola drove us silently back to a house without dancing, without song, without love.

⊹ ⊹

It took time to learn the music of silence.

It took my life.

But little by little, Cassandra Caiola became Mother to me. For I have always lived in the house without music.

God weeps no tears for dead whores, Capri. God weeps no tears.

Little by little, with Sister Constance-Evangeline's compassionate guidance.

God weeps no tears, Capri. God weeps no tears.

And eventually I, too, wept no more. And Cassandra Caiola at last heard me whisper the word she wanted so desperately to hear—

one sweet word of love

And truly, there was no sweeter revenge for Cassandra Caiola than to hear the word *whore* on the lips of Lana Lake's daughter. She made me say it again and again, a record without end, until she laughed and laughed out loud and tears sprang to her eyes, because this was music to her ears like no other music could be. It was the only music I ever heard again.

At least, it seemed that way for a very long time. But in the end it was the song that drew me back. The song that gave me my name and flowed in my veins, the song that drew me back to what I had lost. Back to the house of dancing, and singing, and life.

Back to the Isle of Capri.

Thunder shattered a sky as dark as wet satin. The moon was a weeping eye.

"Is that you?"

Not once had I heard her say my name. *Capri.* She couldn't stand to say it.

"Where have you been all this time? Close the door, it's cold."

I said nothing as I shook the rain from my hair. My hair was a light strawberry blond that had never darkened to the luxurious auburn of my mother's. I hadn't inherited her beautiful hair, or her talent for dance, or her brazen love of exhibition.

Her fiery temper was, in me, a slow-burning ember.

Red flame melting white ice.

Cassandra Caiola sat stiffly in the straight-backed chair that looked down on Lana Lake's bungalow. Living her life through the windowpane as she had for forty years.

Rain sluiced through the leaves of the towering eucalyptus trees. Decades of dead leaves and blue gum mulched into the ground with mounds of peeling bark. The house seemed like it was slowly sinking. Dissolving into nothing.

Some nights, the moonlight danced on the minty leaves like silver drops of water, and the breeze swished through them like Daddy's brushes, and we'd listen to them, Cassandra and I, in our chairs by the window, in the house without music.

And on other nights, like tonight, the wind rattled through the trees and a litter of hard-shelled fruit clattered on the tiled roof like an iron drum, and we'd listen, *ba da da,* in the house without music.

Cassandra's head nodded in memory. Her eyes were almost closed. The sky was clear now, and I stared at her profile in bas-relief, white as marble in the moonlight.

I thought of the angel and its features of stone, and I wondered what was in Cassandra's heart. But for stone angels and dead whores there are no regrets, no remorse, no dreams to torment deep into the night. There is no laughter, no music, no dancing. No dream of an Isle of Capri . . .

In this light, Cassandra's eyes had no color of their own. They were the color of eucalyptus leaves reflected in Lana's bedroom window.

"What's that on your lips?" she demanded.

Crushed red beetles, the juice of wild pomegranates, a whore's lipstick, Napoli spaghetti sauce, something else, something red—

In my mind I heard a shot ring out as if it were yesterday. I saw Lana run screaming into the kitchen, a half-tied apron on her hips, slipping on blood and chili peppers in a grotesque dance, a balance of life. I saw the spreading crimson stain on the floor as she cradled Daddy's head in her lap.

I saw her lips, full and red.

I saw the rich, wet kiss of one who had loved deeply.

I had never kissed nor been kissed.

Now I kissed the woman who had been my mother for forty years.

I kissed her with Lana Lake's fierce burning passion.

I bit her lip until it bled, and then I shoved the plain golden ring hard into her mouth, snaking it around her tongue.

She started to choke. Her hands flew up like twin birds, raking me with the fingers of a murderess, but I didn't feel a thing. The daughters of dead whores never do.

I kissed her again until she stopped breathing, and her last breath amounted to less than the mouthful of air in my ruined paper heart.

Afterward I stood at the window and stared at my reflection.

I stood there for a long time thinking of nothing, nothing at all.

Then I threw the window open wide and breathed in the exotic, peppery perfume of the dripping eucalyptus. I listened to the music of the rain tap-tapping on the tiled roof of the bungalow like a set of coo-coo crazy drum sticks. The wet wind blew branches against the pane and threw dark shadows against the Chinese screen like the sinuous curves of a dragon, and the shadows danced with the moon.

Black Dust

Graham Joyce

alf hidden behind a thicket of hawthorn and holly bushes was a second cave. It astonished him to see it there. As a kid Andy had scrambled over every boulder, probed every fissure and crevice, and swung from the exposed roots of every tree clinging to the face of Corley Rocks. Yet here was a new cave, quite unlike the one in which he'd been holed up for the afternoon. After feeling the mild tremor, Andy needed to get home. But something in this new cave called to him.

Unlike the first cave, a mere split in the rock face which had always been there, this one was dome-shaped, with an arched chamber as an entrance. He drew closer. Squeezing between the hawthorn and prickly holly to get into the cave, it became obvious to him that this second cave went back much deeper. He could see well enough for the first few yards, but after that the cave shadows set hard in a resinous black diamond.

Still it called.

He wanted to move deeper in, but his throat dried and his breathing came short. He rolled his foot in the blackness. A pebble crunched under his shoe.

There was a tiny light, no bigger than a glowworm, swinging at the rear of the cave. It flickered and went out. Then it appeared again. The light shimmered, still swinging slightly from left to right. He heard footsteps shuffling towards him, and then there appeared in the gloom a second light, smaller than the first, and nearer the cave floor. The lights were approaching. Then there was a sound like the low growl of an animal, and it made him think of that dog.

That dog, slavering and throwing itself at the fence, chewing the thick wire mesh. A brute of an Alsatian, but the drooling jaws and yellow teeth had Andy convinced it was part wolf. Andy always kept one eye peeled for the dog while the other, of course, was alert for Bryn's father.

Bryn appeared in his socks. "It's all right," he said. "He's not here."

Andy crossed the swarthy yard and removed his shoes at the threshold of the kitchen. Shoes off at the door because of the coal dust. Everyone. The house and yard once belonged to a coal merchant who'd gone bust, and the cinder path leading to Andy's house was black. The yard was black. The gate was black. The coal dust had even pointed up the cement between the black-red bricks. They had to take off their shoes so as not to trail black dust into the house. Bryn had developed a lazy habit of not bothering to put on his shoes merely to cross the yard, even though his father, with a bunched fist, had once made his ear bleed for this offense.

"Twenty minutes before he gets back."

The boys went through the kitchen. Bryn's mother, Jean, looked up from her ironing. "Still down there then, your dad."

"Yes," said Andy.

"Twenty-four hours now."

"Yes."

"They got oxygen. They got food to them. They'll get him out." She pressed her iron into a collar and a jet of steam wheezed into the air.

The two boys went upstairs to Bryn's room, from where they got the rope, the water bottle, and the tiny brass compass. They didn't want to hang around. Important not to be there when Ike got back off shift. Sometimes when playing table football or lounging in Bryn's bedroom, the door would open quietly and Bryn's mother would whisper, "He's back. Make yourself scarce." And with that they always would.

Once when Andy awaited Bryn in the kitchen, Ike had come in from work and imposed himself in the doorway, glowering. Andy had felt compelled to look away. Without saying a word to Bryn's mum, the big man slumped in an armchair before the fire, and how the chair-springs had groaned. Ike's skin glowed pink with the scrubbing from a recent shower at the pit, but his body still leaked the odor of coal. A smell like a sulphurous gas, steaming off the man as he stared moodily into the fire. He snorted at the coal dust irritating his sinuses, hawked and spat into the fire, and this movement released a fresh wave of hostile gas.

Andy had on that occasion feared that even breathing might cause offense. Finally Bryn appeared, beckoning him away. Outside the door they had both vented huge sighs.

Of course they didn't need the compass to find their way to Corley Rocks. A matter of a mile and a half from the mining estate, Corley Rocks was the highest natural point in the old county of Warwickshire. The ploughed earthworks of an Iron Age encampment mouldered on the flat field above an outcrop of red sandstone rock, and from there you could take in the green belt of land all round. To the south stood the two giant wheels of the pit-head winding gear, and beyond that the spires and smoking chimneys of Coventry.

The dog started up again.

"Shut it," Bryn growled as they left the house. "Shut it." It was exactly the way Andy had heard Bryn's old man speak to the dog, half-song, half-warning, and it was always effective in subduing the animal. Except when Andy or anyone else tried, in which case the dog simply became more inflamed, hurling itself with stupid energy against the mesh fence.

"Do you think that dog is a killer?" Andy said as they walked up the black cinder path away from the house.

"Probably." Bryn hooped the rope across one shoulder. "You carry the water bottle."

The rope was usually for display only. They'd never done any real climbing at Corley Rocks. Everywhere was accessible by scrambling over the smooth, rounded edges of the sandstone. There was only one place where a rope might be helpful, at the sheer face of the rock above the cave, and Bryn was keen to try it. And it had to be admitted: looped across the torso from left collarbone to right hip, the rope looked a treat.

Andy was envious, because carrying the water bottle was shit. But the rope was Bryn's after all.

They had to pass the entrance to the mine, with its weighbridges and security gates. "Don't think about it," Bryn said. "They've got air. And food. They'll get him out."

It was a hot afternoon in August, and by the time they reached the rocks they were sweating and had drunk all of the water. The cave was merely a fissure, a crack opened in the rock face, but it could be reached by the means of small cavities scooped out of the soft stone, ancient hand-holds and toe grips. They climbed up and retreated to the back of the cave, welcoming the shade.

Their schoolteacher had said that traces of prehistoric habitation had been found at the cave: flints, stone tools, bones. Someone had even un-earthed a huge sabretooth, currently being examined by experts at Coventry museum. People had always lived there, it was said, and before that the rocks themselves had been pushed up by fault lines in the vast coal reservoirs under the ground: the very coal that Andy's and Bryn's fathers now mined on a daily basis.

Bryn lifted the rope from his shoulders, causing his T-shirt to ride up. Andy saw below Bryn's ribcage the flowering of a huge blue and yellow bruise. It looked like one of the purple-leaf cabbages his own dad grew in the garden. He said nothing. He knew. Bryn knew he knew. And it was none of his business; that's what Andy's mother had said to his father.

"Not your business, Stan, to go getting tangled up in," Mina warned her husband. "Not your business at all."

Andy's father had wanted to go down to Bryn's house to have words. Bryn had turned up one afternoon while Andy's dad dribbled water from the garden hose on his prize-winning leeks. For the old giggle Andy's dad put his finger over the hose and jet-sprayed the two boys. The giggling stopped when the lads stripped off their wet T-shirts.

"Hell, you've been in the wars, haven't you?" Stan said, turning back to his leeks. Then he did a double take, looked harder, and laid down the hose. Taking in the multiple bruises on the lad's body he stepped closer. "Let's have a look at you, son."

Bryn danced away. "Nothing. Fell off a ladder."

"Come here, I said. Stand still. Christ, son! Hell's bells!" He brushed the wounds gently with his callused fingertips. Then he said, very quietly, "Must have been a good few times you fell off that ladder."

"Yeh," Bryn sniffed.

Andy's mother, who'd seen all of this, came out with a clean T-shirt apiece for the lads. Stan was already halfway down the path. She chased after him. "You're not going down there. Not your business!"

Stan had himself once clouted Andy with a closed fist, but only once, and some years ago. Not a single day had passed when he hadn't regretted it. "I'll be back sharpish."

"You're not going down there!"

Stan pulled up short. "I said I'll be back sharp," he whispered in a way that settled the argument. Andy's mum returned to the back garden, where the boys had their heads down and the hose was still dribbling water onto the leek-bed.

With the dog going berserk behind the mesh fence Stan had knocked on the door and had taken a step back. It was some moments before Ike Thompson appeared blinking in the doorway, puff-eyed, looking like he'd just been disturbed from a nap. His eyes were lined with coal dust like a woman's mascara. He sniffed. "Stan," he said.

"A word in the yard, Ike?" Stan turned his back and walked into the open expanse of the disused coal merchant's yard.

Ike shuffled in the doorway, slipped on his boots without lacing them, and followed Stan across the yard.

The men knew each other well enough. They'd mined the same districts, notably the 42s and the 56s; they nodded to each other whenever their paths crossed; they'd even once been part of the same Mine Rescue Team; and they knew that their boys were good pals. They just didn't like each other.

The two miners stood in the cinder-black yard at a distance of about five paces. The dog was barking mad, flinging itself at the fence. "Your Bryn's up at our house just now."

Ike was a big man. His grizzled face bore the blue signature scars of coal mining, like someone had scribbled on his face with a ballpoint pen. He stood a head taller than Stan. But Stan was trunk-necked with a barrel of a chest and muscle packed like coiled wire. He had his own mining scar, a blue and white star right in the middle of his forehead, like a bullet wound.

Ike lifted a hand to his mouth, squeezing his bottom lip between a coal-ingrained thumb and a coal-ingrained forefinger. "Yup."

"Says he fell off of a ladder."

Ike let his hand drop now he knew what this was about. He glanced to the side, and then back at Stan. "Yup."

The Alsatian barked, and slavered, and seemed to try to chew its way through the mesh fence. "He won't be falling off that ladder again, now will he Ike?"

Ike turned to the dog, and in a low, throaty voice, almost a hiss, said, "Shut iiiiiiiiiittttttttttt." The dog lowered its head and crept back into its kennel. "That it?" said Ike.

"That's about it."

"Right. You can go now."

"Happen I will go. But if that lad should fall off another ladder, then I'll come down here again. And we'll have another talk. More serious."

"Oh aye?"

"Too right, we will. Too right."

The two men stood off each other for another minute. Then Stan said, "I'll be seeing you, Ike."

Stan retraced his steps along the cinder path. He felt Ike's gaze drilling into him at every step.

"Stop thinking about it," Bryn said. "They'll get him out. My old man will get him out."

Andy knew they would get his dad out all right. He just wished everyone would stop telling him. He hadn't been allowed to go up to the pithead, where the wives and grown-up sons and daughters and the rescue teams and the camera crews all congregated, waiting. It had been twenty-four hours since a roof had collapsed half a mile underground, trapping seven miners, one of whom was Stan. The rescue teams had made an early breakthrough, piping air and passing food through to the trapped men, but the rescue efforts had hit a snag when a second roof-fall had threatened. Ike was on one of the rescue teams.

"They're right under here," Bryn said. "Right under this spot."

"How do you know that?"

"My old man told me. He said the seam runs north and under these rocks."

Andy thought about his own dad half a mile directly below him, waiting.

"You're not crying are you?" Bryn said. "Not *crying*."

"Dust in my eye. Dust." Andy's fingers found a flake of red stone. He flung it from the back of the cave into the crack of light, and it dropped, skittering down the slope. "Anyway you wouldn't care if anything happened to your old man."

Andy wished he hadn't said that. Bryn started whipping the end of his rope. "He might be a shit but at least he..."

"At least he what?"

"Nah. Come on. Let's climb the Edge."

The boys scrambled out of the cave and walked up to an outcrop of red stone known as the Witch's Face. Bryn hoisted himself over the chin and nose of the Face and wanted to use the rope to get Andy up. Andy objected on grounds of pointlessness. From there they proceeded to the Edge, a cliff overhang directly above the cave.

At least he what? Andy thought as they clambered up the steep sandstone slopes, between ragged clumps of hawthorn and holly. One day Stan had brought home a second-hand guitar. Andy had pestered Stan for this guitar, but when it arrived he soon found out that the strings cut his fingers to shreds. He'd taken the guitar down to Bryn's house, and he was exhibiting it to Bryn when Ike appeared unexpectedly, standing in the kitchen doorway, sniffing back coal dust. His eyes fell on the guitar.

Ike walked across the kitchen without removing his boots, gently lifting the guitar from the lad. "What you got here then, lovely boy? Let's have a look, then."

Ike sat, effeminately crossed his legs, positioned the guitar across his thigh, and gently thumbed the strings. He played a chord or two and the dog in the yard howled. Ike laughed. "Hear that?" He strummed a few more chords and then picked out a tune. "Christ, these strings stand too high off the frets. You'll never play this, lovely boy. Nice tone, but it's a piece of rubbish."

"My dad got it for me," Andy said, meaning to sound defensive.

Ike laid the guitar down. "Come on lads, get in the car."

"Where you going?" Jean had protested.

"Get in the car, boys!"

Where they went, in Ike's beat-up old Ford Zephyr, was Chaplin's music store. Ike spent most of the journey explaining to Andy how he used to have a guitar—two guitars, even—but when Bryn and his sister had come along, why, there was no time, no bloody time to play them, and he'd always regretted selling the instruments, and now he was going to put that right. He talked like that all the way round the music shop, nonstop; he insulted the shop manager; tried out every second-hand guitar in the store; crooned passionately to other customers; purchased right off two decent instruments for the boys; and had a twenty-minute bash on a Premiere Drum Kit before leaving.

"Where's the swining money coming for those, then?" Jean shouted when they got back.

Ike was all sweetness. He squeezed his wife and kissed her angry mouth. "Music before butter," he said. "Remember that, lovely boys. Music before butter."

Stan and Nina had something to say about it, too. They made Andy take his guitar back. Stan went with him. Stan and Andy stood in the kitchen, with their shoes on this time.

"Why can't I buy the lads an instrument apiece?" Ike said. "Why can't I?"

"It's too generous," Stan said.

"Rubbish. How's that anybody's concern but mine?"

"It's my swining-well concern, too," said Jean. "Where's the money coming from?"

The lads watched this intently. "Boys, sod off into the other room, will you?" Stan said. Bryn and Andy filed out, both still clutching the new guitars by the necks, and closed the door behind them. "Look, Ike, you can't make up for things by throwing money at them."

"What's that? You've lost me."

"The guitars. You can't make other things right."

Ike suddenly understood Stan's point. His face clouded. "I see. I see what this is about, and I don't like it. Tell me, how does one thing touch the other?"

"I'm just saying."

"How the bloody hell does one thing touch the other? If I want to buy the boys instruments apiece, I buy them bloody instruments apiece! Christ, man!"

Stan was man enough to sense he might have made a mistake. "I don't know, Ike, it's too much."

But Ike had soured now. He called the boys back, and while he waited for them he said, "Your lad can carry his guitar home with him or I'll take it in the yard and split it into matchwood, now!"

"He will, as well," Jean put in.

Stan sighed. "Come on," he said to the bewildered Andy. "Bring your guitar."

Ike followed them out. The dog growled from its kennel but Ike silenced it with a thunderous look. "One thing does not touch another," he said, almost in a whisper. "You should know that, Stan. One thing does not touch another."

"Happen."

They'd not gone twelve yards before Ike softly called to Andy. "Practice every day, mind," he said softly, and with a terrifying squint to his eye. "Practice every day."

"I will," said Andy.

On the top of the Edge Bryn fumbled with the rope, securing a Pig's Ear knot as he looped it round a spindly clump of rooted hawthorn. Andy was supposed then to loop the rope around his own waist while Bryn lowered himself over the Edge, preparing to descend to the cave that way—a mere matter of nine or ten feet below the lip of the Edge.

Bryn duly disappeared over the lip, negotiating toeholds and finger grips, grunting occasionally and chattering happily. Andy meanwhile stood with his hands in his pockets, anxiously gazing across at the twin wheels of the pit-head winding gear, wondering how the rescue was proceeding. It was possible to superimpose on the landscape the giant ghost of an old lady crouched at those black wheels, spinning away with some dark and concealed purpose. And it was while Andy gazed across the fields to the distant mineworks that he heard a yelp and felt the rope tighten round his waist.

Andy grabbed the branch of a nearby tree. The rope jagged against the feeble hawthorn, lifting it out by its roots. Bryn yelped again as the rope dropped him another six feet. Then the hawthorn root popped out of the sandy soil, like a pulled tooth. The rope whiplashed at Andy turning him in a complete circle, losing its purchase on his body. The bush lashed at Andy's face as it went past him. It snagged on two fingers of exposed tree root, and Bryn was dumped another six feet. Then the bush tore free and whistled as it went over the Edge.

Andy didn't stop to look over. Instead he hurried down past the Witch's Face and round to the slope in front of the cave, where Bryn lay in a crumpled heap. Blood bubbled at the corner of his mouth.

"Yawlright?" Andy said.

"Of course I'm not all right."

"You're all right."

Bryn groaned. He'd been badly winded by the fall, and he'd scraped his hands and his knees. He'd also bitten his tongue, which accounted for the blood. In the end he'd fallen no more than about twelve feet, and had bounced down the sandstone slope beneath the cave mouth. He sat up, holding his head.

"Hey," said Andy. "Not *crying* are you."

"You shit. Why didn't you hold on to me?"

"You must be joking. You were gone before I knew it."

"Useless. You're useless." Bryn was on his feet.

"It was your stupid idea. Tying the rope to that bush. Stupid. Where are you going?"

"I'm going home."

"Wait. I'll come with you."

"Sod off."

Bryn shrugged off his friend's advances and limped away. Within a minute he was out of sight. "Wasn't my fault," Andy shouted. He slumped onto the slope beneath the cave, knowing he should have gone home with Bryn. While Andy's mother was spending every anxious moment waiting at the pit-head for news of the rescue, Bryn's mother had told him to come for tea. Just as he'd done the previous night, munching on sardine sandwiches when Ike had turned up.

Ike had broken shifts to be part of the rescue team. He'd stood in the doorway, kicking his boots off, all-in. He drew a chair to the table where the boys sat, and without a word to anyone laid his head down by the plates and the butter, leaking the odor of coal and exhaustion. The boys munched on their sandwiches, looking at him. After a while Jean placed a steaming mug of tea on the table and Ike lifted his head. He blinked sleepily at the boys.

"Well," Jean had said.

"Not much," Ike said. He slurped his tea noisily. Then he turned to Andy. "Thing is, lovely boy, he's in a corner with the other blokes and the ceiling is pressed down on 'em, see. And we can't get."

A flat, opened, sardine can lay on the table, next to the butter. He picked up the can. "See how you get this bit of fish stuck in the corner and you can't get your knife into it? Well, that bit of sardine's your dad. In there, look? And the top of this tin is the roof come down on him. Now if we pull out what's holding up the roof, see?" He pressed down a huge, coal-ingrained thumb, crumpling the flimsy metal sheet of the sardine can. Tomato sauce and fish oil bubbled around the scythed edges of the can. "Well. There you are."

Ike carefully replaced the sardine can next to the butter. "Don't you worry, lovely boy. Ike will get him out." Then he put his head back on the table and closed his eyes.

Jean had made a silent gesture that they should leave the table.

Recalling all of this, Andy felt a sob break free deep in his chest and force its way into his throat. He wiped his eye and tossed another pebble down the sandstone slope. There was nothing he could do. They wouldn't let him wait up at the pit-head and there was no one at home.

Then the ground shook. Very slightly. The mild tremor made him grab at the earth, and he thought he heard a muffled thump. Just for a second he'd felt the shock of earth dislodging, and he knew he hadn't imagined it because a couple of tiny pebbles broke loose from the cave and went bouncing down the slope. He wondered if it had anything to do with the pit rescue.

He decided to hurry home. He got up and picked his way down the slopes, barely keeping his footing. He knew that if he went back up to the Edge he could cut across fields and get home faster. His hands trembled.

He was clambering between boulders, over the exposed roots of trees, when he stumbled. That's when he saw the second cave.

Inside the cave, the doglike growl subsided. Then it came again, only this time it sounded like a man trying to clear his throat of coal dust. The two tiny lights continued to swing from side to side. Another, distressed throaty growl made Andy want to get out.

But as the lights floated towards him out of the gloom he recognized the bowl of a miner's helmet. The upper light was a helmet lamp. A miner, face blackened with coal dust, approached him from the dark end of the cave. Hanging from the miner's belt was a Davey lamp, with its tiny flame alive.

The miner stopped and leaned against the wall. Breathing heavily, he tried to clear his throat again. He was struggling. "Hello Andy. Where's my lovely boy then?"

Ike blinked at him in the darkness, his face caked with sweat and black dust. All Andy could see of his features were his teeth and the whites of his eyes. Ike had a rope looped over his shoulder; identical to the one he and Bryn had played with earlier. "Bryn went home."

Ike seemed confused. He closed his eyes and leaned his head against the cave wall. Ike was breathing asthmatically. He seemed to have trouble getting his words out. "Oh. Came to have a word with him, I did. See."

Now Andy could see and hear industrious activity taking place deeper in the cave behind Ike. He tried to look beyond the miner. "Where's my dad?"

"Your old man's all right. I got him out." Ike unhooked the rope from his shoulder and flung it to the cave entrance. "Told you I would."

Andy tried to push past Ike, to get to his dad. "Let me through."

Ike stopped him. Struggling to draw himself up to his full height, he placed a big blackened paw on Andy's shoulder. "No, no, no. That's not for you back there. Nothing to concern you back there. I just came to see my lovely boy. But you say he's not here, then?"

"No. He went home."

Ike slowly lifted a sooty hand to wipe back the sweat from his brow.

Even in the darkness Andy could see it bubbling black and coursing dust into Ike's eyes. He was out of breath. "Tell him I came. Now you run along home, son. Go and see your old man." Andy nodded as the miner turned and retreated, with slow heavy steps, the lamp swinging at his side, deeper into the blackness of the cave. "And tell your old man," Ike called softly.

"Tell him what?"

"Just tell him."

Andy escaped from the cave into the bright summer light. There, lying on the floor was the rope Ike had flung at the cave entrance. Andy picked it up. It was black from the coal, and the gritty dust immediately transferred itself to the boy's hands. He was already blackened from the paw print Ike had left on his shirt, so he hooked the rope over his shoulder and hastened home.

When Andy persuaded the gatekeeper to let him through to the pit-head, he found his mother there, and his father. Stan had already been brought up with the other rescued men. They were all in good shape, but there was no celebration and no rejoicing because one of the rescue team had been killed in the effort of getting the men out.

Andy didn't see Bryn for some weeks afterwards. His mother had taken him, along with his sister, to stay with her family in Wales. When Bryn did return Andy tried to pass on the message Ike had given him.

"What?"

"He came looking for you. Up at the rocks. Your old man."

"What?"

"He left the rope. Do you want it? The rope?"

Bryn wrinkled his nose in contempt. "No."

"But you must."

"Shut it, will you? Shut it."

Eventually, Bryn and his mother and sister moved permanently to Wales.

Andy never said anything about it to his own father. One afternoon he said to Stan, "So Bryn's dad saved your life, then, didn't he?"

"That's what they say, son. That's what they say."

That was the closest they ever got to discussing the matter.

More than once Andy went back up to Corley Rocks to try to find the second cave. He looked hard for it. He never did find it. Though he did have the rope. He hung it on a nail in the garden shed, where it remained untouched for many years, black with coal dust.

October in the Chair

Neil Gaiman

For Ray Bradbury

*O*ctober was in the chair, so it was chilly that evening, and the leaves were red and orange and tumbled from the trees that circled the grove. The twelve of them sat around a campfire roasting huge sausages on sticks, which spat and crackled as the fat dripped onto the burning applewood, and drinking fresh apple cider, tangy and tart in their mouths.

April took a dainty bite from her sausage, which burst open as she bit into it, spilling hot juice down her chin. "Beshrew and suckordure on it," she said.

Squat March, sitting next to her, laughed, low and dirty, and then pulled out a huge, filthy handkerchief. "Here you go," he said.

April wiped her chin. "Thanks," she said. "The cursed bag-of-innards burned me. I'll have a blister there tomorrow."

September yawned. "You are *such* a hypochondriac," he said, across the fire. "And such *language*." He had a pencil-thin mustache, and was balding in the front, which made his forehead seem high, and wise.

"Lay off her," said May. Her dark hair was cropped short against her skull and she wore sensible boots. She smoked a small brown cigarillo, which smelled heavily of cloves. "She's sensitive."

"Oh puhlease," said September. "Spare me."

October, conscious of his position in the chair, sipped his apple cider, cleared his throat, and said, "Okay. Who wants to begin?" The chair he sat in was carved from one large block of oak wood, inlaid with ash, with cedar, and with cherrywood. The other eleven sat on tree stumps equally spaced about the small bonfire. The tree stumps had been worn smooth and comfortable by years of use.

"What about the minutes?" asked January. "We always do minutes when I'm in the chair."

"But you aren't in the chair now, are you, dear?" said September, an elegant creature of mock solicitude.

"What about the minutes?" repeated January. "You can't ignore them."

"Let the little buggers take care of themselves," said April, one hand running through her long blond hair. "And I think September should go first."

September preened and nodded. "Delighted," he said.

"Hey," said February. "Hey-hey-hey-hey-hey-hey-hey. I didn't hear the chairman ratify that. Nobody starts till October says who starts, and then nobody else talks. Can we have maybe the tiniest semblance of order here?" He peered at them, small, pale, dressed entirely in blues and grays.

"It's fine," said October. His beard was all colors, a grove of trees in autumn, deep brown and fire orange and wine red, an untrimmed tangle across the lower half of his face. His cheeks were apple red. He looked like a friend, like someone you had known all your life. "September can go first. Let's just get it rolling."

September placed the end of his sausage into his mouth, chewed daintily, and drained his cider mug. Then he stood up and bowed to the company and began to speak.

"Laurent DeLisle was the finest chef in all of Seattle; at least, Laurent DeLisle thought so, and the Michelin stars on his door confirmed him in his opinion. He was a remarkable chef, it is true—his minced lamb brioche had won several awards, his smoked quail and white truffle ravioli had been described in the *Gastronome* as 'the tenth wonder of the world.' But it was his wine cellar . . . ah, his wine cellar . . . that was his source of pride and his passion.

"I understand that. The last of the white grapes are harvested in me, and the bulk of the reds: I appreciate fine wines, the aroma, the taste, the aftertaste as well.

"Laurent DeLisle bought his wines at auctions, from private wine lovers, from reputable dealers: he would insist on a pedigree for each wine, for wine frauds are, alas, too common, when the bottle is selling for perhaps five, ten, a hundred thousand dollars, or pounds, or euros.

"The treasure—the jewel—the rarest of the rare and the *ne plus ultra* of his temperature-controlled wine cellar was a bottle of 1902 Château Lafitte. It was on the wine list at $120,000, although it was, in true terms, priceless, for it was the last bottle of its kind."

"Excuse me," said August politely. He was the fattest of them all, his thin hair combed in golden wisps across his pink pate.

September glared down at his neighbor. "Yes?"

"Is this the one where some rich dude buys the wine to go with the dinner, and the chef decides that the dinner the rich dude ordered isn't good enough for the wine, so he sends out a different dinner, and the guy takes one mouthful, and he's got, like, some rare allergy and he just dies like that, and the wine never gets drunk after all?"

September said nothing. He looked a great deal.

"Because if it is, you told it before. Years ago. Dumb story then. Dumb story now." August smiled. His pink cheeks shone in the firelight.

September said, "Obviously pathos and culture are not to everyone's taste. Some people prefer their barbecues and beer, and some of us like—"

February said, "Well, I hate to say this, but he kind of does have a point. It has to be a new story."

September raised an eyebrow and pursed his lips. "I'm done," he said abruptly. He sat down on his stump.

They looked at each other across the fire, the months of the year.

June, hesitant and clean, raised her hand and said, "I have one about a guard on the X-ray machines at LaGuardia Airport, who could read all about people from the outlines of their luggage on the screen, and one day she saw a luggage X-ray so beautiful that she fell in love with the person, and she had to figure out which person in the line it was, and she couldn't, and she pined for months and months. And when the person came through again she knew it this time, and it was the man, and he was a wizened old Indian man and she was pretty and black and, like twenty-five, and she knew it would never work out and she let him go, because she could also see from the shapes of his bags on the screen that he was going to die soon."

October said, "Fair enough, young June. Tell that one."

June stared at him, like a spooked animal. "I just did," she said.

October nodded. "So you did," he said, before any of the others could say anything. And then he said, "Shall we proceed to my story, then?"

February sniffed. "Out of order there, big fella. The man in the chair only tells his story when the rest of us are through. Can't go straight to the main event."

May was placing a dozen chestnuts on the grate above the fire, deploying them into patterns with her tongs. "Let him tell his story if he wants to," she said. "God knows it can't be worse than the one about the wine. And I have things to be getting back to. Flowers don't bloom by themselves. All in favor?"

"You're taking this to a formal vote?" February said. "I cannot believe this. I cannot believe this is happening." He mopped his brow with a handful of tissues, which he pulled from his sleeve.

Seven hands were raised. Four people kept their hands down—February, September, January, and July. ("I don't have anything personal on this," said July apologetically. "It's purely procedural. We shouldn't be setting precedents.")

"It's settled then," said October. "Is there anything anyone would like to say before I begin?"

"Um. Yes. Sometimes," said June, "sometimes I think somebody's watching us from the woods, and then I look and there isn't anybody there. But I still think it."

April said, "That's because you're crazy."

"Mm," said September, to everybody. "She's sensitive but she's still the cruelest."

"Enough," said October. He stretched in his chair. He cracked a cobnut with his teeth, pulled out the kernel, and threw the fragments of shell into the fire, where they hissed and spat and popped, and he began.

There was a boy, October said, who was miserable at home, although they did not beat him. He did not fit well, not his family, not his town, nor even his life. He had two older brothers, who were twins, older than he was, and who hurt him or ignored him, and were popular. They played football: some games one twin would score more and be the hero, and some games the other would. Their little brother did not play football. They had a name for their brother. They called him the Runt.

They had called him the Runt since he was a baby, and at first their mother and father had chided them for it.

The twins said, "But he is the runt of the litter. Look at *him*. Look at *us*." The boys were six when they said this. Their parents thought it was cute. A name like "the Runt" can be infectious, so pretty soon the only person who called him Donald was his grandmother, when she telephoned him on his birthday, and people who did not know him.

Now, perhaps because names have power, he was a runt: skinny and small and nervous. He had been born with a runny nose, and it had not stopped running in a decade. At mealtimes, if the twins liked the food they would steal his; if they did not, they would contrive to place their food on his plate and he would find himself in trouble for leaving good food uneaten.

Their father never missed a football game, and would buy an ice cream afterward for the twin who had scored the most, and a consolation ice cream for the other twin, who hadn't. Their mother described herself as a newspaperwoman, although she mostly sold advertising space and subscriptions: she had gone back to work full-time once the twins were capable of taking care of themselves.

The other kids in the boy's class admired the twins. They had called him Donald for several weeks in first grade, until the word trickled down that his brothers called him the Runt. His teachers rarely called him anything at all, although among themselves they could sometimes be heard to say that it was a pity the youngest Covay boy didn't have the pluck or the imagination or the life of his brothers.

The Runt could not have told you when he first decided to run away, nor when his daydreams crossed the border and became plans. By the time he admitted to himself that he was leaving he had a large Tupperware container hidden beneath a plastic sheet behind the garage, containing three Mars bars, two Milky Ways, a bag of nuts, a small bag of licorice, a flashlight, several comics, an unopened packet of beef jerky, and thirty-seven dollars, most of it in quarters. He did not like the taste of beef jerky, but he had read that explorers had survived for weeks on nothing else, and it was when he put the packet of beef jerky into the Tupperware box and pressed the lid down with a pop that he knew he was going to have to run away. He had read books, newspapers, and magazines. He knew that if you ran away you sometimes met bad people who did bad things to you; but he had also read fairy tales, so he knew that there were kind people out there, side by side with the monsters.

The Runt was a thin ten-year-old, with a runny nose, and a blank expression. If you were to try to pick him out of a group of boys, you'd be wrong. He'd be the other one. Over at the side. The one your eye slipped over.

All through September he put off leaving. It took a really bad Friday, during the course of which both of his brothers sat on him (and the one who sat on his face broke wind, and laughed uproariously) to decide that whatever monsters were waiting out in the world would be bearable, perhaps even preferable.

Saturday, his brothers were meant to be looking after him, but soon they went into town to see a girl they liked. The Runt went around the back of the garage and took the Tupperware container out from beneath the plastic sheeting. He took it up to his bedroom. He emptied his schoolbag onto his bed, filled it with his candies and comics and quarters and the beef jerky. He filled an empty soda bottle with water.

The Runt walked into the town and got on the bus. He rode west, ten-dollars-in-quarters worth of west, to a place he didn't know, which he thought was a good start, then he got off the bus and walked. There was no sidewalk now, so when cars came past he would edge over into the ditch, to safety.

The sun was high. He was hungry, so he rummaged in his bag and pulled out a Mars bar. After he ate it he found he was thirsty, and he drank almost half of the water from his soda bottle before he realized he was going to have to ration it. He had thought that once he got out of the town he would see springs of fresh water everywhere, but there were none to be found. There was a river, though, that ran beneath a wide bridge.

The Runt stopped halfway across the bridge to stare down at the brown water. He remembered something he had been told in school: that, in the end, all rivers flowed into the sea. He had never been to the seashore. He clambered down the bank and followed the river. There was a muddy path along the side of the riverbank, and an occasional beer can or plastic snack packet to show that people had been that way before, but he saw no one as he walked.

He finished his water.

He wondered if they were looking for him yet. He imagined police cars and helicopters and dogs, all trying to find him. He would evade them. He would make it to the sea.

The river ran over some rocks, and it splashed. He saw a blue heron, its wings wide, glide past him, and he saw solitary end-of-season dragonflies, and sometimes small clusters of midges, enjoying the Indian summer. The blue sky became dusk gray, and a bat swung down to snatch insects from the air. The Runt wondered where he would sleep that night.

Soon the path divided, and he took the branch that led away from the river, hoping it would lead to a house, or to a farm with an empty barn. He walked for some time, as the dusk deepened, until, at the end of the path, he found a farmhouse, half tumbled down and unpleasant-looking. The Runt walked around it, becoming increasingly certain as he walked that nothing could make him go inside, and then he climbed over a broken fence to an abandoned pasture, and settled down to sleep in the long grass with his schoolbag for his pillow.

He lay on his back, fully dressed, staring up at the sky. He was not in the slightest bit sleepy.

"They'll be missing me by now," he told himself. "They'll be worried."

He imagined himself coming home in a few years' time. The delight on his family's faces as he walked up the path to home. Their welcome. Their love. . . .

He woke some hours later, with the bright moonlight in his face. He could see the whole world—as bright as day, like in the nursery rhyme, but pale and without colors. Above him, the moon was full, or almost, and he imagined a face looking down at him, not unkindly, in the shadows and shapes of the moon's surface.

A voice said, "Where do you come from?"

He sat up, not scared, not yet, and looked around him. Trees. Long grass. "Where are you? I don't see you."

Something he had taken for a shadow moved, beside a tree on the edge of the pasture, and he saw a boy of his own age.

"I'm running away from home," said the Runt.

"Whoa," said the boy. "That must have taken a whole lot of guts."

The Runt grinned with pride. He didn't know what to say.

"You want to walk a bit?" said the boy.

"Sure," said the Runt. He moved his schoolbag, so it was next to the fence post, so he could always find it again.

They walked down the slope, giving a wide berth to the old farmhouse.

"Does anyone live there?" asked the Runt.

"Not really," said the other boy. He had fair, fine hair that was almost white in the moonlight. "Some people tried a long time back, but they didn't like it, and they left. Then other folk moved in. But nobody lives there now. What's your name?"

"Donald," said the Runt. And then, "But they call me the Runt. What do they call you?"

The boy hesitated. "Dearly," he said.

"That's a cool name."

Dearly said, "I used to have another name, but I can't read it anymore."

They squeezed through a huge iron gateway, rusted part open, part closed into position, and they were in the little meadow at the bottom of the slope.

"This place is cool," said the Runt.

There were dozens of stones of all sizes in the small meadow. Tall stones, bigger than either of the boys, and small ones, just the right size for sitting on. There were some broken stones. The Runt knew what sort of a place this was, but it did not scare him. It was a loved place.

"Who's buried here?" he asked.

"Mostly okay people," said Dearly. "There used to be a town over there. Past those trees. Then the railroad came and they built a stop in the next town over, and our town sort of dried up and fell in and blew away. There's bushes and trees now, where the town was. You can hide in the trees and go into the old houses and jump out."

The Runt said, "Are they like that farmhouse up there? The houses?" He didn't want to go in them, if they were.

"No," said Dearly. "Nobody goes in them, except for me. And some animals, sometimes. I'm the only kid around here."

"I figured," said the Runt.

"Maybe we can go down and play in them," said Dearly.

"That would be pretty cool," said the Runt.

It was a perfect early October night: almost as warm as summer, and the harvest moon dominated the sky. You could see everything.

"Which one of these is yours?" asked the Runt.

Dearly straightened up proudly, and took the Runt by the hand. He pulled him over to an overgrown corner of the field. The two boys pushed aside the long grass. The stone was set flat into the ground, and it had dates carved into it from a hundred years before. Much of it was worn away, but beneath the dates it was possible to make out the words DEARLY DEPARTED WILL NEVER BE FORG.

"Forgotten, I'd wager," said Dearly.

"Yeah, that's what I'd say too," said the Runt.

They went out of the gate, down a gully, and into what remained of the old town. Trees grew through houses, and buildings had fallen in on themselves, but it wasn't scary. They played hide-and-seek. They explored. Dearly showed the Runt some pretty cool places, including a one-room cottage that he said was the oldest building in that whole part of the country. It was in pretty good shape, too, considering how old it was.

"I can see pretty good by moonlight," said the Runt. "Even inside. I didn't know that it was so easy."

"Yeah," said Dearly. "And after a while you get good at seeing even when there ain't any moonlight."

The Runt was envious.

"I got to go to the bathroom," said the Runt. "Is there somewhere around here?"

Dearly thought for a moment. "I don't know," he admitted. "I don't do that stuff anymore. There are a few outhouses still standing, but they may not be safe. Best just to do it in the woods."

"Like a bear," said the Runt.

He went out the back, into the woods which pushed up against the wall of the cottage, and went behind a tree. He'd never done that before, in the open air. He felt like a wild animal. When he was done he wiped himself with fallen leaves. Then he went back out the front. Dearly was sitting in a pool of moonlight, waiting for him.

"How did you die?" asked the Runt.

"I got sick," said Dearly. "My maw cried and carried on something fierce. Then I died."

"If I stayed here with you," said the Runt, "would I have to be dead too?"

"Maybe," said Dearly. "Well, yeah. I guess."

"What's it like? Being dead."

"I don't mind it," admitted Dearly. "Worst thing is not having anyone to play with."

"But there must be lots of people up in that meadow," said the Runt. "Don't they ever play with you?"

"Nope," said Dearly. "Mostly, they sleep. And even when they walk, they can't be bothered to just go and see stuff and do things. They can't be bothered with me. You see that tree?"

It was a beech tree, its smooth gray bark cracked with age. It sat in what must once have been the town square, ninety years before.

"Yeah," said the Runt.

"You want to climb it?"

"It looks kind of high."

"It is. Real high. But it's easy to climb. I'll show you."

It was easy to climb. There were handholds in the bark, and the boys went up the big beech tree like a couple of monkeys, like pirates, like warriors. From the top of the tree one could see the whole world. The sky was starting to lighten, just a hair, in the east.

Everything waited. The night was ending. The world was holding its breath, preparing to begin again.

"This was the best day I ever had," said the Runt.

"Me too," said Dearly. "What are you going to do now?"

"I don't know," said the Runt.

He imagined himself going on, walking across the world, all the way to the sea. He imagined himself growing up and growing older, bringing himself up by his bootstraps. Somewhere in there he would become fabulously wealthy. And then he would go back to the house with the twins in it, and he would drive up to their door in his wonderful car, or perhaps he would turn up at a football game (in his imagination the twins had neither aged nor grown) and look down at them, in a kindly way. He would buy them all—the twins, his parents—a meal at the finest restaurant in the city, and they would tell him how badly they had misunderstood him and mistreated him. They would apologize and weep, and through it all he would say nothing. He would let their apologies wash over him. And then he would give each of them a gift, and afterward he would leave their lives once more, this time for good.

It was a fine dream.

In reality, he knew, he would keep walking, and be found tomorrow, or the day after that, and go home and be yelled at and everything would be the same as it ever was, and day after day, hour after hour, until the end of time he'd still be the Runt, only they'd be mad at him for leaving.

"I have to go to bed soon," said Dearly. He started to climb down the big beech tree.

Climbing down the tree was harder, the Runt found. You couldn't see where you were putting your feet, and had to feel around for somewhere to put them. Several times he slipped and slid, but Dearly went down ahead of him, and would say things like "Just a little to the right now," and they both made it down just fine.

The sky continued to lighten, and the moon was fading, and it was harder to see. They clambered back through the gully. Sometimes the Runt wasn't sure that Dearly was there at all, but when he got to the top, he saw the boy waiting for him.

They didn't say much as they walked up to the meadow filled with stones. The Runt put his arm over Dearly's shoulder, and they walked in step up the hill. "Well," said Dearly. "Thanks for stopping by."

"I had a good time," said the Runt.

"Yeah," said Dearly. "Me too."

Down in the woods somewhere a bird began to sing.

"If I wanted to stay—?" said the Runt, all in a burst. Then he stopped. *I might never get another chance to change it,* thought the Runt. He'd never get to the sea. They'd never let him.

Dearly didn't say anything, not for a long time. The world was gray. More birds joined the first.

"I can't do it," said Dearly eventually. "But *they* might."

"Who?"

"The ones in there." The fair boy pointed up the slope to the tumble-down farmhouse with the jagged broken windows, silhouetted against the dawn. The gray light had not changed it.

The Runt shivered. "There's people in there?" he said. "I thought you said it was empty."

"It ain't empty," said Dearly. "I said nobody lives there. Different things." He looked up at the sky. "I got to go now," he added. He squeezed the

Runt's hand. And then he just wasn't there any longer. The Runt stood in the little graveyard all on his own, listening to the birdsong on the morning air. Then he made his way up the hill. It was harder by himself.

He picked up his schoolbag from the place he had left it. He ate his last Milky Way and stared at the tumbledown building. The empty windows of the farmhouse were like eyes, watching him.

It was darker inside there. Darker than anything.

He pushed his way through the weed-choked yard. The door to the farmhouse was mostly crumbled away. He stopped at the doorway, hesitating, wondering if this was wise. He could smell damp, and rot, and something else underneath. He thought he heard something move, deep in the house, in the cellar, maybe, or the attic. A shuffle, maybe. Or a hop. It was hard to tell.

Eventually, he went inside.

Nobody said anything. October filled his wooden mug with apple cider when he was done, and drained it, and filled it again.

"It was a story," said December. "I'll say that for it." He rubbed his pale blue eyes with a fist. The fire was almost out.

"What happened next?" asked June nervously. "After he went into the house?"

May, sitting next to her, put her hand on June's arm. "Better not to think about it," she said.

"Anyone else want a turn?" asked August. There was no reply. "Then I think we're done."

"That needs to be an official motion," pointed out February.

"All in favor?" said October. There was a chorus of "Ayes." "All against?" Silence. "Then I declare this meeting adjourned."

They got up from the fireside, stretching and yawning, and walked away into the wood, in ones and twos and threes, until only October and his neighbor remained.

"Your turn in the chair next time," said October.

"I know," said November. He was pale, and thin lipped. He helped October out of the wooden chair. "I like your stories. Mine are always too dark."

"I don't think so," said October. "It's just that your nights are longer. And you aren't as warm."

"Put it like that," said November, "and I feel better. I suppose we can't help who we are."

"That's the spirit," said his brother. And they touched hands as they walked away from the fire's orange embers, taking their stories with them back into the dark.

Missolonghi 1824

John Crowley

*T*he English milord took his hands from the boy's shoulders, dis-comfited but unembarrassed. "No?" he said. "No. Very well, I see, I see; you must forgive me then..."

The boy, desperate not to have offended the Englishman, clutched at the milord's tartan cloak and spoke in a rush of Romaic, shaking his head and near tears.

"No, no, my dear," the milord said. "It's not at all your fault; you have swept me into an impropriety. I misunderstood your kindness, that is all, and it is you who must forgive me."

He went, with his odd off-kilter and halting walk, to his couch, and re-clined there. The boy stood erect in the middle of the room, and (switch-ing to Italian) began a long speech about his deep love and respect for the noble lord, who was as dear as life itself to him. The noble lord watched him in wonder, smiling. Then he held out a hand to him: "Oh, no more, no more. You see it is just such sentiments as those that misled me. Really, I swear to you, I misunderstood and it shan't happen again. Only you mustn't stand there preaching at me, don't; come sit by me at least. Come."

The boy, knowing that a dignified coldness was often the safest demeanor to adopt when offers like the milord's were made to him, came and stood beside his employer, hands behind his back.

"Well," the milord said, himself adopting a more serious mien, "I'll tell you what. If you will not stand there like a stick, if you will put back on your usual face—sit, won't you?—then . . . then what shall I do? I shall tell you a story."

Immediately the boy melted. He sat, or squatted, near his master— not on the couch, but on a rag of carpet on the floor near it. "A story," he said. "A story of what, of what?"

"Of what, of what," said the Englishman. He felt the familiar night pains beginning within, everywhere and nowhere. "If you will just trim the lamp," he said, "and open a jar of that Hollands gin there, and pour me a cup with some *limonata*, and then put a stick on the fire—then we will have 'of what, of what.' "

The small compound was dark now, though not quiet; in the courtyard could still be heard the snort and stamp of horses arriving, the talk of his Suliote soldiers and the petitioners and hangers-on around the cookfires there, talk that could turn to insults, quarrels, riot, or dissolve in laughter. Insofar as he could, the noble foreign lord on whom all of them depended had banished them from this room: here, he had his couch, and the table where he wrote—masses of correspondence, on gold-edged crested paper to impress, or on plain paper to explain (endless the explanations, the cajolings, the reconcilings these Greeks demanded of him); and another pile of papers, messy large sheets much marked over, stanzas of a poem it had lately been hard for him to remember he was writing. Also on the table amid the papers, not so incongruous as they would once have struck him, were a gilt dress-sword, a fantastical crested helmet in the Grecian style, and a Manton's pistol.

He sipped the gin the boy had brought him, and said: "Very well. A story." The boy knelt again on his carpet, dark eyes turned up, eager as a hound: and the poet saw in his face that hunger for tales (what boy his age in England would show it, what public-school boy or even carter's or ploughman's lad would show it?), the same eagerness that must have been in the faces gathered around the fire by which Homer spoke. He felt almost abashed by the boy's open face: he could tell him anything, and be believed.

"Now this would have happened," he said, "I should think, in the year of your birth, or very near; and it happened not a great distance from this place, down in the Morea, in a district that was once called, by your own ancestors a long time ago, Arcadia."

"Arcadia," the boy said in Romaic.

"Yes. You've been there?"

He shook his head.

"Wild and strange it was to me then. I was very young, not so many years older than you are now, hard as it may be for you to imagine I was ever so. I was traveling, traveling because—well, I knew not why; for the sake of traveling, really, though that was hard to explain to the Turks, who do not travel for pleasure, you know, only for gain. I did discover why I traveled, though: that's part of this story. And a part of the story of how I come to be here in this wretched marsh, with you, telling you of it.

"You see, in England, where the people are chiefly hypocrites, and thus easily scandalized, the offer that I just foolishly made to you, my dear, should it have become public knowledge, would have got both us, but chiefly me, in a deal of very hot water. When I was young there was a fellow hanged for doing such things, or rather for being caught at it. Our vices are whoring and drink, you see; other vices are sternly punished.

"And yet it was not that which drove me abroad; nor was it the ladies either—that would come later. No—I think it was the weather, above all." He tugged the tartan more closely around him. "Now, this winter damp; this rain today, every day this week, these fogs. Imagine if they never stopped: summer and winter, the same, except that in winter it is ... well, how am I to explain an English winter to you? I shall not try.

"As soon as I set foot on these shores, I knew I had come home. I was no citizen of England gone abroad. No: this was my land, my clime, my air. I went upon Hymettus and heard the bees. I climbed to the Acropolis (which Lord Elgin was just conspiring to despoil; he wanted to bring the statues to England, to teach the English sculpture—the English being as capable of sculpture as you, my dear, are of skating). I stood within the grove sacred to Apollo at Claros: except there is no grove there now, it is nothing but dust. You, Loukas, and your fathers have cut down all the trees, and burned them, out of spite or for firewood I know not. I stood in the blowing dust and sun, and I thought: *I am come two thousand years too late.*

"That was the sadness that haunted my happiness, you see. I did not despise the living Greeks, as so many of my countrymen did, and think them degenerate, and deserving their Turkish masters. No, I rejoiced in them, girls and boys, Albanians and Suliotes and Athenians. I loved Athens and the narrow squalid streets and the markets. I took exception to nothing. And yet . . . I wanted so much not to have *missed* it, and was so aware that I had. Homer's Greece; Pindar's; Sappho's. Yes, my young friend: you know soldiers and thieves with those names; I speak of others.

"I wintered in Athens. When summer came, I mounted an expedition into the Morea. I had with me my valet Fletcher, whom you know—still with me here; and my two Albanian servants, very fierce and greedy and loyal, drinking skinfuls of Zean wine at eight paras the oke every day. And there was my new Greek friend Nikos, who is your predecessor, Loukas, your *type* I might say, the original of all of you that I have loved: only the difference was, he loved me too.

"You know you can see the mountains into which we went from these windows, yes, on a clear cloudless day such as we have not seen now these many weeks; those mountains to the south across the bay, that look so bare and severe. The tops of them *are* bare, most of them; but down in the vales there are still bits of the ancient forests, and in the chasms where the underground rivers pour out. There are woods and pasture: yes, sheep and shepherds too in Arcady.

"That is Pan's country, you know—or perhaps you don't; sometimes I credit you Greeks with a knowledge that ought to have come down with your blood, but has not. Pan's country: where he was born, where he still lives. The old poets spoke of his hour as noon, when he sleeps upon the hills; when even if you did not see the god face-to-face—woe to you if you did—you could hear his voice, or the sound of his pipes: a sorrowful music, for he is a sad god at heart, and mourns for his lost love Echo."

The poet ceased to speak for a long moment. He remembered that music, heard in the blaze of the Arcadian sun, music not different from the hot nameless drone of noontide itself, compounded of insects, exhalation of the trees, the heated blood rushing in his head. Yet it was a song too, potent and vivifying—and sad, infinitely sad: that even a god could mistake the reflection of his own voice for love's.

There were other gods in those mountains besides great Pan, or had been once; the little party of travelers would pass through groves or near pools, where little stelae had been set up in another age, canted over now and pitted and mossy, or broken and worn away, but whose figures could sometimes still be read: crude nymphs, half-figures of squat horned bearded men with great phalluses, broken or whole. The Orthodox in their party crossed themselves passing these, the Mussulmen looked away or pointed and laughed.

"The little gods of woodland places," the poet said. "The gods of hunters and fishermen. It reminded me of my own home country of Scotland, and how the men and women still believe in pixies and kelpies, and leave food for them, or signs to placate them. It was very like that.

"And I doubt not those old Scotsmen have their reasons for acting as they do, as good reasons as the Greeks had. And have still—whereby hangs this tale."

He drank again (more than this cupful would be needed to get him through the night) and laid a careful hand on Loukas's dark curls. "It was in such a glen that one night we made our camp. So long did the Albanians dance and sing around the fire—'When we were thieves at Targa,' and I'm sure they were—and so sympathetic did I find the spot, that by noon next day we were still at ease there.

"Noon. Pan's song. But we became aware of other sounds as well, human sounds, a horn blown, thrashings and crashings in the glen beyond our camp. Then figures: villagers, armed with rakes and staves and one old man with a fowling-piece.

"A hunt of some sort was up, though what game could have been in these mountains large enough to attract such a crowd I could not imagine; it was hard to believe that many boar or deer could get a living here, and there was uproar enough among these villagers that they might have been after a tiger.

"We joined the chase for a time, trying to see what was afoot. A cry arose down where the forest was thickest, and for an instant I did see some beast ahead of the pack, crashing in the undergrowth, and heard an animal's cry—then no more. Nikos had no taste for pursuit in the heat of the day, and the hunt straggled on out of our ken.

"Toward evening we reached the village itself, over a mountain and a pass: a cluster of houses, a monastery on the scarp above where monks starved themselves, a *taberna,* and a church. There was much excitement; men strutted with their weapons in the street. Apparently their hunt had been successful, but it was not easy to determine what they had caught. I spoke but little Romaic then; the Albanians knew none. Nikos, who could speak Italian and some English, held these mountain people in contempt, and soon grew bored with the work of translating. But gradually I conceived the idea that what they had hunted through the groves and glens was not an animal at all but a man—some poor madman, apparently, some wild man of the woods hunted down for sport. He was being kept caged outside the town, it seemed, awaiting the judgment of some village headman.

"I was well aware of the bigotries of people such as these villagers were; of Greeks in general, and of their Turkish masters too if it come to that. Whoever started their fear or incurred their displeasure, it would go hard with them. That winter in Athens I had interceded for a woman condemned to death by the Turkish authorities, she having been caught in illicit love. Not with me: with me she was not caught. Nonetheless I took it upon myself to rescue her, which with much bluster and a certain quantity of silver I accomplished. I thought perhaps I could help the poor wretch these people had taken. I cannot bear to see even a wild beast in a cage.

"No one welcomed my intervention. The village headman did not want to see me. The villagers fled from my Albanians, the loudest strutters fleeing first. When at last I found a priest I could get some sense from, he told me I was much mistaken and should not interfere. He was tremendously excited, and spoke of rape, not one but many, or the possibility of them anyway, now thank Christ avoided. But I could not credit what he seemed to say: that the captive was not a madman at all but a man of the woods, one who had never lived among men. Nikos translated what the priest said: 'He speaks, but no one understands him.'

"Now I was even more fascinated. I thought perhaps this might be one of the Wild Boys one hears of now and then, abandoned to die and raised by wolves; not a thing one normally credits, and yet... There was something in the air of the village, the wild distraction of the priest—compounded of fear and triumph—that kept me from inquiring further. I would bide my time.

"As darkness came on the people of the village seemed to be readying themselves for some further brutishness. Pine torches had been lit, leading the way to the dell where the captive was being held. It seemed possible that they planned to burn the fellow alive: any such idea as that of course I must prevent, and quickly.

"Like Machiavel, I chose a combination of force and suasion as best suited to accomplishing my purpose. I stood the men of the village to a quantity of drink at the taberna, and I posted my armed Albanians on the path out to the little dell where the captive was. Then I went in peace to see for myself.

"In the flare of the torches I could see the cage, green poles lashed together. I crept slowly to it, not wanting whoever was within to raise an alarm. I felt my heart beat fast, without knowing why it should. As I came close, a dark hand was put out, and took hold of a bar. Something in this hand's action—I cannot say what—was not the action of a man's hand, but of a beast's; what beast, though?

"What reached me next was the smell, a nose-filling rankness that I have never smelled again but would know in a moment. There was something of hurt and fear in it, the smell of an animal that has been wounded and soiled itself; but there was a life history in it too, a ferocious filthiness, something untrammeled and uncaring—well, it's quite impossible, the language has too few words for smells, potent though they be. Now I knew that what was in the cage was not a man; only a furbearer could retain so much odor. And yet: *He speaks,* the priest had said, *and no one understands him.*

"I looked within the cage. I could see nothing at first, though I could hear a labored breath, and felt a poised stillness, the tension of a creature waiting for attack. Then he blinked, and I saw his eyes turned on me.

"You know the eyes of your ancestors, Loukas, the eyes pictured on vases and on the ancientest of statues: those enormous almond-shaped eyes, outlined in black, black-pupiled too, and staring, overflowing with some life other than this world's. Those were his eyes, Greek eyes that no Greek ever had; white at the long corners, with great onyx centers.

"He blinked again, and moved within his cage—his captors had made it too small to stand in, and he must have suffered dreadfully in it—and drew up his legs. He struggled to get some ease, and one foot slid out between the bars below, and nearly touched my knee where I knelt in the dust. And I knew then why it was that he spoke but was not understood."

At first he had thought there must be more than one animal confined in the little cage, his mind unwilling to add together the reaching, twitching foot with its lean shin extended between the bars and the great-eyed hard-breathing personage inside. Cloven: that foot the Christians took from Pan and Pan's sons to give to their Devil. The poet had always taken his own clubbed foot as a sort of sign of his kinship with that race—which, however, along with the rest of modern mankind, he had still supposed to be merely fancies. They were not: not this one, stinking, breathing, waiting for words.

"Now I knew why my heart beat hard. I thought it astonishing but very likely that I alone, of all these Greeks about me here, I alone perhaps of all the mortals in Arcadia that night, knew the language this creature might know: for I had been made to study it, you see, forced with blows and implorings and bribes to learn it through many long years at Harrow.

"Was that fate? Had our father-god brought me here this night to do this child of his some good?

"I put my face close to the bars of the cage. I was afraid for a moment that all those thousands of lines learned by heart had fled from me. The only one I could think of was not so very appropriate. *Sing, Muse,* I said, *that man of many resources, who traveled far and wide . . .* and his eyes shone. I was right: he spoke the Greek of Homer, and not of these men of the Iron Age.

"Now what was I to say? He still lay quiet within the cage, but for the one hand gripping the bars, waiting for more. I realized he must be wounded—it seemed obvious that unless he were wounded he could not have been taken. I knew but one thing: I would not willingly be parted from him. I could have remained in his presence nightlong, forever. I sought his white almond eyes in the darkness and I thought: *I have not missed it after all: it awaited me here to find.*

"I would not have all night, though. My Albanians now discharged their weapons—the warning we'd agreed on—and I heard shouts; the men of the village, now suitably inflamed, were headed for this place. I took from my pocket a penknife—all I had—and set to work on the tough hemp of the cage's ropes.

"*Atrema,* I said, *atrema, atrema*—which I remembered was 'quietly, quietly.' He made no sound or movement as I cut, but when I took hold of a bar with my left hand to steady myself, he put out his long black-nailed hand and grasped my wrist. Not in anger, but not tenderly; strongly, purposefully. The hair rose on my neck. He did not release me until the ropes were cut and I tugged apart the bars.

"The moon had risen, and he came forth into its light. He was no taller than a boy of eight, and yet how he drew the night to him, as though it were a thing with a piece missing until he stepped out into it, and now was whole. I could see that indeed he had been hurt: stripes of blood ran round his bare chest where he had fallen or rolled down a steep declivity. I could see the ridged recurving horns that rose from the matted hair of his head; I could see his sex, big, held up against his belly by a fold of fur, like a dog's or a goat's. Alert, still breathing hard (his breast fluttering, as though the heart within him were huge), he glanced about himself, assessing which way were best to run.

"*Now go,* I said to him. *Live. Take care they do not come near you again. Hide from them when you must; despoil them when you can. Seize on their wives and daughters, piss in their vegetable gardens, tear down their fences, drive mad their sheep and goats. Teach them fear. Never never let them take you again.*

"I say I said this to him, but I confess I could not think of half the words; my Greek had fled me. No matter: he turned his great hot eyes on me as though he understood. What he said back to me I cannot tell you, though he spoke, and smiled; he spoke in a warm winey voice, but a few words, round and sweet. That was a surprise. Perhaps it was from Pan he had his music. I can tell you I have tried to bring those words up often from where I know they are lodged, in my heart of hearts; I think that it is really what I am about when I try to write poems. And now and again— yes, not often, but sometimes—I hear them again.

"He dropped to his hands, then, somewhat as an ape does; he turned and fled, and the tuft of his tail flashed once, like a hare's. At the end of the glen he turned—I could just see him at the edge of the trees—and looked at me. And that was all.

"I sat in the dust there, sweating in the night air. I remember thinking the striking thing about it was how *unpoetical* it had been. It was like no story about a meeting between a man and a god—or a godlet—that I had ever heard. No gift was given me, no promise made me. It was like freeing an otter from a fish trap. And that, most strangely, was what gave me joy in it. The difference, child, between the true gods and the imaginary ones is this: that the true gods are not less real than yourself."

It was deep midnight now in the villa; the tide was out, and rain had begun again to fall, spattering on the roof tiles, hissing in the fire.

It wasn't true, what he had told the boy: that he had been given no gift, made no promise. For it was only after Greece that he came to possess the quality for which, besides his knack for verse, he was chiefly famous: his gift (not always an easy one to live with) for attracting love from many different kinds and conditions of people. He had accepted the love that he attracted, and sought more, and had that too. *Satyr* he had been called, often enough. He thought, when he gave it any thought, that it had come to him through the grip of the horned one: a part of that being's own power of unrefusable ravishment.

Well, if that were so, then he had the gift no more: had used it up, spent it, worn it out. He was thirty-six, and looked and felt far older: sick and lame, his puffy features gray and haggard, his mustache white—foolish to think he could have been the object of Loukas's affection.

But without love, without its wild possibility, he could no longer defend himself against the void: against his black certainty that life mattered not a whit, was a brief compendium of folly and suffering, not worth the stakes. He would not take life on those terms; no, he would trade it for something more valuable ... for Greece. Freedom. He would like to have given his life heroically, but even the ignoble death he seemed likely now to suffer here, in this mephitic swamp, even that was worth something: was owed, anyway, to the clime that made him a poet: to the blessing he had had.

"I have heard of no reports of such a creature in those mountains since that time," he said. "You know, I think the little gods are the oldest gods, older than the Olympians, older far than Jehovah. Pan forbid he should be dead, if he be the last of his kind ..."

The firing of Suliote guns outside the villa woke him. He lifted his head painfully from the sweat-damp pillow. He put out his hand and thought for a moment his Newfoundland dog Lion lay at his feet. It was the boy Loukas: asleep.

He raised himself to his elbows. What had he dreamed? What story had he told?

NOTE: Lord Byron died at Missolonghi, in Greece, April 19, 1824. He was thirty-six years old.

Insect Dreams

Rosalind Palermo Stevenson

I

...and then the sounds begin to reach her, the violent beating of wings, a breeze rising up, a bird gliding on wing...a vision of mouths, footsteps on the gravel on the walkway, the kicking up of stones, the shifting weight from left to right, vibrating deep into the earth, and moving past...a vision of something sweet, of something sugary, or of a soft secretion, she is folded in upon herself, like a leaf which has fallen and curled...a vision of the garden's weedy waters, of its ghostly portico, its statues, the Dutch moat, a sunflower, roses, and other flowers...a vision, a vision, the cry of a bird again, on wing nearer now, furious spasms in her abdomen, the bird on wing higher, higher, then out of view...a vision of longing, a burning up, a flap of skin to which she must affix herself, to which she must hold fast, hold fast, there is a high wind coming, there is the danger she will be blown away...

Sometime in the night a sound wakes her: a thud as of a heavy object falling, and then someone moaning. Maria Sibylla Merian sits up, but can hear nothing more. The night is long, too long, and the air is stultifying.

Down in the hold of the ship the insect moth, *Phalaena tau,* is dreaming, day or night, it makes no difference, though now it is night. The moth is in chrysalis with the other specimens that Maria Sibylla has brought with her on the journey.

Awake she finds she cannot breathe, her cabin is airless, and the odor is foul even here at the stern so close to the captain's quarters. She comes up to the deck to breathe the air, in the dead of night, alone, a forbidden female figure, solitary, silent, and all the while the ocean reticent, the waves just barely lapping.

Imagine. Imagined. The fragmentary themes that drive her night. The ocean. The Atlantic. The crossing to Surinam. It is an allegorical crossing like the crossings of Moors. The dark faces of the men. The ship, *The Peace,* just barely rocking.

She recalls the ritual dances of certain insects. The way the female becomes bloated and huge. And gives off an odor that is strong and pungent, but at the same time sweet, and the males pick up the scent and approach, half-flying, half-crawling to the female.

Now she stands on the deck of the ship. Induced by her God. Under the ceiling of Heaven. Beneath the planets and the stars. The constellations— Lepus, Monoceros, Eridanus. Love of knowledge. Travel and changes. Danger of accidents (especially at sea). And a danger of drowning.

Heavenly God, it is Your will that guides me. It is Your will that guides the entire universe, that binds all forms together. Heavenly God, take me into that self-same will and guide me to Your perfection.

Does she know Plato's Sea of Tartarus? Where all the waters pierce the earth to the Sea of Tartarus? The sailors believe that if they come too close to the equator they will turn black like the natives who live there. Or that if they sail too far to the north their blood will congeal and turn to ice in their veins. But tonight there is nothing but the black of black waters, the sea of darkness, the stars in the heavens.

*   *   *

Pale woman. Defined by your sex. By your birth. By your birthright. When did the door first open? It was her father's influence, no doubt, the artist Matthaus Merian the Elder. She was a child when he died and her memory of him is imperfect. Papa. Papa Matthaus. The safe, the clean, the eminently sane smell of him.

She holds the cast of the head of Laocoon.

Observe the way she holds the giant head.

Sirs, I will hold this head, the head of poor Laocoon, who warned against the Trojan horse.

She is exceptional, her father tells the men.

Stand over here, Maria Sibylla, over here, stand and hold the head.

It is a plaster cast and heavy for a small child; it weighs at least seven or eight pounds, but she holds it.

She holds it as though it is not heavy, as though it does not weigh seven or eight pounds.

and the canals below the windows
the dead level of the waters
the canals that one can see in all directions

It is the light reflecting on her cup of liquid. A small plate next to it with crumbs. It is one of the mornings in the Netherlands before she makes her ocean crossing. A child brings her insects from the Kerkstraat Gardens. It is a ritual they perform: the child arrives at the door and calls out to the woman, "Mistress."

Ja, what have you brought?

I brought a moth pupa.

Did you pluck it yourself?

Yes, Mistress.

Where did you find it?

I found it in the Kerkstraat Gardens.

Here, come, let me see.

The child, a girl, holds out the inert brown shell of the pupa.

Ja, I see, rolling it delicately over on the palm of her hand.

The child's eye is becoming sharp, a love for precision is developing, a satisfaction in identification of the insects. She is just one of the children who lives around the Kerkstraat Gardens, but Maria Sibylla has taken an interest in her.

Maria. Maria Sibylla.

Sibylla is the woman's middle name, the name passed down to her from her mother.

And the Sibyl closed her eyes and saw events unfold before them, in the darkness a horse falling, its rider going down in battle, and then many horses falling, and many riders going down in battle, and rains, and plagues to cleanse the earth.

Make way, make way.

In Amsterdam it was all excitement and exotica. That was how the fire took hold inside her; it was from what she saw in Amsterdam, brought back by the science travelers. But they were hobbyists compared to her, compared to her deadly seriousness. The fire took hold from what she saw in Amsterdam in the interiors of the museum rooms. The creatures floating as in dreams. The creatures in their cases floating.

There are creatures that no one has seen. Creatures that have not been classified, counted, entered in the journals and the record books of science, whose shapes defy the patterns of logical construction, whose colors are as if from other worlds, self-regenerating, pure, infinite variety and complexity, sketched by God, painted by angels, life miraculously breathed into them, life, alive, free, that no one has seen, that she, she must see.

The air is cold on her face, cold through to her bones.

The night is bearing down on her and she thinks that it will crush her. The way the night bears down on her.

The night bears down and makes her think of dying oceans, of vast bodies of water slowly releasing and losing breath, and of all the life contained down in the oceans' depths, down in those fathomless deeps, and of all the life carrying on with the business of living, and with the business of feeding and mating and dying.

The air is cold on her face. Cold through to her bones. She is out from her cabin. Out on the deck. Wrapped in her folds of black twill.

The ship has slowed down almost to a standstill. There is no wind, light or moderate, no fresh and strong wind, no scant wind, no aft, no large, no quartering wind.

She is steady on the deck, steady on her feet, she has her sea legs, she can walk on them, she keeps her back straight.

The sailors will not look at her. They believe it will bring bad luck to look at her. They believe she is a witch—*die Hexe, bezaubernde Frau.*

She is a woman traveling alone under the protection of the captain, in her sight line the insects of Surinam.

There will be land soon. She can smell it. It is a sweet smell in the air, mingled with the smell of salt. Anticipation of arrival. The first rays of the sun. Thin and tentative. The slow lifting of the darkness.

Surinam. Soor i nam. State of the kingdom of the Netherlands on the northeast coast of South America. 55,144 square miles. Capital, Paramaribo.

Paramaribo. Delicious word. Sweet as the sugar cane that grows there, sweet and savage.
Birds tear towards the sun. Their wings on fire like the wings of the Holy Spirit. Tongues aflame for all the earth to see.

She wakes gasping for air, her body bathed in perspiration; her hair is pasted to her head by the perspiration. She pulls the bedsheets off her body, lifts into the mesh netting that envelops her bed, it is the mosquito netting, she lifts her face into it and it feels like a spider's web. She thrusts her hands out in front of her, remembers where she is, what this is, reaches into the blackness to find the seam and lifts away the netting. She locates the candle on her bedside table and lights it. Is guided by its sallow light to the window where she stands looking out, again the night, the moon a harsh orange sliver in the sky.

She is in the bedroom in her suite of rooms at Surimombo—Surimombo is the plantation lodging house owned by the spinster, Esther Gabay. At the time of her stay, there are these three others: Francina Ivenes, the widow, a permanent lodger at Surimombo since the death of her husband some years ago; the physician, Doctor Peter Kolb, who has his practice in the township; and Mathew van der Lee, the young settler, who has come to profit in the sugar trade.

Surimombo. It is a chorus from the slaves. *The race to the end.* Surimombo. Surimombo. Monsoon rain, water washing down the Parima, the fabled river that ran through Paradise. It is the place that was Eden when God expelled Adam. And Eve had no choice but to follow. And now the Parima with its current, the way Maria Sibylla looks in the canoe, she looks large in the canoe, with her back straight, a giantess carrying her insects.

And from the river a disturbance, from deep down under the green-blue bowl of agitation and foment,

Surinam is all rivers: the Nickerie; the Saramacca; the Coppename and the Suriname; the Commewijne and the Marowijne; the Para; the Cottica; the Maroni; the Tapanahoni,

and all around the rolling fields of sugar cane, the way the stalk breaks so that the sweet pulpy insides come dripping out, inviting you to bite, to suck,

it is impossible not to bite, to suck, the rich sweetness.

The sun throws glints of light that catch from time to time the defensive pose of a pupa; still, still, breathless, nothing that moves, nothing that will give rise to movement. It looks like the dropping of a macaw, or like a piece of wood, a bit of broken twig, the pupa waiting to unfold.

It is at the end of the dry season and many times throughout the day, she must wait before she can move on. She must take shelter and wait for the rain to stop.

The jungle forest is open to her, and she keeps step with its pace, with its drifting and continuous movement.

What looks like a centipede, or a snake curled on a branch, is nothing more than the branch itself, its curve, a thickness in the growth of its bark, a guest shrub growing in an enclave of its formation. Meanwhile the creature that she seeks is there, no more than an arm's length in front of her, its eyes focused in her direction.

She is with Marta, her Amerindian slave, who is hardly a slave at all, though one of a dozen slaves included in her lodging fees at Surimombo. Marta knows the names of the trees, the leaves and branches, the larvae feeding on them, the moths they will transform into. She knows the frogs, the spiders, the snakes, the birds, hummingbirds drinking the nectar of flowers, the buds, the fruits, macaws screaming in the trees, winged and magnificent, their colors streaming like the colors in flags, the flags of the homelands, the welcoming flags of homecomings.

Back in Amsterdam she has a friend, a woman who has grown a giant pineapple. From all around people have come to see it, and Mr. Caspar Commelin has written an article about it for inclusion in his science journal. Maria Sibylla writes to Caspar Commelin, and to the other Amsterdam naturalists, the men who are part of the scientific exchange.

Sirs, I have had the satisfaction this day, the 21st of January, 1700, to witness the transformation of a caterpillar, gold and black striped, which I found soon after my arrival here; to witness it become these months later, a butterfly.

She works in watercolors on vellum.

Her vellum is the finest there is, made from the skin of lambs, the lambs unborn, taken early, violently.

+ +

Suppers at Surimombo are served each evening at six o'clock. Esther Gabay takes her place at the head of the table. On the side to Esther Gabay's right are seated Doctor Peter Kolb and Mathew van der Lee. Maria Sibylla is seated opposite them, next to the Widow Ivenes. The food is always plentiful and rich: large bowls of mutton and fricassees, platters of Guinea fowl and vegetables, mullets and snapper, fruits and tarts, alligator pears, guava, and shaddock. Nut meats and oranges are brought to the table last, along with pastries dripping with sugar. The meal is served from left to right. The conversation is animated and jovial.

"How exotic your insects are," says the Widow Ivenes to Maria Sibylla. "Do they ever crawl upon your hand or your wrist? What does it feel like when that happens, the sensation of your insects crawling on your flesh?"

Sirs, the quickening. Life appearing in the egg and nourished there. And then ferocious biting through. The pede, the stage at which I plucked it, plucking too the leaves on which it fed until its transformation into pupa. Profoundest rest. A rest that angels yearn for—and for that time asleep and dreaming. Then beckoned by the dream it starts to stir, the slightest stirring, and then a parting of the cotton that protects the shell, and a splitting and a chipping of the shell itself, until the transformation is complete from pede to winged creature; emerging, blasting, to fly dazed and free and glorious.

Out of a sky filled with sun, out of air that is still and filled with the scent of flamboyant and sugar cane, storms rise up without warning and blacken the Surinam sky. A breeze begins to blow in the darkened light, a moist breeze that takes hold and the sweet smells are carried stronger, and the moisture in the air bathes the face; but then the breeze gathers strength and becomes a wind, and the wind a raging gale, and the gale gains hurricane force. There are signs if one takes notice. Everything becomes quiet. There is a cessation of the sounds of the birds and the insects.

Maria Sibylla is out behind the Surimombo plantation house when her first storm forms in the stillness. She is studying a species of potter wasp which has built its nest upon the ground. She is intent upon recording her observations, and writing the notes that will accompany her drawings, so that she does not take notice of the darkening light. It is Mathew van der Lee who comes running to fetch her—frantic his running—shouting something she cannot hear, stopping just short of knocking into her, he grabs her sketching papers and her charcoals, and, though now quite on top of her, he continues his shouting. They are not back inside the house five minutes when the walls begin to rattle, and the whistling of the wind becomes deep and throaty like a lion's roar, and she huddles low with Esther Gabay, and with the Widow Ivenes and Doctor Peter Kolb, and with Mathew van der Lee, she huddles low.

The storm subsides and the sounds start up again, the rasp of insects, the calls of birds, the screeching of monkeys.

Mathew van der Lee inquires if he might accompany Maria Sibylla on a collecting expedition she has planned to the shoreline in the aftermath of the storm. It is his specialty, he tells her, the seashore; he had been a collector himself back in the Netherlands.

She packs her vellums and her charcoal, her nets and her collecting jars.

She walks erect and keeps her back straight, her shoes are caked with mud, the bottom of her skirt is wet and dragging.

It is light. The sun completely broken through. The hills behind the shore heavy with what the winds have brought, invisible but present, the air laden with it.

"Madame Sibylla," says Mathew van der Lee. He wears a hat in the style of the day, black felt and rimmed. He wears a jacket also in the style of the day, three-quarters in length and black like the hat, and his shirt is white beneath the jacket. They are on the edge of the shoreline along the Paramaribo coast. Maria Sibylla is walking ahead of him. "Madame Sibylla," he says again. "You shall outdistance me if you walk so quickly, Madame Sibylla." He is teasing and young, pleasing and handsome in his white shirt, in his hat, in his jacket.

* * *

Sirs, we sing the creature's praises! The pede perceives the visual impressions around it, not by means of rows of eyes located down along the sides of its body, but through distinctly tiny simple eyes, ocelli, placed on each side of the head.

For a minute she is breathless. Her breathlessness exaggerated in the intensity of the heat. It is so hot she almost cannot bear it.

The Widow Ivenes beckons her to visit in her suite of rooms. The Widow is sitting with a metal plate against her forehead, alternately placing it against the back of her neck. The drapes are drawn. There is a bowl of water on the table by her bed. "I would like to tear these clothes from my body," the Widow says point-blank to Maria Sibylla.

Maria Sibylla has come into the Widow's room with a fan with which she is fanning herself unrestrainedly. It was hand-painted in Italy, but she purchased it in Amsterdam. She offers it as a present to the Widow Ivenes. The Widow takes the fan and heaves and sighs, and heaves and sighs again.

Only Esther Gabay seems to never mind the heat. She carries on in it with the running of Surimombo. Even during the hottest hours, she carries on in it, just as the slaves carry on in it with their work in the sugar fields.

The African slaves go about naked. Or mostly naked. The women naked from waist to neck. The young ones with their breasts taut, their skin the deepest browns, their nipples black, like black cherries on the trees back in Holland. The older women stand with their breasts below their waists in the late day sun. There is a dance the African slaves perform and Maria Sibylla has witnessed it—the Winti, or Dance of Possession—their hips roll as they pass the calabash, drink from the bowl, smoke the tobacco, and then *here Miss, here Miss,* holding out the worm for her to take, *here Miss, here Miss . . .*

꜀ ꜀

That evening there is smoked salmon arrived by ship from Amsterdam. With the salmon is turtle and king fish, grouper and snapper. A beverage is served made of coconut and lime. Hands are washed between courses. The evening meal is like a prayer. Like a service in the church in Paramaribo.

late at night she hears the doctor snoring, she hears him through the walls of the suites of the house, his breath coming in snorts and gasps.

and in the eaves around the house—spiders.

and in her room the smell of the salve she uses to protect her skin. It is something Marta gave her made from the sap of palm leaves. And blood oranges in a bowl. And grapes in another bowl. Her hair is wrapped in cloth. The cloth is cut in strips and woven through her hair. Blood oranges in a bowl next to the grapes.

and what she feels is the heat. The relentless bruising heat.

Sirs, it has been thought the thickened lines of wing venation are veins like those that comprise the network of our own fragile bodies, and through which the moth's blood (made up of a dense white liquid) flows outward each to body parts dependent on receiving it. This proves not the case. The wing venation are solidly composed and act as brace cords for support.

She is in the small forest behind the Surimombo sugar fields. They call it Surimombo Forest because its edges border the plantation. The light is green and indistinct. Her eyes must make an adjustment. The light filters down through the branches of the trees and through the flowers that grow along the tree trunks. A flatworm glides on a moist trail of sludge on the leaf of a giant acacia. The worm is red and iridescent. When she tries to lift it, it dissolves.

God stirs. In any case impels. Nettles. On which the creature feeds. The Mora branch. And its leaves. The Yucca with its red fruit.

* * *

Mathew van der Lee has followed her into the small forest where she is working along its edges. It was by chance, he says, that he caught sight of her, from the sugar fields where he had been observing the harvesting technique at Surimombo. He could not resist, he says, but to see after her, to inquire of her while at her work. I have seen many such plants in the botanical gardens in Amsterdam, he says, pointing to the crimson blossoms of the bougainvillea, but none in the gardens compare to these.

It is said that there were no lovers, only a husband who wound up by menacing—the rumors of his vices—and the whispers of the word *cruelty*—a husband whom she fled in retaliation and defense. A daring act then, at that time, imagine.

But history shall have it there was a lover.

Maria Sibylla is not a child. No. She is a woman already of some years. Though she was little more than a child on the day of her marriage to Johann Graff. But she fled that husband.

On the 21st day of November in the year 1685, Maria Sibylla gathered what was hers and set out for the Protestant Pietist colony at Friesland, and for the colony's home at the Castle of Weirweurd, and for the prefect, Petre Yvon, who then presided there. She set out to join those pious men and women who lived each moment in the love of God and in the denial of the worldly influence. She took her vellums, her charcoals, her specimens, some articles of clothing, some personal effects.

On the morning of the 23rd of November, her husband appeared outside the door of the Castle, where he bellowed out the name of his wife, and where within those walls Maria Sibylla remained silent.

She was staring out her window when he arrived, thinking of the creatures she might find there, wondering how she might conduct her work from this new home, she was seeing God in all she saw, and trusting in God to direct her.

* * *

Graff sought audience with his wife through the personage of Petre Yvon. He demanded that he be admitted inside the walls of the castle. She is mine, he shouted, mine, I will not let go what is rightfully mine.

Only silence for reply.

And though he went down in a rage on his knees and pounded on the rock-strewn ground for three days, eating nothing, and not even drinking water, and though the ground was cold in the strong November chill, and though he made supplication and implored, and beseeched and importuned, and alternately begged and bellowed, she would not yield.

Tropical sweetness now. Sweeter than the sugar cane. Sweeter than the syrup dripping from the stalks cut and bound for refining. Blinding sun. Blazing heat. Leaves of plants so delicate they wither in the sun.

Sirs, the female is fussy in her decision as to where to lay her eggs; she grades each leaf for suitability, rejecting one leaf after another before choosing.

Insects swarm, approaching hungry and curious, the jungle forest stretches before her, sounds, the occasional glimpses of birds. She is on her way to Rama, farther down along the Saramacca. The African slaves walk ahead of her, unsheathing knives flashing, cutting a path through the dense growth of the forest, hacking down the weeds and the saw grass so she can pass through. She has with her bottles half-filled with brandy to preserve dead some of what she finds, but also the mesh cages lined with bolting cloth to take other specimens alive, and to retain for them the natural conditions of their environment, to study their transformations without interrupting them, to observe for herself all the stages of their development. Her head is covered with a wide-brimmed hat. A few beads of perspiration run down from beneath the hat. She wears a shirt under the makeshift overall that she has sewn for her work in the jungle. The Surimombo slaves call her medicine woman. The women bring her chrysalids that they promise will open into moths, and butterflies more beautiful than any she has ever seen, creatures which will whisper certain truths to her, endow her with certain powers. But everything now has begun to draw her attention. It is no longer simply the larvae, the moths, and the butterflies. Now she wants to know frogs, toads, snakes, and spiders, hummingbirds, the parrots and red monkeys screeching in the trees, the habits of the grasses that grow here, the invisible creatures that inhabit the air.

Sirs, for each there is the head, the thorax, the abdomen; the surface of the body divided into platelike areas; there are the mouth parts, the antennae, the feet; and the special hairs that are sensitive to sound.

"Your hands are so delicate, dear," the Widow Ivenes tells Maria Sibylla that night at supper, "one would never guess from looking at them you are a scientist."

Pastries and puddings are brought to the table, jellies and preserved fruits, fruit tarts sitting in transparent syrups, cakes made from nut meats, sweet oranges, yellow pineapples, alligator pears, guava, shaddock.

After supper Mathew van der Lee asks permission to enter Maria Sibylla's study. It is in a ground floor room at the rear—attached to but distant from the other rooms of Surimombo. "Mr. van der Lee. Here, come." Before he is able to say a word, he is directed to a brownish shape in a mesh cage that looks at first as though it might be a curled bit of bark. But then there is the slightest movement. A kind of weaving from side to side, a tear in the wall at one end, a small but violent movement, the tear opening a little larger, and then a little larger still, until a shape is visible inside, pushing forward through the tear, a damp and matted little thing pushing its way through the opening until it has pushed itself fully out, and then sits and rests there for a time. "There, you see," is all she says.

Sirs, there is a heart, as well, I have found it lodged in the frontal vessel suspended from the wall of the abdomen. The tiny heart can almost not be seen. But it is, I assure you, there, and it does beat, good sirs, as does our own.

She is near Para Creek. Marta is with her. They are searching inside the edges of the forest wall, looking for unknown genera of blossoms and strange chrysalises, looking and describing and collecting.

Marta walks ahead, hacking with a machete at the dense overgrowth, the frequent surfacing of saw grass. She points to a branch on a tree. Maria Sibylla approaches, rapid and silent, ah, yes, ja, ja. There is a red caterpillar with yellow stripes crawling along the top of the branch. It is feeding on the leaves that grow there. The movement of Maria Sibylla's hand is sure and quick, scooping the caterpillar from the branch and placing it firmly and unharmed in a jar with a bit of the bark and some leaves from the tree. The caterpillar will be brought back to her study to be kept with the others, the numbers of her specimens growing, in jars with mesh tops, in wire cages, in bottles stoppered with cork.

They turn a corner of the forest into a lush growth of rafflesia, the plant is called the corpse plant because it smells like rotting flesh, the flower is enormous, glowing bright orange, the diameter measured in feet, the thick tubular stem. The Indians extract a liquid from the stem that is used to stop the flow of blood. Marta tells her that it is also used to counteract the bites of snakes, that it quickly reverses the effect of the poison in the bloodstream though the flesh has already grown dark. Marta tells her that the seeds of the peacock flower are used to bring about the menses, that the female slaves swallow the seeds to abort their fetuses, to preserve the unborn child from a life of slavery like their own.

Branches bend and scrape in the breeze, airy and delicate, twisting and turning, continually changing direction, and the shrill shrieks of the howler monkeys high above, flying, torsos twisting and turning, arms outstretched, teeth bared, panting and screaming.

The old woman appears as if out of nowhere, she is all bone and sinewy and nerve cells dancing on the coarse, black flesh of her neck and shoulders, and down along her arms, the heavy bracelets on her wrists, the nerve cells dancing into the bones of her fingers. She is speaking in the Creole that the Dutch call Neger-Englen, and Maria Sibylla can understand some of the words: *tree, hanging or suspended?, comb, bird.* And all the time the old woman is speaking, a sack near her feet is screeching and humping. The old woman reaches inside the sack and firmly holding its neck pulls out a brilliantly colored, huge young macaw. She hands the macaw to Maria Sibylla, who, avoiding its enormous stabbing beak, takes the frantic bird and covers it with a net to calm it. The old woman points to herself and says, *Mama Cato, Mama Cato.* Maria Sibylla repeats the name, *Mama Cato.* The old woman wants to trade for the macaw. She points to the sack filled with supplies that is slung over Maria Sibylla's shoulder, indicating she wants it emptied on the ground. Maria Sibylla tells Marta to take the sack and empty it on the ground. The old woman points to a bright blue piece of salempouri cloth and a green tree frog in a stoppered jar of liquid. Maria Sibylla nods her agreement to the trade. The leave-taking is abrupt; the old woman quickly disappears back into the jungle. Marta steps forward and begins putting everything back inside the sack, while Maria Sibylla continues holding the now-silent macaw.

Mosquitoes swarm and puncture her skin.

Beads of blood form on the punctures.

The blood is trickling where the mosquitoes have bitten.

And then another and another puncture in her skin.

Sirs, a most uncommon discovery. A butterfly exactly one half male and the other half female, the rear on one side being male, and on the other female.

In the Kerkstraat Gardens there had been butterflies, benign creatures, but not so beautiful as these. These are more beautiful, but not benign.

Somewhere the ants are taking down a tapir. The pig does not stand a chance. As the ants dig in. As the flesh falls away. As the spirit of the beast rushes out through its head. The slight whoosh of sound each time she pins an insect. Her back stiff and straight. Inside the house, the light glows from the candles.

"I have looked at several cane pieces for farming," Mathew van der Lee announces during the evening meal. "There are some acres south from here, at the mouth of Sara Creek."

"So far to the south, Mr. van der Lee," the Widow Ivenes responds with alarm. "We will never see you if you move so far to the south."

"You will visit often, Widow Ivenes, and spend your time much as you like."

"The Sara Creek region is not thought safe, Mr. van der Lee," says Esther Gabay. "The runaways are settled near to there."

"It is said the numbers of the runaways are few, Madame Gabay."

"The numbers may be few, Mr. van der Lee," says Esther Gabay, "but the assaults on the sugar farms are many."

"And the expeditions of our soldiers fail most often in their efforts to recapture them," adds Doctor Peter Kolb.

"But there are slaves recaptured every day, Doctor Kolb," says Mathew van der Lee.

"And every day there are more runaways," counters the Doctor, "and more violence against the plantations."

"The violence is not likely to continue," insists Mathew van der Lee. "How many slaves will risk the punishments if caught? —the beatings, the mutilations. There is one of your colleagues in Paramaribo, Doctor Kolb, whose job it is to amputate limbs from recaptured runaways."

"The punishments do not deter the runaways," says Doctor Peter Kolb. "Their sensibility is not as ours, Mr. van der Lee."

"I am not persuaded of that view," says Mathew van der Lee.

"Nor am I, I would agree, Mr. van der Lee," says the Widow Ivenes. And then turning to Maria Sibylla, "What has science to say on the subject?"

"It seems not a matter for science, dear Widow Ivenes."

"What of your work then?" The Widow persists in drawing Maria Sibylla into the conversation.

"My work progresses, Widow Ivenes."

"And extraordinary work it is, Madame Sibylla," says the Widow.

"What is extraordinary," says Esther Gabay, "is that so much effort should be taken in the interest of insects."

"There is greater fortune to be made in sugar cane," says Doctor Peter Kolb.

"My interest here is not in sugar, Doctor Kolb."

"Madame Sibylla's interest is to witness nature and not to mine for its material potentiality," says Mathew van der Lee, staring openly at Maria

Sibylla. "She is an artist and a scientist, Doctor Kolb, and those are the interests which occupy her. Much as my own interest in collecting has occupied me. It is true I now seek fortune here in sugar, but I have not lost interest in the creatures of the natural world."

"Indeed well spoken," says the Widow Ivenes.

Mr. van der Lee. Come see. He moves closer to her and he sees. It is the moth pupa she brought with her other specimens on the journey from Amsterdam so that she might witness the completion of their transformations. There in a cage in the Surimombo study. The moth has broken through its shell, broken out at last from chrysalis, after these months since its ocean crossing. The small, delicate moth clings to the wires of the cage with its wings wildly flapping. It is the *Phalaena tau*, its wings appearing moist in the light from the candles, and the flames flare up and cast shadows on the wall. Of the moth. Of the woman. And the man.

The next day she has an accident. She reaches out for a caterpillar on the leaf of a tree in the forest near to the main house. It is a vibrant blue-black, inky and depthless, two ruby stripes along the sides of its body. Sensing her presence, it lifts its head, raises it high as if surveying, then lowers and lifts it again, and then it stops with its body rigid and its head raised. She quickly cups it in her palm and is met with a stinging pain so severe she can barely open her hand to release the caterpillar into the cage. Her body flushes hot. Her hand swells to twice its size and she can hardly remain standing. There is the feeling of sinking, of wanting to let go to the ground and let sleep come, of wanting the floor of the forest—green and lush like the sofas of dowagers, thick and soft in rich velvets and muted shades of olive—to receive her. She sinks down to the bottom of the tree trunk and waits for the dizziness to pass. Almost immediately an apprehension wells up inside her. She feels a sensation on her legs. She pulls the fabric of her clothing up and sees small black wood ticks that despite the layers of her skirt have in seconds covered the flesh of her lower legs and are swarming towards her thighs and her abdomen. She leaps up, surprises a giant macaw on a branch not far above, the bird lifts its wings and shrieks, the shrieks soar up through the branches, and the bird follows. She leaps up and walks as quickly as she can, though she is still unsteady and somewhat dizzy from the poison still in her body. Breathing is difficult. The air is thick with moisture, it is all moisture, the air turned fluid, a substance not breathed but swallowed into the lungs, the chest cavity fills and congests. She is moving forward, returning to the Surimombo main house, in any case she wasn't far, had not gone far. And to the bathing house where she applies an ointment to her legs and her belly following a washing treatment with a brush and harsh liquids. The skin red now, scrubbed raw. Reclaimed. Clean. The bathing house is cool, the water strained through sieves to keep the sand out, the floor polished stone and cool on the bottoms of her feet, and the small black parasitic insects, all to the last one, fallen to the floor, inert, a little pile at her feet, then washed, washed away by the water. She balances herself, holding on with one hand to the wall of the dressing room in the bathing house, the dressing room with its conveniences, small round soaps in smooth clay dishes, jars of salts for soaking, fragrant oils, fresh-cut peacock flowers, a bath sheet for drying her body, a white muslin robe for wrapping up in, the bathing house itself shaded by palmetto leaves falling like folds of fabric over the wooden structure. Now a lizard appears on the outside of the window, it is one of the small lizards that are everywhere in Surinam. Its body is pressed against the mesh that serves as a screen, the sun's rays make it glow, crystalline, the body transparent, shot through by the sun so that she can see the insides clear and shining, and the long thin vein that runs from its head down to its tail and extends out to each of its four legs and to each of the toes of its webbed feet. Dear lizard, remarkable beast, lit by the afternoon sun, pierced through by a ray of white light, human eyes are blinded by so much light, by so much heat and brightness. She goes over to the window to view the lizard more closely and sees Mathew van der Lee off a ways in the distance; she sees his figure in the white sun, against the bleached out grasses near the sugar fields. He is walking with his hands clasped behind his back. Later, he will ask if he might accompany her again up the coast to the ocean on one of her hunts there for shells. They will set out as if on a picnic, carrying charcoals and vellums, specimen boxes and killing jars. They will walk over sand strewn with branches and mollusk shells, nests of seaweed, dead fish, ghost crabs heaped together on the shore. She will walk erect with her back straight, with her shoes caked with mud and the bottom of her dress wet and dragging. Mathew van der Lee will make a lighthearted comment about the mud on her shoes, and just as he does his own

"It is nothing, Doctor Kolb. It is only the heat. No. Nothing. Or if anything, the heat."

"Yes, the heat. How is your work progressing?"

"Well."

"And your hand? Has it healed from the accident?"

"Yes."

"I am a physician, Madame Sibylla. Will you permit me to have a look at it? You would not want it to fester."

"It is nothing, Doctor Kolb. It was only a reaction to the pathetic creature's venom. As you see, it has completely subsided."

Drums are beating. Drums are beating in the night. The sound of the drums comes from the forest beyond Piki Ston where the runaways have erected their settlements. The drums cannot come from the plantations; on the plantations the black slaves are forbidden to drum, forbidden to send their rebel messages. She has seen what happens to those who disobey. She has seen the bloody stump where a hand once was, and the body flogged skinless, and a raw, pulpy mass where the flesh once was, and the body kept alive in ruin.

She is fatigued. It can be seen on her face, and in the way she comports herself, in the way her breath comes labored, and her eyes appear clouded and distant.

It is the heat. And the poison still in her body from the caterpillar's sting. Night has fallen and the window is covered with moths that are drunk on the light from the flames of the candle. The moths will die, just as she believes that she will die, that the heat of the sun will kill her, that the harshness of this place will end her life. She is still weak, and still vertiginous from the caterpillar's venom.

The venom in her body has increased her fatigue, and her nights are beset by dreams, and by visions that appear and disappear, alternately beautiful and terrifying.

In a dream she is menaced by an animal, it comes around in front of her, an aggressive look in its eyes.

* * *

She is standing listening to the river, the still, glassy surface shining in the sun, the sun's rays rippling on the surface, she is standing looking out to the bend in the river, a distance farther and white waters start to form, the current goes crazy with white waters, a little while more and rapids, a little while more and the water gushing and pounding, crazy water, a little while more and crazy water, dashing against rocks, the falls to take you to the bottom, and the devil's egg, the rock that is perched above the water, the dashing crazy water, the falls are Piki Ston Falls, along the riverbank the monkeys with their perpetual screaming, is it with warning? is it with ill intent? the violent screams of the monkeys, but here where she is standing the river is still, there is no ripple, the sun shines in streaks on the placid surface.

Small, sweeter than the alligator pear, the sweet red fruit of the yucca.

The butterflies are made of feathers. She points to all the tiny little feathers.

In her drawings her themes come slowly into focus, a merest outline, a shadowy creature, and then she adds light.

The theme of primulas with nun moth, plum branch and pale tussock, cotton leaf jatropha, mimicry moth, antaeus moth.

The theme of the lantern fly, meadow larkspur and pease blossom moth, various beetles and a harlequin beetle.

The theme of four dead finches. The birds are pathetic the way she portrays them. There is no question they are dead, quintessentially and permanently dead. Flight no more. For the small brown birds.

And the sun breaking through enormous,

it sears the flesh, the ground, the wooden frame of the Surimombo main house.

* * *

In a clearing in the forest Marta has wrapped herself in salempouri cloth, and the bright blue of the fabric is shining, and she is dancing, she is spinning in front of Maria Sibylla. The dance can stop the fierce thunderstorms and the torrents of the rains, and Marta is dancing to bring an end to the rains.

But the sky is gray, and the heavy rains are again threatening.

There is a crocodile somewhere in the meh-nu bushes with its jaws snapping. There is the sound the leaves make when the wind blows through them. A storm rising up. The scream of the toucani. In the Surimombo jungle there had been a trail of dead toucani. Or had they fallen randomly? And the crocodile is creeping out from the swamp onto the jungle floor. And the rain will cause a lake to form in the jungle.

The leaves of the Ku-deh-deh fortify the heart. Marta holds the fingers of her right hand outstretched above her heart, her eyes are dark and excited as she picks the waxy leaves and crushes them.

And all the while Maria Sibylla is searching among the vines and the creepers.

But what about the moth, the newly hatched *Phalaena tau*? Ah, the *Phalaena tau* has been recently transformed. Has broken through its shell and been released. It was Maria Sibylla herself who released the moth. Into the heat. Into the harshness and the freedom of the jungle.

The *Phalaena tau* has flown to make her own way in the jungle.

And Maria Sibylla is searching for the new moth, the stranger.

Among the vines, the creepers, the rosettes of leaves, the night-smelling orchids, the mora excelsa.

Along the branches of the unnamed tree.

*   *   *

The blossoms are red and the tree is unnamed. And the roots of the tree are buried. In the jungle earth that turns to water. The ground is soft, the leaves are shimmering.

And she is silent now and waiting. The voluptuousness of the time of waiting.

She has been walking for so long her feet are burning, but her eyes are searching everywhere. For you, the stranger, for the promise of what she has come for.

She is looking for you, bewitched by you.

In the green, indistinct light of the jungle. That filters down through the branches of the trees.

The screaming birds, their calls harsh, piercing.

The jungle orchids, the delicate tree orchid, the air-borne orchid with its tentacles dangling, and covered in small white flowers, its musky scent, its mouth that never opens.

She is breathless and her heart is beating rapidly.

The heat pours down but she no longer notices, she is intent on finding you.

You are her loadstone, her wish, her temptation, her consummation.

Entranced she is looking, in a fever she is looking.

For the slanted traces that will lead her to you.

The small paroxysms, the silent heartbeat, the throbbing.

But where is it that Maria Sibylla finds you? So quiet. On the branch of the unknown tree? It is a secret tree, so secret even the Amerindians do not know its name, the Tree of Paradise? The tree of the fall from grace? The tree the serpent wrapped itself around and whispered, offering its fruit, and the leaves stinging like nettles, and you clinging with your tiny feet, having taken hold to suck the sweetness, the snake there with you all the time, all wound around its branches, and you as you had always been, from that first hour, when you were the first one, the first to take hold upon that branch, the first to nourish on that unknown, unnamed genus, and having had your fill of eating to spin and spin the silk that would enclose you, and keep you safe inside that first of all enclosures, protected and unharmed, to sleep for the season of your transformation.

I I

There is a beast, there is a beast in Surinam. A white beast seen prowling in the grasses near the sugar farms. The Indians say it is the jinn of a demon that lives under Piki Ston Falls. That it will come and slash slash with its teeth as large as Waha leaves. That it will come to take its dwendi, its lady mama girl, to make its wild monkey bride, to make its wild monkey bride girl running. It has hair that is white and sticks out like the shoots of white copal; it has hands that are claws and it stands on its legs like a man.

The beast stalks the sugar farms while the day steams with heat, or at night stalks the shanties of the slaves.

It is the slaves who see the beast, but sometimes it is one of the Europeans. Like the white overseer at Plantation Davilaar. The man was relieving himself near the edges of the sugar field when he saw an animal crouched a distance from him. The beast reared up and the man turned on his heels and ran.

"It is only an hysteria of the Africans and the Indians," Esther Gabay tells the others over morning meal.

The serving girl brings trays to the table, sets out platters of ham, baskets heaped high with breads, eggs, cassava cakes, green tea, coffee, chocolate.

"It is only an hysteria," Esther Gabay repeats, "or a fabrication that has been hatched by the runaways."

"Hatched to what purpose, Madame Gabay?" asks Doctor Peter Kolb.

"To stir unrest among the slaves, Doctor Kolb."

"It is more likely a wolf, Madame Gabay," says the doctor. "It would not be the first time that a lone wolf, displaced from the pack, or with its instincts otherwise upset, has been known to attack humans."

"There are no wolves here, Doctor Kolb."

"It is a species capable of turning up, Madame Gabay, of one day simply making an appearance. There are many forces that will drive a pack, or that will provoke a lone wolf, to wander into a new territory."

"I have lived here all my life, Doctor Kolb, and have never heard rumor of wolves."

"They have been known to turn up, Madame Gabay."

"We have never had wolves, Doctor Kolb."

"We may have one now, Madame Gabay."

"What is your opinion?" the Widow Ivenes asks, turning suddenly to Maria Sibylla. "Do you believe it is an hysteria?"

"I believe we should not waste our days with speculation on a creature that may or may not exist. I, in any case, shall not waste my days on it. We must trust in the will of the Divine Being, Widow Ivenes, and in our Fate, and I in my work that it is necessary I continue."

"Will you continue in the forests?" asks Doctor Peter Kolb.

"I shall continue as I must, Doctor Kolb."

"Would it not be wise, Madame Sibylla, to avoid the forests?" asks Mathew van der Lee.

"Would you dissuade me, Mr. van der Lee?"

"For your safety it would be cautious, Madame Sibylla."

"For my safety, Mr. van der Lee, I should never have left Frankfurt am Main for Amsterdam, and later Amsterdam for Friesland, or Friesland for Amsterdam once again, and now made this journey to Surinam. Safe, inside my house, Mr. van der Lee, might I still not fall ill and languish and die?"

She prepares after morning meal to travel with Marta into the forest right outside of Paramaribo. The other slaves have begged not to have to accompany them, apprehensive as they are now of the beast.

*   *   *

Marta, who has begun to copy the makeshift style of Maria Sibylla, wears an overall that she has sewn, and under it a shirt Esther Gabay has given her left behind by a previous lodger. Both women wear hats. Their feet and their legs are well covered.

Marta is perspiring, the perspiration runs in large beads from beneath the brim of her hat and down her face, down her Indian nose with the hint of a bump in it, her nostrils flare, her lower lip protrudes.

Maria Sibylla brings her hand behind her own neck, and reaches down along the back of her left shoulder, she digs her fingers into her flesh, a relaxation from the heat, an easement from the weight of the vellum, the charcoal, the brushes, the nets, and the killing jars.

The women are in a small patch of clearing where the light shines down unfiltered and blinding. They raise their hands above their eyes to see.

Hummingbirds in crimson. In vibrant purples and greens. In vests of metallic colors that gleam and change as the light hits them, or as the birds shift the positions of their bodies. The birds are barely larger than the butterflies. Hovering above the branches and singing in unison. There are some sixty of them at least, and they are singing a mating song. Small and glittering like precious stones. All hovering and in song. Maria Sibylla surmises they are males, it is the striking colors that tell her, the males wardrobed for mating and singing in chorus. The voices are not beautiful—their song does not have the sweetness of the helabeh, nor the lyric quality of the thrush. They make a rasping sound, a thin, high-pitched tone such as stone scraping metal.

The birds come into focus like the details on the canvases of certain paintings, at first mere abstract shape and color and then gradually sharpening, becoming discernable.

A little deeper into the forest and again they see hummingbirds, but these, though alive, are not singing.

They are caught in the traps that the shamans have set for them, their bright metallic colors gleaming in the nets in the sun, but their bodies are limp now, no longer hovering, the birds are caught in the shamans' nets, the blur of wingbeat has stopped and they are trapped, forty or fifty at least, perhaps more in the nets of the shamans.

The shamans have set traps for the hummingbirds. That is their diet, Marta tells Maria Sibylla—to be fed exclusively on the flesh of humming-birds.

And the mating song is deadly for the hummingbirds, to be caught in the nets of the shamans.

The sugar farms veer off in all directions: Machado; Castillo; Alvamant; Cordova; Davilaar; Boavista; Providentia. The plantations with their yearly harvests. With the intense heat of their boiling houses and the slitting of the cane to test for sweetness. And the sugar that is dripping from the stalks. It is the wedding at the Castillo Plantation and it has brought all of the township of Surinam out for the celebration. The bride is the daughter of Castillo and the groom is the elder Alvamant. She is seventeen, while the elder Alvamant is forty-three and twice a widower. The bride is virginal and sweet like the sugar cane.

It is from the Castillo wedding that the famous portrait of the men de-rives: twenty-two of them in all, posed like the Officers of the Militia at one of the banquet tables. Doctor Peter Kolb is in the portrait, seated looking towards the left, and gesturing with his hands in conversation. Mathew van der Lee is also shown in the portrait, his expression animated and turned in semi-profile facing Doctor Peter Kolb. The eyes of the other men stare straight ahead, the groom at center expectant and flushed.

From this wedding, too, comes the portrait of Maria Sibylla dressed in garden silk and satin capuchin. Her mood is high and her skin glows in the heat. She is fresh from one of the wedding dances, it was a cotillion and this done in turns, each with a different partner. She has had several of these turns with Mathew van der Lee.

The Widow Ivenes tells the wedding party her dream of the white beast. In the dream the Widow is a child again. She is leading the beast on a chain and the animal is following docile and quiet, trotting like a little dog behind the Child Ivenes. But then a wind starts up and the fur of the white beast begins to ripple like a lion's mane, and the Child Ivenes and the beast move steadily against the wind, and the beast lets out a ferocious roar and throws its head back, all the while roaring, and the Child Ivenes's hair blows free from her cap.

But the beast is not a dream at the Providentia Plantation. A female slave has been mauled and her infant snatched from her. The woman had given birth the night before, and in the morning fell behind the others at the edges of the sugar fields. The beast appeared out of nowhere and sprang at the woman and tore at her flesh, and the woman dropped her baby to the ground. When she did, the beast stopped its attack and let go of the woman, then grabbed the baby from the ground and ran into the jungle.

The black men are crouched outside the flap door of one of the shanties.

Jama-Santi, the child who was witness to the attack, is brought by the men to tell what he saw. He was in the bushes at the edge of the sugar field where he saw the woman resting with her infant. He saw the beast nearby as if in hiding. The beast came across the field on all four paws, like this, and Jama-Santi moves forward in a crouch to show the men, and then it slashed at the woman, rising up on its two legs until it was taller than a man, and then it knocked the woman to the ground and ran off with her infant.

crocodile man, monkey man, alligator man.

There is a bristling on the backs of the black necks; it goes unnoticed for the moment by the Dutch. There are the words that are repeated in the shanties, by the black slaves speaking in their Neger-Englen.

alligator man, mystery man, crocodile man.

But what more is to be said about the wedding party, about the feasting and the dance, the endless rounds of the cotillions? Or for that matter what more is to be said about the wedding couple? The chaste bride. The expectant groom. Shall we call attention to them now and to the coming of the night with its sweet outpouring like the liquid from the sugar cane? The stalk is slit deep, and the syrup of the sugar is dripping.

Maria Sibylla has gone out behind the main house of the Castillo Plantation and has been followed by Mathew van der Lee. "Mr. van der Lee," she says when she sees him. "Here, come." Her black hair is piled high upon her head, and her shoulders are bare, and she is thin in her garden silk. "Madame Sibylla," says Mathew van der Lee as he approaches her.

They will be returning soon to Surimombo.

It is early evening, just before the nightfall. The day of work is over on the sugar farms. The slaves talk about the beast, they say its eyes are malignant, flashing. And the land moves out from the sea down into the jungle.

It is her desire that is driving her. To seek beyond the limits that would otherwise constrain her. In the morning she goes out alone into the fields, behind the house, into the small forest, alone into the jungle.

From a distance she thinks they are large birds, but as she approaches she sees they are monkeys. There is a brood of them on the ground in the clearing. The monkeys are curious, especially the youngest ones, they approach without fear to smell her out. A baby grabs at the bottom of her overall. But when she steps forward, the baby lets go and runs back to the rest. The adults approach menacing, their shrieks deafening, then all at once they pull themselves into the trees.

When the monkeys clear, Maria Sibylla sees the old black woman, Mama Cato. She has brought cowrie shells and beetles to trade for fabric and a sheet of vellum. Mama Cato is running back and forth in front of Maria Sibylla, shouting something that the Dutch woman does not understand. Then Mama Cato stops her shouting and her running and throws her head back and makes a call like a bird. Her call brings toucans. The toucans are flying all around her, the toucans in flight, flapping their wings above Mama Cato.

When the trading is finished, the old woman moves back into the jungle and the toucans disappear above the trees.

But something else is moving now, a hint of something moving among the trees.

Or is it only the way the land moves out from the sea into the jungles. And the swaying of the branches in the trees.

Are there footsteps? Footfall? When Mama Cato has left her alone in the forest? The sound of thrashing against the jungle growth.

Is it the beast? The white beast stalking? On its diurnal ritual? The heaving and sighing of the beast.

And in the distance the cracking of the whips, the whips cracking back on the sugar farms.

That evening at supper the five of them gather. How familiar now the sight of them gathered. The plates are passed from left to right, the way they have always been passed since the first evening of her arrival. And the lodgers are seated where they have always been seated since the moment they first sat down. The talk tonight is of the beast, of the incident at Providentia Plantation. Since the attack on the female slave there has been talk of little else at Surimombo. And Esther Gabay, for all her fears of its effect to stir unrest among the slaves, is unable to control the conversation, to stop the steady stream of discourse on the beast.

"What is called a beast is sometimes merely a deformity," says Doctor Peter Kolb, "such as the deformity of the mystery people, the Ewaipanoma, who are born without a head."

"But the Ewaipanoma are not a real people," says Esther Gabay.

The moths have come and are beating at the window, attracted by the glow of the candles in the dining room, and the window is covered with moths, just as each night since her arrival the window has been covered with moths, and it is as though nature has conspired with its own ritual, and the window is all movement and pulsation. But look who has come this night to take advantage. It is the spider called a wolf spider because it preys in the manner of wolves. It has come to hunt on the window on which the moths have lighted with such compulsion that even when the spider makes its presence known, the moths are unable to flee. For the moths are transfixed there by the light from the candles, bearded, with their bodies flattened, pressed close to the window. And the window provides a feast this night for the spider.

Or later in the salon, or in her laboratory, or in the bedroom of her suite of rooms where the cocoon of the mosquito netting hangs all around her, and the fabric of the netting is soft and silky to the touch.

Despite the layers of the netting, the mosquitoes puncture her flesh, as they have done many times since her arrival.

But who comes dancing in these hours before she sleeps. Gaunt. Thin. He is thin. Like an insect. Imagine.

Dancing in the hours before she sleeps.

If the beast has sport with you, you die, if the beast touches your mama woman, you have babies that come out with heads like crocodiles, if the beast touches you, you feel red pain rising in your loins. That is what the Indians say. And that is what the Africans also say. The Indians and the Africans are of one mind about the beast. It is only the Dutch who say something different.

The beast is not a joke. The beast kills you. Do you know the beast? Is the beast the Ewaipanoma without a head? How can they live without a head? How can they eat you without a head? It is a mystery. It is a question that does not have an answer. The Ewaipanoma live in the deep jungle. But no one can live in the deep jungle. Only the Ewaipanoma and the Africans and the Indians when they are running. They are like dogs when they are running and they are trying to flee their masters. They are running from the slashing of the whip. The women running too. The women running from the whip. And from the use that is made of them. As many times as is desired. Though not desired by them. And they are like wild dogs the women when they are running into the deep jungle, where the Dutch man tries to follow but gets eaten by the crocodile. But if he finds the dog, oh, no, oh no. If he finds the dog. In the jungle.

The beast has struck and infected with fear the imaginations of the captive peoples, the Amerindians with their russet faces, proud under the whip, and the Africans, too, also proud, and watchful.

The white men beat the slaves with whips, they do not care that they are descended from the tribal princes.

The sudden raids and the enslavements. The spirit cast down a thousand times, a thousand times and gnashings . . . bitter bitter.

But what is the beast? Is it the jinn of a demon hiding under Piki Ston Falls? The falls are high and the water rushes.

Where did the beast come from, appearing out of nowhere? How can the beast appear out of nowhere? Out of nothing? It must come from somewhere.

Here is a white beast: On the Cordova Plantation, Jacob Cordova is punishing a black man for drumming.

But in the deep jungle, past the Nickerie, along the Saramacca River, past the swamp lands with its crocodiles, in the deep jungle that is thick with the liana, there are the settlements of the runaways, there are the fire hearths going and the women cooking at the fire hearths outside the new shanties, and the Dutch man cannot follow here, cannot get past the crocodile and the liana, and the black man is drumming and drumming and drumming.

She is infected now with the malaria from the mosquitoes. The mosquitoes have infected her with the malaria.

* * *

The malaria has her and her eyes are bleary, boiling, the heat has worn her down and the mosquito has overcome her, and she is hollow, her bones are hollow, and her skin has become rough and parched, and hot to the touch, and glistening in the darkened room. Esther Gabay has ordered the thick dark curtains pulled across the window to keep out the light from the sun. And in the dark it is as though Maria Sibylla is glowing, as though her skin is glowing. Her lips have swollen and are thick now, and dry, and her tongue, too, has swollen, and is thick inside her mouth, and her speech is slurred in her delirium, and her words come out in fragments and make no sense. She is saying something about a tulip in the Netherlands, or two river pigs, approaching, and sinking down into silence.

where are you, Maria Sibylla? Mari? Mari? in a thick Dutch accent.

she has a heaviness in her legs, the slowing down of her pulse, the heaviness climbing in her legs.

she cannot breathe, the heaviness has made her breathless.

the fever has made her pale, drawn, brought a dryness to her lips, as if parched, faded, and the air filled up with water draws her body fluids like a sponge, in drops it draws her body fluids from her.

she is in a place that is uninhabitable, it is filled with a substance that she knows cannot sustain her.

there is a tree sloth in her path, hanging limp and in unimaginable pleasure in the shade of a Mora tree.

and her heart beating, hard

and her breath shallow

she is on the Cerro de la Compana, the mountain that is called Bell Mountain, located south of the savannah in Surinam.

* * *

white stones rise up on the mountain, the boulders rise white and can be seen from all directions, rising up on the mountain, where there are no trees, only the boulders that rise up to the peaks.

or she is in her father's study looking at the drawing table, at the scene for a still life set on the drawing table.

it is the book of flowers open

the book of insects dreaming

Maria. Maria Sibylla.

and she is sinking down, inside her fever, and sinking down, and down inside her dreams.

Surimombo with its rolling fields of sugar cane, the way the stalk breaks.

and the pale emptying of the darkness.

she is inside the netting, the mosquito netting that is brushing against her like cobwebs, when she tries to move, when she tries to lift up, when she raises her arm, or turns from her back to her side.

or she is walking with Mathew van der Lee along the seashore.

it is his specialty, he tells her, the shore of the sea.

he is speaking and his breath is continuous, it is the absence of pauses that allows his breath to be continuous.

the African slaves hiding in the old abandoned gardens.

amidst the screaming birds, the macaws that scream loudest, the howler monkeys that roar like the jaguars.

* * *

her eyes are black with the dilation of her pupils, the bites have punc-
tured her, have left deposits deep inside her, the seeds of the malaria have
been planted inside her, and have left her forever assailable.

and Doctor Peter Kolb with his bag of tricks coming in and out of her
room, looking now stern, now grave, now perplexed, now fatigued and
hopeless, resigned as though he has exhausted all that he can offer, with
his bag, with his hands, with his hands thick and sometimes shaking, and
yet the shaking is ignored as he, Doctor Kolb, puts his hands first on her
head, and then at the base of her throat, and on her neck, and on her
shoulders, listening, to her breathing, listening to her labored breathing.

and Mathew van der Lee inquiring of Doctor Kolb, often several times
in a single day inquiring, asking after the progress of her recovery, his own
face blanched and creased with his concern, or sometimes waiting outside
her suite of rooms for the doctor to exit, or at cards in the evening distracted.

but Marta, too, has been coming into the sick woman's room, at night
when the doctor has left, and Esther Gabay is aware of it and does not ap-
prove, but does not stop it. Marta brings liquids to drink and some to ap-
ply as a compress, and some that have been ground into a paste, or infused
in a glass, and in the end these prove the cure.

In the end these prove the cure,

and the world again becomes visible,

and the sun breaks through again completely, to sear the flesh, the
ground, the wooden frame of the main house at Surimombo.

As soon as she is able, Maria Sibylla sets out with Marta, they go no
farther than the small forest behind the Surimombo sugar fields, the forest
is lush with peacock flowers.

Her eyes still ringed with the tiredness left by the malaria, she wears
no hat, her hair falls past her shoulders.

* * *

The world again surrounds her,

the calls of birds, the hum of insects,

on the branches of the trees, caterpillars.

The world again surrounds her and she is working in the forest,

the sweep of her net across the jungle floor,

but while she is working, the slaves are hiding.

The slaves are hiding, wearing hats with gold trim, with iron pots and bolts of cloth, with cowrie shells, sweet oil, candles, pigs, sheep, combs.

And the beast has come sniffing across the sugar fields, and the children hiding in the bushes, or in their hammocks, or in their cribs in the shanties that cannot hold them, and their mothers are saying, oh no, oh no.

The beast has come trotting with the legs of his trousers flapping.

It is on the Machado Plantation. Where the beast is reflected in the eyes of the child Josie. The beast is reflected in the eyes, in the eyes of the black child Josie who has just been purchased by Jorge Machado.

The girl is twelve and already has her menses, she is twelve and thin and delicate, with dark eyes and long legs.

It is on the Machado Plantation, and involves Jorge Machado himself, the look of shock in Josie's eyes, the look of fear, of terror, and then of shame, and the touch of the man who has grabbed her, the man who owns her, the man whose property she is.

The weight of Jorge Machado's neck is pressed against the child Josie's face, and his arms have pinned her arms to their sides, and what he is doing to her, she cannot stop him, his thick neck that is pressed against her mouth, his shoulder that is digging into her breast, his flesh that is pushed into hers, and what he is doing to her,

and her eyes are open and staring.

Where is the mama of the child Josie? The mama is so far away now. And the mama cannot protect her. And the daddy cannot protect her. Where is the daddy of the child Josie?

It is from fear, perhaps from fear and anger, perhaps from the aggrievance to her body, or from the weight of his neck against her face, or from his arms which have pinned her, or the pain from what he is doing to her, the child Josie cannot stop herself she bites Jorge Machado. It is on his neck that she bites him, his neck that has been pressed against her mouth, she sinks her teeth deep into his neck, as he penetrates her,

and his shock to feel it,

and his fist pounding down on her mouth,
and her teeth that are broken, and the blood filling up in her mouth.

He rears up like a beast and brings Josie up with him, and Josie is screaming, and the blood is pouring out from her mouth.

But that is not enough to contain the rage of Jorge Machado.
He has a rage that cannot be contained and he spills it out on the child Josie.
And her screams pour out with the blood from her mouth.

And Jorge Machado is pounding and pounding, with his fist like a hammer he pounds her, and her arms flail against him, she is trying to protect herself with her flailing arms, with her arms that flail against him,

until he twists both her arms in their sockets,
and her arms are hanging limp from their sockets,
until Jorge Machado fully spends his rage and by the savage force of his own massive arms he tears the arms out from the sockets of the child Josie.

-ǂ ǂ-

"There is your beast, Madame Gabay," Maria Sibylla says solemnly, having listened with full attention to the account. "And there is *your* beast, Doctor Kolb, there is the wolf that you suspect with its eyes flashing and with its teeth that rip and tear and rip and tear, and there is your beast, too, Widow Ivenes, your fine white beast that trots behind you like a dog, and it is sitting right beside the beast of Madame Gabay."

That night she dreams that she is on the ship, *The Peace,* that it has come to take her home. The ship sets sail and she is returning to her home in the Netherlands. She is standing on the deck as the ship leaves the shore, as it sets sail out to the sea. She is standing on the deck and there is still light from the sun, but the air is cold. And when night comes she is still on the deck and it is now very cold. In her dream she can see the moon at three-quarters, and the planets and the stars. All those miles away from her.

The next day she is alone in the small forest, Marta is not with her. It is called the Surimombo Forest because it extends along the edges of the Surimombo Plantation and can be seen from the sugar fields.

It is the day she discovers the little-bird spider. It is a tarantula, covered with hair, straddling its prey, sucking the blood out from a tiny bird. The bird is on its back only a few inches from the nest, its head hanging limp between a fork in the branch. Maria Sibylla is transferring the scene to vellum, painstaking and accurate in her rendering.

She has announced that morning during breakfast she will cut short her visit. On its approaching journey back she will again board *The Peace.*

It is the heat that is driving her, she has told them, that is prompting her to cut short her visit, and she is still fatigued from her illness, from the malaria, and she believes that if she remains she will not survive, and all the while the heat is breathing itself into her, hot and needling and insistent like the mouth of an insect.

*   *   *

Footsteps approach, she is vaguely aware, the sound of someone thrashing against the jungle growth, she stops drawing and turns in the direction of the footsteps.

It is Mathew van der Lee who has followed her, who has come to seek her out where she is working.

She stands silent, the sun's rays on her.

You are working.
I am working.
Is it true what you said, you will leave soon?
Yes, true, it is true.
But I thought that you might stay.
I am sorry, I must leave, Mr. van der Lee.
Will you not change your mind?
It is too hot, Mr. van der Lee.
I have purchased some cane fields, Madame Sibylla.
You will soon be rich, Mr. van der Lee.

There is something in the shape of his face, its triangularity, and the impression that it gives, there is something in the expression on his face.

And her face still flushed from the malaria.

It will be difficult to leave you, Mr. van der Lee.

He is thin and his lower jaw protrudes slightly. He has the look of a student long past his student days, he is reserved and yet he is intense, he is somewhat delicate and yet there is a strength to him.

And the heat from the sun beating down.

What is the contradiction welling inside her, the contradiction rising inside her? The heat on the one hand—the insidious armies of ants, the wood ticks that in seconds can cover the entirety of the body,

*   *   *

and on the other, everything is lush, lush, and the clouds tinged pink, and the floor of the jungle is thick and soft, so soft you can sink down into it.

Her hair shines black.

Her black hair falling past her shoulders.

Her beating heart, her breathlessness.

And Mathew van der Lee standing before her.

Maria Sibylla stares, then she beckons him closer, motions him to come closer, closer, quiet, puts her fingers to her lips, quiet, quiet, here, come, Mr. van der Lee, and she shows him what it is that she is drawing, the tiny bird that has been vanquished by the spider, the tameless spider still in the act of ravaging the bird, she shows him first on her drawing on the vellum and then points to the live model on the tree, and they are standing very close now, with their faces nearly touching, and there is the mingling of their breaths in the hot, humid air of the forest, under the branches of the tree, this tree that rises up like an altar, like an altar to which they have brought their supplication, their devotions and their dalliance, their yearning and their desire, and the parrots on the branches high above are screaming, as though the birds are giving voice to the intensity of the drama that is taking place below, to the triumph of the silent spider, and to the agony of the vanquished bird, and to the intentness of the woman and the man, and Maria Sibylla is solemn now, as still as stone, her chest no longer rising and falling with the inhalations and exhalations of her breath, she is no longer breathing, her breath held, held for an impossibly long time, and Mathew van der Lee is so close to her now, and quiet, and he is also barely breathing, his breath also held, until at last in one continuous breath he whispers the words, I thought that I might—I thought that we might, and then Mathew van der Lee goes down on his knees before her.

III

On the deck of the ship there are three figures: Maria Sibylla Merian in ship-dress, a muslin jacket and a chip hat, her body rigid, her face pale; and next to her, her Indianen, Marta, who is dressed much the same as Maria Sibylla, and who is going home with her to the Netherlands; and on Marta's shoulder a macaw perched with its huge wings from time to time flapping, it is the same macaw that had been traded with Mama Cato. The bird has a gold chain fastened to its leg and that in turn is fastened to a heavy bracelet on Marta's wrist, and the bird's feathers are a brilliant mix of yellow and green and turquoise, the yellow is sunflower yellow, like the king's yellow, like Indian dyes and canaries, and the green and the blue are like emerald and cobalt, or a green like Mittler's green, or a blue like indigo, steel blue, sapphire.

IV

To Mr. Mathew van der Lee from Maria Sibylla Merian
Surinam, October 5th, 1701
van der Lee Plantation
Paramaribo

Monsieur!
I have received the gentleman's (your) letter of March 19th and read therein that you are surprised to have received no letters from me.
I have also received your previous letters, as well as animals from you on two occasions. The first time, they were brought by the apothecary, Mister Jonathaan Petiver, but because I was not in need of such creatures I gave them back to him and thanked him, requesting that he write to you, telling you I have no use for such animals and did not know what to do with them. For the kind of animals I am looking for are quite different. I am in search of no other animals, but only wish to study certain transformations, how one emerges from the other. There-

fore, I would ask you not to send me any more animals, for I have no use for them.

I continue my work and am still doing it, bringing everything to parchment in its full perfection. But everything I did not bring, or did not find at the time when I cut short my journey, cannot now, after so long a period, be similarly rendered, or remembered, or imagined. And there are so many wondrous, rare things that have never come to light before, and which I will now not be able to bring to light. For the heat in your country is staggering, and many were surprised that I survived, and I have still not fully recovered from my malaria. Thus all my memory associated with that time—which even then had the quality of a dream—has become now all the more ephemeral in its proclivity to fade. And that is so much so that what I have preserved on parchment remains as the only tangible reality that I can summon of that time.

On the journey back, Mr. van der Lee, the sky raged for one entire week with storm, and I believed that God had set upon me, that he was pursuing me in the violent wake of the ship, and we all held fast upon the vessel as our only hope for life while day and night the storm raged, and the good captain, sallow, soaked, and freezing, did not let go his place at the helm beside the helmsman. Though this I knew only afterwards, as you might guess, for during the storm I was confined to my own quarters, where never previously sick from motion, I was at that time quite ill. For my weakness from the malaria was still inside me, and that along with the tossing of the ship brought back my fever, and in my fever I believed, Mr. van der Lee, that I was beset upon by God, so filled as I was with remorse for all that had happened and perhaps as much so for what could not.

It has been my pride for all my life to rely upon my good sense, and to engage the pragmatic view to carry me, and science to inform me, and God to guide and to protect me. But during those days and nights of storm at sea these went out of balance, Mr. van der Lee, and I came to believe that God was in pursuit of me for my weakness, and that the storm had been sent by His intention to fell me, and that the ship would be destroyed and everyone on board along with myself would perish, unfortunate as they had been to journey with me. I came to believe, too, that the sailors had been correct in their judgment of

me as a witch. And I counted myself fortunate that the trials for witchcraft had been long since discontinued in the Netherlands, and that the
last of these trials (it afterwards being deemed unlawful) had preceded
me by a full 90 years. For were that not the case, I was convinced that I
would surely be among those numbers of unfortunate women who
were hung or burned or drowned. That is how distraught my mind was,
Mr. van der Lee, from the fever and the storm. But then the storm
cleared and the ship proceeded forward on a sea that was again calm,
and we on board all settled back into its more gentle motion and continued that way for the remainder of the journey.

With that my mind, and my heart, too, became restored, and my
days were spent again on deck, where I imagined I could catch the fading scent of the flamboyant trees, and all the other sweet smells of Paramaribo, and Marta, whom I brought back from your land to the
Netherlands, and released from her condition of servitude, continued
to nurture me throughout the journey with infusions of plants. These
skills she had learned from her mother, who in turn had learned them
from a Shaman in her former village of Kwamalasamoetoe, which in
our language means the Bamboo Sand.

It is true I feel a longing for your land. In my ears there is still the
sound of the rivers with their surface waters one minute placid, the
next roiling. And my thoughts in some strange way are still carried forward by the sweep of those rivers.

There is great beauty in your land, I have never denied it, Mr. van
der Lee; there is great beauty alongside the brutal harshness. I saw
many things and many forms of life that I would elsewise not have
seen, and I know you glimpsed and understood them, too. Your land
has a multitude of small insects that are rare, and other creatures, fierce
and strange and beautiful. I observed the habits formed by these creatures, and observed the way they have their own laws and their own
proceedings, and these I regarded as metaphors for our own human
lives.

I saw the swarm of ants devouring the spider, and the spider devouring the hummingbird. The Palisade Tree that is called the Tree of
Paradise, the apple of Sodom that is red and poisonous, the thickness
of the jungle with its tangle of vines, the rats, the storks, the armadillos
and the lizards, the toucans and the parrots—all of these have I seen,

Mr. van der Lee, and they have moved me. I felt, too, the heat that daily burned there, the heat that in the end I believe almost killed me. For the sun burns hotter there than a furnace, and hotter, too, than the strong clear fires used for boiling the sugar cane. But enough has been spoken of that heat.

It is that other heat I wish to speak of now, a heat capable of arousing in some unwilled and wild way. For it was that heat, too, that breathed itself into me, Mr. van der Lee, hot and needling and insistent. And perhaps you will now understand that you wish to recall to me what I have not forgotten.

"What is it you see? What do you see, Madame Sibylla?" How frequently you plied me with such questions, Mr. van der Lee. "What has taken you so far from your home?" you asked. "What keeps you as far? What do you yearn for to the point of dying?"

On that afternoon, Mr. van der Lee, when you followed me into the small forest, the one called Surimombo Forest, you plied me again with these same questions. And with other questions, too, while all the while the heat from the sun was burning me and the moisture in the jungle air was suffocating me. You wore a charm around your neck— untypical of the fastidiousness of your attire—it was a piece of bone, yellowish and slightly curved. You were telling me about the Cerro de la Compana, the mountain that sings like a bell, telling me that it was located south of the savannah on the rolling sandstone hills, and that we must journey there together to hear its bell sound. And I was in the Surimombo Forest and you had followed me and Marta was not with me and I told you again I had already made up my mind to cut short my journey and you went down on your knees before me, down to the leaves on their tiny stems shimmering blue-green on the jungle floor. And the perfume was overpowering from the delicate begonias, the caladiums, the fragile calla lilies, the red passion flowers. And you pushed in against the forest growth, Mr. van der Lee, no longer plying me with questions then, but saying to me instead, "I thought that you might— I thought that we might," and taking me down to the jungle floor with you.

But I must ask you now, as it seems to me I asked you then, there in that staggering heat—what is it that is expected? What can be hoped for now? when it could not be hoped for then?

I could not stay then, Mr. van der Lee, because the heat would have killed me, and apart from that your life on a sugar farm could not be my life. That has not changed. The entrancement that we shared cannot endure. There can be room in my life for only one thing, Mr. van der Lee, for only one thing that is passionate and irresistible. And the rapture that I seek is in the transformations that I study, and in bringing everything to parchment in its full perfection.

A light rain is falling now with the sun still shining. We call that *Leichter Machen,* or the *Lightening.* It is regarded as bewitching light, Mr. van der Lee, and sometimes it is called the love light or the lovers' light, or interchangeably the festival light. And if you stand at some strategic point you can see this light reflected on the waters of the canals still rippling with the falling rain, and to the eye it looks like countless lights reflected on the waters of the canals, and with the outlines of the bridges on each one. It is a fairy scene, Mr. van der Lee.

But when the rain stops, the strange light will disappear, and all will be as normal again, and no one will know what had been seen. There are visions like that, Mr. van der Lee.

I did not answer your earlier letters because there seemed no more on my part to be said, and because I did not wish to give the impression that there was something to be hoped for or expected. I still do not wish to give that impression, Mr. van der Lee.

I write and ask you now to not send animals. For I have no use for them. That is, for the animals such as you sent previously. I wish only to study certain transformations, how one emerges from the other. And I therefore ask you not to send me animals, for I have no use for them.

But if you must send something, Mr. van der Lee, send butterflies, small caligo butterflies, diurnal butterflies and ricinis, sactails, jatrophas, moon moths, peacock moths, send primulas with nun moths, pale tussocks and pease blossom moths, tachinid flies and calicoid flies, owl moths and harlequin beetles, or send lantern flies, Mr. van der Lee, in a box that is filled up with the lantern flies, and make certain they are alive when you send them and can be kept living, so that when I open the lid, Mr. van der Lee, they will rise up like fire, and shoot out of the box like a flame, and that will delight me, Mr. van der Lee, and will remind me of that other fire that one day rose up inside me.

CREDITS

ABOUT THE AUTHORS

Dan Chaon is the acclaimed author of *Fitting Ends* and *Among the Missing*, a finalist for the National Book Award, which was also listed as one of the ten best books of the year by the American Library Association, *Chicago Tribune*, the *Boston Globe*, and *Entertainment Weekly*, as well as being cited as a *New York Times* Notable Book. Chaon's fiction has appeared in numerous journals and anthologies, and won both Pushcart and O. Henry awards. Chaon teaches at Oberlin College and lives in Cleveland Heights, Ohio, with his wife and two sons.

Elizabeth Hand is the multiple-award-winning author of eight novels, including *Generation Loss*, *Mortal Love*, and *Waking the Moon*, as well as three collections of short fiction, the most recent of which is *Saffron and Brimstone: Strange Stories*. Since 1988, she has been a regular contributor to the *Washington Post Book World*, among numerous other publications. She lives with her family on the coast of Maine.

"The Man on the Ceiling" holds the distinction of being the only work ever to win the International Horror Guild, Bram Stoker, and World Fantasy Awards in the same year. A novel expanding and re-imagining "The Man on the Ceiling" recently appeared from Wizards of the Coast's Discoveries line. Melanie and Steve are also past winners of the British Fantasy Award. Their work can be found in *The Magazine of Fantasy & Science Fiction, Isaac Asimov's Science Fiction Magazine*, and in such anthologies as *Outsiders* (ROC), *The Year's Best Fantasy & Horror* (St. Martin's). 2009 will see two more solo novels: Melanie's *The Yellow Wood*, and Steve's *Deadfall Hotel*.

M. John Harrison is the author of *In Viriconium*, which was nominated for the Guardian Fiction Prize in 1982; *Climbers*, which won the Boardman Tasker Memorial Award in 1989; and *Light* (2002), co-winner of the James Tiptree, Jr. Award. His short stories have appeared in many venues, from the *Times Literary Supplement* to *Time Out*, and are collected in *Things That Never Happen* (2002). His latest novel is *Nova Swing* (2006). Since 1991 he has reviewed contemporary fiction for the *TLS*, the *Guardian*, and the *Daily Telegraph*; and young adult fiction for the *New York Times*. He was a member of the Michael Powell Jury at the 2003 Edinburgh International Film Festival. He lives near the river in West London.

The Oxford Companion to English Literature describes Ramsey Campbell as "Britain's most respected living horror writer." He has been given more awards than any other writer in the field, including the Grand Master Award of the World Horror Convention and the Lifetime Achievement Award of the Horror Writers Association. Among his novels are *The Face That Must Die, Incarnate, Midnight Sun, The Count of Eleven, Silent Children, The Darkest Part of the Woods, The Overnight, Secret Stories*, and *The Grin of the Dark*. Forthcoming are *Creatures of the Pool* and *The Seven Days of Cain*. His collections include *Waking Nightmares, Alone with the Horrors, Ghosts and Grisly Things*, and *Told by the Dead*, and his nonfiction is collected as *Ramsey Campbell, Probably*. His novels *The Nameless* and *Pact of the Fathers* have been filmed in Spain. His regular columns appear in *All Hallows, Dead Reckonings*, and *Video Watchdog*. He is the President of the British Fantasy Society and of the Society of Fantastic Films.

Brian Evenson is the Director of the Literary Arts Program at Brown University. He is the author of seven books of fiction, including *The Wavering Knife* (which won the International Horror Guild Award for best story collection) and *The Brotherhood of Mutilation*. His most recent novel, *The Open Curtain* (2006), was a finalist for an Edgar Award and an IHG Award. A novel, *Last Days*, will be published by Underland Press in early 2009.

Kelly Link's debut collection, *Stranger Things Happen,* was a Firecracker nominee, a *Village Voice* Favorite Book, and a *Salon* Book of the Year—*Salon* called the collection "... an alchemical mixture of Borges, Raymond Chandler, and *Buffy the Vampire Slayer."* Stories from the collection have won the Nebula, the James Tiptree, Jr., and the World Fantasy awards. Her second collection, *Magic for Beginners,* was a Book Sense pick (and a Best of Book Sense pick), and selected for best of the year lists by *Time* magazine, *Salon, Boldtype, Village Voice, San Francisco Chronicle,* and the *Capitol Times.* It was published in paperback by Harcourt. With Gavin J. Grant and Ellen Datlow she edits *The Year's Best Fantasy & Horror* (St. Martin's Press). She also edited the anthology *Trampoline.* Kelly lives in Northampton, Massachusetts. She received her BA from Columbia University and her MFA from the University of North Carolina at Greensboro. Kelly and her husband, Gavin J. Grant, publish a twice-yearly zine, *Lady Churchill's Rosebud Wristlet*—as well as books—as Small Beer Press.

Born in New York City, Jonathan Carroll has lived in Vienna since 1974 except for a two-year period in Hollywood, California. His writing has been described as literary fantasy, often with elements of surreal horror. His first novel, *The Land of Laughs,* was published in 1980; among those that followed are "Rondua" books *Bones of the Moon* (1987), *Sleeping in Flame* (1988), and *A Child Across the Sky* (1989); British Fantasy Award winner *Outside the Dog Museum* (1991); *The Marriage of Sticks* (1999), *The Wooden Sea* (2001), *White Apples* (2002), and his latest, *Glass Soup* (2006). Among his many nominated stories and books are "Friend's Best Man" (1987), winner of the World Fantasy Award, and the Bram Stoker Award–winning collection *The Panic Hand* (1995).

M. Rickert grew up in Fredonia, Wisconsin. When she was eighteen she moved to California. After many years (and through the sort of "odd series of events" that describe much of her life) she got a job as a kindergarten teacher in a small private school for gifted children. She worked there for almost a decade, then left to pursue her life as a writer, supporting this folly by working at a series of odd jobs. (There are, of course, mysterious gaps in this account, and that is where all the truly interesting stuff happened.) Her short story collection, *Map of Dreams,* was published by Golden Gryphon Press in 2006, and won the World Fantasy Award.

Thomas Tessier was born in Connecticut and educated there and at University College, Dublin. He lived in Dublin and London for thirteen years, during which time three books of his poems were published and three of his plays were profesionally staged. For several years he wrote a monthly column on music for *Vogue* (UK). His short stories have appeared in numerous magazines and anthologies, including *Borderlands, Cemetery Dance, Prime Evil, Dark Terrors, The Year's Best Fantasy and Horror,* and *Best New Horror.* His first collection, *Ghost Music and Other Tales,* received an International Horror Guild Award. He is the author of several novels of terror and suspense, including *The Nightwalker, Phantom, Finishing Touches,* and *Rapture,* which was made into a movie starring Karen Allen and Michael Ontkean. His novel *Fog Heart* received the International Horror Guild Award for Best Novel and was cited by *PW* as one of the best books of the year. His latest novel, *Wicked Things,* was published in paperback in June 2007 by Leisure Books, and a hardcover edition is forthcoming from Cemetery Dance. He lives in Connecticut, and is currently working on a new novel and completing his second collection of short fiction.

David J. Schow is a short story writer, novelist, screenwriter (teleplays and features), columnist, essayist, editor, photographer, and winner of the World Fantasy Award (short story, 1987) and International Horror Guild Award (nonfiction, 2001). Peripherally he has written everything from CD liner notes to book introductions to catalog copy for monster toys. As expert witness, he appears in many genre-related documentaries and DVDs and has traveled from New Zealand to Shanghai to Mexico City to shoot or produce same. He lives in a house on a hill in Los Angeles. Website: www.davidjschow.com.

Each of Glen Hirshberg's first two collections, *American Morons* (Earthling, 2006) and *The Two Sams* (Carroll & Graf, 2003), won the International Horror Guild Award and were selected by Locus as one of the best books of the year. He is also the author of a novel, *The Snowman's Children* (Carroll & Graf, 2002), and is a five-time World Fantasy Award finalist. Currently, he is putting the final touches on two new novels and a third collection. With Dennis Etchison and Peter Atkins, he co-founded the Rolling Darkness Revue, a traveling ghost story performance troupe that tours the west coast of the United States each October. His fiction has appeared in numerous magazines and anthologies, including multiple appearances in *The Mammoth Book of Best New Horror, The Year's Best Fantasy and Horror, Dark Terrors 6, Inferno, The Dark, Trampoline,* and *Cemetery Dance.* He teaches writing and the teaching of writing at Cal State San Bernardino.

Thomas Ligotti is recognized as a contemporary master in the genre of horror fiction. Conspicuous features of his works include an idiosyncratic prose style and inventive narrative structures as well as subjects and themes of a uniformly grim nature. The recipient of several awards, including the Horror Writers Association Bram Stoker Award for his collection *The Nightmare Factory* and short novel *My Work Is Not Yet Done*, Ligotti is often compared to classic horror writers such as Edgar Allan Poe and H. P. Lovecraft. Ligotti's latest collection of stories is *Teatro Grottesco* from Mythos Books, which also published his nonfiction work *The Conspiracy Against the Human Race*, subtitled "A Primer of Horror in Life and Art." A short film of Ligotti's story "The Frolic" is available on DVD. In addition, Fox Atomic, a subsidiary of Fox Studios, released a graphic novel based on works from his 1996 collection, *The Nightmare Factory*.

Benjamin Percy was raised in the High Desert of Central Oregon. He received his BA with honors from Brown University and his MFA with a teaching fellowship from Southern Illinois University. Ben currently lives in Milwaukee, teaching creative writing, composition, and literature at the University of Wisconsin-Stevens Point. He also writes book reviews for the *Capital Times*. When he isn't hunched over the keyboard, hammering out stories, he enjoys hiking, canoeing, fishing, skiing, and throwing back a few pints with friends and family.

Bradford Morrow is the author of *The Almanac Branch*, *Trinity Fields*, *Giovanni's Gift*, and *Ariel's Crossing*, among other novels, most recently *The Fifth Turning* and a collection of stories, *Lush*. The recipient of numerous awards, including the Academy Award in Literature from the American Academy of Arts and Letters, a Guggenheim Fellowship, the PEN/Nora Magid Award, and the O. Henry Prize, Morrow is also the author of a children's book, *Didn't Didn't Do It*, illustrated by Gahan Wilson. Founder and editor of the literary journal *Conjunctions*, he teaches at Bard College. Bradford Morrow divides his time between New York City and an upstate farmhouse.

Peter Straub is the author of seventeen novels, which have been translated into more than twenty languages. They include *Ghost Story*, *Koko*, *Mr. X*, *In the Night Room*, and two collaborations with Stephen King, *The Talisman* and *Black House*. He has written two volumes of poetry and two collections of short fiction, and he edited the Library of America's edition of H. P. Lovecraft's *Tales*. He has won the British Fantasy Award, eight Bram Stoker Awards, two International Horror Guild

Awards, and two World Fantasy Awards. In 1998, he was named Grand Master at the World Horror Convention. In 2005, he was given the HWA's Lifetime Achievement Award.

Stephen King was born in Portland, Maine, in 1947, the second son of Donald and Nellie Ruth Pillsbury King. He made his first professional short story sale in 1967 to *Startling Mystery Stories*. In the fall of 1971, he began teaching high school English classes at Hampden Academy, the public high school in Hampden, Maine. Writing in the evenings and on the weekends, he continued to produce short stories and to work on novels. In the spring of 1973, Doubleday & Company accepted the novel *Carrie* for publication, providing him the means to leave teaching and write full-time. He has since published more than forty novels and has become one of the world's most successful writers. Stephen lives in Maine and Florida with his wife, novelist Tabitha King. They are regular contributors to a number of charities including many libraries and have been honored locally for their philanthropic activities.

Joe Hill's first book of stories, *20th Century Ghosts*, received the British Fantasy Award, The International Horror Guild Award, and the Bram Stoker Award for best collection. He is also a 2006 World Fantasy Award winner for his novella "Voluntary Committal," which appears in the same book. His first critically acclaimed novel, *Heart-Shaped Box*, was published by William Morrow in the U.S. and Gollancz in the UK.

Ellen Klages was born in Ohio, and now lives in San Francisco. Her story, "Basement Magic," won the Nebula Award in 2005. Several of her other stories have been on the final ballot for the Nebula and Hugo awards, and have been reprinted in Year's Best anthologies. A collection of her short fiction, *Portable Childhoods*, was published in 2007. Her first novel, *The Green Glass Sea*, based on the short story of the same title, won the Scott O'Dell Award for historical fiction and the Judy Lopez Memorial Award for Children's Literature in 2007. It was also a finalist for the Northern California Book Award (Children's) and the Locus Award (Best First Novel). In addition to her writing, Ellen serves on the Motherboard of the James Tiptree, Jr. Award and collects lead civilians. Her house is full of odd, old toys.

Tia V. Travis is a native of Canada and grew up in the prairie provinces of Manitoba and Alberta. She has made two appearances in *The Year's Best Fantasy and*

Horror and was a finalist for the World Fantasy Award and the International Horror Guild Award. Currently she is working on her first novel, a ghost story set in Western Canada. She lives in Northern California with her husband, author Norman Partridge.

In 1988 Dr. Graham Joyce quit an executive job and decamped to the Greek island of Lesbos, there to live in a beach shack with a colony of scorpions and to concentrate on writing. He sold his first novel while still in Greece, and traveled in the Middle East on the proceeds. He is a winner of the World Fantasy Award for his novel *The Facts of Life* (2004); a four-time winner of the British Fantasy Award for Best Novel, for *Dark Sister* (1992), *Requiem* (1995), *The Tooth Fairy* (1996), and *Indigo* (1999); and twice winner of the French Grand Prix de l'Imaginaire for *The Facts of Life and Leningrad Nights* (1999). Joyce has also published children's novels, including TWOC (2005, winner of the Angus Award) and most recently *Do the Creepy Thing* (2006), currently listed for the Carnegie Award. His short stories and novels have been translated into over twenty languages. He has adapted his own work for Hollywood studios and frequently reviews for the *Washington Post.* He lives in England and reports on the bad behavior of "the savages"—his wife and two children—on his website blog at www.grahamjoyce.net.

Bestselling author Neil Gaiman has long been one of the top writers in modern comics, as well as a writer of books for readers of all ages. He is listed in the *Dictionary of Literary Biography* as one of the top ten living postmodern writers, and is a prolific creator of works of prose, poetry, film, journalism, comics, song lyrics, and drama. His *New York Times* bestselling 2001 novel for adults, *American Gods,* was awarded the Hugo, Nebula, Bram Stoker, SFX, and Locus awards, was nominated for many other awards, including the World Fantasy Award and the Minnesota Book Award, and appeared on many best-of-year lists. His official website, www.neilgaiman.com, now has more than one million unique visitors each month, and his online journal is syndicated to thousands of blog readers every day. Born and raised in England, Neil Gaiman now lives near Minneapolis, Minnesota. He has somehow reached his forties and still tends to need a haircut.

John Crowley is the recipient of the American Academy and Institute of Letters Award for Literature and the World Fantasy Lifetime Achievement Award. His critically acclaimed works include *Little, Big,* the *Ægypt* Cycle (*The Solitudes, Love & Sleep, Dæmonomania, Endless Things*), *The Translator,* and *Lord Byron's Novel:*

The Evening Land. He teaches fiction writing and screenwriting at Yale University.

Rosalind Palermo Stevenson's fiction and prose poems have appeared in numerous literary journals and anthologies. Her story "The Guest" was awarded the Anne and Henry Paolucci prize for Italian-American writing, and was selected as *Italian Americana*'s best story of 2005, also to be included in the forthcoming anthology, *The Best of* Italian Americana *in the Last Twenty-Five Years.* Her short novella *Insect Dreams* has been published as a book in the Contemporary Novella series (Rain Mountain Press). She lives in New York City.